VERGUIDE

A BALANCE OF SOULS

$$(\male \div) = (\dagger \rightarrow \infty)$$

ALFRED LEONARD

Published by

**MELROSE
BOOKS**

An Imprint of Melrose Press Limited
St Thomas Place, Ely
Cambridgeshire
CB7 4GG, UK
www.melrosebooks.com

FIRST EDITION

Cover designed by Matt Stephens

ISBN: 978-1-906561- 54-3

Printed and bound in Great Britain by:
CPI Antony Rowe, Chippenham, Wiltshire

A BALANCE OF SOULS

For my wife Trish. My home is where you are.

In life, man must cleave to two things. Firstly, an opinion upon all subjects; and secondly, hopes. For 'tis upon these that a person's character is forged and makes him what he is; or will become.

There is doubt in most things. But on one fact each person can depend; the grim reaper will not be denied his quota; death awaits us all.

By the same author.
'Ampshire Boy.

SOME WHEN IN THE PAST. SOMEWHERE.

My ancestors were a troubled people; disturbed mainly by money and religion; or human greed and the reason to reach for it. These were the two biggest barriers to Verunians' co-existence. There is not a planet in the Universe that will ever be a peaceful, happy and safe place to live until we eradicate both from the necessities of our society.

On my planet, the grasping tentacles of the Church reached out in all directions. Over thousands of years religion had demanded the building of huge, extremely expensive edifices, sometimes draining the local Verunian communities of both sustenance and life. Not a week has passed since records first began, many thousands of years ago, during which the donation plate has not been passed around in one such creation or another.

Billions have willingly donated the extreme sacrifice, their very lives, in the name of religion. Always weak and easily led, despite the education available to almost every Verunian in our society, our people were ever willing to wage war on behalf of their gods. Almost a perverse flaw in the Verunian psyche, they were ever prepared to annihilate the perceived enemies of their religious leaders. A hint of aggression from one faction towards another would inevitably stir up a deeply-rooted instinct to kill amongst the vast majority of the people of Veruni.

For thousands of years we built the monuments to our religions. Those huge - and yes, let us admit it - extremely well built, impressive, yet cold and damp temples, churches and cathedrals. Vast numbers of these rapidly fell into decline and consistent in their response to the appeals from the clergy, Verunians responded without a second's thought; throw some money into the kitty, repair the roof. Surely, our Heavenly Fathers would reward all who donated; and if He does not reward us in this life, then He surely will on the day of Judgement.

No God could be so greedy; so unjust; so demanding of sacrifice or so bloodthirsty. The tersely spoken sentiments were those of Belial First, spoken to me so many years ago. In that strange, underground cave-like place where I had first met him, his voice had been bitter, telling the story of his own original planet where religion had been the mainstay of Verunian existence.

But his most telling argument against religion was that all sin, whether in the form of violent crime or social misdemeanour, was acceptable, providing the perpetrator uttered a few well-chosen terms of regret.

Belial First's voice had taken on a comical imitation of a priest. 'Father, I have sinned. I have murdered my mother-in-law in a spate of terrible anger.'

And the priest's whimsical, bored singsong response. 'Take three times penance and piss up the wall of the church.'

SALADIN. NEW YEAR'S DAY, 2004.

Gentle circular movements of loving fingers on his protruding stomach calmed the crying baby. Just a few weeks old, he was hungry but his mother did not yet deem it time for his feed. His thoughts were still with the soothing feeling of the warm water, after being dunked into his mother's kitchen sink, and the soft and loving touch of the fingers gave the boy a sensation on his skin that was truly delicious, almost ticklish, but not quite sufficiently ticklish as to cause any squirming in his infant body. Thoughts of food were temporarily abandoned, pushed into a backward corner of his mind by the touch of his mother.

Bright blue eyes, overly large, emulating those of a beautiful woman, looked up into the smiling face of his mother. Intensely black hair, sparse over the back of the head but growing quickly, exaggerated the whiteness of the baby's skin; and in his mother's eyes the presence of a full working outfit of arms, legs, fingers, toes and other human male appendages gave her a feeling of a job well done. 'Allāh be praised.' She did not forget to thank her god for his gift.

Yet too young to be alarmed, the baby saw the second person appear above the face of his parent. But this face was totally different from that of his mother. It was not sharply defined - more a hazy outline; and where he would expect to see the facial shapes of nose, ears, mouth, eyes, etc., there was nothing. Nothing more than a blank, blurry outline of a head. The thing had appeared for the first time only a few days ago and the boy was becoming quite used to its presence. Increasingly, as the boy aged, he would think of it as *the thing* and after a few hurtful teasing sessions at school, would learn not to mention it.

But 'the thing' did have a voice. A man's voice. A softly modulated voice that spoke a language that was totally different from the hard guttural sounds of his parent tongue. A voice that would be with him for many, many years; and the voice spoke the words that would lead the boy to his destiny.

TWINS. 27TH MARCH, 1977. EAST TIMOR.

Human emotions can rip the will to live from the breast of any person. Her heart felt as if it was a dead weight in her chest and she continued to scream and sob long after the second child - a boy - had followed his sister into this world. Man can never understand the extreme physical and mental pain of childbirth; nor comprehend the quickness of its passing when a healthy offspring is placed into the arms of a new mother. But for this woman the blessed and most welcome release from her pain would not pass so quickly.

A simple rattan mat was the only barrier between the woman and the dirt floor of her shack, and it was on to this mat that the twins were delivered. Spread-eagled still on the floor of the flimsy building, the woman felt as if the terrible racking pains of childbirth had not alleviated the pain in her heart. Rather it had increased the dreadful soul-consuming emptiness that lived within her through every waking moment of her life.

Not for this mother the comfort of a midwife or doctor; nor for her the support of a loving husband trying to ease her pain and aid the birth with nothing more to offer than the warmth of a large masculine hand. Despite the presence of the elderly inmate, the woman felt totally alone. Alone, empty-hearted; and with newborn twins to care for. Softly she spoke her prayer, for an empty heart has a greater need of God. 'Holy Father, help me in my moment of greatest need. Lead me always in Your footsteps and watch over my children.'

Maria Vinacco felt a strange sensation. She felt suddenly as if she was not alone and a fine needle of hope speared her aching heart.

Closing her eyes, she concentrated hard, hoping and praying that it was a sign from her dead husband that he was aware of the birth of their family. Many times over the following years, often in her worst moments of depression, she would feel this sensation; and would never be able to decide whether she was experiencing a supernatural connection with her dead husband or a religious encounter with the Almighty in heaven.

As time passed, Maria noticed that the ethereal sensations occurred only when she was with the twins.

JOSH TEMPLETON. MONDAY 25TH JUNE, 1984. NEAR BUNGENDORE, AUSTRALIA.

This was the day. Early rising was not the forte of this young man and he had been trying, with a noteworthy lack of success, to practise the self-discipline required for this enormous effort for many weeks. In the years to come, he knew that military life would demand that he be where he was expected to be in good time. The Royal Australian Navy did not take kindly to laggard behaviour and Josh knew that his glib excuses, accepted so willingly by his mother, would not dissuade the naval disciplinarians from awarding him some sort of punishment for poor timekeeping.

And of late, the young man had been burning the candle at both ends. All-night drinking sessions were part of the delicate transition period from boy to manhood, almost anywhere in the world. With little to occupy his mind whilst awaiting this fateful day, Josh had thrown himself enthusiastically into a world of wine, women and song; that triple-edged sword of debauchery that can so easily ruin a young life. And his stash of savings, hoarded away since childhood, had taken a severe battering. Josh was acutely aware of the meaningless nature of this trio of excess. Wine was eschewed by the young Australian man and the beer tasted similar to impure ditchwater after a dozen or so bottles. The women were young girls, displaying an easy carelessness with their virtue, most of whom could outdrink, out-fight, out-swear, and outlast Josh in any drunken sexual encounter; and the word song would most certainly not be used by their neighbours in any description of their noisy renditions of popular and very bawdy vocal offerings.

The month of June in Canberra can be bitterly cold. The soft mattress on his double bed and a heavy duvet tucked around his body made the boy feel as if he was cocooned within a warm, safe haven; sheltered from the wicked world of reality, responsibility, ambition or meaningful employment. Most mornings he was aware of his mother getting up to start the early morning feeding session. There were many hungry animals on the family's property and an animal lover does not often enjoy the luxury of a lie-in. Often, Josh considered jumping smartly out of bed and helping his mother with her routine chores; or even of getting up especially early and making her a cup of tea - 'One of these days'. His intentions towards this good deed were about as sincere as his daily promise to himself; to give up the heavy drinking sessions with his pals. Such promises, made late in the day and crouched over the enormous kitchen table, head in hands, unwashed, undressed and reeking of alcohol, lasted well into the afternoon: at which time a miraculous recovery descended upon him, clearing his mind and making room for *'Just one more night'*.

But this was the day. For the very first time in his life Josh was about to accept the responsibility of rousing himself from his bed. Until this momentous occasion, his mother had never failed to get him up in time for whatever activity the day held in store for him, from school to rugby practice. The luminous face of the alarm clock, from which the strident bells had never before been known to sound, showed 05.30; and Josh groaned. The boy turned over in his bed and looked out of the window. The house was far enough from the public road to render the drawing of curtains unnecessary. 'Bloody hell, it's still dark,' Josh muttered to himself. 'What time does it get light?' Suddenly realising that he knew absolutely nothing about the early hours of the day, Josh felt a brief second of shame. 'At least the bloody *roos* are up and about.' Josh had noticed in the gloom of the early morning that the front lawn was crowded with half a dozen large marsupials, busily chewing on the lush green grass and casually leaving their droppings in their wake. Animal offerings in exchange for food, the presence of which never failed to enrage his father.

A supreme effort saw the young Josh on to his feet. Wobbly legs, aching head, mouth like a gorilla's armpit and bursting for a pee, the boy staggered to the bathroom, bouncing off the walls on unsteady pins. But he had made it - up and about and ready for action. Unfortunately, akin with any other teenager, his ablutions were noisy, lengthy, and totally oblivious of his father's endless reminders. 'Be careful with the water; turn off the lights; shut the doors quietly; and remember that there are other people living in this bloody zoo.' Consequently, his mother had an earlier start to her day than was customary and his father had a real strop going when he left for work. *'Pity those poor blighters at his office today,'* thought Josh.

But this really was the day. And shortly after 08.30, Josh left the house. His father had managed a brief 'See you boy' as he left for work. *'No doubt glad to see the back of me,'* mused Josh, mistaking his father's sadness and brevity for gruffness.

Unable to actually bid her son farewell, his mother had escaped into her own little world with the horses, busily mucking out and feeding as if this was to be a normal day; and not really the day that saw her son leaving the family nest. Of similar mind, Josh was grateful to his mother; he could not actually face saying goodbye.

Avoiding the badly soiled lawn, Josh headed off down the long, twisting drive to the public road where he would wait for his best pal to pick him up and take him to the bus terminus in Canberra's Civic Centre. Abreast of the large pond, lifeless in the stillness of a windless day, Josh turned and looked back towards the house. 'Damn!' There was his mother, sitting atop her favourite horse, hand shielding her eyes from the brightness of the early morning Sun. He saw the Aussie wave, a hand brushing away bugs and flies from her face; but he knew that it was a hand brushing away a tear. His own firmly held emotions got the better of him and he felt the warm tears streaming down his face. 'Shit!' Australia's favourite word blasted from his mouth and fearful of racing back to embrace his mother, he turned and forced his legs to move onwards.

And this was the day that Mr Joshua Templeton became Ordinary Seaman Templeton, RAN. Leaving his home was turning into the hardest thing that he had ever attempted but with his mind open wide in expectation of a world of change, and his heart already heavy with an aching longing, he left his home. But his heart would soon lighten; and he had not the slightest inkling of religious thoughts or out-of-this-world sensations.

MOUNT TOKACHI, JAPAN. SEPTEMBER 2003.

Vespa orientalis. As Queen of her colony she was a huge specimen of what is more commonly known as the Oriental Hornet.

The large black and yellow gasters of her lower body appeared glazed, as if recently doused in water, and they reflected the rays of the Sun in all directions. After her latest marathon mating session, she needed to rest and regain her strength. The bodies of her numerous male suitors lay around her in droves; not one had survived the encounter with the oversized Queen. Her huge body pulsed; content at last that her body was fertilized and ready to start producing a replacement batch of eggs in a few short weeks. A strange humming sound, way above the range of frequencies audible to the human ear, emanated from her nodding, bobbing head. With a body length of almost forty-five millimetres and a wingspan of some one hundred millimetres, she was twice the size of any other insect in her surrounding area.

As an inexperienced, newly fertilized female, she had started to build her nest in the hollow of an old tree many months before, in the early spring of 2003. She remembered the ground leaping and trembling violently, the plume of dark clouds of dust and ash spewing from the mountaintop, and the strange rumblings from what seemed the centre of the Earth. Her whole body had fluttered in fear as the tree fell and she attempted to flee before it struck the ground. But she was not quick enough and the tree, together with the beginnings of her nest, had fallen to the ground, spilling her efforts into a small cave below.

In the months that followed, she had rebuilt her nest inside the cave using chewed tree bark. Each individual cell was painstakingly constructed in horizontal rows to form combs. She had deposited a single egg into each of the fifty sealed cells and after about a week, the eggs had hatched into larvae. The next two weeks were a frenzy of activity for her, foraging for insects and attacking other colonies to feed the ever-growing larvae. Depositing the eggs seemed to give her a newly-found strength and this increasing bodily strength made her bold. She had no option but to make the attacks alone and her initial feelings of fear and trepidation whilst attacking the nest of the wild honeybees had dwindled and died as her body grew larger. Replaced with feelings of elation, and a blood lust fuelled by an urgent need to feed the larvae from her loins, she had revelled in the many killing sprees.

Blood pulsing; heart racing; eyes glazed with concentration and sheer joy; she had pressed home her attacks with devastating finality. Alone, she marched into the nests of her prey, stinging left, right and stabbing deeply, casting the heavily-armed defenders casually to one side. She killed relentlessly, decimating her victims with a deep feeling of joy and satisfaction, even when she knew that she had killed more than enough to provide food for her colony. Once engaged, her natural urge to kill was rampant and could not be assuaged until there existed nothing left to kill.

Eventually the larvae sealed themselves inside their individual cells, slowly morphing into adult hornets and eating their way through their restraining walls. This was her coronation, a time of great joy; and she personally greeted each of her offspring as they slowly emerged into the world.

Rest. The Queen welcomed her inactivity and for many days after the first of her colony had appeared she had remained motionless, regaining her strength and marshalling her thoughts. She now had fifty willing workers to carry out the everyday tasks of caring for the nest and the colony; foraging for food; nest building; cleaning; and caring for future generations. Only one task would she reserve solely for herself; that of producing eggs. As Queen of the colony, this was her legitimate right and only death would prevent her from exercising that right.

Already she felt the internal pains of increasing growth. She did not know why. Every other member of her colony was also growing; they were much bigger than others of their species that they encountered on their hunting expeditions. The huge Queen could find no reason to complain about this strange, abnormal growth. Her colony was bigger and stronger than any other on the mountain and they could feed on whatever they chose.

Despite her small army of willing subjects, she still felt the urge to lead her troops into battle. A warrior Queen, larger than any other insect on the mountain, she led the merciless attacks with a ferocity normally associated with much larger predators.

Man. She knew of these large beings. Although few came close to her nesting site, she had seen them on her foraging flights. The chatter of their method of communications was meaningless and faintly irritating to her at first. However, something strange was happening to her; suddenly she knew their words; she could understand their meaning. She had been dozing after a particularly fierce, satisfying and bloodthirsty raid on an adjacent hornets' nest when the first comprehensible words that she ever heard burst into her consciousness. *'Man is your enemy. Do not fear him, but pass him by. When the time is right, I will have much work for you. Build your kingdom and I will instruct you how to train your subjects into an army.'*

ON THE SURFACE OF THE EARTH, ABOVE THE MAUSOLEUM OF THE VERGUIDE. 4562. (AUC2452).

Cast your mind into the future. Way, way ahead, into the unknown that is man's fate.

The surface of the Earth is bleak and desolate. Neither a blade of grass nor the decaying stump of a long-dead tree can be seen in any direction. The surface is completely flat, for even the hills have been sandblasted into the coarse gritty mixture of sand and pebbles that covers the entire globe. Once green, lush and vibrant, teeming with life of all kinds and a glittering blue jewel in space, with seemingly unlimited sources of water and millions of square kilometres of productive soil: the surface of the Earth is now dead.

At this moment, all is still, an all too brief window of respite from the raging dust storms that almost continually sweep around the surface of our world. Space and solitude, on the surface of our world, is not difficult to find in the year 4562, for very few of Earth's inhabitants venture to above ground levels. Only the very brave and adventurous of its people can muster sufficient courage to attempt survival in the searing heat from the gigantic Sun that engulfs the heavens. Those that do make the effort, despite being invisible to other human eyes and encased in the latest heat shrouds, still feel the tremendous heat and remain for only a few hours at a time.

The Presence gazed around the surface, its mind drifting forwards in time, dreaming of the day when the surface of this once gloriously vivid planet might return to its former blaze of colour. Full Life Span Clone (FLSC) number 310-75-1610 was not recognisable as male or female; the requirement for genital organs had been removed when the messy method of reproduction by sexual intercourse had been rendered obsolete.

As the Presence looked upwards towards the Sun, eyes protected from the glare by a lightweight solar shroud, it took a moment to reflect upon what conclusions earlier generations of Earthlings would have drawn from the frightening closeness of this, their source of all earthly energy.

Gone forever were the misguided beliefs guarded so jealously and fiercely by the Earth's occupants prior to the 21st century, when its peoples would, no doubt, have looked up at the only star in our Solar System expanding with such painful, agonizing slowness in the sky with each new millennium. For those diverse and warlike people would have gazed heavenward and mumbled incantations to some mythical outside agency. They would have wrapped themselves in sombre clothing and consumed small quantities of bread and wine, which they believed symbolized the blood and flesh of the lead character in what must have been the greatest work of fiction ever written.

Earth's occupants were now a drastically transformed species. But each individual clung just as fiercely to their existence as an Earthling, as did their predecessors to their religious beliefs. However, the Earth-person of the 46th century did not associate himself with an area of land on the surface upon which he may have been born, nor did he pay homage to any deity or artefact. He saw himself as an occupant of what is now an ugly, inhospitable planet, at least on the surface; and he worked only for the good of that planet.

Many concepts had changed over the past several thousand years; and here, the Presence had to recalculate the passage of time into the 46th century concept of time.

Man was now intelligent enough to recognise that the mythical characters awarded godly status were nothing more than a clever idea to control what were then the uneducated masses that populated the Earth. Religion, as recognized by any of our forefathers, had died a natural death almost two thousand years ago, as had the practice of identifying oneself as an American, a German or a Frenchman, etc. For those land masses no longer existed.

Torrential storms and rising seas, caused by the melting of the Earth's ice caps, had flooded the globe many years previously, forcing the residents of our planet to find alternative accommodation. At that time, the expression 'global warming' had accompanied the wagging finger of the supposedly infallible, all-knowing scientists and wise men; caused undoubtedly, they cried in unison, by the use of fossil fuels. Not one of these highly educated persons recognised, or even considered, the possibility of the Earth being sucked inexorably closer to its mother star. For such movement by a planetary mass could not be identified by their technology and for many, many years, they pointed their accusing fingers at the use of the Earth's fast depleting stores of fossil fuels. The Earth's people, most of whom still belonged to the dark ages, were fleeced by the fossil-fuel commercial conglomerations who were hell-bent on amassing as much of their ancient monetary systems as possible. Governments of the day were influenced by these vast business concerns, eagerly thrusting their collective noses into the pigs' trough by exacting exorbitant taxes from the masses for fossil-fuel products. History would not treat them kindly, for it is recorded that the profiteers, both individuals and governmental groups, are regarded as monsters who misused a global resource in a mindless quest for financial gain.

Deep in thought, the FLSC allowed its mind to cast itself backwards in time. It saw that the average occupant of the Earth in the 2nd millennium AD was not just a greedy person but also a vain and covetous animal that gave little thought to the feelings of his or her fellow human beings, let alone the safety or well-being of their planet.

Future archaeologists will regard the period from zero to 2100 AD as homo sapien's Machiavellian Man. A period during which his cunning, unscrupulous attitude and amoral nature blended perfectly with his quarrelsome tendencies. His tiny brain, with its finite capacity for storage and retention, had developed little from early Cro-Magnon Man. Manipulated by his leaders, both political and religious, he was little more than a lemming, following blindly along mankind's path to final annihilation, sublimely content with his portion of daily bread, handed down to him by his leaders.

Notwithstanding Machiavellian Man's other faults, foremost in his character defects were his vicious and warlike inclinations. For thousands upon thousands of years, the people of this once beautiful planet had waged war amongst themselves. Not in defence of their planet; not always in defence of their lives; and certainly not always in defence of their freedom and liberty. What then might explain this mass execution of so many Earthlings? What might be said or written to justify such wanton disregard for human life to the people of the 46th century? Surely, there can be no logical reason? It must therefore be a human madness? A weakness in the human mentality? Some long forgotten missing link in the DNA chain, when man evolved from the apes? Perhaps, way back when the bipedal primate Australopithecus first walked the Earth, a cytotoxic T cell[1] gained prominence in the human brain? But no, unfortunately no such convenient justification is available.

Much more sinister was the true reason. Religion. That mindless belief in some supernatural being. A supernatural being capable of creating and controlling the Universe and everything within it. This was the root cause of early man's bloodthirsty encounters. A child-like belief in fairies, goblins, super heroes, mythological monsters, ghosts and the supernatural. And there lay the problem for a 46th century Earthling. For how could such a deity so strongly deny the anthropocentric[2] order of nature? If such a deity created man in His own image, then He must have been a cruel and violent person. Surely, if Our Lord made man in a true (and by extension one assumes an exact) likeness of himself, then he must have had the same limited lifespan as His followers. But if He lives forever, as by popular religious belief and dogma mankind was led to believe, then He obviously cheated on the human race. If man is indeed a true and exact image of Him, then He cast off the mortal links with this life after having lived His three score and ten, long, long, ago and is comfortably ensconced in heaven with the rest of the Holy Trinity. If He is long gone, He will of course never return, unless one accepts the possibility of reincarnation.

Mankind was led to believe in a holy state after death, whereby man's soul toddled off to heaven for a rest, to await rebirth, and that

---

[1]Cytotoxic T cell. A killer cell.

[2]Anthropcentric. Regarding humans as the universe's most important entity.

there exists no pool of additional souls available. Hinting that the only way to achieve salvation and transmigration was to be a good and loyal follower of God, during what was a fleeting moment of life.

Machiavellian Man might have argued that in the event that an existing soul returns to this Earth in a defective body, or a body that becomes defective through disease, etc., then such practices as euthanasia should have been encouraged rather than scorned. Reasoning might suggest that if in life a person had contracted a painful and intrusive illness, better to press the button, take an early bath and get into the return queue nice and early. Savings on archaic health services, social security budgets, etc., would have been enormous.

But if Machiavellian Man had accepted that humankind was made in a true image of their heavenly father, and that they all sprang from Adam's randy episode with Eve, then what of poor old Mr Darwin's theory?

The Presence found it difficult to comprehend the beliefs and actions of his ancestors and felt a moment of deep regret for the countless lives lost in the senseless worship of a seemingly endless list of deities and for the woeful ignorance of its predecessors that even applied anthropomorphism[3] to some of its religious icons.

A metaphorical shudder passed through the invisible body of the Presence. Its powerful databanks supplied the information about his forebears but the systems, no matter how powerful, could not make it comprehend how such a creature as Machiavellian Man could be quite so morally base. Such beliefs and behaviour were anathema to the 46th century Presence, where altruism, empathy, tolerance, freedom of choice and the simple belief in one's total commitment to the safety and well-being of planet Earth were the bedrocks of its society.

With the shudder came a realization that it had been on the surface too long. Already a feeling of extreme discomfort had started to permeate throughout its invisible body. Allowing its mind to drift back into the past was one of its greatest failings and this time its preoccupation with the times gone by had dragged it into a region of great danger.

At this time in Earth's history, the huge Sun was both an enemy

---

[3]Anthropomorphism.   Attribution of a human form, human characteristics, or human behaviour to nonhuman things.

and the provider of all earthly energy. Unknowingly, the Presence had allowed its concentration to wander. The anti-gravity system had assumed the fallback setting of levitate and the Presence, cocooned within its heat-shroud, had risen to some three thousand metres, a dangerous height. A simple thought process instructed the heat-shroud system to return to datum level; that is the first level of safety below ground zero.

As the shroud descended to safety, the Presence felt a moment of extreme sadness, as it did on every occasion that it had to descend below ground. However, this moment of regret was always quickly confounded by the joy it felt when confronted with the familiar vista of its magical underground world.

AUTHOR'S NOTE.

In the telling of this story, I will use a literary convenience that I have dubbed the Thread.

It will be used at the beginning of most chapters to achieve several aims. To introduce a new section or fill a gap from an older section; to explain events, places, and ideas; or to prepare the reader for a change in direction of the story.

As such, the introduction that follows can be regarded as the first Thread.

INTRODUCTION.

Mankind's safety on planet Earth is under threat and the future holds a multitude of problems for the human race. At the beginning of the 21st century, many people would argue that the single potentially most destructive threat to our planet is global warming. Others might consider that there are more urgent threats to the continuation of life. For example, more intelligent mutating viruses, more virulent forms of immune deficiency diseases or the possible hell of an airborne bubonic plague.

And yet others might consider yet more threats which might endanger life on our planet: nuclear warfare, the final depletion of the world's supply of fossil fuels, the ever-spiralling increase in the cost of government or some cataclysmic event such as a collision with some yet unknown space object. All of these threats are real; they exist today.

But there is a greater danger. Over population. The populations of both China and India already exceed one billion and planet Earth struggles to provide sustenance for some six and a half billion souls. A conservative estimate suggests world population levels of ten billion by 2050 and possibly as many as twenty billion by the beginning of the next century.

Maybe our planet is capable of producing sufficient food to sustain twenty billion people. But is there enough water? All terrestrial life depends on this liquid. To maintain a decent quality of life a human being requires approximately eighty litres of fresh water each day. The Americans, the largest users of fresh water in the world, use around three hundred and eighty litres per person, per day, more than four times the daily requirement. Taking a middle line, if each person uses one hundred litres each day, the world will have to provide some two thousand billion litres of fresh water every single day of every single year from the year 2100 ad infinitum.

Already the hugely overcrowded south of England suffers from water shortages. And this is without the expected influx of immigrants and refugees in the near future.

CHAPTER 1
THE BEGINNING

THREAD:

Sometimes the most innocent of activities can land a person in the strangest of circumstances.

SINGAPORE. 1962.

'Thy name is Belial.'
 I heard the words, spoken quite clearly. But the spoken word was not quite how the information passed into my mind. It was more a sensation of the words and the information was not passed to me word-by-word but rather as a block of information which mimicked the clicking sounds of a very fast teleprinter.

I felt no alarm. I was warm, comfortable and as far as I could tell, uninjured. It was not dark, and the temperature was pleasantly warm. The surface on which I lay was dry and soft. I heard no more, drifting back into unconsciousness.

In the year 1961, I was serving with the Royal Navy in Singapore. Based at the Royal Navy Wireless Telegraphy Station, Kranji, I was a leading radio operator working shifts in this then active communications centre (comcen). The only given name that I answered to in those days was that of Victor Yewly, nicknamed Volly - short for volatile Victor.

Most naval personnel win a nickname at some time or another. Many are antonyms and sometimes this nickname can stick to a person throughout a naval career span of some twenty-two years. Mine was awarded because of my imperturbable nature. I was extremely easy going and rarely lost my temper or got upset about anything. Seen as having a slow wick, I was difficult to rouse and calmly accepting of all taunts and jibes. Usually I explained my sweet nature by pointing out that I had, for several years in the RN, had the piss taken out of me by experts!

I was twenty-two years of age. Of slightly below average height - circa one point seven metres tall - and weighing in at about seventy-five kilograms, stockily built and with dark hair which I kept at just above crew-cut length. And there was little about me in terms of identifying features, neither large scars, tattoos nor abnormal features marked me as me.

Comcen Kranji was an almost autonomous outpost of HMS *Terror*, which was the main naval establishment in Singapore, located near the dockyard. It was situated a few kilometres along the Bukit Timah road - which provided the main road link between the causeway across to Malaya and Singapore City. At the time, Kranji was a much sought after posting for naval communication ratings.

I had been in Singapore since April 1961, at first unaccompanied by my family. This initial period of lonesomeness was not by choice but for two very good reasons; firstly that my wife was expecting our first child in May and secondly because the Navy did not ship out wives and children until proof of accommodation was provided.

My first problem in finding a place to live was judging just when to commence rental. My wife Tracey was not due to deliver our first baby until about the middle of May and the child would not be allowed to fly until it was about six weeks old. Ideally, therefore, I needed to find somewhere from about the end of June. Finding such accommodation on a crowded tropical island like Singapore, with a large contingent of resident British forces, was particularly difficult and I had searched for several weeks before finding a bungalow in the nearby village of Serangoon, one of the more popular areas for serving personnel.

The circumstances surrounding the discovery of this rather special bungalow, in such a select area, were unusual. Earlier in my naval career I had served on the frigate HMS *Redpole*, the Navy's then navigational training ship, based at Portsmouth. One of my shipmates at that time had been a senior electrical rating who maintained the serviceability of the ship's radio transmitters and receivers; one REA1 Jack Prewlot.

Towards the middle of June, I had been instructed to report to HMS *Terror*; there was some problem with my pay. Consequently, on one of my rest days from shift work, I had bummed a lift with the driver of the naval tilly[4] making a mail run into the base. This tilly delivered and collected the mail and various other items to and from the naval base and dockyard on a twice-daily basis and was extremely useful to personnel who did not own personal transport. Once at *Terror*, and having plenty of time to complete my business, I ambled down to the pay office in the bright sunshine, enjoying the immaculate presentation of the establishment.

Shift work is a tiring business and with nothing to occupy my mind I was feeling dozy. Decidedly lethargic, I was gazing around at the others in the room and could feel my chin dropping on to my chest. The door to the pay office opened and the next in the queue stood up and made his way through the open door. The man exiting the office was none other than Jack Prewlot. We shook hands and exchanged enough information to explain each other's presence at *Terror*. Accompanied by his wife, Jack had been in Singapore for well over a year and had recently been allocated a married quarter. He was moving out of a bungalow in Serangoon and was willing to introduce me to the owner in the hope that I might take over the rental.

Meeting the owner had been a very pleasant event. He was a very rich and polite Malayan and we met in the soon to be vacated bungalow. This extremely friendly gentleman readily agreed to transfer the rental to me and, whilst I had his attention, I raised the possibility of transferring the property to official status by asking the Navy to accept it as a naval hiring. This meant that the property would have to meet certain standards, following which the Navy would undertake to pay the rent and guarantee continued occupancy, deducting a nom-

---

[4] Tilly. Naval mini-bus.

inal amount from the current occupant's salary.

What a stroke of luck! Both in meeting Jack and finding accommodation in which my family and I could spend the whole of our time in Singapore, without the disrupting business of moving. A few weeks after this stroke of good fortune, on Monday 3rd July, 1961, my wife and new baby daughter Alicia joined me on the beautiful tropical island and we all settled into what is called, in Navy terms, a married accompanied draft.

Kranji worked a four-watch system, each watch doing what was known as the forty-eight about. The system involved four teams of men, or watches in Navy speak, and covered a rotational four-day period. Working day one from 12.00 to 20.00 - the afternoon watch, and on day two from 08.00 to 12.00 - the forenoon watch, and again that same night from 20.00 to 08.00 - the dreaded all-night-on; with days three and four off duty.

My watch was C watch. It consisted of a radio supervisor in charge of the watch, with three leading radio operators, twelve or so more junior operators and four Asians. The RS in charge was Archy Turpin, obviously nicknamed Dick. The two other LROs, besides me, were Victor Collins, nicknamed Jumper, and William Stiles, 'Call me Nobby'. The others in the watch had a colourful and descriptive mixture of nicknames from 'shit-face' to 'shagger' - don't ask!

Each of the four watches was an individual, closely-knit community. Each community had no choice but to work together but they also on many occasions chose to play together. Off watch activities, apart from inter-watch sporting contests, included a whole raft of events, from sightseeing outings to bottle parties and banyans. Such occasions were organized on a fairly regular basis and most of the watch would make every effort to attend.

Time passes very quickly in happy circumstances. About a year after the arrival of my family on Friday 18th August, 1962, Nobby Stiles, being the banyan organiser, made arrangements for a day out on one of the many uninhabited islands around the coast of Singapore. Choosing to arrange the expedition on the watch's second day of rest, since most people are by then fully rested following the long twelve-hour night shift, the list of takers included all but two of the watch. Each attendee was expected to donate twenty dollars towards the cost of boats, booze and food, a trifling amount at eight dollars to the pound sterling. Beer cards, permitting the purchase of a set monthly allowance of duty-free beer, were also collected from each person to enable the purchase of bottles of the local Tiger and Anchor beer from the Naafi shop in Serangoon.

The banyan was scheduled to start from a place called Punggol Point (known to Kranji's sailors as Pongo Point), where small boats were available for hire to ferry groups to the neighbouring islands. At the stipulated time, everyone arrived in their cars, mainly old bangers, with families and whatever provisions they had been told to bring. Nobby brought the booze, loaded into the back of his Ford Consul, with his wife and son crammed into the front passenger seat. Several of the group had brought large aluminium baths filled with ice, into which the bottles of beer would be placed when the group arrived at their chosen island.

The large crowd at Pongo Point attracted the attention of the local boatmen and they crowded around hoping for a fare. Nobby, an old hand at negotiating with these boatmen, made his selection from the available boats, selecting those that looked the most seaworthy, and made arrangements for the whole group to be ferried across to Coney Island. Money did not change hands until the return trip; the local boatmen had notoriously poor memories, particularly if they were paid in advance, and were not averse to forgetting to come and get you.

The chosen island for our latest banyan was a new one for the watch and everyone was looking forward to this new adventure, particularly the children. A trouble-free crossing over flat-calm waters saw the entire watch deposited on the soft sand of the beach about forty minutes later. Everyone was enjoying themselves immensely, even so early in the day, and all, including wives and children, helped with carrying the small mountain of provisions beyond the high water mark, clearly marked by a dark line of rotting vegetation washed high up the beach. Our illustrious leader, Dick Turpin, usually carried out the duties of chef and he busied himself getting a fire going and setting up a homemade barbeque, one or other of the watch assisting him when he yelled for help - or another beer.

It was a most glorious day. A hot Sun with a slight breeze, just sufficient to keep the temperature below cooking level. I could see the children splashing around in the shallow water, a paler, softer blue slowly darkening as the water increased in depth. Very few brave sailors ventured past this dark blue line; strangely, many feared deep water, myself amongst them. I could see Tracey undressing Alicia. When not splashing around in the shallows with her mother, or being carted around the island on my shoulders, the baby would spend the day protected from the burning Sun under a large umbrella.

For some time I lay on the beach topping up my tan. I had already consumed a couple of bottles of the strong Anchor beer and was feeling a tad woozy. Unlike most sailors, I was not a heavy drinker. Don't get me wrong - I did enjoy a pint or two, or three, maybe four, but that's my limit; and I could not handle strong spirits. In Navy grog I could find no pleasure; the one hundred and fifty percent rum, although diluted by two parts of water, left me half pissed and the taste was pretty grim too; more like liquid molasses than rum. Fortunately, as far as I was concerned, whilst serving in Kranji and living out of barracks, I was not entitled to the daily issue of the potent brew.

The hot Sun was burning into my back and I knew that if I extended my bronzy-bronzy session any longer I would be in serious danger of a severe dose of sunburn - I had fallen into that trap some years before on my first visit to the tropics and I had no wish to repeat that painful experience.

Looking around at my watch *oppos*[5], I could see that most had now returned from their cooling dip in the sea and were flopping down on towels or lilos. Some of the young mothers were still in the shallow water playing with their youngsters and one or two of the older mothers were trying to coax their offspring into the shade for another application of sunscreen. Next to me, Tracey was dozing, for she had to take every opportunity for rest as it came along, driven always by Alicia's needs.

Quite why I do not know, but I suddenly had an overpowering urge to go walkabout. I did not want to disturb my wife so I got up, drifted across to Dicky Turpin and told him that I was off to do a bit of exploration; just wander around and see what I could find. Our elderly leader, he must have been all of thirty-five years old, knew me well. I enjoy nothing more than poking around on the beach with a stick, lifting any rock or log to see what wildlife lives beneath, and

---

[5]*Oppos*. Friends in Navy speak.

Dicky just nodded. 'Don't be too long, or you will miss the scran.' He tossed the words at my departing back.

The island was not very big, roughly circular with a diameter of no more than five hundred metres. Except for one or two lovely sandy beaches, the whole circumference of the island was covered with an almost impenetrable covering of mangrove swamp, the dense bushes and long roots intertwining a metre above ground level. During the long night watches in the comcen, I had often passed the small hours chatting with the Malayan operators and they had often brought up gruesome local legends from Singapore's chequered history. One such legend involved an island off the coast, similar to the one that I was currently traipsing around, stick in hand, poking hither and thither.

The legend, very briefly, was that of a lost burial chamber. Apparently, in the year dot the people of Singapore believed that dead bodies attracted the strange and deadly viruses that everyone knew floated around in the air, waiting for a human host. Fearful of disease and pestilence raging through their population, the living immediately transported their dead to a nearby island for burial. Legend had it that deep caves existed on some of the islands, with secret entrances known only to the headmen of the local kampongs. The caves were so deep that the diseases could not escape. Sometimes, and here I had noticed that the eyes of my Asian friend took on a sterner look, not only the dead found their way into these chambers. Listening to the elderly Asian operator telling me this story, his eyes wide with spiritual awareness, I though it all a load of tosh!

Just for the shortest of moments, my mind froze at the memory of those local legends and I stood up and looked around me. I could have sworn that I had heard a soft moan or the call of an animal or sea bird. The noise was not repeated so I pushed it from my mind and continued with digging at the root of a mango tree. The sand was very soft and I had got down to about a foot deep already, thoroughly enjoying myself more and more the deeper I got. In moments such as those my mind usually returned to its boyish state; I became very excited and my imagination soared skyward as would a rocket; pirates, buried treasure - yahoo! I was going to be rich!

My mind was solidly locked-on to the fairies' frequency. I had already bought a new car and a new house, and a glamorous new wardrobe for Tracey; I had more money than you can shake a stick at. In the process of designing a special wardrobe for Tracey's shoes (I knew that most women do not have much affection for shoes but Tracey would buy a new pair every day if she could afford it), I heard the noise again.

Similar to the soft, sighing sound of the wind. But different, unlike any sigh that I had heard before; more akin to a rippling sigh - at the time I thought it sounded like a sigh interrupted, almost imperceptibly, by very fast Morse code. It was slightly louder this time and I turned my head toward the source of the sound. Nothing, or at least nothing that I could see.

'Belial, o chosen one, art thou with senses?' The soft, slightly Jewish-sounding voice interrupted my reverie. Semi-conscious, I had been trying to retrace my steps to this moment in time, hoping for some explanation for my present confusion. The voice annoyed me greatly and I fancied that it obeyed my unspoken thought, *'Keep silence!'* - a fine naval command, short and concise, used to keep the *erks*[6] quiet when on parade. Closing my eyes tightly, I forced my mind back to reviewing my most recent actions; for some reason it was tremendously important that I understand the circumstances surrounding my being where I was.

I had been considering returning to Tracey and the rest of my watch on the beach. Yes - slowly my mind drifted back in time and whilst I was looking around I noticed a large copse of palm trees. The gently swaying stand of trees was about two hundred metres away and, unless my eyes were deceiving me, there was also the shape of a building. Odd, yes - but I had heard from my Asian *oppos* that the Japanese, during their occupation of Singapore, had built rest and recreation facilities on some of the islands for their troops. Perhaps this was the remains of one such rest camp.

Glancing down at my wrist I wanted to check the time. When on foraging expeditions I am totally out of it; time is meaningless and I can spend hours just poking around. The watch was not on my wrist. Of course! I had taken it off when sunbathing. Being a tad vain I am fond of getting an all-over tan if I can; or at least as all-over as good manners and taste dictate. Goodness only knows what the time must be. I could not see any of my compatriots and there was no sign of

---

[6]Erks. Ordinary sailors.

smoke from the direction in which I thought my group had settled but it was still full daylight.

The lack of smoke was some indication of how much time had passed. The barbeque fire must have reduced itself to hot coals, ready for cooking, and I decided that I had left Tracey alone for far too long. About to make my way back to the beach I turned - and that is when I heard the noise again, a little louder and more insistent. OK, so I'm a slave to curiosity and pushing aside my parental responsibilities, I headed off towards the stand of palm trees, intent on exploring whatever ruins might remain there.

Although I knew that I really should not have been doing it, I pressed on towards my goal. As I entered the copse of palm trees, I was amazed to see the ruins of what must have been a quite substantial building. Most of the walls were still intact but doors, windows and the roof were long gone. Moving into the enclosure I could see that the floors had been concreted; unusual in that part of the world where more natural materials were usually used for flooring. Not only that, but the concrete was remarkably thick, probably two hundred millimetres, much more solid than it needed to be. Giving the matter a little thought I assumed that the Japanese had built the place and that they must have had a plenitude of sand and cement! However, what struck me as odd was that the concrete was broken - and I don't mean just badly cracked. It was smashed, as if some tremendous force from below had hurled the concrete base into the air. Large pieces stood at all angles, some standing on end and reaching for the clear blue sky; the area had all the appearance of an earthquake.

This was my own personal heaven. Huge lumps of concrete to investigate; there was bound to be a great deal to interest me here. Parental duty now dismissed entirely from my mind, I set off into the haphazard scene of destruction. More time was frittered away as I meandered aimlessly from one lump of concrete to the next. Suddenly, in my peripheral vision, I saw a large and beautifully coloured lizard scuttle across in front of me, disappearing behind one of the largest lumps of flooring. Such a wonderful specimen of wildlife was a bonus and I dashed after the creature, determined to get a closer look at it. As I raced around the upturned mass of stonework, and I remember thinking it was almost as high as a door, the deck opened up beneath me; and I dropped.

Alfred Leonard

I have no idea how far I fell but the journey seemed to take several minutes. Maybe my mind just stopped working whilst I fell and it just seemed a long time. As I fell something struck me as very odd. The sides of the shaft were smooth, almost as if they were made of marble, or rubbed smooth by constant use; and what I thought was a deep outer shine appeared to be an inner translucent glow. That was my last memory and whatever happened after that mattered little; for I at last felt ready to face up to whatever had been trying to attract my attention.

No sooner had I decided that I was ready to listen than the voice started again. *'Belial, I wilt speak with thee, arise from thy slumber and behold me.'* From this point on I will dispense with attempting to repeat the speaker's quaint and antiquated mode of speech, mainly for the sake of clarity but also because it spooked me somehow.

CHAPTER 2
BELIAL FIRST

THREAD:

We are not the only occupants of our Universe. Unbeknownst to man, there is an 11th planet in our Solar System.

CONEY ISLAND, SINGAPORE. 18TH AUGUST, 1962.

My first priority - now that I was once again fully conscious - was to check that I was intact. I sat up and looked down at my body. When I had left Tracey on the beach I had been wearing swimming shorts, a T-shirt and a pair of flip-flops on my feet. Lying on a raised dais, shorts and T-shirt were still intact but my footwear had disappeared. Having fallen for such a long period of time I expected to be quite badly injured, if not dead; but as far as I could tell I was completely unscathed. Not a mark on me. Looking upwards to where I expected to see the roof of the cave I could see nothing; a trick of the eye maybe, or a hint of great height. But there was no sign of daylight.

My eyes soaked up my immediate surroundings. I still could not see who had been talking to me. There was not the slightest indication of life; but scattered around the floor below me there was considerable evidence of death. Bones, skulls and pieces of broken timber, piled up about a metre deep; clear evidence that at some time this place had been used as a burial chamber. However, I felt no fear, apprehension or dismay; I was completely at ease with both my situation and the detritus of the burial ground. My feelings were of relaxed comfort, perfectly content; neither hungry nor thirsty - satiated was exactly how I felt.

I stood up - but that's not entirely true either. I had the notion to stand, the better to survey my whereabouts, but before brain could engage muscles I was on my feet. My first thought was that I had received a knock on the head in my fall but I had no physical indication of such an injury; no bumps, abrasions, aches or pains. *'Pull yourself together, Volly. You must be going do-lally!'* My thought provoked a girlish chuckle from my as yet unseen companion. But here I was standing up and as I looked around the gigantic cave it looked bigger than the whole island. Slightly closer than the roof, I could just make out the surrounding walls but they were a long way away. At first I could not understand it; if the cave was bigger than the island then some of what was above me must be water. Yet the cave was completely dry and warm; strange indeed.

Distracted for just a few moments, and wondering how such a place could exist below sea level, I turned back to inspect the pile of bones. Sitting at my feet was something that had not been there before. The object was totally still, as if made of stone, but as I gazed down upon it the shape and consistency began to change. From what appeared to be a solid blob, the shape took a different form. Taller, slimmer and, as it changed its shape, it quivered and became, in parts, transparent. The shape shimmered like light from a flickering candle and it appeared to be struggling to hold a solid form. Still silent, the shape continued to change very slowly until finally it took on the appearance of a small child, about seven years old.

Frail arms and legs were perfectly formed, complete in every detail, right down to the carefully trimmed finger and toenails. The body was a bright white, similar to that of an albino, and the skin had obviously never been subjected to sunlight. Atop the blob, the head was a different kettle of fish. Not human in any way recognisable to another human but similar to the head of a vulture without the large beak. Deep blue and shiny. The top half of the head was perfectly smooth without the slightest wrinkle or hair follicle. Whilst the bottom half contained what must have been a zillion tiny eyes, covering both the bottom half of the face and what might have been a neck. Except that there was not a neck, not as such; the broad band of eyes around the whole circumference of the head sat squarely on the shoulders of the small body and, of those that I saw in that first glance, all seemed to be looking in different directions. Of other orifices in the head or body I could see no sign; not ears, mouth, nose - and as my own eyes drifted downwards, I could see no sign of genitals.

I was not alarmed. Nor was I surprised to find this naked apparition beside me; it was as if I expected it to be there, part of something about which I had been forewarned. It did not turn its head towards me; nothing moved on the body; but I heard the slightly sibilant voice speak once again. Perhaps it would be more accurate for me to say that I did not actually hear any sound emitted from my new friend; and I did know for an absolute certainty that it was my friend. Let us say, for want of adequate words to describe it otherwise, that information was passed into my brain, not word by word but in large filo-fax sized lumps, transmitted in super-fast Murray[7] code.

It was odd. I had of course heard of computers and the birth of the digital age. But up until a few seconds ago I was not especially *au fait* with computer terminology. And I suddenly understood about digital streams of information and databases; realising that the transfer of data had passed from my friend, directly into my brain in just that way. My brain had been formatted like a digital compact disc and I had no difficulty in accepting this form of communication. Capable of continuing my own thoughts, over and above the transfer of information at a higher level, I realised that my new friend had been preparing my brain to accept whatever information he wanted me to have. I use, and will continue to use the term he, but of course without any clue otherwise there was no way of deciding my friend's gender more accurately.

The stream of data continued to flow into my brain and I understood the process more and more as each moment passed. A more accurate description of the download was that data was burned into my memory. I felt as if my brain had been compartmentalised and

---

[7]Murray code. A code used in automatic telegraphy in the 1960s.

the information was being carefully filed away in the correct folders. Over and above the transfer of all these compartments of information, the creature told me its story.

My new friend claimed to be a resident of a planet called Veruni and before I start his story it is necessary to explain some of the facts transferred to me.

CHAPTER 3
VERUNI

THREAD:

Arcano caelestia; celestial secrets. The people of Earth have been known by many names in their long history. Earthlings, Gaians, Geians and of course by Verunians as the Avoi-Shun. Similarly, the Earth itself has been known, as far as we know, as the Blue Planet, Gaia, Ge and Lazulum. Thought to have been formed a few million years after the Sun's fires first started to burn, it is therefore a little over four billion years old.

That is four thousand million years. Against a human lifespan of some seventy years, the concept of such vast time-spans by the human brain is difficult to comprehend. In fact the human concept of time, that each second passes and is gone forever, is flawed. Time, in Verunian celestial concepts, does not pass. If we accept that our tiny Solar System is the smallest factor within a space community, and that that system is part of the Milky Way Galaxy, which is an infinitesimal part of our known Universe, then we must also accept that our Universe is possibly just the smallest factor within another, much larger space community; *ad infinitum*. At present, space technology can show us only those celestial bodies that have, so far, returned reflected sunlight. Some of that light has travelled for billions of years. But what of those as yet undiscovered, celestial bodies that are tens of billions of kilometres distant? Maybe the light, having left the Sun some four and a half billion years ago, is still travelling towards these distant bodies and may or may not be seen for billions of years to come.

In 1930, Pluto was discovered, and in 2003 the 10th planet in our Solar System will be first sighted. Both are further away from the Sun than any other previously discovered planet; clearly they have not just been born. They were always there; the reflected light from the Sun just took longer to return. But there may be another explanation for the sudden appearance of some planets, based upon the Verunians' radical concept of time.

Infinity - two parallel lines that never meet. But to gain a different concept of time, bend those parallel lines and join them into two concentric circles. Assume that our Universe is part of that circular corridor of infinity, as the Verunians describe the space between the two outer lines. The central core might contain uncountable billions of other circles of infinity, all on different planes and interlinked like a writhing tangle of snakes. In our circle of infinity it can be seen that time passes only as long as it takes anything in that circle to reach its starting point; then it starts again. Given some cataclysmic event it is also possible that dead or dying stars might be forced out of their corridor of infinity into a neighbouring corridor, bursting into new Galaxies or Universes as pieces of space debris as they break up and leaving behind Black Holes in the wake of their sudden appearance. If such disintegrating planetary bodies should enter our circle of infinity, they will at some time in the future start to reflect light from our Sun and will become visible from Earth. Hey presto, a new planet.

SINGAPORE. THE CAVE OF BELIAL FIRST AND EXTRACTS FROM THE DATA TRANSFERRED TO ME. 1962.

As everyone knows, the Universe is made up of an unknown number of Galaxies, each containing many thousands of stars, with each star or stars combining into separate interacting systems with their own orbiting moons. Our Galaxy is the Milky Way and, as part of that, our own Solar System, probably some thirteen billion years old, has only one known star; the Sun. Currently orbiting around the Sun are its ten known moons, travelling at tremendous speeds through space in an anticlockwise direction. These moons are the planets of our Solar System, namely Mercury, Venus, Earth, Mars, Jupiter, Saturn, Uranus, Neptune and Pluto, listed in order of their relative distance from their mother star. Added to this list in 2003 will be the first sighting of 2003UB313, which will subsequently be declared as the tenth planet in our Solar System in 2006 and named Eris.

It is also common knowledge that Earth's moon is believed not to have any orbiting moons of its own. To place Veruni in space imagine it as the Moon's moon; but it does not actually orbit the Moon. It remains fixed, out of sight from Earth, half a million kilometres from the Moon's surface. If you can imagine Veruni permanently fixed to the Moon by a flexible beam, the whole rotating around the Earth so that Veruni is never in view from Earth, you then have a pretty good idea of how my new friend's home behaves in space.

Veruni is man-made. Or at least manufactured by Verunian man. These strange-looking aliens created their own planet many billions of years ago. They had good reason for this forward planning - their existing star, located in our nearest galaxial neighbour of Andromeda, was slowly dying. Preparing to migrate from their original dying star, the Verunians devised a method of using powerful space-bulldozers to sweep up billions of pieces of space debris - gas, dust, and ice, the remains of some gigantic supernova. The end product was, at first, a barren and lifeless Veruni - named after their original homeland. In terms of time, if one accepts that the planets in our own Solar System were created some thirteen billion years ago, followed by the birth of our Sun some nine billion years later, then the Verunians' new planet was created one billion years after the birth of the Sun.

Two billion years later, after careful husbandry by the visiting Verunians, their new planet was ready for occupation. It was similar in size to Pluto, the second smallest planet in our Solar System. Gravity on Veruni is similar to that of the Moon, at one sixth that of Earth, and under Verunian care their new planet blossomed into a densely forested, fertile landscape. With abundant salt-water seas and rainfall, together with a protective atmosphere, it was a careful reproduction of Earth.

Many of the plants and materials were actually taken from Earth during the regular foraging expeditions by Verunian space vehicles and the samples that were collected were taken back to Veruni to be modified and prepared for propagation on their own planet. On rare occasions Earthlings were taken for study by Verunian scientists and a disastrous experiment occurred in earth-year zero AD when a Verunian scientist was left on Earth in what was to be the first and last effort to make direct contact with our human race. Unfortunately, the experiment was a complete failure because the aggressive and hostile Earthlings misinterpreted the good and simple deeds of the Verunian ambassador; they deified the ambassador and put him to death.

From that moment on, the Verunian Guidance Committee decided to avoid and shun the planet that they called Lazulum, named after the deep blue of the lapis lazuli gemstone that they had mined and studied. The people of Earth were to be avoided at all costs and all contact with its people shunned; and they dubbed us the Avoi-Shun.

'So how did Veruni remain hidden from Earth's space probes?' My question had been nothing more than a fleeting thought but Belial First had instantly provided an answer. Verunian technology is many light years in advance of that on Earth and they developed various cloaking systems to keep the existence of their planet hidden from our eyes. The cloaking system took the form of an invisible Verunian spacecraft, stationed between each earth-probe and Veruni, in such a way that the eyes, cameras and sensors within the earth-craft could see everything except their planet.

This sophisticated and highly intelligent life form no longer wished to become involved in inter-planetary activity. Nor did they wish to have further direct contact with the devious and dangerous Avoi-Shun; their watchword became secrecy. They could not, under any circumstances, draw attention to their existence in the Solar System. If their space-craft, which became heavy in the gravity of the Blue Planet, left any indication of their landings, then such marks were obliterated or disguised, sometimes by insignificant replicas of Earthman's decorative crop circles and at other times by larger events such as Verunian-generated earthquakes or tsunamis.

In the one billion years that followed, the new planet progressed much as Earth has done. However, being closer to the Sun than Earth, global warming gradually raised sea levels to such an extent that the whole of Veruni's surface fell below sea level. Over yet further millen-

nia, the intense heat from the Sun dried up the seas and the whole surface of the planet turned to desert, the fine sand blown in every direction by the perpetual hurricane-force solar winds.

The cause of this global warming was not the use of fossil fuels
but solely the heat from the Sun. Three billion years ago, Verunian
scientists did not appreciate that the heat output from the Sun was
still increasing and will continue to rise for the next two hundred billion years. In fact, Verunian experts have concluded that Earth's global warming problems have very little, in galaxian terms, to do with
burning fossil fuels. For these finite earthly resources will eventually
dwindle away; but the problem of global warming will remain. The
reason given by my friend was the continuing rise in temperature of
our star.

Verunian predictions foresee the Sun's temperature continuing to
rise and the rate of increase will rise more steeply in the last few billion years prior to the Sun's output reaching its zenith. During these
final few billion years, the rise in temperature is expected to be by
about 0.1 degree Celsius every decade; and the rising temperatures
will produce a significant increase in the number and magnitude of
those most dangerous, and unpredictable, solar events; solar flares.

As far as the long-term future of the Sun is concerned, those same
experts predict that it, together with its Solar System, will inevitably
suffer a shared fate. After the Sun reaches its hottest point, it will gradually cool over a period of some five hundred billion years. Eventually,
akin with every other organism in nature, it will die; and its destiny
is to remain a gigantic blob of space flotsam until it is ejected from the
Milky Way through a Black Hole. Unless they are lucky enough to be
sucked into the magnetic field of some other star, or their inhabitants
are clever enough to develop the technology to manoeuvre their celestial body, the people occupying the planets of our Solar System will be
forced to commence space hopping to survive; just as the Verunians
have been doing.

To the Verunians, the lifeless surface of their planet was not a
problem, they simply moved underground, designing and building
the systems necessary to provide energy and food. This resourceful
and intelligent race provided a system of dissipating and diffusing
the power from the Sun and would, eventually, return Veruni to its
former green and vibrant appearance. Based upon the predicted life

of our Solar System, Verunians had a rosy future and some seven hundred billion years available to them before they needed to space hop once again. But no, there was a much greater and more urgent problem; they needed to space hop within the next one thousand years. Consequently, there was insufficient time to create another planet.

A new problem but with the same root; the Sun. With their gift of second sight, Verunian mediums had foreseen a gigantic solar flare, millions of times larger than ever seen before. Occurring in about 3010 earth-time, the flare will commence on the far side of the Sun, away from Veruni, Earth and the Moon; but the unprecedented power of the solar seismic waves produced by this solar flare will ripple around the surface of the Sun and burst out, still with incredible force, towards Veruni. By an extreme stroke of bad luck, Veruni will, at that precise moment, be at the nearest point to the Sun in its orbit and the planet will take the full force of the shock. A reprieve for both the Moon and Earth, whose inhabitants will be only too aware of the power of the seismic waves. They will witness the apparent enlargement of the Sun and struggle to find reasons for their salvation.

However, the seismic blast will overwhelm the Verunian station-keeping systems and push the planet out of the Sun's magnetic influence. Cast adrift into cosmic obscurity and certain destruction; and in the process of which returning the planet to its origins; separate particles of gas, dust, and ice - space debris.

Recognizing their sudden vulnerability, the Verunian Chairman, after considerable discussions with his Guidance Committee, decided that Lazulum provided their best chance of survival. With an expected one thousand years to achieve their goal they had many options in establishing contact with the Earthlings. Despite their dislike for the idea, they could have jumped into one of their spacecraft and nipped down to Earth, had a word with the combined world leaders and negotiated a deal. Earthlings, however, were bastards and they could not be trusted. No more able to honour a treaty than urinate into the wind, they were the Avoi-Shun and the very idea of making contact was not a pleasant one.

Having monitored every scrap of intelligence that managed to pass through Earth's ionosphere into space since man first managed to walk erect; the Verunians knew all they needed to know about the Avoi-Shun. Earth leaders knew about their planet's growing problem of overheating. Yet each year the people of the Earth argued about which colour should be regarded as 'in fashion' and huge amounts of their monetary systems and valuable resources were committed to draping the human body in different styles of clothing, instead of directing their money, time, effort and resources towards saving their planet.

Barbarians still, the mentality of Earthlings remained in the dark ages. They still lived in their own individual countries; they were insular and thought only of self-gratification, continuously waging war both amongst themselves and with the inhabitants of other land masses. Each individual country clung desperately to the existence of various fictional super beings; God, Jesus, Allāh and Buddha, to name but a few. A world of sybarites[8]; to the individual Earthling, the greatest joy was to out-do his neighbour or to extract money or some personal gain from individuals, government agencies or commercial conglomerates, preferably dishonestly. Missing entirely from the human psyche was a notion of global-self and most depressing of all, from the Verunian point of view, was that they would never see themselves as an Earthling, an Avoi-Shun, or a Worldman, but were intent upon clinging forever to their own individual national identities.

To the Verunians, the people of Earth had not yet reached a level of intelligence to render them suitable co-habitants of a planet. Annihilation of the Earthlings would have been simple. Verunian weapons, fitted only in their spacecraft, were far more devastating than anything on Earth but war and its associated destruction of life was anathema to the Verunian people.

Thus the Verunian Guidance Committee devised a plan to share Earth in the year 3010; but they would need inside help to achieve this. A guide must be selected from the Earthlings, whose task it would be to steer the planet's populations towards Earth's deterioration to a dead planet. Earthlings must be forced to witness the inevitable devastation of their planet, just as Verunians had witnessed theirs. The Verunians could, of course, install the necessary cloaking, diffusing and dissipating systems to reduce the Sun's output and protect Earth. But they knew that forcing the Earthlings through the traumatic events of global meltdown was the only way to force them to

---

[8]Sybarites. Devoted to luxury and the gratification of sensual desires.

accept their new Verunian co-habitants on Earth.

The Verunians' own move underground, although forced upon them by the heat from the Sun, was not a painless exercise. Their own underground accommodation did not provide for a limitless population and draconian birth control measures were put in place to ensure that their population did not exceed the available living space. The Verunian Guidance Committee had known some five hundred million years ago that their planet would eventually die from solar heat and had carefully prepared themselves for the event. The population of Veruni was little more than fifty million, all that it was possible to transport from their original dying star which had supported a population of some fifty billion. The remainder of the original Verunian population had dispersed around the Galaxies, not from any desire for galactic domination but to give themselves the best chance of survival. Each dispersed group agreed to venture forth alone, not knowing the destination of the other groups of star men, to ensure that in the future a dying planet's population would not suddenly attempt to join another group and, in the process, overwhelm the capabilities of that planet.

Earthlings might regard the original Verunians as a race of eudaemons[9]. Their appearance was similar to Earthlings, although much smaller, none being more than one metre in height. At first they propagated themselves in the same way as humans and their population had peaks and troughs produced by a natural birth rate; but the overall trend was that of a gradual decrease in their numbers.

This peaceful race were exceptionally intelligent and their technological competence increased year by year, enabling them to obtain various resources from different parts of our Galaxy. Crops thrived and the Verunians enjoyed an idyllic lifestyle on their fertile planet; at least until the seas started to rise.

Given ample warning of this event by their second sight abilities, they moved underground and developed systems to provide heat and rainfall for their living requirements and their crops. They also started a radical programme for procreation, that of cloning, with the eventual aim of sustaining a controlled population. Over several hundred millions of years, their human frames were changed anatom-

---

[9]Eudaemon. Benevolent supernatural being.

ically. They no longer needed genitals for breeding and these were dispensed with. They no longer needed arms or legs, since all movement was achieved by levitation; however, limbs were retained for the sake of appearance. With the passage of time, lungs, stomachs, anal passages, mouths and noses became redundant since the Verunians took all their nourishment and life sustaining essentials directly from the drastically filtered sunlight that they allowed to reach into their underground living spaces.

All disease was eradicated; there were no disagreements; no employment other than the care of the infant clones; the maintenance of the super-computers that controlled the minutiae of life; the furtherance of science; and the administration of the Guidance Committee.

Verunians aged much more quickly than Earthmen and a normal life span lasted for about sixty years. But they chose to clone their replacements as infants to give the illusion of a normal life span. However, age-related deformities, together with an associated deteriorating condition of the Verunian body, increased dramatically after about fifty years and a policy of voluntary euthanasia was enforced on the fiftieth anniversary of cloning for every single member of the population. Their total population was never allowed to exceed fifty million people; planet hopping with greater numbers would be impossible, even for them.

All newly-cloned arrivals were preprogrammed with a complete database of knowledge, sufficient for them to lead a useful life in the utopian world that had been created. The information included the history of Veruni; the details of the formation of their Universe and the billions of other Universes; together with all necessary technical and life-sustaining knowledge that they would need during their fifty years of life. They were thus all equal, with a single seat of power; or rather a single decision-maker as head of their Guidance Committee, since not much in the way of control or government was needed.

To all intents and purposes, the planet Veruni had a rosy future; they could look forward to a long and settled period of existence for the next one thousand years.

Trouble rarely encroaches upon human existence in single catastrophes. And the same adage could be applied to the Verunians. Back in the 1950s, Verunian scientists had discovered another dagger of disappointment concerning their plans to join us on Earth. Once again the time-span had been changed but this time the reason was not the old enemy, at least not entirely. For it was the hostile nature of the Avoi-Shun that was destined to be the primary cause for the Verunians' latest enforced change of plans; and it appeared that a much earlier intervention in Earth's future would be required or Earth would no longer be available to accept them.

For all the vicissitudes of life there is an answer. To the Verunians, life underground had solved most of their problems. Beneath the surface many of man's more volatile acts become more difficult to practise. Warfare; the underground cities were self-contained and protected from airborne attack, and the movement of large bodies of men and equipment was not possible. Terrorism; individual communities could be sealed off and the production of weapons more easily discovered by sensitive monitoring sensors, and thought-monitoring surveillance equipment made tracking any such intentions much more simple. The dangers to health from direct exposure to the Sun were eradicated; and natural calamities capable of producing high body counts were virtually non-existent. The dangers from air, sea, road and rail accidents no longer existed; and Verunian-man developed a softer, more tolerant nature when the pressures of modern-day living were removed.

But the reality of the Verunian dream to mould Earth into their way of life must wait for a very long time; the Earthlings had a few more tricks up their sleeves, unintentionally designed to frustrate the plans of the Verunians.

To add to our proposed future co-planetarians' confusion was yet another tricky ingredient, destined to unintentionally throw a spanner in the ointment. Although they had tremendous powers of foresight, it was not possible to see the actions of an individual until about fifty years before that person actually existed. And the actions of two, as yet unborn, people would contribute towards the end of life on our world.

Similar to a fantastic comic-book scenario, the list of man's future excesses of violence were laid before me. Without intervention, Veruni had discovered that Earth was scheduled to die in the year 2111.

The 20th century on Earth was a bloody period in the history of humankind. And most of the events of the 21st century, through which Earthman will blunder blindfolded and bleary-eyed, with little care and even less attention, were no more than a long-term continuation of existing 20th century conflicts. Collectively they would account for the loss of billions of lives but humankind had been programmed to accept, almost without comment, such wasteful destruction of Earth's manpower.

But the Verunians could see the cumulative effect of three major events. Nuclear warfare in a relatively confined area of the world will break out in the 2040s. At the time, our physical world will appear to shrug off this violent confrontation but the hidden penalty will not delay too long to materialize.

Similarly, a second nuclear battle, on a much bigger scale, will occur in the 2080s and this will be the main factor contributing towards Earth's fiery end. Entered into the history books as World War 3, this will be a dispute between China, the world's only superpower, pitted against the combined might of the Islamic world. In dispute will be two national ideals that the protagonists had long hungered for; control of the Earth's diminishing supplies of fossil fuels and global domination.

And the final cataclysmic event will occur in the year 2111 when the combined effect of these two nuclear strikes will create a split in the Earth's surface. This gigantic separation of the world's tectonic plates will occur in California and extend to the very core of our planet. Earth, an unstable mass, will break up and disappear into oblivion. And following collisions with the greater portions of the disintegrating Earth hurtling out of control through space, the catastrophe will take the Moon, Veruni and the other terrestrial planets, Mercury, Venus and Mars, with it.

This was a terrible setback for the Verunian Guidance Committee. Foiled by the firecracker that is the unpredictable nature of natural childbirth, the Verunians realised that they would need help from the Earthmen much earlier than originally planned.

The search for an individual that might understand both Veruni's and Earth's predicament continued for many years. Over time, this person became known to the Verunian Guidance Committee as the Verguide. From the final shortlist of candidates, my name was chosen to help the Verunians save our world. Volatile Victor Yewly was to become the Verguide.

And that was why I was sitting on that raised dais, absorbing what sounded remarkably similar to a load of codswallop. 'Me! Volly - chosen as the saviour of the world! Give me a break! Why me?'

In response to my strangled cry, Belial First told me that some four thousand years before; a fact-finding spacecraft had visited Earth. In the process of gathering a few human specimens, one of my ancestors had been impregnated by a Verunian. It had been a spontaneous impregnation, breaking the strict rules of Verunian culture at that time; and the Starman had paid the ultimate penalty. But the deed was done and my birth-line was to retain a diminishing percentage of Verunian blood for eternity. In recognition of this fact, I was to be awarded a Verunian name of special significance; I was to be known to the Verunian people as Belial.

Again I did not have to ask the question, Belial First simply replied. *'Yes, Verguide. We are related, distantly maybe, but we are kinfolk.'*

'But how the devil could I be expected to achieve the Verunians' aims? Just one man against the combined might of the world.' I was getting quite used to the system now and I waited for Belial First to answer my unspoken thought.

Whilst not quite up to the standard of Superman, I was apparently to be given some very special abilities to assist me in achieving my mission. An invisible protective shield that would surround my body whenever I needed it; immense bodily strength on demand; the gift of second sight and the ability to read the thoughts of others; and the exciting capability of being able to project my mind to another place and overlook a person or place. 'And,' Belial First completed his list of goodies out loud, 'you will be allowed to project your second-self forward in time.'

It was obvious that Belial First was struggling to explain this almost supernatural ability and his voice took on a dream-like quality as he explained further. 'Think of it as your alter ego, Verguide. Whenever you wish you will be able to move through time, taking all of your existing senses with you. In what your fellow Earthlings might describe as an out-of-body sensation that you will find most useful. With practice, your alter ego will be able to cause objects to move and obey the commands of your mind, much as would a poltergeist.' A thoughtful pause from Belial First, and I sensed a warning; and the inevitable but.

I was not wrong. 'But Verguide, there are restrictions that you must be aware of. You will be allowed to project your alter ego forward through time, until the year 2130, always returning from the future to your solid form. We, the Verunian Guidance Committee, have imposed this forward limitation because there are events in the future that even you will find difficult to comprehend and which we at this moment in time are unwilling to explain. Neither will you be able to delve into the past, for we have discovered that therein lies a temptation to alter the future that is difficult for any human to suppress. Whilst in this state of bilocation, you will be able to convert your alter ego to solid-form; but be especially warned Verguide, do not materialise for too long whilst in the time yet to come, for it is dangerous to both your alter ego in the future and your solid form in the present. The transfer of information is almost complete, Verguide. And I too have only a few more points to make. You must learn to trust me Verguide. Learn to trust the power of your brain, for it is infinitely more powerful than man is yet capable of understanding. Control of your brain will increase over the years as you gain more and more knowledge of its machinations. It is capable of projecting you forward in time to a known future, and has retrospective capabilities that are almost unlimited.'

At the time I did not fully appreciate the meaning of this particular statement from Belial First; and it would be well over a hundred years into the future before I would be able to make any use of it.

In addition to my powers, Belial First promised two more items in support. If necessary, a Verunian emissary would be sent every fifty years to update the technology included in my brain; and secondly, that when they eventually joined us on Earth, no harm would come to its existing inhabitants. How I used the powers invested in me was left entirely in my hands; any method was acceptable as a means to achieving my task as the Verguide.

Which reminded me, *'What on Earth was I supposed to do as the Verguide? What was my task?'* Within the mind-boggling story that had been related to me, there was little that a simple mind such as mine could actually grasp.

The most effective orders for military men are those short and sharp statements that are shouted very loudly and are clearly understood by both the person with the big mouth and the people with the delicate ears. Belial First answered my final silent question. 'Your primary task as the Verguide is to avert World War 3. A secondary task is to control the expected population explosion over the next century. In time, the people of your planet will realise that life on the surface will become untenable and when the time comes you, as the Verguide will have a further task; to lead your fellow Earthlings towards a state of existence that is enjoyed on Veruni, namely living underground in peace and harmony. To do whatever you can to soften the aggressive and anti-social nature of the human beasts and mould them into gentler beings, similar to our race of Verunians.'

'*Not a huge task for a Royal Navy leading radio operator then!*' Expecting a speedy conclusion to this weird dream, my Navy-trained mind was turning reality aside with humorous flippancy. And even Belial First did not provide a response to this thought.

But what I took for a dream was not yet ended. Throughout the transfer of all this bumf into my brain, either the available light in the cave had increased or my vision had improved considerably. Looking around me, I could now see that my Verunian friend and I were enclosed within a perfectly smooth circular enclosure, reminiscent of the inside of a silky round balloon. The dais was floating in mid-air and the bones and detritus from the sea had disappeared; obviously a figment of my own imagination in response to the stories from my Asian compatriots. My body felt very light and even the slightest pressure from my hands lifted me bodily off the dais; and somehow I knew that the structure and general ambience had been formed to mimic the planet Veruni.

Belial-First confirmed my assumptions and told me that, in fact, the structure was deep under the Antarctic Larsen B ice-shelf, protected from discovery from anything or anybody on Earth. There was no opening in the ruins on Coney Island; it was simply a way of guiding me to the area in which I could be transported to this cave and for my briefing as Belial - the Verguide.

Other facts leapt into my consciousness. The construction of the cave was so simple, in terms of Verunian technology, and just the merest concentration on my part gave me the details of how it had been constructed. The Sun could be a powerful enemy but when its power is harnessed correctly it can also be a supreme benefactor. Its power had been used to burn the cave into the ice-cap and to reseal it; and it was lined with a new metal, stronger than anything else yet discovered on Earth, that would prove of great value to Earth's people in the generations to come.

Unnoticed by me, the digital stream had ceased, the download was complete. When next I looked down, my Verunian friend had gone.

CHAPTER 4
REALISATION

THREAD:

Most people will have experienced vivid dreams. Fantastic events and magical moments seem so real when one's actions are controlled only by the mind. Defined as a sequence of mental images during sleep, these stories of the mind can be benign, intensely erotic or sometimes downright malignant; and are of course completely inconsequential. But their most troublesome characteristic is that they are sometimes extremely difficult to remember.

Not so mine.

SINGAPORE. 1962.

The noisy, lapping sounds of the waves breaking on to a sandy shore eventually dragged me back to wakefulness. The sea must have got up a bit while I had been asleep and the tide had risen, because I found the sounds quite intrusive. It was pitch dark, as black a night as only the Far East can produce. It had obviously rained very recently since the bulbous clouds occasionally obscured the stars from view. Around me the ground was wet and soggy; and the large concrete sections of the ruins took on a more threatening aspect.

I felt no discomfort, neither excessively hot nor cold; neither did I feel any pain, headaches, scratches or bruising, hunger or thirst. My mental state was one of perfect calm, troubled only slightly by my most recent memories; but I could not understand why I was still on the banyan island in the middle of the night.

The dream had been fantastic and obviously very long and, much as my mind fought to recall and evaluate what I had dreamed, it faded. As in the case of most dreams I forgot about it and forced my mind to concentrate on making some sense of my present circumstances.

Struggling to my feet, I started moving away from the ruins. 'One day,' I promised myself, 'I would come back and investigate them further.' It had certainly been great fun poking around in the ruins; and I never did find that lizard. As I cursed the blackness of the night the clouds cleared and the stars bathed the island in the half-light of the Moon. The whole island felt much more menacing at night, the more so when I discovered that I was alone.

The remains of the barbeque were plain to see, as were the numerous footprints deeply embedded into the sand. Under a gently bent palm tree, I noticed a rattan bag that someone had left behind when they departed from the island, possibly for me in the hope that I might return from wherever I had been hiding when the time came for my watch *oppos* to return to the mainland.

Yes! A few sandwiches, some fruit and two bottles of Anchor beer - great! Suddenly I was both hungry and thirsty. Unscrewing the top of one of the beers, I guzzled down half of one of the pint bottles in a single, mighty swig. Sandwiches followed the beer into my rumbling stomach; and I saved the fruit for breakfast. Surely someone would be back tomorrow, to have another look for me?

Refreshed from my late supper, I lay down upon the cold, wet sand. Sleeping is never a problem for a watch-keeper and I fell into a deep, dreamless sleep. Neither thoughts of space, worldly problems nor odd-looking supernatural beings disturbed my slumber.

Feeling on top of the world, I awoke at about 09.00 the following morning. Somehow I just knew that a passing vessel would call into the beach in about fifteen minutes time on its way to Pongo Point loaded with its catch from a fishing expedition. Time enough to eat the fruit, have a few sips of beer and ready myself to leave the island.

Alfred Leonard

As predicted, a fishing vessel, little more than an open canoe under a small sail, hove into view around the corner of Coney Island. Not in the least bit surprised by its appearance I stood up and raised my arm, in the international sign of recognition and peace to the two Malayan fishermen as they lowered their scanty sail and allowed their boat to sidle gently on to the sandy beach.

Most Singaporeans spoke excellent English and I told them that I had got hopelessly drunk, fallen asleep and been left behind by my friends. Obviously fond of a few beers themselves they nodded and smiled in sympathy at my tale and offered me a lift to Punggol Point, which of course, I accepted gratefully.

Bit of a dodgy trip, from Coney Island to Pongo Point, in that small boat with its extremely low freeboard, and I was concentrating hard on not making any sudden movements, which might overbalance the flimsy craft. Concentrating so hard that I did not notice the large party of naval and army personnel until the boat did a one-eighty turn and the two Malayans reversed the boat on to the sandy beach at Pongo Point.

Intended obviously as a search party, they would now serve as my reception committee awaiting my arrival and no doubt some sort of feasible explanation for my whereabouts during the previous night. Quickly I assessed the situation. I was going to need an excuse for my absence much sooner than I had anticipated.

Immediately, and without any conscious effort on my part, a story entered my mind. The words seemed to fall unbidden from my mouth and I explained that whilst intent on completing an exploratory survey of the island, I had crossed to the far side and there found an abandoned boat. Seemingly intact but too heavy to drag across the sand; I had decided to attempt to paddle it around to my watch-mates. It would make a fine diving platform if we could find some way to anchor it. Unfortunately, the prevailing current had taken the boat away from Coney and I had tired myself considerably in my attempts to return to shore, eventually giving up and falling asleep in the drifting boat. When I awoke it was dark and the boat had drifted back to Coney on the incoming tide. 'I found the food and drink and decided to await rescue,' I finished lamely.

A simple story and one with very few loopholes to trip me up under closer scrutiny. My story was accepted and Dicky Turpin gave me a lift home to my waiting wife Tracey. Naturally very relieved to see me, Tracey fussed around providing a hot meal whilst Dicky and I sat on the front patio talking about everything except my night of absence. As yet I had not found the time to think about the incredible dream and dismissing the whole episode from my thoughts, I returned to my normal life of a watch-keeping communicator at Kranji.

My old Ford Prefect was in dock. On a recent trip to the beach, Tracey had been sitting next to me with Alicia on her lap. Travelling quite slowly up the hill out of Serangoon village, we were heading for a day at Changi beach. It was raining, probably just a short shower, and visibility through the windscreen was poor because the old car was fitted with air-operated windscreen wipers. Every time the accelerator was pressed to increase revs when climbing hills, or attempting passing manoeuvres, the air-pressure dropped and the wipers were virtually useless.

At that time we had acquired a small family pet called Pepe, a multi-coloured, multi-breed mongrel puppy, hundreds of which roamed the streets of Singapore in a feral existence. This soft-natured and very friendly little dog loved Tracey and it would follow her everywhere. Obeying every command, it even sat untethered outside the shops, oblivious to other passers-by or animals, quietly awaiting Tracey's return.

The little dog's favourite resting place was on Tracey's lap but on this day Pepe's position had been usurped by Alicia and the dog made continuous efforts to climb over, or between, the two front seats to reclaim its rightful place. Eventually, Tracey got quite annoyed with the dog as it tried to scramble over the back of her seat and screamed for me to control it. Honestly, I took my eyes off the road for just a few seconds, reaching for the dog - and the next thing I knew the car was at the bottom of a mossie-ditch, those deep rainwater drains so prevalent in Singapore. Looking out of the windows of the car, all I could see was concrete in all directions, which brought back some weird memories.

Fortunately, the car had come to rest almost perfectly level and I was able to open my door and clamber out. Tracey managed to hand Alicia to me and wriggled out of the same door. With my precious cargo safely on the pavement, I trudged off towards the local garage for a crane and tow-truck.

Whilst the car was undergoing repairs, Dicky was giving me a lift to and from Kranji. A most distressing state of affairs for me, because Dicky was an appalling driver. Mindless of speed limits, other road users or the prevailing weather conditions, it was foot to the floor-boards; and the devil take the hindmost!

It was thus that a few weeks after my sleepover on Coney Island, I found myself in Dicky's car for another white-knuckle ride on our way to Kranji for the afternoon watch. I was feeling particularly refreshed because Dicky had awarded me a standoff during our last all-night-on shift and I had therefore been off-watch for some seventy-odd hours.

Roaring along the Mandai, that infamous stretch of road that follows the outline of Seletar reservoir and eventually joins the Bukit Timah road, Dicky was doing his Italian impression and giving the car some wellie. The road, reputedly built by allied prisoners of war during the Japanese occupation, had been deliberately engineered with reverse cambers on all the bends and the dangerous corners had undone many of Kranji's tired watch-keepers returning home, particularly when the roads were wet.

Despite Dicky's breakneck speed, we were overtaken by a speeding Jaguar on a long right-handed, gently tightening bend. A very dangerous manoeuvre, since the bend was blind, and Dicky was furious. He hated being passed at the best of times but for it to happen in such dangerous circumstances left him fuming and he threw his arm out of his rolled-down side window and shook his fist at the departing Jag.

'Look at that crazy git,' Dicky stormed, banging his hands on the rickety steering wheel. Seeking to mollify him, I added my own tuppence of wrath, aimed at the errant driver of the disappearing Jag. 'What a twat, I hope his tyres explode. He will end up in the jungle at that speed.'

What an odd coincidence; no sooner had I uttered my words than the Jaguar came into view in front of us. It was still travelling at great speed and approaching one of the hairpin bends close to the corner of the reservoir. Suddenly bits of rubber, smoke and metal flew from the side of the car; the Jag hit the high bank and somersaulted into the large trees bordering the dense jungle. As we approached, the car burst into flames and we could see the driver, a young white woman, engulfed by the rapidly spreading inferno. We both leapt from Dicky's old car and raced to the woman's aid. But we knew that our efforts would be futile; the fire was just too fierce and kept us at bay. However, I had managed to get close enough to notice that the front offside tyre had burst.

Matelots are naturally cynical people and the nagging thought that I may have wished, and therefore caused, the woman's death bothered me not a jot; but I did upon reflection consider the whole experience a bit weird.

A passing motorist had sped off towards Sembawang village to raise the alarm and we waited until the emergency services responded to the accident. Having offered our statements to the police, we continued on our way, arriving at Kranji only a few minutes late for our afternoon watch. In retelling the events of the accident, I made much of my extra-sensory powers of manipulating mere mortals and took great delight in being responsible for the blown tyre. Sailors also have an excessively macabre sense of humour and none thought less of me for claiming such responsibility. 'Stupid cow deserved all she got,' was the general consensus of opinion.

During that afternoon watch I carried out my usual duties of router, that is the person who allocates the correct destination indicators for each addressee of a message, enabling subsequent comcens to identify quickly their actions in respect to each message. There are literally thousands of these routeing indicators listed in several naval communications publications. Most of the more commonly used indicators I knew by heart and I did not have to refer to the appropriate publication listing them. But today, as the afternoon wore on, it seemed that I knew them all. Thinking nothing of this, I assumed that I was on particularly good form. I was pretty sharp and I took my work very seriously but it did occur to me later that night, when I was lying in bed reviewing the day, that my knowledge of the various communications publications had improved dramatically. *'I'll see what tomorrow brings'* was the last thought that lingered in my head as I drifted off into another dreamless night.

The next morning I was up at 06.30 in plenty of time to take a quick shower before breakfast. Tracey was already up and attending to Alicia and at the same time trying to conjure up a couple of hard-boiled eggs. Today I had the forenoon watch, which would be followed this evening by the dreaded all-night-on. My white shorts and naval white-front were placed by the side of the bed by Tracey, ready for me to jump into. And I mean jump into! Our Amah was rather more liberal with the starch than was absolutely necessary and my shorts had to be pried apart, stood on rigid legs and stepped into!

It was a great life in Singapore. Tracey was particularly keen on the assistance from our Amah, who did as much as Tracey wanted her to do; washing, ironing, cleaning, baby-sitting, shopping - anything really, but in the whole of our time on that wonderful island, Tracey was not able to persuade our Amah to ease up on the starch.

Shortly after I had wolfed down my *cackle-berries*[10], I heard the peep-peep of Dicky's car and, having kissed both Tracey and the baby, I sauntered out to the waiting vehicle.

First thing in the morning is not a time for conversation and both Dicky and I made our way towards Kranji in agreeable silence. As the car passed the entrance to Seletar RAF Station, Dicky put his foot down when the road straightened for about half a mile or so. By the time we entered the outskirts of a tiny village, little more than a scattering of wooden-framed huts along the side of the road, we were doing a fair old rate of knots.

'Watch out for the pig,' I yelled, as a vision of the fully-grown animal dashing out of the huts at the side of the road entered my head. 'What bloody pig?' Dicky chuckled, just as the pig raced in front of the car. There was no way Dicky could have taken avoiding action; the pig ran blindly into the side of the car, so intent had it been on escaping whatever fate had intended for it.

An impressive bang accompanied the impact with the pig. The car swerved across the road and hit a ramshackle old lorry coming the other way. The head-on collision was at a combined speed of about 140 km/h and both Dicky and I hurtled through the windscreen into the front of the lorry. The scream of tortured metal seemed to ring in my ears for several minutes after the collision but stopped as soon as I picked myself up from the side of the road.

Having dragged myself slowly to my feet I stretched and carefully checked that all my limbs and other body appendages were still in place. Not a mark on me; neither scratch nor bruise and hardly a

---

[10]Cackle-berries. Navy speak, hard-boiled eggs.

hair out of place. When I found Dicky he was no longer recognisable as Dicky; he was just a mass of torn flesh and blood. Decapitated, his head was lolling in a nearby ditch, eyes wide in total shock and disbelief.

The lorry driver, a Malayan, lay comatose on the road; alive or dead I knew not and to my eternal shame, cared less. My reaction reminded me of a little ditty that Belial First had used to illustrate man's easy acceptance of the mega-deaths of other human beings. He mentioned an incident where a motorway pile-up had caused the death of sixty-three people and newspaper articles had reported that all of the cars were repairable, hinting that the twisted remains of the vehicles were of more value than the lives of their occupants.

Totally calm - it was not for nothing that I was known as Volatile Victor - I grabbed one of the local village men who had appeared from nowhere. Dozens of them, crowding around the dead pig, angrily waving their fists at me, completely oblivious of poor Dicky spread across the front of the ancient green lorry, like marmite on green toast.

The villagers were more concerned about their bloody pig than for any of the humans involved in the collision. As I shouted at the man I had grabbed, yelling for him to leg-it up to RAF Seletar and report the accident, I was also very aware of the anger of the mob closing in on me. Vague memories of some story of a couple of Army chaps hanged by village men after a similar incident some years ago returned to my mind and I moved across to guard Dicky's head; that gory trophy would be denied them.

Almost all the village men were armed with their long-handled machetes, the ubiquitous local tool used for trimming grass and who-knows-what-else. This group advanced menacingly towards me; I knew I was deep into the brown stuff and for a moment I thought of flight. Fast and fit, with bags of excess endurance, I knew for certain that I could out-run this lot.

However, the thought of picking up Dicky's head sickened me; I just could not do it and, not about to leave it for these angry people, I stood my ground. The advancing line of six spread out in front of me, gripping their machetes, and lifting them to about head height in a classic prestrike attitude. The biggest of the group took a wild swing at me and a soft thud of the strike was clearly heard. But the blade had not made contact with me; for some strange reason it had stopped just a few centimetres from my body. In the blink of an eye I had grabbed the handle of the machete and started to lift.

The man was strong, I'll give him that, and his wiry frame managed at first to withstand my gathering strength. He was looking down at me as he sailed above my head, a look of complete astonishment and pain in his dark-brown eyes. The large Malayan, still clutching his prized machete, finally returned to earth fully twenty metres behind the threatening mob. For the briefest of moments my legs turned to jelly. Was this another dream?

Having witnessed their friend flying over their heads, the remaining five villagers decided to attack *en masse*. Once again I must have lived up to my nickname, for when the RAF police arrived my armed antagonists were sleeping peacefully, or moaning in agony, around the gruesome scene. Total silence had descended on the accident site and the remainder of the onlookers from the village were eyeing me carefully, probably assessing their chances of overwhelming me with superior numbers.

Senior British politicians demanded that dealings with the local population should always be conducted in a softly-softly diplomatic manner. The RAF police knew this but they also recognised a volatile situation; and the RAF Sergeant in charge was magnificent. Wading in fists flying and followed loyally by his two Corporals, they dispersed the crowd, who simply broke and ran under this unexpected onslaught.

Watching from the side of the road as the emergency services cleaned up the mess; I waited until the RAF Sergeant eventually returned to ask what had happened. Feigning agitation I explained as best I could and asked him if he would inform Kranji of the accident. Finally, given a chance to assess my condition, the Sergeant seemed surprised that I was not injured. My clothing was pristine and there was not one single spot of blood on me.

Clearly I could not explain how I had escaped injury. 'Just lucky,' I offered. Glancing around at the still unconscious would-be machete men, the Sergeant raised an eye in question. 'Don't really know,' I croaked, pretending to lapse into post-accident distress syndrome. 'They seem to have had a bit of an argument amongst themselves.'

'You are luckier than you know,' mused the Sergeant, 'these people can be vicious bastards when they are roused.'

Confusion whistled around in my head. I had foreseen both the pig and the resultant accident. Immediately the strange and vivid dream that I had experienced on the island returned to me; I needed to be alone to think things through. A sense of fear and uncertainty almost overwhelmed me as I realised that what I had taken for a dream was clearly not the case; I actually had some of the powers that Belial First had babbled on about.

Calmness returned to my reeling senses, first things first; distract the Sergeant from any further questions. Once away from the accident scene I could use the age-old excuse of loss of memory to avoid any leading questions. Feigning once again, I staggered and sat down with my head held in my hands, giving what I hoped was a good impression of the onset of shock.

There really was nothing wrong with me and I was quite fit enough to continue on to Kranji and complete my shift. But if I could convince the Sergeant to take me home I could send Tracey off to the shops and sort out my thoughts. 'Do you think you could fix me up with a lift to Kranji?' I asked. Mulling over my question for a few seconds, the Sergeant looked into my eyes, felt my brow and finally replied. 'You ought to go to Changi hospital for a check-up really; but you don't have any signs of internal injury. And you don't look too bad, so I intend taking you home. Delayed shock can be a bugger,' he continued, 'and if you feel groggy overnight or in the morning, see a naval doctor for further advice. I will let the Naval Patrol Headquarters in *Terror* know and they will inform Kranji.'

Sitting in the back of the RAF Land Rover on my way back to Serangoon, I deliberately continued my sham of feeling a tad groggy, to the extent that I needed help walking up the drive to my front door. Tracey went loopy, forced me to take a shower and go to bed where I remained dutifully, all that day and through the night.

Not that I slept much. Dozing for short periods during the afternoon, I lay awake most of the night listening to Tracey's gentle snoring and not so gentle grinding of teeth. Losing a night's sleep was a fair trade for the opportunity to think. Assuming that all of Belial First's story was true, and I now had good reason to believe it so, then I needed a plan, or plans - at least something to get me through the next few weeks.

A host of questions occurred to my swirling brain. First among which was, *'What would I need to do if I was to even attempt to complete the Verguide's tasks?'* Nothing - the response to my thought was a blank screen in my head and for a moment I felt similar to an expectant cursor on a computer screen; waiting for answers that I could not as yet provide.

'Christ, this is like pulling teeth,' I thought as ideas slowly entered my mind. Belial First had promised me that all the information I needed was downloaded into my brain. Clearly my antediluvian mental faculties had not yet learned how to access the information and it was going to be a slow process of trial and error. But ideas were coming to me; remain anonymous, out of the public eye; use my newly acquired skills carefully and discriminately; and above all else - don't rush, take my time.

Perhaps a trial project, see what happens. No icon has a larger following than that of money. I will have need of money, enormous wealth and a system of managing it. And the money must not suddenly appear, for such sums as I would need must be accumulated over a considerable period of time and must be seen to be acquired legitimately. But as a trial run, any amount of money will do. Whether I use my powers, imaginary or not, the monetary gain must look genuine. So look into the future, maybe predict some numbers for the Singapore State Lottery or enter a ticket - nothing to lose and all to gain.

Having made this simple decision my mind started to drift off in other directions, thinking of other measures I might adopt. I suddenly realised that this was a mistake; I must force my mind to accept only those measures relevant to the short term and, brain complying, I finally drifted into sleep.

When I awoke, having missed the all-night-on, I had another forty-eight hours of my own time ahead of me. A grilling from the Naval Patrol HQ seemed inevitable but despite Belial First's promises I could not foresee that event. Perhaps my second sight was limited to the more important events; or still in its infancy but growing with each new day. 'We'll see,' this short statement seemed to act as a trigger for my mind and further thoughts of my future were sidelined.

Above all else most women respect and demand honesty from their partners. As far as I knew Tracey and I had no secrets and I hated lying to her. But I had no choice, I dare not confide in anyone - I had heard enough stories about the Netley Naval Mental Hospital to convince me that it was not the holiday destination of my choice. But I had to continue my charade of shock and mild injury; nothing serious of course, no headaches or pains. And certainly nothing that would involve a hospital appointment or closer scrutiny.

Leaving Tracey in the cacophony of street traders, over-stocked trading houses and milling humanity that made up Serangoon shopping centre, I pushed Alicia in her small pushchair up the hill to the local garage to see if the repairs to my car had been completed. No problem; the car gleamed on the forecourt awaiting my arrival, proclaiming to all and sundry that the owner spent a great deal of time polishing the old wreck. It is at least something to do when you have time on your hands and Alicia loved splashing in the spilled water.

Repairs cost one hundred dollars, quite a large sum of money in 1960s' Singapore. Luckily, I had recently claimed my quarterly home-to-duty travel expenses so I did have a few spare bucks. Excited at a car trip with her daddy, Alicia happily jumped into the front passenger seat, leaned forward with her podgy arms on the dashboard and gazed out of the windscreen.

For some bizarre and unknown reason I felt a great need to have a look at the crash site. With Alicia as my co-pilot I drove the familiar route past the Seletar housing estate and the entrance to the RAF base. There was very little traffic on the road and I slowed almost to a stop at the crash scene.

The lorry was gone, and the road and roadsides had been cleared of all debris. Not a sign of the terrible accident remained, except for a few shallow scrapes on the road; not so much as a few skid-marks. Dicky had not even had time to hit the brakes.

A few kilometres down the road was a fishing pond into which I turned, letting Alicia have a run around while I enjoyed a quiet beer at the ramshackle bar. Peace and solitude can be an effort to bear for a one year old and it was not long before Alicia wanted to move.

Back in Brockhampton Drive, Tracey had not yet returned; she was probably in some shoe shop, working her way through the entire stock. Alicia loved her paddling pool and I filled it from the outside tap and sat contentedly watching her play. Somehow the last few hours of family life had concentrated my mind and I resolved that whatever happened in the future I must make sure that Alicia's life did not suffer because of anything that I might do.

By lunchtime Tracey had returned but I had still not been approached by the naval authorities. Always have a plan, my motto from childhood, and I decided to visit Dicky's wife in an attempt to console her in some way. I had put off this unpleasant action all morning but I knew it was my duty to explain about the accident and answer any questions in the best way I could. If by then I had still not heard from *Terror* or Kranji, then I would walk down to a phone in Serangoon shopping centre and give the Chief in the comcen a bell; see how the land lay.

Very few of the bungalows occupied by Kranji's watch-keeping personnel were fitted with telephones, for a very good reason. Such a convenience would make it too easy for the Chief to get hold of you for extra work or filling in for someone's absence in emergencies. Much better to remain incommunicado; a ruse passed on to me by Dicky.

Knowing that Dicky and his wife had not been able to have children, I thought it might soften the blow if I took Tracey and Alicia with me. My sweet-natured little girl enjoyed nothing better than visiting; and she loved a cuddle with her Aunty June. They lived in an adjacent road called Braemar Drive, which ran parallel with our own Brockhampton Drive. It was little more than a short walk and we set off just after lunch; but the journey actually lasted ages because Alicia wanted to walk.

Similar to walking a puppy, Alicia was very inquisitive and she made numerous detours and stops, investigating everything she set eyes upon. Very similar to me in so many ways, she was happiest on the beach, poking under the stones and rubbish from the sea.

I was not looking forward to seeing June. In fact I was not at all sure that I should be visiting her. Perhaps it might be better to leave it to the naval authorities? Whatever, the die was cast and we knocked on the front door which was closed for the first time in my memory. A very haggard and distressed June opened the door and fell into my arms. She was quite a large woman, big-boned and buxom, but I lifted her into my arms like a child and carried her into the house, away from the prying eyes of the Chinese neighbours.

We stayed for several hours, during which I had the good sense to answer her questions and refrain from making any other comments about the accident. Nothing we could say diminished the grief that she was feeling and I could hear her accusatory thoughts. *'Why is he still alive? Why was my Archy not spared?'*

Despite the depressing circumstances, I was elated at my being able to read another person's thoughts and I remained locked into June's mind. I was therefore prepared for her next question, 'Who was driving the car?' June knew that Dicky and I sometimes shared the driving, no matter which of the two cars was being used, and I assured her that it had been Dicky behind the wheel.

For some time June sat quietly, cuddling Alicia, but to be perfectly honest, I was relieved when it was time to take our leave; and I winced when I heard Tracey offer the weeping woman a spare bed at our house if she felt the need. Men find it difficult to deal with an abundance of weeping and wailing, preferring to bottle up their grief and find other outlets for their anger at the loss of a loved one; and fortunately June refused the offer.

For the next week I was awarded sick leave. Quite how this occurred I have no idea. I was simply told by the Chief at Kranji to stay at home. During this period I had little spare time to contemplate my tasks as the Verguide and I was still extremely doubtful about the whole episode.

But I had no time to relax. I was up to my ears in organizing Dicky's funeral and packing up June's possessions in preparation for her return to the UK. No doubt the most difficult task of all for me was that of dissuading June from taking a last peek at her dead husband's remains. Dismembered, disembowelled and decapitated; what I left at the side of the road bore no resemblance to my good friend. Although the least damaged, the head was badly lacerated; the right ear and eye were missing and the mouth, which was split vertically and devoid of teeth, hung in a lopsided drunken grin. No matter how clever the mortician, any reconstruction would not be a sight suitable for a distressed wife and I could not allow June to see the terrible state of her husband's remains.

During the many meetings with June leading up to the funeral I had seen the desire to see her husband one last time forming in her mind; and I formulated my own simple plan to deflect her intention. Time to drag a white lie from the White Witch's hat. I told June that Dicky had not died instantly at the crash scene; he had lived long enough to make me promise not to allow June to see his broken remains. Who would contradict me? Apart from the angry villagers and a small group of RAF Police, I had been the only other person at the scene; and I knew that no one was about to describe to this griev-ing woman the exact condition of her husband after the crash.

Inside June's mind I could see that my plea fell on grateful ears. In truth, she had been dreading seeing what remained of Archy and I planted a thought into her mind that it would be much less painful to remember him as he was.

Maybe there was something in what Belial First told me. In what I saw as a revelation of my strengthening powers, I could almost see my thought transmit itself between us; like a stream of data in a flash of light, unseen by human eyes. An involuntary startled movement caused my body to flinch when I realised what had happened. I had instigated a thought in another person's brain, steered a person's actions in a specific direction according to my will. *'Gordon bleeding Bennett!'*

Immensely calmed, June sailed through the trying business of Dicky's funeral. Each time she remembered her husband, which was often, she saw him as the tall, energetic Cornishman that she had stood next to on the day that they had married. Not once did the dreadful thoughts that had plagued her in the first few days follow-ing his death return to her; those painful thoughts of a torn and bro-ken body following a head-on collision were suppressed by the power of my own mind.

Much later, whilst waiting at Paya Lebar airport to board her flight back to the UK, I whispered to her that given the power of foresight, which I inherited from my mother's gypsy connections, I had looked into her future and seen her with a new husband and three beauti-ful children. As she climbed the steps to the aircraft, she suddenly stopped in the doorway, turned, looked directly at me and waved. She had heard quite clearly my last thought directed towards her. 'Good-bye, have a good life,' transmitted through some unknown dimension.

Life pretty much returned to normal. As the senior LRO at Kranji, I was promoted to acting local petty Officer and handed charge of my watch until a fully qualified replacement could be flown out from the UK. Taking charge of the watch was nothing new to me. I understood the workings of the comcen completely and I had deputised for Dicky on several occasions. Fully qualified in terms of recommendation, education and sea-time requirements, I had recently sat the provisional examination for petty Officer at Kranji's Signal Training Centre. A final qualifying course at HMS Mercury when I returned home would confirm my temporary promotion.

Navy life suited me and I suited the Navy. Recently I had decided that if I had some hundreds of years to live, then my first existence would be a full pensionable career in the RN. At present, I had no intention of changing my life based solely on what might have been a particularly powerful dream. And I resolved to continue my life for a while and see how things progressed. Enjoying my newly awarded promotion - the additional perks, freedom and respect - pleased me immensely and I was determined to push myself as far as I could go along my chosen career path.

Before his death, Dicky had been a guiding light to me; an old sweat leading a young and promising communicator through the complex matrix of naval regulations which might eventually lead to early promotion. His most recent suggestion was that I should consider becoming an Officer. If nothing else, such a recommendation guaranteed fast-track promotion to petty Officer and chief; and since becoming an LRO I had discovered that it was much easier to be in a position to give orders, rather than to receive them.

The trick was achieving the recommendation; it was not awarded to any no-hoper that asked. Selection boards were convened occasionally, when enough suitable candidates warranted the bringing together of several very senior naval Officers, to assess the worth of the would-be candidates.

Several Admiralty Fleet Orders, the means by which the controllers of the Navy disseminate changes to rules and regulations, together with their requirements and information, gave me all the details I needed. A quick visit to a young petty Officer, who served as Kranji's secretary, told me that a board would be convened in about three months' time in HMS *Terror*. Just enough time for me to get the ball rolling.

In the Navy, everything stems from a formal request - 'To see the Captain to be considered as a candidate for promotion to Special Duties Officer'. Initial recommendations were made at ship or establishment level and, given that initial recommendation; endorsements are rubber-stamped through the chain of command for a final decision. Having made many similar requests in the past, I knew how to give a good account of myself when appearing before my captain. Blessed with my natural calm and composure I could project a confident and purposeful attitude and, when I wish to, I can discard the lower-deck vernacular, speaking fluently and intelligently.

Influencing my captain's decision was not necessary; I could see that he had already made up his mind before I had marched smartly into the room. Such foreknowledge gave me enormous confidence and after only a few brief questions he gave his decision, 'So recommended and forwarded'. I had successfully cleared the first hurdle.

Eyes firmly on my future, I allocated little time towards speculating about the bigger picture. Over the next few weeks I needed to concentrate on the immediate present leading up to my Officer selection board. Naturally, I missed little opportunity in asking to see some of Kranji's Officers for private interviews, the better to prepare myself for whatever questions the selection board might ask. Favourite amongst these questions were those concerning naval history, the great naval leaders of the past and their battles, and not yet willing to trust fully my psychic powers I spent some time reading up in Kranji's small library.

As the day dawned for my board, I was due the forenoon watch. But an order to attend a selection board overrode all else. My highly polished little Ford Prefect carried me to HMS *Terror*, where I sat amongst several other candidates outside the Captain's conference room, awaiting my call to be interviewed. Seeking to gain any advantage available to me, I had already made up my mind to try out another of my supposed powers. There was very little chance that I would be first to be interviewed; such events were usually carried out in alphabetical order and I should be the last man in.

Sure enough the first candidate, looking extremely apprehensive, white-faced and trembling visibly, passed through the imposing, richly decorated and ornate doors to face his ordeal. As soon as the door closed behind the candidate - he was doomed to failure, I just knew it - I willed my mind to follow him into the room. It just happened! Suddenly, some part of me was hovering above what remained of me in the waiting room; and I looked down at myself in awe and wonder. My solid-self was performing quite normally, no one wished to talk since they were all lost in their own worlds of fear and trepidation, but I could see my eyes blink and the occasional nervous crossing and uncrossing of my legs.

Never a vain person, but for the first time I saw myself as others see me. Not too bad really, a completely normal and healthy man in the prime of life. But for the first time I noticed something very odd. I had led an eventful childhood and had won the small scars of life with whatever honour I could muster; but the scars had gone, not a blemish on my body.

No time for any closer inspection; could I actually move that part of me that floated in the air and could anyone else see it? The merest hint of intention in my mind and I flitted across the face of one of the other candidates. Not a flicker of cognition, nor a breath of air to mark my passing. Down to business then; let's see how the poor unfortunate's interview was progressing.

Senior Navy Officers do not reach high office by means of right, unless of course they are related to the big house. They are all highly intelligent men, superbly motivated in the service of their Queen and Country and, to a man, they are born leaders. After many years engaged in the business of leading, these men knew how to catch a man off-guard and, noticing the nervousness of the first candidate, they did not ask him to sit. Leaving him to stand for a few minutes might produce a shake or wobble at the knees, a sure sign of uncertainty and lack of backbone - a commodity most highly regarded among naval Officers. The Board gave this young man an extra few minutes on his feet and their patience was rewarded.

The unfortunate lad had no option, sit without being bade or collapse in a sniffling heap on the deck. Close to tears, further questions were unnecessary; since everyone in that room knew that the boy had failed. But like a cat playing with a half-dead mouse, the selection board made absolutely sure that the less than able candidate would not reapply by submitting him to a barrage of questions.

This was exactly what I had hoped for. Navy selection boards, akin to most other personal interviews, usually follow the same pattern. Ask the same questions of each individual candidate; the better to judge the replies and weed out the weakest. Forty minutes later it was all over for number one contender. He would have to wait for about six weeks before his failure was confirmed. But I had all the information that I needed and I returned to rejoin the rest of me in the waiting room.

Clearly I was destined to be the last interviewed. No problem, I had expected it. Lunchtime came and went; the selection board traipsed out of a rear door to the conference room, no doubt on their way to a slap-up meal and a few glasses of tipple in the wardroom. Myself and one other remaining candidate were not invited to join them and were left to fend for ourselves. We bummed a sarny and a cup of tea from *Terror's* signal office and wandered aimlessly in the hot Sun, waiting for the return of the selection board.

Before the board reconvened, I was chatting to the other candidate. He asked me if I had been to a selection board before. Obviously fishing for some help I decided to give him a hand; he looked a good sort and I thought, *'Why not?'* I gave him a few clues about likely questions, told him to relax and be as natural as possible. 'Don't try any airs and graces, these old farts can see right through that,' I advised him.

Buoyed up by this insight, the penultimate candidate was called for interview. Emerging just twenty minutes later he was smiling, gave me a thumbs up and clattered down the stairs, elated with his obvious success. *'Don't get too cocky Volly.'* I reeled my souring confidence in a peg or two and strode on command in front of the board.

No less a personage than the Commander-in-Chief Far East Fleet had decided to chair this selection board. A newly-promoted and recently-appointed vice admiral, he was in the process of wielding his new broom amongst his fleet. The Captain of HMS *Terror,* together with three other Captains flanked the Admiral. Striding purposefully across the wide room I stood in front of my peers, saluted and awaited the order to sit. Either they were weary of their games or they were full of lunchtime pink-gins; either way I was immediately invited to sit.

Totally confident and relaxed, I crossed my legs and refrained from crossing my arms in front of me; a sure sign of a defensive nature.

Always polite, I threw in plenty of 'sirs' with my answers, pausing for feigned thought before replying to a question, and allowing my eyes to traverse the line of staring eyes in front of me.

Nobody likes a smart-ass and I deliberately cocked-up my answer to one question; giving the wrong answer to the question asked by a somewhat bleary-eyed four-ring captain.

'What newspaper do you read, Acting RS?'

'The Times, Sir.'

'Who is the editor of the Times?'

'Don't know, Sir.' Best not to appear to be too perfect.

The final question from the selection board almost threw me. It was not one that had been asked earlier in the day when I had eaves-dropped on the proceedings.

'What is your understanding of time in the Royal Navy?' The question was from the Admiral, a bloody silly and very vague question; or a very shrewd question designed to mislead me. The Admiral knew that I was a communicator and I knew that he wanted me to mention the 24-hour clock and the importance of using GMT on all signals; and maybe throw in something about the significance of accurate timings on position and enemy reports. My name was already at the top of the passed list, so just for a laugh I tossed old Belial-First's definition of the corridors of infinity at them.

The entire board were skilled navigators and they tutted and sighed. 'Unconventional'; 'An interesting thought'; 'Bloody nonsense'; and the Admiral got himself into a bit of a tiz-was and would have scratched my name off the passed list had I not stayed his hand. *'The lad's answer had at least been innovative,'* the thought burst into the Admiral's mind, as he decided to leave my name at the top of the list of successful candidates.

Not surprisingly, I was immensely pleased when, a few weeks later, I was sent for by Kranji's Officer-in-charge, and told that I had passed the board. Of course I had to fabricate a certain amount of surprise at this news but I played out the role of a grateful Officer candidate. As such I knew that I would be carefully watched over the next few years, not to mention given most of the more unpopular jobs. I would be expected to volunteer for almost anything, from taking charge of shore patrols to organizing sports events, fund-raising, social events, liaison with the public; all the jobs that Jack-me-tickler normally goes to extraordinary lengths to avoid.

With the course of my naval career safely set on the accelerated promotion track, I had done as much as I could for now; all I needed was the passage of time and a successful conclusion to several advancement courses when I returned to the UK.

Following my success at moving into the invisibility dimension, I was now pretty much convinced of Belial-First's story; his predictions; and the actuality of the many powers that he had transferred to me.

Over the past several weeks since Dicky's death and the departure of his wife to the UK, I had devoted whatever spare time I could muster to making an outline plan towards the year in which WW3 was due to commence. Although I felt somewhat foolish in making such a plan, only time would tell whether I was wasting my time; but if a Verunian ambassador turns up in fifty years' time then I can ask some more detailed questions. If he doesn't then I will assume that it was some elaborate hoax by a wandering space-person intent upon creating havoc in the cosmos.

Presumably if I am to live on for hundreds of years I should not age, and only time, once again, will decide that. However, I had roughed out a basic plan taking me up to and beyond the 2080s, when World War 3 was predicted by Belial First. Whilst formulating my plan I realised what a great deal of living I had to do. One of my major doubts was that my existing body might age in the normal way and the thought of what one hundred and eighty years or more might do to the whole human corpus left me cold. Belial First would have some explaining to do when next I met him.

My plan was simplicity personified. Complete my naval career until about the mid nineties; and during that time amass as much money as I possibly could. At some point around the turn of the century I would have to think about taking on another identity, assuming that my physical appearance did not change. And await the arrival of the Verunian ambassador in the year 2012 to update my skills.

Belial First's description of WW3 meant very little to me. Politics, diplomacy and national intrigue were definitely my weak subjects; and the fact that China and the Muslim world might consider going to war to contest fossil fuels and global domination flew straight over the top of my head. In its present state, my brain could not deal with such issues and I knew that many more years of experiment and study were needed before I could contemplate any actions towards the fulfilment of my tasks as the Verguide. As far as World War 3 was concerned, it would have to wait for a radically different me.

My powers seemed real; but I was deeply troubled. Who knows the hallucinatory powers of the human mind? From a very early age I had suffered from an imagination that was quickly stimulated; an imagination that analysed, probed and gnawed at every new experience that life hurled at me. Maybe my perceived new powers stemmed from a deeply-rooted deficiency in my brain striving for dominance within me; or a confidence that flew in the face of reality that instilled in me the belief in such powers being possible; or a psychological mismatch that struggled between the Jekyll and Hyde facets of every human organism.

However many times I examined my doubts, I could not deny that certain strange events had occurred. There is not a sane man alive who has suffered the pain of my uncertainty; or at least not one that is coherent enough to tell the tale. And for the sake of my sanity I had to attempt a final experiment. Should the experiment prove successful then I would have no other option than to accept and believe the whole business; and make some detailed plans for the remainder of my first lifetime.

Funds, money, dinero, the filthy lucre. Without doubt I was going to need a great deal of man's greatest desire; and it had to be obtained legitimately. Financial wizardry was another skill that I had not yet mastered and I knew naught of the ramifications of dispersing illegally obtained money in the financial markets of the world. Similarly, I knew nothing of the art of disposing of stolen treasures or of the methods to convert stolen items into cash. Given that my powers were real, I could walk into any bank, jewellers or private house and steal whatever I wanted; but realising the value of the stolen items was a different proposition. The Singapore State Lottery was my best bet.

Drawn every three months, the latest draw was due in two days' time. Plenty of time for me to amble down into Serangoon shopping centre and buy a ticket. Similar to radio-bingo, tickets were sold for three months prior to each draw and people bought them by the millions. The average oriental person believes with total conviction in fate and adores nothing more than a small wager; and the lottery attracted virtually the entire adult population of the island as hopeful punters. Tickets were sold at most retail outlets over the entire island and cost five dollars each. After the Singapore authorities had deducted their gaming tax and administration costs, the remaining fund was distributed amongst the winners.

It was not rocket science. Each five-dollar ticket consisted of a card containing fifteen numbers, divided into three lines of five numbers, from the range one to ninety-nine. Notwithstanding ties, only two winners were possible; the first to reach a line of five numbers and the first to complete a full card.

Monday evening at 19.00 signalled the start of the current draw. The first ten numbers drawn were broadcast on Singapore radio and repeated every evening until Friday. In the unlikely event that a winner was forthcoming in the first week, the claimant had until midday Saturday to stake a claim. Both claimant and winning ticket were required to make a valid claim, which had to be made in person at the lottery central office at the Chinese National Bank in Singapore city. The winner, or winners, was declared before the second set of ten numbers was announced on the following Monday. And so on, until the winner of the full card was decided.

Of more interest to me, in my bid to win the jackpot on the next draw was the *modus operandi* surrounding the selection of the numbers for each draw. A surreptitious visit to the lottery central office during the week preceding the first night's draw provided me with the answer. Inside the LCO I found just two men, sitting in the office practising their method of producing the numbers. Simple really, nothing high-tech about this, just the usual bingo-caller's bag containing ninety-nine small metal discs, each imprinted with a number. One of the chaps casually dropped his hand into the bag, selected a number at random from the bag and handed it to the second chap, who placed it on a magnetic board and clearly enunciated the number into a microphone.

Whilst experimenting with what I thought of as my invisibility, I had noticed that whatever I touched usually remained visible; unless I willed it otherwise. On the Monday of the draw for the first set of ten numbers, travelling once again in my invisibility suit, I called at the LCO to put my plan into action. My hopes that the same two men would be conducting the draw were realised and I waited for them to check that all numbers were present, sweep them into a bag and leave the room for a break. They must have gone for an extended tea-break because the two men did not return for a couple of hours, which gave me ample time to remove the ten discs which corresponded to ten of the numbers on my ticket. There were a couple of spare bags lying around and I placed my selected discs into one of these.

As the draw commenced I was sitting opposite the disc selector, in front of whom was the bag with the eighty-nine remaining discs. Pushed close alongside this bag was another, invisible to both men. The radio announcer made the appropriate remarks prior to the draw, theatrically giving the bag a noisy shake close to the microphone, and replaced it on the table. Placing the second bag on top of the first and with a hand on each bag I could now control which was visible at any given time. The rest was easy and at the end of the evening I had ten numbers ticked off my ticket and no one the wiser.

Not about to be greedy, I had selected ten numbers that would not produce a winning line for the smaller prize. The three million dollar jackpot would do just nicely as a foundation for a greater fortune.

Two weeks later the airwaves and newspapers were full of the news. The Singapore state lottery had been won in record-breaking time. Previously, the quickest full-ticket had been produced after twenty-six numbers; the winner of the latest draw had produced a record that might be equalled but could never be beaten. Jackpot in fifteen numbers.

Armed with my winning ticket I took a taxi into Singapore city to collect my winnings. For once I did not wind-up my old Ford Prefect; I could certainly afford a taxi and I might as well live it up a bit. Very shortly I would be the proud possessor of three million very pretty Singapore dollars; £375,000 sterling - and very nice too. To put that amount of money into perspective, I estimated that a four-bedroomed, detached house in the home counties of England would cost between four and six thousand pounds.

I had not expected there to be any other winning tickets; and I was right. Handed my cheque by the Chairman of the lottery committee, I held it for about thirty seconds before passing it over to a grinning bank manager; disposal - three hundred thousand pounds to be transferred to a UK bank deposited in Tracey's name; the remaining six hundred thousand dollars to remain in Singapore in my name. There were to be no objections from the Singapore government about the amount of dollars leaving the country, since state lottery money was regarded as being of a different colour and not subject to the normal export controls. Tracey did not yet know of our good fortune but I wanted the bulk of the money in her name; I just did not know what was ahead of me, my future could be a little uncertain.

Enlightenment, belief, understanding, comprehension; often these pressure-releasing emotions enter the mind like a flash of lightning. Mountainous seas of doubt had beaten relentlessly on to the beach of my uncertainty. Having a calm nature does not absolve the human mind from doubt. And it seemed as if I was beset from all directions; my doubts had left me feeling bruised, besieged, engulfed and pressurized to an extent that I had never before reached.

My feelings must have mirrored those of a rabbit, cornered in the blackness of its burrow. Huge and bulging eyes are not much use in complete darkness and the trembling rabbit relies upon its other senses; those of hearing and smell to detect the presence of danger. Loud in its sensitive ears is the sound of approaching tiny feet, padding quickly towards her; and exploding into the analytical sensors of her nose was the advancing aroma of the ferrets. From all directions came the smell, growing stronger with every soft footfall; and the tempo of the rabbit's heart increased to marching-band proportions.

During the early morning after my lottery win, I was disturbed by Tracey's loud grinding of teeth. In the lightning flash of acceptance my troubles and doubts left me. What is that second, inner part of a person, that religious fanatics call the soul? That unknown part of all of us that makes us what we are? That vague, indescribable, innate, integral core that when nurtured by a stable and loving family produces a rational human adult; or a monster if maltreated during its formative years.

The mountainous seas of doubt subsided and unlike the rabbit, my own soul was lifted by my sudden and total conscious acceptance of Belial First's story.

Obtaining the funds had finally convinced me that the revelations of Belial First in the cave-like structure were not a dream. It was real and I had no choice than to believe the rest of his story. Finally, I accepted it as fact. For a few minutes I lay in awe of this knowledge before my much-diluted Verunian genes reasserted control over my feelings. Don't panic; bags of time; be careful and plan every move.

In keeping with the leisure pastimes of most people, I read the local papers; listened to the news on the radio stations in Singapore; and I had even watched the TV news whilst stationed at home. But I was not knowledgeable in global affairs; issues such as oil reserves and consumption of fossil fuels, gross national products and the value of a nugget of solid gold missed the top of my head by a country mile! But experts were thick on the ground and with the means to great fortune literally at my fingertips there would be no need for me to do or learn everything. Given time, a team of experts could be assembled to provide whatever I needed; projections, forecasts, hypotheses, detailed knowledge - the whole can of worms.

Already many of my more senior fellow communicators could foresee the enormous advantages in the dawning digital age and were talking of global networks of inter-linked supercomputers. Most certainly, I would need several people on my team capable of keeping abreast of, if not formulating, new technology, hardware and software in the digital field.

But to start the ball rolling, I firstly needed the services of a good financial advisor. An accountant, recruited initially to manage the six hundred thousand dollars lottery winnings that I had deposited in the Singapore bank; but if my choice of individual proved good enough, he or she might head up my team.

CHAPTER 5
THE TWINS AND THE SHARK

THREAD:

In the months and years following my acceptance of Belial First's story, I carefully evaluated some of the information downloaded into my mind. Much of this information appeared to be of little use to me; Verunian history, culture, methods, aspirations, technological details, etc. But from this evaluation arose a better understanding of the powers that had been invested within me.

Verunians live in another dimension of time. As such they have lived the years that is Earth's future; up to our year of 3050, shortly after the predicted solar flare incident.

What initially appeared to be an ability to travel freely in time was, in fact, a misconception on my part. Their ability to move in time was restricted by the extremities of their existence. Verunians could move back in time at will but only forward as far as the years of their own existence allowed. My own time-travel capabilities had also been restricted by the Verunians; forward only to a preset time in the future, returning always to the present. I cannot go back in time.

My initial understanding of my invisible cloak was also not entirely accurate. More a double existence; an ability to project my alter ego out of its human container and move freely as an unseen but separate entity. The solid carcass left behind appears completely normal and functions in the usual way; apart from a reduction in mental and physical capabilities: a zombie-like attitude and appearance, resembling that of a village idiot, which can usually be explained by complaining of having a heavy cold, a flu bug or a virus. It is only the alter ego that moves through time. It is possible to materialise in a different time but it is energy absorbing for the time traveller and can only be sustained for about twenty minutes. Belial First's warning about the dangers associated with allowing my alter ego to materialize whilst separated from my solid self was also tested over a period of time. And I found that whenever I materialized, my solid form drifts into unconsciousness at the same time, much the same as a person fainting, and it is best attempted when the solid body is sleeping.

The alter ego retains the full strength of its solid counterpart. It can cause items to move, appear or disappear at will; and it is also possible to vary the degree of visibility. Mind-games, whereby I was able to influence a person's decisions and actions, required my alter ego to be in the same general area as my subject.

There are many words to describe an alter ego; shadow, doppelganger, double, mirror image, twin, shaded-image, other-self, clone, spitting-image, second-self, etc., but Belial First referred to his alter ego as a biphan, a binary phantom image of his solid self. Other people cannot actually see my alter ego but if I move and they are looking at that exact spot, they may see a disturbance in the air; a shimmering, distorted image, or a rippling in the air, resembling transparent wrinkled paper. And some, perhaps those more in tune with the world of mysticism and fantasy, might well be aware of something in the air, a presence that not one of them could ever adequately describe.

It seemed also that some of my powers were of much more use than others. But far and away the most useful capability was that of being able to cast my mind wherever I pleased. Over time I came to describe it to myself as overlooking: an ability that allowed my mind to roam the world, similar to an eavesdropping space monitor, zooming-in to whatever target attracted my interest.

For many years I searched, overlooking the brightest minds in the world, assessing the possibilities of their joining my team in the years to come. But there also existed a drawback with this ability; whilst I could look I could not cause an effect. To do that, I had to use my alter ego.

TIMOR. MARCH 1988.

The Timor Sea is known as a major breeding ground for tropical storms and typhoons. One such storm had been born over the cold, deep waters of the Timor Trough and was beating its way steadily towards the northern Australian coast. Cyclone Hanna, a ferocious storm whipped into existence by the rising cold air fusing with fiercely hot and humid air circulating from the equatorial regions, was just a few days old. This storm was intent upon repeating the success of a predecessor, cyclone Tracy, which had flattened Darwin, capital city of the Northern Territories, on Christmas Day 1974.

Reacting much as would a cork in the wake of an ocean liner, the little girl was tossed about in the raging storm of the Timor Sea. The huge waves towered over her head and she had to cling tightly to her twin brother in their mutually supportive effort to stay alive.

About a mile off the Cobourg Peninsula of North Australia, which is north east of Darwin across the Van Dieman Gulf, the huge waves dissipated only slightly in the relative shelter offered by the eastern shore of Lingi Point; in the deep waters of Blue Mud Bay, they were still frighteningly large to the two young children.

In her fierce determination that both would survive this nightmare, Ana Carla Vinacco clung to her brother Jose Vincente. The first to be born by little more than ten minutes, Ana was recognized as the elder and took the lead in all things. Between them they had little clothing left, most had been discarded in their efforts to remain afloat; and both had discarded much worn, waterlogged canvas shoes and long-legged shorts, fearing that even so little weight would hamper their chances of survival.

They had done well to find each other in the raging seas after the ship had turned turtle. It seemed that a miracle had dragged Jose through the seas to Ana's side. Body temperatures were falling drastically and frozen fingers could no longer grasp at slippery arms. The two eleven year old children were finally separated again and Jose slid down the side of a huge wave, disappearing from Ana's view. Huge droplets of tears were unnoticeable as they appeared in the large, dark brown, fathomless eyes of the beautiful girl; the sea instantly washed them away. Distraught, she twisted her lithe young body in the sea, desperately searching in every direction. Suddenly she saw him, visible in the air above the gaping metre-long width of the Great White's mouth.

The scene was implanted in her memory for the rest of her life, crystal clear as in a digital photograph. The huge white-death, seven metres in length and weighing about two thousand kilograms, had risen from seventy metres below the raging surface; and as it broke through the surface tension of the sea in a maelstrom of bubbles and froth, the force of the displaced water forced her brother into the air. As the ragged-tooth, apex-predator of the deep slowly sank into the water, it held its fearsome mouth open, waiting for its prey to succumb to gravity.

Ninety days earlier this most feared shark in the seas had left the west coast of Africa and started its nine thousand-kilometre journey to Australia. Most of the journey had been close to the surface but on occasions the huge Great White had plunged to almost a thousand metres in search of food. Only twice on that long journey had the shark found sustenance. On both occasions it had been the carcass of a long-dead whale and whilst the shark was by no means a fussy eater, it preferred its usual dish of pinnipeds. Passing through the Clarence and Dundas Straits the shark, nearing the end of its twenty-year life span, had picked up the electrical fields of the many bodies in the water around the stricken ship. From thirty kilometres away the message was clear to the ravenous predator; food and plenty of it.

The hungry beast honed on to the slowly sinking hulk. From a depth of about fifty metres it started to evaluate targets using its enormously sensitive olfactory organs. Weary of the carrion of the sea, the shark saw above him the outline of a pinniped. What appeared to be an agile young seal, flipping itself playfully on the surface; an *hors d'oeuvre* to his liking. Immediately commencing its killing manoeuvre, the shark effortlessly gained depth and thrust upwards with tremendous force, blasting its tiny prey into the air.

The cold-blooded killer crunched down hard on to its victim as it fell back into its gaping mouth. The pressure of its bite could cut a full-grown man in two without the slightest effort. But on this occasion the shark got a nasty surprise; its long, sharp and enormously powerful teeth, built for ripping and tearing, did not sink into soft flesh but struck what the shark took to be a floating log. Hard and unforgiving, the shock wave rippled through the long body of cartilage and the shark instantly ejected its expected delicacy back into the sea.

Certain that her beloved brother was doomed, Ana could not believe her eyes as Jose sailed through the air towards her, landing in a tumbling splash within arm's length. Reaching out she grasped him close, just a few seconds before the rough hands of the seaman from HMAS *Wogga* pulled them both into his ship's cutter.

CHAPTER 6
THE TWINS ESCAPE

THREAD:

My overlooking wanderings had indeed brought the twins to my attention. But before them I had found their parents. And even before that I had latched on to the mother of the twins, identifying her as a highly intelligent, free-spirited individual who might be of some help to me in the future.

Indonesia - comprising almost fourteen thousand islands, of which only three thousand are inhabited by its one hundred and eighty million population. This massive archipelago lies scattered around the Java, Banda and Celebes Seas between Malaya and Australia. Two-thirds of its huge population occupy the fifth largest island of Java and eighty-seven percent of the population follow the Islamic faith.

The country had been governed since the mid-1960s by suppressive dictatorial rulers. Successive leaders had persecuted the neighbouring native Maubere people of Timor after invading that country following Portugal's abandonment of their former colony in 1975. Before they left their colony, Portugal had instilled Catholicism into ninety percent of Timor's population, which occupied the small island measuring a mere four hundred by sixty kilometres.

A long and bitter resistance campaign would eventually see East

Timor achieve its independence shortly after the turn of the millennia. During this struggle, the lack of national resources and few opportunities for employment left little money to arm the resistance fighters, many of whom resorted to arming themselves with weapons captured from the opposing Indonesian army.

EAST TIMOR. 1975.

During the period of East Timor's resistance to the Indonesian invasion, many Maubere women and children were interned in concentration camps. Forced labour, starvation, torture and sexual abuse prevailed; and was regarded as part of life by the persecuted. One of those persons so interned was the woman who eventually assumed the married name of Maria Ana Vinacco.

Born in the small fishing community of Manatuto, a few kilometres east of what is now East Timor's capital of Dili, Maria was the product of a viscous rape of her mother by an occupying Japanese Officer in 1943. Following this extremely brief but brutal encounter, Maria was born in 1944. An exceptionally pretty child with milk-white skin, she had inherited the natural beauty and bearing of the Maubere people from her mother and the intelligence of the Japanese from her father. A gifted child, she blossomed in the settled and secure environment during her island's colonial years.

Not quite ever recovering from the trauma of her rape but still a devoted Catholic, Maria's mother did not accept her many suitors in the years that followed. Feeling less than whole and somehow tainted, she chose instead to devote her life to her daughter. Jobs were scarce and Maria's mother lacked any educational qualifications or special skills. That left her with two options: prostitution or to found some small business of her own.

Setting up a small business requires capital, she had none. But what she did have was a strong body and a steely determination to support herself and her child. Laundry, only the well-to-do could afford to transfer the effort of cleaning clothes to someone else, and Maria's mother spent her days trudging around the town drumming up new customers; and her evenings washing and ironing.

The business grew slowly and life became a little easier for Maria and her mother. When the time came, Maria attended the local Catholic school where she was quickly identified as a brilliant academic. Blessed with an intelligence quotient at almost genius level and a virtual photographic memory, she absorbed information at a fantastic rate. The child waltzed majestically through her high school period and qualified as a medical doctor at the Dili University of Medicine.

By 1975, the year in which the Portuguese decided to up-stumps, Maria had been married for the past eleven years to her husband Roberto Jose Vinacco, another doctor of medicine that she had met at medical school. For some unknown reason, and despite intensive tests and trials, their union had not been blessed with children. A fact that Maria's mother, desperate for the joy of grandchildren, regretted until the day she died.

History reveals that Indonesia's invasion of Timor followed the departure of the Portuguese in 1975; and its new President, Suharto, the self-styled Father of Timor, commenced his country's ferocious campaign of suppression amongst his new subjects. Over the following years this despot is alleged to have stripped the country of its assets and amassed a personal fortune of several million US dollars. In the process, some two hundred thousand lives would be lost, countless tortured and many women raped and sterilised.

At the time of the invasion, the two MDs were in private practice in Dili. It was to the capital that the couple had moved following the death of Maria's mother. Comfortable in their small house and with an expected lifetime of happiness in front of them, they were brutally ripped apart in 1976.

Husband Roberto had patriotically joined the resistance movement against the Indonesian occupation; not in any war-like manner but by providing free medical support when asked. Summarily tried and shot after one of the earliest skirmishes of the struggle, Roberto faded from the memory of those for whom he had provided support and left his wife to fend for herself. He died just a few weeks before Maria discovered herself to be pregnant, dying before he knew that his lifelong wish for children was to become reality.

Under suspicion by association, Maria was arrested and incarcerated in one of the concentration camps built amongst the impenetrable jungle along the Laklo River. Unlike many others of the inhabitants, Maria did not enter the camp destitute. The two highly intelligent doctors had anticipated the invasion by Indonesia and had invested their total monetary worth, which included a quite considerable legacy from Maria's mother, into a single diamond. The marquise cut white diamond, ablaze with fifty-eight facets, had a street value of about twenty thousand US dollars and represented Maria's foundation for future years.

Maria was ready when the door flew inwards off its hinges, almost immediately followed by the uniformed Indonesian military police. A small boy, acting as street lookout, had raced ahead of the police and warned her of their imminent arrival. Maria had instantly swallowed the diamond; it would reappear as nature demanded, to be hidden away or swallowed once again in the event of any further threat.

Even covered in the filth of the jungle and clothed in rags, Maria was still a most beautiful woman. At first, whilst heavily pregnant, she was spared the sexual demands of the guards. Delivered of twins directly on to the dirt floor of the flimsy wooden shelter in which the captives lived, Maria was overjoyed when both were pronounced healthy and whole on 27th March, 1977. Joy, tinged with sadness flowed through her and she prayed that Roberto could look down upon what would have been his pride and joy; and the fulfilment of a good life.

Deep within herself Maria felt a terrible fear. She knew that the guards would now see her as available and she resolved to do whatever was demanded of her. She dare not risk displeasing a single guard, all of whom were prone to hand out the ultimate punishment whenever they pleased. Caring little for herself she regarded her own life as over and her main concern was to survive long enough to see her children reach an age when they could care for themselves.

Making friends with other inmates was a dangerous business. Guilt through association was a common reason for punishment or death and idle conversation was avoided. She worked each day in the camp's sweatshops, producing cotton goods for sale in the market places of the world; and a fortune for her masters in the process. Or in the camp kitchens and laundries provided for the guards, Maria did whatever was asked of her; demurely accepting the protection of an Indonesian guard in return for services provided. Although her protector provided her with the food she needed for her babies, he was not a senior member of the guards and Maria suffered her share of casual, drunken rape from his more senior colleagues.

For ten long and painful years Maria lived the life of the persecuted and whilst her own beauty faded, the perfection of her children continued to shine through the depressing drudgery of their surroundings.

Choosing names for her twins had not been difficult for Maria. The elder of the pigeon-pair she called Ana Carla after her own mother; and the younger by about ten minutes she called Jose Vincente, after her dear husband. Now ten years old, they were beautiful; not just in Maria's eyes but in the eyes of all that beheld them.

Protective guards had come and gone; Maria had lost track of the names of most of her temporary husbands. The latest was an older man, a Sergeant. He was kindly towards her and seemed genuinely fond of both her and her twins; so much so that she had not had to submit to a rape for several months. In truth she no longer considered the enforced sexual act as rape, it was a way of life to her; something that all women in her environment endured. It just happened, a depraved act of an invading army that was a meaningless, mindless few minutes in the course of another backbreaking, tiring and dirty day in a seeming eternity of degradation and poverty. It provided food, life, survival; and a continuing chance to care for her family.

Every night as Maria lay in the makeshift bed with her protective Sergeant, she groped for an answer for the fear gnawing at her insides. It was December 1987 and her children were ten years old, ready in the eyes of many of the guards to satisfy their cravings. Young boys were no less safe than young girls in this remote camp. The guards preferred to find satisfaction for their sexual proclivities amongst the inmates; and only the very young, or the very old were safe.

Reaching the end of his military service, the Sergeant had lost his wife some years earlier and felt a real fondness for his newly-found family. In contrast to his compatriots, the Sergeant was a big man and his very size deterred many of the advances towards Maria and her children. But their safety was by no means assured and Maria kept her children close about her whenever she could; drunken guards had an eye for the main chance at any time of the day or night.

A few weeks later, just after the dawn of the New Year in 1988, the kindly Sergeant lying alongside his Mauberian woman whispered a question. 'Would you like to leave this camp?' Maria's intelligence had prepared her for most events, almost a gift of foresight she could usually predict an outcome for a developing set of circumstances. But she was totally unprepared for this question. Not in her wildest dreams did she foresee such an occurrence. Fearing any response, she lay quietly for several minutes. *'How far can I trust this man?'* she asked herself. Yes, he treated her with kindness - gentleness even - and a degree of respect missing from her life for so long; and he seemed genuinely fond of her children. He provided food and protection and he was nearing the end of his service life.

Faint heart never won a chance of freedom, and Maria decided to gamble the lives of herself and her children; and she whispered the single word, 'Yes.' The utterance of the word left a dent in her soul and carried with it a desperate craving for freedom; not for herself but for her beautiful children. Fear was her constant companion; she dare not risk asking questions. He must have some plan and Maria waited as patiently as her thumping heart would allow for her Sergeant to make his meaning more explicit.

People smugglers, dubbed Coyotes in America and feared as Snakeheads in China were making a fat living from offering the chance, however slim, of escape from persecution. Rumour had it that one such people smuggler was presently in Dili, recruiting for passengers on his latest venture, that of landing a boatload of refugees on the northern coast of Australia. All of this information, whispered by her Sergeant, filled Maria with something that had been missing from her life for many years; hope! But they would need money. The Sergeant had a little, saved up from his army pay over many years, but it would not be enough to cover the cost of four people seeking passage to a new life. At the knowledge that the Sergeant intended coming with her, Maria's confidence soared and she suggested that if they could reach Dili then she might be able to raise sufficient extra money for their passage; hinting at help from relatives. Reluctant to fully trust the Sergeant, Maria refrained from mentioning the diamond; only herself and Ana were aware of its existence. But she intended using it to barter for inclusion in the Snakehead's illegal endeavour.

Just four weeks later during the silent hours of a stormy February night in 1988, Maria crouched by the side of a jungle path a few hundred metres from the camp enclosure. Leaving the camp had not been a problem; security was non-existent since few inmates made any effort to escape. Those that did were usually quickly rounded up by regular patrols, handed in by quislings or died in the terrible jungle conditions, usually from snakebite.

Her Sergeant had left the camp two days before, ostensibly on a rest and recreational visit to Dili. He had, however, left Dili immediately and trekked back to the camp to collect Maria and the children. Still fit and strong, he had no doubts about his own ability to make the long march; he was more concerned about the capabilities of Maria and the children to complete such a long slog, since he intended taking a sweeping route to Dili that would see them spending up to a week or more in the jungle. Travelling mostly by night he hoped to evade capture or injury and make contact with the people smuggler as close as possible to the boat's departure date.

All of his information came from the bars in Dili and, whilst he had not actually met the Captain of the boat, the man had been pointed out during a recent visit to the city. The Sergeant could not act or negotiate; he would be under immediate suspicion should he make any contact whatsoever. He must wait until the last minute and let Maria make the arrangements. Latest information indicated that there existed no method of selection for the passage; instant obedience of the Captain, a willingness to risk all and the ability to pay were the only criteria.

The family had waited in the thick jungle for many long hours. Nervously Maria had made several lone trips to the narrow path along which the Sergeant was expected to return from Dili. 'Be as the fawn, hiding from the hyena,' she instructed her children before leaving them, holding each of the beautiful faces between her hands and looking deeply into their eyes.

No sound was heard but suddenly an arm fell around Maria's shoulder and she had to screw down tightly on to her vocal chords to prevent the scream from reaching her mouth. She could not suppress all sound, however, and she hissed that most feminine of gestures; a quick inhalation of breath that is so annoying to most men. Her Sergeant was a large-boned man but his silent approach had taken Maria by surprise; and despite being soaked to the skin and as cold as charity, her heart flipped. Her man had not failed her, the dice were rolled and she called upon the Vicar of God to protect them in their bid for freedom.

All four were wearing sturdy clothing, which had been provided by her Sergeant - strong boots and jeans, tied with string at the ankles to prevent the many jungle creatures from crawling up their legs.

The journey was not nearly as hazardous as anticipated. They had plenty of time to reach Dili and could afford to rest during daylight hours, concealed from view in carefully selected dense patches of jungle. They ate and drank whatever the jungle provided to supplement the meagre rations that the Sergeant had managed to bring back from Dili. Well used to surviving on starvation rations for many weeks at a time, both Maria and the children suffered little from hunger; however the Sergeant's huge frame was accustomed to larger portions but he made no complaint.

Approaching Dili, they could see that the suppressive policies of the occupying forces had left many houses abandoned on the outskirts of the town. Those considered not fit for occupation by the invading army were left to rot in the humid atmosphere of the island. In the same vein as a leopardess hiding her cubs, Maria carefully briefed the children to remain hidden from view and to answer no call other than that of their mother; after which the two adults left the children and ventured into the crowds of Dili.

Maria had not seen the city for many years and she wanted to assess the feelings of the people and the changes to the city but she dare not distract her focus from the immediate future; and concentrated on her forthcoming discussion with the people smuggler. The diamond was hanging from a single strand of leather, tied firmly around her waist under her jeans. She might have to expose some of herself when removing it in front of the smuggler but such an action was of no consequence to her - so many had laid their eyes on her body that one more would make no difference to her feelings.

Long, frustrating hours drifted by with no sign of the Captain of the boat; and both Maria and her Sergeant began to fear that a boatload of willing passengers had already been found. But late in the afternoon the man, with two of his crew, entered the packed bar. Maria was now anxious to return to her children and she wasted as little time as possible. As soon as the trio had been served she stood and headed towards the toilets. As she passed the people smuggler she lowered the front of her jeans, bent down and appeared to pick something from the floor. Straightening she looked the man straight in the eye, opened the palm of his hand and dropped the diamond into it. A huge risk, she knew, but she could think of no other way of making contact without drawing too much attention to her association with her Sergeant. The people smuggler would no doubt have carefully scrutinized every occupant of the bar, searching for customers and informers alike. His was a dangerous business and his watchword was caution. He would certainly have noticed Maria with the Indonesian and although both were clothed as civilians he would still be suspicious. Maria hoped that the valuable diamond would override his suspicions; it could not fail to pique his curiosity. Should the Captain of the boat refuse to return the diamond, her Sergeant would kill all three with his concealed pistol.

Passing by the table on her return from the toilet she once again paused at the side of the people smugglers. A chair was pulled from an adjacent table and Maria sat, waiting for the Captain to speak. Acting the role of an experienced prostitute, the couple appeared to be negotiating the cost of her favours; but in the process the diamond was returned to Maria and a deal struck.

Under the command of Captain Horatio Xeves, the ship, a small and ancient freighter of about eight hundred tonnes, had already seen some sixty-odd years of service plying the waters of the South China seas. Originally the *Tsang Tao*, the vessel had been renamed the *Tetum* after the official language of the Timor population. A cunning deception, probably in the hope of disguising the fearful condition of the ship from its would-be passengers.

When the ship left the coast of Timor, from a point just a few kilometres east of Dili, it was loaded to the gills with human flotsam. Some four hundred souls were crammed within and on top of the leaky vessel, which had to be continually pumped of seawater to avoid floundering. Among these four hundred were Maria, her Sergeant and her two children. Never again would Maria have to worry about concealing the diamond; it was safely installed in a safe in the Captain's tiny cabin.

Living conditions onboard were atrocious. Within two hours of sailing every toilet on the tiny ship was blocked, the doors locked

Alfred Leonard

and nailed by the crew to prevent further use. Passengers reverted to the use of buckets for both washing and toilets, slopping the contents over the side when they had finished. Not all of this human detritus landed cleanly in the sea; most slid down the sides of the vessel in a disgusting smear of human excrement, adding a crazy zigzag camouflage to the ship's paintwork. Within hours of sailing there was not a clean part of the ship available for sleeping or eating and the smell of so many mainly unwashed bodies, packed in close proximity, was almost unbearable.

Packed into every nook and cranny were the possessions of the passengers. The preboarding instructions, which called for a maximum of one small container, suitcase or kit bag per person, had been conveniently disregarded by some of the more wealthy refugees; and large was the pile of discarded containers in the deserted cove from which they had departed, heaved unceremoniously overboard by the crew. Forsaking clothing except for an additional T-shirt and shorts, Maria had packed food in each of the four rucksacks that the family had brought with them. She anticipated that the journey would take about three days, given a speed of advance of about eight knots, but being extra cautious she still rationed their food so that it would last much longer: just in case.

The storm broke during the afternoon of the third day. At first a single black cloud in a clear blue sky, it developed at frightening speed. Ferocious winds from the north drove the tiny ship southwards through the enormous seas for several hours. Many were lost overboard having failed to lash themselves to some part of the ship that would support their weight. The huge Sergeant tore their jeans into strips to make a lashing strong enough to hold them and tied the family to the foot of a small mast.

Navigating, for the Captain and crew, was a nightmare for the heavy seas and strong winds made it almost impossible to keep the tiny ship on course. The shipload of refugees missed the Dundas Strait, between Melville Island and the Australian Cobourg Peninsula, by just a few degrees; the winds had blown them further east and they sailed into the relatively sheltered but still very rough seas of Blue Mud Bay.

During March 1988, an incident occurred off the northern coast of Australia that threatened the good name of that country in the eyes of the world. So heavy were the reporting restrictions imposed that not one newspaper would risk running a report of the vague hearsay that swept around the journalistic enclaves of Darwin, Sydney and Canberra.

An old ex-Royal Navy Leander class frigate, HMS *Charybdis*, had been sold to the Royal Australian Navy in 1983 for virtual peanuts. Renamed HMAS *Wogga*, it had served well as a navigational training ship but was nearing the end of its useful life. Operating in the Arafura Sea, in the vicinity of North West Crocodile Island, on 8th March 1988, a signal was received over the now ageing satcom equipment that a suspected illegal entry vehicle (SIEV) had been spotted heading across the Timor Sea towards Australia's northern coast. *Wogga's* orders were to intercept the SIEV and prevent the ship unloading its human cargo.

Newly promoted to Commander and in command of HMAS *Wogga*, James Mason-Dixon, RAN, was regarded as a high flyer, destined for great things and the heady heights of flag rank. A navigational expert, the Captain of *Wogga* had proved his expertise on several previous sea-going appointments but this was his first command. Just four weeks previously the crew of *Wogga* had watched their well-loved previous skipper leave the ship for emergency medical treatment and had seen their new captain swagger up the gangway an hour later to take his place.

The signal to action was a stroke of extreme good fortune to Mason-Dixon. He had bitterly resented being appointed to this bucket; however he was determined to make the most of his first sea-going command in the hope of better appointments in the future.

The daily sea-going life of a navigational training ship is one of intense boredom, followed by several months of the same. Endless dreary days of attempting to instruct *snotties*[11] in the intricacies of navigation. After a single month, Commander Mason-Dixon, who insisted on retaining his hyphenated name in the face of opposition from Navy high command and the general practices of the Australian people was totally bored.

---

[11]Snotties. Very junior naval Officers.

Alfred Leonard

Not for long did the man occupy the seat of power on the bridge of HMAS *Wogga* before his despotic treatment of the young Officers striving for comprehension earned him the nickname of 'masochistic hyphen dickhead'. There had been many occasions when the Commander had been overheard berating a young *snotty*. Simple good manners, a regard for the feelings of others and naval protocol demand that such minor slaps on the wrist be delivered in private. But Mason-Dixon cared little for time-honoured principles and delivered his admonishing chastisements in front of the on-duty bridge personnel, jabbing a hard finger into the chest of his victim in a crude attempt at highlighting a point. Not surprisingly, his crew despised him.

'Port thirty, steer three-five-five, increase revolutions to maximum.' The Captain burst on to his bridge and assumed command. The sharp commands were issued, having ignored the usual requirement to relieve formally the Officer of the Watch and oblivious of the fact that 'hands to dinner' had just been piped.

Port thirty is an excessive wheel command, even for a warship. *Wogga* reacted in a sudden burst of power and heeled over sharply to starboard. Below decks most of the crew lost their plated dinner; and cups, plates, soup, and vegetables flew across the ship as she heeled dangerously in the violent manoeuvre, all broken crockery to be replaced at the crew's expense.

Wogga hugged the tip of Croker Island, steaming at maximum revolutions into the violent storm. Radar operators in the operations room had picked up a contact and the Captain, hell-bent on obeying the instructions from his masters concerning his first operational mission to the letter, launched his ship into the teeth of the storm. Not one of the off-watch crew was standing; all had strapped themselves into their bunks, fully clothed and with survival suits as pillows, awaiting whatever God in His Heaven held in store for them.

The ship's movements were unbelievable. Two and a half thousand tonnes of warship felt as if it was climbing up the side of a mountain. The steepness of the climb was frightening even to the most tested of mariners; but the strange, brief moment of peace as the ship sat on the crest of each mighty wave, followed by the sickening drop, was sheer agony. In the seconds that it took the ship to fall into the ocean, mimicking a leaf on Niagara Falls, all hands had but one thought, '*Will she make it this time?'* The almighty crash, juddering and squeals of distress from the ship as she struck the bottom of each wave put the fear of the unknown into all onboard. Out of bounds to everyone during bad weather, it was total madness above decks; wire and whip aerials had been ripped away and the portside sea boat had been torn from its davits.

In the midst of this chaos, the Captain sent for the helicopter pilot and asked if he would consider flying out to identify the radar contact. It was fortunate indeed for the pilot that the final decision to fly, or not to fly, remained with him; for the Captain would not have thought twice about ordering the helo into the air.

By the time *Wogga* breasted Vashon Head, the SIEV *Tetum* was slowly drifting into Blue Mud Bay; and a little under two hours later the frigate had the freedom seekers in sight. Fortunately for all, the seas had died down considerably in the shelter of the bay and *Wogga* slowly edged within hailing distance of the *Tetum*.

As the frigate hove into view some of the refugees dived overboard and attempted the swim to shore. Although no one on either of the two ships ever knew, not one person made it. Every single one was devoured by the small flotilla of sharks that had been following the *Tetum* for two days, attracted by the smell of the vessel. The perseverance of these creatures was well rewarded when bodies fell overboard during the storm and again when others attempted to swim ashore. Each occasion prompted a feeding frenzy, which saw the bodies torn to shreds, blossoms of blood spots staining the surface of the sea with each violent strike, usually whilst life, but no longer hope, still beat within the stricken Mauberians.

Mason-Dixon was extremely satisfied. His ship was a testament to the skill of her British builders. She was a shambles but she had survived the anger of the storm and the mad dash to its present location. Looking across at the reason for the mad dash, the Commander could see the freshly washed sides of the old freighter and what remained of the hastily-added *Tetum* painted in red along the side and around the stern.

However, he was agitated. Some of the refugees were jumping overboard and any number might reach Australian territory to claim political asylum. This must not be allowed to happen. It would cause extreme embarrassment to the Australian government and be the cause of intense annoyance to Commander Mason-Dixon, since he would have failed to complete his orders. A senior naval Officer he might be but he panicked. He must prevent these people from reaching shore. As far as he was concerned his whole career depended upon what happened over the next few hours. Already visions of his admiral's flag were fading in his mind; and he acted instead of thinking.

'Action stations surface; man four point five gun; gunnery Officer to the bridge.' The orders streamed from his fevered brain and he added almost immediately, 'Ah, Guns. At my command two shots across her bows,' as the Gunnery Officer appeared miraculously at his side. 'Aye Aye, Sir,' and Guns was gone, returning to the operations room to take command of his gun's crew over the ship's gunnery intercom system.

At the call to action stations, the ship's First Lieutenant, colloquially known as the Jimmy, reported to his Captain that the ship was closed up at action stations. Lieutenant Commander Eddie Moran, nicknamed Steady Eddie because of his easy-going unflappable nature, was about to leave the bridge to return to his own action station in the damage control office; when he overheard the Captain's orders to Guns. *'Wrong!'* The single word hammered into his brain; the Captain's actions were totally unsuitable for this situation. Firing on a ship in peacetime, even warning shots, was strictly against the RAN's rules of engagement. *'Why did the Captain not know this? Put Wogga between the SIEV and the shore and fend her off. Wogga had enough power to overwhelm the engines of the old freighter.'*

'Sir, a quick word in private if you please.' The request fell on deaf ears and a head already full of the hero worship expected from a grateful nation.

'Not now, First Lieutenant, say your piece or get off my bridge!' The Jimmy had no choice and voiced his objections to the proposed action; objections plainly heard by the whole bridge staff. The Captain was adamant; he would not countermand his order, which left the First Lieutenant with no other option than to draft an entry for the ship's log, countersigned by the Officer of the Watch as official witness. In naval parlance, the Jimmy had cleared his own yardarm.

'Main Gun loaded with high explosive; ready to shoot, Sir,' Guns informed his Captain over the ship's intercom system.

'Shoot!' ordered the Captain, that single imperative sealing the fate of the dejected looking SIEV. The huge bang reverberated around the ship causing almost the entire crew to start. They were taken completely by surprise; at action stations they may be, but dealing with an SIEV should not involve gunfire.

The rancid aroma of cordite permeated the whole ship and many of the crew retched at their first taste of the disgusting smell that lingered in the mouth for hours afterwards. Clearly visible through the bridge windows, the shell fell exactly as programmed; one hundred metres shore-side of the *Tetum*, the puff of water into the air followed the explosion in the still choppy seas.

'Shoot!' The order to fire the second warning shot was given. But on this occasion fate conspired with nature to frustrate the best intentions of man. At the exact instant that the shell was fired, *Wogga* slipped into the dying remains of a large wave, and the shell sped on its way; aimed directly at *Tetum's* midships, just above the water line.

Onboard *Tetum* all was chaos. Captain Xeves was in a quandary; he did not know whether to attempt to beach his ship or order the refugees over the side. The intimidating frigate had been yelling incomprehensible commands over a loudhailer for some time but he knew what they wanted; stay away from the shore. Out of his depth, he also did not know whether he wanted to stop his crew from encouraging the refugees to jump overboard in a last-ditch bid to escape. Sometimes, he knew, a prolonged waiting game achieved the best results and he ordered the engines to be stopped, intending to await developments.

The first shell from the frigate caused more panic amongst the asylum seekers. The Captain was unperturbed; he knew it was just another ploy in a much bigger game. When the second shell struck his ship amidships, it exploded in the galley area just above the water line. High explosives in a four point five shell blew the sides of the freighter to smithereens, leaving a gaping hole and numerous dead and injured. Dozens more dived or fell on to the White Death's table; the insatiable feeding-machines declined not one and the water around the *Tetum* turned red with blood. The exploding force of the shell also blew a hole through the bottom of the vessel; she split in two, rolled alarmingly to port and slowly started her last journey to the bottom of the ocean.

Alfred Leonard

Emerging into the relative quiet of Blue Mud Bay, the seas had sub-sided and Maria had loosed the ties that bound her family to the mast; but they had not strayed far from their safe place. The devastation from the frigate's shell snapped a large spar from the wooden mast, which swooped downwards, still attached to a strong length of rope in a looping swing. The spar removed the head from her Sergeant, who had been sitting in front of Maria, and buried itself in the chest of his Mauberian mistress. Both died instantly and neither saw the twins fall into the sea. Maria had seen the approaching spar but she made no attempt to remove herself from its deadly path; for deep within herself she carried a horrible secret. Her body was infected with that most awful of venereal diseases, syphilis. She instinctively knew that the Australian authorities would insist upon a thorough medical examination for any of the illegal immigrants that managed to make it to the shore; and that such an examination must surely reveal her con-dition. The very thought of other people, and particularly the twins, becoming aware of her predicament filled her with a soul-consuming loathing; the discovery of her own secret would also reveal that she had transmitted the deadly disease to the Sergeant and she could not face that. Now was a good time to die. She had given her children the chance of a new life. *'Please, Holy Father; let them survive.'* This was the final thought of Maria before she left this earthly life; and as with every other mother, her last wishes were for her children.

The burly leading seaman in charge of *Wogga's* cutter reached back into the sea to pull the second child to safety. He could see that this was a really lovely girl; her small breasts were clearly visible through the remains of her wet T-shirt, signalling the approach of woman-hood. The seaman had witnessed the attack from the gigantic shark and had marvelled at the small child's incredible luck when the mon-ster had rejected its meal. Hopeful of rescuing more people from the sea, he circled for some time. The marksman in the bows of the cutter blasted away with his rifle at the flashing bodies of the blood-enraged predators swimming around the floating remains of the SIEV. It was a sickening sight, body parts, blood and gore forming a human soup on the surface of the sea; but not a sign of life from the limbless carcasses. The two children were to be the only survivors and the

Leading Seaman was angry; his Captain had extracted a terrible price from the refugees on the old freighter in exchange for his desire to please his masters. *'You murdering bastard!'* The thought echoed continuously around the burly seaman's head and he did not know how he was going to prevent himself from giving the target of his anger a meaty smack in the mouth when he returned onboard his ship.

No more signs of life were found in the sea and the seaman looked over at the two children. One of his crew had bundled them into several blankets and wrapped them with an old tarpaulin. Both looked white with shock, tears flowing freely down their cheeks. Their eyes cast frantically amongst the human remains in the sea looking for a well-loved face that they knew, but could not yet accept, they would never see again.

In the general hum of machinery and warmth of *Wogga*, Ana and Jose remained silent throughout their meal. Their rescuer stood guard outside the small master-at-arms office, telling everyone that they were getting dried and dressed; and steadfastly refusing to allow anyone to see them. He wished to delay the inevitable questioning for as long as possible, allow them time to speak to each other and decide their story; and to get some hot food inside them.

Meal eaten, or rather consumed in a frenzy since they were so hungry, the twins whispered to each other. In the short period of time that it took to eat the meal, Ana had come of age. She knew that she was the stronger of the two and that she must now assume the responsibilities as head of the family. Only too pleased to leave everything to his sister, Jose submitted to her leadership; and to avoid conflicting stories Ana had told him to refuse to speak, pretending post-traumatic stress. The twins had inherited academic brilliance from their parents and both were highly intelligent. They had thrived under the private tutelage of their mother over the past eleven years and their only weak subject was that of current world affairs; an obvious result of their incarceration in the concentration camp on Timor.

But these two beautiful children, perfect in every way except maybe for a hint of malnutrition, were not the only persons onboard *Wogga* suffering from the stress associated with a traumatic experience. Commander Mason-Dixon knew, without a shadow of doubt, that in the instant that the second shell was fired, his career had ended. A vision of himself, entering the room where a row of heavily gold-braided Officers were convened for his court martial, and seeing the accusing, unsheathed sword pointing menacingly at his belly, had taken permanent residence in his mind. At some point in time, most demi-tyrants expose their necks to the descending guillotine of circumstances beyond their control. And for Mason-Dixon, his hopes and dreams disappeared from view, like a cloud driven before the wind; and with them went his bombastic attitude towards life.

A totally different man stood in his shoes; just a few seconds after the shell blasted the hulk of the old freighter, together with its human cargo, into eternity. Subdued in the ruins of his failure, he began to descend into the depths of despair and self recrimination, branding himself a cold-blooded killer; which in the eyes of his crew he most certainly was.

Commander Mason-Dixon sent for his First Lieutenant, having first endorsed Eddie Moran's objection in the ship's log. He handed the log ceremoniously to Moran, signifying for all intents and purposes the hand-over of command of his ship. The Captain went down to his day-cabin, a rare event for a warship's commanding Officer whilst at sea, and there, and until the ship docked in Darwin, strove to write his report of the incident. The only decent contribution that the Captain managed to make in the whole sorry story was included in the final paragraph of his report in which he pleaded for the Australian government to grant the two survivors political asylum.

Born on 10th December, 1966, Josh Templeton, the burly rescuer of the two Timorese children, had been in the RAN for a little over four years. His parents, Hayley and Rodney, had emigrated from the UK when Josh was just nine years old. At first the family had lived in Tuggeranong, a suburb of Canberra in the Australian Capital Territory (ACT). But as the years progressed they managed to purchase a thirty-acre plot in the Bungendore area, a small community on the outskirts of Canberra. Here they lived, happily caring for the menagerie of horses, dogs, cats, chickens, ducks and geese about the property. Rodney had worked hard and achieved much since the family's arrival in their chosen new country and was now the financial director of a large agricultural company, based in the ACT.

When Josh decided to join the RAN, his mother was at first delighted with her new-found freedom and immersed herself in her favourite pastime - getting involved in the local equine sporting scene. Despite her busy lifestyle looking after her own horses and getting involved in various gymkhanas and other horsey events, Hayley was getting a little bored with her virtual solitary existence. Rodney worked late most weekday evenings, she was left on her own for long periods, and she was considering fostering children or even adopting, to give her some added interest in life.

It was through her son's involvement in the SIEV incident that Hayley Templeton heard of the two Timorese refugees, recently orphaned during their family's attempt at asylum. No sooner had the gangway been deployed from *Wogga's* quarterdeck, than Josh was on the phone to his mother.

He knew that his mother was somewhat bored with her lonely existence on the small farm and he also knew that he wanted to help the two children that he had pulled from the sea. Josh was by no means a religious man but he knew that something with more influence than fate had been abroad on the day that he had pulled the only two survivors into his boat. More than help, he wanted to care for them and protect them; and since he was as yet unmarried then the only person he would entrust with their care was his own mother.

A seed was planted into Hayley Templeton's mind; and as her son related the events of the children's harrowing experience, the seed took root and grew within her heart. A very determined woman when roused, Hayley set her own targets and agendas; nothing swayed her from her chosen endeavours and husband Rodney usually complied with her wishes. Extremely well connected, both amongst the large landowners and with senior members of Canberra's central government, Hayley made her plans. She believed firmly in the old idiom that claims: it is sometimes better to know someone, than to know something.

Four months later, at the end of June 1988, two young Timorese children, remarkably similar in their facial characteristics, stepped off the train at Canberra main line station. They were dressed warmly against the chilly winter winds gusting off the nearby hills of the Great Dividing Range and were looking for faces that they had learned to trust and love. In civilian clothes, Josh stood on the platform, towering over his tiny mother; casting his eyes anxiously up and down the length of the train. Both children broke into a run when they saw the faces for which they had been searching; Jose ran straight for Hayley and Ana dashed into the arms of Josh. The new family Templeton climbed into the battered old Land Rover and headed off through the side-streets of Canberra, out past the airport to a surprise welcome party.

Ana and Jose Vinacco, granted a permanent settlement visa within a year of joining their adoptive family, changed their names by deed poll to Ana Maria and Joseph Robert Templeton; both felt a deep desire to include their parents' names in their own. Attending private schools within a week of their arrival at Canberra, their teachers were gobsmacked at their academic prowess, far in advance of any other pupils of their own age. Both had IQ equivalents bordering on genius.

CHAPTER 7
AN UNPLEASANT TASK

THREAD:

By 1976, still in the service of Queen and country, I had been promoted to the rank of Lieutenant.

Since our return from Kranji in 1963 I had undergone a qualifying course for petty Officer, and a long and gruelling period of instruction to qualify as a special duties Officer; the whole interspersed with the odd sojourn to sea duty.

UNITED KINGDOM. 1976.

Tracey was comfortably established in a large country house in the village of Hambledon. Located midway between Petersfield and Portsmouth, at which naval dockyard most of the ships I might be required to serve in would be based, and within commuting distance of the Navy's Signal School, HMS *Mercury*. We had scoured the area around Portsmouth to find a house that suited Tracey, since I tended to leave such decisions to her. The house came with about five acres of land in the form of large gardens and a couple of paddocks. Alicia loved horses. Now a lovely teenager, she had done so since she was about four years old - hence the reason for buying a property with some attached land.

We had been forced into paying considerably more than the property was worth; but since it perfectly matched our needs we had little choice other than to dig deeply into our well-stocked pockets. Land and location do not always mix and there were a number of other bidders but since this particular house was perfectly located and had just the right amount of land, we felt justified in out-bidding all others.

Despite our attempts we had not managed to produce further offspring. Good health, as promised by Belial First, had been my constant companion; but I often wondered whether my biologically-altered status mirrored that of the Verunian people in this one small way. 'Was I sterile?' The thought often occurred to me over the years.

Still an attractive woman, Tracey had retained her youthful looks. She was blessed with a small bone structure, slightly taller than average, and kept strict control over her weight. However, at nearly thirty-five years of age, she was beginning to show some signs of ageing; the odd grey hair and an almost imperceptible puffiness around her facial features that was discernible only without a layer of feminine slap. As of yet I had not had to use any ageing preparations to hide my unchanging appearance; everyone simply thought that I was one of those lucky people immune to the ravages of advancing years. But it would not be many more years before I would have to consider making some changes.

In the early summer of 1974 an unexpected event took place. With my long-term plan in mind, that of using this, my first life, to raise funds and select a team to assist me in my task, I had for the first time had to use my powers in the destruction of another human being.

Whilst serving in Kranji in 1963 and having manipulated the Singapore lottery, I had acquired the services of a young financial advisor, as yet unknown and untried, to manage my hoard of Singapore dollars tucked safely in a Singapore bank. Using my powers of concealment I had visited the University of Singapore to check the records and grades of the soon to graduate young accountants.

The worldwide futures market of the sixties dealt mainly with trade in agricultural products and was a vastly different enterprise than that of a 21st century world. But as everyone will be well aware, it was still very much a volatile place in which to invest money and what I was looking for was a brilliant financial brain that I could influence; and help with my powers. With neither the time nor inclination to remain in Singapore for what I saw as a long-term business venture, I needed the first member of my team urgently.

A young Chinese student at the Singapore Institute of Commerce, one Kenneth Lim, was due to graduate in late 1963. Destined to be the top man of that year he had been a gifted student and revelled in the minutiae of financial rules and regulations. To a middle class family, he was born shortly before me in 1940. A very small man in stature, little more than one point six metres tall, quiet, studious and without obvious flaws or vices, I had been overlooking him for some time. Engaged to an older Chinese girl, Kenneth hoped to marry as soon as he graduated, set himself up in business or obtain a well-paid job, and fulfil the demands of his future parents-in-law.

A few months prior to his graduation, I had made arrangements to interview Mr Lim at the Institute of Commerce. The Institute's principal had been only too pleased to accede to my request and I sat in the library dressed in extremely expensive civilian clothing awaiting the arrival of Lim. Always excessively polite, he answered my personal questions about his family; he knew that I had come with the possibility of employment and was anxious to make a good impression.

Briefly I outlined my circumstances; lottery winner, large funds available for investment, requirement for a Singapore-based financial consultant working exclusively for me - and followed up with a most generous package of remunerations. In his first year I offered to pay him twenty thousand Singapore dollars and ten percent of the profits. At his disposal, I would place half a million Singapore dollars for investment in the hazardous futures market, trading mainly with the United States and Japan, in oil, electrical goods, shipping and clothing. As the large numbers tripped from my tongue, I saw the glint in Lim's eyes. This was my man.

The young Chinese, speaking in excellent English, thanked me profusely for my offer and accepted immediately. It was a much more generous offer than he could expect to receive in any of the other financial institutions on the island; a fact of which I was well aware. His heart was already hammering away in his chest. He could not believe his luck and he was anxious to dash off to tell his sweetheart that they could now afford to marry.

Over the next eight years up until 1971, Kenneth did a remarkable job. His strong work ethics, dedication and desire to make his fortune turned my half million into ten million dollars. Occasionally I fed him some insights of my own but he had been largely on his own; and I was hopeful that he would remain in my service for many years to come. In the process he had amassed a tidy sum for himself and was living very comfortably with his wife and three young children in a large, secluded house in Sembawang village.

The money generated for me by Kenneth's hard work continued to grow steadily and remained lodged in the Bank of Singapore. Project money was how I viewed it, a nest-egg set against future requirements; possibly in my second lifespan. Certainly the money was superfluous to my everyday needs. Tracey and I lived very comfortably on my naval salary and the returns from safe UK investments for the bulk of the lottery win. We did not lead an extravagant lifestyle but we also did not want for much.

To some men the acquisition of even greater amounts of money becomes an obsession; and Kenneth was just such a man. His greed for more was fuelled by a major change in the futures marketplace in 1971. Up until this time foreign currencies had been pegged to an international gold standard; but this had now been abolished and the currencies of the world were allowed to float. An international money market (the IMM) was inaugurated and futures trading began for the same world's currencies.

This was a turning point for Kenneth and for me. For Kenneth was a genius when trading in currency exchange, helped in no short measure by my own abilities and powers. In three years my account at the Singapore Bank had doubled to twenty million dollars; a very healthy and not inconsiderable profit - but about five million dollars short of my own estimates.

Becoming increasingly more suspicious, I was considering spending a few weeks of my Navy leave in travelling to Singapore, both to overlook Kenneth on a more regular basis and in the hope that my physical presence might set the man back on the straight and narrow.

But a surprise communication from Veruni changed everything.

Belial First had told me that direct communication between us would be impossible for the foreseeable future, mainly because the Moon permanently blocked Veruni from Earth's view and provided a shield which blocked their existing technology. However, in the intervening years, Verunian scientists had continued to work towards providing a path of direct communication between themselves and their Verguide.

Previously, the Verunians had little use for conventional communications systems; their telepathy was good for about fifteen thousand kilometres and covered most of their everyday requirements. But communicating with me posed a different problem. Positioning geostationary relay satellites in space, or around the circumference of the Moon for any known communications method, had been discarded for fear of discovery by the Avoi-Shun. Consequently, Verunian scientists had, for some years, been working on a new system of isolating a beam of sunlight and transferring their thought waves along it; a hot-wire with a difference.

To this end they had harnessed their only source of power, the Sun, to drill a hole through the centre of the Moon. A mere one millimetre in diameter and almost three and a half thousand kilometres in length, the concentrated beam of sunlight that it carried was centred on a footprint covering the south of England.

'Belial.' At first I thought I was dreaming again. The voice was similar to that which I remembered from twelve years ago - but how could it be? I was not in Singapore, neither was I in any large cave-like location. I was lying in my bed early on a sunny July morning in 1974. Tracey had gone down to make a cup of tea and I was mulling over my probable trip to sort out the problem of Kenneth in Singapore. The well remembered buzz in my head as information was transferred to me - I knew it now to be a digital stream - was commonplace in our new digital world.

Vast amounts of information were passed to me in a fraction of a second but it would take my relatively prehistoric brain several weeks to analyse it all. Of special interest to me of course was the setting up of the new communications system. Installed specifically for communicating with the Verguide, it was initially a simplex system to me but as my new skills developed I would eventually be able to ask the Verunians for help and advice using a duplex, two-way system.

Basically the Verunians concurred with my long-term plans. They updated my skills and powers and informed me that nothing had changed concerning the fate of either planet. A real boon to me was the updating of my overlooking capability. Previously, it was necessary for my alter ego to be standing within a few kilometres of my subject in order to read thoughts, or influence decisions; but after the upgrade I could obtain the same results when simply overlooking from a greater distance. Quite what the greatest range was I had no idea but it was certainly good enough for me to experiment on Kenneth in Singapore. I had no difficulty whatsoever in forcing him to get up from his desk and close the door to his study or open the drawer in his desk.

My feeling that Kenneth was not being as honest with me as he should was confirmed when I forced him to open every compartment in his desk. I watched him release the secret drawer and made him withdraw the small ledger. Just as I thought, the figure embezzled totalled a little over five million dollars. Gazing down at Kenneth's little red book, I felt sadness engulf me. There was no need for Kenneth to cream off the money for his own profit; he was rewarded far in excess of anything that he could have achieved without my funds to invest and not once had he been brave enough to risk his own gathering fortune. The next few years would return huge profits for those with the necessary capital and knowledge, however obtained, from speculation in the money markets of the world. Already I could see the advent of the Stock Exchange in the early 1980s, where the value of companies could be traded on the S&P500.

A dilemma then. What to do about Kenneth? Yes, he was a young man, and yes, he had a young family; but he had profited greatly from his association with me and merely to fire him was, to my mind, not sufficient punishment. The loss of his job would not cause him much concern; he certainly had enough money to last him for the rest of his life and his knowledge of the futures market would reward him handsomely, even if he was forced to use his own money. No, he had to go. It would provide me with an additional benefit, for it would allow me to try out my new overlooking capabilities and to test my ability to dispose of someone without fear of discovery, reprisal or punishment. So I made my plans to kill Kenneth Lim.

The meticulous records that Kenneth maintained clearly indicated myself as the owner of the bank account that he used for his transactions. My intention was to kill Kenneth and leave the hidden ledger to be discovered by the police. This would most certainly implicate me as the prime suspect; therefore matters must be arranged to ensure that I had a cast-iron alibi for the time of his death.

Although my updated overlooking skills enabled me to influence what a person did or thought, it would require the presence of my alter ego in Singapore in order to end the man's life.

Consequently, some days later, I informed my staff at Comcen Fort Southwick that I would be spending the weekend of 6th and 7th July, 1974, in my office, ostensibly writing up quarterly staff assessments; and that I did not want to be disturbed. Occasionally during large naval exercises, I remained at the comcen overnight and had a bunk in my office for this purpose. There was very little chance of anyone disobeying my order not to be disturbed; my office was deep underground at the far end of a long passageway system and no one, apart from my two assistants who would not be returning to work until Monday, ever ventured down there. Completely self-contained, with a small kitchen and bathroom, it was a wonderfully quiet retreat, ideal for concentrating on a particular project.

Quite how anyone finding me might react, in the semi-conscious state in which I existed when engaged abroad in alter ego mode, I knew not. One fine day it might be interesting to find out. If anyone did manage to get into my locked office, they would find me lying on my bunk; present but not quite all correct. Presumably a doctor would diagnose some sort of coma and I would be transported to the RN Hospital at Haslar.

Early on Saturday 6th July I walked into the comcen, spoke to the on-duty supervisor and made sure that he entered into the turn-over log that I was staying in my office for the weekend. Underlined, the supervisor had added his own comment, 'The old man does not want to be disturbed.'

Actually taking the opportunity to write up some staff assessments, I remained in the office until about 11.00. Deeming it time to act, since the time converted to 19.00 Singapore time, I willed my alter ego to transport itself to Kenneth's house on the island.

I found him beavering away at his desk and for a few minutes I watched him work. TV shows and films show the hero or the villain taking human life in a routine, off-hand, disinterested way; and most other people accepted loss of life in the same casual way - unless of course they were directly involved. But for me, taking a human life was not a matter to be taken lightly and I dreaded taking this drastic step. But the man knew me well, he was privy to details of my financial dealings and he had access to all my funds on the island. Simply sacking him might convince him to drain vast amounts from my accounts before I could stop him; and he could prove a problem in the future.

But I must not delay. I felt that if I stayed my hand much longer I might chicken-out completely. As a boy I had thought nothing of stretching the necks of game caught on hunting expeditions with my father; but this was different.

By transferring a thought into his brain I caused him to remove the secret ledger from its hidden drawer and, as he sat looking in a puzzled manner at the little red book, I slipped the garrotte of thin wire around his neck and pulled hard; pressing my knee into his back for added pressure. Not a sound came from Kenneth but he died a horrible, choking and bloody death. The garrotte bit deeply into his neck, for in my inexperience I had pulled much too strongly and when I looked at his face I could see that his eyes were bulging, almost popping out of his head. Quickly I checked that the hidden compartment was open and made sure that the secret ledger was on the desk, fervently hoping that Kenneth's wife Helen Lim would not realise its importance and dispose of it.

As for the money that Kenneth had purloined from me, I took no further interest. At least it salved my conscience a little knowing that Helen and her children would be well provided for.

There was no profit in remaining in Singapore but I wanted to spend some time overlooking the following few hours, after the body of Kenneth was discovered. Having reconnected my alter ego to my physical body, I remained on my bunk at Fort Southwick, overlooking the Lim household.

The Singapore police were baffled. No sign of forced entry into the crime scene could be found; there were no signs of a struggle; and nothing untoward had been heard by Helen Lim or her children. All the investigating detective inspector had in the way of evidence was a blood-soaked body with obvious neck wounds; and a nagging suspicion of assassination. The wounds were very similar to those left by the infamous garrotte, which was a favoured killing weapon for the many different Chinese sects who constantly waged war amongst themselves.

Late Sunday afternoon I left the comcen, having spoken once again to the duty supervisor. No comment was made and I knew that no one had attempted to contact me during my alter ego trip to Singapore.

Over the next few days I received several phone calls from the Singapore police and from the Bank of Singapore. Both officials were extremely polite for I was the holder of some of the largest bank accounts on the island. My acting skills were increasing year by year and I had no difficulty in simulating surprise and deep regret at Kenneth's death. Naval humour got the better of me at one stage I'm afraid and I gave the Inspector a nasty fright when I demanded that the culprits be brought to justice; for such demands from wealthy European entrepreneurs could not be treated lightly. The poor chap had no real answers for me and although he promised to make the case his number one priority, and gave vague hints of assassination, Chinese cults and a long term investigation, I could see on his desk the case file, already marked 'case closed'.

The Bank Manager, Mr Charles Lee, was well known to me. At least his voice was, because of the many telephone conversations over the preceding years. After the usual platitudes concerning Kenneth, I asked him if he might assign a personal account manager to manage my funds; a service for which I would gladly pay. The dollar signs flashed across his eyes, he had the very man.

His youngest son Paul had just graduated from university and would be the ideal candidate. My request would provide Mr Lee senior with a perfect opportunity to recruit another member of his family into the bank. Using my best businesslike voice, I told Mr Lee that the choice was his to make; but I insisted that whoever he appointed, it must be under the strict understanding that my financial instructions must be obeyed to the letter. In addition, a private telephone line was to be set up to Paul Lee for my exclusive use. The number must never be engaged and should be diverted to Paul whenever he was away from his office. Twenty-four hours a day contact was what I needed.

All things considered, the demise of Kenneth had probably saved a considerable amount of money, since my initial terms of employment for him had been exceedingly generous. However, I had learned from that mistake and would restrict my future employees to good salaries but a much lower share of the profits.

CHAPTER 8
TIMOTHY YEWLY

THREAD:

Well over ten years have passed since 1974. These I spent learning how best to use my updated skills, making plans for my change to a second existence and in selecting a small team to help me fulfil my task as the Verguide.

To this end I continued to keep an occasional eye on gifted people throughout the world. Of the half dozen that I regularly overlooked, the most promising candidates appeared to be Maria Vinacco and her children. It had been sheer luck that I had been overlooking her life shortly after she gave birth to the twins.

By the year 2000, my target date by which I must commence a new life, I knew that Maria would be too old to be of much use to me. But the birth of her twins was a gift from heaven for both of us; for I saw in them such levels of intelligence as are rarely seen in the human brain.

Overlooking the Vinacco family much more often than any other possible recruits became routine for me. There was little that I could do to improve their personal circumstances. Determined not to use my powers in changing individual lives too much, I could do little more than ensure that death did not visit them before the natural order of such things; and again, I could only provide this protection whilst overlooking them.

However, I remained with the family during their escape from Timor and was able to protect the twins during their time in the sea and the encounter with the shark. Using my updated power of projecting a protective shield to others, I had enclosed both children within its sheltering embrace, which gave the shark such a nasty surprise when his pinniped turned into a log.

Sadly I was unable to help Maria; I was too busy protecting her twins. But I also knew that there was no point in prolonging her life, for she had already given up hope. Human dignity and self respect had been ripped from her over the years in the concentration camp and she had given up on life. When mind and body were at their lowest ebb, she felt too as if her religious convictions had failed her when she discovered her sexual disease. But she was at least spared the terrible knowledge that what she had contracted was not syphilis but a forerunner of a devastating new disease that was destined to sweep the world in the new millennia; an immune deficiency disease that would claim the lives of hundreds of millions in the years to come.

ENGLAND. 1990S.

Following the twins' ordeal and their subsequent good fortune in finding the kindly Templeton family, I had continued to keep an eye on them. As the world approached the new millennium I knew that they were well cared for, well loved and nearing graduation from Canberra's excellent university system. It was almost time for me to recruit them.

As the world approached the turn of the century, my most pressing concern was that of vacating my existing life and clearing the decks for lifetime number two. Sadly, in 1996 and having reached the age of fifty-five, which is the normal retirement age for naval Officers, I had to leave an occupation that I loved and take up a civilian role. Deciding to use my time in making plans for my rebirth, I set to.

As the years go by in a loving relationship, most people do not notice the signs of deterioration in their partner. Tracey had aged well and was still a most attractive woman; but I had been fighting a battle to add years to my appearance for some considerable time. Constantly dying my hair grey was an onerous chore, particularly since I had to be so secretive about the process. A full-set, that is a full-faced beard and moustache to non-pusser[12] people, can age a man considerably, and I had elected to add such facial camouflage to my armoury of age-disguising techniques. However, the beard was not a good idea and after a few months of itching and scratching, I shaved it off.

Always in good health, I nevertheless took to complaining about various non-existent aches and pains, whilst steadfastly refusing to seek medical help, blaming my problems on old 'father time' and a sailor's natural disinclination to visit the sickbay.

Our only child Alicia had married in 1981. Through the years after their marriage, her husband, accountant James Ridout, soon came to realise that his wife had a problem, which she attributed to having spent the first two years of her life in a tropical climate. SAD, or Seasonal Affective Disorder, a form of winter depression generally known as the 'Winter Blues', made Alicia's life a misery during England's cold winter weather.

By mutual agreement the couple emigrated to Australia in 1992 and had settled nicely into a large five hundred acre farm on the outskirts of the ACT, close to a small town called Braidwood. The move to a sunnier part of the world was obviously beneficial to Alicia, who produced three daughters in quick succession. Kacey in 1993, was followed by Ruby in 1995, and finally by Lydia in 1997.

Alicia's move to the antipodes had been a purely fortuitous event for me. I did not influence her decision in any way but it did provide me with an excuse to visit them on a fairly regular basis over the past few years; and of course whilst there I was closer to the Templeton twins.

Alicia had been horse-mad since she was a small girl and her own three girls were destined to be no less keen. It was inevitable that one day Alicia would meet up with the Templetons at the many horsey events in and around Canberra and at one such event I was introduced to the twins. At that time I did nothing to indicate my interest in their future, merely intending that the Templeton family be aware of my name.

---

[12]Pusser. Anything naval.

Formulating a plan for a second lifetime had consumed an enormous amount of my time. My plan required that I suddenly become the proud father of a fictitious son. Shortly after our return from an Australian visit in 1996, I informed Tracey that I had been contacted by a young woman claiming that her son had been fathered by me. Blunt and brutal? Yes. But my forthcoming death would be much more easily borne by Tracey if her love could be dampened by the knowledge of an old love affair of mine; particularly a recently-discovered dalliance.

Explaining the birth of the boy was a painful business for me. Tracey had been a most wonderful wife, lover and companion; but I could see no other way. The story that I told her was that I had been tempted into a brief liaison with a woman in Plymouth whilst my ship had been undergoing repairs in the dockyard in 1974. The child, a boy called Timothy, was born the following year and took the name of Yewly since I had been named on the birth certificate as his father. The woman involved, and I did not name her to Tracey and neither did she ask, had not intended to contact me preferring to leave it to the boy to decide whether or not he wished to find his father later in life. Two years ago the woman had contracted cancer of the breast and had decided to tell her son about me before she died. Hence the recent contact.

The tears in Tracey's eyes almost unmanned me. She was devastated. But she was a sensible person and quickly understood that my pretended liaison had been a one-off. After a time she forgave me but our relaxed and trusting relationship was never quite the same again.

Planning for my change of life had been ongoing for a considerable number of years. By 1995 I had managed to ensure that all the relevant information concerning the birth of my fictitious son was filed in Plymouth's Registry Office. I had a birth certificate, medical record card and a national insurance number; everything I needed to obtain a passport and assume a new identity. Timothy Victor Yewly, born 3rd March, 1975, was to become the new me and my heir to the Singapore billions. All that remained for me to do was to introduce my son to various bank managers, arrange for my own death and seamlessly assume the role of Timothy.

Shortly after my admission to Tracey, I told her that I was going to

Singapore to terminate my business activities there. She knew that I had some money left in the Bank of Singapore and that I had been dabbling in the futures market; but she had no idea how much. Travelling by scheduled flights in the normal way, I returned once again to that magical island. On arrival I checked into a good quality hotel, made arrangements to see Paul Lee the following day and thought only of obtaining a tasty evening meal and, if I could somehow overwhelm the terrible jet-lag, get some rest.

Paul Lee, now manager of his bank, was delighted to see me. And so he should be since I was currently the largest private account holder on the books of his bank. My account had risen from about twenty million dollars in 1974 to a staggering two billion. At current rates of exchange that figure converted to about half a billion pounds sterling. Pleasantries and preliminaries completed, I gave Paul my instructions. 'Please make the necessary arrangements to have a copy of my final will and testament stored here. Additionally I wish to transfer ten million pounds to a UK bank, in Timothy's name. And I think it is time for you to meet my son, since he will be the sole beneficiary of my local assets in the event of my death. In the meantime, my son is to be made a joint account holder of all my existing accounts. Perhaps you could find time to see us again tomorrow?'

My wishes, Paul assured me, would be complied with immediately; and he made an appointment to receive the two of us the following day. As I was leaving his office, I turned as if suddenly remembering something. 'Oh, Paul. I might not be with Timothy; I have some other important business meetings that might last longer than planned.' Paul Lee was all attention, 'Not a problem,' he assured me, shaking my hand and executing a most elaborate and obsequious bow.

I dared not use my alter ego system to call upon Paul Lee. The chances of being found in a coma-like condition were much greater in a public hotel and I did not want to draw any such attention to myself. The next day I left the hotel in the time honoured fashion by depositing my key at reception, adding that I expected to be out all day. Having exited my taxi in the centre of the city I ducked into a public toilet and emerged a few minutes later as Timothy Yewly.

Paul Lee was as polite to my son as he had been to me. Carefully monitoring his brainwaves I could see no suspicion in his mind, just the thought that, '*The boy bears a striking resemblance to his father*'. The necessary documents were lined up on the expensive desk for my signature and I had simply to sign them as Timothy Yewly. Chatting about the bank's association with my father Victor, I spent an amusing half-hour with Paul, eventually agreeing that, 'Dad has obviously been delayed. I'll ask him to call in later today or tomorrow morning to countersign the documents.'

Several weeks later I called into my UK bank and repeated the exercise. Timothy would be welcome at both banks from now on and had access to huge funds in both the Far East and the UK. I had no wish to continue trading in the futures market for the time being; and such investments that were made on my behalf by my two account managers were to be strictly low return but totally safe. It would be a few years yet before I recruited the Templeton twins, one of whom would become my fund raiser, dabbling in the world-wide futures market once again.

The next step was the death of Victor, allowing me to live permanently as Timothy. Neither Tracey nor Alicia wanted to meet my newly-found fictional son, much to my relief since it would have been difficult to arrange such a meeting; and I had no wish to use any of my powers upon my family. The fact that I accepted Timothy as my son came as no surprise to Tracey; she had always known of my wish for a son and had blamed herself for failing to produce more children.

Some weeks later I explained to Tracey that I intended leaving the residue of my Far Eastern accounts to Timothy in my will. Knowing that she was herself a very wealthy woman, and that all our UK wealth would be left to Alicia, she accepted this decision quite readily. 'It will give the young man a small start in life, some small compensation for spending the early years of his life without a father.' Tracey's words may have been intended as an indication that she was slowly beginning to accept the expansion of our family. But I saw the comment as a double-edged sword, subtly hinting at my careless impregnation of the boy's mother and subsequent failure to be a father to my unknown son.

My intention was to arrange my death in the year 2000. In the intervening few years I spent more and more time away from my UK home. Tracey did not mind since she spent many months each year with Alicia and our grandchildren.

From the time of my skills update my powers had increased considerably and I had become quite adept at using and controlling them. More and more I appeared as Timothy, building up a range of friends and acquaintances, instilling memories of school and college days into the memory-banks of various people. Blanking the thoughts of others and replacing my own thoughts into their minds was now a reflex action on my part, as was the power to influence their actions and movements.

During one particular period, I overlooked Number Ten Downing Street for several weeks, listening-in to cabinet meetings and personal discussions between the Prime Minister, his cabinet, advisors and visitors. At the time I had no specific axe to grind and I did not influence any major decisions; simply changing the Chancellor's decision to raise fuel tax in the autumn budget. Used as a small test of my increasing powers it worked perfectly and had the nation known of my deed I would most probably have been feted as a national hero.

The ability to project a protective shield to anyone, anywhere in the world, was tuned and tested during this period; and I had used it on several occasions for purely personal reasons when protecting my family from harm. At that moment in time my powers were seldom used but I had no doubt that in the future they would be brought into use much more frequently.

But arranging my death was my immediate concern. In achieving this aim a body was my most urgent requirement. The thought of killing again to provide this need filled me with revulsion; I could not do it without a very good reason. It would be much less of a strain for me to steal a cadaver from a morgue or hospital. To this end I started overlooking various places at the beginning of the new millennium. A ghoulish business indeed, checking the contents of morgues and wandering the wards of hospitals and old people's rest homes, anywhere that there was a likelihood of my finding a suitable body. The condition of the body did not matter too much. I intended that it would not be found for a few months and that the face would be disfigured; but it would be found with my wallet and watch, dressed in my clothing and, of course, as Timothy, I would undoubtedly be required to identify the body.

Early March 2000. I had found a body, similar in size to me lying in a morgue in Sheffield. The body was in good condition and was about fifty years old. The previous owner had taken quite good care of himself but had died of a sudden embolism. Fortunately, the cadaver was free of glaringly obvious features such as tattoos or scars that might survive the three months of deterioration that I had planned for it. As an added bonus, the man had not been married, had no surviving family and no one was expected to come forward to claim the body.

When next the mortuary attendant opened drawer number eleven it was empty and a few seconds later he could not remember why he had opened it. I had erased all memory of the occupant from his brain and all records from the morgue. A discarded mortuary wheelchair came in very handy and I had trundled the body out to my hired van and bundled it into the back. Over the next two days I drove down to Portsmouth and my intended destination.

To the left of the M27 when approaching the channel ferry terminal can be seen a graveyard of World War 2 submarines jettisoned after a lifetime of service and slowly rotting away in the salty water awaiting their turn to be transformed into razor blades. It was a simple matter for me to swim up to one of these hulks and secure the body beneath the submarine, where it would lie for about three months until I was ready for it to be discovered.

A few days later I boarded a cross channel ferry to St Malo. Having parked my car in the cavernous car deck, I made my way through the throngs of travellers to reception to hire a commodore class cabin, seeking to be remembered as much as possible by the crew. Early the next morning the ferry had docked at St Malo and I disembarked in my car, drove around the town and out into the countryside and re-embarked for the journey home later that same day. Once again I upgraded my cabin; had a good evening meal; tipped the waiting staff outrageously; and returned to my cabin.

In the morning when the ferry docked at Portsmouth, I was not to be found. A forlorn and forsaken sight, my car sat alone in the middle of the huge car deck and my alter ego watched in amusement the antics of the other car drivers in trying to negotiate the car, obviously abandoned by some idiot who had not responded to the ship's announcements to attend his vehicle.

Some three months later it was time for the body to be discovered. In the dead of night I simply untied the cadaver and dragged it up on to the nearest beach. My watch, wallet and clothing had been on the body for the whole time that it was attached to the old submarine and I made a point of checking that each item was still attached before I left the scene.

Tracey was in Australia, where she virtually lived, seeking to spend as much time as possible with her grandchildren. The telephone call from the Portsmouth police telling her of my death gave her a feeling of loss, but not a sufficiently strong enough emotion to produce a tear or two. Indeed, since I had told her about Timothy, and despite her expressing her forgiveness, most of her feelings for me had gone. She felt little more than a quickly passing moment of sadness and a brief rekindling of happy memories of the years during which we had been so happy together. Somewhere she had a number for her husband's newly-discovered son. *'Now what was his name?'* She thought. *'Ah, yes - Timothy,'* and she searched through her address book for the number that she had hoped never to use.

Sitting comfortably in the small flat that I had taken as Timothy's residence in the city of Winchester, I waited for the call from Tracey. When the phone rang, I answered in the usual way, giving no indication that I knew of the death of my father. The conversation was brief; one-sided; business-like; and emotionless. 'You may or may not know that your father's body has been found. The Portsmouth police have all the details and if you ring them I am sure they will be only too pleased to explain the circumstances of his death. I will not be coming to the funeral but I would be grateful if you will make whatever arrangements are necessary in the UK; and to let me know if you need anything from me.' Tracey was glad to end the call and for some strange reason took great delight in slamming the phone back on to its cradle.

The police told Timothy that the body was most probably me, since my personal belongings were still attached. As Timothy, I agreed to travel down to Portsmouth to identify the body and the police were only too pleased to close another missing person's file. The body was handed into the care of a funeral parlour and was duly cremated two days later.

During the following weeks I received a huge pile of letters and e-mails of condolence, in response to the announcements I had arranged in various national newspapers. Naturally, I replied personally to all, explaining the quick cremation and hinting that there would not be a memorial service since father had expressly forbidden it. Transferring the accounts to me was simplicity itself; a short telephone instruction to each bank manager, both of whom knew me personally, telling them to make whatever arrangements they thought fit. Death duties made a huge dent in my fortune but I was not in the least put out about that; the money would be regenerated many times over in the next few years.

At that moment in my life the small flat in Winchester served my needs as a temporary residence. But it would not be suitable in the long term and I started to search for a more suitable place for me to both reside in and mould into an operational base.

To this end I purchased a large estate in the rural hamlet of Abbotstone in Hampshire. It was deep in the English countryside, about seven kilometres from the small market town of Alresford, famous for its watercress. In excess of two thousand acres, it was in a sorry state. The main residence, tied cottages, machinery and the land had been neglected for several years whilst the elderly and childless owners had drifted into senility - and death.

Such estates attract a great deal of interest when they come on to the market and a number of pop stars, sporting idols and icons from show business were somewhat miffed to have every offer gazumped by an unknown bidder.

Money makes all things possible, especially when backed up by very special powers, and I had no difficulty in obtaining the necessary planning permission to demolish the existing main residence. The house was to be rebuilt in a beautiful valley about a kilometre away from any main highway, on the remains of a previous house that had fallen into ruin many, many years before.

Outline planning permission was given for a replica Georgian manor house on the surface but with an underground facility below it. Playing the part of an eccentric young millionaire with more money than sense, I gave the impression of a person fearful of nuclear war; and one who wanted to build a life-preserving area to counter such an event.

A huge pit was excavated under the site for the manor house, some fifty metres deep by about two hundred square. The base and outside walls were to be ten metres thick and all internal partition walls two metres wide to support the twenty-five metres of solid concrete separating the above ground area from that below. It was a massive operation, commissioned in late 2000 and intended to be ready for occupation three years later. Reached by a lift system, installed in the cellars of the manor house, the facility had its own power system connected to the national grid and with powerful automatic back-up generators located in a separate chamber some fifty metres from the main living areas.

Huge food and water storage systems, air filtration plants and sewage systems were installed; cosmetic systems added largely to convince the local council that I was indeed building a nuclear bunker.

In addition, a large shaft, some five metres in diameter, was installed at one side of the underground accommodation; sealed and covered with a strong safety-glass top at ground level. The shaft allowed the Sun's rays to reach inside the complex and using a series of large mirrors the sunlight was reflected around the entire underground area. Unknown to all, I also added a Verunian solar-energy system, the controlling core of which was a small cluster of industrial diamonds which, when lined up by the Verunian software in my powerful computer systems, provided all the power and heating required in the complex.

As a nuclear bunker, the site would not be used very often, except maybe for routine tests, etc., but as an operational base for the Verguide Team it would be in use on a daily basis and would use a great deal of energy; the use of which could easily be identified by the local electricity supply company.

Over the next year or so I intended letting it become known that I had decided to venture into business, mainly trading on the world's stock exchanges. The ruse was to explain the appearance of my team, the increasing use of the bunker and the considerable size and usage of the bandwidth I intended installing for connection to the world-wide network. Over time, my usage of electrical power would also increase and I had arranged a sophisticated software programme that monitored the use of power, increasing and decreasing the use of conventional energy as required.

CHAPTER 9
SALADIN

THREAD:

In the years before the early 2020s there had been very few serious incidents of political extremism on mainland UK. Of those that did occur, some were successful and some were not. Isolated, almost uncoordinated bombing attacks on London's transport systems took place in July 2005, again in July 2011, and repeated in 2022; but a completely organised and sustained period of attacks awaited the arrival of a new leader and a new extremist group.

ENGLAND. EARLY 21ST CENTURY.

The young boy's mind was filled with Islamic historical hero worship. Stories of Osama bin Laden's militant Sunni organisation filled his mind and the boy was devastated when the notorious *al Qaeda* leader was killed in an Air-India crash in 2009. An incident that many believed had been perpetrated by a joint MI6/CIA hot operation, whereby the four hundred and twenty-five other souls onboard the jumbo jet were sacrificed in order to rid the world of what the Western World considered to be a fanatical despot. Although the Egyptian

Ayman al-Zawahiri inherited the mantle as leader of bin Laden's group, it was never able to repeat the successes of the late 20th and early 21st centuries.

The young boy was fascinated by the Law, which is a broad interpretation of the meaning of *al Qaeda*, and his heart thrilled at the stories involving the destruction of infidels and non-believers across Africa, the Middle East, Europe and the Far East.

Bin Laden's followers, those of the *Wahhabism* or *Salifism* understanding of Islam, mourned his passing for several years and would never forgive the Western World for the lack of a body to place in the elaborate shrine that they built in Medina. Maybe future archaeologists will find the empty Muslim reliquary, placed centrally within the impressive *mihrah*, pointing significantly towards Mecca, and wonder at the reason for the lack of human remains.

The boy read avidly of other Islamic extremist groups, whether Sunni or Shiite. Of Hamas, that troublesome Palestinian Sunni group that was a constant thorn in the buttocks to the Israeli nation. Formed in 1987 by Sheikh Ahmed Yassin, their group name Hamas means zeal; and zealous they were in their attacks on Israeli targets, both military and civilian. The boy's mind fumed in indignation at Israel's occupation of Palestinian territory and his whole mind and body supported the struggle by Hamas to remove their enemy from the West Bank and the Gaza Strip. Completely besotted by hero worship, the boy always thought of these Muslim religious fighters as soldiers and he was never in his lifetime to use the word 'terrorist'.

Living in England, he was sheltered from any danger from bullets, bombs, tanks or troops. He knew nothing of the actualities of war; and the fact that so many human beings died bleeding and screaming did not occur to the boy. His young boy's mind feasted on the fact that his sister group of Islamic warriors - the Shiites - were also fighting a battle against the infidels in Lebanon. Sayyad Hassan Nasrallah's army, *Hezbollah*, followed the dictates of Ayatollah Ruhollah Khomeini, leader of the Islamic revolution in Iran in 1982. The impressionable young boy soaked up the stirring words describing the aims of this group: 'Dedicated to the eradication of western imperialism; the transformation of a multi-confessional state into the worship of Allāh; and the complete destruction of Israel'.

Even at such a young age the boy already dreamed of saving the world, the obliteration of every other religion on the face of the Earth and the total destruction of the world's infidels. He knew that the word *Hezbollah* meant the party of God and he constantly daydreamed of his own fame in the years ahead as leader of the greatest Islamic group of warriors in history, fighting with such fervour that the whole world would gasp in astonishment.

Born of Kurdish parents, both Sunni Muslims and originally from northern Iraq, this boy was Saladin-Hakim Salah; born in Birmingham on 29th October, 2003. He was destined to become known to the world by many names; loved by billions; and feared by as many again.

After their arrival in the UK, his parents Abdul Salah and Axin Jaleel told a consistent story to those that asked. A story of pain and suffering by their families over many years. A story whereby they had made their escape from persecution at the hands of Saddam's Shiite regime, passing through the Sangatte Gap at Calais in January 2003, just before the Gap was closed by the British and French governments. In truth, the young lovers had little real fear of persecution but both, at the tender age of eighteen and from the same Iraqi village, had used the international excuse of persecution when they made their bid for a life together in England; escaping from something they feared yet more than persecution - arranged marriages that neither wanted.

Repeatedly since he was a young boy Saladin had listened to his parents reliving their tortuous journey into Dover. They spoke of an adventure, told in thunderous voices with frequent praises to Allāh, a quest by two young people searching for a new life. The weeks in Sangatte were harsh but there was no shortage of food or blankets; and frequent trips into Calais and the surrounding villages produced a rich reward for those with sufficient daring.

The French, much akin to the British, as the two young people would soon discover, were generally ambivalent towards the invading army of asylum seekers and confronted by aggression they usually capitulated and handed over whatever cash or valuables they had in their pockets and handbags. Acting as a team, the young Kurdish lovers refused to join any of the established gangs and hierarchy at Sangatte, preferring to act alone in the absolute surety of one's support for the other.

The attacks were swift. Calculated to frighten their target into stunned inactivity for the precious few seconds required to relieve them of their valuables. At almost any time of the year the restaurants and bars in Calais are packed with evening revellers, many of whom are tourists returning *en pied* to their hotels after a satisfying French meal, their senses dulled by too much *vin de plonque*. The method of attack by the young Kurds never varied and neither did their choice of targets - invariably a couple. Always approaching from the front, they gave the impression of being a courting couple, very much in love and with their arms wrapped around each other.

Their victims saw no threat in the approaching lovers and usually moved to one side to let them pass. But it was then, having passed, that Abdul turned and wrapped an arm around the neck of the man, pushing the woman to one side and pricking the man's neck with the point of his knife. Stunned by the swiftness of the attack, there was little resistance whilst Axin's practised hands emptied the man's pockets. The attack was over in just a few seconds and the female member of their target usually handed over her handbag, especially when confronted by a knife-swishing swarthy young man with dark skin and a terrible grimace on his face.

During the couple's stay at Sangatte, Abdul and Axin had acquired a considerable sum of money. The couple's hoard was in British pounds since the Holding Centre's clandestine capabilities included both *bureau de change* and fencing arrangements for stolen valuables. The cost of a ferry or train ticket was easily within their means but they had no documentation; and the cost of procuring fake passports and visas was prohibitive.

Only one option remained. They must make the dangerous journey, as had so many of their fellow asylum seekers before them, in, on or under a vehicle passing through the Channel Tunnel. But Abdul was fearful for Axin's safety and had no wish to join the massed invasion of the Calais railyards at the entrance to the tunnel desperately searching for somewhere to cling on to as the train slowed before descending underground. Such hit or miss tactics were fraught with danger and not for him so he searched for another way of making the crossing.

Consequently, he made several trips to the nearby hypermarket where he spent long hours studying the bulky articulated lorries, parked up whilst their drivers shopped for cheap washing powder, beer or cigarettes - a ready source of additional income for the more unscrupulous drivers. He was looking for a transport company that operated a large number of vehicles and that were easily identifiable by their striking livery.

Amidst the snow showers of a freezing cold day towards the end of January 2003, Saladin's parents made their move. They had left the Holding Centre the previous evening; it was much easier to leave the camp under the cover of darkness and a cold night in the bushes surrounding the lorry park at the hypermarket was a small price to pay. At this point in the telling of the story Abdul always paused, allowing his wife to include in a slightly breathless voice that Saladin had been conceived that night.

Hidden from view inside the tightly bunched clump of bushes, the escaping couple waited until the hypermarket opened and the lorry, coach and car parks began to fill. It was easy for them to slip from their hiding place and mingle with the crowds of happy shoppers, all seeking some bargain to boast about on their return to their homes.

By mid-afternoon there were three Bri-Trucker lorries parked up, their drivers killing time before completing the short journey to the train terminal. Abdul had noticed during his previous fact-finding visits that Bri-Truckers, unlike most other British transport operators, employed a larger proportion of women drivers; and this fact suited his needs perfectly.

As each of the three brightly-coloured lorries had approached the lorry park, Abdul had searched the cab with his sharp eyes to determine the sex of the driver. So far none had been female. Undeterred, the would-be escapees bought burgers and drinks from the mobile food vendors dotted around the parking areas. Time was on their side and they were quite prepared to spend another night or two under the bushes.

Good fortune usually shines upon the patient, however, and shortly before 15.00 a flash of bright colours from the traffic roundabout on the approaches to the hypermarket signalled the arrival of another Bri-Trucker articulated lorry. Somehow Abdul knew that Allāh had blessed their enterprise and his heart had already increased its beat-rate before his eyes confirmed the good news; the driver was female.

Having skilfully reversed the huge vehicle into one of the few remaining and narrow parking slots, the driver stepped down from the cab. Abdul was expecting to see a burly, mannish figure but was surprised when a slightly built and obviously very female driver came into view. Dressed in an overly tight sweater that emphasised the size and shape of her breasts, she was disdainful of the cold temperature and carried a small leather jacket, slung carelessly over her shoulders. Jeans and high heels completed her ensemble and she sauntered across the lorry park towards the shopping area. As she passed close by, Abdul was especially pleased to spot the flash of a golden ring on her wedding finger.

Now was the time to pray to Allāh and the young couple sat on a pavement edge in the coach park, pretending to be waiting for their coach driver's return. Whilst the pretty lorry driver was away from her vehicle they prayed continuously, for it was essential that the young woman return alone to her vehicle.

Abdul already knew all he needed to know about the layout of the impressively large driver's cab on their chosen method of transportation into the UK. Hidden from view behind the driver's seat was a curtained-off area. This space contained a bunk and various storage places that the driver used when taking tacho-enforced rest periods whilst parked-up in the numerous lay-bys throughout Europe.

Two pairs of eyes gazed constantly at the never ending flow of humanity exiting the main doors to the hypermarket. Both immediately picked up their target as she emerged, freshly showered, powdered and painted, leisurely drifting back to her lorry - Allāh be praised, alone. Fearing that she might make an immediate departure, the young Kurds fell in behind the driver and followed her back to her cab. As the young woman searched for her keys in her leather jacket, Axin closed the gap to her side.

In preparation for their escape to a new life the Iraqi couple had been practising English for some time. Over the past few months they had little else to do, other than make the effort to speak and think using the English language. By no stretch of the imagination could they be considered as fluent but they could make themselves understood and as Axin engaged the driver in conversation, Abdul dashed forward and held a rag soaked in a mushroom-based amatoxin[13]. Wrapped

---

[13]Amatoxin. Mushroom-based poison.

tightly in Abdul's strong embrace, the pretty driver's struggles lasted but a few seconds before she slumped in his arms, dazed and robbed of her senses. Quickly they lifted the white-faced woman into the driver's cab, and themselves climbed into the bunk-space behind the driver's seat, supporting the woman's body until she began to regain some control over her befuddled senses.

Abdul was worried. He did not really know if the home-made amatoxin was potent enough to kill and he waited in silence until he felt the muscles in her arms begin to twitch. He massaged her arms and whispered 'We will not hurt you but you must do as we tell you.' Over and over he repeated the short sentence until she pulled forward, forcing herself out of his restraining grip.

Gentle probing with well-rehearsed questions revealed that the driver was married to an active service soldier, presently serving in Iraq and attached to a multinational group providing protection for a weapons inspectorate team. A fact that drew an ironic chuckle from Abdul who was well aware that a second armed conflict was brewing in his country and was expected to kick-off in the next month or two.

Whilst on her trips to Europe the driver left her two children with her mother. Driving the lorry was her only means of boosting her husband's income sufficiently to support the mortgage on the family's home in Northampton. Reconfirming his promise that she would not be hurt, Abdul told her that they intended to travel to Dover in the bunk space and that she was not, under any circumstances, to leave the cab or give any indication of her passengers' presence.

A dark hand containing a long-bladed knife appeared in front of the driver's eyes and the voice that threatened its use was filled with menace. 'You die first if we are discovered.' Visions of her children passed across her mind; she knew that she would obey whatever instructions came from the menace behind her. Abdul reinforced her determination to obey him by pointing at the photograph of the two babies hanging from the driver's rear-view mirror and he promised that, 'If you betray, I spend rest of life tracking down and killing two babies.' In the face of the ferocity in the dark man's voice the female driver could make no response; she was struck dumb, unable to speak or respond in any way. His final, chilling promise, 'To cut out their hearts and stuff them into the babies' mouths so that your family will know it was me,' frightened the poor woman rigid. Axin had confiscated the driver's handbag and had removed details of her name, address, telephone number, driving licence details, etc., but she did not take any of the driver's personal cash or the large amount of Euros provided by Bri-Truckers for emergencies.

Young and extremely attractive, the driver was well known to both the British and French customs and immigration authorities at Calais. Breezily greeting each official with her usual dazzling smile and chit-chat, she played her part well, displaying the stiff upper lip and backbone of the British people when faced with adversity.

Formalities completed, the lorry joined the line of other vehicles waiting to board the train and tensions increased dramatically inside the cab when a delay of forty minutes was announced. Always a quick thinker, Axin suggested that the young driver join them in the bunk space. The apparently empty cab and drawn curtains would suggest that the driver was taking a nap and did not want to be disturbed by any of the other drivers. The ruse worked perfectly and they remained in total silence, a *ménage* of mistrust and fear, until the sound of other engines being started signalled that the boarding procedure for the train had begun.

There is precious little room in the open-sided lorry carriages on the tunnel trains and all drivers are expected to leave their cabs and use the facilities of a separate rest room. However, some drivers chose to remain with their vehicles, contrary to all health, safety and fire regulations; and the trio remained in the bunk space during the short forty-five minute journey to Dover.

To all intents and purposes the journey was over, since all customs and immigration checks were completed at the Calais end of the tunnel. The large Bri-Trucker lorry disembarked from the train at Dover, left the terminal and headed north on the M20 towards London.

Ecstatic at the success of their venture, the two Iraqis hugged and kissed; and praised their heavenly master. But they remained out of sight for the short journey to the Maidstone service area, where they left the frightened driver to continue her journey alone. The female driver, relieved to be free of her captors, was at first angry with herself for complying so easily with the wishes of the illegal immigrants and intended informing the police of the whole sorry story as soon as possible. Anger and determination fed her resolve for some minutes, until a more rational mind recalled the menace in Abdul's voice. At which point she wisely decided to keep the incident to herself. She would not tell another soul and the story would accompany her to her grave. On no account would she place her babies at risk.

For the two illegal immigrants the journey north to Birmingham was virtually uneventful. Travelling from town to town by bus, they neither aroused suspicion nor were challenged in any way. Two days after leaving the Bri-Trucker lorry at Maidstone the pair arrived in Birmingham and headed straight to an address given to them during their stay at Sangatte. This was the home of a well known Islamic arranger, who helped large numbers of illegal immigrants to obtain the necessary paperwork to enable them to remain openly in the UK. The efforts that this man made were not repaid immediately, for he preferred a small down payment, followed by a lifetime of regular monthly contributions towards his fighting fund. Small essentials such as British passports, birth certificates and national insurance numbers were easily arranged. As were the basics of life in terms of housing: work - not essential but available if they wanted it; a marriage ceremony; and, almost as important to the two Iraqi newlyweds, the intricate details of how to screw as much money as possible out of Britain's extremely generous, and leaky sieve of social security.

Nine months later their son was born. Saladin-Hakim was the apple of his parents' eyes and the couple lavished attention on their baby. Over the years he proved to be an extremely intelligent boy. He excelled at school and seemed to absorb knowledge effortlessly. The family led a trouble-free life in their chosen city and there was certainly no need to find employment, for what the social services could not supply was easily made up for by a very occasional night around the restaurants in the East End of London. They had not lost the slick skills required to relieve a happy couple of their valuables and they visited all the surrounding large cities in the Midlands; and even risked a few attacks in Birmingham to muddy the water for the police.

However, they were careful not to injure any of their victims. They were well informed about the inadequacies of the British police, who would much rather sit in their patrol cars waiting for motorists to speed, park or use some hand-held device in a manner that attracted a nice fat fine than chase after some minor hoodlums shimmying a few evening diners: and which had the added benefit of boosting a constable's monthly quota of crime prevention.

Strangely, Mr and Mrs Salah developed a burning hatred for the British people, despite their obvious happiness in their son and their comfortable life in Birmingham. They were not mistreated in any way, nor were they attacked, vilified, teased, tormented, ignored or abused. Maybe a little insular in that they lived by choice in the streets occupied almost exclusively by other Muslim immigrants but on the occasions when they ventured further afield they were treated cordially and afforded the usual courtesy that one Briton displays to another.

Abdul felt somehow betrayed. He had not been received in his adoptive country with open arms and a brass band and, over time, he began to feel resentful. He could not really explain his feelings, not even to his beloved Axin, and certainly, later in life, not to his son.

For a few short years at his junior school, Saladin-Hakim wished that his parents had gone the whole hog and given him a westernised name. He felt totally different from most other boys in his school. His parents had told him that he was a Muslim, and therefore different, and whenever he was involved in the normal rough-and-tumble and teasing of school life, he recalled the stories his parents told him of their escape to this country.

The young boy had not yet developed his own hatred towards his adoptive homeland. Quite the opposite, since he was a friendly, likeable boy who made friends easily, from both his own kind and amongst the British boys. It is arguable that without the vitriol fed to him in constant doses by his father, Saladin would have blended into British society quite happily.

But hardly a night passed without his having to listen to his father lambasting the British, the Satanists (USA), the French and just about the whole of the rest of the world. More and more his parents allocated blame for all of their perceived woes on to an indefinable source, 'The British!'. A very young Saladin could never quite fathom who the British were but this brigade of brigands were certainly very nasty people, since his parents' hatred for them was deeply rooted. The British seemed to be involved in all things and eventually the boy came to his own conclusions for this group of unhelpful people, who appeared to go out of their way to enrage his parents, placing obstacles in the path of all his father's aspirations.

And Saladin's own resentment increased year on year. The more so as he gained access to the internet and learned more and more about the persecution in his own Iraq and, as with his father, he laid the blame squarely on the shoulders of the western powers - Europe, the USA and more especially Great Britain: 'The bloody British!'

Mind warped by his parents' extreme bitterness towards their new homeland, Saladin progressed towards manhood in the decade or so of years from 2010 to 2025; and the developing man became aware of a troubled world.

From around the globe illegal immigrants flooded into Europe and the British Isles looking for a better life; and the numbers escalated to almost locust proportions. From a figure of some six hundred thousand in the early part of the 21st century, the numbers increased to almost two million each year.

Palestinians were squeezed out of their country by continued Israeli occupation of the West Bank, the Gaza Strip and the Golan Heights. And with Israel's eyes gazing longingly north to the Lebanon and west into Egypt in search of new land it was likely that the flood of humanity escaping such expansionist dreams would increase even further.

From the dissolution of the USSR in 1991 and until the gigantic Russian rebirth in 2015, the Middle Eastern Stan countries continued their rocky road to political chaos. Weak governments were supplanted every few years by the ever growing power of various drug barons and local warlords. A considerable number from the populations of these countries found themselves unable or unwilling to live under such troublesome conditions of severe hardship and repression; and their only available option was to make a break for a better life.

Bosnia and Herzegovina with its population of Serbs, Croats and Bosnians spread in a mismatched tapestry throughout its borders continued its see-saw existence; and in the process spilled tens of thousands of refugees towards the relative safety of their western neighbours. This volatile region of the world, harbouring a population of Muslims, Serbian Orthodox and Roman Catholic believers, was destined for many such conflicts during the 21st century; and the flow of refugees flooded and ebbed like a huge wave, as the region's unrest intermittently flared and settled.

The young Saladin's heart filled with pride when pestilence, disease, crop failures, political unrest and religious belief set the Horn of Africa alight with the flashes of exploding ordinance in 2018. His own group of Sunni Muslims in Somalia saw their herds of cattle, their main national resource, dwindle to alarming numbers, dying from lack of feed and water. Their eyes swivelled west to the country of their neighbours in Ethiopia, fuelled by the invective from their warlord leaders.

Billions of the world's dollars had been hurled willy-nilly into these two countries over many years but the largely nomadic tribes saw little of these dollars and their existence was still precarious. Instead, the coffers of the warlords overflowed with money and they amassed huge armies, equipped with modern, sophisticated weapons that few of their own technicians had the brainpower to understand, let alone maintain and use effectively.

The Islamic grand plan was to unite the Muslim populations of both countries and evict the Christians and all other African religious groups into the barren lands of Somalia, retaining the vast area of Ethiopia as their own Muslim-only land. This was to be the first of the world's conflicts to produce a country occupied wholly by a population worshipping the same religion.

At fifteen years of age, Saladin witnessed the deathknell of the western world's peace-keeping organisations, since both NATO and the United Nation's Security Council felt powerless to intervene, preferring once again to adopt a fence-sitting posture. The boy was thrilled when the mighty USA, itself facing threatened oil cuts from the Middle Eastern Islamic countries, refused to take a unilateral stance and stepped back from confrontation. Without the means to escape by sea, many of the Christians fled west and north into Europe. However, the majority from Somalia were intercepted and annihilated by the Ethiopian Islamic forces before being able to make an escape. Those that managed to escape added to the general influx of refugees into the UK and mainland Europe.

As an older man aged nineteen, his whole being fumed when the mighty Satan flexed its muscles. Fearful once again of losing its supply of oil from the Middle East, the USA convinced Iraq to support a trilateral attack on Iran in 2022, supported by its lapdog Great Britain.

Under the guise of suppressing Iran's build-up of nuclear weapons, the United States managed to convince both supporting countries to defy Security Council resolutions allowing Iran to build a small number of such weapons; and to make a pre-emptive non-nuclear strike.

This short incursion into a powerful Islamic country left the western alliance with a severely blooded nose and led to yet more persecution of the Iraqi Kurds when their Shiite countrymen took bloody reprisal for the Kurds once again deciding to support Iran during the Western powers' invasion.

And the subsequent mistrust throughout both Iraq and Iran between Sunni and Shiite provided a real setback for the rest of the world's Islamic leaders who, following the unification of Muslims in Ethiopia, had begun harbouring hopes of a unified Muslim faith throughout the world; and which in the fullness of time, might achieve their eventual aim of world domination.

The vast majority of escaping Kurds headed for Europe. Some crossed into Ethiopia (renamed Islamia in 2018) where they encountered a fate much more terrible than they had hoped for, since they were quickly rounded up and put to death. Of those few hundred thousand that made the crossing into Islamia, not one was to survive; and each was to suffer a horrific death by stoning, perpetrated before a multitude of onlookers in specially built arenas throughout the country.

Saladin also witnessed the dawn of a new mobile communications era. Details of conflicts and acts of extreme cruelty were readily available on the worldwide communications network, Freinet[14], to which anyone owning one of the ubiquitous and very cheap voice operated Pewi[15] systems could connect from any point on the surface of the Earth. This satellite-based system, completed in 2019, provided free access to anywhere and anyone and was used exclusively by the world's media and by various international governments and organisations to disseminate information to the masses and, more importantly, for crime prevention and detection.

The powerful satellites, originally deployed by the USA and China

---

[14]Freinet. Freedom of Information Net.
[15]Pewi. Personal Wrist Information.

Alfred Leonard

for military purposes, and subsequently declared a world resource after pressure from various commercial and crime enforcement enterprises, covered every inch of the globe. Linked to the world's gigantic databases, they were capable of zooming on to a pin-head, and provided continuous cover of the world's more gory confrontations.

Replacing a wristwatch, the Pewi terminals provided numerous other facilities, such as time (in any time zone of the world), navigation, voice communications, data transfer, calculating machines capable of solving the most complex of mathematical equations, dictionaries, foreign language interpretations and information on any known subject on command. When plugged into a vehicle it provided a heads-up display in the windscreen.

Saladin also welcomed a change to his own religious order. The Shiite branch of Islam have always had an established religious hierarchy - from Mullahs to Grand Ayatollahs. But the Sunni branch of Muslims had not found a need for such a system and had no such recognised forms of religious significance.

The Pope speaks for the Catholic Church; the Archbishop of Canterbury speaks for the UK's Christian followers; the Dalai Lama represents the Buddhists; and the Grand Ayatollahs speak for the world's Shiite Muslims. Sunni Muslims populate huge areas of the world in vast numbers and are by far the largest group of Muslim worshippers but they do not have a single voice through which they can express their feelings on the world stage. Recognising this shortfall in 2018, the Sunnis finally decided to install dedicated Islamic preachers in the thousands of mosques throughout the world and a nominated chain of command supporting them.

In each place of worship (*Masjid*) one or more prayer readers (*Imām*) would be permanently nominated, and given the title of *Masjid-Imām*. A *Grand Masjid-Imām* would be appointed to oversee up to one hundred mosques; *Faqihs* oversee ten *Grand Masjid-Imāms*; *Grand Faqihs* supervise up to ten *Faqihs*; with a single worldwide leader designated as the Rasul-Allah.

Of these Sunni religious leaders only one would be allowed to interpret Islamic law and make any changes; and that one person was to be the Rasul-Allah, whose decisions reached the multitudes through the established hierarchy.

As Saladin entered his late teens, his own near genius intelligence and the hatred bred into him over his formative years enabled him to become the youngest Masjid-Imām within the UK's Muslim community. Unheard of previously in the history of Islam, this young nineteen year old man had developed the oratorical skills of Winston Churchill and his vitriolic speeches in mosques all over the UK saw his meteoric rise through the religious ranks of his followers.

It was at one of his early speeches, during a visit to Liverpool, that the young Saladin heard a voice in the crowd cry, 'Saladin, Rasul-Allah' - an expression, and soon to be Islamic blessing, that he filed away for future use. He was destined to progress to the rank of Grand Masjid-Imām in 2024, to Faqih two years later, to Grand Faqih in 2028; and to the pinnacle of Sunni Muslim religious hierarchy in 2030.

As boy and man, Saladin still saw 'the thing'. As a child his mother had explained that it was his guardian spirit, the Angel of Light. And since Muslims believe that angels are made from light, then her son's must be a particularly powerful entity, since the face was almost entirely light. As a young man he had been ridiculed too many times to mention it to his compatriots. But it still appeared occasionally - mostly when he had almost forgotten about it. As man fully grown, he would use it to strengthen another claim at a time when no one could challenge his word.

Hatred for all things non-Islamic, so deeply felt that it produced physical pain in the young man's head, was the underlying theme in all his speeches. His main argument was that a Muslim be gentle and non-confrontational only when not under threat or attack. This argument was hammered home by the well-spoken young Masjid-Imām by teaching his followers that a Muslim living in the midst of infidels is always under threat; and by extension Muslims need not obey their creed's demands for normal polite social behaviour.

His interpretation of the Qur'anic statement 'Fight in the cause of Allāh those who fight you, and slay them wherever ye catch them' was that it gave free reign to attack the enemies of Islam whether they be non-combatants or not; which flew in the face of the generally accepted interpretation by the celebrated Islamic scholar Ibn Kathir.

Through the auspices of Freinet, he interpreted most of the persecution around the world as an attack on Islam. And these attacks were not against Islamic armies but against non-combatants. He saw himself as the promised one, sent by Allāh to lead his people to their rightful place as rulers of the world. Despite his rapid rise to fame within the Muslim community, Saladin's immense ego demanded satisfaction on a global scale. He had devoured the history of his extremist forebears in the various old-world militant organisations of terror such as al-Qaeda, Hamas, Lashkar-e-Toiba and Hezbollah, not one of which had managed to establish a strong base within the geographical limits of Great Britain. Saladin saw it as his task to establish a new organisation and to make it the strongest and most feared Islamic extremist weapon the world had ever seen. But such dreams of greatness are not realised without certain materialistic support, mainly that of money.

In obtaining sufficient funds to start his own extremist organisation, the young Masjid-Imām convinced the senior Islamic leaders in the UK to modify slightly the Third Pillar of Islam. This Third of the basic Five Pillars calls for the paying of alms; basically a slightly amended Robin Hood principle of taking from everyone for the benefit of all.

However, the modification required the imposition of a Muslim tax, or *zakat*, and all Britain's five million Muslims were required to donate. After just one year the kitty stood at some twenty-five million pounds and in 2022 the UK had its own Islamic army, al-Shamshir[16], led by Masjid-Imām Saladin Salah - an organisation that was destined to be responsible for some of the worst atrocities against humanity that our planet will ever witness.

A small newspaper article early in 2022 brought this man to the attention of the world. It outlined the remarkable achievement of a young nineteen year old Muslim being promoted to Masjid-Imām in Birmingham. I had been overlooking Saladin since he was a baby and this article was the first indication of approaching success for my efforts. He was clearly someone that I might manipulate and use over the following years and I decided to keep a much closer eye on him in the years ahead. Reading his thoughts I could see that he was ambitious, bigoted, heartless, cold-blooded, ruthless and already a killer whilst engaged in minor radical activities in Ireland, aimed at rekin-

---

[16]Al-Shamshir. The Scimitar.

dling the age-old strife between that country and the mainland.

Over time I had fed into his mind the words for many of his speeches, led him through the steps to change the Third Pillar and influenced the senior Islamic leaders to accept this man and his new ideas that cast such a thrill into their hearts. Into his mind I fed the belief that he was indeed the Messenger of God. In time he came to believe that my voice was the voice of Gabriel and I outlined his path to martyrdom, paradise and a seat next to Allāh in heaven; not, you will notice, at the feet of his divinity, but next to him, signifying equal importance.

A natural leader, with heavenly blessings of good looks and intelligence, Saladin stood just one point seven-eight metres tall. Slightly built with blond hair and startlingly blue eyes, he sported a traditional beard, which hung the length of his fist below his chin but without a moustache. Except when preaching his vitriolic sermons to his followers he wore western clothes, forsaking traditional cummerbund and turban for casual jeans and T-shirt.

At the tender age of eighteen, he performed his own circumcision as part of a private ceremony to signal his rite of passage to manhood, in the same year completing his pilgrimage to Mecca. One of his abiding principles from that moment onwards was that his closest Lieutenants should complete the *hajj* at the same age and kiss the sacred Islamic Black Stone, embedded within the Kaaba in the great mosque in Mecca, which was given by God.

As a Muslim mystic and preacher, the fame of the still young Saladin spread throughout the world over the next decade or so. Similarly, the new extremist group al-Shamshir became widely known. Extremist acts remained relatively low key, sufficient only to build up the confidence of his growing army of seekers-of-paradise; those ready and willing to die for him and their cause. Al-Shamshir accepted responsibility for any and all acts of extremism, no matter where in the world the act was perpetrated, but the actual identity of Saladin as the leader of the group was known to only a few of the more senior members of the Birmingham mosque and the Islamic leadership in the UK.

Of these, none would dare to expose him, for all believed that the young cleric did in fact possess a direct line to Allāh, which he demonstrated on so many occasions during his speeches and sermons. Wearing the traditional chador, a dark robe that covers almost all the head and body, he adopted a characteristic pose with head dropping to his right shoulder. The charismatic preacher would stop in mid sentence and hold the first digit of his right hand to his lips in a plea for silence. After just a few seconds of listening he was able to expose some minor failure of his Muslim hierarchy in not adhering strictly to the Five Pillars - failings to which they freely admitted, accepting and endorsing the Grand Faqih's strong, personal relationship with the Almighty.

In this way, he brainwashed his superiors into accepting his word as law and in 2031 he finally managed to implant the Sixth Pillar into Britain's Islamic law - *Jihad*. The very existence of this Pillar was a strictly controlled secret within Britain's Islamic community. But the crowds went wild with excitement when, at the end of the newly pro-moted Rasul-Allah's speeches, he raised his arms slowly from the waist to high above his head, with three fingers exposed on each hand. His own personal signal promising Allāh and his people that *jihad* would live within his heart, until global domination was achieved.

Of those whose tongues were in the slightest way suspected of being capable of either identifying Saladin as the leader of al-Shamshir or speaking of the Sixth Pillar, none survived. Saladin had simply to think of that person and he or she was shortly afterwards found gar-rotted in their beds.

I was kept particularly busy and growing increasingly sick of kill-ing and was particularly grateful that I now had a team to help with this messy and distressing task.

CHAPTER 10
MECCA

THREAD:

The winter of 2021 was a particularly hard one. Prolonged periods of heavy snowfall reduced the country to a standstill. After years of ever-increasing global warming, the cold snap came as a complete surprise to one and all; not least to the highways agencies and county councils, between whom the responsibility for keeping the country moving was shared. The usual excuses about the wrong type of snow and ice that did not conform to normal consistency brought transport systems to a standstill.

The United Kingdom and especially the densely occupied south of England, had not throughout history managed to come to terms with snow; and, as history will eventually disclose, never shall.

Like blades of grass, new towns had sprung up all over the south of England, occupying enormous acreages of Greenfield sites. During the first two decades of the new millennium, population density increased to levels never before achieved in any other country in the world. The reasons were twofold. Firstly, to satisfy the voracious appetites of successive greedy governments, each bending their collective knees to the dictates of the European Council and forever demanding more and more in taxation to support their own, and Europe's, expensive social policies; and secondly to comply with disastrous

European legislation imposed upon Britain to accept more and more of the world's refugees.

At one time a major superpower, the once mighty British Empire, as with all other empires before it, finally slipped almost unnoticed into history by the turn of the century. The largest empire in recorded history, holding sway over large areas of North America, Africa, India, Australia and the Far East handed over Hong Kong, its last major overseas territory, in 1997. Also obliterated was the concept of Atlanticism, the buddy-system and doctrine of transatlantic cooperation between Great Britain and the United States of America - wiped out by order from Brussels - and the British parliament looked exclusively towards Europe for support.

The young Saladin spent long hours leading up to the bleak winter of 2021 in prayer and deep meditation. Onlookers got the distinct impression that he was talking with his deity; often he spoke out loud and without fail his utterances terminated with cries of, 'Allāh be praised,' which echoed around the mosque. The eyes of senior Sunni mosque leaders had already earmarked the young Muslim to complete the *i'tikaf*, which required the young acolyte to spend ten days of exhaustive, in-depth study of the Qur'an and Islam in general. Such detailed and intense study was designed to launch his religious career.

At eighteen years of age he was currently slightly incapacitated, recovering from his self-performed circumcision. For he alone had wielded the surgical knife, stretching his prepuce as tightly as he could and making a quick slashing movement, having firstly, and somewhat rashly, closed his eyes. In a few weeks' time, at the beginning of December, 2021, he would complete the *hajj*.

MEDINA, SAUDI ARABIA. EARLY DECEMBER, 2021.

Five young Muslims stepped off the glistening A380 aircraft at Medina. They were tense and anxious to continue their journey. The interminable formalities of claiming baggage; passing through immigration and customs exasperated and irritated every single one of the eight hundred and fifty-three passengers that had recently disgorged from the huge aircraft.

Finally reunited with their baggage and feeling a little uncomfortable in the heat of the taxi rank outside the terminal building, the quintet waited patiently for their turn at the head of the queue for transport. The breeze felt the same as a hot-fan to the thickly-blooded westerners.

The first visit to a foreign country for all five of the Muslims, it was also the first time that they had felt entirely responsible for finding their way in life. But they were eighteen; a new generation; the world was theirs to claim; they were three metres tall and, Allāh be praised, it was their God-given right to do just that. And this, their *hajj* or pilgrimage to Mecca, was the fulfilment of their principal obligation as Muslims and the completion of the Fifth Pillar.

Bolstered by their feelings of this God-given inheritance and the solemn, religious and somehow menacing ambience of Medina, they toured the city. Basking in the baking heat of Saudi Arabia, *Al Madina Al Monaware*[17] is home to some one point three million Muslims.

Possibly the two most religious sites within the city of Medina are the shrine of Muhammad$_{pbuh}$[18], the Prophet's Dome; and the Quba mosque, the very first Islamic place of worship. The long queues to gain entry to these popular sites took most of the day to clear and it was late in the day before a very weary Saladin rested on his prayer mat in the coolness of the Quba mosque.

The name Saladin seemed to reverberate around the minds of Britain's Muslim leaders, no matter how hard they tried to stem their thoughts. Consequently, he was already held in great esteem by the elders of his mosque, and his *hajj* had been funded by his Sunni peers. He could have asked for some preferential treatment, travelling in a little more comfort and avoiding the crowded, single-class aircraft, the queues and the constant attacks from squadrons of flying insects. But he had been determined to complete his *hajj* in the same way as any ordinary Muslim and in the next few days he was to be rewarded beyond his wildest dreams.

---

[17]*Al Madina Al Monaware.* The enlightened city.

[18]Author's note. Muhammad. Muslims are required to add the suffix 'praise be unto him', or pbuh, whenever the Prophet's name is used. I have continued this tradition as a mark of respect.

From Medina the group continued to Mecca, where they completed the ritualistic seven circuits of the Kaaba inside the Great Mosque and touched the black stone, having pushed through the milling crowds tightly packed around the huge religious symbol.

Wherever they travelled, the phalanx of young Muslims maintained the same formation. Saladin in the centre, with a Lieutenant in front, at the rear, to his right and to his left. And so they were arranged within the dim interior of the Great Mosque in Mecca. Saladin could hear the voices of his closest associates, quoting directly from the Qur'an, parts of which they had all memorised, word for religious word. But Saladin himself had gone one step further. Considered a *Hāfiz*, he was already one of a select group who had committed the entire Qur'an to memory; his mind seemed infallible and capable of instant recall whenever he needed it.

In the peaceful interior of the Great Mosque, Saladin's whole body lost contact with his prayer mat, such was the shock of the first revelation. Ear-shatteringly loud, the vibrant and demanding voice screamed into his brain; and into the minds of the whole congregation.

'I am the angel Gabriel. *Hajji* Saladin-Hakim Salah. Blessed one, do you hear me?'

'I hear you O Gabriel, my Lord.' A strange peace settled over Saladin as his ringing voice spoke the words. Every single person in the crowded mosque heard Saladin's reply; and all in turn received a message that a new Messiah was convening with their maker. The silence that followed was long and hard to bear but not one amongst the assembled worshippers dared utter a sound. It was an intensely religious moment for all of them and all believed that they had been especially chosen to be present at this momentous occasion; and to witness the events that followed.

'You are the chosen one,' continued the voice, loud in the silence of the mosque. That of a skilled raconteur, the voice echoed in the expectant silence; and Saladin soaked up every word.

'I charge you to add these words to the Book of Muhammadpbuh. The Shiites are an abomination amongst Allāh's faithful. In the fullness of time my faithful and true Sunnis will rule Islam. When the time is right I will call upon you, Saladin-Hakim, for you are destined to become my Rasul-Allah on Earth, and when my wishes are finally fulfilled you will be required to reinterpret the Book of

Muhammadpbuh.'

'Allāh be praised,' from the congregation.

'Your tasks are to fight to retain our beliefs and to lead God's chosen people to salvation, in the time of the great flood.'

'Allāh be praised.' The response in the mosque was louder, stronger, gaining in confidence.

'I will be with you always; to help and guide you. Call on me and I shall answer.'

'God is great.' The massed Muslims were really getting into the groove.

'Fear naught. Answer to me alone and I will protect you.'

'Allāh be praised, God is great, there is but one Father in Heaven.'

Long minutes of total silence followed, until very slowly, as if in ultra-slow motion, the congregation arose from their prayer mats and encircled the young Saladin. They fell to their knees and chanted 'Rasul-Allah, Messenger of Allāh', repeating the incantation over and over. Their belief and acceptance of the words that had been spoken were absolute; and Saladin's new fame started to spread around the Islamic world. Resembling an all-consuming bushfire, the religious flames of his importance within the Islamic world swept ever onwards, brushing aside all argument or doubt.

The new salutation of Rasul-Allah was pure excitement to the young Saladin, if a little early in his religious career. But a single doubt lingered in Saladin's mind. '*What could Gabriel have meant by his expression, in the time of the great flood?*'

It would be almost a lifetime before Saladin found the answer to his question.

CHAPTER 11
RECRUIT TWINS

THREAD:

Having successfully and seamlessly changed over to a new existence as Timothy Yewly - and having seen the laying of the foundations of my underground complex at Abbotstone - I was now ready to recruit the people that I had selected to become the Verguide Team.

At the same time I decided to meet Tracey and Alicia, hoping that they would accept me as a member of their family and not be too shocked by my extraordinary likeness to my father.

AUSTRALIA. 2003.

The long trip to Sydney seemed to take forever. Most tiresome of all was the long leg to the Far East and I resolved in future to chop up the journey into three separate legs: out to the Middle East; on to the Far East; and then the final leg to Australia.

Finally kissing the Tarmac at Sydney, I waited in the slow-moving queue of very sweaty and extremely tired travellers to complete the immigration formalities. Finally I strolled through to the domestic terminal and waited as patiently as I could for my flight to Canberra.

I hated flying in the old Dash-8 propeller-driven aircraft; I was not the most confident of flyers at the best of times, despite the number of hours I had already spent aloft.

The tiny aircraft was buffeted around in the high winds and I was immensely relieved when it slammed on to the runway at Canberra. The hire car was waiting for me and since Alicia's farm involved a long trip along dirt roads I had specifically asked for an off-roader; and the Land Rover would withstand the hazards of the Australian back roads with no problem whatsoever. The hotel looked comfortable and I settled into my room for a rest before making any attempt to contact my relations.

For the next couple of days I cruised around Canberra, getting used to the layout of the city once again. Although as her father I had visited Alicia many times over the years, we had spent most of our time out at the farm at Braidwood. Consequently I did not know the ACT that well. Firstly, I wanted to locate the exact whereabouts of the Templeton property for, although I had overlooked it on many occasions, its actual physical location was somewhat blurred in my brain. The trip to the small settlement of Bungendore and continuing up over the hill towards the main highway to Sydney brought me to the thirty-acre site, set nicely on the slope of a small hill. Not yet ready to approach Hayley Templeton, I drove past the entrance for about a kilometre, turned around and drifted past again.

There was not much to be seen from the road. The house was virtually hidden from view behind some very high conifers and at the end of a long, twisting driveway. Several horses could be seen, grazing on the sparse grass, but as far as I could see there was no other sign of life. However, it was not the right time to simply turn up on her front doorstep and announce myself; I needed a more subtle introduction and to achieve this end I must face my first wife and daughter.

The following day I set off along the well remembered route towards the farm at Braidwood. It was a beautiful Australian day; bright, hot sunshine and a deeply blue sky that stretched into eternity above me. In no particular hurry, I stopped at the picturesque picnic spot at Warri Bridge and indulged myself with a cooling paddle in the rippling waters of the Shoalhaven River as it meanders its way towards Braidwood.

The impending meeting with Tracey invoked conflicting feelings inside of me; I felt a stomach-churning mixture of expectancy and dread for the coming reunion. A thoroughly upsetting feeling that partially tainted the serenity of my surroundings. But I was hoping to form some sort of relationship with Tracey and Alicia and I could not be at all sure of my reception.

The broad main thoroughfare through Braidwood, with its timeless old-world buildings flanking each wide pavement, reminiscent of early wild-west towns in America, had changed not a jot since my last visit. I deliberately slowed the Land Rover, the better to soak up the pleasant ambience of the place as I passed through.

Leaving the main highway at Braidwood I headed east towards the Budawang National Park. I cruised through the isolated settlement of Mongarlowe and slowed the Land Rover considerably as the Tarmac road ended. Several kilometres of pot-holed dirt roads brought me within sight of the Ridout property and I pulled over for a few minutes to freshen myself up and prepare myself for the forthcoming confrontation. Deliberately, and somewhat unkindly, I had planned to make my visit a complete surprise, mainly because I was still unsure of how my first family would receive me.

In the distance I could see the familiar sight of the main house and outbuildings, set amongst the shade of a stand of tall eucalyptus trees. It looked an idyllic site and certainly one that I would have chosen personally. In the paddocks on the gently sloping hillside, which looked richly green following recent rainfall, I could see several people circling on horseback. But I was too far away to identify anyone. Most probably Alicia's three young daughters having their horsey instincts firmly implanted by their mother. *'But remember Volly,'* I cautioned myself, *'as Timothy you have not been here before, so be careful.'*

There was no other sign of life but I knew that several large dogs were kept as pets and deterrents to the feral foxes and dingoes that roamed the area. Nudging the Land Rover into drive, I headed along the twisting dirt road down to the homestead. My approach had not gone unseen, for both Tracey and Alicia's husband James were waiting at the front entrance when I pulled up in a cloud of dust.

Hair bristling along their spines, four muscular cross-breed dogs, part dingo and part bull-mastiff, stood tall and attentive, growling ominously as I stepped down from the car. Fortunately they were held in check on stout leather leashes by James who, seeing that I was alone, tied the dogs to a large metal ring set into an old tractor tyre and shooed them into wooden kennels. I heard a gasp from Tracey and she collapsed into the dust. It was several minutes before we could revive her. Obviously my uncanny likeness to her dead husband had unsettled her badly. Refusing my help, James yelled for his wife, effortlessly lifted his mother-in-law and carried her into the cool interior of the house. I followed, as much to get out of the fierce outback Sun as to escape the drooling mouths and vicious eyes of the dogs.

Sitting quietly, I looked at Tracey whilst James went in search of a cool glass of water. She had changed considerably. Obviously she had aged but at sixty-two she had retained her classical high-boned features and her body had not yet succumbed to the spreading phenomenon as did the bodies of most elderly ladies. Held in place by an Alice Band there were very few signs of grey in her hair; her legs were still long, shapely and slim; and she had a soft golden tan. She most certainly belied her years.

The few brief moments that I was left alone with my wife passed too quickly, as Alicia and her all-female brood burst through the door and a storm of wailing and waving of arms erupted at the sight of their grandmother lying on the settee. Totally unnoticed, I sat in the large leather armchair and waited for some calm to return to the family. James brought another glass of water, just as Tracey started to come around and she sat up, sipped at the water and glanced around the room until her eyes settled on my face.

Not a word was spoken. We just sat staring at one another, both totally oblivious of the general melee from the remainder of the family.

'Well, I am afraid I seem to have stirred up a storm,' my words attempted to lighten the situation. It was remarkable - and typical of Tracey - for she regained her composure after only a few seconds. 'You must be Timothy; and you are the image of your father when I first met him.' She spoke very softly, as if almost overwhelmed by her memories of the love she once bore for a body so achingly familiar as the one before her. A quick 'Shoo!' - aimed at the girls - and she stood abruptly, having made a decision; and slowly she walked over to me, arms outstretched and pulled me to my feet. She embraced me firmly and whispered 'Welcome' in my ear.

Alfred Leonard

Following their matriarch's show of acceptance, the remainder of the family, one by one, came over to shake my hand, or give me a hug. The three girls, actually my granddaughters, were introduced to me. Kacey was ten, Ruby eight, and Lydia, the baby of the family, was six. All three had inherited their grandmother's good facial bone structure and were tall and willowy; obviously destined for great beauty in later life. I loved them dearly and wanted desperately to hug and kiss them as my granddaughters; and I had to squeeze down hard on my raging emotions.

A very pleasant evening followed. Sitting on the wide veranda, behind fine-mesh insect barriers that failed dismally to prevent some of the more persistent creatures from finding a route inside the house; and dogs, cats, fly-swats and sprays, worked overtime in a losing battle to reduce their numbers. It is said that if every one of Australia's twenty million population were to destroy ten common houseflies each day, the species would be extinct in a year.

Meaty steaks followed, cooked to char-grilled perfection on the barbeque, with a crispy-green Waldorf salad; washed down with several glasses of an excellent local Sauvignon. James could hardly believe how the four dogs had suddenly taken a liking to me. They sat, gazing up at me as they nuzzled around my feet, clearly accepting me as a member of the family. My inducement powers extended into the animal kingdom and I had no difficulty in planting thoughts of '*I like this man*' into their minds.

Later in the relative peace after the girls had been sent to bed, I sat on the wide veranda with Tracey and Alicia, enjoying a cold beer and outlining my life. They listened intently, interrupting only occasionally with the odd question and, by the end of the evening, had totally accepted me as family.

It was time to broach the purpose of my visit. Speaking quietly, I explained that I was looking for exceptionally qualified university graduates to aid me in my business organisation; and that I was, in particular, looking for young people who had no real family ties and would therefore commit themselves totally to myself and my activities. Whilst outlining my requirements I had been inserting thoughts of the Timorese twins into Alicia's mind and she suddenly blurted out, 'I might know just the people!'

Listening intently, I remained silent whilst Alicia, aided by Tracey, told me the story of the Templeton twins' arrival in Australia. How academically brilliant they were and of their present difficulties in finding suitable employment. Finally, after displaying some uncertainty at employing foreign immigrants, I agreed to meet the twins as soon as Alicia could set up a meeting. It had got quite late and Alicia asked me to stay the night after promising to phone Hayley Templeton the following morning. Feigning jetlag, I announced my intention of turning in and James showed me to my room and shook my hand warmly, before bidding me goodnight.

Since my powers had been bestowed upon me by Belial First, I had not at any time used them for any nefarious self gratification; but tonight I knew that I could not resist the opportunity. The choice between overlooking and using my alter ego was quickly made; in the darkness and confusion of what I had planned, materialising might produce greater rewards.

Moving carefully through the house towards Tracey's bedroom, I came upon the four dogs lying on their comfortable raised-platform beds, flanking the passageway on the first floor. They looked up at me, sensing my presence but unable to see me, and I had to calm their instinct to warn the household; and all four flopped back on to their beds with a gentle whimper.

Each of the eight bedrooms had its own en-suite bathroom and Tracey was just emerging from hers when I entered the room. Naked, and drying her hair with a gentle kneading action of her hands, she looked almost flawless. Small, pert breasts; a flat and firm stomach; and long unblemished legs bore witness to a lifetime of exercise and care. A simple T-shirt completed her night-time outfit and she lay on the bed and picked up a book and a pair of plain reading glasses. I remembered how frustrated I had become, all those years ago, when she had insisted on reading before attempting sleep, no matter how late the hour or how tired she or I might be. Standing at the end of the bed I gazed at her, unable to drag my eyes away, and I feasted upon the sight of my one true love; realising how lonely I had become during the years of our separation. Obtaining a new wife and companion must be one of my first tasks, as soon as I had recruited the twins and set them on course into the future.

Photographs of me littered the room, together with photos of Alicia as she grew into womanhood. A new wife for me was essential but

I must not forget Tracey's happiness and I resolved then and there to arrange for a new husband for her. She deserved some happiness as she teetered towards her final years. I knew that she had many more years to live; she was not destined to leave this earthly life until 2021 when she would be eighty years old.

It took only about fifteen minutes of reading to condition Tracey's mind for sleep. She used the reading activity as one might use a sorbet in the mouth, cleansing the mind of old thoughts and conditioning it for the next day's activities. As the light was extinguished and she turned over for sleep, I lowered myself on to the bed next to her. The temperature in the room was comfortable, neither too hot nor too cold, and Tracey did not use any outer coverings. She simply pushed the thin duvet off the end of the bed, just as I had done so many times in the past. The house was very quiet, except for the odd bump and sigh from the dogs on the landing; and Tracey quickly dozed off into a gentle slumber. Whilst she slept my hands discovered once again the familiar outline of her body and she twisted and turned as her passion climbed to almost forgotten heights; for like myself, she had abstained from any sexual contact since I had died.

Her mind screamed for wakefulness but I retained a firm grip, convincing her that what was happening was just a dream. In such a controlled state she thought nothing of the weight of my body as I lay on top of her squirming body, penetrating fast and deep. We made love for almost an hour before I left her, sleeping peacefully in what was to be the first undisturbed night's sleep that she had managed for many years.

Continuing with my pretence of jetlag, I was up early the next morning, showered, shaved and sitting in the large family room: the bright Australian Sun was already hot through the high floor-to-ceiling windows. I had already prepared coffee and tea and Alicia immediately started to lay out the breakfast table, chattering away to me as easily as she would have done to a natural brother. The three girls burst down the stairs, trailed by the four dogs, and dashed noisily outside for a mad run around the wide expanse of lawns. There was no sign of James and, in answer to my question, Alicia told me that he had left during the early hours of the morning for a business meeting in Sydney.

Early breakfasts did little for me, I found it extremely difficult to eat so early in the morning, and I had already finished my slice of toast and a second cup of tea when Tracey entered the room. A flushed face with a bright, happy smile confirmed to me that she had total recollection of the previous night's lovemaking. Despite her recollection being that of a dream, it had all felt so very real. An early morning shower had been even more necessary for her this morning, for the dream had been so lifelike that it had left her with ample evidence of her body's natural response to the erotic dream.

The young man, sitting gazing at her with the exact same features and eyes of her first, and so far only love, had invoked a turmoil of emotions the previous night. She felt reborn somehow, alive and tingling with anticipation, and when she searched her mind she realised that her feelings towards another man, who had been showing some interest in her for some time, had also changed. *'Perhaps she was ready to start another relationship?'* she asked herself. She was certainly still capable of the physical aspects of such a relationship, as she had proved so convincingly last night. A deep blush revealed her thoughts and my mind was firmly entwined with hers when she made the decision to saddle her horse and ride over to visit one of her neighbours. A widower two years her junior and, at sixty, still a fine figure of a man. His name was Anthony (never Tony) Jarvis and he owned two thousand acres of stud farm that stretched almost as far back as Braidwood. Hardly able to stifle my laugh of pleasure, I read her thoughts of staying for lunch, supper and a wicked, *'What the hell, breakfast too!'* I knew that Mr Jarvis was in for a wild night and I finally felt at peace with my transition from first to second life. But whatever happened, Tracey must never discover that she was about to become a bigamist.

With a firm hug and an invitation to call anytime from Tracey, she left to saddle her horse; and I reminded Alicia of her promise to call the Templetons. As soon as the telephone was answered, I knew I was in for a long wait. Chatting on the telephone was one of the few pleasures available to women whose lives were lived in the backwoods of Australia. The two women settled into what was to become a marathon three-hour conversation; both using loudspeaker phones, shouting their heads off as they moved around their kitchens, preparing whatever was required for lunch, dinner and the household pets.

Not wishing to appear intrusive or to interfere in any way, I ambled down to one of the many large ponds a few hundred metres from the homestead and sat on a dilapidated wooden seat, watching the kangaroos and other wildlife going about their daily business of gathering sufficient food.

The conversation, which I continued to overlook, included a wide range of subjects, from personal women's problems to a choice bum sighted on a new member of the horsey brigade. Most of the conversation was of little or no interest to me and my mind drifted to a new place that I had discovered over recent years. A place of complete inactivity; where I was not aware of the passage of time or the actions of others around me. Almost a monitoring state, from which I could recall all that had occurred but had been unaware of it actually happening. During such peaceful retreats from the world I sometimes lost control of my alter ego, which when freed from my physical body flitted away to find more interesting subjects to overlook; and such was the case today, an occasion that I would very shortly have great difficulty in explaining to an inquisitive granddaughter.

Lydia climbed on to my lap. She reached down and lifted my unresponsive arms around her, snuggling close. 'I thought you were dead,' I heard her say.

Before I could reply I heard my name mentioned. Instantly I returned to attentive overlooking of Alicia's telephone conversation. She was explaining my unannounced visit and told of my likeness to her father and of how the whole family had taken an instant liking to me. The response from Hayley Templeton, at the news of my interest in the twins, was tinged with mixed emotions. However, she was a practical woman. She knew that the twins would continue to find it difficult to obtain good jobs around Canberra; and possibly anywhere else in Australia. In truth she could not understand why the twins were having so much trouble, since most of the population of Australia were immigrants of some kind or another and employers rarely showed such antipathy towards applicants of any creed or colour; but still the twins had failed to progress beyond the initial interview stage for any vacant post.

Despite their brilliant minds, obvious intelligence and impressive degrees, they had both found it difficult to find employment that matched their talents. A westernised name, together with first class honours degrees, ensured that they both easily won through to the interview stage when applying for jobs; but their Timorese background always seemed to be the stumbling block. Naturally, any good job vacancies were much sought after around Canberra and those on offer attracted a huge number of applicants. Somehow, prospective employers found it difficult to accept the Timorese applicants despite their attractive faces, exceptionally good manners and intelligence; and always there were other candidates who were - more Australian.

My intervention at each of the twins' interviews was unknown to Hayley Templeton. A great deal of time and effort on my part was expended to ensure that they were not selected for any of the posts for which they applied. The doubts chasing each other around in Hayley's mind were transparent to me and I introduced a thought that perhaps she had done as much as she could for the twins; and perhaps it was time to help them even more by letting them go. I heard her agree to see me the following day and turned my attention to the little girl sitting on my lap.

'No little Lydia, I am not dead,' I finally replied, hugging her close to me.

'But where were you?' she cried. 'You frightened me because your eyes looked like my pony's eyes when he died.'

'Oh, I was probably just away with the fairies, dreaming of home - probably just jetlag.'

We sat idly watching the ducks and geese landing on the *dam*[19]. The flight path brought the heavy birds over a circle of high conifers, followed by what must have been a bottom-squeezing swoop down to the water. Each landing tickled the humour of the little girl, as the birds pushed their webbed feet forward to cushion and slow their contact with the water. Her high-pitched giggles pleased me immensely.

'Do you watch the birds every day?' I asked her.

'Pretty much, Granddad.' Her typically Australian reply did not surprise me. But her addressing me as granddad certainly did. *'From what unknown depths of childish understanding had she deduced that I was her grandfather? Maybe from the photographs in her grandmother's bedroom?'* I thought, quickly deciding to ignore her comments; let sleeping dogs lie.

'But where were you when you were with the fairies, Granddad?'

---

[19]Dam. An Australian pond.

This child was not about to give up on the notion of a new grandfather, nor easily accept my liaison with any fairies.

'What price am I paying, missing out on watching this lovely child grow?' my secret thoughts continued. In cricketing terms the question was a wide ball; and I should have let it pass me by.

'Well,' I replied, lowering my voice to a whisper, 'I am really a goblin, from fairyland, and I have come to your home to grant you a wish. Sometimes goblins have to phone home to keep the boss up to speed. We can only do that when we are dozing; and we must be alone.'

The child was reaching an age where her belief in Santa Claus and the tooth-fairy were wearing thin. But still wishing to edge her bets and not completely discard the notion of such beliefs, she struggled to accept my explanation. Failing to get her head around my words, and not wishing to upset either Santa or the tooth-fairy, she finally grasped the crux of the matter. 'Only one wish, Granddad?'

Before I left the property, Alicia gave me a yellow reminder tab on which was written the address and telephone number of the Templetons and told me to call on them the following day.

As I crested the hill, which overlooked the beautiful valley containing the homestead, I stopped the Land Rover and looked back, hoping for a final glimpse of the girls; but there was no one in sight, just four burly dogs languishing in the shade of the veranda.

That evening, after dinner in the hotel, I rang the Templeton number. The telephone rang for some time before being answered by a breathless Hayley Templeton. She had obviously been working in the fields. The loud and bubbly voice of Hayley Templeton greeted me and while I introduced myself I planted a vague memory of a previous meeting into her mind; a somewhat confused memory of someone who looked identical to Alicia's father.

We spoke for some time and Hayley told me that Ana had a part-time administrative job in a garage owned by one of her friends and Joe was scratching a living doing as many shifts as he could at the local pizza parlour. Brother and sister were happy in many ways. The Templetons ensured that the pair lacked for nothing, at least in terms of the basics of life, but what they could not provide were jobs that suited their talents; and both yearned for more demanding ways to earn a living.

Briefly I outlined my offer of employment for the twins in the UK and waited for Hayley's response. Alicia and Hayley were firm friends, both being very keen members of the local horsey set, and of course Alicia had related the story of her newly-found half-brother Timothy on several occasions. However, Hayley remained uncommitted and undecided, and made no comment about my suggestion of the twins moving to the UK. But as our conversation continued, she began to feel much more relaxed about the twins leaving home; departing Australia and travelling to the other side of the world to find their way in life no longer seemed too bad an option.

Positive feelings about this man, who had so suddenly come to her rescue, began to enter her mind for, if truth be told, she had been reaching the end of her tether, she also suddenly realised, about the twins actually finding suitable employment that matched their capabilities. Our conversation ended with an invitation for me to call the following morning, at which time Hayley promised to have the twins and Rodney present.

Feeling particularly satisfied with my efforts so far, I left the hotel and took myself on a night-time sightseeing tour of Canberra; ending up on the shores of Lake Burley Griffin enjoying the cool of the evening. In such peace and solitude I was able to rehearse my approach to the twins and the Templeton family. I wished to make no mistakes, for despite my powerful talent of influencing the thoughts of others, some individuals of extreme intelligence were occasionally able to overrule my implanted wishes. The offer that I was about to make to the twins was to be a very generous one; an offer that they could hardly refuse, and I was confident that they would accept.

Early to breakfast the next morning I was partially wrong-footed when I found Josh Templeton waiting in the hotel's dining room. We had not met previously but of course I knew who he was after overlooking the rescue of the twins from the Timorese boat incident. Allowing my eyes to pass unhesitatingly past Josh's face and continue their casual glance around the dining room, I headed for a small table near the window. Whilst ordering my breakfast I felt the presence of Josh approaching my table and I stood to take his outstretched hand as he introduced himself.

Josh was a big man, almost two metres in height and powerfully built; and he towered over me before we sat. An invitation to join me for breakfast was readily accepted, during which Josh told me that he had now left the Australian Navy and was attempting to establish a fence-building business in the ACT and surrounding area. Following a telephone call from his mother the previous evening, Josh wanted to satisfy himself of my intentions towards the twins. Clearly, his mind told me that he considered them to be his brother and sister and was extremely concerned about my proposal to offer them employment in the UK.

As our conversation progressed, I could see that Josh was not at all happy about his future life in Australia. The treatment of the SIEV had sickened him. The Nimby attitude of the authorities destroyed forever his faith in the Australian leadership and the only ties binding him to his adoptive homeland were those metaphorically dangling from his mother's apron.

The big man was also not at all happy about his own choice of occupation. The heavy physical labour associated with building fences, sometimes in the intense Australian heat, was not a problem to this giant of a man; what worried him was that deep down he wanted more from life. He had grown to love his Timorese brother and sister and was intent on persuading me to withdraw my offer of employment.

Anticipating his words, I turned his mind into a turmoil of indecision by suggesting that he too accompany the twins. I could certainly find suitable employment for this man. Temporarily at a loss for words, Josh stood, grunted and left the room, heading for the toilets for a few moments of quiet reflection and to regain his composure. When he returned and without further question or discussion, he agreed to my offer. He would accompany the twins if they too decided to return to the UK with me.

Later that morning I drove up the long drive to the Templeton property. Huge clouds of dust billowed behind the Land Rover and I was surrounded by a welcoming pack of cats, dogs and the whole Templeton family. It was extremely hot and I was glad to enter into the coolness of the single-storey, air-conditioned building.

Almost before my backside had touched the seat of the chair, Josh had shoved a bottle of ice-cold beer into my hands, enclosed within the ubiquitous stubby-sock that prevented the dripping bottle from depositing the melting ice on to my trousers.

The twins had grown into amazingly attractive people. Both at the same height of about one point seven-five metres, their delicate features and softly-brown, almost golden complexions highlighted the deep brown of their eyes and jet-black hair. Sitting around the large kitchen table, the conversation shifted and swayed aimlessly in the general chit-chat of social intercourse; until I asked them if they had considered my offer of employment.

As always Joe looked to his sister to take the lead; and Ana, in her beautiful lilting Aussie twang, said simply, 'Yes, we would very much like to accept your offer.' This immediate statement of acceptance almost caught me off guard once again. I had expected to be asked for some details of job descriptions and salary at the very least; but the twins had obviously discussed the situation overnight and had reached a mutually agreeable decision. Their thoughts were plain to me: *'At least there would be more opportunities in the UK, even if their employment with me proved not to their liking.'*

Not wishing to outline my plans in front of the Templeton seniors, I invited the three younger members of the family to dinner with me that evening. After taking my leave I hoisted myself to my feet in preparation of leaving. Almost immediately the four dogs, each of whom had been slumbering noisily on their raised canvas beds, leapt to their feet and launched themselves through the badly lacerated fly-screen across the patio doors, barking and howling in their efforts to be first on to the front lawns and into whatever car might be leaving the property. One particular dog, obviously a few cents short of an Aussie-dollar, headed straight on to the large circular front lawn and raced around in ever decreasing circles, chased by a much smaller animal snapping at its heels, until finally collapsing into a gasping, tongue-lolloping heap under a shady tree. Hayley explained that a previous owner had kept the dog in a very small pen for its first few years of life, its only exercise had been to wander around in circles and every time the dog left the house it followed this strange ritual of chasing itself around the lawn.

Back at my hotel I made the necessary arrangements for dinner that evening, booked a table for four and made a particular point of asking for it to be served in a private corner of the dining room.

Later that evening as I strolled once again into the plush eating area, I realised that I need not have bothered. The dining room was huge, and there were few others ready to eat so early in the evening. In retrospect, asking Josh and the twins to join me at 19.00 had been a very good idea, for there was little chance of our being overheard in the impressive room.

As I entered the dining room I tutted loudly in distaste. Clearly emblazoned on the door was the sign, 'Salon de diner' - obviously the work of some witless Australian wonder to impress foreign visitors. Sitting alone at my table gazing out over the beauty of Lake Burley Griffin, I laughed out loud when I mentally corrected the sign, 'Tucker room' - such an honest Australian description would have impressed me much more.

Glancing at my watch I noticed that it was already 19.15. My guests were late and I began to wonder if a change of mind had taken place. Feeling weary from jetlag, the heat of the Sun and my daytime activities, I could not muster the energy to overlook the trio; and resigned myself to waiting as patiently as I could. To pass the time, I strolled over to read the plaque on the wall of the tucker room, which listed some interesting facts about the lake and Canberra in general. Apparently the lake was formed by damming the Molonglo River and Canberra was designed by an American after whom the lake was named.

My reading was disturbed as the door swung inwards and I was out of sight as Josh and the twins entered the dining room. 'We're not late,' cried Ana in delight. 'He hasn't arrived yet and we can have a quick look at the menu before he turns up.' The beautiful smile faded from her face when I coughed, she turned towards me and said, 'Oh, you are here,' and I noticed that her face had reddened in embarrassment.

In total contrast to my own smart casual dress, my guests wore jeans and loose fitting tops. Such obvious disregard for the dress code of the 5-star restaurant was totally unacceptable to the officious-looking *maitre d'* who came barging through the dining room doors, heading for my table with a stupid raised-eyebrow expression on his face. *'We cannot allow such casual dress in our restaurant,'* I could read his thoughts as he lumbered across the room. Thinking quickly, I imposed the thought of a $50 tip into his mind and without breaking step the head waiter deftly picked up a handful of menus and continued to our table.

Throughout the meal I asked my guests many questions. As a future employer I felt entitled to do so. Maybe it was a little unkind of me, because I knew the answers to most, but I deliberately asked questions of the twins that they would find difficult to answer. Their knowledge of their father, of their grandparents, school days - that sort of thing. How they came to be in Australia, the jobs that they had applied for, what their hopes were for the future. I sympathized with their failed efforts to find posts in their adoptive country that were more suitable to their impressive qualifications, hinting in no small way to the fact that they were being treated as little more than illegal immigrants, whilst all the while knowing that it was I who had thwarted their applications and interviews.

Most of their many questions I dodged, apart from describing their individual posts as assistant, financial advisor and minder, and I tried to keep them interested without giving them too much information. To Ana, I explained that my large Hampshire estate needed managing and that several large projects were about to be entered into; millions of pounds would be placed in the care of Joe, and his task would be to increase that amount as much as possible; and for Josh I simply mentioned that where large fortunes are involved, there also lurk those unsavoury people who might wish to interfere with the smooth running of events and his would be the job of protecting the twins.

The evening passed quickly and it was not until I was trying to wade through the enormous portion of pudding that I got down to the arrangements for the flight to the UK. The internal leg from Canberra to Sydney would be on a scheduled sky-bus service and I hoped that we might check-in our luggage straight through to Heathrow. 'Oh, I have already checked with the airline, and that is standard procedure.' The female drive to organise and manage everyone's lives is strong even in younger women and Ana had already started her job as my assistant. Clearly intending to take charge of everything she added, 'And it will be best to remain in the domestic terminal until our international leg is ready to board. It gets so busy in the international departure lounges.' She did not speak a final comment but I saw it in her mind *'And the shops are so much nicer ground-side.'*

'The public departure lounges will not be a problem for us, Ana,' I added, smiling broadly. 'We are travelling first class. Except, of course, for the thirty-minute hop to Sydney.'

Providing a traveller makes an effort to be early at check-in for every leg of a worldwide itinerary, air travel is not at all stressful. As a retired Royal Navy Officer, and especially a retired communications specialist, I made every effort to be early for every appointment.

Our journey to Bangkok went like clockwork, where we disembarked from the comfort of our first class seats to stretch our legs in a mad dash through the terminal building. Turnaround time at Bangkok was severely limited, with just enough time to have a quick look around the shops before making our way through the departure formalities.

Ana was excited and wanted to find a postcard and a small present for her adoptive mother. At twenty-six, she was quite capable of looking after herself and I thought nothing of her dashing off on her own to look through the female sections of the many designer outlets. 'We had better start thinking about returning to our gate, Josh.' As I spoke I turned to look at Josh but he was gone.

Galvanised by an ear-piercing scream, Josh was sprinting along the corridor, heading for the source of the commotion. Shoppers of all shapes, colours and sizes were bulldozed out of his way; and I could see the agonising worry in his mind.

Not especially conscious of the milling crowds of window-shoppers traipsing around the shops, Ana was lost in a world of her own. Most women seem to lose all sense of time when hunting for bargains and she had learned from her adoptive mother how to haggle over prices on the numerous shopping expeditions around the vast malls in Australia. Bright lights, catchy music and an aura of contentment cradled the young woman as she browsed. Almost anything the heart desired was on sale in the huge international airport, from expensive jewellery and clothing to bunches of oriental flowers; and she was in her element.

But whilst travelling around the world, there are those predators who regard a young unaccompanied person of the opposite gender as a potential partner for a casual dalliance of a sexual nature, particularly those with a free-and-easy Latin mentality. And the handsome young Italian considered himself to be every woman's dream. Cutting Ana out of the crowd as his target for today, the would-be lover made his customary advance, sidling up behind his victim, gender area nudging gently against the rounded buttocks of the female form, whilst making some casual comment about the goods on display.

But what the unfortunate young Italian did not know was that Ana was damaged goods and she abhorred unexpected contact with another human form. Phobias are the most common mental anxiety disorder amongst women and Ana's phobia was diagnosed as *Andras Psilafitos Phobia* - an irrational fear of tactile men.

Wistfully dreaming of her adoptive mother, Ana was in a world of her own, mind totally engrossed in making a selection from the vast number of cards on sale. The young man's whispered words were unheard, as in one fluid movement she flipped from normal everyday behaviour to a fully-dredged panic attack, turned and kicked the smiling sexual assassin in the crotch, screaming at full-lung capacity.

Any help from Josh was unnecessary. As he burst into the shop his eyes took in the scene in an instant; Ana was crouched by the shop counter, trembling uncontrollably in fear and loathing, and her amorous suitor was crouched on the floor - *hors de combat* - hands desperately trying to ease the pain of the full-blooded kick.

'You bastard!' Two words summed up Josh's opinion of the man who had attacked his sister, although if truth be known, his feelings for his adoptive sister were rather more than brotherly love. A red mist descended over the Australian's eyes; giant, sun-tanned hands grasped the fallen sex-offender, lifted him effortlessly above his head and hurled the body to the rear of the counter, narrowly avoiding taking the hapless shop assistant's head with it.

Without a word he stooped and picked the woman up like a baby, turned and left the shop. No one attempted to stop Josh as he carried the fretful young woman through the departure formalities, nor asked him to pay for the damage to the shop; but much later as I dozed in my seat on the long leg to Heathrow, I saw the unfortunate young Italian parting with large sums of money.

For those with nothing to hide and a British passport, customs and immigration procedures at Heathrow are quite informal. Obtaining the necessary passports for the twins had been simple; a couple of application forms a few weeks before and a little mind-bending had been all that was needed, and I handed the twins their new passports just before we touched down. Josh had retained dual citizenship and therefore still had a British passport and of course had no problems passing through immigration.

My People-Carrier was parked in the long-term car park and I threw the keys at Josh after I had unlocked the doors.

Over the years I knew that Josh had made several trips to the UK to visit grandparents and other relatives and I was pretty sure that he remembered his way around the country. 'Might as well start earning your keep Josh. You can drive - and I hope you know the way out of the airport.'

'Where to Boss?' Josh asked.

'Abbotstone is our destination, Josh. I will navigate if you are unsure at any time.'

'Well for Christ's sake don't fall asleep, or we will be going round and round in circles for the rest of the day,' the ripple of happy laughter from Josh heightened everyone's mood.

Driving up the long drive to the estate at Abbotstone I gazed ahead and the sight of the imposing house cheered me considerably. No longer alone in my task, I had a team, the members of which I knew would become a family to me; the Verguide Team.

CHAPTER 12
RETURN OF THE DIAMOND

THREAD:

Three years pass, during which the Verguide Team settle into life in England. In the back of my mind I know that there is a task that I feel duty-bound to complete.

Following the devastating effects of the second shell from the *Wogga*, all was chaos on board *Tetum*. In the few minutes between the shell exploding and the *Tetum* turning turtle, Captain Xeves strove to make himself heard over the noise of the vessel breaking up and the screams of the doomed passengers as they blundered from handhold to handhold, searching for any means of prolonging their lives.

'Take your chances in the sea,' he screamed the words over and over again, knowing deep in his heart that he, his crew and most if not all of the passengers were about to meet their maker. The last thought of the somewhat grandiosely named Horatio Xeves, just a millisecond before he felt his guts ripped open as the great white finally crunched deeply on to its supper, was that of a glittering diamond, still safely locked in the Master's private safe, now lying on the seabed off the coast of Northern Australia.

ENGLAND. JUNE 2006.

The wreck of the *Tetum* lay at the bottom of Blue Mud Bay, in about seventy-five metres of shark-infested sea. Finding a specialist wreck-diving firm capable of deep-diving to this depth was not difficult and at my very first attempt I managed to find a firm that employed a couple of penetration divers, those highly-trained individuals capable of entering a wreck and recovering items from it.

Gordon Archey's firm was the first hit when I entered 'Australian Penetration Divers' into my computer's search engine. A quick telephone call arranged a meeting. Mr Archey was only too happy to accept my invitation to a meeting in London, especially since I offered to fund first class travel and accommodation for him and his diving team leader.

Gordon (Gordey) Archey was typically ex-RAF and I recognised him immediately as I arrived at the Dorchester in Park Lane, between Marble Arch and Hyde Park corner. The Grill Room was a favourite meeting place for me. The dark red tartan upholstery and drapes enhanced the crisp whiteness of the tablecloths and a lunch of thinly sliced smoked salmon with freshly-baked stilton bread, followed by traditional British roast beef, and the whole washed down with several bottles from the hotel's impressive wine list, emphasised that I was a man who could afford the best in life.

After initial introductions and idle chitchat before the meal was served, conversation dried up whilst the two Australians satisfied their gargantuan appetites, somewhat embarrassingly requesting, 'Another round of that thinly sliced meat for starters'!

During the chitchat, Gordey told me that he had left the RAF in 1981 and had emigrated to Australia with his mother. Still single, he was short, very fat, balding, on the plus side of the half century and sported an enormous handlebar moustache. Before eating, he slipped on a pair of battered spectacles, the rims of which were stained green with mould from continual sweat and long usage. He did not offer the additional information, that of being drummed out of the RAF for petty theft, but I read it in his thoughts.

The penetration diver, Jeremy Mextby, nicknamed Ginge for very obvious reasons, was tall and skinny, a beanpole of a man aged about mid-forties. His shock of bright red hair drew a watcher's attention away from his squinting eyes and he kept his gaze downwards to hide a severe case of lazy-eye syndrome. Also describing himself as ex-RAF, the pair had met in Sydney in the late 1980s and had teamed up as a diving team shortly afterwards. Self-trained, they produced impressive references from various clients, all of which appeared genuine and, apart from a feeling of distrust, I had no reason, at that time, to doubt their professional abilities or honesty.

But as the meal progressed, I could smell a rat. The smell of this particular rat was growing more pungent; and my feeling of distrust deepened as each course followed on from the previous. Ginge's predilection for hiding his squint by gazing at the table was mirrored by his senior partner when making statements that were not quite accurate. After the meal was completed, they both consumed several portions from the sweet trolley - cheese and biscuits, several cups of coffee, and rounded off with three pints of lager. I decided that despite my reservations about their honesty, I also needed these men to recover the diamond.

Keeping the existence of the diamond in reserve, I outlined the loss of the *Tetum*. Carefully I explained that the whole illegal immigrant incident had been suppressed by the Australian government; hence the existence and site of the wreck was known to none, other than the Royal Australian Navy of course. My knowledge of diving was very limited; even more skimpy is my familiarity with deep diving, and I asked the two experts if seventy-five metres posed many problems for them. Before replying Gordey sucked in his breath between his teeth and, on conversational solid ground, raised his eyes to mine. He spoke at some length about the expensive equipment that would be required to reach the wreck, adding, after dropping his eyes to the tabletop, that he expected the whole process to span about two weeks.

Two sets of eyes flicked greedily towards my face when I mentioned that there existed a small Captain's wall safe; located beneath the Captain's bunk, and it was that which I required them to recover. Instantly I knew that they both desperately wanted to know what was in the safe and I toyed with them for a few minutes, asking for the safe to be recovered intact and handed to me unopened. Eventually I allowed myself to be persuaded that it might not be possible to retrieve the safe undamaged and unopened, and I told them that the only item of interest to me was a small diamond. 'How much is the diamond worth?' asked Gordey, by now sweating profusely and gazing around to attract the attention of the waiter, intending to ask for another round of lager. I decided to over-inflate the value of the gem and dropped my voice to a whisper. 'About half a million Australian dollars,' I replied. Silence followed this piece of information as both assessed just how much they could demand from me for the diamond's recovery and I let them stew a little until the beers were delivered.

'Thank you Peter,' I addressed the waiter. 'A wonderful meal as usual,' and handed him my Diners Card adding, much more loudly than was strictly necessary, 'add twenty percent for yourself!' When the receipt was produced, I casually slipped it into my top pocket without a glance at the details, informed Peter that we had a little more business to discuss and that we would not yet be leaving.

Forehead wrinkled in concentration whilst he completed the numbers game, Gordey could hardly wait to blurt out his diving fee. 'Yes, I think fifty thousand dollars should pretty much cover it,' a slight pause and, 'American,' he added lamely, securing an additional thirteen thousand pounds sterling for his greedy afterthought.

They could have asked for much more and I would have agreed to pay, for I had already decided that these two greedy individuals would not survive after they had served my purpose. Overflowing the honey-pot, I handed them a small attaché case containing five thousand pounds in used notes as a deposit and promised the balance in local currency when I arrived in Australia to collect the diamond.

The beer and wine had dulled the wits of the two divers. But Gordey was still searching for an important detail, a question that he needed to ask. It was on the tip of his tongue but he could not recall exactly what it was. Suddenly it came to him and he was so anxious to speak the words that he forgot his mouth was full of beer. 'But how do you know there is a diamond onboard the ship?' Gordey choked as a mouthful of beer splattered across the table. 'Because it is my diamond,' I lied. 'A family heirloom that I was forced to use to cover a temporary hiatus in cash flow.'

During the following few days I overlooked the pair as they visited old stomping grounds in and around the Home Counties. They had decided to stay on for a few extra days, particularly in light of their forthcoming windfall, and as they sat on the return flight to Sydney, I knew that there was little left of the deposit, most of which had been wisely spent in London's West End!

Their whispered discussion during the flight was extremely enlightening to me. I had, of course, suspected treachery and their talk of how quickly they might get a duplicate paste version made of the diamond confirmed my fears. There was no point in my cancelling the recovery agreement. I had already disclosed the location of the wreck and pinpointed the exact position of the small Captain's safe. Dealing with them after they had completed the dangerous recovery of the diamond would be a pleasure!

Bobbing around in the gentle swells of Blue Mud Bay, the small inflatable dinghy with its powerful outboard motor made an adequate dive boat. The divers were completely alone; not another soul could be seen along the shoreline. A faint splosh as Ginge flopped backwards into the warm sea. He was agitated and his deep-rooted fear of sharks caused him to feel for the reassuring cold metal of his harpoon gun, looped by a strong lanyard to his dive belt. A fighter pilot in the sea, his eyes continuously searched above and below, and his brain focused on a single thought. Not of the diamond, nor of how he might spend his forthcoming share of the profits of this dive, but that he would have sight of the familiar outline of the huge predator before it attacked. Next to him as he descended was a wire cable which dropped vertically to the seabed, attached to which were the two spare cylinders of Trimax gas, his emergency supplies in the event of unforeseen eventualities. *'Three hours in these dangerous waters,'* the thought did little to alleviate Ginge's fears. He would certainly earn his share of the rewards and, as he sank ever deeper, his fears deepened in parallel with the increasing darkness and numbing cold.

Descending through the clear water, Ginge saw nothing, not another living thing, only the reassuring cable with his failsafe gas supplies disappearing into the blackness below. A capable and experienced diver, Ginge nevertheless felt the usual dreadful apprehension that overcame him as he descended from murky sunlight into the black depths of the ocean. The transition never failed to both unman and unnerve him completely; and the feeling when he looked down into the blackness into which his boots were fast disappearing, created churning waves of panic in his chest. Reaching upwards, he switched on his diving lamp, which was attached to his helmet, and automatically felt for the spare dangling from his diving belt.

A slight thud and he had touched bottom. Instinctively he looked down and saw a gentle cloud of sand blossom from under his feet. *'Time to see if the wreck was in sight,'* he thought, as he switched off the helmet lamp and turned on the powerful handheld lamp. Unbelievably the wreck was no more than five metres in front of him; they had struck pay dirt on their first attempt! With this good fortune, Ginge, now totally businesslike, strode towards the wreck and looked through the gaping hole in what was the bottom of the *Tetum*.

What was left of the ship was lying on its side and Ginge saw that access to the Captain and crew's quarters was not going to be difficult. He simply pulled himself up a ladder, passed through an open hatchway and followed a short corridor to where he knew the Captain's cabin was located, just below the bridge. Despite the short distance that he had to travel inside the wreck, Ginge did not neglect to set his distance lines that would guide him to the wreck's exit. It was not difficult to become disorientated, particularly as dust became disturbed into vision-distorting clouds and the cold bit ever more deeply through the diving suit.

But over and above his apprehensions, Ginge felt elation. This job was going to be a piece of cake; the safe was spotted instantly as he entered the small cabin. Evidently someone had removed the paneling just before the ship went down, making his job just that much easier. A few hefty blows with his axe removed the small safe from the timbers to which it had been bolted and Ginge made his exit from the wreck and, after observing the necessary decompression stops, returned to the surface.

Relief flooded over Ginge as he hauled himself out of the sea and into the gently bobbing diving dinghy. The dive had been completely trouble-free without the merest glimpse of a shark. *'Easy money,'* thought Ginge, *'wish all dives were as simple as this one!'* He felt no reluctance or distrust as he handed the safe to his boss; the thief's bond of trust was strong between them.

Having travelled down to Australia in my alter ego state, I was waiting for the two divers when they returned to Gordey's house on the outskirts of Darwin. The house had been quiet all day as I lay on Gordey's bed overlooking the diamond recovery operation and keeping the sharks at bay. Loud snores had occasionally been erupting from the adjacent room for most of the afternoon; Gordey's mother having a catnap.

Laughing and shouting in their joy at a successful dive, the two friends entered the living room noisily. The antiquated safe had been no match for a hammer and cold chisel and swiftly gave up its contents into the greedy hands of the two divers.

I was standing behind Ginge as he removed the diamond from the safe. A bundle of soggy currency was the only other occupant; it was casually discarded by Gordon. Handing the beautiful gem to his partner, Ginge let out a soft sigh of satisfaction. He always felt extreme elation, a feeling that non-divers could never experience, when he retrieved articles from the deep. 'Better than sex,' he murmured as he handed the gem to his teammate. Gordon smiled, or at least his fat face fell apart in what served as a smile, at his partner's words.

At that moment, Gordey's mother entered the room with cups of steaming coffee. At eighty-two, she was still very active and her enormous body wobbled as she shuffled breathlessly across the room. She cast a disinterested glance at the diamond in her son's podgy hand and, without a single word, turned and left the room. It was my first sighting of the old woman and she was the ugliest human being that I had ever seen. Unkind acquaintances of Gordey often speculated how such an ugly woman could have arranged conception, for the photographs of the younger woman showed that it was not advancing years which had distorted the woman's features; they had forever been so! All who surmised at the details of the conception agreed on one thing; the man must have been completely blotto when the deed was done. A more kindly thought entered my own mind. *'For someone long deprived of a soft female body, almost anything on two legs or four is probably better than nothing,'* a feeling neatly expressed in the old salts' adage *'any port in a storm!'.*

Faces aglow with excitement, the two men gazed at one another. When Gordey placed the fake alongside the glittering original, it was difficult to tell the difference between the two. 'How much have we made?' The voice of Ginge was almost reverent in its intensity as he asked the question that had been sitting at the back of his mind for so long. Gordey thought for some moments. 'Well…fencing the diamond should bring at least a quarter million Oz; and about eighty thou' from that useless bloody pomme. I'd say about a hundred and fifty thou' each I reckon, Sport!'

Leaning casually against a sideboard I had until now remained a silent observer. Earlier that day I had removed an old revolver from the drawer in the sideboard, and had spent some time cleaning and loading the weapon. Confident that it would fire, I walked across to the table and lifted the original diamond.

As soon as my hand closed over the gem, it disappeared from the two divers' sight. They both gasped and looked at one another; where had the diamond gone? 'What the…where's it gone?' Gordey's voice was strangled. 'Which is this?' picking up the fake. 'The bonzer one or the duff one?'

They both fell to their knees and began feeling around the floor and, presented with such tempting targets, I could not resist giving each a resounding kick on the most sensitive parts of a male torso. Screeching in pain and confusion the two lay on the floor, hands pressed firmly into their private parts, eyes bulging with fright and flooded with tears of pain. Very slowly, as their moans subsided, I allowed the revolver to come into view and I whispered, 'Hello boys, you must remain very quiet because I do not intend to speak loudly since I have no wish for your mother to become involved in this.'

Cloaked in its protective shield, I allowed my alter ego to speak out loud and I thanked them for retrieving the diamond, adding that had they not been greedy, they could have made a nice little profit. 'And maybe even stayed alive!' I added ominously, revealing my intentions.

Total silence. Huge eyes looked beseechingly around the room; they could not comprehend what was happening. They could see the gun aimed rock-steady at them and had heard my voice; but they could see no one. They knew they were in great danger and they also suspected their fate, and they pleaded desperately for mercy. I toyed with the idea of allowing myself to materialise but forced myself to remain ultra cautious. 'You do understand why I must kill you both?' I threw the question at the pair, who were still curled up on the floor. They gave it a good go really, both blaming the other for their attempt at swindling me, and I listened quietly as the accusations grew more heated. Surely, the old woman would have heard the ruckus and should soon be shuffling along to see what was going on?

But I left it too late. No sooner had I dispatched Gordey and Ginge with clean shots through the forehead than the door flew inwards. The old woman was an unstoppable battering ram and the door flew off its hinges and sailed across the room. In her hands was a double-barrelled shotgun. Without a glance around the room or a sight of any target, she blasted off two cartridges, flipped open the weapon, reloaded and fired again. A skilled handler of the weapon, the blasts continued until she had expended about a dozen cartridges in all directions. The room was a mess, her squinty eyes were glazed with a fiery hatred and somehow I just knew that she knew! Fortunately for me, I had not unshackled my protective cloak and I remained motionless as the firing stopped.

The old woman looked shocked when she finally allowed her eyes to fall downwards to her son and huge, fat tears welled up inside them. Arthritic hands, covered in liver-spotted, wrinkled skin felt for a pulse in both the bodies. Long years of celibacy and loneliness sometimes contribute towards acute awareness and she spoke in a quiet and controlled voice: 'Blast you! You can go now. You have done your worst.'

Not until she left the room did I move. As quickly as I could I placed the revolver into Ginge's hand. There was no need to clean the weapon, for I did not leave fingerprints in my alter ego state. To complete the picture I placed the fake diamond into Gordey's hand. The investigating team would no doubt conclude that the two men had argued over the diamond; Ginge had shot Gordey and then turned the weapon on to himself when he realised what he had done.

The safe and bundle of still soggy banknotes I left in the room; it would give the Australian police something to chew upon and I almost laughed aloud when I imagined the interview with Gordey's mother. 'I'm telling you constable, it was an invisible man, his body must be in that room somewhere because I blasted the place to hell and gone!'

Once again I had not found the taking of human life an easy option. Despite my powers making the deed relatively simple, I had extracted the extreme penalty only as a last resort. Reasoning with the two petty crooks would not, I am sure, have achieved a satisfactory result for me. The pair would no doubt have tried to convince me that the fake diamond had been the only one found in the wreck of the *Tetum*.

Seeking self-approval of my actions I resolved that the pair had certainly deserved their punishment for their attempt to steal the diamond, not to mention their callous decision to renege on a business agreement. And it was not beyond the realms of probability that some careless, booze-induced tittle-tattle might lead the authorities to the twins.

Much later, I promised myself that I would continue to overlook Gordey's mother and maybe find some way of supporting her during her remaining time on Earth.

CHAPTER 13
TWINS' POWERS

THREAD:

Recovering the diamond had been the fulfilment of a promise that I had silently made to Maria Vinacco so many years before.

Ana had taken over the running of my affairs, such as they were, employing staff for the house and estate and generally running my diary. But she was not fully employed and whenever I read her thoughts, I could see that she was doubtful if her role in my organisation would be sufficient to keep her interest.

The younger of the twins immersed himself in my financial affairs and spent long months in the financial cities of the world. Certainly, whilst he was involved in the business of making money he was quite happy; but when alone I could see the turmoil within him. I was powerless to help him but I hoped that what I had planned for him, and his sister, would ease both their minds.

Nominally in charge of security, Josh had very little to occupy his time during the first few years of his return to his birth-land. As an organisation, we had absolutely nothing to hide in terms of secrets, nor much to steal in terms of valuables. Visitors to the house were made welcome, whether they be expected or simply drop-ins strolling around the estate. Apart from our private apartments, we encouraged an open-house policy.

To provide myself with some interest in life I concentrated on planning the first experimental underground city. Within the data banks installed into my brain by Belial First was all the information I needed; but it would be totally impossible for me to manage the entire project on my own. A team of experts from all the academic disciplines was essential; from local planning to engineering; science; architecture; law; agriculture; chemistry; biology; metallurgics; mineralogy; meteorology; etc. The list was virtually endless and it was time to enlist some additional help.

ABBOTSTONE, ENGLAND. MARCH 2007.

Personally, I was in a bit of a quandary about how to proceed with my plan, the next phases of which might involve my getting into politics and commencing deeper underground exploration. But my biggest problem was that I had not yet told the team of the grand plan.

Causing China and the Islamic world to pull back from the abyss of World War 3 was my primary task as the Verguide. In order to achieve that aim I must find ways to deter the global ambitions of the antagonists; and such measures as I chose to use must be introduced at the right time.

My secondary aim was population control, keeping the world's population within the bounds that could be accommodated under the surface of the Earth; and I hoped that achieving this secondary aim might also lead to reaching my primary aim. Population control can be achieved in several ways but each involves the annihilation of large numbers of people. But the process of incurring large-scale body counts might give the conflicting sides pause for thought, something else to occupy their minds; and might just enable me to kill two birds with one stone.

Preparing sufficient accommodation below the surface would be another conundrum; and the world's technology was not yet ready to tunnel as deep as would be necessary.

The other three members of the Verguide Team knew naught of Veruni, Belial First or me for that matter, and I desperately needed to bring them up to speed. I needed them with me, their total support, and with a complete knowledge of what had occurred so far.

Spring was definitely in the air; it was 27th March, 2007, the twins' thirtieth birthday. Somewhat selfishly, I decided to give them a present that would be of enormous help to me. As a team, they had settled into their new roles very quickly and as a team they seemed, on the whole, reasonably happy, living together in the new estate house at Abbotstone.

The personal relationship between the four of us was a little strange. In reality, I was sixty-six years of age and very much the father figure. However, Josh, at forty-one years of age, was by far the biggest in physical size; but since I had not aged, he also looked the oldest.

The baby of the family, Joe, still looked to his older sister for support and guidance and it was to her that he went first, whenever he was troubled. The very beautiful Ana had become the rock of the team, sorting out the teams' personal problems and dealing with her own duties with consummate ease.

But whenever I tuned-in to the Team, sitting around the big kitchen table taking a meal or lounging in the big armchairs during long winter evenings, I sensed an atmosphere of uncertainty, insecurity and an almost unidentifiable lack of purpose. They needed leadership, clearly-defined objectives towards a common goal. But most of all they needed knowledge.

The two thousand acres of the estate were managed by a professional estate manager who was responsible for the upkeep of the whole estate which included the house and gardens. My only stipulation was that in farming the land, at least five teams of heavy horse should be used. In truth, apart from annual staff Christmas parties, I rarely saw the man; Joe managed the farm budgets and Ana dealt with any queries that the manager might have.

For me, in terms of fulfilment, progress and life's little rewards, all play and no work makes Jack a poor boy. And with very little to occupy my time I continued to spend long hours overlooking various people around the world - presidents, kings, religious leaders or a passing face or event that aroused some interest in me - and I could usually be found in a coma-like doze during those long periods.

For much of the time I kept a watchful eye on my family on the other side of the world and had even considered trying to influence Tracey and Alicia to return to the UK with my grandchildren. I had even worked out a reason for my proposed actions, that of having the large acreage at Abbotstone turned over to farming by shire horses. I thought that the mention of my daughter's favourite animal might entice the family from the sunny climes of Australia; and that she might jump at the chance of running the agricultural business of the estate. But each time I overlooked the family they looked so happy and content that I had forcefully to stifle my plan.

My thoughts turned elsewhere, to developing underground explo-ration to even greater depths and to decide what might prove more useful, actually entering into the political world or relying upon influ-encing those already established in that field.

Before any attempt could be made to build an underground city, we would need office space and possibly accommodation for several hun-dred staff. Loath to coerce the local planning department into approv-ing further building on the estate, I decided to build underground.

Our team planning meetings were always very informal affairs and usually took place over breakfast, lunch or dinner. Thanks to the Verunians, I had a very retentive memory; facts, figures and conver-sations usually came instantly to mind whenever needed. However, despite the twins' formidable natural intelligence, they could not pos-sibly retain sufficient detail as our operations became more and more complex. And one of the Team was suffering badly from poor mem-ory; Josh was beginning to lose some of his mental agility - not that there had been an enormous amount of it in the first place!

So it was that on this wet and windy 27th March, 2007, I had arranged for the twins to receive a very special birthday present. Our live-in housekeeper, Mrs Amy Jupp, a thiry-five year old divorcee with two children, who ruled the house and the rest of the domestic staff, had prepared a rather special evening meal. In the dining room, the large table had been laid with five place settings, a fact that was instantly pounced upon by the twins as they entered.

'Who is coming to dinner?' Ana's voice had a hint of excitement and expectation and she looked around the room, expecting to see a fifth person.

Always the quiet one, Joe looked at me. He dropped his chin to his chest and peered at me over the rim of his spectacles, a quaint mannerism that I had come to know so well.

'What's going on?' Josh burst into the room; he was always ready to eat.

Throughout the day, there had been little in the way of recognition of the significance of the date; a few 'Happy birthdays' from staff and visitors seemed to suit the twins well enough. Much as did I, they loved a party, but abhorred being the centre of attention; and I saw them both cringe as their eyes took in the decorations on the table. Nothing too elaborate, just a few birthday cards in front of each of their place settings and a small pile of presents for each of them. In the centre of the table were two large cut-glass cake stands. On one of these stands sat a small birthday cake and on the other was an even smaller jewel case.

'Let's eat.' I spoke the words and lowered myself into the seat at the head of the table. The twins sat to my right and Josh took the seat on my left. We were all dressed casually in jeans, light sweaters and I even had my old well-worn slippers on.

'What's for starters?' Josh was hungry, and he smiled his huge friendly smile at Amy Jupp as she wheeled the hostess-trolley into the room.

'Let's eat dinner and do the presents bit afterwards. Is that OK with everyone?' I looked around at the others. They all looked into my eyes and smiled compliance.

'We cannot start yet,' said Joe, 'we are one short,' nodding at the vacant chair.

'In complete contrast with Josh, the fifth setting is for a small person with a tiny appetite; and he will not be joining us until the end of the meal.' They all looked a bit puzzled but accepted the situation and got stuck into the meal.

The usual subdued tit-bits of everyday conversation continued throughout the meal, interspersed with items of business, decisions and any comical events that had occurred on the estate.

Finally, when Amy Jupp brought in the coffee for the three Australians and tea for me, since I could no longer for some inexplicable reason endure the smell of coffee, I asked her to ensure that we were not disturbed for any reason until I phoned down to the kitchen later in the evening.

The whole team looked at me with questioning faces as I gave my instructions to Mrs Jupp. When she had left the room, I waited in silence for a couple of minutes and asked Josh to lock the door.

'Bit odd, Boss.' Locking doors was something that did not normally happen in the main areas of the house. But he hoisted himself on to his feet and headed over to lock the door.

'Whatever happens over the next few minutes, do not become alarmed; there is no danger. You are about to see something that no other person on Earth - apart from me - has ever seen before. And I stress, once again, there is no threat to any one of us, so remain calm.'

All three of my dinner companions had been gazing intently at me and all jumped when a child-like voice piped, 'Good evening everyone.'

Three sets of eyes turned instantly towards the sound of the voice. Ana screamed that quick, piercing sound that threatens to shatter the eardrums of everyone in range, particularly when it is totally unexpected.

'What the…' The sound of Josh's chair, hurtling backwards as he pulled himself to his feet, caused me to start uncontrollably. Now we were all jumpy!

'Bloody hell, Josh! Put that away!' Miraculously, a pistol had appeared in Josh's huge hand. I had no idea that he carried such a weapon and I decided not to question the legality of his obtaining or carrying it.

Joe, as usual, had kept his own counsel, preferring to think and evaluate before acting. He was gazing at the being in the chair and he was the first to address it.

'Good evening to you,' said Joe. 'I am afraid that I am unable to offer you any salutation, since I am also unable to determine quite what you are.'

With obvious care, Josh stowed his armoury into his clothing but could not resist giving the secret compartment a pat with his hand, indicating that it would not take him long to rearm himself, should the need arise.

At Joe's quiet greeting, we relaxed a little and sat looking at Belial First.

Belial First looked at me and nodded. Telepathy is so much easier than speech.

'Please forgive my theatrics.' I paused and looked around at the Team, a huge grin on my face.

'Please allow me to introduce Belial. Belial First to be precise, from the planet Veruni.'

I gave them a few moments to soak that one up and continued.

'As we of course all know it is the twins' thirtieth birthday today. And I have a rather special present for them. Please do not speak another word, remain completely silent, all will become clear.'

Belial First took control of our minds for some considerable time. For me the digital stream was now a second language but I could see the others struggling at first to cope with the mass of information, transmitted at such tremendous speed into their newly-formatted brains.

After many minutes of total silence the piping, child-like voice spoke again.

'Goodbye Verguide, goodbye the Team and enjoy your birthday cake.' Belial First took his leave and the fifth chair was, once again, empty.

Silence pervaded the room, total silence; not even the ticking of a clock could be heard. The kind of stunned silence that accompanies a thoughtless gaffe in social etiquette, or the revelation of a terrible family secret such as an unexpected birth or death.

Ana was the first to speak. 'Is it all true, Boss?' Her soft voice still retained the Australian twang, even after several years in the UK.

She looked at me with those huge, deep-brown eyes. I could see the wonder in them and, slowly but surely, comprehension, understanding and belief. The Team had seen nothing of my powers, for I had kept them tightly under control whilst in their company. Yes, there had been some comments about my knowing their thoughts before they had a chance to speak them; but they had no knowledge of my true capabilities.

'I'll give you a hand to fill in the application for your old-age pension.' Joe could hardly restrain his laughter as he spoke the words. 'You old boys can often feel challenged by bureaucracy and filling in a form can be quite a chore for you.'

As part of Belial First's information transfer, I had asked him to include the details of my life. They now knew everything about me; how I had watched over them, and influenced their lives.

'Could you not have saved Mother?' Ana asked the inevitable question, her voice filled with an aching sadness and longing.

'I have no secrets from any of you now.' I was watching their faces very carefully.

'You can all look back at what I have done, analyze, evaluate, second guess, whatever. But what is done, is done. There can be no going back. There are obviously parts of my existence that I still find difficult to deal with, particularly concerning my wife. I have learned to accept my role as the Verguide and I intend doing everything in my power to achieve the eventual aim of the Verunians; and more importantly ensure the safety of our planet.'

'As for your mother, you already know the answer - that I was so busy looking after you two that I did not have time to overlook your mother; and you all know her medical condition.' I added unnecessarily.

'And my natural feminine inquisitiveness has been satisfied without having to look inside the rather obvious box next to the cake!' Ana's face glowed, she had already accepted the challenge, already come to terms with the extraordinary events of the evening, her new role in life and her exciting new powers.

Ana and Joe were smiling outwardly but their eyes were filled with the wetness of tears. The twins looked at one another and Ana reached forward to open the box. The lid of the box was fully hinged and Ana allowed it to fall on to the cut-glass cake stand, revealing the beautiful marquise-cut diamond beneath. Ablaze with its fifty-eight facets, the white diamond reflected lights from all parts of the room and it appeared that it too had indeed travelled from another planet. The glittering jewel had been a talisman or a beacon of hope for their mother throughout the years of captivity; and the minds of the twins turned inwardly as one to memories of the past.

Quite naturally, they wanted to be alone with their thoughts. Josh unlocked the door and followed Joe from the room. Pausing, Ana turned, walked very slowly back to my side, placed a hand on each side of my face and kissed me softly on the lips.

'Thank you,' she whispered and was gone.

'We have much to do.' Joe spoke the words a few days after Belial First's visit.

All three of the Team had been quiet, reserved and thoughtful over the past few days. So much so that I was beginning to regret my asking Belial First to reveal every tiny detail. But at the same time, I knew that they were experimenting with their new powers.

Telepathy, we all agreed, was the most useful for everyday activities. Poor Mrs Jupp, she never did discover how she sometimes just seemed to know that Ana, Joe or Josh wanted a snack or a cup of coffee.

With their newly-found powers, many personal dreams had been shattered. The knowledge that Josh carried a torch for Ana had been with me for some time but he now finally knew and accepted that his love for her would never be reciprocated; at least not in the way that he wished. Notwithstanding some very special circumstances, we all knew that the twins might never marry; they had been too badly scarred by their experiences in the prison camp.

The twins had not escaped the attentions of the guards as their mother had so fervently hoped and both had undergone both sexual and physical abuse. But they also welcomed the understanding that their mother did not know of this abuse; they had not really been sure of this fact until now. The knowledge gave them both great peace and a wonderful warm feeling in their hearts when they thought of their mother. She had endured extreme conditions and extreme harshness but had managed to keep her children alive, even in the face of her ritual daily pleas for heavenly help falling upon deaf ears. No child could expect more of a mother under those circumstances.

Deeply rooted phobias would plague Ana for the rest of her life. She would never be able to accept a man, not physically, for even with her newfound powers, she could not blot out the image of her first brutal sexual experience. Neither could Joe, who, deep inside his still troubled mind, was not really sure whether he was male or female. Religiously, they both trotted off to their doctor twice yearly for a check-up, for they were both dreadfully afraid of having contracted some terrible sexual disease which might only manifest itself at some unforeseen moment in their lives. And at this moment in time, they both knew that they could never, under any circumstances, risk passing on this disease to partners or children.

Maturing years, intelligence, knowledge and the indefinable element of human logic should overcome most of the troubles that haunt the mind of a child; but fear of the unknown lingers in the mind forever. They were the untouchables and could not be dissuaded otherwise, no matter the eminences of the physicians or the wisdom of the speaker. At least not at this moment in time but maybe their birthday present might change their minds later in life.

Also uppermost in Ana's thoughts was the realisation that her growing fondness for me must be contained within the bounds of an avuncular relationship. Over time feelings change and my earlier thoughts of needing a second wife had long-since ceased to have any practical purpose in my life; and I had resigned myself to living a monastic existence for as long as life lived within me. Ana knew that I would never remarry. I was a one-woman man and Tracey still filled my heart.

Within the bounds of personal relationships, being given the ability to read another's mind is a double-edged sword. Especially so when the arrangement is one-sided because it is terrible to know the truth of a loved-one's innermost thoughts - and even more especially so when one is fully aware that one's feelings are not reciprocated. When both have the ability to see the innermost thoughts of the other at any time, then it is possibly manageable, since there can be no lies, half-truths, innuendoes or ambiguities.

Also free from these human traits were our planning meetings. From the moment the Small Person, as the Team often subsequently referred to Belial First, installed the information into the Team, an obvious air of relaxation and confidence descended upon us. We could each read the others' minds; we knew exactly what the others were thinking. We could transmit these thoughts over great distances and at incredible speed. We could overlook each other; predict each other's actions, all useful tools for the future.

I felt intense sorrow for the Team; for I knew that they would miss something very special in terms of human relationships for the foreseeable future. Most would not know the deep love that can exist between a man and a woman, a love that leads to the commitment of marriage. Nor would they know the love that parents feel for their children, or the very special joy of a grandchild.

But we also all knew that it was not I that had robbed them of these pleasures. For the twins, life had been especially unkind to them during their formative years and their human hopes and dreams had been doomed to failure long before they had met me. Belial First had shown each of them what the brutality that is fate had reserved for them had they not joined the Verguide Team.

Tall, willowy and with an exquisite figure, Josh had been destined to marry a local beauty Queen. Within two years of their marriage this lovely, young and sylph-like woman, the victim of a very rare brain condition, would metamorphose into a foul-mouthed harridan, her twisted spine permanently bent at the waist in a never-ending gesture of submission and a pea-sized brain rapidly reducing her to a condition of non-existence. Mercifully, Josh realised, he had been spared that experience; and also the drudgery of caring for his wife and baby son who was also destined to suffer the same fate as his mother.

Not much better news for the twins. Their lives should have already ended when, whilst attempting to recover their mother's lost diamond, they were destined to become involved with the Timorese underworld of vice and narcotics. Their demise would have been a particularly horrific and bloody encounter, at the hands of a sub-human assassin employed by the mob, when the diamond was discovered to be missing from the wreck of the *Tetum*.

Belial First had not spared the details. Not for any vindictive reason but simply because he could not tell a lie, neither could he fabricate alternative scenarios to soften the truth. He saw only what might happen, exactly how it happened and without any garnishing whatsoever.

Soaking up this information had kept the Team quiet and thoughtful and I was more than a little relieved when Joe spoke those few words.

'Yes indeed, we do have a lot to do,' I replied rather formally, with the first smile that I had been able to muster for some time.

The Team was all present at breakfast. Mrs Jupp - always Mrs Jupp - she had made her wishes quite clear to me at the very first interview for the post of housekeeper. 'I would prefer to maintain a degree of formality in our dealings,' she had said somewhat stiffly, 'especially in front of the other members of staff.'

Ana had pleaded with me not to employ her, 'She is much too

English, formal, and reserved.' But I had seen something quite different and I knew that she would remain with the Team for many years, devoting her time to serving us and to the education of her children. I could also see something else, for Mrs Jupp too was damaged goods. She would never remarry, not wishing to risk the violence and terror inflicted upon her during her first attempt at legal cohabitation.

Things were back to normal. I brightened immediately. The Verunian influence was powerful, very powerful, but it could not entirely understand the human psyche or the ramifications of the human brain. Possessive of a lesser degree of mental acuity, Josh and I had slipped without thought or resistance into the Verunian mindset. But at near genius level the brains of the twins operated on a different plane and they may well have succeeded in overriding the Verunian brain-ware, robbing me of the two most important members of the Verguide Team.

Joe and Ana had been watching me and smiled at my thoughts.

'No danger there, Boss,' Ana reassured me.

'And please don't ask us to call you the Verguide, or Belial, or some other cosmicality.' Josh occasionally invented his own words but his meaning was quite clear to us all.

'Boss will be fine.' I regarded the term as an Aussie endearment, of sorts.

Buried deeply within their new brain-ware was a detailed description of my plans, the Verunian plans and the plans of anyone brought to mind. However, being human, we all loved to talk about things and initial plans are not always perfect; we all agreed that daily discussions would be beneficial.

'So what is the Team's next project? Build underground or politics?' Joe preferred to get straight to the point.

Over the next hour or so we agreed that it was too soon for both. As far as my political career was concerned, it was too soon for the elections in 2010 and I could not make a move until about three years before the 2015 general election. Early plans involved the formation of yet another political party and I intended that it was to be radical in the extreme, with policies to entice the masses to my banner.

But I also did not want a long period of what had become normal political shenanigans; that is lying; discussing; questioning; doubting; fence sitting; backbiting; and back-stabbing. All of which might be used by my political opponents to cloud the issues before an actual election. Obviously, should I decide to embark upon a political career, I had every intention of using the Team's not inconsiderable powers to achieve success; and would certainly behave in the most underhand and devious manner demanded by my political status. For after all is said and done, politicians the world over understand only one method of behaviour; and I had no wish to disappoint them.

More than pleased to put this part of my future life to one side, at least for the present since I was not much looking forward to a very public lifestyle, I turned to the underground project.

This second alternative, that of digging into the mantle of the Earth, was also quite out of the question at that time. It was not, however, too early to start investigating and planning the possibility of living below the surface of the Earth.

But as an eccentric billionaire I might well wish to fritter away a few million pounds on enlarging my underground nuclear shelter and establishing a study centre to investigate the reasons for global warming; and we had agreed that this ruse would suffice when recruiting the army of experts and advisors for our project.

To provide the level of protection from a violent surface of the Earth predicted by Belial First, man would have to go deep to find a safe place to live, deep into the mantle. Notwithstanding the fact that the Chikyu Hakken[20] mission would attempt to retrieve samples from the Earth's mantle, shortly after the twins' birthday, we all felt that any attempt to tunnel to that depth at the present time would be regarded as insane. We intended instead to build an underground town, at about two hundred metres below the estate house at Abbotstone, a test bed for the future.

There was much to do, indeed. As second-in-command of the Team, Ana would of course drive the project; and in so doing she blossomed. Dealing with the intricate details of a large project was her forte. Totally dedicated, she threw herself into the enterprise and became involved in every aspect, recruiting, purchasing, planning, scheduling, man-management and welfare. No detail was considered of so little importance as not to demand her attention.

An outline planning application to the local district council was

---

[20]Chikyu Hakken. USA, EU, China, South Korea consortium, drilling to seven kilometres into Earth's mantle.

returned with a large red 'APPROVED' stamped carelessly across the document. Initially, the application caused consternation amongst the council planners, most of whom thought the whole idea a complete waste of money. Many people had built small underground complexes but this was the first they had seen on such a large scale. They eventually concluded that, since the building of the proposed expanded nuclear shelter and study centre was to be built beneath a Greenfield site, planning approval was unnecessary. But the stated intention was to provide underground accommodation for several hundred human beings and the council stipulated that we must comply with normal building regulations.

Powerful drilling machines were designed and built. Capable of drilling a tunnel with a ten-metre diameter, they were very similar to those used in the construction of the Channel Tunnel. The eventual complex in plan view resembled a double string of sausages. Each compartment, one hundred metres long, was linked by a smaller five-metre diameter passage to the next adjacent neighbour.

In maintaining the illusion of building a structure to house a team of experts dedicated to solving one of the perceived threats to humanity, the Team gathered together to christen the complex at the end of the first day's drilling. The actual christening ceremony was performed by Josh, standing above the huge hole descending vertically into the Earth and adding a touch of subconscious Australian naval humour to the proceedings.

'I hereby christen thee Volly's Folly,' urinating solemnly into the dark hole.

Inappropriate, humorous? The name stuck.

Over the many years that followed after its completion in 2012 and throughout the years of its use, the name did stick. Volly's Folly became a household name around the globe.

Unintentionally and eventually, Volly's Folly actually returned a profit. The public became enamoured with the site. Schoolchildren on educational visits and coach-loads of experts from all persuasions flocked to Abbotstone.

But the visitors saw only a small proportion of the complex, the vast majority of which was accessed by separate entry systems within the main estate house and would provide accommodation for the team of experts yet to be recruited, for what became known to us as the Mantellium project.

CHAPTER 14
TRACEY

THREAD:

We all lose someone at some time in our lives. But why is it that the worst moments in one's life seem to happen at the dead of night? Fear, regret and a deep sadness washed over me and I knew that Tracey was gone.

AUSTRALIA. 2021.

Sleep had deserted me. Lying in my bed at Abbotstone I had been keeping an eye on Saladin; I had a feeling that he was planning something momentous in the near future. But my interest was instantly diverted to the other side of the world when I had the sensation that something had happened to Tracey. Immediately I focussed upon the imposing farmhouse in Australia, set within the large acreage of mainly scrubland that made up the estate of the late Anthony Jarvis, Tracey's second husband.

In the centre of a large, airy and sunny bedroom, the body of an old woman lay on the bed. Silver hair spread over the high pillow and neatly folded sheets covered the body from head to foot; but she had departed this life so recently that no one had yet thought to cover her face. Around the bed sat her daughter and three granddaughters, all four with a striking resemblance to their matriarch.

Outside the wailing dogs seemed to sense the death of their mistress, yelping and jumping up at the door in their efforts to gain entry. Inside the room, an air of cold and dampness seemed incongruous in the dry Australian outback; and a feeling of deep sadness pervaded the senses of those occupants that still lived.

It was difficult to restrain an almost overwhelming desire to materialise in the room. These five women were part of me, a part of my life that I had forfeited many years before. But I dare not and I kept my distance from the body of my wife until the room was empty and the house silent. Even then, I found it impossible to move closer and I just sat and looked at her. She had been many things in her life but to me she had been a most wonderful lover, wife, friend and companion. I was struck with how old she looked and I realised that when a couple grow old together they do not notice the creeping ageing process in their partner.

Within Babylonian mythology there is a goddess whose spheres of influence include fertility, sexual love and war. Her name is Ishtar and the grouping of humanity's driving forces associated with her is most interesting, since in all marriages there is some degree of both sex and war. In terms of the first driving force of fertility, Tracey and I could have wished for more; but of the latter two, we certainly had our fair share.

Memories. Those images stored, and sometimes forgotten, at the back of the mind that support us in our darkest moments, returned to me.

Our first meeting, when I felt her slim hand in mine, and fell hopelessly for the slim and vibrant teenager, so full of life and hopes for her future. She had been a slip of a girl with a deep well of love bubbling to the surface, just waiting to be lavished on her family, an inexhaustible supply of love that can only be found in a few very special women. A woman who gives of herself, especially her time and skills, always there and ready to help in any way she can.

Monday 3rd July, 1961, the day that she had stepped from the aircraft in Singapore and handed our infant daughter into my arms. The tiny face seemed to recognise me; the child smiled broadly and an instant bond was formed that would last a lifetime.

The trim outline of Tracey in her jodhpurs and riding helmet on our little smallholding at Hambledon. Where we spent so many happy years; such an insignificant, tiny figure perched in the saddle of the huge horse but capable of controlling the beast's every movement.

Remaining any longer was impossible for me, already the tears were streaming down my face and I felt empty. 'Goodbye my love,' I whispered and willed a return to Abbotstone. I could not stay for the funeral. Tracey had her immediate family near to her and they were much more entitled to the privilege of such a public farewell.

But I was a changed man; life had lost meaning and direction for me. Over the next several months, my life was unbearable. Confining myself to my study, I lived a reclusive, cloistral life. Mrs Jupp stomped in and out of my study carrying food and drink, most of which remained as she left it. I found it difficult to swallow and the sensations of mere hunger and thirst had deserted my body. After a while, even she stopped berating me and resorted to loud sighs and tuts of disapproval.

It was difficult to concentrate on anything whilst in my emotional doldrums and I must have appeared slightly gaga to the twins. Deeply enervated I wallowed in my grief and sought only those things that would deepen my selfish depression.

Sometimes that vicious, predatory singularity that is nature can wear a kindly, forgiving face; and in some circumstances can provide a corresponding heart-lifting zenith for every depressing nadir. For me, my constant bubble of despair was burst by the birth of my first great-grandchild, named Tracey Elizabeth and borne to Kacey just three months after the death of her great-grandmother; thereby restoring the balance of souls on Earth.

CHAPTER 15
ROYAL MARINES, AFRICA

THREAD:

Way back in the first decade of the 21st century, access to global information was provided by way of the international information network, or Internet. Those with a burning desire for information and sufficient funds to afford the capital costs of hardware were further saddled with an ongoing monthly running cost to use the facility; and if they were wise, the additional cost of protecting themselves and their personal information with a proprietary internet security package.

Of the newly connected users, a very large majority spent long hours surfing the net during the first few months, followed by years of virtual inactivity. But some were hooked. They became known as nerds, addicted to trawling through the millions of websites reminiscent of a deep sea fisherman wading knee-deep through his catch searching for who-knows-what. Others used it to cheat and steal and to annoy their fellow man, obtaining personal data illegally and using this information to clone credit cards, bank statements and identities. Yet others used the net for their own lewd gratification, seeking to corrupt the young and innocent.

Mankind was like an internet of flesh and blood to me, and whilst casting my mind around the world, I too became a nerd, a hidden, cosmic nerd.

The highs and lows of human life were laid out before me, in stark reality. Although my alter ego, whilst floating through the book of life saw it all in a pale, insubstantial outline, almost not of this world, I still seemed conscious of the events unfolding before me. Not doors, walls, curtains or clothing blocked my view, and I saw the best and worst of humanity. In time, I came to regard this vision of life as simply daydreaming, where a series of images passed through my mind; but not of my own actions, wishes, or desires but witnessing the thoughts and dreams of other people in real time. Whilst my unfocussed mind was engaged in a non-specific wandering mode, the feeling was of a wild, weirdly and unfamiliar nature; distorted in shape and outline, fuzzy around the edges; hazy, as with a faint hint of predawn mist obscuring the view of a distant object.

Often I felt as if my wanderings were controlled by an outside agency and I suspected that it might well be the Small Person directing me towards someone, or something, that could assist me in my task as the Verguide. Certainly overlooking Maria Vinacco, her twins, and Josh had provided me with a perfect team of accomplices.

But why my mind focussed on Jake, I do not know. Maybe it was the complete and utter heartache of the man, his inability to find peace of mind and sleep each night, or his troubled dreams when he finally succumbed to extreme exhaustion.

Or maybe it was a preknowledge of his being involved in a major event in the future, what was to be the most dastardly act by a political extremist group in history.

In reading the following chapters, please note that Royal Marine jargon is shown in italics as is the case for any foreign language; and a decode is shown at the end of the book.

AFRICA. NOVEMBER 2023.

The worry gnawed at his guts; in *bootneck* jargon, he was *sweating neaters*. The intense anxiety was permanently churning him up; he could not concentrate and at times he was completely oblivious to the physical discomfort of his surroundings. When he looked down at his hands, dappled from the sunshine seeping through the towering jungle above him, he could see that each hand was crowned with a line of jagged, pure-white knuckles.

'Get a grip, you rat-faced *ooloo wallah.*' Jake Hildreth, Corporal Royal Marines, spoke softly to himself in reprimand. He knew that he should not be uttering a sound, for although the *comms* system in his helmet was switched to listen-only, he was well aware that sound travelled great distances in the jungle.

'*Heads up,* time to *turn to,*' the voice of his squad Sergeant sounded in Jake's helmet. The *Corps* of 2023 never ever, under any circumstances, removed their battle helmets when in the field. For through the helmet came the instructions from command, whether from their own Squad Sergeant, the Platoon Lieutenant, the Company Major or, in exceptional circumstances, from the *old man* himself. It mattered not how great the distance between the groupings of his unit, 1 Assault Group RM. Squads, platoons, companies - all were intralinked at the lower levels and interlinked upwards through the chain of command to brigade HQ. And every single individual, from the lowest ranking *sod-buster* through the Platoon Major, had the capability of conversing with the battalion Lieutenant Colonel. Every single Marine knew of the individual channels linking this formidable fighting group and of the satcom footprints that provided such first-rate communication facilities.

Voice-operated, a Marine simply spoke his *comms* requirements inside his fully-enclosed helmet and the system did the rest, using a completely unbreakable one-time encryption method.

'Speak channel one,' or '*tut-tut*' with the end of the tongue against the roof of the mouth, brought up the most commonly-used channel linking his squad. A range of sounds had been introduced, unofficially and at squad level, to be used during those times when silence was paramount. A quiet and extended '*ssss*' forbade any sound, until a whispered '*yap-yap*' was heard.

The squad had been resting. They had left their parent carrier, the sixty thousand tonne HMS *Queen Elizabeth*, by helicopter at 03.30 that morning. The *birds* had carried them over one thousand kilometres to within seventy of their final destination. Since *hitting the deck* at a little before 07.30, the squad had *yomped* the thirty-five kilometres to their present location in seven hours of non-stop flog. Good going for a newly deployed squad straight out from the UK and through the diabolical and sometimes impenetrable jungle.

Some of the Marines were overweight and unfit from months of easy living ashore and had *hoisted inboard* many a jibe from their Sergeant during the trek. 'Move your sorry arse, you *fat knacker.*' The only response to a request for a quick *stand-easy.*

A fit squad of *Royal Machines* would have eaten up the ground and covered the same distance in a little over five hours. But of course the modern Marine did not really *yomp* anymore. He still walked, or marched over the ground, but he did not do it with a heavy load. He carried only lightweight weapons, ammunition, body-armour and poncho, most neatly stowed in small pouches attached to his weapon-belt. Everything else he needed came from the air, dropped from high altitude with pin-point accuracy. The *crabs* took great delight in announcing over the squad's radios 'Scran up, you *junglies,*' as a container of hot meals or ammunition landed gently amongst them.

At their Sergeant's command to *heads up* the squad slowly roused themselves. Despite their inexperience in the field they were well trained and made very little noise whilst preparing to *leg it* again. A few soft sighs and groans but not the slightest tingle or jangle of metal against metal; their kit was made of the finest water and wind-proof material and their weapons of the lightest and strongest plastic material ever produced by man. Without exception, they were the best-equipped troops on the planet.

Jake tried desperately to calm his churning stomach. The lewd and vivid scenes that plagued him must be cast from his mind, at least until night came.

Breaking down their *bivvies* took but a few minutes. A simple task of crawling out from beneath their ponchos, rolling them up and stuffing them into a small pouch attached to their weapon belts. Each Marine had a primary task, that of checking the equipment of his *oppo.* In addition, some of the squad had other tasks. Some were assigned to skirmish the site to ensure that nothing was left to betray their presence, others to checking *comms,* navigation, medical status, etc. Jake, as a senior Corporal, was assigned the task of recovering the perimeter defence. The long line of fibre-optic cable, laid on the ground around the unit's campsite, was virtually invisible. This defence gave off a slight electrical charge if touched, sufficient to deter jungle nasties such as scorpions or snakes and which at the same time passed a warning bleep into the helmet of the on-duty sentry.

Alfred Leonard

The old lion was weary. At ten years of age he felt so weary that his bones ached. Just fifteen days had passed since he had lost his final battle to retain his pride. Over the years the battles for control of his domain, his females and his good life had been many and frequent. But he had been strong, unbelievably strong, and he had seen off his many challengers, whether singly or in coalitions for a very long time.

The final encounter with a huge male that seemed to tower above him had been brutal. He should have died. And had he not had the brain-power to break-off and run, he most surely would have, for the solid power of his opponent drained his own strength like the blood gushing from a gutted antelope. He was also fortunate that his successor was extremely anxious to get amongst his harem, to commence the gory business of killing the youngest cubs and claiming his just rewards from the females in his new kingdom.

For several days the deposed king rested up, licking his wounds. He did not eat and rarely drank and was driven by one all-consuming desire - stay out of sight and escape. Hunting for food was not one of his skills, he had had a team of lionesses to do that job; and why work when you can lie in the Sun but still claim the lion's share when a kill was made?

Each day the old lion remained hidden from sight. At night he moved ever further away from his kingdom; he had no desire for a second encounter with the powerful beast that had deposed him. During the fifth night he had literally bumped into the young lioness. Lithe, sleek, smelling evocatively of past pleasures and enormously amorous, the female feline's first thought was to flee.

It had been several weeks now since she had been evicted from her family. The pride's alpha matriarch had mistreated her since birth and her otherwise sleek hide was festooned with scars, cuts and abrasions. She had suffered badly during her two years of life and her hunting skills were adequate but by no means perfected. Always pushed to the end of the queue at a pride's kill, demoted even further down the line to a position below that of the new cubs, there was precious little left for her to eat. Since leaving the pride she had fared considerably better as far as food was concerned, catching a variety of small prey. At about one hundred and forty kilograms, she weighed about half that of the old male, who had literally trodden on her sleeping body, and it was only the weight of his right fore-pug resting on her tail that had restrained her initial urge to flee.

Instinctively she had known that he was a nomad, exactly the same as she was. A smell of age surrounded the still large body of the male carnivore but her heightened senses and almost irresistible urge to mate suppressed this first impression and concentrated instead on the sheer maleness of his presence.

The old lion curled his upper lip, the better to expose his Jacobson's organ to analyse the chemical signals radiating from the female. The sexual signals burst into his brain and his sixth sense interpreted her readiness to mate.

An almost gentle grumbling, from deep within the old male's body, calmed her. She hoisted herself slowly to her feet and nuzzled closely into his shoulder.

Recognising the highly fertile condition of the young lioness, the deposed king nudged her gently. Instantly she offered herself in the mating position and the heart of the old male soared when he mounted her. Perhaps all was not lost.

Five days later he almost wished that he had never encountered her. She had repeatedly insisted upon his attentions, time and time again, up to forty times a day; and now he could hardly stand. He lay down in the coolness of a dense stand of long grass, hoping fervently that she was finally satisfied. At least for today and until she left to hunt during the night.

She snuggled him to wakefulness. At first he thought that she intended extending their numerous copulations through the dark of the night. But the foul smell that invaded his senses instantly changed his mind. He had not smelt the pungent aroma for many years but he had not forgotten the pain of the bullet searing his rump from his first encounter. The hateful smell that pervaded his nostrils was that of man; and he licked thoughtfully at the long ago healed scar.

Of one thing he was quite sure, best to stay well away from this two-legged predator that seemed able to kill with effortless ease and at great distance. He pushed himself against the young lioness. She flopped back to the ground and he curled his long body around her.

Alfred Leonard

Sergeant Brian, Blacky Blackstow, was not of the new school of Royal Marine. He did not subscribe to the modern free-and-easy interaction between senior and junior ranks. On the day that he had replaced the double-stripes of a Corporal for the triple-chevrons of Sergeant, Blacky Blackstow had severed all contact with the Corporals' mess. He was quite happy for more senior Officers and other ranks to call him by his Christian or nickname. But woe betide any junior other-rank that took the liberty of addressing him by anything but Sergeant, sarg', or sar'nt.

Numbering some thirty-five Royal Marines, his squad formed part of 3 Platoon, which itself made up part of 2 Company of 9 Assault Squadron. Unusually he was not the leader of his squad, at least not in terms of rank. A very junior second Lieutenant had been drafted in, to gain experience. 'Wet behind the ears, and a waste of space,' Blacky was often heard whispering his withering comment about the baby-faced Officer.

'We're ready to move, Sir.' Blacky's almost unheard 'sir', said it all.

'Sweepers out,' Blacky dispatched his scouts, a Marine stationed on each flank at about two hundred metres.

'Ginge and Pokey, take point,' he sent his advance guard forward.

'Custard, check the *bivvy* and watch our arse.' Jake raised his arm in acknowledgement.

'Move out,' the squad fanned out in pairs and continued their *yomp* towards their final destination.

Jake watched his comrades depart. He was alone in the jungle and as he peered around he began to feel slightly on edge. He could not explain this uncomfortable feeling; it was just a slight tingling up the ridge of his spine, almost that of being watched by unseen eyes. Jake did not very much relish being alone in the jungle; it always unnerved him. Shrugging off this unsettling feeling, Jake cast his eyes around their temporary camp.

Some of the more recent replacements to the squad may well be a tad green but they were obviously well trained. Not a sign of their presence during their recent rest period could be seen.

Rwanda is a relatively small African country, west of Lake Victoria and just south of the equator. Its hilly terrain and once fertile soil has provided sustenance for its people for many years. Known as the land of a thousand hills, it is landlocked and wedged between Burundi, Uganda, The Democratic Republic of the Congo and Tanzania.

Its simple blue, yellow and green striped flag flies proudly over its capital Kigali. Almost the entire population, numbering about twelve point five million souls, relied upon agriculture for their food; and the vast majority existed at below subsistence levels. With little other than agriculture to sustain its people, the only methods of generating national income were from exporting coffee and tea and attempting to attract tourism to a troubled country.

Without proper management, soil does not remain fertile for ever. An ever increasing population created densities rivalling those of the south of England. An uncertain climate and decreasing soil fertility combined to produce chronic malnutrition and endemic poverty.

Mineral deposits were miniscule. And throughout its sometimes violent and chequered history, the Hutu, Tutsi and Twa tribes, which made up the vast majority of the population, had managed to live together through varying periods of war, hate, dominance, suffering or forbearance.

In the decade between 2010 and 2020, the population exploded once again when most of the two to three million Hutus returned to their homelands, having fled following the war in 1994.

The country struggled on, always heading towards disaster until in 2021 a young farmer in the Ruzizi river valley blew up a huge rock that had stubbornly refused to be moved for hundreds of years. The young Tutsi had heard the family stories of this defiant rock since childhood and had saved long and hard to beg, borrow, steal or purchase what he considered to be a sufficiently large enough charge to blast the rock to kingdom come. Overdoing it somewhat, the explosion blasted the rock into a million pieces and left a small crater about five metres deep. In the farmer's eyes the rock resembled the multi-coloured, glittering effect of a huge firework, the like of which he had seen on one of the television screens on display in Kigali's shops.

Through the exploding cloud of shattered rock the Sun seemed to flash in all directions. And the young farmer sighed in satisfaction and clapped his hands and jumped with joy at the pretty display. He sat on the edge of the crater, waiting for the dust to settle. Slowly a thin layer of dust covered the skin of his exposed arms and legs.

Bright yellow spots of rock and others with a strange, clear almost blue, brilliance.

Eyes slowly enlarging in awe, the young Tutsi almost gagged when realisation dawned upon him. Gold, diamonds! The gods of the jungle had smiled upon him; he was rich!

And all around the crater he could see signs of more. He slid into the deep hole, rubbed his bare feet into the soft soil, and exposed a seam of solid gold; so brilliant was the flash of sunlight, reflecting from the treasure trove, that the young Tutsi had to cover his eyes.

In the months following that discovery, the country's battle for dominance and control of the newly-found vast mineral deposits had renewed with dreadful ferocity.

The ecstatic Tutsi farmer had died within a week of his discovery. As had the rest of his family. His land had been forcibly acquisitioned by the country's Tutsi-controlled military and sealed off against trespassers. But hiding a discovery of this magnitude was impossible and the stories echoed around the corridors of power in Kigali. In what was termed a reprisal against Tutsi greed, the Hutu tribe quickly re-established their *interahamwe* guerrilla squads that, in reality, had never actually been disbanded. At first in small skirmishes, the Hutus picked at Kigali's defences. Hutu military leaders knew that the key to controlling their country's newly-found riches lay in control of the capital and its airport.

Dancing in the dust, stark naked, eyes glazed with strange hallucinatory mixtures gleaned from the jungle plants, the Hutu headmen took every opportunity to harangue their *interahamwe* groups, exaggerating past mistreatment by the Tutsis to the nth degree. The minor confrontations quickly escalated into all-out warfare. Casualties were high in both camps, since the population was an almost 50-50 split between the opposing sides.

The ruling Tutsi government believed that women softened the aggressive tendencies of men and had therefore introduced a policy of equal numbers of men and women members of parliament. Whatever the veracity of this belief in the softer nature of women, the policy certainly did not achieve the expectations of the Tutsi government. In confirmation of this hemline theory the female members danced in parliament's impressive chambers, waving cudgels, knobkerries, swords and axes; their voices trilling the war-songs of Africa in those high falsetto voices that only African women seem capable of producing. Their voices urging the menfolk to ever greater efforts to defeat the hated Hutu, who were intent upon stealing the gift from above, those vast gold and diamond deposits so recently discovered.

Britain no longer responded to the almost unending calls for financial or military help from the Dark Continent. But by a strange quirk of fate, the present holder of the defence portfolio in Whitehall had a secret, a hidden fact which she very much did not want the rest of the British cabinet to become aware of.

Extra-marital relationships have always been a part of being an MP, or so it seemed to the common man. However, Mrs Joanna Hinchcliffe-Sunderland, Member of Parliament for Hickstead East, had taken not one but two lovers. Twins; African; strapping young men of just eighteen years of age, both of whom cared not a jot for the plain features and late middle-aged plumpness of their mistress who shaved her wobbly jowls more often than did the boys.

She provided accommodation, food, protection and as much money as they needed to fund their drug-related habits. Both had giggled insanely when they had first heard the fine English adage that one does not look at the mantelpiece when one is poking the fire, and thought how perfectly the adage described their present *ménage a trois*.

Unbeknownst to the rotund Mrs Hinchcliffe-Sunderland, the twins came from a very large and extended family in Rwanda. In fact the incumbent minister of education, in the Rwandan government, was their uncle. Joanna would have been well advised to remember a commonly-known expression intended as a guiding light to all aspiring politicians.

'When dodging the arrows of innuendo and libel,

Be as the priest; and love only spouse and the bible.'

And maybe if she had instructed the boys more carefully about keeping one's secrets to oneself, she might have saved herself from her fate. For she was quite correct in assuming that her affair was a little known secret at home in the UK but it was a much different matter in Kigali. The whole of the Rwandan cabinet knew of the affair and the First Minister had filed the information carefully away; he instinctively knew that it would be of use at some time in the future. And so it had proved.

Tutsi government forces were well trained, well equipped and generally well led. But any army performs poorly when pitted against guerrilla operations. It is almost impossible to predict from where the next attack will come. An indirect and much edited feed from the American's spy satellite systems provided complete coverage of the country; but this gathered useful information only during daylight hours. Rwanda was not offered information from America's top-secret night-vision system; for the very existence of that technology was tightly controlled within the shores of that giant continent.

Hutu forces were rapidly gaining the upper hand. They had already managed to surround the capital and had taken control of some parts of the airport. The First Minister was worried, very worried, and he had racked his brain for a method of re-establishing his tribe's stranglehold on the country. And then he had a very strange dream and remembered his twin nephews. He had immediately sent the boys' uncle to London; time for Mrs Joanna Hinchcliffe-Sunderland to pay the first instalment in the cost of her nightly romps.

The First Minister knew that the final instalment would demand a much higher price from Mother Nature in the form of a painful death from AIDS. But that information was not to be passed to the UK's Minister of Defence; it would be a nice surprise for her ladyship, after she had convinced the British cabinet to provide military assistance.

Each individual Marine knew his mission. As a squad they had attended numerous briefings and *O groups* conducted by the *sneaky beakies*, before leaving the carrier *Queen Elizabeth*. Phase one of Operation Gold Dust required number 2 Company, of the 9th Assault Squadron, split into two platoons consisting of four squads, totalling some three hundred and twenty royal Marine commandos, to clear the countryside of rebel forces. Their mission: to capture Rwanda's capital and support the ruling Tutsi government. Mission specifics: each squad to be dropped from helicopters at preliminary muster points surrounding Kigali, at a distance of some seventy kilometres from the city centre. On day one, each squad was expected to cover the fifty kilometres to a holding point, twenty kilometres short of the city centre, neutralising any non-government troops that they may encounter. At the holding point they would wait in ambuscade, until ordered to push forward into the city, mopping up any Hutu guerrillas attempting to escape.

It was a textbook operation. The Parachute Regiment, otherwise known as the Red Devils, made up of seven hundred steel-helmeted red berets, completed a fast-descent night drop into Kigali airport. In the blackness of the African night, the superb discipline and fighting capabilities of this crack British regiment of *maroon machines* proved their value.

Within an hour all opposition had passed through their respective departure gates, either en route to whatever heaven or paradise their religion had promised them or on foot and at a great rate of knots into the surrounding hills and countryside. Phase two of Operation Gold Dust had been achieved.

The lioness had left her mate sleeping, snoring heavily in the stand of dense grass. She had raised her young body effortlessly to the standing position, sniffed at her sleeping mate and left him to commence her hunt for food. She too had tasted the smell of the humans but she did not fear the smell, as did her spouse.

In the darkness she had made several unsuccessful attempts to creep up on wild pigs and other small prey. Failure at hunting did not bother her too much; she knew that she would not be successful every night. But she did find the body of a baby gazelle, still wrapped in its cloak of placenta and foetal membranes, obviously still-born.

Hunger was not tearing at her stomach; she had eaten only the night before. Scraping dust and fallen leaves over the carcass, she concealed it for later collection. For now her curiosity had been aroused by the smell of the humans and her mate's obvious concern at the overpowering aroma. Long strides ate up the ground and she quickly closed the gap between herself and the group of humans.

From the vantage point of a small hillock, the young lioness looked down into the Royal Marine *bivvy*. Her sharp hearing isolated the distinctive grunts of human snoring, amongst the familiar sounds of other night noises, and her keen eyesight picked up every involuntary twist and jerk from exhausted muscles and nerves stretched to breaking point. She did not move closer to the group; instinctively she knew that to do so would be dangerous.

But she was now becoming anxious; she had been away from the old male for too long. She had watched the group stir into activity and had even considered taking a closer look at the lone man, carefully inspecting the camp-site. Her eyes were riveted on the man. She watched his every move until he too followed after the departing group. Worryingly for the lioness, the group of men were heading off in the direction of her mate. She must move quickly, circle around the group and warn him.

'Secure, and silent running.' Sergeant Blacky Blackstow's hushed command to cease their current *yomp* and quietly establish a camp for the night overrode the thoughtless 'Secure' command from the Second Lieutenant, which had broken the silence inside the helmet of every Marine in the squad. 'Bloody OD,' Blacky thought, 'why did they have to assign this *plum-percy* to me?' Every *bootie* was of the opinion that the majority of Officers were play-soldiers, tuppence short of a shilling and sadly lacking in common dog. *'But this little runt,'* thought Blacky darkly, *'was about as much use as a bloody airy fairy.'*

Night quarters differed little from the rest camp of the afternoon. Fires were not necessary since a hot supper and hot drinks would arrive shortly, courtesy of *crab-air*. Ponchos provided whatever would be needed in terms of shelter throughout the night and the ingenious design of a Marine's helmet negated the need for a pillow.

Once again the perimeter defence was set, everyone knew what was expected of them and the guard rota had been decided long before they had left *Queen Elizabeth*. Helmets were firmly closed and visors locked in the down position, which prevented sound going out but did not interfere with normal background noises coming in. From within the helmet, *comms* were so good that individual, group or whole squad conversations could take place at a simple voice command.

Jake Hildreth was lucky; he had not drawn one of the short straws that signified a Guard-Commander duty for this night. A whole night's sleep, *ace*! He was looking forward to a restful night.

Tired, exhausted, *bombed-out, down on your chin straps*; bootnecks had many different words to describe their weariness. Jake was all of these and more. The squad had *yomped* twenty-five kilometres since their last rest period. Every nerve-jangling step had been a nightmare of tense alertness. Waiting for attack from almost any direction; blundering into an ambush; or falling victim to what appeared to be hordes of snakes, scorpions and other jungle nasties. Never mind the possibility of confronting one of the larger predators, an encounter feared by all. Just a quiet, 'Sunday afternoon *bimble*,' as Blacky had described the long and exhausting hike.

That gentle stroll had seen the minute hand of Jake's watch complete over seven more rotations since they had left their last *bivvy*; it was past midnight before they had reached their holding point.

Compo rations were a thing of the past; the hot supper was excellent. The only part of the meal that was missing was a couple of cans of beer; and every man-jack of the squad would have given a month's pay for a chance to use their *church keys* on a cool can of the amber liquid.

Two hours later Jake was suffering once again. In his dream he saw his wife climbing the stairs to their bedroom; followed by a strange man. The man's face was hidden from his view. He watched in morbid fascination as the couple paused at the door of his bedroom, wrapped their arms around each other and kissed passionately. The hands of the stranger were all over his wife's body, kneading her erogenous zones, inflaming her sexual senses to levels that Jake knew only too well existed. Jake's body twitched and jumped in spasms and he mumbled incoherent utterings into his closed helmet, his anguish clear to any onlooker. He was sweating profusely and his hands were clawing at the wet earth.

He awoke with a start, the sky was ablaze with lightning and the rain was falling in solid sheets of water. Jake's extreme reaction to his dream had somehow dragged him from the shelter of his poncho. The crack of thunder directly overhead seemed to jar his body and the earth itself appeared to jump and crackle in time with the tremendous storm, the like of which Jake had never before seen. The lightning was continuous; it filled the sky and lit up the surrounding countryside as if it were full daylight. *'Bloody typical,'* thought Jake, *'they have arranged this fiasco right in the middle of Rwanda's rainy season.'*

Alfred Leonard

They took a lot of flack, from every member of every armed service, everywhere in the world. Whomsoever *they* might be. But it was definitely 'they' who were responsible for every badly planned operation; every piece of bad luck or misfortune; and every mistimed escapade allotted to all who wore the *globe and buster* on their berets.

Jake was badly rattled. In the lightning capital of the world he stood, stretched his aching muscles and lurched a few metres away from his *bivvy* to vent his tanks. He looked at his watch, almost 02.45. The rain did not bother him, no matter how heavy the downpour, or for how long it might last, he knew that his kit would keep him warm and dry. There was still a little lukewarm tea in his flask. He sipped thoughtfully at the reassuring beverage, glanced around, peering into the darkness of the night whenever the lightning stopped for a few minutes. Sleep was needed, he knew that he must try to rest once again; tomorrow could well bring more exhausting activities.

Beneath the *bivvy* all was calm; strangely there was no wind with the storm. The thunder and lightning continued for some time and then faded away, rumbling intermittently into the distance. Jake's tortured thoughts refused to give him solace and kept him from sleep. Even whilst awake, and no matter how hard he fought against it, his mind seemed determined to continue the dream; and his senses whirled in anger, confusion and disorientation until he was unsure of what was fact or fiction.

Hot totty, *all the fours, a sex gannet*; Jocelyn was a nymph. A sexual athlete, ready to drop 'em at a moment's notice. Jake's mind tormented him and ruthlessly thrust away any chance of sleep.

'Next train from platform two, Exeter and London only.' The announcement over British Rail's tannoy system at Plymouth station listed the only two stops for the next departure.

The announcement always tickled non-local users of this station, because of the broad west-country accent of the announcer. Exeter, a short word when spoken in normal English mode, but when extended into a long and mispronounced 'ex ek ee ter' by the *janner* voice used to record the automated voice system, it sounded quaint in the extreme.

The train had left Plymouth a little after lunch on a fine spring afternoon many years ago. It was early May in the year 2005 and Jake had been onboard making his way to Liverpool for a rare visit to his parents. The carriage had been almost empty for the first part of the journey to Exeter and Jake had drifted in and out of sleep throughout the journey.

Sleep came easily to the young nineteen year old Marine. He was a fine figure of a man, heavily built and with a deeply-black skin. Tightly curled, jet-black hair crowned the heavy Negroid features of his face. But the skin of his face had a yellowish tinge, a very slight abnormality that had won him his nickname of Custard. The nickname did not bother him, *bootnecks* and matelots took great delight in awarding confidence-withering nicknames and strange diminutives. Cussy, Custy, Bustard, Bussy and countless other derivatives sailed majestically over Jake's unconcerned head. He had passed through the gruelling *bootneck* training regime and had had the Michael extracted on a thousand occasions. 'You can't crack me, I'm a rubber duck,' Jake had chuckled at his favourite riposte.

The surreal peace of the journey to Exeter was shattered by the arrival of a giggling bevy of Portsmouth's fairest maidens. By chance they had chosen to find seats in the almost empty carriage in which Jake sat. Across the aisle, directly opposite the young black man, the bevy of beauties took their seats and cast their eyes over his impressive bulk. One of the group, dressed in the shortest of short miniskirts, gave Jake a *glimp* of tiny, lace-edged knickers as she swivelled in her seat and faced him.

'Hello,' she said. 'I'm Jocelyn.' And after a very brief pause, 'What's your name?' Long blonde hair, with just a hint of curl framed her pretty face.

But she looked very young, *'No more than sixteen,'* thought Jake. 'I'm Jake.' He was not really shy but he had always found it difficult to act really casually around women, especially really young women.

The Pompey lasses burst into fits of laughter and giggling when Jocelyn quipped, 'Not Jake the rake?'

It is difficult to see a black person blush. In Jake's case, it was more evident than in others of his colour; his yellowish tinge displayed a definite pinkish hue.

The general banter continued for some time as the fast-moving train sped along the continuously welded tracks, weaving its way through the undulating landscape and dark red soil of Devon.

Conversation dried up. Most of the young girls dropped willingly into dreamland no doubt reliving the excesses of the previous night's hen party. Jake had become bored with casting surreptitious glances at the group, always hoping for a glimpse of breast, thigh or whatever else might pop into view. He turned his attention to the countryside and turned his thoughts to previewing his forthcoming homecoming. The return of the prodigal son it most certainly would not be. Yes, Jake had left home against his father's wishes but his lifestyle had not been wasteful, or lavish and extravagant; and neither was he repentant.

It was to be a surprise visit. He could change his mind at any time during the journey. 'Just give me a good excuse,' Jake had whispered his plea. But the whispered comment had been heard by Jocelyn, who had crossed over to the seat opposite Jake.

'What did you say?' Her whispered question brought Jake back to the present.

'Nothing much,' he replied. And there was no way on this Earth that he could stop his eyes from dropping to her legs, splayed slightly and revealing a tantalising glimpse of bright red panties.

Jake licked his lips; his mouth had suddenly become a desert and his desiccated tongue and parched throat tried desperately to form words. Jocelyn was only seventeen. But she had already enjoyed six glorious years of sexual activity. At times she did not trust her own body, for its cravings sometimes left her gasping. She was always ready for a fling, anywhere, anyplace; and many was the young Lothario that had attempted to fulfil their dreams behind the proverbial bike shed.

She crossed her legs, forcing Jake to look into her eyes. She was ready now, her nerve-ends were screaming with suppressed passion; and she just loved the look of this fit-looking young man.

Ten minutes later they returned from the toilet. Jake could not believe what she had done to him, squashed inside the small public loo. Her actions had been those of a depraved woman but Jake had to admit that his own had been little better.

The brief trip down memory lane had calmed Jake. He grimaced in the darkness, forcing himself to his feet; no point in attempting sleep anymore, it was zero five *ring bolt* and Sergeant bloody Blacky Blackstow would be ringing the *time out* bell very shortly.

Going about the business of squaring away his *bivvy*, Jake reviewed his troubled thoughts. The issue of their first meeting, twin girls, were gorgeous bridesmaids at their wedding, three years later. Jessica and Jerusalem. From where the hell Jocelyn had dragged that name, Jake did not know but his wife had a thing about names beginning with the letter 'J'. *'Probably why she set her cap at me,'* thought Jake. Beautiful, coffee-coloured little angels and Jake patted the breast pocket of his shirt where a copy of his favourite photograph permanently resided.

The one thing that he never regretted was the birth of his two little daughters. He had known what his wife was when he had married her; had known that she could not live without a daily dose of manhood; and he knew full well that if he was not there to provide it, then she would look elsewhere. And what was he making such a fuss about? It was only sex, probably little more than another mundane, meaningless bodily function to Jocelyn. Whatever, Jake knew that he had no other options. Stomach it or lose his beautiful babies. *'I'll see the doc,'* thought Jake, *'perhaps he can help me get through the nights.'*

Daylight arrived early so close to the equator. Feeling drained from his sleepless night but much better, Jake called for *crab-air* to deliver breakfast.

Late in the previous afternoon, the lioness carried the long dead carcass of the baby gazelle to her mate. The old male cuffed her roughly around the face and dragged the carcass away; there would be precious little left after he had taken his majority share. But the lioness had other things on her mind and she watched her mate devour her offering of food. He would have great need of the renewed vigour that the food would provide.

The two big cats felt safe in their stand of tall grass. The sweet water in the nearby river valley and a meagre supply of small animals provided all their needs for the foreseeable future. The human smell had not come any closer to their hide and they spent most of their time either mating or sleeping.

Alfred Leonard

The long *yomp* had taken its toll on the squad. All suffered some degree of blistering to their feet and most felt drained and dehydrated. They were all gratefully anticipating a day or so of rest, waiting for the order to begin the squeeze on Kigali. General intra-squad nattering revolved around the subject of their march. To a man they were elated at their success; for some it had been the first real-time *yomp* of their military career.

It was a bizarre sight. Blanco-white bodies, stripped to their *shreddies* and lying in the African Sun but still with their helmets glued to their heads. Getting bronzy for leave, servicemen were permanently involved in dreaming of their next leave and making some preparation or other towards it, from saving money or buying *rabbits* to getting a tan.

Most had enjoyed several hours of *gonk*. They had washed their sweaty bodies as best they could, using the moist and still warm *nappies* dropped with their breakfast. The doc, an ordinary member of the squad trained in first aid, had treated the minor scratches and blisters; and most were sitting around, chatting and cleaning their weapons. There was little danger of a sneak attack; they could relax in the knowledge that random patrols and their perimeter defence would warn them of any unexpected visitors.

'Begin phase three,' the order from *Queen Elizabeth's* operations room was heard only by the squad's Second Lieutenant and Sergeant. It had suddenly got dark a little after 18.00. Frighteningly quickly it had changed from full sunlight, to dusk, to darkness, much akin to drawing the curtains at home. And the jungle noises increased in volume once again, almost in joyous anticipation of the forthcoming night's mauling and killing.

'Sarn't Blackstow,' the voice of the young Lieutenant had a new timbre. He had meticulously updated the *troop bible*, listing the various aches and pains of his squad, and made copious notes about each individual's performance so far; he had also cleaned his own kit and he was ready to move.

'Get the men ready to *snurgle*, we *dig out blind* in ten minutes.'

'Ripper.' Blacky acknowledged the order from his leader; perhaps there was a little more to this *snotty* than he had bargained for.

Deforestation in the south accompanied the increasing needs of man and the loss of natural habitat had forced many animal species towards the north of Africa into the desert regions where man could barely survive. The chemical signals from others before them, had kept the two lions heading ever northwards.

Panthera leo times two were dead to the world. The female had no wish to hunt this night. The extended mating sessions over the past few days had left her weak but finally satisfied. Only time would tell if their numerous, frantic and sometimes painful couplings were destined to bear fruit. She was in an almost hypnotic sleep, a deep, body-renewing slumber that would restore her youthful energy in the morning.

The old male was long past caring about anything; even the rumbling hunger in his belly could not keep him awake. Long eye-lashes and ears flickered at almost every jungle noise but nothing short of a charging elephant would awaken him. He knew that he was not long for this world; but at least he would be going out with a bang!

'Whoever had dubbed this country as the land of a thousand hills, might wish to have a recount.' Jake thought that he must have scrambled up at least a million since they had started their sweep towards the capital.

Over recent years, Rwanda's leaders had appeased the suppliers of financial aid by agreeing to large areas of reforestation in small areas of unfertile soil, despite the need for more and more agricultural produce to feed the growing population.

The jungle recovers quickly from the predations of mankind and it was thus that Jake's squad found the going so hard. For the young Second Lieutenant, the compass pointed only to the west; and he kept the squad hacking at the thick jungle for many hours at a time, displaying a stoic determination not to follow the easy route along the course of the river. Few and far between was a clearing in the jungle, a place to take a proper rest and organise a refreshment drop.

Per mare per terram. Jake thought of the *bootneck's* motto. By sea: by land. A fine motto indeed, concisely and perfectly describing the role of the Royal Marines. But Jake had already had a bellyful of *per terram* and his thoughts drifted to the warmth and comfort of his mess deck on *Queen Elizabeth.* He was completely away with the fairies, lost in dreams of a warm shower and a gigantic portion of steak and chips.

Two things happened almost simultaneously. The squad emerged into a large clearing; and the air buzzed with incoming fire.

The loud and rapid explosions came as a total shock to the squad and the newer members were about to discover if their waterproof trousers were impervious to dampness produced from within.

'Down!' Blacky's calmly whispered command produced an instant reaction from the squad. All dropped to the ground. 'Return fire!'

Modern British rifles did not go bang, bang, bang. They made the phut, phut sound of compressed air escaping through a tiny hole. What the weapons lacked in meaningful sound was more than compensated for in their devastating effect. In the hailstorm of bullets fired by the squad, branches, trees and anything else in their path was literally pulverised. Night vision was almost perfect through the commandoes' visors; and their weapons did not give the enemy any indication of their positions.

'Belay!' Absolute silence followed the order to cease firing. Not a single bang was heard from the guerrillas' obsolete weapons.

The attacking group of guerrillas had disappeared as suddenly as they had attacked. But not without cost. Fifteen guerrilla bodies were lined up and digitally photographed. The photograph was uplinked to the satellite and was being studied in *Queen Elizabeth's* photo analysis room within twenty minutes of the attack.

The squad suffered only one casualty. The Marines' helmets were good, very good. But even they could not survive multiple strikes on the same spot. Three strikes in the blink of an eye. The first shot had dented the helmet, the second a split second later had just penetrated the outer covering of the helmet and the third had passed through the brain of Sergeant Blackstow.

On this occasion Jake drew the short straw. He was sent out with four others to reconnoitre; and make sure that their attackers had left the immediate area.

During Jake's absence, the Second Lieutenant had a long conversation with command. The upshot of which surprised and delighted Jake on his return.

'Battlefield promotion, Sergeant Hildreth.' *'Blimey!'* Thought Jake, *'A battlefield promotion! They are about as rare as hairs round a brown-hatter's arse.'* In the final analysis, Royal Marines are but simple sailors, albeit with more brawn than brain, and the crude analogy leapt casually into Jake's mind.

The jungle did not resound to the ululations of bereaved *bootnecks*. Sergeant Blackstow had not been a popular member of the squad but what Sergeant is? In fact there was little evidence of grieving. The squad had a job to do. Everyone knew the risks; everyone knew that casualties were inevitable; and everyone knew that they might be next.

Crab-air dropped a *coffin-shute*. And Sergeant Blacky Blackstow was bundled somewhat unceremoniously into the bag. Before it could be zipped up Jake ambled over and casually removed the small embroidered triple-chevrons from Blacky's chest. He zipped up the body-bag, released the inflated balloon and watched as the recovery ropes floated into the darkness of the night. *Crab-air* would recover the body before they left, plucking it from the jungle as easily as picking an apple from a tree.

The surprise attack had taken place in darkness at about 22.00. After a brief conference Jake and the *snotty* decided to rest in the clearing for the night. They had made much better progress than the other squads squeezing inwards towards Kigali and were ordered to hold their present position until daybreak.

The old male nomad lay curled in the long grass. His back was bent in a round arch, his head resting on his rear hind quarters. Gasping for air, he was barely conscious; but he knew that he was alone again. A gentle breeze stirred the now sparse mane around his face, once so gloriously thick and black. In search of new horizons, and the possibility of joining another pride, the female had snuffled up to him, a final gesture of affection, and she was gone.

Drifting in and out of sleep, his confused mind could not differentiate between past and present. At one moment he was young again, amongst his pride, the king of all he could see. The next moment he returned to the present time and his body ached. The now dissipated muscles of his legs twitched and throbbed, as would a man with a very bad dose of the flu. Not long now, he knew that his time was near; and from somewhere deep inside his mind he also knew that his species would not for much longer roam freely over his homeland.

Man's encroachment into the once fiercely guarded national parks of Africa had already seen the numbers of large predators dwindle alarmingly. Less than five thousand kings of the jungle currently existed in the whole of Africa; and most of those eked a living in the northern desert regions.

A sudden flick of his long tail was the only indication of his anger at this thought. He sank once again into that dark place; a place where all his pain and suffering disappeared and his heart sang again during his joyous dreams.

A lancing pain shot through his body, as the old lion once again opened his eyes. For a few seconds he could not comprehend what had disturbed him. And then the abominable smell hit his senses. Man. Very close; too close.

In his newly-found position of power Jake found it difficult to stop issuing orders. The squad's *comms* channel buzzed with his instructions. Unlike Blacky, who maintained a fixed position within the squad, Jake opted for a roving commission. Appearing from nowhere he snapped at the heels of his command, like a good sheepdog. Also unlike Blacky, Jake would never make a good leader of men. He found fault much too quickly and praised not at all.

He had roused the squad at 05.00 on day three of their holiday in Africa, put in a call for breakfast and ammunition and began a humiliating inspection of weapons. No Marine ever mistreats his rifle; over time it becomes another appendage to his body and the daily maintenance and cleaning routines are carried out meticulously.

Blacky, securely trussed in his zipped-up body-bag, had gone home. Most of the squad had heard the chopper flying low over their position during the night, picking up a parcel for delivery to the family of the late Sergeant Blackstow. 'At least it will save the Chancellor another pension,' one of the squad quipped when Blacky's absence was first noticed. The young Second Lieutenant winced at this remark. *'Some people resort to attempted humour in the direst of circumstances,'* he thought; but the comment tickled his own sense of humour and he realised that he was slowly becoming institutionalised.

They had left their *bivvy* at a little after 06.30. It was extremely hot and humid. More of the heavy thunderstorms were forecast for later in the day. Sweat trickled down trouser-legs, hot and aching feet squelched inside boots and soaking-wet hands found it difficult to maintain a grip on weapons. The jungle's blood-sucking annelid worm was everywhere and seemed to appear on hands and arms as if by magic. The leech's suckers, at both ends of its body, clamped the dreaded creature to its food source and the predatory worm gorged on blood until removed with a hot cigarette end.

Calling for a *stand-easy* at 10.00, Jake ordered the squad to de-leech in pairs. Most Marines carried snacks to munch on between main meals, together with a flask of water or cold tea. And crab-air was the finest *maître d'* in the world, circling overhead in the stratosphere, never failing to drop whatever was required.

Newly promoted, Jake could not prevent his eyes from continuously glancing down at the chevrons on his chest. He had washed away the bloodstains as best he could and he would replace them as soon as he returned to the *Queen*. He was thus engaged when the huge beast reared up in front of him.

The dying predator had very little peripheral vision. As is the case with all large cats he was blessed with two eyes that faced forwards, towards his prey. Despite the pain, he had forced his head to turn in every direction searching for the source of the hated smell that offended his senses so strongly.

Thunderstorms were brewing and already the sky was filled with huge cumulonimbus clouds. The wind, usually his greatest ally, was a fickle messenger of doom. As boisterous as a playful cub it changed its direction of approach continually, never settling long enough for him to judge direction and distance to his enemy. And man was his enemy, of that the old lion had no doubt.

Unsure of what to do, the old lion waited. Panting occasionally in the heat, he peered through the long grass, first in one direction and almost immediately in another.

His patch of grass was in the centre of a jungle clearing, most probably created by large families of elephant many years before. Suddenly he heard footfalls - from behind him! In one final effort of strength, willpower and hatred, the old lion turned toward the direction of attack and reared up on to his hind legs. At fully two point five metres above the ground, his head towered above the man. In the split second before the man moved, the lion saw his own reflection in the visor covering the man's face. It confused him; what was a man doing with a lion's face, some new sorcery dreamed up by this hideous creature?

The man dropped instantly to his right, revealing another man immediately behind him. The old lion could not hold his threatening stance any longer and he literally dropped on to the shoulders of the second man. Naturally conditioned reflexes urged the lion to strike for the throat. But the target area was too small and his gaping mouth enclosed the man's head. The bite pressure of a fully-grown male lion is incredible. But the long, darkly stained teeth did not penetrate the helmet of Jake's number two.

Following closely behind his new Sergeant, the Marine was on his first tour of duty and he too was daydreaming. His eyes were on Jake's heels but his mind was far, far away. He saw Jake fall to the right, lifted his eyes and gazed into the jaws of death. To the young Marine it seemed to take an eternity for the darkness to take him; everything happened in heart-stopping slow motion.

The huge body of the lion crushed him to the ground; the gaping, foul-smelling mouth descended over his helmet. Brain screaming with hatred, the huge feline felt a terrible anger and an intense desire to kill this man. The huge beast made one final, supreme effort; he flicked the body of the man as effortlessly as would a terrier killing a mouse. Jake's number two was still alive. But only just. He had felt his spine snap in several places and a strange half-light was settling over him. He saw his mother and his two sisters and tried desperately to lift his arm to wave goodbye to them.

He lived long enough to hear the phut-phut from Jake's rifle which dispatched the lion to its final hunting ground and felt the weight of the huge body fall over his own.

CHAPTER 16
THE BEGINNING OF THE TERROR

THREAD:

During the second decade of the 21st century, Her Majesty, Queen Elizabeth II, finally vacated the throne of England, handing the House of Windsor to the next in line of succession. To many of her subjects she had been a Queen without equal and had been a clean-living, strong-minded and deeply religious role model throughout her life. Without exception the whole nation mourned her deeply. For however long man would allow himself to occupy this planet, she would hold a unique place in England's history; that of occupying the throne of Great Britain for the longest period in British history and for being the last of the long-lived monarchs.

For fate held in store a terrible end for some of her successors. By some unfortunate coincidence, Her Majesty Queen Elizabeth II died about the same time of year as another famous leader, who had lived over eight hundred years before.

Way back in the mists of time, a revered 12th century Kurdish Sunni Muslim also died. This famous leader, renowned in both Muslim and Christian worlds for his leadership and military prowess, founded the ruling *Ayyubid* dynasty of Egypt, Syria, Yemen and Iraq. The general displayed a remarkably chivalrous and merciful nature during the war against the Crusaders. Regarded as a *Waliullah* (friend of God) by the Sunni sect of Islamic believers, he died at Damascus on the 4th March, 1193. His tomb exists today in the *Umayyad* mosque; and his name was Salah al-Din.

ENGLAND. EARLY 2025.

The recently promoted Grand Masjid-Imām, Saladin-Hakim Salah, would become twenty-two years of age on 29th October, 2025. It was January. The warm Sun belied the fact that Britain was in the depths of winter. Birmingham's packed streets were throbbing with shoppers and the noise seeped into the cool and quiet interior of the mosque.

Saladin was deep in thought. Six of his eight *hajji* Lieutenants were seated on the floor around him. They maintained complete silence whilst their leader planned their next operation.

Four years previously the eighteen year old Muslim had completed his pilgrimage to Mecca. Quickly promoted to the religious rank of Masjid-Imām, he had convinced the UK's Islamic leaders to introduce a *zakat*, a tax on every Muslim in the country. The proceeds from this taxation were to be placed at Saladin's disposal, to further the aims of the Islamic religion in Great Britain. Such funds, however raised and whoever raised by, were usually intended for a hidden agenda. And such was the case for this money, the hidden agenda being Muslim political extremism.

Islamism expects that its followers should lead a clean, healthy and trouble-free life. They must not lie, steal, kill, gamble, lend money for profit, wager, eat pork, consume intoxicating liquor or commit adultery.

But Saladin had other ideas. In order to stir up extreme levels of discomfort for the British government, sufficient to create a sociological anomic situation, the whole Islamic population of the UK mainland was declared to be a Dervish army. But this army was not to whirl, dance or howl; they would be a nuisance Dervish army. Where the anti-establishment policy of social disorder flew in the face of expected Muslim behaviour, the perpetrators were excused by way of an irade, issued by the incumbent Rasul-Allah himself. This stated that the Nuisance Dervish Army engaged in such anarchic activities would not be barred from paradise. For the men, in particular, this meant that the company of pure women, the *houris*, would still be available to them in heaven.

By the end of 2023, Saladin had twenty-five million pounds sterling in his war chest. Mosques all over the UK mainland were ordered to instruct their flocks to commence a campaign of civil disobedience. Ethnic rioting, mugging, robbery and mayhem were considered viable acts of civil disobedience, anything short of murder. The Islamic community were actively encouraged to engage in as many non-violent activities as possible, in a re-enactment of the Peasants' Revolt of 1381. The aim was to overwhelm the police, civil authorities and the courts, and to climb up the collective nose of the British public as far as they possibly could.

Social disobedience is a multi-faceted enigma. Hundreds of thousands of recusant Muslims throughout the UK combined to cause havoc and chaos; and the many facets of this particular challenge to the leadership in Westminster was both varied and extreme.

Almost every aspect of social life in the UK was targeted, with the aim of committing as many offences as possible.

Individual, irritating offences using vehicles are easy to commit; parking offences; deliberate speeding; using mobile phones unlawfully; running a vehicle without insurance or MOT; abandoning old cars in the street when of no further use; filling up with fuel and leaving without paying which created endless problems for police authorities dealing with complaining garage owners; and disrupting the flow of traffic by blocking roads. Refusing to pay car tax; council taxes; TV licences; bus, train and tube fares; rent; mortgages and utility bills. Refusing to complete tax returns, censor forms and voting registration forms. The choices were virtually endless.

Group offences such as mobbing and ransacking department stores, food stores and shopping malls; blocking city centres and motorways with tractors, lorries, cars and vans; holding endless late-night rallies where huge crowds of noisy, banner-waving people took part in riotous behaviour through towns and villages, tormenting the rest of the community trying to sleep.

Wanton waste of essential utilities was also encouraged; leaving taps running reduced reservoirs to dangerously low levels; and leaving gas and electricity appliances running continuously overwhelmed the national grids.

For the big business organisations, utility companies, government and law enforcement agencies, and fire-and-rescue services, it was a costly exercise. For the common man it was inconvenient at first but he would pay later when the costs were passed down in increased local, direct and indirect taxation. Inconvenient and tiresome, for the British people are orderly and well trained in one particular aspect of human existence; they know how to stand in line, politely queuing to await their turn. And it was a specific instruction from the leader of al-Shamshir that the Muslim nation of Great Britain display a more bullish attitude towards this distinctly British characteristic. 'Do not wait in line, barge to the front of the queue. For this will infuriate the British people.'

In defiance of their leader's instructions to adhere to a non-violent strategy, heavily armed gangs of teenagers rampaged through the cities, on the transport systems and in pubs and restaurants in a carbon-copy of hooligans *steaming* during the early years of the 21st century. Terrible injuries were inflicted on the innocent public, which threw Saladin into a tremendous rage and he kept his retribution squads busy in exacting a heavy price from the ringleaders. However, any associated financial gain from the practice of *steaming* was gladly accepted at the country's mosques on completion of each raid.

Every town and city across the mainland of the UK suffered in one way or another. Very few of the British Christian population, and including those of other beliefs and persuasions, escaped some upsetting experience or other. Be it a hectoring from gangs of Muslim teenage boys, a rough and tumble of older ladies by groups of teenage female *hoydens*, or becoming inadvertently involved in an affray.

Rioting was a particular favourite of this Dervish army. Town centres were rendered no-go areas all over the country, particularly in the evenings, and in the residential areas at various times throughout the night, riots were especially designed to disturb the peace and tranquillity of the neighbourhood. The rioting groups, sometimes several hundred strong, marched wherever they pleased, carrying banners declaring their intention to create a single form of worship in the UK. Screaming abuse at the British government and the British infidels, with liberal invocations of the first line of the *shahada*, they chanted;

'There is no God but Allāh and Muhammadpbuh is the prophet of Allāh.'

Splinter groups consisting of twenty to thirty people would break off from the main group of rioters, and run amok through the shops, offices, gardens, etc., inflicting as much damage as possible on the buildings as they passed through. Breaking windows, smashing down doors, tipping over stock, anything that was in their way was torn down or smashed.

The Dervish *iblis* continued their crusade of civil unrest for almost a year until late in 2024 when the British government finally ceased discussing the problem. By this time literally billions of pounds worth of damage had been wreaked; the reputation of Britain as a safe investment opportunity had been reduced; and the stock exchange no longer registered much in the way of reaction to the numerous Black Mondays.

Saladin, his team of eight Lieutenants and the more senior British Islamic leaders, achieved far more than they could have wished for, even in their wildest dreams.

For the current British political leadership was weakened from prolonged pandering to the whims of the European mainland. With very little say in how Britain was governed, the British lap-dogs might occasionally manage a slight tug on the leash in protest at the demands from Stuttgart, where the brand-spankingly new European Union headquarters building was currently located.

Brussels had lost the battle to continue hosting this money-gobbling organisation in 2017; they could not muster sufficient votes against the combined German and Italian vote, supported by a very reluctant but pressurised British vote, to relocate. At least this move saved the annual two hundred million Euro cost of moving the entire kit and caboodle between Brussels in Belgium and Strasbourg in France for four days every month, as demanded by the original Treaty of Amsterdam.

During the July to December 2017 period of Britain's reign as President of the European Council of Ministers, aka the Euro Summit, the constitution of the EU was changed to allow Germany to fulfil the role of Permanent President of the Euro Summit (Stuttgart PPES) - further testimony to the power wielded over Britain's government. Dreams of a Fourth Reich were still strong in Germany and the demand from the PPES to Britain's leaders was unambiguous, 'Get the Islamic problem sorted!'

Appeasement was the answer from the coalition of Liberal and Labour politicians that ran the country. Various bread-and-circus type proposals were offered to the Islamic leaders; tax concessions, which included the zero rating of any previous business-taxes associated with the country's many mosques; allowing *zakats* to be considered as a legitimate expense and therefore tax-deductible; the reintroduction of a marriage allowance whereby the Muslim community could claim tax benefits for up to four wives; and the whole tax concession package backdated for ten years.

Strangely, the Prime Minister baulked at the Chancellor's original suggestion of, 'Up to four wives and as many concubines as can be proven to be resident at the claimant's household.'

Freedom of immigration to the relatives of the British Islamic organization was also on offer, together with a simplification of the rules and procedures governing such immigrants, to such an extent that simply signing a list of names supported any application. The granting of British citizenship and the issue of a British passport within six months of arrival into the country was an additional part of the deal.

But crucial in this list of inducements was the repeal of all legislation restricting the wearing of ethnic clothing and the formal acceptance of the right of Muslim men to keep their women hidden away from prying eyes, which allowed for the wearing of *yashmaks, burkas, chadors, turbans, jibbahs* and *djellabas*. The final bribe on offer was that of allowing Britain's Muslims to celebrate Friday as their holy day and day of rest; and allocating Sunday as a normal working day if they wished. All British companies and employers were required to fall into line with this proposed new policy.

On this bright sunny day in January 2025, Saladin was in a happy mood, basking in the success of his nuisance Dervish army. Following that hugely successful anti-social campaign, he was searching for an auspicious date on which to launch his next attack on Britain's lower classes. And it was as a plebeian lower class that Saladin saw the Christians and Roman Catholics, who formed the bulk of the remainder of the population of his island.

Always theatrical, he had already decided upon his next attack but feigned deep thought and intense concentration to impress his

Lieutenants. There were no flashes of light, or any other indication of divine intervention; the answer seemed to spring into his head. The memory of Salah al-Din, after whom he had been named, sprang into his mind and he recalled that the great leader had died on 4th March, 1193. And there was something else in his memory banks about the early spring, but he could not bring it to the forefront of his thoughts.

Mind off with the *houris*, Saladin found it difficult to concentrate on the same subject for any length of time and his thoughts constantly flipped to that of his latest concubine and the delights in store for him this night.

A slight shuffling could be heard. One of his Lieutenants had rearranged his backside on the hard floor and an unpleasant aroma filled the room, accompanied by a definite hint of curry. Lambent blue eyes hardened and Saladin glared at his group of trusted assistants. But Saladin could not for long remain angry with his trusty cronies. A huge smile spread across his face and he recalled the words of his father, when still a small child. 'You are called Saladin, which means righteousness of the faith. You must always remember this.' As a small boy, Saladin had not a clue what the words implied but his father had spoken them with such religious awe that Saladin had not had the heart to ask for enlightenment.

The slight disturbance had dragged his mind from his duties for the coming night and he remembered the other significant events associated with early spring of recent years. One of which was the demise of the very old, highly revered Queen Elizabeth II, who had died during that early part of the year. And one particular date had since been recognised as a national holiday and for this particular year Saladin knew that street parties had been planned all over the country. And as a special salute to his predecessor, the newly-crowned head of the House of Windsor had arranged for the Royal Marines to stage a special beat the retreat on Horse Guards parade.

'*Bismillah.*' The first word of the Koran. An invocation of the name of Allāh; and often spoken by Muslims before beginning a new venture or activity. 'So be it,' Saladin spoke aloud. It was a signal to his Lieutenants that their leader had come to some decision; and that they could now move or speak.

'Tell us, Rasul-Allah, we implore thee.' *Hajji* Abu Tamimi, the leader of Saladin's First Scimitar, was prone to flowery speech, particularly on what he considered auspicious occasions. 'Tell us, Lord. How are the swords of Islam to be used against the crony of the great Satan? How will we earn our passports into paradise as glorious Muslim *shahids*?'

'*Bismillah!* Our next attack will take place on the 4th March.' A slight pause to allow his Lieutenants to soak up that information. He knew that it did not give them much time to carry out his instructions.

'Abu, my friend and First Lieutenant, arrange for the helicopter to be brought to London. Make sure that it is well hidden until it is required for use.' Saladin knew that he could rely upon the leader of his First Scimitar to get the most important job of his planned operation completed correctly and on time. 'Aye, Lord Rasul-Allah, blessed favourite of the mighty one.' Abu Tamimi always gave a formal acknowledgement of his leader's orders. And in their minds, the Scimitar leaders had already promoted the Grand Masjid-Imām to Rasul-Allah.

'Ramzi, we will require five thousand death-rain. See to it.' *Hajji* Ramzi Choudary, Commander of the Fifth Scimitar and not to be outdone by the much-favoured Tamimi, lowered his mouth to the floor and lightly kissed the ornately patterned stones. 'As you wish, my Lord,' he whispered.

'I will require one more Scimitar.' Saladin allowed his eyes to dwell upon each of his four remaining Lieutenants, finally coming to rest on the beautiful, almost feminine face of *Hajji* Ramzi Mahmood, who led the Sixth Scimitar. '*My honey-pot.*' Saladin recalled the almost countless times that this beautiful man had attracted equally attractive females to his side and who had quickly stood aside when his master deigned to make a selection. 'The Sixth Scimitar will be responsible for programming the death-rain. My wish is that half will explode on my first command and the remainder on my second command.' Ramzi Mahmood raised his long eyelashes, and gazed upon his lord and master. 'Your wish is my command, O Lord.'

'As for the rest of you, make yourselves available to the three active Commanders. Do whatever is required of you.' 'Aye, Lord.' The remaining three Scimitar Commanders chorused their acquiescence to their leader's orders.

JAKE.

Bloody horses. They polluted the air in the barracks with their stench. Sergeant Jake Hildreth was not a happy man. He was thirty-nine years old and rapidly approaching pensionable age. With less than a year to demob, he would have preferred any posting rather than his latest. 'Bloody nursemaids to a bunch of *airy-fairy bandies*.' Jake had a very low opinion of Royal Marine bandsmen and saw his latest job as a poor ending to his military career.

A few years previously, around the beginning of the second decade of the 21st century, a new unit had been formed within the Royal Marine Corps. Ministry of Defence officials had decided that the military bands were easy targets for dissidents. Consequently, a new unit had been formed, staffed by senior (for senior read older and probably past their best) *bootnecks* nearing the end of their time in the service.

This new unit formed a ceremonial guard for the tri-service military bands. They were billeted in Knightsbridge barracks in Hyde Park, London, aka Hyde Park barracks. Each and every member of this unit was expected to be immaculately dressed whilst carrying out their duties and to be available to travel the country wherever a military band was performing.

Jake would have liked to serve his *run-down period* lazing around the Sergeants' Mess at Deal, acting as course instructor to a bunch of very green new recruits. Anything would be better than spending most of his time decked out in full *blues*. And as for the Hyde Park barracks, well that was just the icing on the cake! Jake could not stand horses and the stench of horseshit was everywhere. The Household Cavalry were nothing but a bunch of *snappers*. Jake did not know which offended him more; the sight of the horses raising their tails and dropping their smelly bits all over the barracks or the sight of the fat arses of the riders spread across their horses' backs. His only consolation was that he would not have to soldier on for more than a few months.

Jake knew that civvy street was going to be hard going. Apart from marching smartly and being pretty handy with a rifle or bayonet, Jake had no other skills. Quite what he was going to do to earn a living after demob he did not have a clue. No need to worry about that for a while though; he would leave the Royal Marines with a goodly sized lump sum and a fairly healthy pension for the rest of his life. *Beer coupons* would not be a problem for some time to come.

Lying in his *pit* in his cabin, Jake was having a private *drip-session*. Morosely engaged, he was reviewing his life, which usually involved revisiting the worst parts and going over and over the times during which he considered himself hard done by. This usually put him in a foul mood and gave him an excellent excuse for spending the entire evening at the bar in the Sergeants' Mess, finally staggering back to his cabin to fall blind drunk into his *pit*.

Neither fortune nor favour had smiled upon Jake Hildreth. He had taken for his wife the biggest bloody whore that Pompey had ever produced; he had been passed over for promotion so many times that he no longer bothered to read the quarterly advancement notices issued by the MOD; he had received more *green-rubs* than a billiard ball; and he was as sure as *eggs was eggs* that some military calamity would befall him over the next few months that would kiss goodbye to his hard-earned pension.

To rub salt into fate's cruel lacerations, that bloody *snotty* from Rwanda was now a full-blown captain. 'Captain bloody Reggie Pertwee, two years under his belt and he's a bloody Captain!' Jake screamed to the ceiling in frustration. The little toad had stolen all the glory. 'Don't bother writing a report if you don't want to, Sergeant. I will draft one, and you can countersign it if you wish.' The bastard had known full well that *Custard* found signing a cheque difficult enough, never mind writing a report of a military operation. Another *green-rub* for Jake, that same toady captain was now the Officer Commanding his present unit. 'Why me, Lord? Why me?' Jake giggled when he remembered the next line in his favourite joke, when a huge finger appears in the sky pointing directly at him and a deep voice from heaven replies, 'Because you give me the shits.' Good humour well and truly restored, Jake picked up his *Egyptian AFO* and continued reading.

Only two hazy spots of sunshine shone down on Jake 'Custard' Hildreth. By some strange quirk of maladministration, he had not had to forfeit his three stripes when the Rwandan conflict had ceased. Such battlefield promotions are rare indeed but actually continuing in the new rank after hostilities have ceased is an even greater rarity.

Wisely, Jake had kept his head down and his nose clean. He carried out his duties to the very best of his limited ability. He was careful not to upset anyone nor tread on anyone's toes and just hoped to remain in the Sergeants' Mess. It would have been nothing less than purgatory to be forced to return to a lowly Corporal's status.

Little angels. His twin girls had grown into real beauties. They constituted the only other tiny piece of sunshine in Jake's life. However, they must have inherited a few of their mother's genes since both had produced triplet boys a few weeks before their 15th birthday. Jake had questioned his angels closely, attempting to discover the names of the man, men, boy or boys that had so thoughtlessly impregnated his little angels and carelessly walked away to find other prey. Both girls had shaken their pretty heads in bewilderment, 'Don't know Dad, it could have been any one of a dozen boys. We've always shared *everything.*' Portsmouth County Council had wanted to provide a small flat to each of the unmarried girls but they had stood their ground and insisted upon a comfortable four-bedroomed detached house to share.

Bored with the repetitive sexual content of his reading material, Jake threw the small, bright-blue pamphlet in the general direction of his waste paper basket. At times such as these when he had no real duties to perform, he had little control over his mind. Almost always, his thoughts returned to Rwanda, seemingly drawn in some macabre way to the horrors of that short but very bloody little war.

A double phut-phut from his rifle had downed the huge beast. Firing from the hip his aim had not faltered and he watched the suddenly limp carcass of the lion fall on to his comrade.

'Man down,' Jake spoke inside his helmet and waited for a response from his squad Officer. 'Hold your position; we will be with you in five,' the plummy voice replied. The idiot had not even asked what had downed the man.

Whilst he waited, Jake hauled the heavy dead weight of the lion from his *oppo's* chest. There was a great deal of blood. The body no longer retained the outline of a man; the spine must have been broken in several places because legs and arms seemed to be in the wrong places. Peering at the lion, Jake saw that his shots had entered the lion's body just behind the front shoulders. 'Must have been a clean heart shot,' he mumbled to himself, immensely pleased at his expertise.

Bursting into the clearing from the surrounding jungle Jake was exasperated to see that the squad had bunched up behind their Officer. 'Bloody idiots,' he whispered again to himself. It finally dawned on him that his place was with the squad; taking point had been a mistake.

Quickly he sorted out his charges. Two were sent forward, two were sent back down their trail and flankers were sent out in pairs to the left and right. Blushing furiously, the Officer did not contradict his Sergeant's decision. He knew that he had been remiss in allowing the squad to bunch.

The body of the fallen Marine was hastily zippered into a *coffin-shute*. Jake made the call for *crab-air* to pick up the parcel and the squad, now down to thirty-three men, continued their mission towards the city of Kigali.

Again from nowhere; bullets suddenly whipped around them, taking them by surprise. Their attackers had allowed the two point men to pass unmolested and had waited for the main group to close before opening fire. The squad was in extended line and the initial unexpected raking of automatic fire felled four Marines.

'Down, return fire.' Jake gave the order. The sounds of the squad's rapid fire could hardly be heard, overwhelmed by the continuous firing of their attackers' older and much noisier weapons. The action lasted barely five minutes.

Total silence followed as the attacking guerrillas fled back into the jungle. A few minutes later firing could be heard at the rear and Jake knew that the fast-departing guerrillas had mopped-up his rearguard whilst making their escape.

Whilst the squad waited for the RAF to drop more body bags, Jake and the young Officer convened an *o-group*. 'We are down to twenty-seven,' the *noddy* Officer's voice was plummy and precise, as he spoke to his Colonel onboard the *Queen Elizabeth*. 'But we have accounted for thirty guerrillas so far, Sir, and I am sure that we can deal with whatever they throw at us.'

'You must push on, Reggie.' The voice of the Colonel sounded worried, thought Jake. 'We cannot send you any replacements as yet,' continued the Colonel. 'But as soon as they are flown out to the *Lizzie*, I will bring you back up to squad strength.'

'We can manage, Sir. We would like to push on with our mission.' Jake was not given any chance to influence or challenge the decision of the inexperienced young Officer. 'Very good. Well done, young Reggie.' The Colonel concluded the brief conversation.

A rash decision indeed. One that would cost the lives of another dozen Marines over the next twenty-four hours as the weakened squad pressed forward. The swift and deadly attacks and ambushes continued throughout the night and into the following forenoon, when they finally reached the outskirts of Kigali. The squad had lost twenty of its thirty-five Marines and had sent almost fifty of their opponents to the happy hunting grounds.

Miraculously, both Reggie and Jake survived. '*Reggie!*,' thought Jake, Blacky had not mentioned the given name of their intrepid leader. '*Suits the little twit down to the ground!*'

SALADIN. HELICOPTER TO LONDON.

Hajji Abu Tamimi could not fly a helicopter; neither could he drive a large articulated lorry. But he knew someone that could and he was the leader of his Scimitar; and delegating was so much easier than doing.

After some exhaustive enquiries, a suitable aircraft was identified as one of a new design by the Israelis. It was very small, very fast and very agile. Fitted with the latest lightweight ramjet engines, it was especially capable of dealing with both ground troops and tanks.

Known to the Israelis as the BATY7, it had already been subject to several modifications in its short life. It employed a radical new design that provided virtual silent running, reducing the scream of jet-engines to a noise resembling that of a flock of birds. Purchasing such an aircraft from the Israeli government was not an option; the Knesset would never condone the sale of their latest helicopter that used such groundbreaking new designs. And there was a much less troublesome and far cheaper method of obtaining one.

Stolen to order from the factory which produced it, situated just south of Tel Aviv in a town called Bat Yam, the aircraft was immediately flown out to sea. A few kilometres off the coast of Israel, floating in the warm waters of the Mediterranean, waited the cargo vessel *Condura*. Owned by al-Shamshir and completely legitimate in its trading patterns and cargoes, the vessel regularly shipped whatever its parent extremist organisation required. The helicopter was immediately dismantled and packed in small wooden crates that would eventually find their way to a large highland estate along the rugged coastline of Gruinard Bay in Scotland.

Just south of Ullapool, this site had been the focus of intense but unseen activity for several years. Underground complexes had been built, by al-Shamshir sympathisers, to accommodate equipment, workshops and laboratories - everything which a well-organised army of active extremists could ever wish for. The workforce, together with whatever supplies were required, arrived from the sea. Not a whisper about the underground facility ever reached the outside world; anyone considered a risk to the security of the site simply disappeared.

After completion of the building work, the underground laboratories were occupied by unmarried Muslim men. These were the experts, the designers, the men capable of providing whatever Saladin wanted to complete his missions. They lived in the complex; all their personal needs were in the complex; they were fanatics, deeply religious and with no need of women and they were happy to dedicate their lives towards global domination. No matter how bizarre Saladin's demands, something was usually found that could be modified or rearranged to fit the bill.

Two of Saladin's Scimitars were always on site, with the Commander of the lowest numbered Scimitar assuming overall command. Presently the Seventh and Eighth Scimitars were taking their turn at overseeing the smooth running of the factory; and the Commander of the seventh, Omar Babar, was making the decisions.

Softly running machinery could be heard throughout the cozy underground weapons-producing facility. All was peaceful, ordered activity and the brightly lit interior glowed like sunshine on a spring day. In the corner of a large hangar, the helicopter was being dismantled and packed into the same boxes in which it had arrived at the site.

'*Hajji*, do you want any weapon-pods for this job?' Senior engineer, helo pilot, and truck driver all rolled into one, Parveen Rauf was a crucial member of al-Shamshir. *Hajji* is a pilgrim, one who has made the sacred trip to Mecca, but it can also be used as a title. Every soldier of al-Shamshir addressed the Scimitar leaders as *Hajji*.

The two people were alone. Had they not been they most certainly would not be discussing the mission. 'Not for this trip,' Abu Tamimi replied. 'All we know at the moment is that the death-rain will be used.' Thoughtfully he gazed over the head of his old school friend, 'And I guess we can assume that the target is in London, since that is where Rasul-Allah has ordered me to take you and the little bird.'

Groundhogs, fag-ends or nail-bombs; death-rain had many aliases used in the general day-to-day conversations between al-Shamshir's armament handlers. The weapon had not previously been deployed and it would prove a devastating killing device over the next decade or so.

The original idea for the weapon had once again originated from an Israeli invention. Devised, tested, trialed and discarded by the Israelis, the weapon had been intended as a possible crowd disperser. But al-Shamshir's weapons laboratory could see a use for this system and had stolen the idea and modified it to suit the needs of their master. About the size of a cigarette with a weighted and sharply pointed end, it was deployed from the air on to precise target footprints. As each individual fag-end strikes the ground, a small charge drives the tiny missile below the surface.

What was to become a nightmare for the world's security services, the death-rain can be programmed to activate individually by the simple pressure of someone walking on it; or detonated remotely as one single explosion to provide a murderous controlled blast. Blasting upwards and exploding a split second later inside the victim, the bomb caused massive damage to the human body. Many victims were disembowelled and few survived the massive trauma.

'Maybe I could take a few rapid-fire pods, just to give London a bit of a strafing.' As quickly as the thought entered the Hajji's head, it was dismissed. Saladin did not appreciate fine tuning of his own plans and such acts of initiative were usually rewarded with a one-way ticket to paradise.

The exquisite features of the young woman standing in front of him softened and her curvaceous lips opened into a stunning smile; she had guessed his thoughts. 'By Allāh's holy book, she's a pretty creature,' Abu thought. He had always wanted his old school friend, lustful intentions and feelings about which she was perfectly aware but had steadfastly refused to satisfy. So far. And they both knew that Abu would never give up hope.

The boxes would leave the estate on 2nd March, 2025 tucked away in the back of a Land Rover, a tractor and trailer or any one of a dozen or so different estate vehicles. Via a circuitous route, the crates would be reunited in the interior of a very large, purpose-built articulated lorry. Here, the tiny aircraft would be reassembled, ready for its mission over London.

The comings and goings to the estate did not attract any untoward attention. As a highly successful shooting estate, conference centre, expensive de-tox facility for the rich and famous and management training school for the up-and-coming leaders of industry, it had a regular stream of visitors.

'*Bismillah*, it is done.' Parveen's soft voice sent another ripple of excitement up the spine of Abu. 'When do we leave for Liverpool?'

The once bustling motor factory looked deserted and forlorn. Gone forever were the acres of shiny new cars, lined up in neat rows ready to be shipped to franchises all over Europe. Only one of the giant assembly rooms remained and that had a very different use in 2025. The once giant car manufacturer had made billions from this factory but that was all in the past. And Liverpool still mourned the closing of the factory, for it had been one of the biggest employers in the city.

Ancient, dilapidated and covered in dents and scratches, the old double-decker bus ground slowly into the forecourt and came to a screeching halt in front of the sorry looking building. The front near-side wheel was on the pavement and the bus tilted alarmingly to one side. Onlookers could just make out the faded outline of the building's previous occupants, in large letters above the high sliding doors that gave access to the cavernous interior, FORD.

Giant 'L' plates were emblazoned all over the old bus. Signs posted on all four sides proclaimed the fact that the bus was a passenger-carrying vehicle and that the driver was under training.

'Get off the bloody kerb, you thick southern twat.' It was the end of another long, frustrating and exhausting day for the speaker, whose heavy Scouse accent extended the syllables in the word kerb and almost dropped completely the sound of the letter 'r'. Xaviar James Adlam always introduced himself as Scouse Adlam and not one of his present crop of would-be bus drivers knew of his real Christian name.

From 09.00 to 18.00, Monday to Friday, he travelled around Liverpool and Birkenhead, with occasional trips up the coast to Southport whenever he feared for his sanity most.

Short, no more than one point five metres in his raised heels, thin, almost bulimic; he appeared to be a very insignificant person. But he possessed a wicked tongue and a vocabulary of insults that would have impressed any American drill instructor. He lavished these insults on his trainees whilst they learned to judge the dimensions of the large bus and to master the manual crash-gearbox. It was almost impossible to find a passenger-carrying vehicle on Britain's roads that had a manual gearbox and most of the nation's population would not know what a crash-gearbox was. Quite why the law still required bus drivers to learn this obsolete skill, Scouse could never explain.

Having reversed the ancient Tilling Stevens double-decker bus from the pavement, the trainee stepped down from the cramped cab. His back was soaked in perspiration and he was mightily glad to be out of the cockpit. 'Which one of you tossers is going to put the bus to bed?' Scouse glared at his students. None volunteered. Without power steering, the job of reversing the cumbersome vehicle up the narrow road to the entrance of the disused factory was a nightmare. The group of trainees to a man sighed with relief when Scouse let them off the hook. He was weary; sitting in the bus all day, screaming instructions and abuse at his charges, was a very tiring business. He was in dire need of a few pints before returning to his empty, lonely home.

The driving school also provided training for the drivers of lorries or heavy goods vehicles. Green with envy, the group of trainees watched as a large articulated lorry was reversed up the narrow entrance, disappearing into the dark hole of what was now used as a garage for the training vehicles. The manoeuvre had been completed with consummate ease. 'Like a skunk up a bear's asshole.' The quip from Scouse was followed by a happy chuckle.

This was another of al-Shamshir's legitimate cover businesses. Scouse reversed the old bus into the building, switched off the engine and stepped down from the cab. Mechanics were everywhere, changing wheels, repairing the many parts damaged by the students during the day and generally keeping the vehicles fit for the road.

The work was low paid, the rewards even lower than the meagre pittance that Scouse happily handed over to his local pub each week. Most of the mechanics were Muslims, a fact that did not bother Scouse one little bit; he had nothing against them or any other immigrants that came into the country. He knew they were good workers and he had seen some of them working through the night to keep the vehicles in good working order.

Scouse did not dally long in the maintenance area. His growing thirst usually dragged him away after the briefest of conversations. 'Working late again tonight then, Taffy?' Scouse struggled with the pronunciation of the mechanics' real names and called every one of them Taffy. No offence was intended by Scouse and none was taken by the Muslims, very few of whom understood more than a few words of the Liverpudlian's strange mode of speech. The Muslim mechanic pulled his features into a sardonic grimace and nodded an affirmative. 'G'night then,' said Scouse, who turned and hurried off to his local.

At the rear of the busy garage and screened behind giant tarpaulin screens was a large lorry, already coupled to its sizeable trailer. Both lorry and trailer were almost new but their appearance very much belied this fact. Devoid of company names or logos, the cab of the lorry looked well worn and was covered in a haze of road debris. The trailer was equally non-distinctive, just another of the several hundred thousand that transported the nation's goods around the country.

But both lorry and trailer were in tip-top mechanical condition; the number plates were clean; every switch and light had been checked and rechecked; and every single tyre had been carefully examined to ensure that they complied with Ministry guidelines. There was not one single item that would attract the attention of a bored traffic cop.

During the night of 2nd March, 2025, the helicopter was reassembled in the nondescript trailer. Rotors folded and firmly strapped down, it fitted comfortably inside its ride to the capital. During the following night the tiny aircraft would make its journey to London, by way of the M6 and M1, and parked-up in a well-used lorry park near Vauxhall Bridge. Here, the helicopter would wait, surreptiously guarded by the First and Fourth Scimitars, concealed from view until required to make its first flight.

On the heavily congested motorways, sticking to the speed limit was not a problem. The powerful engine of the lorry was capable of well over 140 km/h but the engine was heavily governed and would not exceed the 80 km/h national speed limit for HGVs. Not that Parveen would ever dream of exceeding any speed limit: a) it would attract too much attention; and b), *Hajji* Abu was behind her, concealed in the rear of the cab but watching her every move. Not that there was much of her body on view to her lecherous leader. Every inch a lorry driver, she wore an old pair of jeans, a roll-neck sweater and a scruffy sheepskin coat, topped off with a well-worn baseball cap.

The attractive lorry driver knew why the Scimitar leader had elected to accompany her. Whoever did so would have to spend the night with her, tightly squashed together in the small bunk at the rear of the driver's cab. She also knew that the randy Abu would make an attempt to seduce her. He had already made it abundantly clear that her refusal to cooperate might well force him to give Saladin a less than accurate account of her part in the preparations for the operation.

She had one more card that she could play, if she really wanted to? Abu was an attractive man and a favourite of Saladin; she could do much worse than to become his mistress, concubine or wife. *'Wait and see,'* Parveen gave herself some good advice.

THE NIGHT OF THE 3RD MARCH, 2025, LONDON.

The inside of the cab was rank with the smell of human habitation. The youngest member of Abu Tamimi's First Scimitar lifted the protective leather cover concealing the bright red lever and pulled it. The young man had seen the trailer complete its precision-smooth transformation on many training sessions. The roof folded into the front wall of the trailer and both sides and the rear wall lowered slowly to the ground. The tiny aircraft slid silently to the rear of the trailer and its rotors unfolded smoothly as would those of a butterfly preparing for flight. As the ultra-quiet engines burst into life, Abu and Parveen sat in the cramped cockpit, their heads encased in flying helmets.

Parveen did not wait for instructions. As soon as the machine was ready for flight, she lifted the single collective that controlled her bird and started the mission. At 03.00, some of London's residents may have heard the ultra-quiet engines but few people witnessed the aircraft lift vertically into the night sky.

She was angry with herself. Abu had timed their arrival at the lorry park so that they would arrive during the silent hours of the previous night.

Not especially tired from the long drive, the huge lorry was simplicity itself to drive and effortless to control or manoeuvre but she needed a shower and she was hungry. *Hajji* Abu was busy deploying his Scimitars, ensuring that they were stationed to ensure that the lorry would enjoy sufficient surrounding space to allow the launching of the bird. How they achieved that end was left up to them and several newly-arrived drivers, foolish enough to argue with the strangely-dressed parking attendants, would be found rotting in their cabs.

She was also excited. Thoughts of the next few hours had been racing around her brain throughout the journey. *'Submit to Abu? Should she or should she not? Did she want to, or did she not? Would he respect her if she did? Or would he discard her as he would a used condom?'*

No chance of a shower. But the Scimitar had brought hot food and wet, still warm towels with which to bathe. In the rear of the cab, she stripped off her clothes, washed herself as best she could, combed her hair and wrapped a large bath towel around her body. She had decided.

The door of the cab opened without a sound and closed with a meaty thump. Tamimi pulled back the curtains which were hiding the sleeping compartment from his view. Exquisite! Dark skin glistening in the moonlight, Parveen's long jet black hair reached down to her waist, resembling a black shawl. She was beautiful and Abu's mouth was suddenly dry; he wanted this woman so much.

The little bird was a dream to fly. Powerful but quiet engines lifted the aircraft with ease. Its two passengers remained totally silent. Locked in two delivery pods strapped beneath the aircraft, the deadly death-rain rattled gently in response to the slightest aircraft vibration.

'Why was she angry?' Such was Parveen's skill at piloting the small bird that she could allow her brain to drift over other recent events. She knew full well why she was exasperated. Abu was a fully-grown, strong and virile man, in the prime of his life. She had given herself freely and had expected an hour or so of lovemaking from her ardent

pursuer. But it had all been over in the briefest of twenty seconds. And the experience had left her body feeling unsatisfied, still highly erotic and extremely sensitive to the touch. Abu had been so small. She was not quite certain whether, during the entire brief encounter, penetration had in fact taken place.

Such is the way with a man. Having given the woman the time of her life, Abu had instantly fallen asleep. Wrapped in his arms his beard had tickled her back for the remainder of the night and his loud snores testified to his body's relaxed and satiated state.

Throughout the following day, Abu had proclaimed his love. Parveen would be his number one wife, the head of his harem, the *Begum* Tamimi. A Muslim man can take for wife any woman he chooses, except for pagan women. But this is not the case for a Muslim woman, who has no choice but to marry a Muslim man.

Parveen had no quarrel with Muslim law, she was quite happy to spend her life with a man who sang from the same hymn-sheet as did she. Memories of the previous night filled her mind. *'No! A thousand times no!'* She could not face a lifetime filled with such fumbling inadequacy.

So she had played her final card. During the previous evening, she had interrupted Abu's description of their life together, as man and wife. 'Saladin,' she had whispered. 'What would he think of us, cavorting in the back of a lorry during a mission?' The mind of *Hajji* Abu Tamimi, Commander of al-Shamshir's First Scimitar, friend and confidant of the Grand Masjid-Imām Saladin, froze in mid sentence. For several long seconds he could neither think nor speak. *'What in God's holy name was the woman talking about? Was this some form of threat? Was it to be blackmail?'* The thoughts tumbled around inside his head. He needed time to think and without a word, he sprang down from the cab of the lorry.

Helicopter flights over London are not rare. The celebrities of the day could afford to avoid the incredible congestion within the city of London. Almost every one of these financially well-endowed personages enjoyed the ease of travel that an airborne vehicle provided. Leaders of commerce and industry, radio and television presenters, and many other wealthy people, started their working day very early indeed. Consequently, helicopter movements were quite common, even at 03.00, and Abu and Parveen went about their gruesome business unnoticed.

Abu had briefly considered sweeping around in a large half-circle, to approach their target from the east and hide the direction of their launch pad from any onlookers. But he had listened to Parveen's reasoned decision to fly directly to Horse Guards Parade, drop their weapon load and make their escape.

She had argued that they needed little more than a few hundred metres of altitude to achieve their aim; and at that height, the chances of being picked up on radar were remote. London did not yet have the latest night-vision satellite surveillance system that provided the likes of New York and Washington with 24-7 coverage.

All was quiet in the cockpit of the helicopter. Abu had refrained from speaking about their personal relationship, apart from a curt, 'It's not over, we will speak again after the mission.' Which left Parveen in a dilemma and which added to her anger. *'Had she made a dangerous blunder? Turned Abu into an enemy?'* Once again, she could only wait and see.

Flying low over St James's Park, the little bird planted a small diversion. Still flying low, it then proceeded towards Horse Guards Parade, where the two main weapon pods were fired. Death-rain peppered the parade ground, burying themselves up to three centimetres below the surface. There they would lie, completely undetectable to even the most sensitive of sensors, until detonated at Saladin's command.

Flanked by the Old Admiralty and Old Treasury buildings, Horse Guards Parade is only a couple of hundred metres from Downing Street, the home of the British Prime Minister. Recently cobbled, the parade ground shimmered in the heat of the early March morning. Already the heat waves distorted the vision of St James's Park. Hundreds of specially invited spectators filled the areas around three sides of the parade ground and every nook, cranny, window and rooftop was crowded with onlookers.

JAKE.

At last. Jake ordered his squad to halt and waited for the bands to reach their start positions. His feet ached, his head throbbed and he was soaked with sweat.

The original plan for his escort squad was to surround the parade ground, a protective ring of armed Royal Marines. But that bloody wazzock of a Captain had been determined to wield his new broom. The Colonel had welcomed Captain Reggie Pertwee's suggestion that the Royal Marine escort could be used to enhance the performance of the bands, by completing complicated counter-manoeuvres amongst them. 'More like a bloody circus,' was Jake's opinion.

The United Kingdom's newly-crowned monarch had ordered the entire House of Windsor to witness a nation's salute to a revered Queen. Not one dared to decline this royal command or to cry-off under some excuse of ill health or other engagement. For the day was designed to be both a national salute to a dead Queen, and an attempt to overturn the nation's deepening disenchantment with the Royal Family.

And so it was that the royal enclosure was crowded with princes, princesses, dukes and duchesses by the dozen, all chirping merrily amongst themselves. Also present in this reserved area was the Prime Minister and representatives from each political party and various sporting idols of the day. Oblivious to the mass of common humanity, the occupants of the royal enclosure could not find the strength to respond to the unending waves and resounding cheers. And they were even less inclined to comply with the ceaseless demands of the assembled media representatives, turned out *en masse* for this prestigious occasion. All requests to smile, wave, hold hands, blow a raspberry or fart in the wind were steadfastly ignored.

At the first sound of the massed bugles, Britain's prime minister lifted himself to his feet. As a retired Commandant General Royal Marines, Phillip Savin had donned full dress uniform to take the salute from the troops as they marched past. Bedecked in row upon row of medals, he had elected to stand, straight, firm and proud, during the entire performance.

Thirty minutes later, the PM was regretting his rash decision to stand. His legs were rapidly turning to rubber. The heat was astonishing, despite the canvas cover hastily erected over the royal enclosure that morning. But his discomfort was nothing to that of the marching military formations. The heat from the cobbles penetrated the thick soles of regulation army boots and seemed to melt the marrow in the bones of those that wore them.

A brief hand signal from the PM. An order to the Parade Colonel to cut short the proceedings and commence the finale. He had stood for long enough in the infernal heat and he knew only too well of the agony of the performing troops.

He would never know it but by that brief hand signal Mr Phillip Savin had signed his own death warrant. But he would not be the only recently-released soul to search for the gateway to a better existence.

THE ATTACK.

The cool interior of the mosque in Birmingham was in complete contrast to the intolerable heat of central London. Saladin's dreams of the delights of his ever-growing harem were smashed to smithereens by the sounds on his television.

The parade was not scheduled to end for another thirty minutes and the Prime Minister's decision to bring the proceedings to an early conclusion had almost caught him out. He would have to hurry. His hand reached out and picked up the small remote control. He looked down at the three buttons, marked *wake-up, maim, kill*.

Scattered around the room sat the invited guests of Saladin, specially selected to witness the hand of Allāh smiting the infidels. These were the Muslim leaders who had been guilty of slight transgressions and who were destined to suffer the wrath of their leader. The voice in Saladin's head had identified each and every one of them. A few choice words from Saladin during the forthcoming carnage would make the audience well aware of their fate and leave them squirming for a few more weeks and would add enormously to Saladin's personal pleasure.

Saladin watched the face of his prime minister and saw him flinch as the *wake-up* button was pressed. The TV microphones picked up the ripple of explosions in St James's Park. The small diversion planted by the tiny helicopter exploded and Duck Island disappeared in a huge mushroom of soil, trees, water, feathers and dead ducks. The massed bands were the best of Britain's military and they marched on through the sound of the explosions whilst the police and emergency services raced towards the lake in St James's Park.

A few minutes later a terrible smile spread over the face of Saladin.

His eyes darkened in colour and took on the glint of the fanatic. It was time. His finger pressed *maim*.

The massed bands were well into that most stirring of marching music, "Heart of Oak", the official march of the Royal Navy, composed by Dr William Boyce and with words by the 18th century English actor David Garrick. *'Come, cheer up, my lads, 'tis to glory we steer, to add something more to this glorious year'*. The glorious year referred to was of course 1759-1760, during which British forces were victorious in battles with the French at Quebec City, Canada; Quiberon Bay off the coast of France near St Nazaire; and followed a few months later by the Battle of Wandiwash in India.

The wingless mercenaries took flight like a plague of locusts. Tiny messengers of pain and death, the death-rain exploded from the ground beneath the feet of all who stood on Horse Guards Parade. In that fraction of a second, the tiny bombs detonated upwards into the soft underbellies of their victims, there to explode a millisecond later. Blood, guts, bits and pieces of the human body, clothing, weapons and band instruments burst into the glorious sunshine. The onlookers gasped in shock, the explosion had been so *contained*, only those on the parade ground had been hit.

TV cameras continued to roll and the whole country stood in shocked silence at the gory scenes. The screams and groans from the injured were heartbreaking in the sudden silence. However, in such circumstances the most common human reaction is a desire to aid the victims.

People from all walks of life raced to the side of the fallen and started to administer whatever assistance they could. Hundreds of square metres of ground, covered in an ever growing puddle of blood and human detritus, made the journey on to the parade ground difficult and many slipped into the mess, only to rise up and continue, covered in blood, to give support to the injured. These macabre scenes would give many a young viewer troublesome nightmares over the coming years.

The bright blue eyes watched the scenes carefully. His whole body seemed to glow with satisfaction and he felt an overwhelming sense of achievement. His place in history was assured as the must successful Muslim leader that had ever fought for world domination.

He waited a few minutes more. Give the dying infidels a few minutes more of life and then he, the rightful Rasul-Allah, leader of al-Shamshir, would administer the *coup de grace*. Not so much regarded by him as a mercy-blow; more a deathblow, a final tramping under foot of his loathsome enemies.

Long and slender, the cool finger hovered above the *kill* button. Not a flicker of doubt, remorse or regret showed in the cold eyes of the watcher. Now! The finger pressed the button and the staring eyes watched more closely as the TV cameras panned over Horse Guards Parade.

For long minutes the motionless figure watched the carnage. His eyes did not move from the sights before him when his lips moved to form the chilling words, aimed at the traitors in the room. 'Look into the eyes of your neighbour and there you will see the terror that foreshadows your death; for you have failed al-Shamshir and your faith and you must prepare to make your case to the devil.'

This second explosion, every bit as devastating as the first, ripped through fallen and helper alike. Life was extinguished in every supine body, the flame of life put out by a single finger, as if the Holy Father had pressed His digit to a candle in heaven.

One of the TV cameras had found the PM. He had not been killed outright by the first explosion and was lying on his back in front of the royal enclosure. Royal and celebrity bodies littered the shaded area, in various bodily conditions between earth and heaven; or hell. The camera remained fixed on the PM's face, covered in blood and with his right eye dangling from a thin thread. His mouth formed words but no sound came from his throat; his vocal chords had been severed. The words would puzzle and perplex most of the country's lip-readers until finally recognised by an Oxford don. '*Annus horribilis, actum est.*'

A horrible year indeed for the retired General and for him it was most certainly all over. But unlike his well-loved Queen, Phillip Savin would not be able to use the first two words as part of a Christmas message or to explain the poor performance of some unfortunate political colleague at a state opening of parliament. However, he did at least achieve a place in history, as the second British prime minister to have died at the hands of an assassin.

JAKE.

Jake felt the pain. Deep in his lower abdomen. He fell to the ground, sorely wounded but still alive. In such circumstances, a man's first reaction is usually concern for his testicles.

Jake's heart flipped; where once had been solid oval shapes was now a mess of blood and skin. Also gone was his penis, a favourite plaything from his earliest memory. Lifting his eyes, he turned his head and saw his Captain a few metres away.

Reggie's stomach had been blown apart and what remained of his intestines billowed out of the grotesquely distorted body, like a bunch of purple grapes. Jake had little time to spend thinking of his Captain; he was desperately feeling around for his missing private part. Deep within him, he was still hoping that some clever surgeon might reattach his pride and joy to his torn body when the second explosion ripped through the morning air.

Jake died instantly; he would not know the joy of walking out of his barracks into Civvy Street, nor would he need to worry again about what to do with his life when he did. He had gained his freedom in a different way.

THE RETREAT.

On Britain's M1 motorway a few kilometres north of Milton Keynes, is the Newport Pagnell service area. Parked in the lorry park was the al-Shamshir truck that was returning the helicopter to its hiding place in Liverpool. Abu and Parveen had eaten a light lunch and were returning to the vehicle, ready to continue their journey.

Both were silent, strangely subdued instead of elated at the success of their mission. Parveen's unanswered statement still hung in the air between them. Abu had given the matter a great deal of thought. He had offered this woman everything he had to give - his love, his wealth, his position in Islamic society and last but by no means least, the rank of *begum*. Such wealth and status on offer did not seem enough, however, and Abu had wracked his brain for a reason why. In a flash of divine inspiration, all became clear to the Muslim *Hajji*.

Obviously she had feelings for another. Her mention of Saladin had clearly given her game away. She had her eyes set upon a higher status in life; that of number one wife to their leader. All of these thoughts supported Tamimi's latest decision.

The woman could not be allowed to speak to Saladin who would, Abu decided, not look too favourably upon his First Lieutenant cavorting in the back of a lorry whilst on a mission.

Parveen felt many things. Numbed by the ferocity of their attack on what was the country's greatest asset - the Royal Family; sickened by the gory scenes portrayed on the television; fearful of Saladin's punishment should a poor report of her performance reach the great man's ears; upset and confused by Abu's continued silence; angry at herself for submitting to his advances; and still frustrated by the sheer incompetence of the man's bedroom efforts.

But she did not feel much when the stiletto slipped between her ribs. Her beautiful eyes flew wide when the tip pierced her heart; she died instantly.

Abu smiled ruefully. Killing was nothing; he had taken many a life. It would be a cool day in hell before he offered himself to another woman. *'Ungrateful bitch!'* And he had plenty of time to arrange for the disposal of the body and to invent some plausible story for Saladin.

CHAPTER 17
FERRY

THREAD:

Sporting pastimes. Some people take part as a means to escaping the stress of modern living; others do so to escape the constant, irksome and harassing attentions of a spouse; yet others join in to test their mettle against the skills of other mortals; there are some who do it for gain; and yet more who use it as a method of social interaction; but the vast majority enjoy sport simply to take part.

The choice of sports available to modern man is as wide as the lists of mind-boggling rules and regulations that govern them. Golf is considered to be one of the more simple pastimes. Chuck a small, white, dimpled ball on the ground, give it a good whack with a lump of metal on the end of a stick, chase after the ball and do it again. Keep doing this until the little white, dimpled ball falls into a small hole. Simple? Indeed it is, until the player picks up the rulebook, wherein lay the source of many a minor disagreement - argument - shouting match - punch up - leading to all out war!

Saladin liked to keep his Scimitars busy and he knew that attacks on any form of holiday transport were relatively easy to arrange and produced a huge number of complaints hurled accusingly at a government that had not a chance in hell of protecting every individual train, bus, ship or aircraft.

Alfred Leonard

CAEN TO PORTSMOUTH FERRY.
EARLY OCTOBER, 2027.

It had been an extremely bumpy return trip across the English Channel. *La Manche*, as the French have it, had been particularly unkind to the group of golfers, few of whom travelled comfortably by sea. And the Froggy Captain of the huge ferry had also been less than kind. All thirty golfers were unanimous in attributing their discomfort to the driver of the ferry. Piling on the knots into the teeth of the force six storm had moved the vessel in the most alarming fashion; not to mention the mixed contents of their bloated stomachs.

Four days of non-stop partying, during which he had consumed numerous large portions of spicy *moule* and *sauce gastronomique*, washed down with several gallons of French *biere a la pression*, was playing havoc with Mick Fuller's bottom end. But he was not the only one suffering from this problem, a fact that other travellers could attest to, having sampled the obnoxious smells and nasty green haze that settled over the bar area on the giant ferry.

Spending most of his working life crawling around the dark, dismal and confined spaces of various government buildings, the retired computer engineer could tolerate almost anything that this life could throw at him. As a member of an elite group of geeks that maintained the computer systems of various international communities and hugger-mugger organisations in the rats-nest of embassies in England's capital, he had learned over many years to deal with the strange behaviour, language and customs of a whole host of different races and creeds.

Unlike many of his golfing society, Mick was not a trophy hunter. He suffered from an appalling lack of hand-eye coordination and had a golfing swing that had tested the patience of many a golfing professional. Over the years Mick had handed over hundreds of pounds to these teachers of golf but none had managed to override his deeply instilled muscle memory.

His tolerance had been hardened in the furnace of taunt and ridicule over many years. Mick could stand the continual verbal mistreatment from his golfing friends concerning his golfing skills but he was not of an especially competitive nature. 'I'm here for the food and booze,' was his usual response to some snide remark about his golfing prowess.

On a good day with a strong following wind, Mr Fuller could out-drive any six year old junior golfer. Using his driver off the tee, he was capable of launching his ball an incredible distance of some sixty to seventy metres. Assuming he managed to avoid a whiffy[21], he usually managed to strike the ball quite well and the distance was usually achieved. Where the ball went, however, was an entirely different question; and usually somewhat of a mystery. Ever the good-natured playing partner, Mick spent most of his time tramping through the long grass and ditches; delving into the copses amongst the trees; poking into the streams, rivers, and lakes; or digging for some long-lost treasure in the sand bunkers. 'Nature Boy' was one of his many nicknames.

Another of our golfing hero's nicknames was Air Shot, or the Wailing Wizard, for Mick was never, ever, found to be at a loss for some perfectly good reason for his golfing inadequacy. 'Please stand still when I am teeing up, you Tossers - I saw a bird in the corner of my eye - my hand slipped at the top of my backswing - the ground's too wet - it's too muddy - my glove's a bit worn - I've got a hole in my shoe - new grips, not broken in yet - the Sun's in my eye - I lifted my head - I wish you twats would watch my ball - please God, why me? - these are not my most favourite conditions - someone got me paralytic last night.'

Leaving Portsmouth on the overnight sailing to Caen on a Wednesday night and returning on the Sunday, the golfing trip included three days of golf. Thursday and Friday were fun days, involving team games where individual performance did not matter too much. Saturday, however, was traditionally championship day. The day on which every man played for himself, battling fiercely for the many prizes on offer, including the accolade of GEEGS champion golfer.

Many a man had frozen in fear and trepidation on the first tee of championship day. Many more had found it difficult to focus on the small white ball after the previous evening's revelry. Friday night was always a night of heavy drinking. Staggering legless back to their rooms at about 03.30; dragged from sleep at 07.00 for an early drive to

---

[21]Whiffy. Air shot, or failure to strike the ball.

the golf course; teeing off from about 10.00; the punishing schedule left most players feeling less than confident in their chances of striking the ball.

And Mick had known that he was not on his best form. At his very first attempt to tee off he had missed the ball. Manfully ignoring the guffaws and comments from his fellow society members, he lined up and retook his stance. 'Would someone kindly hold the ball still?' Mick had been here before!

And then there had been that bunker. 'Shall we putt out while you are trying to get out of there, Mickey?' 'Don't dig too deep, Michael.' 'Shall I fetch you a cigar, Mike?' The group also included a number of other Michaels and remembering whom to call what was also somewhat difficult after a night of intense alcohol consumption.

'Snidey gits,' thought Mick. And after three or four additional attempts to hoist the annoying little ball out of the bunker, Mick thought indignantly, 'I've only had fourteen strokes at it.' But he was ever conscious of delaying his playing partners. 'Yes, you twats go ahead. I'll have a couple more goes and then I'll pick up.'

Another year of shame. Mick had known it when he had seen his ball float majestically into the bunker on the first. 'Bloody silly place to put a bunker,' he had whispered to himself at the time. He had known at that moment that his name would not be included in the long list of prize winners and that he alone would be vying for the wooden spoon.

The Captain of the golfing society was a complete pillock. Mick dreaded the moment each year when the Captain lowered his voice in that condescending manner during the prize-winning ceremony. 'And finally, for the seventeenth year in succession, the prize for most golf goes to - Mickey Fuller.'

The weight of the infernal wooden rabbit was a constant reminder. Tucked into the bottom of his overnight holdall, the wooden spoon prize was a large, carved, wooden rabbit. When he arrived home, Mick would follow his annual routine of heaving the bag and rabbit up into his loft; and there it would remain for another year. He fully expected to take the despised trophy to his grave. And this year he intended drilling a hole in its rear end and stuffing a miniature golf club up it!

'Yes,' thought Mick, standing at the rear of the ferry. '*I can tolerate many things. But I cannot abide drunken pillocks indulging in a sing-song!*' And, as the caterwauling had started Mick had left the bar, seeking a quiet spot to lick his wounds.

The ferry had slowed. It had passed Outer Spit Buoy just offshore from Southsea and the movement of the ship was now much more stable. '*And the second thing I cannot stand,*' Mick's thoughts continued, as another of his golfing society moved to his side, '*is bloody know-it-all ex matelots.*' Retired RN Rob Morgan welcomed any opportunity to air his knowledge of anything naval, ear-holing anyone and everyone within listening distance. Mick had suffered this non-stop description of the warships in the harbour several times over the preceding years; their names, pennant numbers, weapons systems, displacement, etc. The list of details seemed endless. Mick was much too polite to move away, and had to listen to the diatribe once again. '*Bloody bleeding ears again this year,*' he smiled at his silent thought.

With a naturally suspicious nature, Mick suspected that his comrades had started the sing-song on purpose - to drive him to the upper deck and into the sights of the mouthy sailor.

But by some great good fortune, the incredibly boring monologue of naval hardware suddenly ceased. Robby Morgan had seen something that had thrown him out of his stride. Racing towards the stern of the ferry were ten Jet-Skis. They had appeared from nowhere and were racing towards the stern of the ferry in two lines of five. The obviously skilful riders had complete control of their small personal watercraft and by the time they had raced along each side of the ferry, completed a full turn and repeated the manoeuvre, the attention of those on the upper deck of the ferry was firmly focused upon them. Climbing the sides of the large waves and descending back into the depths, all the while performing various twists and turns, was a mesmerizing sight.

Dressed in black wet-suits, their heads encased in bright red crash helmets, the two teams of riders were putting on a dazzling display of skill. Crashing through the churning sea thrown up by the huge vessel's propellers in an intricate synchronized pattern produced rounds of cheering from the enthralled onlookers. A particularly dangerous looking manoeuvre involved the riders approaching close alongside the ferry, reaching in and touching the side in a game of tag. The slap of the hand on the side of the ferry could be heard above the noise of the ship's engines, wind and general noise of end-of-journey chatter. After ten meaty thumps from near the water-line, the jet-skiers raced away towards the jetties in the inner harbour and, much to Mick's displeasure, the monologue started once again.

The journey from harbour mouth to the innermost berths of Portsmouth harbour can take upwards of thirty minutes. As the huge ferry turned about, in preparation for its reversing manoeuvre into its unloading dock near Whale Island, the upper decks were thronged with people. The stairways leading down to the car-decks were crammed with other travellers, anxious to be first to their vehicles. A general feeling of goodwill prevailed; people were happy to be out of the storm, on relatively solid ground again and keen to be on their way.

The rippling sound of muffled explosions startled many of these people. Apart from those too drunk to care, every one felt the shudder run through the hull of the ship. Five gaping holes appeared along the port side of the stricken ferry. Finding a new path of least resistance, the seawater rushed into the gigantic lower car-deck, greedy in its rush to engulf everything in its path.

The giant ship heeled over swiftly, unbelievably quickly, hurling those on the upper decks into the cold waters of Portsmouth harbour. Between decks in the lounges and waiting areas, all was chaos. Bodies in every state of injury and confusion were piled in droves, those on the bottom of each pile struggling to lift the suffocating weight of others that had fallen on top of them. Frantic shouts for help mingled with the metal-tearing screams of the ship, as she turned even further to port, seemingly intent upon settling on the seabed.

Those that had been thrown overboard were struggling to reach safety. Anywhere out of the way of the swiftly turning vessel that was toppling towards them. Few were strong swimmers and those that were made a swift escape from the descending hulk of the ferry. Some helped those that could not swim, or who were struggling badly. But the scene was one of confusion; the water was cold and it quickly numbed the muscles of those in the water.

Soggy, water-logged clothing hampered movement and slowed

the desperate efforts of the weakest to keep their heads above water. But there were too many bodies in the cold harbour and the ship was rolling down towards them so very quickly. Most of the screaming ceased when the huge upper works of the ferry crashed on to the struggling mass of humanity and the sea turned red with blood.

Ten minutes later, amongst the general confusion, screaming, bleeding, crying and dying of those passengers still inside the hull, a further five explosions ripped along the starboard side of the heavily listing ship.

'It will ensure the maximum loss of life,' *Hajji* Omar Izzadeen, leader of the Fourth Scimitar, had informed his leader at the final planning meeting for the ferry operation.

Never again did Mick feel able to bemoan his luck at the presence of the old matelot. Not a strong swimmer Mick was struggling badly in the cold water of Portsmouth harbour. At the first explosion, a strong right arm had propelled him over the side of the ferry. He sank deeply below the surface and at one point, he thought that his downward plunge would not stop until he hit the bottom. Struggling madly under water, his breath lasted only a few short seconds; he thought he was a *goner*.

He smiled now at the thought, breathing normally again and being towed to the shore by the old naval man, for the word *goner* was some sort of military reference to a lost golf ball, heading for the out-of-bounds area. Most golfers referred to this occurrence as an oscar brown, or OB; but Rob Morgan had a penchant for inventing his own names for misguided golf shots. And *goner* had some connection with a blitzed German dam in some British air strike during the Second World War. Mick was a trifle confused but he was sure that bouncing bombs had something to do with Rob Morgan's explanation of his golfing terminology.

Nevertheless, he felt safe now, somehow knowing that he was in capable hands and would survive. Sadly, Mick did not yet know that there would be insufficient numbers to stage further forays into France for the geeks' golfing society and that their discordant choir would never again serenade the ferry passengers between Portsmouth and Caen. Mick, of course, would mourn the former but not the latter.

CHAPTER 18
RASUL–ALLAH

THREAD:

It is rare to find a person with a true photographic memory. A person who is capable of recalling almost anything that he chooses, and at will. With my help, Saladin gave the impression that he forgot nothing and had total recall.

Throughout the 2020s, Saladin worked tirelessly to improve his knowledge of Islam. Ten days of intensive study during his *i'tikaf* had been the first step on to the ladder of Sunni Muslim religious hierarchy, during which he had confounded his teachers with his deep knowledge and understanding of the Qur'an. And for ten long years, he devoted many hours in stirring up dissatisfaction with the interpretations and Islamic social decrees, issued by the incumbent Rasul-Allah.

SAUDI ARABIA. 2030.

Opposites rarely agree and in order to win an argument, the contrary interpretation must be more convincing than the original or vice versa.

An unrelenting series of conflicting Islamic theological arguments were leaked over a period of many years by Saladin's growing band of supporters. In support of these authority-diminishing tactics, the offensive camp had many tools from which to choose: misleading headlines, bad press, innuendo, character assassination, sly hints and downright lies; but the most damaging was probably misquotation.

Those whose lives project them into the civic spotlight are often expected to comment on various items of public interest at the drop of a hat. And for those with a particular axe to grind, such moments provide a wealth of opportunities to repeat words that a person thinks are said, or wishes to hear. Correcting misquotes can be an absolute swine for the speaker.

By continually highlighting Saladin's mental ability to retain information and his infallible capability of accurately recalling events from that stock of retained knowledge, allied with a continuous smear campaign, the effectiveness and efficiency of the present Rasul-Allah was repeatedly dragged into question. Given sufficient time, it is certainly possibly to chop down a large oak tree with a penknife; and on every occasion when the leadership of the present Rasul-Allah was challenged, the name of Saladin was associated with it. Not directly, of course, but in a sly, cunning and roundabout way that hid the true intentions of Saladin from the observer.

'You are the true Rasul-Allah, Lord.' So spoke his trusted Lieutenants. 'We who heard the voice of Gabriel by the Great Stone at Mecca know that it is true. Only nod my Lord, and I will take my Scimitar to destroy the imposter who sits on the throne that is truly yours.'

The words, spoken many times by his Scimitar Lieutenants, never failed to raise the hackles on the back of Saladin's neck. He knew his destiny; but he also knew that the imposter must die by his own hand: any connection between himself and the demise of the current Rasul-Allah would be disastrous and douse forever his dreams of global dominance.

Notwithstanding this knowledge of the consequences of such action, Saladin also knew that arranging the imposter's death would be so easy; a Mullah Penny Black in the false eye of one of his own loyal *Fuqaha*[22] paying his annual obeisance to his Master would do the trick.

---

[22]*Fuqaha.* Plural of Faqih.

In his mind, he saw his supporters as legion, Saladin's Legion. He felt an affinity with this word; he loved the historical association and the religious awe that filled his mind whenever he used it. Any one of his legion would fight to the death for the honour of skipping along the smoothly cobbled path to paradise and at the same time propelling their young lord on to the throne of Rasul-Allah. The associated loss of an eye would be a small price to pay.

A few degrees south of the Tropic of Cancer, in the historic Saudi Arabian region of Hejaz, lies the city of Jeddah, nestling on the coast of the Red Sea. In the spring of 2030, a tall, painfully thin man named Khadem al Sadr, spiritual leader of billions of Sunni Muslims around the world, twisted and turned on his simple bunk. Nearby lay the plain white cope that identified the man as Rasul-Allah, folded carefully when he prepared for sleep.

Fretfully Khadem twisted and turned, searching for that most elusive of conscious states to a dog-weary man; rest, peace, oblivion, the darkness and healing state of sleep. Within his own private inner sanctum, the adytum of the Floating Mosque, located near to the centre of the second richest city in the world, the holy man was troubled.

This most revered of Sunni Muslims was under attack. And the attack had been determined and unremitting over the past eight or more years. An intelligent man, completely at home in the complexities of his Qur'an; a quiet man, not given to explosive demonstrative oratory exhibitions; a peaceful man, ever willing to turn the other cheek; a loving man, who saw all of Allāh's children as his own; a generous man, who handed over every single riyal in donations to his religious coffers; and above all else, a Muslim man, complete and sincere in the true sense of the word. A man who lived what he preached, gentle, non-confrontational, a slave to truth; and a man who saw leadership as a gentle guiding hand for his people, his decisions tempered by the controlling influence of the Islamic Century Committee consisting of one hundred Grand Faqihs from around the world.

Confronted with more than one free slot, most men find it difficult to decide which space to occupy in a car park. Conversely, complex decisions that controlled the everyday behaviour of billions of Sunni Muslims were reached only after months of brain-blistering discussion; and the Rasul-Allah bore the final responsibility for every uttered word. Metaphorically, his back was torn to ribbons on a daily basis; each word he uttered was examined from every conceivable angle, his intentions interpreted and challenged in a thousand different ways, and as each day ended it left his mind in a whirlpool of turbulent emotions.

Of late, this good and gentle man had been hallucinating. Always in the dead of night, and within a few minutes of finally reaching the blissful release of sleep, the visions came to him. Constant in content, the picture in his mind was that of a mythical presence, sitting high above him on his throne, dressed in simple clothing, reaching out his arms to his faithful messenger. Soft and persuasive the lilting voice affirmed Khadem's goodness and congratulated him on his work as God's Messenger.

Sometimes the voice highlighted a poor decision or praised him for a better one but always as the vision gradually faded the final message was clear: Allāh had need of a stronger leader, a man of steely resolve and a man who possessed a natural ability to lead.

Whilst not clearly stated, Khadem knew what was required of him. His earthly occupancy of the throne of Allāh must be given up; and he knew that the occasion of his death was the single event that could provide a vacancy.

Sodomy and bestiality are regarded as abominable crimes. Some believe that the taking of one's own life should also be added to the shortlist of man's most immoral acts. And a brain starved of rest, attacked from all angles during every hour of the day and night, is susceptible to almost any suggestion that might alleviate the existing pain and uncertainty.

Khadem al Sadr was an intelligent man, acutely aware of the direction from which his persecution was being coordinated. From the accursed land of England; that tiny nation, that had meddled so often in the affairs of his religion. But on this occasion, the threat would not come from a crusading Christian on a white horse but from another of his own faith.

Al Sadr was also a man of the desert and he knew that when the leopard and the jackal contest ownership of a scrap of meat, it is not often that the leopard goes hungry. Assailed by doubts, indecision and a desire to believe the visions of his Lord Allāh, the tormented mind of Khadem saw himself as the jackal, the Throne of Rasul-Allah represented the scrap of carrion and Saladin was the strong, muscular, undeniable leopard.

In his heart, he knew the answer; his gentle nature was no match for Saladin. At the moment of his death, as he kicked the chair from beneath his feet, Khadem al Sadr spoke the words that had sustained his faith and the only words that had any true meaning for his tortured mind.

'*Lā ilāha ill-Allāh, Masha Allāh.*' There is no god other than Allāh, God has willed it.

CHAPTER 19
POLITICAL INTRIGUE AND INFLUENCE

THREAD:

An increasing demand for oil and gas from the steamroller that was China's spiralling productivity, allied with the carefree attitude of western nations in burning the natural resources of Earth, allowed Mother Russia to give birth to a new era.

This rise in Russia's fortunes was further fuelled by ground-breaking, innovative technology that enabled engineers to reach the reserves of fossil fuels buried beneath the Central Siberian Plateau; and gave the slumbering bear the means to reawaken its aggressive nature. The eyes of the Kremlin turned towards their old dominions and the unstoppable Red Army was loosed upon the Stan countries to the south.

Intended as a trial run to gauge the resolve of the western peace-keeping organisations, Russia launched a devastating missile attack on Afghanistan.

But the Kremlin had a much bolder goal for this strike towards the equator. They wanted a gateway to the Indian Ocean; and Pakistan would therefore have to fall under Russian leadership. The largest of the Stan countries and the natural barrier between the bear to the north and the southerly countries barring the way to the Indian Ocean, Kazakhstan capitulated in seventy-two hours, followed quickly by Afghanistan.

Pummelled by highly trained and well-led tank regiments, which were supported and supplied by Squadron upon Squadron of Russian helicopter gun-ships, the remainder of the Stan countries followed suit and fell like a house of cards. The Russians and Afghans had never been friendly neighbours and the red-blitzkrieg vented its spleen upon its old enemy, with a vicious pounding that left most towns and cities razed to the ground.

A brief pause along the mountain ranges that made up the western border of Pakistan allowed the advancing Red Army a short respite, a chance to resupply and complete minor repairs, before the final push east across the Indus river and south to the sea.

To the Kremlin leaders it was a moment of pause, designed to see what the western world was prepared to do about their latest unsheathing of the Bear's claws. The answer was - nothing, nada, absolutely zilch. Not unsurprisingly to the Russian leaders, after the deathly silence following their trial run into Afghanistan, the machinations of the Western World's peace-keeping organizations had slipped into disarray, discord and a disproportionate disinclination towards military action.

Diplomatic notes, costly world-summits convened all over the Western World, and the verbal banging of war-drums does not a retaliation make. But more specifically, the self-centred national interests of each cooperating western nation had, with one single stroke, nullified years of planning and effort.

There is not a modern army on the face of the Earth that can function without an efficient communications system. And the Western Alliance could no longer communicate; their systems had degenerated into a hopelessly incompatible mismatch of hardware, software and the basic requirement for an international language.

Immediately following the lightning war over the Stan countries, the Western World metaphorically bowed its head and immediately recognized the fresh new face of the phoenix that was the Communist States of Soviet Russia. Many world leaders hoped for a consequential reduction of strife and mistrust in what had always been a deeply troubled part of planet Earth; others sucked in a short, sharp intake of air between their puckered lips and waited.

The Soviet Duma had funds and they had a huge army already

tempered by the harsh realities of battle. They also had a brand new naval base at Karachi that would prove invaluable to their growing seagoing might. Already the cavernous silos were being built, large enough to conceal the keels of twenty-five new nuclear submarines from the ever-circling space spies of the capitalist countries to the west.

Time also was on their hands. Time to turn their minds to other deeply held national grievances. First among these was the deeply-rooted general mistrust of the Western World and its power-hungry, money-grabbing, interfering leaders. Russia could now afford to rekindle the flames of its national characteristics that had for so long been suppressed; namely a fierce competitive spirit and a determination to be first in all human endeavours.

In double-quick time, the message flashed out from the Kremlin. The games were on again, the competition to be first to explore the rest of our Solar System and to bring those far-off worlds under Russian influence; the race to build new weapons of warfare and to extend the use of such weapons into space; and who knows - maybe the first nation to achieve that heady pinnacle of global domination.

For the people of the Earth their rewards would come from the *menu a prix fixe*, namely the return of the cold war and the associated feelings of uncertainty, fear and the cold and clammy expectancy of nuclear warfare. For the leaders of the protagonist country, the returns were of a much finer nature. Selected from the *a la carte menu*, these included the well-remembered, delicious feelings of playing with fire; of brinkmanship; of gambling with the lives of countless millions; and maybe of another term of office awarded by a grateful nation.

In terms of space exploration the years of cooperation and sharing, and of peaceful coexistence, disappeared almost overnight. The most fruitful decade in terms of cementing international relations was the ten years from about 2002 and the end product of this accord had been the continued expansion of the International Space Station (ISS).

This beacon of man's cooperation reflected the Sun's rays, as did every other occupant of space in our Solar System, but the ISS was man-made and it shone as a tribute to mankind's capabilities when acting as one. Permanently manned from the early years of the 21st Century, it had been much enlarged over the years up to about 2010 when public pressure from around the world demanded that a limit be placed upon the vast amounts of money required to complete the project. Financed mainly by the cooperating nations of America, Russia, Japan, Canada and Europe, the ISS cost hundreds of billions of dollars in financial terms, dollars that the vast majority of mankind considered could have been better spent.

But man is a complex organism. And national aspirations can quickly dim a shining light of mutual achievement and cast it into the darkness of grasping greed, forever stunted by the mire that is isolationism. Petty arguments, akin to the antics of children in the school playground, about who-paid-for-what, who-owns-what and who-can-decide-what combined to overwhelm the original international agreements. So much so that by the time of Russia's expansionist aggression, the ISS had become an unmanageable, vastly expensive white elephant.

Neglected, unused, useless - like the single remaining sock from a pair, the ISS continued to orbit the Earth sixteen times a day, travelling at about 28,000 km/h at a height of three hundred and thirty kilometres above the surface of the Earth.

Few shuttles visited the space station and the infant space tourism enterprises fizzled and died as would a faulty firework. There were just too few people on Earth with up to a quarter of a million dollars to spend on a space flight, particularly when it was finally admitted that the body of Mr Average cannot withstand the turmoil of space flight as effectively as that of a highly trained astronaut. Many of the ultra-rich, first-time space-flyers suffered extended periods of severe sickness, stomach pains, a general impairment of their senses and an apparent quickening of existing or developing symptoms. The novelty of space flight for the masses withered and died under astronomical costs, medical suspicion and the will-o-the-wisp that is public opinion.

But the hardware that was the ISS was not dismantled. And the Kremlin had its own plans for it.

THE KREMLIN. SPRING, 2018.

Newly empowered as the President of the Communist States of Soviet Russia (CSSR), Vladimir Voloshin just loved his new, internationally-recognised title.

Moscow, CSSR. In the deep guttural sounds of the Russian tongue it had a certain lyrical ring to it; it sounded of power, influence and domination over a population of many millions of people.

Inside the elaborately decorated central committee room of the Kremlin, Vladimir sat quietly. Despite his languid, almost uncaring body signs, his ears were focussed upon the words of his defence minister. Heavy, deeply-veined hands tapped impatiently on the surface of the table and deeply set eyes studied the pictures of earlier Russian and Soviet leaders scattered around the ornate walls of the huge room. Some in military uniforms with their overly large hats and rows of polished medals: and others in sombre civilian dress, hatless and free of any sign of achievement or public accolade.

'Yes, yes, yes, Comrade Kusnetsov. I hear your pleas to adhere to international agreements and conventions.' The dry palm of a heavy hand pounded flatly on the shiny surface of the giant table, around which the twenty members of the latest Soviet Central Committee sat. 'But we must use our newly-found wealth to strengthen our defences. We must build. To complement the mighty Soviet army we must build a new maritime force that will be the envy of the world. Build a striking force of aircraft that can out-fly anything in the air. And we must, above all, be ready to defend whatever we might claim in space and defend against whatever might attack our nation *from* space. To do this we must know how effective our weapons are under space conditions. The tests will therefore go ahead as planned.'

'The Americans will not take kindly to our flouting intergovernmental agreements. Maybe we are underestimating their will to respond to a more...' Kusnetsov paused, searching for a suitable phrase, '...personal and explosive situation.'

Moscow, CSSR knew for certain that his way was the right way. Only last night he had heard the voice again. *'But no,'* he thought, correcting himself, *'it was not a voice that he heard, more a series of vivid dreams.'* And always these dreams had pointed the way ahead for

Alfred Leonard

him; led him to high military rank; predicted the rise in fortunes for his nation; outlined the strategies that led to the overwhelming of the Stan countries to the south; placed him at the head of the military might that was destined to achieve their nation's desire for a gateway to the southern oceans; and subsequently to the head of this table.

The room was silent. Kusnetsov had finished his final plea for caution. All eyes dwelt upon their President. He sat, dressed in a sombre business suit in which he did not feel entirely comfortable, eyes vacant and cast into the future. A heavy-set man, wide of shoulder and immensely broad at the beam, he would have felt much more at home in his old military fatigues.

Already his insights into the future had witnessed the incredible effects of a nuclear explosion in space. Unhindered by any atmosphere, the explosion had blasted outwards, searching for infinity, to distances of billions of kilometres. Existing space debris, including small asteroids and meteors, rushing to fill the void became contaminated by radiation and passed on to wreak havoc wherever they landed.

'Enough! We haggle and vacillate like old women in a bread queue. The nuclear test will go ahead in space as planned.' Voloshin had reached the limits of his patience and it was time for some leadership. 'Defence will make the arrangements for the test. Finance will make available whatever funds are necessary. And to make the test more realistic, I will choose a target.'

The President of the CSSR was a fit forty-two years of age. He rose from the table with graceful ease, and without word or gesture, left the room. Vladimir Ivanovich Voloshin was happy to talk all day and all night on military or practical matters. But the ramifications of the high finance world left him cold. He would leave those matters to the squinty-eyed public servants that he had left around the table.

As a stepping-stone to Mars and beyond, the ISS did not look very impressive. To the populace of planet Earth it looked to be exactly what it was. A collection of extremely expensive lumps of hardware blasted into space, hastily bolted together as if it was some childish Meccano construction, to sit forever, gazing down on Earth like some ever-hungry deity, fed from the bottomless pit that is man's search for knowledge.

During the course of its building programme, countless millions of human beings were dying from a lack of clean water or food, brought about by the frightening increase in global warming or dying from a whole raft of diseases such as AIDS, cancer, heart problems and those brought on by drug abuse. Most of the world had been involved in some war or another and dissident factions by the dozen screamed loudly their revolutionary rhetoric whilst engaged in their bloody pastime.

And what did the leaders of these dying people do to alleviate these basic human problems? Much as would a dog-weary coalminer, pissing his weekly pay up the wall of his local boozer on a Friday night, they spent billions of dollars on a toy in space.

To the CSSR, the ISS was a target of suspicion. The tricky Americans might have installed almost anything in the parts donated by a generous White House. A less devious western mind may well have scoffed at such ideas but the Russian mind is distrustful of almost everything and who knows what eavesdropping equipment might be in use by any one of the contributing nations.

Acts designed to inflame the feelings of one's perceived enemies achieve their greatest impact if carried out on an auspicious date; the President of the CSSR was very much aware of this fact.

To the crew of the CSSR's first top-secret space-attack vehicle, the ISS was nothing more than another target. Greenwich Mean Time is always used in space, and it was 13.30Z on the 20th November, 2018, exactly twenty years from the date that the first part of the ISS was launched from Earth. Their craft, the first of a new space-destroyer series, designated Korolev Class Attack Vehicles (KLAV1s), used the very latest Starmaker rockets.

The CSSR Air Force had taken control of the cosmodrome at Baikoner, in what had been Kazakhstan, and had built a new space control centre in Western Siberia on one of the many small islands created by the mighty river Ob, as it flowed northwards from the Altay Mountains to the Arctic Ocean. Known to the Soviet space community as Obcon, this new space-control facility was designed as a first-line backup to the existing facilities of Star City near Moscow and had been nominated to control the nuclear test mission.

'Klav1 this is Obcon, target designated as Mission Specific 704; aka the ISS.'

'At last,' breathed the female pilot. She, as Commander of Klav1, and her co-pilot had waited long, boring hours since their launch from Baikoner, circling in space, about three hundred and fifty kilometres above the Earth, waiting for instructions to complete their mission. They knew that the intention was to detonate a nuclear device in space but they had not known at what they would be shooting.

'Obcon from Klav1, roger, target designated Mission Specific 704, wilco.' The hands of the Klav1 pilot flew over the keys of the computer systems, setting coordinates, times, firing points, etc., all designed to achieve a first-time strike. There were no signs of hesitancy or fear in the practised hands of the cosmonauts; they were well trained and had a mission to fulfil. However, a constant companion for the space-destroyer's crew was the underlying uncertainty of just what might happen in the next few hours. Their systems had already informed them that the ISS should be in range to fire their missile in about seven hours. Plenty of time to manoeuvre their craft into a favourable firing position.

Their missile, loaded with a nuclear warhead, was not set for a hot-detonation; the missile would be fired in the general direction of its target, where it would circle until ordered to strike and detonate. Theoretically this should give the Klav1 plenty of time to get out of range and avoid the radiation storm. But this was a first, an untried and unproved mission, and both crew members knew that their fate relied upon all parts of everything going as smoothly as clockwork.

Returning from her work in the small village of Chawton, in the County of Hampshire in southern England, Corinne Streeter was angry. The bloody car had jerked unsteadily to a standstill, leaving her stranded on a nasty stretch of narrow road outside the village primary school. Taller than the average British female, Corinne stood almost two metres in height in her bare feet. Equally as high was the level to which her fiery temper could take her in times of stress, or when clearing up the mess produced by the inadequate efforts of her staff; or anything that did not do exactly what it said on the label.

Already late from her work at the nearby Chawton Library, Corinne had been the last to leave a presentation evening. It was dark, past 21.30, and it was a cold November night - just the circumstances to propel her temper to new heights.

Totally oblivious to the odd passer-by, the tall woman kicked viciously at the wheel of her car. 'Come on! You useless pile of crap. Don't just sit there, do something.' To add insult to injury and further inflame her extreme irritation, her mobile phone whimpered and died. The pain from her right foot, having just managed to travel the couple of metres from the ground, registered in her brain. 'Bastard, bugger,' the invectives worsened as they streamed from her mouth and ended with a childish, 'bloody biggy-boggies.' With the final words her mood lightened, the childish expression always transported her to a happy childhood and memories of a mother that she had adored.

Calmly the tall figure locked her car and raised her face to the heavens, searching maybe for a sign of forgiveness for her fuming outburst. It was a clear night, the Moon shone brightly in the night sky and the uncountable stars flickered an indecipherable message around the Universe. 'A hard frost tonight,' she whispered to herself, speaking quietly in awe at the sight above her.

But what was that? A huge explosion of light in the sky. Close, it felt close. And there, a shooting star - no, another, and yet more. 'Bloody hell,' she shouted, 'there are thousands of them.' They were quite the most beautiful fireworks that she had ever seen, eclipsing the giant rocket displays she had seen a few short weeks before at Alton's Guy Fawkes celebrations. The blast came about two minutes later, knocking her to the ground, more in shock than in physical reaction.

Pieces of the ISS of all shapes and sizes, now little more than space debris, entered the Earth's atmosphere. This storm of radioactive debris produced an aurora borealis effect in the skies, a myriad of coloured lights twisting and turning around the heavens that mesmerised the watchers below.

Most onlookers surmised that it was a natural phenomenon; others assumed the Earth had been in collision with a passing asteroid or meteor; yet more considered that some experimental air or space craft had blown up as it left Earth's gravity; and a few put their fingers on the button.

But not the crew of Klav1 or the Kremlin leaders or anyone else on Earth could possibly know the terrible train of events that had been triggered by this event. And many decades were to pass before the monstrous aftermath rained its destruction upon Earth.

CHAPTER 20
STRIKE INTO EUROPE

THREAD:

The whole world now knew the identity of the leader of al-Shamshir. But as Rasul-Allah he was untouchable, a fact that Saladin had known decades before when he had first chosen the name of his extremist group. Al-Shamshir, the Scimitar; even this *nom de guerre* was chosen as a means of inflaming the world's security services and giving heart to the billions of Muslims around the world.

Rasul-Allah; al-Shamshir; a stone in the shoe of the planet's infidel security organisations; but a shining-light of hope and glory to the Muslim multitudes.

The years since his elevation to the throne of Rasul-Allah had been good to Saladin. Using his uncanny knack of being able to identify those who opposed his leadership, he had quickly established control over the world's Muslim population, weeding out those that disagreed with his policies and interpretations and replacing them with others whose beliefs more closely matched his own.

Extremist activities continued throughout the UK mainland, intended as an attempt to destabilise the established political framework of his homeland.

The first decade of the 21st century had been particularly rewarding. The attacks that he had masterminded on the country's transport

246

systems and on the royal family, together with the period of Muslim rebellion, had achieved much in depleting the confidence of the British people in their existing political systems and leaders.

But Saladin thought it entirely unfair that the people of his homeland should bear the brunt of the suffering and that dog-shaped chunk of Europe, west of the Carpathian Mountains, contained countries overflowing with non-believers, fully deserving of a bloodletting visit from his Scimitars. Not the least of which was one particular country that had afforded a most un-Gallic welcome to his parents so many years before; France.

MILLAU BRIDGE, FRANCE. OCTOBER 2035.

Trafalgar Day, 21st October, 2035. Cold and damp, the ground covered in a heavy early morning dew. At 04.30, it was still quite dark, although the Moon, when not obscured by burgeoning clouds, made an effort to light up their surroundings.

Off to their left was the arterial road route, the A75 motorway that links Paris to Barcelona. Still wet from the previous night's heavy storm, the road was already busy with passing traffic and the steady whoosh-whoosh of fast-spinning rubber wheels had kept the whole attack group from sleep for most of the night.

Silent and tense, the eleven men that made up this attack group of al-Shamshir remained perfectly still. Consisting of the four-man teams of the First and Second Scimitars, together with their leaders *Hajji* Abu Tamimi and *Hajji* Azzam Abdullah, and the eleventh man was none other than Rasul-Allah. Although they could not be seen from the road, they all remembered the chilling words of their illustrious leader, Saladin, Rasul-Allah.

'Total silence is paramount.' Spoken the previous evening and followed after a dramatic short pause by: 'We will communicate with hand signals only.' And the intensely blue eyes had burned to their very souls as he added, after a much longer pause. 'You all know the penalty for disobedience, discovery, or failure.'

To a man, the two Scimitars felt highly honoured. Their well-loved leader had elected to accompany them on this, the first of many such raids on the mainland of Europe.

A slight rustle of noise and all eyes swung towards their leader. Saladin stood, stretched, yawned silently and urinated where he stood. He leaned across to touch Abu Tamimi, who gave the hand signal which meant *'Wake your opposite number and check equipment'*.

Almost as one the bodies began to rise. They too stretched cramped muscles and gently rubbed stiff limbs into action. All were dressed identically in the very latest British army issue camouflage battledress, their faces blackened above beard level.

The group had assembled the previous evening just before midnight in the wide valley cut by the river Tarn over millions of years. Beneath the towering uprights of the Millau Bridge is a small copse of trees and it was there that the rendezvous had been ordered.

The highly trained and disciplined teams had each travelled to France via different routes, using various means of transport and stolen identities. They wore everyday westernised travel clothes and carried minimal hand baggage containing only the simple necessities for survival and hygiene.

Painstakingly a little at a time, all other equipment and explosives had been smuggled into the country during the preceding months. Saladin's Islamic Army, as he chose to refer to his multitude of ordinary law-abiding, hard working but intensely religious and patriotic Muslim supporters, had not failed him. They had ferried in the new American special services limpet-mine that in a few hours' time would bring down the mighty bridge above them.

Despite the blackness of the early morning, Saladin could see the outline of the bridge towering above him. Heavy rain had started to fall once again and the wind had increased in its ferocity. As he craned his head backwards to look up at the bridge it appeared to shift, almost imperceptibly, from side to side and he could hear the wind moaning through the huge cables supporting the bridge. The bridge's movements gave him a giddy, nauseous moment and he quickly lowered his head.

'The wind is a sign of support from Allāh.' Saladin's mind continually searched nature for such signs of heavenly condonation for his actions.

'Whoever had designed the new camouflage suits had done a very good job,' reflected Saladin. They were completely impervious to water and

wind; covered the entire human body, including head and feet; and vented excess heat and perspiration.

The attack team were ready to move in just a few minutes, sufficient time to tighten bootlaces and check that nothing was left in the surrounding overnight campsite. They did not carry weapons, they would not be needed on this or any other of Saladin's operations for the team was expected to make a bid for paradise if discovered by the authorities or apprehended. They all carried a means of escape in the form of a suicide pill.

Each of the five-man teams carried two limpet-mines and a bag containing a dozen spares. It would take just a few minutes to attach them to the central supporting tier of the immense structure above them. A two-hour time delay would give the attacking group plenty of time to disperse before detonation. Saladin's pockets were empty. He was merely an observer and had accompanied the attack group in the face of the strongest opposition from his own Islamic council.

Before making his plans for this attack, Rasul-Allah had thought very carefully about the statement he wished to make to the world. *Le Grand Viaduc de Millau*, opened in 2005 and built at enormous cost by a private consortium, was not due to revert to state ownership until 2045 at the earliest. However, the French Government had decided that the profits from the bridge had far exceeded their expectations and had announced their intention of reclaiming the income from the bridge commencing December 2035. Saladin knew that it would infuriate the French to discover that they would firstly have to rebuild it.

Since the late 2020s, the French as a nation had won the reputation of being the 'cry-babies of Europe'. They made long, vociferous and sympathetic meows about the misfortunes of other nations, from both extremist groups and natural causes, but found themselves collectively unable to provide much in terms of material aid. However, when the misfortune occurred on French soil, or involved France in any way, their cries of woe resonated around the globe, demanding aid, support and the most heinous punishment for the perpetrators and for the authorities who had so pathetically failed to foresee the calamity.

Following his planned demolition of the Millau Bridge, Saladin knew that the demands from the French government would resound around the world and give many a world leader a few sleepless nights.

And in the process catapult his fame towards the heady realms of legend.

In single file, the group left their concealment and followed their leader towards the central pier of the bridge. Almost torrential, the rain was driven into their bodies by the ever-increasing power of the wind. The splatter of huge raindrops falling on to the sparse foliage was deafening to the group of tense attackers. Their footfalls, squelching through the mud, made loud sucking sounds that all could plainly hear, even above the sound of the wind.

They did not consider themselves to hold extremist views; to them every person not a Muslim was an enemy and, as such, a legitimate target in their quest to impose Islamic beliefs on the infidels of the world.

However, this was to be the first of a series of Saladin's hammer blows against the Christian nations of Europe. He considered himself to be the sword of Allāh and he intended a reign of terror throughout the rich countries of Western Europe over the next few months and years.

His sword would fall on many targets, particularly during the Christian festive season. Actions that would claim countless lives, cause severe damage, and inflame the feelings of his countrymen. Such actions would invoke a gentle, admonishing, symbolic wagging of the finger by Christianity's feeble leaders, accompanied by eulogies for the mass deaths, spoken in soft voices, using words designed to soften the hardening fist of hatred in the guts of Europe's population, imploring forgiveness for the perpetrators.

'We must turn the other cheek,' Saladin could already hear the pacifying declaration by the Archbishop of Canterbury. 'Our Lord will find an answer.'

The base of the huge concrete pillar was enormous in diameter. Saladin had a brief moment of doubt and he wondered if the small limpet charges could do the job. But he had witnessed the power of these tiny explosive devices; he knew the destructive power that just a single charge could produce. Weighing a little over two kilograms, each member of the team carried two. Ten charges were attached to the huge tower at head height, and by the simple process of standing on each other's shoulders, another ten about two metres higher. Apart from its small size and destructive power, the most useful attribute of the limpet mine, known colloquially by US servicemen as the Slug, was that it would adhere to almost any surface, wet, dry or covered in ice.

Fumbling any part of this operation would attract dire consequences from their eagle-eyed leader. Each of the group had practised this part of the operation on numerous occasions and all went according to plan. In a matter of three minutes all the charges were set, and timed to explode at 08.30.

Loss of life was not a priority in this attack; a statement was what Saladin wanted. At precisely 08.31, one minute after the limpet mines exploded, the French DGSIT[23] was destined to receive a phone call, claiming that the destruction of the French government's next source of income, the Millau Bridge, would occur at 09.00.

The difference in time between actual and claimed detonation was Saladin's own additional twisting of the knife. As soon as the claim was confirmed, Saladin knew that the message would fly around the world that al-Shamshir's Islamic extremist group, led by Saladin. Rasul-Allah was capable of carrying out extremist attacks in Europe. Ominously, the message would include a warning of future attacks, involving the death or mutilation of thousands of Islam's enemies throughout the world.

Saladin could not resist the temptation to watch the result of his group's endeavours. Parked in a small lay-by, he waited to the side of the D41 road that followed the course of the river Tarn. A kilometre short of the hamlet of Peyre he sat nervously twiddling his fingers and praying silently. The wait seemed interminable and despite the storm raging around the large and comfortable MVW car, Saladin had a clear view of the bridge.

At 08.15, the torrential rain suddenly ceased and the wind dropped to a gentle breeze. Low in the eastern sky the weak autumnal Sun burned through the clouds but gave little warmth despite its enormous size and brightness. Rare are the signs of Allāh's pleasure, particularly for those who doubt his presence, but this was surely a sign from paradise; and the heart of Rasul-Allah leapt with joy. Oh, how he wished that he had kept his Lieutenants with him. For a verbal description of this moment would have girded the loins of the few

---

[23]DGSIT. General Directorate for Internal Security and Terrorism.

faint-hearted amongst his followers, particularly if told by someone other than himself.

Nevertheless, the opportunity once afforded by heaven must not be overlooked and he took a few moments to describe the moment on his Pewi, always careful not to include any information other than a description of the general ambience of the day.

Tempus fugit, but slowly, and at 08.29 the plush leather and walnut trimmed interior of the car seemed to wrap itself around him. It had become very hot inside the vehicle and Saladin pressed the button to lower the window. His hands shook a little as he reached into his pocket for the spare Pewi, purchased in Glasgow the previous week and registered to a fictitious Polish immigrant.

Amazingly blue eyes focused on the centre of the bridge, he tried hard not to blink for fear of missing the moment. Hand shaking slightly he held his personal Pewi out of the side of the car; it would record the entire event.

A gentle bleep, bleep, from the car's internal alarm system resembled a loud clap of thunder to Saladin as that final, never-ending minute ticked to an end. 08.30 and Saladin saw a cloud of dust and debris blossom from the base of the central tower of the bridge, followed almost immediately by the muffled sound of the explosion.

Nothing happened for a few more seconds, during which the wire-suspension system attempted to hold the weight of the bridge. Suddenly a cable snapped, the whip-crack clearly heard by Rasul-Allah, followed by another and another. The northbound carriageway dropped about a metre and a fully laden coach, a heavy articulated lorry and a fast moving car in the outer lane headed for the side of the bridge, hit the retaining walls and came to a standstill in a mess of twisted metal.

Two sections of the bridge, some three hundred metres north and south of the damaged support, dipped crazily earthwards. Vehicles of all shapes and sizes careered into space in a macabre, unrestrained bungee-jump.

Bored drivers travelling at speeds far in excess of the legal limit had very little warning of the disaster awaiting them; and for some time the number of vehicles that simply drove off the edge surprised the gawping extremist leader. His demonic laughter echoed inside the car as he thought how the falling vehicles reminded him of coconuts tumbling off their stands at an English fairground.

Inside the car, Saladin realised that all was quiet. The normal susurration and general hum of passing traffic had suddenly ceased as the two sections of the bridge collapsed into the valley below.

Out of Saladin's sight, the carnage beneath the bridge was a terrifying sight. As the falling vehicles hit the ground, they detonated the remainder of the limpet mines that had been scattered around the area by the Scimitars. The explosions caused further shock and confusion, enormous loss of life and mutilation to those that had survived the drop.

A few kilometres back up the motorway a large French lorry poodled along in the nearside lane. Travelling at the obligatory speed limit of 80 km/h the driver was bored rigid. He had been behind the wheel for almost four hours and it was almost time for a breakfast stop.

Gaspard Briand was forty-three years old, still a bachelor and had no intention of ever getting married. Implanted firmly in his brain were too many memories of bloody battles between his own parents to risk matrimonial status. Dog weary, he had been on the road for almost twenty-four hours since leaving Liverpool and his concentration was wavering; but he loved his chosen profession and lavished care on the big Renault tractor-cab.

Controlling the progress of his huge truck was automatic to this man and his mind started to wander, thinking about the forthcoming engine and brake service that the truck would need in a few days' time.

Suddenly aware of a coach some fifty metres in front of him, he shouted aloud, 'Damn, too close,' suddenly realising that he had not noticed any brake lights on the coach reflecting their shimmering redness on the wet road. Too late, he knew it, as he pressed his foot on to the jake-brake, pulled the transmission brake to the full-on position and jammed his other foot hard on to the foot brake.

Eyes glued on the coach in front of him he saw it lurch to the side and disappear out of sight. Frightened and shocked he could not comprehend what had happened. He felt an enormous jolt and peering into his off-side mirror he saw the rear-most of his two trailers, loaded with brand-new cars, jack-knife into the outer lane of traffic, ripping the connecting dolly from its sister trailer. Eyes bulging with fear and the preknowledge of impending disaster, he kept all braking systems engaged and as a last resort, slammed on the hand brake.

A broken cable whipped across the road, followed by the whine of a shockingly loud twang, which narrowly missed Gaspard and slashed into the trailer behind the cab. The weight of the strike slowed the lorry as it slid towards the abyss in front of him.

The cab-over-engine design of his lorry gave him a good view of the road ahead and he watched with growing dread as the front wheels of his cab, smoke billowing from each wheel with the heat of braking, dropped over the edge. The dead weight of the trailer saved him and the vehicle came to a grinding halt, teetering over the edge, the cab at ninety degrees to the trailer.

Seat belts were for wimps as far as the French lorry driver was concerned, for they restricted as well as restrained movement, and he had fitted a large elastic band to the end of his. When the truck came to a sudden stop, Gaspard had been driven forward and he sat, dazed, badly shaken by the experience and with blood filling his right eye.

Raising his eyes heavenwards, he thanked Him above for saving his life. He unhooked the elastic band on his seat belt and pushed open the door of the cab. Slowly, carefully, making no sudden moves, Gaspard eased his way out of the cab and started climbing back towards the trailer to the relative safety of the road.

In his peripheral vision, he saw several cars burst over the edge of the precipice and disappear from his view into oblivion. He almost made it and was desperately hanging on to a handhold at the rear of the cab.

A soft thud attracted his attention and he saw the crumpled side of a small car slide over the edge, having sideswiped his lorry. The collision did not move the lorry forward but the tremor from the shock of impact sounded a death-knell deep within the mind of the hapless Gaspard. His feet lost their grip on his tenuous foothold, he felt the full weight of his body transfer on to his arms and he hung suspended over that frightful drop for several minutes.

Slowly, his mind in a whirl of indecision and fear, the once strong muscles in his arms and shoulders turned to jelly. Shaking uncontrollably, he knew he was doomed and, as the blood finally drained from his fingers, he could hold on no longer. As he dropped towards certain death, he looked up at his cab in which he had spent so much of his life. He saw the cab separate from the trailer and it was following him to the ground; he surmised that the fifth wheel had finally given up the ghost.

Suddenly resigned, Gaspard discovered to his extreme surprise that he was not frightened. Gazing upwards, he saw the outline of a woman, naked above the waist; launch herself over the edge of the bridge. Her skirt billowed around her body like a parachute and her huge breasts flattened against her breastbone with the force of the wind. Their eyes locked together, the woman's young face smiling, welcoming death and the certain release from whatever had been tormenting her.

Later, when the scenes were played over and over in news bulletins all around the world, the more macabre of viewers zoomed into watch her face as she fell and saw the peace settle over her features as she mouthed the words, 'Thank you!'

Contrary to popular belief, the shock of facing certain death does not always hasten that event and Gaspard was aware of his surroundings all the way down. The seemingly never-ending fall seemed to last for an eternity. It all happened in accentuated slow motion and Gaspard's feeble efforts to flap his arms to escape from the truck, which was dropping at shocking speed towards him, were hampered by a sudden inability to move a muscle.

'Merde, mon dieu.' Whichever God that Gaspard cried out to in his final bid for salvation was not listening for Gaspard was still alive when the weight of his beloved cab drove his shattered body deep into the soft earth.

Saladin had watched the driver of the truck as he lost his grip on the cab of his lorry and fell to his death and almost burst into laughter when he saw the young woman run towards the edge of the road, tearing frantically at her clothing and launch herself into eternity.

Some few minutes after the two sections fell very slowly and ungracefully into the valley, mimicking a ballet dancer crumbling during a performance, the remainder of the bridge started to wobble alarmingly. Other strands of wire began to snap, removing the tops of high vehicles and anything else in their path. Despite the wobbles, the rest of the bridge remained intact and slowly the traffic came to a standstill. The queues reaching back north and south as far as the eye could see.

Already he had taken a tremendous risk by delaying his departure from the scene. With a feeling of deep satisfaction, the new Messiah quickly set the Pewi to transmit the pictures to the French press association and dropped the unit outside the car.

He also dropped a small lipstick container. It might just provide some extra, time-consuming work for the French authorities, not to mention some confusing evidence when they tracked the associated DNA from both pieces of equipment, to a very small and very sweet monkey at a zoo in Delhi.

Reluctantly he left the scene and headed in a northwesterly direction. A private jet awaited him at an airfield just north of Rodez.

CHAPTER 21
THAMES ATTACK

THREAD:

In any large city, there are people about at any time of the day or night. Whether they be party-goers returning from some celebratory bean feast or jet-lagged tourists struggling to deal with the crossing of many time-zones, wearing out the carpets in their hotel rooms by wandering from room to room and gaping out of the window for some inspiration to pass the time, or wondering whether to risk the wrath of the hotel staff by demanding room-service.

Whether they are night-workers banned from smoking in their work-place, sneaking a crafty drag at a cigarette, or the numerous bag-people and general detritus of humanity that make their home in any inner city.

London was no different. During the darkest hours of the night in any city in the world, the streets seem deserted. But there are people about, lying in doorways, sheltering on or below park benches, or sleeping in the open parks - covered in an old overcoat or a flimsy layer of discarded wrapping paper, newspaper, or cardboard box. Some cuddle a pet cat or dog for additional warmth; others cling to the remains of an empty bottle, a last empty syringe or the rapidly fading memories of a lost life.

Christmas Day, 25th December, 2040. Saladin was now thirty-seven years old, his beard already showing signs of grayness but his bright blue eyes still glowed with a fanaticism that controlled his every thought and action. Over the past few weeks, he had held many planning meetings with the leaders of his eight Scimitars.

Even the two Scimitars from the weapons laboratory in Scotland had been ordered south. For many of his Lieutenants these meetings had been boring in the extreme but they had been especially careful not to display any such boredom or disinterest. They all knew that their leader had the most uncanny knack of knowing exactly which of them allowed their minds to wander; and the punishments for such lapses were extreme indeed.

Saladin had planned a Christmas present for his Christian countrymen.

LONDON, ENGLAND. 25TH DECEMBER, 2040.

Eyes sore and aching with tiredness, Saladin had been at his local mosque in Birmingham since 01.30. He had made an attempt at sleep for a few hours before that time but had failed. His mind was in turmoil, for this was to be his first attempt at a coordinated, full-scale attack on England's capital. In common with all other military leaders, he was fraught with doubt about his planning. Had he missed anything? Had he given his Scimitars sufficient time to make the attack and still make good their escape? Would the yet untried bazookas perform effectively? Were his selected targets the best available? How much coverage in tomorrow's national newspapers would be allocated to his exploits? Would he finally surpass the reverence in which his peers held earlier Islamic extremist leaders, Bin Laden especially? For his was not necessarily a Holy War, or a real attempt to impose Islamic dominance throughout the world. He gave that impression to all and sundry; but deep in his own heart, he listened to the voice of his mentor and saw only fame and fortune for himself. Saladin! The greatest Islamic leader since Muhammadpbuh.

Kneeling on his prayer mat and facing east towards Mecca, the fears and doubts continued to haunt him. Seeking confirmation of the exactness of his planning and to calm his fevered and doubting brain, he prayed for the magical words from above. And the moment that he heard the words, he knew that tonight's efforts would be rewarded with justifiable success.

'*Calm your fears, Saladin.*' The voice, deep, rich and with a very faint Australian accent, came into his mind. Saladin sighed loudly, he was instantly calmed. The attack would go faultlessly, of that he was now absolutely assured.

The conversation with the voice of Gabriel continued for some minutes, during which details of various police, military and homeland protection surveillance operations around the capital were relayed to him. Using his group's personal satellite system, zoned-in to cover a footprint of the Thames area of London and protected by his own crypto-system, he would now be able to guide his teams to their targets and aid them as much as possible in their escape.

The conversation with his Lord ended with Saladin's usual plea for a personal appearance. The request was always denied but the denial did not deter Saladin from making the request.

'Almighty Gabriel, praised above all other Angels, grant me the wish of your appearing before me.' And Josh had to suppress a huge guffaw, as he saw the vision in Saladin's mind. That of Gabriel, a tall, but slightly bent figure, with an unfashionably long beard, obviously extremely aged and dressed in the ubiquitous Arab djellabah. Strangely, Saladin's vision did not show a spotless djellabah but an off-white robe stained in many places and with a rim of dirt around the hem. And, most importantly, and this was the reason for Josh's suppressed laughter, Gabriel appeared before Saladin and appeared at a much lower level than the eyes of the Muslim leader.

At this vision, Josh made a mental note to speak to Volly the Verguide, his own personal nickname for me. Maybe they had pandered too closely to this Muslim firebrand's ego? Maybe it was time to bring him down a peg or two? An idea took shape in Josh's mind; perhaps a personal visit might be possible?

Matching perfectly the character of its leader, the al-Shamshir communications system was egotistically one-way. Saladin passed on the good news about the successful conclusion to tonight's activities.

'Gabriel has spoken with me this night.' At these words, all eight Scimitars turned solemnly to the east, fell to their knees and made obeisance to Allāh and Rasul-Allah. Each of the eight Lieutenants raised their heads to check that all members of their own Scimitar remained with their heads bowed; they would not hesitate to inform their illustrious leader of any misconduct.

Each group was standing on the edge of the river Thames, on the Isle of Dogs. They were surrounded by their inflatable rafts which were the latest Royal Marine design and equipped with the nearly silent running Wankel engines. As far as they were aware, they were unobserved. They had agreed with a suggestion from Saladin that all groups should embark from the same point and at the same hour. All groups should then complete their mission at about the same time.

Opposite the man-made aquatic centre, on the southern edge of the Isle of Dogs, is a long, sloping ramp. Squeezed between two huge, high-rise blocks of flats this entrance to the Thames had been saved from development because it was reserved for access by river police, water ambulance services and fire-fighting organisations. Gently sloping from the main road it was littered with broken Tarmac and dry-waves of small stones and rubbish washed up from the tides.

Benjamin Abel, formerly a well-to-do city slicker and previously immensely successful whilst trading on the London Stock Exchange, was asleep in the doorway of one of the ground-floor flats. He did not feel the chill, despite the cooler temperatures of England's winter. Late the previous evening he had managed to lift a handbag from an ever-so-slightly tipsy female couple returning from a Christmas Eve celebration. The contents of the handbag totalled a mere £534; the reward for his daring raid could not be classified as rich pickings. And his first thought was not that of satisfying his belly-rumbling hunger for food but of the number of refills that he could purchase for his already overworked hypodermic needle.

Ben had self-administered his last injection shortly after midnight. He had wandered into the doorway of a block of flats, wrapped his old raincoat around his thin, emaciated body and fallen into a deep, dreamless sleep. He did not dream of Santa Claus bringing him beautiful presents, or of frolicking with his family on Christianity's most holy day. For he could never again dream of any family connections; he had been disowned several years previously after systematically stealing from each and every one of them.

But something had disturbed his drug-fuelled slumber. He heard it again, a scuffling on the slipway leading down to the water. He had no idea of the time. He knew it was early morning because the London night was jet black, not a sign of the Moon in the totally overcast sky. Crawling on his belly, he edged towards the side of the slipway. He had little interest in what had disturbed him, just as long as it was not someone sneaking up on him to steal his last hit. He would need that in the morning to help him face another day of street-wise activity, scheming and stealing, trying to find the necessary funds to fuel his ever-demanding hunger.

Peering over the wall, he saw several ominous-looking shapes. His half-open eyes, filled with the mucous of sleep and partially blurred from his evening of hard-hitting, struggled to focus on the scene before him. A small giggle burst forth from his throat and he saw what he took to be a group of penguins, huddled together on the stony ground betwixt water and slipway. Confused, drug-induced hallucinations; Ben was well used to those! But this was something completely different; a group of penguins, their skins gleaming in a short burst of moonlight. And the group had their own boats.

'For Christ sake, what do penguins need with boats?'

Ben had spoken aloud. A mistake that would cost him dearly. The dark shape of one of the penguins stretched itself to its full height and to Ben's befuddled mind seemed to cross the dozen or so metres between them in the twinkle of an eye.

'Hello, little penguin, what...' The first blow to his temple stunned Ben. He tried to open his mouth to scream. *'Why does this bloody penguin want my last hit?'* This was his last thought before he departed this world.

'Bismillah!' A long arm was raised high into the air above his victim's head and *Hajji* Abu Tamimi, the leader of the First Scimitar, struck downwards, hard and fast.

'Poor bastard.' Tamimi spoke in English, as he turned the piece of infidel trash over with his toe. 'Probably done him a favour,' he whispered to himself, and attempted a cruel, tyrannical smile in the characteristic way of his leader.

In the absence of Saladin, Tamimi assumed the role of group Commander. When the eight Scimitars separated into their individual groups, he would lead Scimitar one.

The killing of the junkie had provided a welcome release of tension for Tamimi. But there was no visible sign of this release and not a sound came from the group. Tamimi, ever the trusted First Lieutenant, remembered Saladin's orders. 'Leave no trace or evidence of your passing.'

Tamimi picked up the long, sausage-shaped stone that had battered the life out of Benjamin Abel. This was not the place to discard such crucial evidence. He would stow it safely in his boat and drop it overboard far down-stream. He knew how clever the law enforcement authorities were and how much information they would glean from such a seemingly unimportant piece of evidence.

Second-in-command to the great Rasul-Allah, Tamimi knew that he would have to report the killing of the homeless bagman. His illustrious leader seemed always to know of operational events that did not coincide with the well-rehearsed plan. But his misgivings had to be firmly pushed to one side; there were more important events on which to concentrate. And it was almost time to commence the attack.

The luminous face of his watch showed 03.55; in five minutes they would embark on another daring plan devised by Rasul-Allah. An attack on targets on both the north and south banks of the River Thames. Each Scimitar had been allocated its own specific targets, just two per Scimitar, a bridge and a building.

Each of the eight Scimitars had a supply of the latest al-Shamshir modified limpet mines. Based upon the American's Slug but specially adapted for firing from a portable bazooka-style launcher, these limpet mines stuck to any surface on contact. Each Scimitar carried twenty mines and two bazookas. Expecting misfires and software errors when fired from an unstable, wobbly boat, they would fire ten at each target.

Tamimi's First Scimitar would take the two most important targets. The British Houses of Parliament, located in Westminster Palace, and Tower Bridge.

Hajji Azzan Abdullah would lead his Second Scimitar to attack the

Homeland Protection Department (HPD), the headquarters of which were located in Lambeth Bridge House (LBH), and Lambeth Bridge itself.

Launching the limpet mines at the International Protection Department (IPD), on the south side of Vauxhall Bridge, and at Vauxhall Bridge itself, would be the Third Scimitar, led by the young *Hajji* Anjem Uzair.

The Fourth Scimitar would make an attempt on the London Eye and on London Bridge. Its leader *Hajji* Omar Izzadeen had not yet been blooded in battle and would be watched closely by Saladin.

Under the command of their over-zealous Lieutenant, the Fifth Scimitar was ordered to bomb St Thomas' Hospital and Blackfriars Bridge. The oldest of Saladin's Lieutenants by some three years, *Hajji* Ramzi Choudary could be relied upon to press his attack in the face of almost any opposition.

Really spectacular targets had become hard to find by Rasul-Allah and his planners but they had decided to allot bridges as the primary targets for the last three Scimitars, with secondary targets selected at random.

For the Eighth Scimitar, under the leadership of a somewhat suspect *Hajji* Shuja Khyam, the primary target was Southwark Bridge and the secondary was scheduled to be the headquarters of the London Fire Brigade, housed on the south-bank almost opposite Lambeth Bridge House.

Hajji Omar Babar, it was said by his compatriots, would follow Saladin into hell. He would not, his Scimitar hoped, be required to demonstrate such loyalty this night. For the Seventh Scimitar was assigned the London TV centre and Waterloo Bridge. And Babar's troops knew full well that nothing, short of death, would deter their leader from pressing home his attack.

Saladin's favourite, the slightly built, almost effeminate *Hajji* Ramzi Mahmood, led the Sixth Scimitar. With facial features as beautiful as any woman and similarly free of hair, Mahmood attracted women like flies around animal droppings. He was the only member of Saladin's close team of Lieutenants that was beardless, a very special concession from Rasul-Allah who preyed upon the flock of pretty young things that pandered to the handsome *hajji's* every wish. The leader of this Scimitar was not a fearless fighter and would not press

Alfred Leonard

an attack too hard if challenged. His targets were therefore the easiest. Chelsea Bridge; furthest downstream and HMS *Belfast*.

Saladin had, rather rashly, argued with the voice that he accepted as Gabriel. He had been ordered to leave Westminster Bridge as the only route across the river. But he desperately wanted to destroy it. Gabriel had been stern in his reply.

'Saladin. I made and named you Rasul-Allah.' The tone of the voice had set the hairs on the back of Saladin's neck a-tingle. He knew that he had over-stepped the mark and wisely remained silent.

'We will leave the bridge intact. The congestion and confusion generated by the whole of London's road users attempting to cross this bridge in the weeks and months ahead will also further delay and harass the city's rescue services.' And, after a slight delay, a very ominous, *'Hear my words, and obey.'*

Saladin had dropped his forehead to the floor in deference, *'Bismillah*, so be it my lord Gabriel.'

At the Isle of Dogs, Tamimi was whispering a short prayer to his attacking force. 'God is great; there is but one God. Allāh be praised, and we rejoice in the words of his true prophets, Muhammadpbuh who sat at the feet of our Lord; and Rasul-Allah who is destined to sit at the right hand of Allāh.' Saladin had trained his Lieutenants well and the new Muslim invocation was spreading like a raging forest fire throughout the Islamic communities around the world.

'After today's attack, the name of Rasul-Allah will fill the mind of every true believer in Islam. His name will shine brightly, like a new star in the heavens.' And, thought Tamimi, *'My own fame and fortune will grow with his.'*

Each of the eight Scimitars clustered together around their boats. All looked at Tamimi. They had proclaimed their allegiance to the one true superhuman in whispered tones and awaited the signal to commence their assault on their adoptive nation's capital.

Patiently the attack groups of al-Shamshir waited. They watched as Tamimi's eyes filled with a glaring, fanatical glint. Tamini raised both arms in the air, in an imitation of Saladin, with six fingers pointing to the heavens: *Jihad.* Al-Shamshir wanted to scream in recognition of the sign but wisely screwed tightly down upon their vocal chords.

Many people saw something of the eight boats, silently phutting upstream from the Isle of Dogs, four on the north side and four on the south side. But not a single person thought much of the sightings. Of those that saw the odd boat, most considered that the British were an odd group of individuals, strange in their habits and hobbies, and dismissed the sightings as some crazy fishing expedition on Christmas Day.

Police Constable Jim Newgent could well have scotched the whole attack, had he not been fast asleep dreaming of cavorting with his next-door-neighbour's wife. He had parked his patrol car between two over-nighting coaches parked illegally on the embankment. His intentions were to have a quiet snooze for about ten minutes, wake the unsuspecting coach drivers and give them a good ticking-off and a parking fine. But Jim was dog-tired, after a day of caring for his four young children, whilst his ever-fruitful wife languished in hospital delivering the fifth.

Had he been awake and alert, he would have seen at least three of the attack boats, clearly silhouetted in an infrequent, brief moment of moonlight. Unfortunately for Jim, his career took a sudden nose-dive; he would never make Sergeant, he had missed a golden opportunity. Forty-eight hours after the attack, infrared satellite imagery provided by the American's CIA would show the patrol car parked for over two hours alongside the embankment with a clear view over the Thames. It would also show the eight attack boats, chugging slowly past in front of Jim. When the constable's event-log was later scrutinized, in the presence of no less a personage than Jim's divisional police Commander, he was mortified to hear his own written comment read aloud, '04.00, QAP.'

'Quiet and peaceful!' The red-faced Commander was clearly furious. 'You must be f - f - f,' - the Commander was desperate to swear, but he had his very pretty young assistant in the room - 'Flippin-fick.'

'Quiet and peaceful! My Christ, eight terrorist boats in front of your eyes, loaded to the gills with bazooka bombs, intent on creating hell and havoc.'

The Commander had a most unfortunate muscle defect around the left side of his mouth which caused him to dribble slightly when he lost his temper. Spittle flew in all directions. The Commander was really rattled and warming nicely to the dressing-down that he had planned for his unfortunate Officer. 'And on my bloody patch too! On my patch! My patch!' His voice seemed to leap an octave with each statement. He was the most senior of London's divisional Commanders and there would soon be a vacancy for commissioner. Such dreams of the gleaming badges of rank on his shoulders and of a much-increased pension began to fade. 'And you ruined my bloody Christmas, you excuse for a bloody, uh, uh.' The Commander just could not think of a suitable epithet and finished his comment with a weak, 'Wanker.'

'If I had my way, you would be hung, drawn and quartered. But I can't. Can I?' The Commander cast a hopeful glance at his assistant, maybe she had been able to find some more severe punishment to apportion, since last they had spoken. 'All I can do is return you to the beat. And a bloody happy new year,' the Commander yelled after the departing Jim.

To the ears of the Scimitars the bazookas made a loud hissing sound as the small, pear-shaped missiles were fired. Very little skill was required in firing the system; it was controlled entirely by the GPS inbuilt within Freinet. Simplicity itself, it was just a matter of entering the correct numerical sequence into the tiny computer; holding the bazooka at an approximate angle of eighty degrees; a quick prayer for the guidance of Allāh; and pressing the button. Within the annals of human warfare there was little to applaud in terms of noise, explosion, flying debris, screaming victims or smoke. The tiny missile rarely missed its target when fired from a stable firing platform. Splattering against walls, windows, doors or any other surface, they flattened into a pancake shape and absorbed the colour of the surface that had intercepted their flight.

Each team fired their twenty missiles, there were no glaring mishaps, no misfires, and in the dark of the night and to all intents and purposes it was an uneventful trip up the Thames. The attacking force continued slowly up the river to Richmond. Here they dragged their boats from the water, deflated them, and loaded them into the waiting fleet of vans, small lorries and large estate cars, all of indeterminate age. Sympathetic drivers emerged from parks, hedgerows, flats, houses and anywhere else that they had been able to find as accommodation for the night. Making as little noise as possible they started their engines and drifted away into the various suburbs of southwest London.

Lambeth Bridge House, the headquarters building for the HPD, never sleeps. During the wee small hours, the adrenaline-rush of fevered activity might dwindle to a barely noticeable facial flush but there is always someone in the building ready to respond to whatever situation might arise. The organisation had grown enormously since the beginning of the 2020s in response to an increase in acts of political extremism around the globe.

England was seen as a haven for the discontented of the world; her borders were wide open, with little in the way of immigration control. Successive weak governments, the demands of an omnipotent European Parliament and a multi-racial, multi-religious population, who were well represented in the country's parliamentary system, allowed almost anyone to enter the country.

The cost of maintaining the departments was enormous and the budgets for the HPD, together with its sister department IPD, represented almost twenty-five percent of England's tax revenue. Originally dubbed military intelligence, the two new protection departments had nothing to do with the military and not a lot to do with intelligence when it came to thwarting the antics of al-Shamshir.

Successive Chief Presiding Officers (CPO) waged constant war with the Chancellor, through the Home Secretary when fighting their corner. Each year more staff were required, computers and equipment became more and more expensive to maintain, replace or protect from the ever-increasing skills of the world's hackers.

'Blood-suckers.' The current Home Secretary had her own, somewhat unfair, nickname for the two departments. Prone to severe blushing, which covered her entire face, neck and probably her whole body, since all that was visible down to and including her massive breasts glowed with redness whenever she was under stress. And fighting for additional funds for the two protection departments was her own personal nightmare. Until that is, some newsworthy success catapulted her name into the daily news-sheets, reawakening her dreams of Number Ten.

During the Scimitar's attack, Lambeth Bridge House had a very special person in attendance. The youngest ever Section Presiding Officer (SPO), Naomi Smith, was the newly-promoted head of Z1 section. Responsible directly to the CPO for England's safety from homeland-based threats, Naomi was reading her way into her new post. But that was not the real reason why she was at her desk in LBH at such an unsocial hour. She was awaiting a telephone call.

In front of her was the contact telephone that had been the reason for her remarkable progress around and up HPD's promotion cone. Naomi had been receiving the calls for some five years and the telephone line had been moved from room to room with each step of her rise to the top level of management. Such telephone lines were known within the HPD as 'speak, and listen'. The hard-wired landlines had been in use for many years and were still used in preference to more advanced means of communications such as Freinet or personal-footprint satellite terminals.

And such was the importance placed on the information that Naomi received, that she preferred to await such preplanned calls in her office; the facilities to deal with the information were more readily available in LBH.

The young SPO had ample warning whenever important information was expected. A preliminary call always preceded the hot-call and Naomi kept the old-fashioned, bright-orange telephone instrument on her desk to remind her of the importance of such calls.

The procedure never varied. Three rings, after which Naomi pressed the 'receive' button on her work-console, spoke a single word 'Speak' and listened for the voice to pass whatever information was available. The speaker always identified himself in the same way and information was passed in the exact same format each time. Always a man's voice, it identified the caller and this was always 'Verguide', followed by the date and time group, month and year in phonetic equivalents. This was followed by the place, amplified if necessary, and the expected attack or event time.

Naomi was tired; her designer-spectacles complemented her attractive face. But the spectacles were new and they pinched the bridge of her nose, leaving dark impressions after many hours of use. Removing her spectacles she rubbed her tired eyes. And with a reflex flicking of her long, superbly styled blonde hair, she stood up from her desk, stretched her tall slim body and walked over to the window overlooking the Thames.

A movement on the river caught her attention; she lowered her gaze and swivelled her eyes to the left. She was looking through the large, overhanging trees near to Cleopatra's Needle.

One of the weird effects of the much vaunted 'global warming' debate was that extremely mild winters allowed trees to retain their foliage for much longer. She saw nothing more and her mind wandered for a few seconds.

One of a pair, she had always admired the Egyptian obelisk and her memories of school days reminded her that the ancient stone edifices, one of which stood on the north side of Lambeth Bridge, were erected originally in the ancient Egyptian city of Heliopolis in about 1500 B.C. London's prize was erected in 1878, its twin found its way to Central Park in New York a couple of years later.

The leaves and branches of the trees were distorting her vision, playing tricks on her tired eyes. She saw many shapes and her always-active mind was conjuring up all sorts of fantastic shapes. She saw what she thought was a boat, almost as you would see a potato etching, in black on a white sheet of paper. The boat appeared to have an archer, kneeling in the centre of the boat aiming his bow at the bridge. Her mind almost returned to normality in time; the boat looked too real and she was about to reach for her spectacles and concentrate more fully on the image when the phone rang.

The distinctive ring-tone of the Verguide. Instantly she ejected the image of the boat from her mind. There was no time to replace her tiny ear-set; she simply lifted the receiver, 'Speak.'

'Verguide: Two five zero four three zero zulu December four zero, London, Thames-side targets, imminent.'

Far too late the warning. The head of Z1 reacted with incredible speed. Firstly a quick call to the Duty Officer. 'Go to condition Zulu Active.' Within thirty minutes LBH would be swarming with homeland protection staff and the somewhat ponderous, well-trodden procedures would grind into activity once again.

Sleepy-eyed river police commenced their noisy sweeps of the Thames. The over-exuberant crews, anxious to be seen to be doing something, zoomed up and down river close to the riverbanks at speeds that precluded seeing anything other than an impressive wake at the stern of their police launches. But whatever they were looking for was long gone; they saw and found nothing and at 07.00 they were stood down.

Throughout her personal call to the Chief Presiding Officer, Naomi knew for certain that she had missed a vital warning, a warning that might have enabled more action to be taken by the authorities and might have saved more lives. She had failed. There *had* been a boat on the river, a very suspicious boat, and had she ordered the capital's police forces to commence their search further upstream, instead of their usual starting place around Westminster Bridge; they may well have caught a few of the bombers red-handed.

Naomi did not mention her somewhat blurred sighting, not to the CPO nor in her subsequent file reports. Such doubtful reports could well blow-up in one's face and ruin a very promising career. She had followed procedures; she could live with that.

And it was so much easier to include a long-winded, scathing chapter on the inadequacies of the London river police and her proposals to improve their efficiency, including, of course, the funding required.

There was little sign of life from London's north bank. Tamimi sat in the stern of his boat preferring not to risk mistakes by steering the boat himself. He hugged the shore; the outgoing tide was much more severe in mid-stream. Much more quickly than he expected the distinctive shape of Tower Bridge loomed overhead. Saladin's words echoed in his brain. 'We want maximum damage, disruption and chaos. Loss of life is of secondary importance.'

He gave the hand signal to load and prepare to fire and his four-man team sprang into action. The shooter shouldered the unwieldy bazooka. Number two stuffed the first pear-shaped limpet mine into the rear of the weapon, and tapped the shooter on the shoulder to confirm that he was locked and loaded. Number three prepared a second mine, while number four cast his eyes in a constant lookout and prayed that he would not be called upon to use the reserve bazooka.

The bridge was coming up much too quickly; they were in danger of over-shooting their target. They must fire five limpet mines approaching the bridge and five having passed beneath it. Tamimi gave the order to let loose, a thundering smack on the shoulder of his shooter. Much too hard, the shooter almost leapt from the boat and his finger squeezed the first limpet away. Where it went or where it landed, the shooter did not care! He relied totally on the software of the system to do its job and, although the launch angle was very acute, the limpet actually corrected its flight and slapped meatily on to the side of the bridge.

Eight of the ten mines found a resting place on Tower Bridge. The remaining two dropped into the water and floated away towards the English Channel. The leader of the First Scimitar was fuming. The rest of Tamimi's squad was grateful for the darkness of the winter night, for looking their Lieutenant in the eye would have been a very hard thing to do. Tamimi knew that he had not controlled the boat as best he could but in his defence he later pointed out that firing from a small, bobbing boat was not as simple as firing the mines from a rock-steady, land-based platform.

The tiny boat continued down-stream. Its occupants relaxed after the mines were fired at the bridge; they felt confident now, and calm, and found time to ask Allāh for his help as they approached the Houses of Parliament. As the boat drifted over towards the imposing building, the hugely impressive face of Big Ben showed the time to be 04.00 and started its chimes, the noise of which frightened the life out of Tamimi's shooter.

Already locked and loaded, the shooter's finger jerked uncontrollably back on the firing trigger. Once again the system's software rescued the shooter, correcting the missile's flight, and it landed sloppily, in the shape of a flying omelet, on the face of Big Ben itself. Nine other mines hit the target and Tamimi opened the throttle on the boat and headed upstream.

They saw no sign of the other attack boats. A good sign from Tamimi's point of view, since it meant that none of the boats had met any serious problems and had obviously loosed their weapons somewhere. The whole group knew that returning with unfired mines would be fatal: the closeness of one's relationship with Saladin did not necessarily guarantee immunity from the most severe of punishments.

First Scimitar was now silently gloating at their success. As the number one Scimitar their performance was all-important, especially if they wished to retain the number one spot. They allowed their boat to coast quietly to the river's bank at the preplanned spot from which they would make their escape.

As the boat nudged the grassy water's edge dark shapes emerged from all directions. Without a word they were handed replacement clothing and they quickly discarded their wetsuits. Before they had time to dress the boat was gone. Removed from the water and stashed in a waiting England Post van, it disappeared from the team's sight. Not one of them knew the boat's final destination.

The five-man First Scimitar separated without a word. They walked to the nearby blocks of flats and rows of terraced houses, amongst which they each found a loyal follower of Rasul-Allah and a safe haven for as long as necessary.

It would be several weeks before the al-Shamshir attack group reformed as a unit. The team leaders would report to Saladin within a few days, which gave them ample time to compose their reports. Naturally each and every report contained a description of a fault-less attack; all limpet-mines fired directly at the targets and the boats under complete control at all times.

A green Christmas is said to make a fat churchyard. The expression is thought to allude to the fact that a mild winter does not kill off the bugs and viruses that traditionally allowed Mother Nature to control the population. But in 2040 the churchyards were to be filled for quite another reason.

As one, at precisely 09.30 the one hundred and sixty time-delayed limpet mines exploded. A single mine would have been sufficient to bring down a large section of a bridge or an external wall or the roof of any one of the buildings attacked. Every target received at least seven mines, sufficient to cause incredible damage.

Most of London's Thames-side residents rushed to their windows, anticipating an unannounced firework display. The explosions were not loud. Muffled by soundproofed windows they sounded innocent, not at all dangerous. But when the sight of the bridges and buildings falling into the river and streets registered upon the people of London, their hearts sank.

What was going on? It was incomprehensible. Some looked sky-ward, expecting to see the flash of fighter-bombing aircraft flashing overhead. Others thought that WW3 had started. Or was this some extremely dramatic, expensive, London civil defence exercise, planned in such bad taste on Christmas Day?

Most were totally unaware of the extent of the damage or loss of life. It was not until much later in the day, when a temporary satellite TV system was brought on-line, that the true story unfolded before the eyes of the country. London bombed! And on Christmas Day! Not even Hitler's unrelenting bombing campaign during the Second World War had managed to inflict so much damage in one strike.

The dead exceeded even Saladin's wildest expectations. The exceptionally mild winter weather had brought many of London's population on to the embankment searching for a breath of fresh air. Children playing with new bikes, pedal cars and other toys; young mothers taking their new infants for a walk along the embankment; hordes of local residents making use of the Eye whilst the capital was virtually empty of tourists; the wards of St Thomas' full of visitors, crowding around the sick-beds of their loved ones.

The Fire Brigade headquarters was totally demolished and all tenders out of action, and the brigade were unable to respond to the calls for help that streamed into their operational command centre.

Big Ben, together with the top fifty metres of the tower, languished on the bed of the Thames.

In LBH Naomi Smith was lucky. She had left her desk to attend the call of nature just a few minutes before 09.30. The loos were located at the rear of the building and she was sufficiently low in the building to escape the blasts on the roof. She did not escape completely, for the building was dangerously unsafe and she sustained considerable injuries whilst attempting to vacate the building. LBH would be out of action for many months and the department would lose an enormous amount of information since all its rooftop satellite receivers, and most of its broadband cables, were destroyed. Unfortunate indeed also for the reputation of the Home Secretary, who had managed to shave tens of millions of pounds off the annual budget for the two protection departments by closing down the out-of-town back-up sites.

In a quiet alcove of the Birmingham central mosque, Saladin watched the media broadcasts. He was totally alone, not wishing to hear comments from anyone until he had watched the news reports. He had been beside himself with frustration throughout the night. Gabriel had seen fit not to provide him with a detailed description of each attack.

He knew only of Tamimi's effort. However, the newscasts reported hits on all planned targets and some isolated explosions elsewhere. Saladin quickly deduced what had happened. Tamimi had already reported that the shooter in the number one Scimitar had probably missed the bridge with two of his missiles and quite obviously others had missed as well, since reports of explosions at the Thames barrier and further down river indicated that at least eight of the mines must have failed to find their designated targets.

The gory scenes on London's bridges, in the hospital and along the embankments were manna to the ego of the would-be supreme prophet of Allāh.

England's news media had a field day. They had not had such a story for many a decade. Reputations could be enhanced this day. Most of the capital's reporters were galvanised into action. Christmas Day; family celebrations; church attendance; all were cast aside. The story was in central London and that is where they must be. Public transport and taxis were taking a day of rest. The only way into the city centre was by car, by boat or *en pied*. Within an hour of the first newscast, owners of small boats were making a fortune providing transport across the river.

Some canny owners recognised the panic in the eyes of reporters, desperately trying to get to the scene, and charged obscene sums of money for the short passage from one bank to the other.

Resembling a dog worrying a very large bone, the media chased their tails for days after the event, going over and over the same original pictures, interspersed with occasional private footage purchased from home movie makers who had just happened to be at the right place at the right time and had survived the blasts.

Saladin soaked it up. He refused to leave the small room in which the large screen filled one entire wall. By the simple process of relaying the pictures from his Freinet Pewi on to the screen, he could watch the results of months of planning in cinematic proportions.

Only occasionally did he respond to the gentle tap on the door, signifying that food and drink had been left for him.

CHAPTER 22
AUSTRALIA

THREAD:

The work to complete the construction of the underground complex at Abbotstone finally came to an end in 2012, on time and within budget.

During this period, the twins were kept extremely busy. Ana and her administrative assistants slowly surmounted the mountain of paperwork and problems associated with driving such a huge project and Joe continued with his task of amassing the greatest fortune in the history of mankind.

But Josh was by no means fully employed. Acting as a back-up to the twins for most of his time, he nevertheless seemed to be enjoying his life in the UK. With the means to overlook whomsoever he chose, he kept in touch with his family in Australia; and we both spent long hours surfing humanity.

Of course, he was well aware that when the Verguide Team required a termination to aid our cause, then he would be the man to take that life. As yet, he had not been tasked to do so but he knew that it was only a matter of time; and his innermost feelings mirrored my own, when I too had faced the same dilemma - could he do it?

Under what circumstances can one human being intentionally take the life of another?

AUSTRALIA. 2013.

The speed limit indicated forty clicks per hour. A ridiculously low figure. Everyone knew it was a silly rule; everyone knew it existed; and equally everyone completely ignored it. All agreed that it would make much more sense, and probably attract more adherents, if the speed restriction applied to set school arrival and departure times. But this speed limit was in effect all day long.

The two small girls were immaculate. Dressed in eye-catching yellow tops and with bright red skirts reaching down to below their knees, they were a picture of health, life, happiness; and the eye-bulging inquisitiveness of the very young.

At just five and a half years old, Rebecca Burgon and her best friend Rachel Stills stood in the playground of Clifftops Primary School. Set in a quiet superb of Canberra, this small, private school catered for the children of the up-and-coming middle classes of this bustling and rapidly expanding city.

At one-sixteenth Aboriginal, Rebecca knew that she was somehow different from most of the other girls in her school. She looked the same as them. Her blonde hair, blue eyes, soft milky-white complexion and upright, slim shape combined to proclaim that she was a normal white girl. But she knew that there was a problem. Although her daddy looked no different from every other daddy that brought children to the school, her mummy was certainly different from most other mummies. Tall and slim with a graceful figure, her mummy had the strange, dull-brown curly hair of the Aborigines; and slightly rounded, somehow heavy facial features, which confirmed her ancestry.

Rebecca was far too young to be aware of racial differences. She would not have been aware of there being a problem, had not Daddy told her: 'You are a real white girl and don't listen to what the other girls might say.' He said it every day, either at breakfast or on the way to school on the days that it was his turn to drive her in his shiny new ute[24].

Certainly neither of the two friends was concerned with racial differences. Of much more importance to them was how to sneak out of

---

[24]*Ute*. Small open-backed pick-up truck.

the playground without attracting the attention of Miss Simons. The girls called her 'The Bulldog'.

When on playground duty, the enormous bulk of Miss Simons could usually be seen overflowing the arms of a dilapidated old rattan chair, in the shade of the wide veranda. Occasionally the huge head on the thick neck of The Bulldog would drop, very suddenly, as if pole-axed, to be followed almost instantaneously by loud snoring. The girls usually laughed with sheer glee when the spittle started to flow from The Bulldog's gaping mouth because it reminded them of their dogs slobbering over the anticipation of a juicy bone.

'She will nod-off, Becky. I just know she will.' The playmates waited quietly and patiently. 'And the *joey* was still there this morning.' Rachel whispered after a slight pause, her strong Australian accent sounding somehow strange in one so young.

It had been several days ago when Rachel had first seen the baby kangaroo. She had been sitting in her usual place in the back of her mother's Land Rover, gazing with complete disinterest out of the window.

The journey to school was the same each morning and after six months of this boring, repetitive journey, Rachel was familiar with every natural feature of the twenty-kilometre trip. She knew every tree, *dam*, rock, building; almost every animal in the open countryside and in the small *paddocks* close to the residential properties on the approaches to her school.

Rachel's eyes had drifted lazily, almost unfocused, over the surrounding landscape. At first the sight of the kangaroo and the baby *joey* did not register in her brain. By the time she had realised what she had seen, it was too late. Mummy had driven by.

The very next morning Rachel was much more alert. She was ready, concentrating hard out of the nearside window when the stretch of bush-land came into view. 'Please God; let the *joey* be there again.' She whispered the quiet appeal to her reflection in the car's window. 'What did you say, Darling?' Mummy asked. 'Just counting my blessings,' Rachel replied. She had heard her daddy use this expression many times and she knew that it always pleased her mother.

There! A large kangaroo in almost the same spot. And with a little *joey* peeking over the edge of its mother's pouch. Rachel could hardly contain her excitement. She reached down and removed her seat belt; she needed to stand up for a better view. 'Sit down and put your seat-belt on.' Rachel's mother screamed the command and at the same time brought the car to a screeching halt at the side of the road. Trembling with suppressed anger Rachel's mother got out of the car; she walked slowly around to the nearside rear passenger door and opened it slowly. Rachel was struggling to reconnect her seat belt and she looked fearfully into her mother's eyes as she opened the door. 'It's alright Darling,' Rachel's mummy said. 'But you frightened me. Promise me that you will never do that again.'

Rachel nodded her head and frantically tried to stem a sudden flood of tears by thrusting a plump fist into her right eye. 'I'm sorry mummy,' she sobbed quietly, 'but I could not see the *joey* very clearly.'

Never again did Rachel repeat her error. This morning she had seen the kangaroo again. It was in the same location, at the rear of a neat line of single-storey buildings, set amongst the shade of lofty eucalyptus trees. 'Is the *joey* still there mummy?'

'Yes darling, it is. I can just see its little head peering out from the pouch.'

It was at that precise moment that Rachel devised her plan.

Clean, shiny, almost new, the car was a dream. The huge eight-cylinder engine hummed powerfully beneath his right foot; the power was incredible, and nothing he had met today could stay with him off the lights. The interior of the car was immaculate, obviously the pride and joy of some very keen car enthusiast. Recently hoovered and polished, the car's interior clashed horribly with its driver.

Brynn Sylvester, Rocky to his gang of cronies, was the epitome of teenage angst. At just eighteen years of age he was unwashed, unshaven and totally unacceptable in ordinary, decent society. His hair was long, below shoulder length, dirty and greasy. His teeth, black and misshapen from years of smoking, had not had a close relationship with a brush for many years. His clothes, like his body, reeked. Bathing and laundering were for the sissies of this world and he would have been mightily offended if some kindly soul had removed his clothing during one of his many out-of-body periods and given them a free wash.

Brynn's eyesight was poor, as was his hearing, and his sense of smell had long since faded. Large and extremely smelly stains on his jeans also testified to a rapid decrease in the efficiency of his bodily functions.

A junky. Rocky knew what he was. He had been a crack-artist since he was twelve. His sister, just two years his senior, had left her *equipment* lying around one afternoon after school. Rocky had found it and decided to give it a go.

Rocky chuckled to himself. His memory was deserting him as well! He could not remember his sister's name. She had died two years ago, at the tender age of eighteen.

Brynn looked down at the speedo, almost 200 km/h; 'Christ, this baby can motor.' He had spoken out loud. 'How much gas left?' He continued to speak above the sound of the motor beneath him. 'Was it Julia? Or Julie? Didn't it start with a J? Hope this bloody car gets me to Dixon[25]. Get out of my way, you asshole!' He screamed the words and rammed his hand on the horn, flitting into the nearside lane to overtake some old biddy in a white van.

Offending both his eyes and senses, Brynn hated white vans. The drivers of such vehicles seemed to have a common personality, consistently bad-tempered and bullish in their driving habits. Exactly as did motorcyclists, they took enormous risks and always seemed to get away with their bad driving. Not once in the five or so years that he had been borrowing cars had Rocky ever considered himself a bad driver. He toyed with the idea of sideswiping the van, just to shake the old biddy up a bit. But, he decided just in time, it was a bit too early in the day for such pranks.

The massive dark silver Ford held the road as would an F1 racing car. On the main highway approaching the ACT, just north of Canberra, Rocky was having a whale of a time. The car did not require very much effort to keep it on the road. What bends existed were gentle and there were no traffic lights, intersections or roundabouts. The car hurtled down the gentle incline approaching the outskirts of Australia's capital, passed the 100 km/h sign, indicating a reduction of speed was required from the 110 km/h limit on the highway.

Numerous other signs appeared on both sides of the road, com-

---

[25]Dixon. A suburb of Canberra.

pletely distracting the first-time visitor. 'Welcome to Canberra, sister City Nara Japan', '50 km/h speed limit within the ACT unless otherwise indicated', and many more. Within a few hundred metres, the eighty sign appeared on the nearside; Brynn ignored them all. He knew there was a roundabout coming up but he loved to approach such road hazards as fast as he possibly could; the smell of burning rubber and the whole-car feeling of instability gave him a magical buzz.

Normally the boy would have continued down the main highway towards Canberra's Civic Centre. There was always great fun to be had running the red lights of the many traffic signals down Northbourne Avenue. But today he decided to hang a left and take a slightly more roundabout route to his destination. If he was really lucky there might be a good-sized kangaroo crossing the road, perhaps with a *joey* in its pouch. Clipping these large animals whilst avoiding a full-on collision was an art; and the rewards for timing it just right were enormous. The sight of a kangaroo in his rear-view mirror pirouetting in the road never failed to reduce him to fits of laughter.

But no such luck on this day. The road was deserted and Rocky gunned the motor. He saw the sixty limit coming up and once again ignored it, pressing his foot a little more firmly on the accelerator. A few hand-brake turns, hard front-end braking and violent twists on the steering wheel left impressive black tyre-marks on the road; not to mention the overpoweringly strong smell of burning rubber from the cloud of smoke hanging in the air.

Today, however, they remained completely silent. Their combined prayers had been answered. The Bulldog had nodded off. Now was their chance.

Silently, the two young friends watched The Bulldog. Slowly, the huge head dipped. For a second or two the girls thought that she had fallen asleep. 'Bollacks, bunyips and botheration!' Becky whispered one of her mummy's naughty expressions and both girls tried desperately not to giggle. The Bulldog's head slowly lifted and her eyes swivelled around the playground. The eyes of each girl were glued on their target; they dare not even blink. Again the head dropped; they waited and this time it fell deeply between the over-flowing swells of

The Bulldog's ample bosom. Deep back-of-the-throat snoring erupted from the bloated, sweating body.

The girls exchanged a glance. The adventure was a go. Today they would see the *joey*. The two friends raced around to the side of the school, crept between some dense shrubbery and located the small hole in the fence. They had found the hole some weeks ago during a game of hide-and-seek; and today they had a use for it.

It was an exceedingly tight fit. But the athletic young bodies were capable of twisting and turning in every direction. Both managed to squeeze through the tiny gap in the school's defences and breathless with excitement they dashed to the end of the road.

Large white lines painted across the road and a central safety island marked the school crossing. Protected by a 40 km/h speed restriction from 08.00 till 16.00 each day, the crossing was well known to the local users; and well marked for everyone else.

'We must be careful,' Becky, still whispering, advised her friend. Both girls remembered only too well the careful instructions that they had already received about crossing roads, both from parents and school staff.

'Yes,' replied Rachel, 'we will go to the island first and then cross the other bit.'

Stooping very low to the ground the girls safely crossed the first half of the road. Crouching on the island behind the bollards, they paused. 'When I say go, we'll do the other half but stay low and follow me.' Rachel gave the instructions and grasped her little friend's hand. 'Go!'

Rocky was slipping rapidly into his terrible depression. He needed a fix and soon.

The inside of the car was still immaculate; he had not had time to stop for drinks, fast food or chocolates, the remnants of which usually littered the inside of any vehicle that he used for more than a few hours. Comfortably cool, the air-conditioning was superb. He was in a rare good humour. The sight of the dancing kangaroo had cheered him a little. The crystal-clear memory of the huge marsupial writhing on the side of the road was fresh in his mind. But Rocky was not aware that the incident had happened several weeks before. Within a matter of a few seconds he had already forgotten that there had not been any animals in his path today.

The speedo read ninety-five. 'I must be getting bloody old,' he shouted at the top of his voice; and pressed the throttle once more. As the needle leapt to one hundred and forty, Rocky saw the forty sign and the school crossing signs. He knew they were there, he had travelled this route on numerous occasions; but he had never once seen hide nor hair of a child.

'Bloody silly rule,' he muttered under his breath and glanced down at the speedo once again. As his eyes lifted lazily from the car's instruments, his eyelids felt strangely heavy and he had to focus the whole muscular effort of his body on his eyes.

A soft, almost unnoticed thud; a blur of red and yellow. Rocky thought that he had hit a stray football from the nearby school. And then he noticed the small red blobs on the windscreen. His befuddled mind could not comprehend quite what had happened. How could a football be filled with what he assumed to be red paint?

Josh had been dozing in Volly's Folly. He suddenly shot upright, fully awake. His mind had been wandering, as it did on many occasions. In overlooking mode he had seen the large silver Ford, speeding down the highway towards his hometown. For some inexplicable reason, and for some time, his attention remained with this one vehicle. However, his mind had started to drift away from the car.

At the thud of impact with the two small bodies, Josh regained full consciousness with instant tears in his eyes. He felt a moment of extreme sadness, followed almost immediately by an all-consuming anger.

Whatever Rocky had hit, stopping was out of the question. Whatever it was would have to find its own salvation. He was already overdue for his fix and if he did not get to the gang's HQ pretty soon, there might not be any left for him.

The car sped on, the driver oblivious of the pain, misery, heartache and loss that he left in his wake.

The two colourful shapes lay in the road. No longer hand-in-hand but still very close together. Like two discarded rag dolls, lying in a spilled pot of red paint they lay motionless. Rachel managed to turn her head and looked into the face of Becky. Eyes wide open, Becky returned her gaze but they were a strange, muddy, lifeless colour; and they did not blink.

The blossoming red liquid under Rachel's head spread in an ever-increasing circle. Rachel felt light-headed and she closed her eyes. She suddenly felt very tired and wanted to go to sleep. In her mind she saw a long black tunnel with brightly-coloured signs and symbols, much the same as her favourite alphabet breakfast cereal. She did not think of her parents; she did not think of Becky; neither did she think of the little *joey*. Her final thought in this life was, *'The Bulldog is going to be very angry when we get back to school.'*

Pumped full of venom, nerve-ends screwed tight and with the red mist of road rage overwhelming the normal actions of a sane person, the old biddy in the white van had been desperately trying to stay in contact with the speeding joy rider. He wanted a few choice words with the little dickhead. 'Ah, trying to get away from me eh,' he shouted to himself as he watched the Ford turn off the highway at the roundabout. Old biddy knew the speed restrictions as well as the next man because he lived in one of the shady bungalows opposite the school.

But he was incensed and his rage swept away all normal behavior. He wanted only one thing, to catch the little road rat and maybe even give him a slap or two.

The white van approached the school crossing. It was travelling much too fast. The driver saw the lumps in the road but by the time he realised what they were it was much too late.

Rachel did not see the life returning to Becky's eyes nor did she feel the plump little fingers wrap around her hand.

The speeding van hit the two bodies. They were hardly more than babies and the van bulldozed the returning spark of life out of the mangled body of Becky.

Deep. Very deep. The person in the dark silver Ford had slipped into the depths of hell. Sudden muscular movements, tremors and shivering shakes moved from limb to limb as would a golfer with the yips; his eyes flickered rapidly, blurring his vision and reminding him of the old-fashioned black-and-white movies that he had seen; and his drug-filled imagination hallucinated almost continuously. His brow and scalp felt white-hot one second and freezing cold the next; he could not control his hands and his feet trembled on the pedals of the car; he could feel warm and slimy secretion running from his nose and hear a tremendous drumming in each ear.

'Delirium tremens.' Brynn Sylvester knew the words. Normally associated with alcohol abuse, this medical condition is more commonly known as the shakes.

Proudly Brynn had displayed his first symptoms to the other gang members several years before and danced in joy as his comrades shouted, 'The shit's kicking in, Rocky - go for it, man!' He had been heavily built, chunky and muscular then, well nourished by a loving mother; and such physical characteristics had earned him the nickname of Rocky. But that was before he had become hooked.

The controls restricting the use of drugs had been relaxed several years before. Their use had escalated around the world; people found it much easier to deal with the pressures of modern-day living when under the influence of a few happy concoctions and drug usage became more of a religion to its growing numbers of young participants.

Even more worrying to world leaders was the tender age at which new disciples flocked to this new calling. The school playgrounds around the world are newly seeded each year with a fresh crop of impressionable young minds, forever seeking to comply with the taunts to try some new potion or other and keep up with everyone else. And the dross of the world does not see a child when selling their goods; they see only another source of income to stoke the fires of their own private hell.

Much to the joy of Rocky's gang, the powers-that-be finally capitulated at the turn of the century in what was probably the world's first global policy of appeasement. Cannabis was downgraded to a class C drug and was quickly followed by many others; the use of drugs was regarded as a personal choice and the offence considered little more than a peccadillo. Downgraded and decriminalised by an enlightened society that had reached a point of no return, a world of do-gooders had failed miserably to find a single workable method of controlling its use. And added to a crazy global idea of criminals' rights, there just did not seem to be an answer.

More and more previously-dubbed illegal substances were used openly and freely; any public place was considered appropriate, from restaurants and bars, to schools and churches. The world of the drug-user is one of words that are virtually unused, unknown, or misunderstood by a non-user. Narcotics; hallucinogens; psychedelics; deliriants; recreational stimulants; sedatives; nootropics; smart drugs; heroin; opium; cocaine; marijuana; khat; LSD; rohypnol and GHB; which may be ingested orally, inhaled, injected or shoved up the rear as a suppository - and all of which are associated with a breakdown of the human body's immune system and an early death.

Booted out of his family home a few months after his fifteenth birthday, Rocky was already a well-established member of the Fries. To his family he had become a demon, a person that his parents no longer recognised. Little of value was left in the family home and Rocky no longer bothered to call at the house; he knew that he had milked that cow completely dry. On the infrequent occasions when he met his mother, she always burst into tears and wailed, 'You will end up like your sister, Brynn.' The vision in her mind each night, as she prayed for Christ's forgiveness and mercy for her son, was not that of an unkempt, dirty and smelly drug-addict but that of a beautiful small boy, with his chunky body and hopeful eyes. 'Not me, Mum. I don't use the stuff.' Brynn had managed to fool himself but not his mother.

Home Units, or massive blocks of tiny apartments, were built in and around almost every major conurbation in Australia from about 2010 to house the continuous stream of refugees from all over the Far East. These buildings quickly deteriorated into slums and were inhabited mainly by those unwilling or incapable of finding work.

Amotivational Syndrome or AS - everyone who lived in that accommodation knew the words, if not exactly what they meant. For they were the current buzzwords that milked a few extra dollars from the Welfare Officers. An apathetic condition stemming from drug abuse and associated with wild mood swings and violence. And those dishing out the State's cash were unwilling to argue with these people; it was much easier to hand out a few extra dollars, secure in the knowledge that they had a good chance of safely reaching the car park each evening.

Supported by a less than generous welfare state, living in these communities became a career choice for those incapable of doing any better and a lifestyle choice for those who had not the inclination or wherewithal to make any attempt to improve their lot. And it was within one of these large Home Units that Rocky's gang had their headquarters.

At the first wild thrill of excitement coursing through veins, arteries and the mind, a potential drug abuser makes a pact with the devil. But Lucifer is a hard taskmaster and drives a hard bargain that is tipped in his own favour. The cost for spending eternity at the court of The Prince of Darkness is paid in time. In exchange for several short years of pain, suffering, dirt, disease and an early departure date to hell, the Antichrist will provide a few brief periods of extreme out-of-body experiences and the cunning, stealth, meanness and total disregard for other human life necessary to obtain the means to reach that depth of degradation.

In the Verden, Josh was angry. His thoughts about drugs and the devil made perfect sense to him. The death of the two little girls had shaken him to his core and he badly needed to take someone to task.

Not especially spiritual, Josh was selective with his belief in religion. When life was running smoothly and there existed no troublesome clouds on the horizon, the gentle Australian ignored the existence of his Heavenly Father. But when life became troublesome, or he was doubtful about a certain course of action, Josh was a fervent user of prayer and missed not one night without speaking with his maker, asking for guidance or divine help.

A sudden realisation swept over the big man. Ambivalent, as a religious persuasion the term fitted him perfectly. Still working himself into a fine old stew, Josh allowed his thoughts to wander once again. Speaking aloud, he mused, 'The Pearly Gates are indeed studded with precious stones, but they are not there for decoration, or to please the beholder. Those elaborate gates are there to distract those waiting in line for permission to enter, for such people will be proud of their lives on Earth, holding their heads aloft, and waiting for a first sighting of a long-lost loved one. Allowing their eyes to cast downwards to the foundation of the gates, reveals a sight that might well confuse an ardent supporter of religion. For there can be seen the multitude of souls who were led astray, those who sinned against society, the mass murderers, serial killers, child abusers, drug addicts, despots and tyrants. These are the people who were told as infants that Our Maker is all-merciful, a deity who forgives any confessed misdeed; and who now waits patiently for a sign of that forgiveness. And they are the same people for whom God's forgiveness will be denied; for there is little point in having a hell unless it is made use of.'

'I must be getting old,' Josh continued, 'for never before have I indulged in such philosophical meanderings.' But he could not shake the feeling of despondency that descended upon him when he considered that the Holy Father was capable of withholding His forgiveness. 'If the whole world is God's church and every human being is part of His congregation, surely such an unforgiving nature demeans Him, and all those made in His image?'

With a huge sigh, Josh lifted himself from his comfortable chair. A knock on my study door and a single hand followed by Josh's face appeared around its edge. 'Won't be gone long, Boss. I have a problem that needs fixing.' A London taxi driver does not faff around when manoeuvring in heavy traffic. Indicate and move, and sod-em-all! Josh was much the same, state an intention and he was gone.

Racing up the stairs of the huge block of apartments, Brynn was in a terrible hurry to get a fix of some sort. Strong, muscular legs propelled him effortlessly up the flights of stairs and his sturdy lungs felt not the slightest strain. In his own eyes, he did not see the travesty of his own body as he stumbled up the staircases, bumping from wall to wall, ripping skin with each contact with the rough brickwork, gasping for air and the terrible sound of the bells that were now ringing continuously in his head.

Fries were the cheapest source of a calming influence for his jumping nerve-ends. The drug produced an ataractic reaction, a tranquillising calmness and peace of mind. Embalming fluid was easy to come by, if you knew where to look, and smoking a cigarette dipped into this fluid provided a wonderful feeling of dizziness, disorientation and a sense of carefree indifference to the world and everyone in it. The drug-soaked cigarettes also made women easy to control and more susceptible to suggestion; not that the women with whom Rocky mixed needed any stimulant to dispense their favours. The latest rape drug was well known to the Fries gang; none could spell gammahydroxybutyrate and very few could pronounce it but all knew of the existence of GHB. The rich-boy's rape drug had a most useful side effect: a victim recognised the physical symptoms of having been raped but the drug wiped any memory of it from her, or his, mind. But the Fries gang had no need of such aids to sexual conquest at their level of society.

And the embalmed fags were readily available in the Fryingpan, the gang's headquarters. Stealing cigarettes was easier than obtaining embalming fluid and fries littered the apartment, testament to the skills of the gang's fag-hags.

'Hey, Rocky's back! How you goin' pal?' Inside the flat all was peaceful serenity; most of its thirty or so occupants were somewhere on Satan's mountain, scrambling for that Elysian place of total oblivion. The greeting did not receive a reply, neither was one expected. Covered in blood and eyes glaringly white as the pupils of his eyes disappeared into his forehead, Rocky staggered into the room. Sometimes an addict finds it difficult to manipulate his fingers and picking up small items is almost impossible. Rocky fell on to his hands and after some minutes of rubbing his face around the filthy floor, managed to suck a fry into his mouth. Recalcitrant fingers were no less capable of striking a match and Rocky crawled to the nearest candle, prelit and stuck on every available surface around the apartment, always ready for such an eventuality and giving the dismal interior an incongruous impression of the interior of a cathedral.

And to the Fries gang it was nothing less than a temple; to them it was the most important room in the whole world. And next door in the apartment's smallest room, the bishop's throne hummed in the bright Australian sunlight, as it satisfied the needs of those that had great need of it and were capable of reaching it. For the fries had a nasty side effect which demanded constant trips to the loo.

'Life is sweet. And the world really is a wonderful place.' Rocky was high, flying with the birds, breasting mountain tops, swimming in the depths of the oceans, floating effortlessly through space and knee-deep in every mind-blowing concoction known to man. Hair flowing in the wind and dressed in the finest grunge clothing that was *de rigueur* for the young of the world, fit and healthy once again, Rocky was flying towards something that he could see but not quite recognise.

He knew that he desperately wanted to see whatever it was but each time he came within focussing distance the object moved away. Time for some sneaky moves, like the heroic jet fighter pilots in the films that the young Brynn had so much loved as a child. Climbing higher and higher, ever higher to the limits of flight, Rocky pushed himself upwards until his body stalled and the dive began. A dive that was endless, screeching through the air at tremendous speed, he was faster than a streamlined bullet and, just before he reached the ground, his body levelled out and approached the distant object.

'Shit! Christ man! It's the Grim Reaper.' Rocky returned to reality with a shock, his heart was pumping so hard that he thought it might jump out of his chest; his body was twitching again and his naked skin tingled as a light breeze wafted over him.

His first thought was not for his missing clothes, nor of the filth that encased his naked body, nor indeed, of the deep craving in his guts; it was the memory of the creature at which he had finally managed to sneak a look. With powerful wings on each shoulder, the giant, hugely muscled body towered above him, his scythe-of-death raised high in expectation of imminent use.

But it was not the outline of this fearsome creature that bothered Rocky, it was the face. Encased within a dark hood the face was almost indiscernible but what could be seen had forced a further eruption from his bowels. Deep, black eye-sockets, containing hypnotic eyes with huge white irises surrounding a blood-red pupil; a fleshless nose filled with thick hairs that squirmed like a nest of rattlesnakes; and a huge mouth filled with needle-sharp teeth - but not just a single set, there appeared to be layer upon layer of them, descending into the creature's throat.

Rocky reached out a shaking hand, searching for a fry; his need was all-consuming, for the vision of the creature had rattled him as never before. As his fingers finally managed to grasp the fag, a heavy foot crashed down upon his hand.

Rocky could not believe it. He was awake for Christ's sake! The creature should have disappeared into the confines of his imagination; but the foot was real, heavy and bloody painful. The sad specimen of humanity giggled uncontrollably; the foot was real, encased within a shiny brown leather shoe, and in the shoe Brynn saw the reflection of a person that could not possibly be him. His eyelids felt heavy, reminding him of wet *wagga blankets*[26], and he struggled to lift his eyes to the face of the giant before him.

'Hello, my friend.' The voice of the giant was soft, friendly; and the face was not the hideous mask of death from his dreams. The voice had an Australian twang to it but it sounded different - anglicized, that of someone who had spent many years away from his parent land. For several seconds the giant waited but Rocky was incapable of uttering a sound. His neck and eyes hurt from the effort of looking upwards; the face was changing, slowing contorting features turning into the grotesque creature in his dream - and Rocky's whole body stiffened into an immovable skeleton of fear.

'You pretty-much sickened me today.' The timbre of the voice had changed, matching perfectly the fiendish features that Rocky could now see clearly. 'You killed those two beautiful little girls. You mowed them down in your stolen car. You cut off their lives as carelessly as you would stomp on a red-back spider.'

'Yo, light me a fry man.' Brynn's need was overwhelming his fear and the large man knew that it was time.

Rocky felt cold. Sitting up on a bare, bony and very soiled rump, he could feel the pressure of a large knee in the centre of his back. When he looked at his legs, he could see his heels drumming on the floor.

Brynn did not know that he was dying; he did not feel the thin wire of the garrotte slice cleanly through his throat nor wonder at the

---

[26]*Wagga blankets.* Two sacks cut open and sewn together.

sticky substance that fleetingly warmed his chest. For the first time in many a long year, his thoughts were no longer centred upon feeding the gnawing hunger in his mind.

His whole being seemed to drift back in time, to a time when, as a small boy he sat on his mother's lap, her warm arms wrapped around him in a loving embrace, listening to his favourite story. The soft voice from the warm body of his mother spoke of Kadaitcha Man, the Australian Aboriginal hero empowered to carry out the punishments handed down by aboriginal courts to wrongdoers. And Rocky was puzzled; he was a good boy, his mother was always telling him how good he was. So why was Kadaitcha Man punishing him?

Dropping the limp body of the drug addict to the floor, Josh stood upright. Human life was special to him and he had been worrying for some time about his ability to extinguish the light of awareness from a person's eyes. Inside the mind of his boss, he had seen his destiny; he was to become the hit man in the Verguide Team. Not especially squeamish he did not flinch from this task, recognising a job that needed doing and understanding that such drastic measures would be taken only when absolutely essential to the successful completion of the Verguide's task.

But this had been for him a milestone in his life; he had not previously taken a human life and really did not know if he could do it. Looking down at the small pile of flesh and bone at his feet, Josh realised two things. Enclosed within the widening circle of dark-red blood, the monster that was Brynn Sylvester had been easy to kill. The body reeked of recidivism and Josh knew that no amount of social finance, care and personal willpower could have prevented the young man from continuing on his downward slide to the devil's lair. The boy had killed indiscriminately but worse he had killed unknowingly; even at the time of his death, the boy had not realised that he had extinguished the two little candles of life.

Secondly, Josh realised that he had materialised. He was in full view of those others in the room who were in any way in charge of their faculties. Dangerous ground, he knew the perils both to his alter ego in this stinking room and to his physical self in Volly's Folly.

'How long have I been visible?' Josh wondered, instantly returning

Alfred Leonard

behind the curtain of invisibility. He could already hear the TV reporters, heads to one side and grinning in doubtful amusement: 'A drug addict was killed today in a tenement building of nefarious reputation near to the Civic Centre. Witnesses speak of the deceased screaming of Kadaitcha Man and the huge body of the assailant - which disappeared before their eyes. And now the weather for Canberra and New South Wales.'

But the drug addict had not been alone in causing the death of the two girls. White van man had played his part, Josh decided, and he too must pay the piper.

The old biddy was totally pissed. Collapsed in his old armchair, TV blaring forth and the room thick with cigarette smoke, the old man was floating in a sea of hate in the frowsty atmosphere. The hate was for himself, directed deeply inwards. How could he have allowed the weasel in the flash car to wind him up so tightly and so easily? Yes, he had been driving the white van for many long years and he had witnessed some of the worst cases of road rage in the fluid mass of traffic within the city of Sydney. Yes, he had been on the road for many hours that day; he had struggled to pass the never-ending line of huge trucks on the highway, only to face the same dilemma with the same trucks after stopping for the demands of nature. Yes, he was tired, frustrated; and no matter what he did he could not dampen the incessant road noise from the wheels of his van that seemed to so easily mash his senses. But deep in his heart, he knew that it was he that had killed the little girls and he also knew that he would never be able to forgive himself.

Somewhere in the foggy recesses of his mind, the old biddy heard the TV newscast about Kadaitcha Man, the death of a drug addict and the word garrotte.

No resistance was offered as he felt his head being lifted from the back of the armchair and he felt only a resigned sense of relief when the cold, steel necklace fell into place.

CHAPTER 23
MUSLIM MUTINY

THREAD:

During the winter of 2040-41, the attacks on Thameside targets in central London were not the only unpleasantness in store for the British people.

Anything or anyone originating from the mainland of Great Britain has been traditionally known by the generic term British. The growing number of ordinary Muslims who considered it their duty to submit to the commands of Britain's most active extremist group became known as Saladin's Army. But they did not necessarily originate solely from within the shores of the United Kingdom. These normally peace-loving citizens were able to move around Europe with little inconvenience in terms of border controls, immigration or customs formalities. From all points of the European compass, they answered the call from the leader of al-Shamshir when during November of 2040 the call from the Birmingham mosque went out for volunteers.

Young and old, they responded. By road, rail, air and sea. Resembling a gently flowing river, the stream of Muslims ready to do their bit for their cause trickled into the towns and cities of Britain's midlands. This was the heart of the country's Muslim community, from where a single brain gave birth to a campaign of terror; and one hundred and fifty thousand willing disciples sought the accolade of ghazi, a warrior who has fought for Islam against non-Muslims.

ENGLAND. NOVEMBER 2040.

Like a bush fire, the call went from mosque to mosque. 'Rasul-Allah calls *you*; Allāh will love *you*; the infidels will curse and fear *you*; paradise awaits *you*; and *Azreal* will swiftly sever *your* soul from *your* body at *your* death; *you*, the chosen ones who will answer the call of Rasul-Allah.'

The call also went out from the minarets of thousands of mosques all over the European mainland, called out as part of the *Azan* by the *Muezzins* five times each day. And the final word of Rasul-Allah's call burned into the hearts of those who could not refuse the call - '*Jihad!*'

History had taught the thirty-seven year old Saladin a great deal. He had read the books, seen the videos and films, and avidly consumed the biographies relating to the Second World War. During the dark months of 1940 and early 1941, Hitler's *Luftwaffe* had hammered home its relentless blitz of Britain's towns and cities. One hundred years after this bloody encounter, Saladin planned another such blitz for the people of his adoptive homeland; and he intended that it be equally as bloodthirsty and vindictive as the first.

The bright flame of fanaticism that fired Islamic imagination and invention provided the needs of al-Shamshir. Saladin's army of followers had the technical expertise and manufacturing skills to produce anything he required in his fight for world domination. And the man himself was now famous the world over; faceless to most; feared by all; and his oratories full of fanciful fanfaronade: he had become a fabulously faceted fable.

In his headquarters at the Birmingham mosque, Saladin was ringed by his Lieutenants. As always, amen corner was silent, waiting for their leader to give them some hint of his plans. They knew that something was happening. Rasul-Allah must have had some further divine inspiration; he had that glint in his eye that foreshadowed some preknowledge of events.

'The Irish Rebellion of 1641; the Irish Easter Rising; the English Revolution of 1642 between the Roundheads and the Cavaliers.' Saladin was musing and whispering his thoughts, casting his mind back through time; searching for some parallel that might perfectly explain his next venture. 'The British Muslim Mutiny?'

'We have an army. And soldiers that rebel against legal authority are mutineers. Islam is still regarded as psychologically anomic in the United Kingdom. It is time for an anarchic response; we will be lawless, show no respect for the Christian infidels and flout the established social order of this country. *Bismillah,* our attack will be two-fold. England will have a Muslim Mutiny, perpetrated by my loyal followers in this country.' Saladin smiled as he thought how nicely the phrase would extend the long list of revolts by the peoples of the world. 'And at the same time we will let loose our European brigades on a killing spree. The British people will learn how great the might of Islam within their homeland is and all will tremble as our legions march on their capital.'

'Issue the fatwa whereby Britain's Nation of Islam will rise up and march as one to the capital. Arrange for the care and accommodation of our supporters from Europe, spare them no expense and see that they want for nothing. Order our weapons factory to devise a simple but effective bomb. Something small that can be deployed safely, and quickly hidden amongst the normal everyday trappings of life. We must ensure that our European brigades have plenty of these special bombs, for theirs will be a very special part of our great campaign.'

Rasul-Allah had looked pointedly at the leader of his First Scimitar. '*Hajji* Abu Tamimi, trusted one; have the weapons team design such an explosive device. Something that can be concealed in almost any everyday item. I would prefer the device to explode at random times during both day and night, about two hours after being deployed and armed will suffice.'

'Have you chosen a name for this weapon, my Lord?' asked the ageing Tamimi. Silence followed his question; all eyes were centred upon their leader. 'Mullah's Penny Blacks!' A huge grin had spread over the face of Saladin as he remembered that Britain had issued its first postage stamp, with a similar name, exactly two hundred years before. His version would, he was certain, leave a greater impression upon history and by using the term Mullah, the name had the added advantage of implicating the Shiites and a hint of the Middle East.

Further instructions followed to the remainder of his Scimitar leaders, for each would have a specific task in both phases of Saladin's brutal Christmas card to the people of England.

Forehead puckered in thought, Saladin completed his instructions.

Alfred Leonard

'The march of the Muslim Mutiny will take place between the 1st and 23rd of December, 2040. Our people will march *en masse* towards London; they will march slowly; create as much disruption as possible; block the arteries of this country; bring the capital to a standstill; and demonstrate our willingness to act as one. Our European contingent will commence their attack to coincide with the January sales. *Bismillah*, make it so.'

And so it was that throughout the wee small hours of Friday 30th November, 2040, thousands of coaches deposited an army of Muslim supporters from all over the midlands into the city of Birmingham. On Saturday 1st December, some one hundred and fifty thousand Muslim souls left their departure points and started their walk to the capital. Slowly the streets of Birmingham ground to a halt as the initial small bands of marchers gradually joined into larger groups; and these larger groups snowballed into a solid mass of people.

At the M42, the army divided into three separate groups, each of around fifty thousand people. Each separate group headed for the capital using the A1, M40 and M5, and each group would fan out around the M25 before approaching central London from the north, east and west.

The coaches had been commandeered and filled with water and food, and these both formed a vanguard for the three advancing armies and protected their rear.

The chaos caused on the motorways and main roads leading to the capital created a rippling effect on the other main transport arteries feeding London. Traffic ground to a standstill over the whole of the south of England, rail systems became hopelessly overloaded and towns and villages were inundated with traffic attempting to bypass the congestion on the main routes.

Children all over the south of England cheered each evening when graphic pictures of the advancing Muslim armies were relayed to Freinet and television systems. Schools were closed; it was no longer possible for most children to make their way to the schools and when they did, there was a shortage of teaching staff to supervise them.

Food stocks ran low in towns and cities all over the country as the resupplying delivery lorries could no longer get through the bumper-to-bumper congestion; and the supermarket shelves looked bare and deserted.

Attempts by the military to stop the advancing hordes were easily sidelined by the fluid nature of the formations. Where roadblocks were set up, the Muslim fanatics simply took to the fields and rejoined the main roads a few kilometres further on. Numerous celebrities, famous people, politicians and senior police Officers stood in the road in front of the flood of people, pleading with them to turn back. All failed, they were totally ignored and quickly removed from harm's way by their escorts.

At night, the Islamic revolt camped on the road, slept in the buses or accepted the hospitality of the local Muslim community. Occasionally, as one, the mass of humanity vacated the motorways and allowed the traffic to move for a few hours, only to reblock the roads at will. This stop-start tactic seemed to inflame the British public even more and fuelled the fires of many local confrontations.

In their wake, the advancing armies left a trail of litter and human waste, discarded carelessly and deliberately in another attempt at nauseating the other members of England's society. Huge piles of rubbish and human faeces spattered the roads and roadside verges and small rivers of urine disappeared into the roadside drains or adjacent fields, creating a disgusting and offensive smell that lasted for weeks after the passing of each army.

The stores of central London were destined to suffer a huge loss over the shopping period leading up to Christmas 2040. Shoppers stayed in their homes; central London was not the place to be. In the seven days leading up to the 23rd December, the armies converged into the centre of the city.

As a last minute gesture, the Prime Minister made his own plea. Appearing on Freinet, he appealed to the Muslim leaders to halt their march. But his pleas, as did all those made before him, fell upon deaf ears. The march would not end until the time decreed by Saladin, midnight of the 23rd December.

During the last day before Christmas, the nation breathed a sigh of relief. Like the song of the nocturnal whip-poor-will at daybreak, one hundred and fifty thousand Muslims seemed to fade quietly away before the dawn of Christmas Eve. They had made not a single demand on the political leaders of Britain, nor did they block the roads on their return to Birmingham. They simply headed to prear-ranged safe houses in and around the capital; and in slow time, as the traffic of England started to move again, made their way back to their permanent or temporary accommodation to await the next phase of their leader's plan.

But the country's relief was to be short-lived. For the massed walk was simply a prelude to the Christmas Day bombing of Thameside targets and the havoc in store for the New Year.

Tuesday 1st January. New Year's Day, 2041. *Auld lang syne* in the shape of the old year was dead and buried. It's the birth of a new year and the beginning of the January sales; time to hit the plastic. This day had settled into the history of Britain as a fixed public holiday, a day of rest, relaxation and a time to replace the gluttony of food and drink with over indulgence of a different kind - retail therapy. A day in the United Kingdom when the celebrations of Christmas come to an end; the beginning of a new beginning; a time to gird one's loins, look to the future and make an attempt to achieve personal promises, expressed in demanding, personal new year resolutions.

Most of Britain had seen in the New Year. They had watched the midnight firework displays; jumped around their living rooms; hugged and kissed everyone within reaching distance; screamed, 'Happy new year,' to all and sundry; and opened another bottle of something intoxicating.

The January sales were on and the Muslim Mutiny and Christmas Day bombings of England's capital had ended. Consequently, there was a relaxed sense of alertness amongst the people in the towns and cities across the United Kingdom. Public transport, shops, pave-ments, restaurants, cafes, bars; the public meeting places were buzz-ing with swarms of humanity, their minds befuddled by too much good cheer.

Unnoticed amongst these throngs was Saladin's European army. But this Muslim army did not linger long; they were totally uninter-ested in the bargains on offer. Their orders were to arm and deploy their bombs and vacate public buildings by ten o'clock.

The carnage started at a little before 10.30. Loud in the mid-winter sunshine the explosions rattled across the country, as would a chain of signal fires. Small, compact and powerful enough to kill anyone within a distance of a few metres, the bombs could be deployed in or on just about anything. About the size, shape and thickness of a postage stamp they could be stuck to any surface.

Inside discarded drink bottles and cans, sweet and ice cream wrappers, fast-food cups and containers, empty packets of cigarettes or matches and attached to a variety of transport and admittance tickets - the opportunities to deploy the weapon were unlimited.

Saladin's army took great delight in inventing numerous places to stick the bombs. Dressed as charity workers; sticking a bomb on the lapel of everyone who made a donation and randomly depositing the innocuous looking devices whilst supposedly accidentally nudging individuals in the mass of shoppers.

To date, the pinnacle of man's efforts to satisfy his dreams of self-annihilation is the development of nuclear weapons. From the moment that the United States of America launched Little Boy and Fat Man on the Japanese cities of Hiroshima and Nagasaki, the scientists of the world have been frantically searching for methods of miniaturising these weapons.

At the turn of the 21st century, a nuclear device could be accommodated within an ordinary suitcase. By 2030, the space required had been further reduced to that of an innocent sandwich box. As recently as 2038, scientists and weapon designers within the framework of Saladin's army managed to make an astonishing breakthrough. Within the space of a few weeks they managed to reduce the required space to a matchbox and then to a postage stamp.

Of course, the explosive power of these small nuclear devices was not great. But it was certainly as powerful as a hand grenade, capable of killing people close to the explosion and bringing down the supporting pillars and walls of buildings.

The tentacles of Islamophobia entwined Britain's national conscience and for six long months the killing spree continued. Casualties were counted in mega-deaths; damage in mega-billions of pounds sterling; the excuses from government to cover their backsides in mega-lies;

and the inability of the police and homeland protection departments to find the culprits in mega-scratching of heads, mega-lamentations and mega-requests for additional funding.

Undertakers grew rich and fat on funerals as the people of Britain grew gaunt and thin with worry; building contractors grew rotund and wealthy on repairing the damage, whilst company assets and private bank accounts dwindled in the face of an extended Islamic extremist campaign; the fame and fear of the unseen assassin that was Saladin grew with each day that passed, whilst the public's confidence in Britain's law enforcement departments mixed with the blood of the dead and dying, and washed slowly away.

The one-sided war left a short-term gain and a long-term legacy for one particular British institution. The National Health Service had been buckling at the knees for decades. Rising numbers of immigrants from Europe, added to a sharply increasing national birth rate, had all but overwhelmed the capacity of this international benchmark in public health.

Many of the senior managers of the NHS felt personally responsible for the millions of deaths. For years, they had prayed for a solution to their worrying problems - a paucity of pounds sterling, a dearth of drugs, a diminishing quality of staff and the never-ending nightmare of finding enough space. Their Lord in Heaven had answered their prayers and to the NHS managers the millions who had died were analogous to a fat man loosening his belt after a particularly gargantuan meal. And now those same managers felt a terrible guilt and many would take that guilt to the grave.

The long-term legacy was not immediately apparent. Naturally, the Homeland Protection Departments had immediately become aware of damaging levels of nuclear radiation following the attacks, since such tests were a routine part of initial scene-of-incident tests. Consistent in their lack of faith in the common sense of the British people, the government chose to hide the truth, slap D-notices on the press and remind civil servants of their responsibilities under the official secrets act. A farcical, if typical, decision and one that would see the incumbent TorLibLab coalition government struggle to retain public support for the rest of its term in office. Saladin's Fabian-policy had been extremely effective; the non-stop succession of bombings and minor skirmishes had sounded the death knell for the British government.

But the long-term legacy could not remain forever hidden and it was to take its own toll over the next decade. The period of the walking dead is defined as that period of time between a body being exposed to radiation, to the lapse into coma and death. Over time, the short-term gain of the NHS was obliterated by the vast numbers of radiation sufferers who once again overwhelmed the health services. Sufferers of acute radiation syndrome endure first-degree burns, blood disorders, immune deficiency resulting in an increased susceptibility to bugs and viruses, and intestinal bleeding. Not to mention massive diarrhoea, loss of water in the body and that well-known conveyor of souls to the stairway to heaven - radiation induced cancer.

In a macabre twist to the tail, Freinet ran an advert for several years after the viscous campaign of violence under the heading 'All good Christians go to heaven. Buy a Penny Black from your favourite Mullah; all the postage you need'.

CHAPTER 24
GREAT MUSLIM WAR

THREAD:

Most of the supporters of Islam born during the last seven decades of the 21st century were either Sunni or Shiite. They followed in their parents' footsteps and adhered for life to whatever religious persuasion into which they were born.

During this period it was very rare for a follower of Islam to convert to a different denomination. They were fiercely loyal to their chosen religious persuasion but similar to every other human being in this world, their spiritual convictions were generally stronger than their political or national convictions; and changing sides from a political or national point of view was not usually a personal problem.

In terms of numbers, the followers of Islam were second only to those of Christianity. But as was the case with most other social or religious beliefs, Islam had a problem. It was a religion of division with two distinct denominations, one Sunni, the other Shi'a, and had been so for many centuries. And this division was Islam's only weakness. Although all were Muslim, the two denominations differed only in their individual interpretation of the Qur'an, which governs their everyday lives - and their choice of political leadership.

Throughout the first four decades of the 21st century, the populations of Islam's Middle Eastern strongholds of Iran and Iraq had fluctuated. As with chaff blown by the wind, the devout Muslims were blown across the continents of Asia and North Africa in all directions. The reason? An accident of birth. Simply because they happened to be born Sunni, Shi'a or Kurd.

By 2040, the huge country that is Iran had forcefully ejected its tiny proportion of Sunni Muslims and was populated, almost exclusively, by some one hundred million Shi'a. Persecuted, discriminated against and treated as a lower caste, almost ten million Sunni had left their native Iran and fled to the adjacent Sunni heartlands of Iraq or continued onwards to find a new life in whatever country would accommodate them.

During the same period, in a tit for tat pogrom, a growing Sunni dominance in Iraq had forced its population of about eighteen million Shiites to flee into Iran.

Kurds had been shunted in all directions, mainly north across the Taurus Mountains into northern Turkey, and many more moving even further west settling wherever they could in all countries of Europe. Seen as lesser Muslims, these mainly Sunni worshippers who do not wholly support the religious and social dogmas of Islamic life - for example, their women do not wear veils - were not really welcome in either the Sunni or the Shiite camps.

Both Sunni and Shiite leaders were still wistfully dreaming about taking Africa as a continent for their own. Hugely inventive, the Sunni leadership under Rasul-Allah had ordered the development of a method of hoovering up the remnants of radiation left after a neutron bomb attack. They hoped to have a great need for this technology after what they saw as a decisive victory over the Iranian Shiites.

Maybe such a victory might also be seen as the sign from Allāh that they had been waiting for.

The scene was set for a confrontation, an attempt to achieve dominance within the Islamic community. All that was needed was a man with the necessary vision, determination, ruthless streak and unlimited resources to wage war.

Alfred Leonard

IRAQ. SATURDAY 27TH APRIL, 2041.

A few short kilometres northeast of Mosul, a dark-skinned man sat on a low hill overlooking the river Tigris. Not overly tall but heavily boned and muscular, his body remained totally still, not a muscle stirred; and brightly blue eyes, glazed and unfocussed, gazed over the scene below him.

Firmly entrenched in its ivory tower, the mind of this man was completely detached from the everyday preoccupations of mankind. At thirty-eight years of age, Saladin was a fine figure of a man and his seemingly uninterested hawk-like eyes missed nothing as he gazed down at the gently flowing river.

Six of his trusty Scimitar Lieutenants sat some distance apart, looking up at their leader in awe. They too remained totally silent, hardly daring to draw breath; for they each knew that Saladin was communing with his heavenly advisor.

Further out, set in a wide circle, were the members of the six Scimitars, looking outwards across the valleys to the mountains beyond, searching for approaching danger.

It was early morning, the air was frosty and the sand beneath their feet felt cold and wet, almost as if it had been freshly doused with freezing water. Ordinary militiamen wore the off-white ankle-length shirts, known as *thawbs*, supplemented for warmth with a camelhair cloak - the *bisht* - and with the traditional *keffiyeh* headdress of chequered cotton held in place by a knotted cord. The only concession made to modern-day warfare was the sturdy American-style combat boots.

In contrast, Saladin and his Scimitars wore jet-black hooded copes, topped by heavy sheepskin coats. Russian-style fur hats pulled firmly over their ears and brightly shining black boots completed their distinctive uniforms. The black of their garb marked them as special, untouchables, the elite, the chosen ones; and ensured that their orders were obeyed instantly. In a few short hours, the heavy outer clothing would have to be discarded as the daytime temperatures soared to over fifty degrees Celsius; only the knee-length leather boots would remain in place.

'*Listen carefully, Rasul-Allah.*' The voice entered Saladin's mind, a voice that he had grown accustomed to, and he knew that he could depend upon the truthfulness of the words that were to follow.

'Listen! Can you hear the noise of the advancing armies? Can you hear the sound of Allāh's might let loose at your command? Concentrate and I will show you how the true and faithful Sunni armies will purge the world of its Shiite enemy.'

For many long minutes the voice of Gabriel continued. *'Huge armies will descend upon the Shiites of Persia[27].'* Into Saladin's mind entered the vision of gigantic armies on the march, each individual face tilted towards the heavens and set in a rictus of religious fanaticism. Strangely, and despite the vastness of the human assemblage tramping through the deserts, not a speck of dust flew in the air.

'The Sunni armies of Allāh will be recruited from true Muslims in North Africa. They will combine with similar armies formed in the Land of the Two Holy Mosques[28] and will follow their tank regiments into Mesopotamia[29]. There they will rest in the Fertile Crescent, form-up into their attacking formations and await your command to advance. Once given, your final command cannot be rescinded; the attack will go forward to its final conclusion. The armies will thrust through the Zagros Mountains into Persia to mop up what is left of the dissident Shiites who had the temerity to tamper with the words of Allāh, committed to memory by the Prophet Mohammadpbuh and drafted as Allāh's laws and instructions in the holy book.'

BED/0109.

The crew called it the tumble dryer. The command area of a modern main battle tank was tiny in comparison to the size of the vehicle. It was also very hot and uncomfortable since the vehicle tended to roll around a lot when crossing uneven terrain. And the air-conditioning usually blew hot air during the fierce heat of the day and freezing cold air during the lower night-time temperatures.

For most western countries, the tank had been discarded as a weapon of war. It was just too vulnerable to a variety of attacks; from other tanks, helicopters, land mines, missiles and close-in enemy personnel. But to the Middle Eastern countries, who still envisaged war-

---

[27]Persia. Iran.

[28]Land of the Two Holy Mosques. Saudi Arabia.

[29]Mesopotamia. Iraq.

fare as involving huge masses of infantry, the battle tank was retained as one of their main weapons, mainly, it must be admitted, as a means of instilling mindless fear into enemy foot soldiers.

But one country took a different view. The war-machine that was Saudi Arabia in the 2030s was forced to take a lead in developing a new model of this fearsome weapon. Oil revenue provided the sinews of war and the bulging coffers were so large that they could not be depleted by any excess of personal or national indulgence.

Years before the Saudis would simply have thrown huge amounts of cash or sympathetic oil concessions on to the bargaining table and taken whatever happened to be available from the world's brokers of arms. But since the western nations had dumped the tank from their military line-up, they had no other option than to build their own.

Built on the hovercraft principle, they were trackless, powered by twenty-four small jet engines to provide lift and thrust. And the multi-directional thrust from a number of these engines could be used to deter close-attack from ground troops or to create dust or sand camouflage. In the right conditions, the vehicle was capable of travelling at up to one hundred kilometres each hour.

The crew of BED/0109 were all small men. The tanks took their name from the only race of people that can survive in the *Rub' al Khali*, that huge area of virtual wasteland in the heart of the country, that sea-of-sand, otherwise known as the Empty Quarter. The Bedouin people seemed to thrive in the harsh desert conditions and the BED tanks were designed to do the same.

Small in body and small in mind; it was often also thought that the crews of these tanks must be empty headed and definitely lacking in brain cells when volunteering to wage war in them. But many men did volunteer and the main requirement for those especially selected was that they be vertically challenged and small-boned in stature, for such men were the only ones capable of operating within the cramped conditions of the tumble dryer.

Most junior rank volunteers were displaced Muslims from further east, undernourished from birth, without family ties or national pride, careless of their lives and, refused work-permits, grateful for any chance to earn a living.

'Will we have to wait here long before we are ordered to move on, Captain?' Asking the question was the smallest of the crew of three,

Jalal Al Saher. He was the driver of the tank and unlike the other two crew members, he had no other function. The day was hot, despite the early hour, and Jalal was sheltering in the shadow provided by the tank, lying on his stomach and occasionally sipping contentedly at a cup of thick, black coffee.

As far as the eye could see, the Saudi-built tanks filled the area around the small town of Rafha, near to the Iraqi border. Parked tightly together in neat Squadrons, the crews were resting and preparing their mobile battle weapons after a long rail and road journey from their barracks in Jeddah.

Soon now, the engines would ignite for the day's testing and tuning, the air would fill with dust, sand and the fumes from aviation-fuel and the simple act of taking breath would become one chest-burning heave after another.

'Already we are nine hundred tanks strong.' Another small man answered the question. Standing a touch over one point five metres tall, this was Second Lieutenant Abdul Karim Bashir. Recently graduated from the Officers' training college at Riyadh, the term 'captain' was music to his ears and gave him a distinctly over-inflated estimation of his worth. He never tired of hearing his crew address him as such and he longed for the day when his brave deeds, solid leadership and fearless dedication in driving forward in an attack would lead him to be awarded the three pips on his shoulder.

Gazing down at his reclining crewman, Abdul continued, 'When the rest of our battalion arrives we can expect some orders.' Second Lieutenant Bashir was well aware of the orders for his battalion but he still remembered one of the lessons from his training course. 'Do not divulge too much information to your men. The rank and filers are renowned gossip-mongers and they will sneak off into the desert to trade information for a woman, money or food at every given opportunity.' The young Lieutenant gazed around the tank, 'And where is that lazy good-for-nothing Armourer?'

Absent from the speaking group was Mizanir Jinnah. 'He has gone into the desert,' Jalal gave the traditional response that demanded no further questions be asked. It was universally accepted within the desert communities that when a man goes into the desert, he should be left alone to complete whatever ablutions might be necessary.

'Umm!' The Tank Captain was doubtful, suspecting that his

Armourer was malingering in the sick-call queue, but kept his own counsel. 'And tell our illustrious Armourer that I have my eye on him. I will be back at ten hundred hours. Make sure you are both ready for today's test firings.'

There was no distinction in rank between the driver and Armourer, they were both privates, but the Captain always acknowledged Jalal to be the senior man because he was two months older. An accident of birth, that had caused Jalal much pain and stress since he had joined his present tank crew, for the absent Mizinir was indeed a wastrel. 'As Allāh is my witness, I will do for that bastard Jinnah before this campaign comes to an end,' Jalal made his silent promise.

In the plush surroundings of an old-style Bedouin tent, Second Lieutenant Bashir listened to his Squadron Commander. 'We are almost ready.' Using a short wooden baton, the diminutive Major stabbed at the large map to his rear. 'Battalions massing along the Iraqi border are almost up to strength. At Turayf, Al Jalamid, Ash Shu'bah, Lawqah, Al 'Uwayqilah, Ar'ar and here at Rafha. Ten thousand tanks will shortly be ready to strike. Within a week, our troops will arrive and we will receive the order to advance. Get your men and machines on top line. Failure is not an option.' The dark, almost black eyes of the tiny Major stared at the fifty Tank Commanders of his Squadron flanked around him, expressionless and soulless like those of a cobra. 'Whichever Tank Commander fails to complete this mission will stand against a wall, with his back to Mecca, and I will personally blow his head off, dismember his body and cast his stinking, cowardly remains into the desert as food for the wildlife.'

Several hours later the Squadron meeting was still going strong. Bashir had not returned to his tank at 10.00 as planned, he dared not excuse himself from the operational planning meeting. Over and over again, the little Major drummed his requirements into his Tank Commanders.

'At the go signal, we will leave Rafha and make our way across the Iraqi border. We will follow the valley of the Sha'ib Firk into the Fertile Crescent, cross the Euphrates and Tigris rivers, and make our way to Ali ash Sharqi, which those of you who have bothered to study your maps will know, is about one hundred kilometres from the foothills of the Zagros. Here we will wait until the signal to invade is received. The journey through the mountains to Iran will be a dangerous period, where we will be exposed to air attacks from the Iranian air force. But our bristling little hedgehogs - the Major's favourite description of his tanks - will be able to deal with them! Our first target inside Iran will be Esfahan, from where we will turn south to Shiraz, thence our final push to Bandar-e Abbas in the Straight of Hormuz. Other battalions will make a similar approach across the Zagros Mountains into Iran and spread in all directions to cleanse our new lands of the Shiite desecraters of the Qur'an.'

All hearts took a slight jolt at the mention of crossing the two mighty rivers in Iraq, for they all knew that their tank's abilities fell somewhat short of its impressive specifications; and they were all equally certain that their fierce little Squadron Major would, of course, spurn any bridge crossings.

'I fully expect that we will not have much mopping up to do,' the Major continued. 'As you all know, massive air and sea attacks will precede our clearance operation. These attacks will rain down on the major cities and troop concentrations, missile sites, airfields, etc., and it is most likely that there will be little resistance left in the country by the time we arrive.'

'*Bullshit!*' thought Lieutenant Bashir. '*If anyone here believes that such strikes will obliterate the Iranian defences, then their brains must be addled by the heat of the Sun.*' They had all read of the safe, underground havens that their own military had built under the sands of the Empty Quarter; and they were pretty certain that the Iranians would have done something similar.

'We are the First Squadron of our battalion and therefore we will lead the charge over the Zagros Mountains and descend like avenging angels on to the offending Shiites of Iran.' With these final words, Major Parviz Tanweer dismissed his Tank Commanders.

SALADIN.

As the huge Sun climbed higher into the sky, the men on the hill overlooking the Tigris grew uncomfortably hot and discarded their nighttime clothing. The temperature rose higher and higher and there was little to alleviate their discomfort except for the prevailing south-easterly wind, known as the *sharqi*, which could blow continuously for several days, gusting up to 80 km/h and often raising huge dust spirals reaching to several thousand metres.

Saladin appeared oblivious of the conditions. Even the smaller dust tornadoes that danced around the hills and valleys did not disturb his quiet contemplation of the valley below. Yes, he could hear the approaching steel-armada, still out of sight but close now, very close.

Resembling a hesitant camel emerging from the dark shade of a sand dune, the first tank suddenly came into view. It was difficult to make out the outline of the vehicle; it was painted to blend in with the terrain in a haphazard design of beige, tan and black designs.

Having briefly glanced at the specifications of the tank, Saladin had expected that its jet engines would be blowing sand and dust in all directions; but this was not the case. As the tank made progress across the sandy terrain, the highly effective side-skirts returned any disturbed material to the ground, leaving little evidence of its passing except for a smooth, even surface.

In less than fifteen minutes, the valley below was crowded with several hundred tanks. Each tank carried a cadre of ten foot-soldiers and as the tanks ground to a halt and settled gently on to the ground amidst the diminishing howl of slowing jet engines, the men leapt from the rear hatches and lay prone on the ground. The eyes of each man looked up the hill, searching for their earthly Lord.

Saladin knew that this was but one small part of the huge invading army that would strike east into Iran. But in this single group was the Army General who would give the order to start the invasion; and Saladin sat beneath his colourful umbrella, protected from the intense rays of the Sun, and waited for the General to come to him.

Army General Shuja Mawahhid did not bend his knee, or bow, to many men. Resplendent in his khaki desert fatigues, his trousers tucked into the tops of his boots, he looked every inch the panzer Brigade Commander. For this occasion, he also sported row upon row of medals, awarded to him for his sterling military service to his native country of Saudi Arabia; and nothing whatever to do with the gold cord that held his keffiyeh in place, signifying that he was a cousin to the Crown Prince.

Under thirty years of age, short and as fat as a pregnant donkey, the General stood by the side of his lead tank. Sweating profusely, he searched the hillside for Saladin's tent, assuming wrongly that the young religious leader would be so encamped. Eventually he spotted the colourful umbrella under which Saladin sat and estimated the walk to be about a kilometre and a half. 'Too bloody far in this heat,' the General whispered his agonised complaint.

The blue eyes of Rasul-Allah looked down on the perspiring General. It would be a long hike for the fat Saudi royal and Saladin settled more comfortably on his rear end; and waited. He had no intention of making this any easier for the army man and quickly quelled any inclination to walk down and alleviate the man's obvious distress.

'*Start the engines, and take me up the hill.*' The intention entered the General's mind and the words almost escaped from his mouth but before he could utter a sound the words were stamped firmly back into his throat by a squeal of sound that overwhelmed his senses; and the metallic sound resembled the drawing of a thousand sabres from their scabbards - but much louder.

'*Walk to Rasul-Allah, General Muwahhid. Throw yourself to the ground in obeisance before the man who is appointed as Allāh's Messenger on Earth and the leader of my Sunni faithful. Such a respectful gesture of homage may well save your head, for already you have delayed The Prophet too long. He reads your thoughts and if you wish to keep your tongue, look not for the tuft hunter[30] in Rasul-Allah.*'

A gurgling chuckle bubbled from the chest of Saladin as he watched the little fat man throw himself to the ground, his hands over his ears, trying to block out the sound of the voice echoing through his head. '*The show of deference is a tad early,*' thought the Sunni leader, '*but better early than not at all.*'

BED/0109.

'*Bismillah,* let Allāh guide us, and for God's sake keep us the right way up, and out of the water.' This was his Tank Captain's simple plea

---

[30]Tuft hunter. The aristocracy once wore gold tufts or tassels on their caps in Universities; and a tuft hunter was a toady to these.

before giving the order to move, whenever they set off for each day's operations.

The words hardly registered in Jalal's mind, he had heard the words so many times before. They had been on the road for several weeks and the memory of the quiet days camped at Rafha revolved around in his mind, reminding him of a paradise lost.

The tiny driver of BED/0109 bent forward in the shell of the tank. Touching the warm steel with his lips he whispered his own daily prayer. 'Allāh be praised. Let all engines start; let all systems work; let us meet no enemy today; let us have smooth ground to cross; try to keep the tired-assed Jinnah awake; keep the evil bastard Bashir off my back - and above all, let there be no water to cross.'

Quite why he made these daily pleas, Jalal Al Saher did not really know. Lacking in race memory to help him, his early days were more akin to those of a camp dog than of a human being, scavenging in the filth of the campsites searching for scraps of food. Of parents, brothers, sisters, family of any kind, the man had no recollection. From his earliest memories as a toddler, he simply followed the band of people that walked.

These were not nomads but displaced persons, fleeing from something - to somewhere - the details of which were mercifully missing from his memory banks. Salal knew only that each day the people walked and he either kept up or perished. He prayed to Allāh but knew nothing of the person or deity with that name. He did not understand the conception of a heavenly entity and had always assumed that Allāh was the King of Saudi Arabia, the land in which the people suddenly stopped walking.

As a child, listening to the words of others had been his only schooling and he had painstakingly taught himself to read and write during his early teens, stealing books and writing materials from wherever he could find them. In his head he identified himself as a Muslim and he had known how to complete the forms to impress the recruiting Sergeant when he had volunteered for military service - marking Sunni in the appropriate places. But the real reason that Salal made his daily pleas was that it left him feeling somehow better to have asked.

Major Parviz Tanweer, their Squadron Commander, did not have the remotest connection with the Saudi royal family and therefore

BED/0109 was not part of the General's Tank Squadron. Jalal did not therefore get a chance to see Rasul-Allah, even from a distance. And this was something that he dearly wanted to do, a chance to meet a real superhuman, to have a picture of a person in his mind when he prayed must be similar to how he imagined it must be to have a memory of a mother and father. Someone or something to relate to a picture in his mind's eye when he asked for help and guidance.

'Rasul-Allah has given the order to move. Forward Saher, follow our fearless Major.' The words thrilled Jalal and he felt a sudden, intense feeling of love towards his spiritual leader. No such loving feelings for his Tank Commander, however, who accompanied his orders with a savage kick into his driver's back; and Jalal cursed those early 20th century tanks where the only means of communication amongst the crew was by such kicks; and cursed even more the cruelty of the modern Tank Commanders who continued the practice for fun.

Every day was a monotonous repetition of the previous days and weeks. Eyes glued on the screen in front of him, Jalal's sole task was to keep formation with the tank in front. Whilst transiting from point A to point B, and with a junior second Lieutenant in command, it was their tank's role to follow, a fact for which Jalal was always grateful. For this was easy, providing nothing went wrong with the engines, he simply set the system to maintain a set distance from the tank in front and tried to remain alert in case of any malfunction.

Problems for Salal would only occur when the Squadron deployed into their fighting formations, because that would be when the big-booted-bastard behind him had to start making decisions and giving orders.

'River crossing ahead.' The dreaded words from his Tank Commander flooded into Jalal's consciousness. 'Oh no,' he groaned, 'not again!' He ached to scream some abuse or criticism of his Squadron Major but could only mutter under his breath, 'Why in Satan's name does the little bastard not use the bridges?' The Major was probably all of a single millimetre taller than Jalal but in the tank driver's mind he was a much smaller man.

BED/0109 had made several river crossings in the last few weeks. All such crossings filled each and every tank man with a sweaty-palm dread while anticipating the manoeuvre and a sickly, bowel-loosening fear during the actual crossing. And the Major did not pussyfoot around when such a hazard came across his bows, he liked to see the tanks immersed completely as they entered the water; and woe betide any of his subordinate Commanders who decided to reduce speed.

At a little over 50 km/h the Bedouin hit the water. Seat straps bit deeply into Jalal's flesh as his body shot forward at the sudden deceleration and his knees cracked painfully on the console in front of him. Whoosh - the sound of the water flooding over the tank sounded loudly in his ears. There was little room inside his driving position and Jalal imagined himself in a metal coffin at the bottom of a desert well.

Every spare millimetre of space was used for storing ammunition and most parts of his body cracked against some nearby hard thing as he was jolted around. Boots cracked into his back, a double kick! The Lieutenant must have slid forward, panicked and pushed his booted feet into Jalal's back to stop his forward slide. *'You miserable excuse for a human being. One day I will take great pleasure in feeding your balls to my camel.'* Jalal's love for his Tank Commander knew no bounds.

The Bedouin tank is adept at operating in water, is totally watertight and virtually unsinkable. The words in the tank's handbook jumped into Jalal's mind, followed instantly by a sudden thought *'And so was the bloody Titanic!'* In the desert, for both man and machine, sand and dust will find its way into every orifice, no matter how small. But water is even more efficient at confounding man's ingenuity; and the words tank and watertight do not sit well together.

Already there was about one hundred and fifty millimetres of water inside the tank, swilling from side to side as the vehicle groped for the far shore. Water dripped from overhead, ran down the bulkheads, sloshed around his feet, obscured his vision and gurgled like loud watery farts each time the tank wallowed in the wake of some other vehicle. 'Death where is thy sting?' Jalal screamed the words in total frustration, looked into his rear-view mirror and for the first time in living memory, saw his Tank Commander smile. In that single moment, the crew of BED/0109 became a team; and never again did Second Lieutenant Abdul Karim Bashir use his boots on a tank driver.

SATURDAY 8TH JUNE, 2041. SALADIN.

Literally hundreds of helicopters and fixed wing aircraft were required to keep the thousands of tanks supplied with fuel, ammunition and victuals.

Throughout the passage across Iraq the tanks had made daily user checks of their weapon systems and were expending ammunition and fuel as if there was no tomorrow. And the small-statured members of humanity, which made up the crews of these weapons of war, grew smaller still, since fuel and ammunition took precedence over food and water. Salal was careful each evening to sleep with his boots beneath his head, for it was often said that a Saudi tank crew would eat anything and boot-stew was better than nothing at all.

Such re-supplying flights provided Saladin and his Scimitars with plenty of opportunities to hop, skip and jump in front of the invading tank Squadrons. During the preceding ten days the advancing Squadrons had hurtled from the Zagros Mountains on to the Plateau of Iran. They had reached and taken Qom and today the attempt to take Tehran would commence.

'Very appropriate,' Saladin considered his choice of day to be a stroke of genius. It was the day on which Muhammadpbuh had died and on this day Saladin would mark the moment in time in yet another way. For it was to be the day that the Muslim nation became united into a single denomination and ruled by one leader.

Senior clerics of the Sunni Muslim faith preferred the word guided in place of ruled but in Saladin's mind there was no doubt; he would rule; and already Gabriel had shown him a vision of the future where he was the single acknowledged ruler of a planet. The vision disturbed him somewhat because what little he could see of the planet over which he reigned supreme did not resemble Earth too closely. But, of course, it could be no other, so he did not worry overly about it.

He and his Scimitars had leapfrogged to the front of the General's column. A few kilometres south of Tehran international airport, he waited once again for the overly fat donkey to appear at the head of his column.

Over the past weeks the efforts of the ground forces of the Iranian Shiite resistance had been mainly spasmodic and weak. And the country's air forces displayed a similar reluctance to commit in any great strength. Although usually extremely effective in destroying tanks, most of Iran's tank-killing helicopter crews refused to fly against the BEDs. The pilots knew that the tanks were too heavily armed and could engage the attacking helicopters long before their own systems got within effective range.

However, some air attacks had been launched at the invading tank columns and the invaders had not escaped unscathed. As far as infantry was concerned, only lightly garrisoned barracks had so far been encountered and these had been quickly overrun.

Most of Iran's elite troops had drawn in their horns and retrenched in the Alborz Mountains, together with hundreds of thousands of civilians fearful of remaining in their homes, preferring to make a stand at the side of their military elite or make their escape from the country. From these positions, and with their backs to the Caspian Sea, they must fight to the death or surrender.

Saladin knew this and he also knew that he did not want his troops to falter at the last step. The Shiite Ayatollahs must all perish and he needed a strong man to lead the final charge against his enemy.

'Shit!' General Muwahhid was the first to spot the man standing in the middle of the road in front of his column. 'Bloody fool! Do not stop driver. Run the imbecile down.'

Some innermost intuition must have been watching over the foolhardy General this day, at the last moment the black garb of the man in front of him gave meaning.

'Rasul-Allah! By the beard of Allāh, what a fool I am.' Viciously, the General booted his driver. 'Stop, you heap of sheep shit! Stop the tank now!' Saladin did not flinch and the tank veered over to the side of the road and came to an abrupt halt.

The General was furious. *'What a stupid thing to do. Stand in front of a bloody tank. The man's a maniac. I'll give him a piece of my mind.'* The angry thoughts flashed through his mind as he hoisted his well-fed frame from the tank. All thoughts of obeisance, or deference, had been driven from the General's thoughts as he strode up to the waiting Saladin. 'What do you think you are doing, you bloody oaf. I could have run you down had I not recognised you at the last moment.'

Spittle flew in all directions; such was the force of the words being shouted from the brightly red face. Without a word, Saladin stepped forward and shot the General between the eyes.

From out of nowhere his Scimitars surrounded the second tank and dragged an unfortunate Colonel into the open air. Feet dragging deeply into the sand, the blackly clad men dragged the battalion's second-in-command to Saladin.

The Colonel was no fool, he instantly fell to his knees, bent his lips to the sand and kept his words and his thoughts to himself. Soft words rained down upon the Colonel's back. 'You are now my Tank General. Rip the insignia of rank from the fat pig over there and take charge of the final attack. You have one task; drive the Shiites out of our new lands. If a single Ayatollah survives this day you will feed the camel dung flies tomorrow.'

BED/0109.

The three men living within BED/0109 had coalesced into a superb, highly-trained team. The river crossing had been a turning point in their relationship. Even the lazy Jinnah had morphed into a proficient Armourer, who was capable of operating the computer systems that found, acquired and destroyed hundreds of simultaneous targets.

Their fighting machine had acquitted itself well in many battles and had downed buildings, bridges, aircraft and the never-ending attacks by marauding suicide squads intent upon taking at least one tank to paradise with them.

It had even sounded the death knell for the antiquated battle tanks that the Iranians had dragged out of retirement. Their Bedouin tank seemed to lead a charmed life, the engines never faltered, they always managed to replenish their ammunition and fuel, and even their meals had improved now that their Skipper - as they now called him - filched extra rations from the Officers' supplies.

War is a fairly pleasant business when on the winning side and up against little opposition. Uncomfortable and frightening at times to be sure, but, thought Saher, *'Certainly not the ghastly nightmare that I had been expecting.'*

TEL AVIV, ISRAEL.

A young mother, still in her teens, sits upright in her bed. A wide smile lights up her face and welcoming arms open wide, reaching for the boy that she had introduced to this world only fifteen minutes before. The pain of the birth was long forgotten, it had faded to the back burners of her brain, forced there by the unexpected and over-whelming joy that had suffused her body when she felt the boy slip from her womb.

Bright sunlight floods through the windows and silhouettes the body of the nurse carrying her child. In the mind-numbing euphoria of the few minutes following the birth, the young mother had watched the Sun creep inexorably towards her bed. Now, as she looked up towards the window, the nurse carrying her son walked into the ward. On one side of the nurse, the head of the boy was clearly outlined by the strengthening sunlight behind them; and the young mother had the distinct impression of a halo encircling the head of her son.

Brighter than she had ever seen before, the sunlight seemed strangely different, whiter maybe. Motherhood certainly changed the way she looked at the world.

'Perhaps the boy will grow up to be an important person, destined to lead our country into the future.' Her thoughts probably mirrored those of every other mother since time immemorial. Of one thing she was certain, as long as she drew breath the boy would want for nothing.

The young mother would never know. Almost immediately the ear-popping explosion filled her world. She did not live long enough to hold her son, nor feel the express train of a wind that followed the bang and blew through the hospital obliterating all in its path.

GRAND AYATOLLAH'S BUNKER, MOUNT DAMAVAND.

The terminology of nuclear warfare is fascinating. Mega-deaths describe the death toll. Latest nuclear weapons had a definite nuclear footprint, which is described as the area outside which survival is greatest. Each footprint can be precisely defined and can cover any area from that small enough to take out an individual ship or village; or large enough to wipe out a chosen land mass of any size.

Nuclear shadows are described as those areas within a nuclear footprint that are sheltered from a nuclear blast.

Amongst the world's nuclear armoury the neutron bomb is the clever bastard. But neutron bombs are exploded high above their target, which are described as airbursts - and below these air bursts there exist pitifully few protective nuclear shadows. And prevailing winds carry the deadly radiation for many kilometres outside the immediate blast area. Unless you are unlucky enough to be caught directly below an air blast, as was the Israeli hospital in Tel Aviv, you can expect to live a little longer after the initial explosion.

However, one's personal expectation of a normal lifespan, together with one's perception of a reasonable quality of life, good health and *joie de vivre*, requires serious readjustment. These intensely dirty bombs kill people by extremely high levels of radiation. They kill every living creature touched by its lethal rays, except maybe for the cockroach, but do little damage to the infrastructure surrounding the target area.

Buildings suffer little damage, save the odd blasting out of a few windows, and doors are prone to provide a few magic carpet rides. They are, in effect, the epitome of nuclear weaponry and were, by the mid-2020s, on the wish list of every country on the face of the Earth.

These bombs are usually delivered directly from high-flying aircraft or remotely by missile. But one country had gone a step further.

Deep within the Alborz Mountains in the northern areas of Iran sits the impressive heights of the highest peak in the Middle East. A dormant volcano, Mount Damavand reaches a little over five thousand six hundred metres into the sky. To the east is the beautiful green valley of the river Haraz, which winds its way to the Caspian Sea to the north. It is from this valley that access is provided to Iran's top-secret war operations complex and fallback administration centre buried deep within the mountain.

Accommodation for about a quarter of a million troops was provided in and around the mountain. It was here that Iran always planned its final defence and the troops had been arriving for many weeks, abandoning their traditional defensive positions in the certain knowledge of being overrun by the advancing Sunnis.

Underground shelters housed several thousand aircraft, both fixed-wing jet fighters and helicopters. Vast amounts of ammunition, missiles, food and spare parts filled the cavernous storage areas, deep within the mountain.

The man was old, very old, with the brightly white hair of an octogenarian. His beard was long; simple corded sandals seemed glued to his feet; he wore the crisply white robes of a Grand Ayatollah of the Shiite Muslim faith; and sported large metal-rimmed spectacles that enhanced the glare from his eyes.

For the past eleven years he had ruled Iran. He was a strong leader and brooked no breaching of the detailed rules associated with his faith. A Muslim's life is engulfed in rules and regulations, which find their origins in the Qur'an, but a Grand Ayatollah can change the interpretation of these regulations and such a man who also wields political dominance can therefore tighten or loosen the stranglehold on his people at will.

This particular Iranian leader had never been known to relax his grip on his people's throats. It was said that he would prosecute on a person's thoughts, if only he could read them.

Consequently, the country's prisons, remand homes and other establishments of penal reform were always jammed full. But unlike other countries, there was never a lack of space within these institutions; the firing squad was a useful tool in freeing up space for a never-ending flow of transgressors.

For the people of Iran there was one simple rule: know and obey *all* the rules of Shiite Muslim society. In the courtrooms throughout the country there was little need for defence attorneys, juries, witness boxes and the paraphernalia of western nations' legal systems.

Any traffic offence, from parking more than a hundred and fifty millimetres away from the kerb to manslaughter at the wheel of a vehicle. Any personal malpractice from urinating in the street to murder Any religious violation from failing to pray the prescribed number of times each day to gesturing with one's finger at the local Mullahs. All were rewarded with death.

Maybe not an instant death but at some time during a long prison sentence all inmates knew that, eventually, it would become their turn to face the twelve dark holes of the firing squad; feel the fetid warmth from one's own voiding bowels running down shaky legs; and wait for the noise that you know you will not hear.

Some leniency was allowed to the armed forces. So it is not surprising that so many of Iran's young men elected a partial guarantee of reaching old age; all-out war notwithstanding of course.

Iran was an oil-rich country and could afford to pay its military well; it could also afford to produce its own weaponry, and for what it could not itself produce, there were plenty of petro-dollars available with which to make a suitable purchase from a myriad of unscrupulous gunrunners around the globe.

Generally, the other nations of the world were well aware of the highly trained, deeply motivated military that Iran had built up over many decades. They were also well aware of Iran's weapon systems and knew if and how they might counteract their use. For many years, the western world in particular had been keen to limit Iran's growing nuclear capability.

But Iran had grown too strong to listen to western demands; and international agreements are easy to make and even easier to circumnavigate. In short, Iran had little to fear from the rest of the world. Only the religious awe of an avenging Mahdi could defeat them; and that is exactly how the ordinary people of Iran and the largely uneducated military personnel viewed the approaching army of Rasul-Allah. And the knowledge slowly sapped their national confidence and gnawed away at their will to fight.

'My loyal friends. I welcome you to our doomsday room.' Each of the twelve senior Ayatollahs, which made up the Iranian cabinet advisory team, clasped their hands in front of their faces in the traditional gesture of prayer and dipped their heads in deference to their leader. Similar in some respects to the Pope, the Grand Ayatollahs of Iran ruled for life, evoked deep respect from their flocks and were considered by the Shiites of Islam to be Allāh's current representatives on Earth.

'It may well be that Allāh has deserted us. Maybe our forefathers were wrong in their interpretations of His words. Perhaps it is I, or maybe my own reasoning, that has angered our Lord in paradise.' Long pauses separated the spoken thoughts of the Grand Ayatollah and his wrinkled face showed the signs of the massive strain that the old man had been subjected to over the preceding few months.

The outline of his features seemed fuzzy and blurred, almost as if they had merged into a flat sheet of brown-paper; his eyes were dull and lifeless; and mucus dripped constantly from his nose. With a casual, poorly aimed Australian-wave at this dripping appendage, he continued.

'Our people are fearful. Our armed forces are doubtful of their ability to repel the invading Sunnis from the west. Is it not ironic, that our greatest fear has always been of the Western World? The Great Satan that is the decadence of the United States of America has always been recognised as the source of our most feared anticipation of danger. Who would have imagined that the attack on our homeland, and on our beliefs, would come not from the western Christians, but from western Muslims?' The mind of the old man was wandering and he found it extremely difficult to suppress whatever thought entered his head; he felt an almost uncontrollable compulsion to speak each and every thought.

Many long minutes of silence followed his last words. During the utterance of his philosophical musings, the twelve cabinet members had pushed themselves to their feet, in a perfectly timed rising Mexican wave. Moving extremely slowly they had clustered around their leader and now looked down upon the head of the Grand Ayatollah in a gruesome caricature of expectant death and decay.

Shaking with fear and trepidation, the right arm of Iran's political and spiritual leader reached out and lifted a solid gold flap in the centre of the table.

BED/0109.

The 1st Squadron of the 2nd Saudi Tank Battalion that was Major Parviz Tanweer's had received new orders. Following a hastily arranged briefing of his Squadron Commanders, the forty-two surviving tanks turned north.

In great good humour, Major Tanweer had decided to be lenient with the junior Tank Commander who had so carelessly allowed his tank to fall out of the advance as they approached their primary target of Esfahan.

New orders had thrilled him to the very core of his being. Personally summoned by his old friend and new General of tanks, he would be awarded the signal honour of taking part in the final annihilation of their enemies. Already he could feel the weight of a Colonel's pips on his shoulders and the bright red flashes on his lapels.

Five hundred kilometres give or take, as the crow flies. Most of this distance across the notorious Dasht-e Kavir desert, known in the western world as the Great Salt desert, which stretches from the Alborz Mountains in the north, to the Emptyness Desert in the southeast.

The Major was desperate to make the rendezvous scheduled for eighteen hours hence. Cooped within their metal coffins, he knew that daytime temperatures would soar to over sixty degrees Celsius, a temperature in which humans found it difficult to draw breath.

The Squadron would have to average a little over thirty kilometres each hour to make it. A heart-pounding race against time but he would push his crews to the limit and, he thought ruefully, he would have to leave any stragglers and forego the joy of feeling the end of his revolver touching live flesh before he gently squeezed the trigger.

A recently-discovered rapport within BED/0109 gave this tank a better than average chance of making the mad dash to the north. Each member of the crew supported the other two; and almost unique amongst the entire Tank Corps, each could perform the duties of the other. Additionally, their Skipper had risked his life by lightening the load of ammunition and taking on extra rations of water.

Inside the command module of the tank it was hot, noisy and very uncomfortable. An untrained body could not possibly tolerate the cacophonous noise from the jet engines or survive the bone-shaking, muscle-stretching rolling of the tank across the never-ending sand dunes.

To add further grist to their extreme discomfort, salt crystals found a way into the interior of the tanks. As would miniature leeches, they stuck to the sweaty skin of the tank crews, burning large areas of exposed skin, particularly those who made the cardinal error of attempting to dislodge the coarse crystals.

'Miz. It's your turn to drive, take over from the Skipper.' Using his fingers, Jalal prodded the comatose Armourer and threw a water bottle in the general direction of his brother-in-arms.

Sleeping was impossible in the moving vehicle but with practice it was possible to switch off the brain and gain some rest, even in the most extreme of conditions. The simple action of lowering heavy eyelids, dropping a head that feels ten times its normal weight on to a chest and the removal of the stress of concentrating can be relatively restful. Unable to lie flat, the small men tossed and turned in their seats attempting to find some relief from the strain of bent limbs, as would a weary passenger suffering in an aircraft's economy seats.

Like a snowstorm, indications of the expected Iranian air attacks appeared on the screens of the attacking tank formations. 'Scatter!' The single word command instructed the tank formations to spread out, make as small a target as they possibly could and prepare to defend themselves.

The fingers of the Commander and Armourer of BED/0109 flew over the keyboards. Each knew the tank's attack and defensive systems as well as they knew the backs of their own hands.

Communication satellites in space gave the Saudi tank crews a clear picture of the impending battle. The system identified the number of airborne attackers and allocated targets to the ground forces. The onboard tank system suggested suitable weapons for each target, based upon whatever ammunition remained unexpended, and gave the human operator a list of release options. Satellite and tank exchanged information continuously, updating remaining resources and targets as the battle progressed.

Apart from the occasional grunt, curse or guttural command following some violent manoeuvre or minor mistake, the inside of Second Lieutenant Abdul Karim Bashir's tank remained chatter free.

'Have you found somewhere yet?' The Skipper shouted into his microphone. 'Not yet, Skipper.' Jalal replied. 'But wait, there is a flat piece of land coming up that looks OK - about three minutes.'

BED/0109 settled to the ground on to her skirts. From the air, early in the morning, in poor light conditions and stationary, it would be almost impossible to spot. Radar repulsing panels were powered up which would help to hide them from the swooping aircraft.

In a blinding blur of flashing explosions and trailing smoke trails, the weapons left the tank. Reminiscent of an exploding armaments depot or a gigantic firework, ordinance exited from every weapons-pod, each in a different direction towards a target in the sky or on the ground. They were in the first wave of tanks and had been instructed to discharge their entire store of ammunition in a single, mind-blowing broadside.

Successive waves of tanks would push past them, fully loaded to take care of the slower moving helicopter formations and any infantry that might be foolish enough to join in the battle.

In the clear blue sky of the approaching dawn, the Iranian pilots dragged their joysticks this way and that. Pushing their aircraft above and beyond the design capabilities of the airframe, they pulled fiercely in every direction, twisting, turning, ducking and diving in their attempts to get within range of a target.

Tensing their muscles to fight the extreme forces of gravity in the tight turns, and frustrated beyond belief, they prayed for sight of something to kill.

But such violent aerial activities tend to burn fuel at an alarming rate and in a final gesture of defiance the pilots pointed their aircraft to the ground and discharged whatever methods of attack remained available to them. To the pilots it was something, their missiles were capable of sub-dividing on firing, and with each sub-division the many smaller missiles were capable of hunting on their own.

The missiles looked for heat and metal; and on the ground there was plenty of that. Many tank crews had panicked in the face of such a determined and heavy aerial attack and had failed to light-up their anti-radar systems or kill their engines. Men streamed from the rear compartments of the tanks and huddled in uncertain groups under whatever cover they could find; they would take no part in this battle but many would pay the ultimate price as a heat-seeking Iranian missile found something warm.

Thirty minutes of continuous firing and BED/0109 was out of ammunition. It could take no further part in the battle until re-supplied, except as a transporter for its disgorged infantry troop.

The three small men sat in the relative silence of their tank, shell-shocked and suffering from temporary deafness; eyes streaming from smoke; faces glistening with sweat and grime; hands shaking in fear as their adrenalin levels slowly dipped to something approaching normal; pulses racing; and muscles twitching in nervous reaction to the strain of the last half hour.

'How did we do?' No one answered the Skipper's question; no one heard the words, not even the speaker. Miraculously they were all in one piece, they had somehow survived the flights of missiles descending from the sky.

Mizinir Jinnah looked down at his screen. Only seven confirmed kills! 'Bloody hell, those Shiite pilots must be good.' His whispered words of salute to the men in the air were, once again, unheard.

He could not control his muscles, his lower jaw seemed to have developed a twitch and his teeth rattled together; no matter how much he strained, he could not control it. He tried to put his hands over his eyes, to stop the rapid, annoying blinking but his hands shook so much that they simply rubbed salt and grime deep within. In response, huge tears erupted from each and when Jalal looked across at his Armourer, he thought that he was crying.

A terrible smell of human excrement filled the tank's interior but not one man made any complaint or pointed an accusing finger at another, they had each felt the venting of their human storage tanks when their vehicle had been slammed into the ground by the force of their first all-round broadside aimed at the attacking aircraft.

Each man had made the same assumption; they had been hit and each expected to be blasted into eternity.

BAGHDAD.

Near the town of Jasimiyah, to the northeast of Baghdad, a young boy stands on the shores of a small lake. At eleven years old he is old enough to shepherd his father's flock of sheep. In truth there is little to occupy his days, apart from daydreaming about his heroic defence of the herd in the face of imaginary attacking leopards.

The sheep ignore him, intent only upon trying to find something to eat from the sparse, unforgiving landscape. Once nomadic, his people now occupy a settlement within sight of the city of Baghdad. Evidence of their uncertain future; and perhaps testament to their disbelief in setting down permanent roots, lies in their tented accommodation.

Something catches the boy's interest in the sky immediately above the nearby city. At first he assumes it is another piece of nature taking flight in the prevailing summer winds. But this is different. Although it is very high it is dropping rapidly and gaining in size with every second that passes.

Instantly blinded by the sudden flash of the nuclear explosion, the boy falls to his knees. He cannot understand what has happened to him but amid the deep blackness he hears the sound of the explosion. His last thought on this Earth is a memory of his father, completing his goodnight ritual: 'Blow out the candle before you sleep my son.'

GRAND AYATOLLAH'S BUNKER, MOUNT DAMAVAND.

Beneath the golden flap was a large red button, covered by yet another metal cover. Lifting this second flap, the old man relaxed his finger to the side of the button.

Unbeknown to the world in general, Iran had developed a nuclear system that was about to astound, and turn green with envy, every other military Commander on the face of the Earth.

Most modern countries could afford their own communications satellites and some outputs from these satellites fed the global Freinet system.

In most Muslim countries, the Freinet output was heavily censored before being released to the general public. Some of the more autocratic countries forbade the wearing of the Pewis and allowed their people access only to their own national systems. Most of the armies of the Middle East were also banned from using the international Pewis, restricted once again to national news broadcasts.

Iran had contributed towards the international system. Enthusiastically, the Iranian leadership had offered to finance the launching of several of the systems suspended in geosynchronous orbit above the Iranian equator. These satellites were slightly larger than those built by the western nations and they were the butt of many jibes and caustic comments about their size - and the technological failure of the Shiite Muslims to make them any smaller.

But hidden within these satellites was a system that would have driven fear and mistrust deep within the other nations of the world: the world's first nuclear system housed in space.

The Grand Ayatollah fiddled with his spectacles. He pulled at his hair and whiskers, touched his ears and rubbed his chin, anything to keep his hand away from the red button. He had made his decision and no one on this Earth could gainsay that decision. An elderly person requires little sleep but this man had lain awake almost every night for the last several weeks, struggling with a decision.

This very morning the attacking Tank Squadrons had entered the foothills of the Alborz Mountains. Large operations boards, consisting of detailed computer-controlled terrain models, clearly showed the horde approaching the Shiites' final defensive position like a colony of ants returning to their nest.

The order to commit the remaining aircraft in a last ditch offensive had been given shortly before first light. Of the remaining infantry brigades, permission was given to any group that wished to find their way to paradise whilst making an attack on the heavily armed tanks.

Iranian infantry brigades are hard-fighting men, as much at home close-in with the knife and bayonet as they are at distance with a rifle, and terrible hand-to-hand skirmishes were ongoing.

As each flight of aircraft or squad of soldiers had left their underground barracks, the old man had stood in his command room, tirelessly blessing each individual enterprise. In the full light of day he could see the crashed aircraft, the tanks smoking and burning, the bodies littering the valley as far as the eye could see.

Even now he could see the helicopters falling from the sky. Here one exploding in mid-air; there another spiralling out of control towards the hard ground; and yonder yet another with a broken main-rotor struggling to maintain height and direction; and still more smashed to smithereens on the top of a Saudi tank.

Unable to suppress a tear, the Shiite leader had watched the desperate imitation of a kamikaze pilot as the helicopter was flown straight into the tank.

After weeks of thought, one basic premise of Muslim logic forced the Shiite leader to his final decision. 'Allāh wills it.'

Panislamism had been his own dream for many of his eighty-four years and in many ways he welcomed the final outcome of the conflict. All things Muslim, and modern Islamic law that governed every aspect of Muslim life, had been dominated by the young Rasul-Allah over the most recent decades. *'Rasul-Allah has the ear of Gabriel; I personally have heard him speak; and his wisdom and heavenly connections have long troubled my own beliefs.'* Such pearls of religious wisdom seemed to flood into his brain, always during those dark, lonely and frightening hours when the world sleeps. At times he suspected the presence of Nasruddin, the Muslim mythological trickster that appears in Muslim folklore, attempting to confuse his weary brain.

'Bismillah, there is but one God.' And the Grand Ayatollah pressed the button, releasing the care of the entire Muslim world into the welcoming hands of Rasul-Allah.

BED/0109.

Sheltering around their tank, the crew and foot soldiers of BED/0109 were struggling to defend themselves against a large number of Iranian National Guards. With a deep bayonet wound in his stomach, Mizinir the Armourer was struggling to prevent his intestines from flopping on to the ground. For some inexplicable reason, the thought of his insides being sullied in the sand frightened him more than the possibility of another stab from the bayonet.

Still a united team, the tank crew had remained close together. But in comparison to the tall and powerful Iranian Guards they might as well have been schoolboys. All three were drenched in blood and weary beyond belief when, in mutual understanding, they linked arms and rolled behind the skirts of their tank, much as would children taking shelter behind their mother. Here they would await their fate.

Amidst the sound of many footfalls and the joyous laughter of rampaging troops, the skirts of the tank were lifted and long bayonets prodded the air around the cuddling group. Death by cold steel was not something that Jalal had ever envisaged; he had always assumed that he would meet his maker inside his tank. His eyes were riveted on the overflowing stomach of Mizinir and he saw the flash of the explosion in his peripheral vision.

GRAND AYATOLLAH'S BUNKER, MOUNT DAMAVAND.

Inside what the Iranian leaders called their doomsday room, all was silence. As the finger of the Grand Ayatollah depressed the button, he felt uncertain about whether or not anything had happened. There was no reassuring click, sound, hiss or pressure release to indicate that his action had achieved anything. They could only wait.

Blasting through the ionosphere towards the receptors in space, the digital signal could not be deterred. Within the geostationary satellites, electrical circuits opened and closed, and the zeros and ones of a digital language sent the pre-programmed missiles on their way.

The intentions of a political leader can often be altered where computer programming is involved. The intention of the old Shiite was the mass suicide of those in and around the mountain called Damavand. But nuclear warheads require the intervention of computer programmers to convert the wishes of political leaders into the correct syntax. And the programmer had his own ideas about dying. He was quite happy to lay down his life for his country, especially whilst so close to his religious leader, but he was not prepared to go alone.

The red button would release a single warhead from space. But that warhead contained six missiles, each of which could be targeted to a different destination. Two of the Messengers from Allāh fell directly overhead in the Alborz Mountains; two others exploded over Tel Aviv and Baghdad; and the last two developed some unknown malfunction and fell into the Arabian Sea.

IN THE VALLEY OF THE RIVER HARAZ.

Traditionally Muslims are buried within twenty-four hours of death; the body is not normally encased within a coffin and the corpse must be laid on the right side, as if facing Mecca. The top of the grave must not be heaped high but must be level with the surface of the surrounding ground.

But no such courtesies could be afforded to the fallen in the valley of the river Haraz; in most cases it was impossible to match up the parts.

And so it was that a few days later, several scrawny desert foxes sniffed appreciatively at the lumps of meat littering the valley. Always first on the scene for a feeding session, they kept a wary eye out for other, larger predators, particularly wolves and leopards, which roamed the mountainous regions of northern Iran.

Lying amongst this carnage, completely unsullied and undamaged, lay an Army General's baton and the recently discarded red flashes of a Colonel; neither would be any use to the shattered remains of the two human beings that had craved so desperately for such rewards.

And a few metres away was a pair of grimy army boots. Jalal had no further need of them.

CHAPTER 25
A LITTLE NATURE HELPS

THREAD:

The politics and national aspirations of the countries of our planet had changed little during the first half century of the third millennium.

Any such worldwide politics and policies were centred around three major entities: the Superpower of Atheist China (SAC), as the world's only superpower; the Muslim Alliance, growing stronger with each year under the guiding hand of a strong figurehead; and the United States of America, whose strength was diminishing in the growing power of the former.

Although Chinese leaders dreamed their dreams of claiming new lands and laid their plans, they did so mainly to occupy the minds of the country's senior military advisors. As political leaders, they leaned more towards protecting Earth for the benefit of the Chinese.

They had metaphorically been banging their war drums for some considerable time, ever since they had reclaimed Taiwan without too much chest beating from the International Community back in 2031. At the time, the thought of taking on the Chinese military had forced even the mighty USA to take a backward step.

The trend in China over the past half century had been to disparage any religious beliefs; the old Buddhist, Taoist, Christian and Catholic churches had been viciously suppressed by the Chinese leaders and a firm line of atheism was implanted into the national psyche.

The Chinese nation had developed a burning hatred for the deeply religious Muslim nations throughout the world, who themselves were seeking world dominance. It was a volatile recipe for conflagration, the belief that deities do not exist versus a conviction that there exists only one true religion and one true Lord Almighty; and it was only a matter of time before the two camps decided to settle their argument.

Rich in all things, China had found the time and resources to increase the size of its military might, even during the period which included the building of their new capital. This huge military increase was formed of an almost equal number of men and women, highly trained, superbly equipped and dedicated to their country's national aims; China's forces were formidable indeed.

But wading forth into battle to conquer another country would not be the task of military humans, neither would it be their task to occupy and control the people of a conquered country. Their task was that of a human advance guard, to destroy any religious artifacts or buildings, raze all towns, cities and any other nationally identifiable feature of the conquered, and mop up every human that survived an earlier relentless and remotely-controlled aerial bombardment.

Such a huge build-up of military might was of course contrary to all 21st century international agreements and treaties, as was their associated and clandestine increase in small, battlefield nuclear weapons, nicknamed Baby Bok Choy by the Chinese because of the missiles' resemblance to this cabbage-like vegetable.

Assuming correctly that both the Muslim Alliance and the USA cared nothing for a raft of non-proliferation treaties; China was not the only nation to ignore a declared intention to reduce their nuclear arsenals.

Of the three known major nuclear powers, all three went to great lengths to hide their weapons of destruction from the International Community and similarly all three nations buried these arsenals deep underground to protect their clandestine activities from the spies circling the globe.

Cleverly, and with the full knowledge of the city's occupants, China's arsenal of Baby Bok Choys was hidden in a separate layer deep below their new capital.

For the Muslim Alliance, formed after the Great Muslim War of

Alfred Leonard

2041, the deserts of the Middle East provided ample site opportunities for their armoury of Messengers from Allāh. The dictatorial Muslim leader, Rasul-Allah, had long hankered for a nuclear arsenal and these weapons of mass destruction were manufactured in large numbers, funded by the petro-dollars that the rest of the world were forced to cough-up on a regular basis.

And the Muslims shared the same dream as did the Chinese, that of a world full of their own kind, worshipping the same deity in Heaven. But the Muslim nation was still divided in geographical terms and the Grand Faqihs of Rasul-Allah's inner cabinet of advisors turned their eyes south towards the African continent.

What a prize, what a home for the people of Allāh - and what a foothold for world domination! The dark brown, soulless eyes of the Muslim religious leaders, resembling the greedy eyes of China, focused on their prize. On a much bigger scale, they made their plans to sweep their military might like a descending scimitar from Casablanca to Cape Town. Genocide on such a vast scale did not disturb their national conscience, for Allāh would be with them.

Messengers from Allāh raining down on the continent would quickly eliminate all human life and, after a simple decontamination process, rebuilding by the invading Muslim nations could commence. Their plans were made, evaluated, remade, re-evaluated, over and over again since shortly after the Great Muslim War but the Grand Faqihs found it impossible to agree on the timing; all awaited a sign from Allāh. Not even the great Rasul-Allah seemed capable of making a decision and continually consulted his Grand Faqihs, amongst which Josh and I fed conflicting information, ensuring that agreement would never be reached. Despite many signs being identified by the argumentative religious leaders, not one sign had yet satisfied their collective expectations.

As for the USA, their Battlefield Mothers were stored in the United Kingdom, buried deep below Salisbury Plain. Using this strategy the Americans sought to claim, if not prove, that they were not part of, and had no knowledge of, nuclear activity in Britain. Housing America's weapons was the price that the British people were required to pay for the possibility of a new aircraft carrier being supplied to the Royal Navy by the USA.

Both countries were still bogged down in the archaic military doctrines of the 20th century, where these giants of the sea were seen as the only method of policing the world. Hugely expensive to build, maintain and operate, these sea-going monstrosities were about as effective as a bow and arrow against the remotely-controlled air power developed by China.

But current opinion and expertise in both Britain and the US of A was dominated by their senior military Officers. Fixed firmly in the past, the mindsets of these Officers was as dogmatic as their predecessors when arguing for the continuation of battleships two hundred years previously. They knew that a Navy without ships would not require captains, admirals and thousands of sailors to command, and they clung doggedly to their belief in the carrier as the only means to justify their existence.

Despite the claims of the Americans concerning the capabilities of their carriers, a single aircraft dropping a single Baby Bok Choy would eliminate the ship, leaving not a sign of its existence on the surface of the sea. Both countries had wasted enormous amounts of money and resources in producing these military toys during the preceding century and the latest version, the American's CVN-22, followed on from the CVN-21 with little more than upgrades to radar; sonar and communications systems; and an increase in displacement from just over a hundred thousand to one hundred and fifty thousand tonnes. And it was no more able to defend itself from air attack than had been its predecessor.

In achieving my secondary task as the Verguide, that of reducing the spiralling population of this planet, I was not alone.

Apart from the body count engineered by man himself, glibly excused by couching the carnage in grandiose expressions such as global domination; expansionist dreams; ethnic cleansing; religion; or experimental mishaps when groping for some new weapon to kill even greater numbers of mankind, or plain and simple greed; there were yet other elements working closely with me.

And sometimes these other elements were capable of killing with an awesome efficiency that outstripped man's feeble efforts.

Supporting me in my quest to exterminate the peoples of the world were two other enthusiastic assassins, whose efforts never tired nor whose inventiveness ever faltered - natural phenomena and Mother Nature.

And sometimes the effects of these two instruments of death can be increased dramatically by the careless intervention of man, which contributes greatly towards their efficacy as killing machines.

JAPAN. JULY 2056.

The small man stooped low and left his *chisel* house. In the background he could still hear the sounds of his wife playing softly on the *mukkuri*, a musical instrument which sounded much the same as a western Jew's harp. The house was a traditional *Ainu* building consisting of a simple wooden frame covered with bulrush and grass, supplemented with whatever else the forest might provide, and crowned with a thatched roof.

The doorway was low and although the middle-aged Japanese man was quite short, he still had to bow at the waist to avoid bouncing his head on the doorframe.

The man's name was Tatsujiro Yamada. He had lived on this small five hectare plot of land for every second of his forty-eight years of life, inheriting it from his own father some three years previously in 2053.

An intensely bitter man, Tatsujiro Yamada lived with a permanent downcast and morose expression on his round face. By nature the Japanese people are an intensely inoffensive race but Tatsujiro did not share this national trait with the rest of the Japanese population; and he freely offered an explanation for his miserable countenance by blaming it squarely on to his wife's inability to produce offspring. An inability for which he punished her, unmercifully.

An idyllic haven, the small farm was located on the slopes of the Tokachi Mountains, on the northernmost of Japan's four islands, Hokkaido. Dependable soil and abundant rainfall produced sufficient food for their needs and could easily be augmented when the need arose by a few deer taken each year from the surrounding forests. Whatever excess the farm produced was sold at market in the nearby town of Urahora.

Claiming ancestry back to the original *Ainu* settlers on Hokkaido, he was a boastful man. Proud of his claimed ancestry he did not regard himself to be strictly Japanese and told all and sundry that his wife's infertile body was due to her pure Japanese blood. No matter how many doctors told him that the real reason for his wife's inability to conceive was his low sperm count, he steadfastly refused to accept responsibility and treated his wife as little more than a slave.

On this warm summer morning in 2056, one of the hottest of the year, he had been woken by a strange rumbling to the north. Lazily he allowed his gaze to swivel toward Mount Tokachi and was not surprised to see a large cloud of ash blackening the sky. In no way perturbed by this sight he knew that the restless volcano had been bubbling and rumbling for as long as he could remember.

It had been back in February, 2003, over fifty years ago, when its longest volcanic tremor had lasted about half an hour. What Tatsujiro did not know, as did not the rest of the Japanese population, was that during that half hour tremor a small earthquake had also occurred on the slopes of Tokachi.

Almost undetectable on the Richter scale the tiny earthquake had opened a small slit in a rocky outlet, some fifteen hundred metres below the summit. The opening was quickly blocked when a rotting pine log fell into the opening, sealing from view the small cave below.

No more than a few metres in diameter, the tiny cave, filled with trapped radiation from the Second World War atomic bombs, had become a new home to a colony of about five hundred Giant Asian hornets, whose nest had dropped off that same rotting pine tree half a century before.

Year on year for the next fifty odd years, up until the time Tatsujiro glanced up at the smoking volcano, the colony of giant wasps had mutated. From comparatively large insects of about twenty-five millimetres long they mutated to their present size of about three hundred millimetres, with a wingspan of almost a metre.

Each year the colony had widened its entrance to the small cave to accommodate their burgeoning body mass and, unlike normal giant hornets, they survived the bitter cold of Japan's northern island.

In that time their numbers had increased to just over two thousand and they had carefully increased the size of their cave dwelling as their population increased. During this enlargement process, further deposits of sealed radiation were released from the many cracks and crevices deep within the mountain. Almost a circle of obsession, the urge to grow, enlarge and build never failed to find the hidden deposits of the means to their ever increasing size.

Usually secretive, the colony restricted their feeding activities to the hours of darkness and over the past few years had wiped out almost every other individual wasp or bee in the surrounding twenty-kilometre radius of their home. With their growing numbers and dwindling food supplies, the vicious creatures had been forced to find other sources of sustenance and of late had found the blood of animals or birds, of any shape or size, to be quite acceptable.

The leader of the colony, a huge Queen almost twice as large as her male colleagues, had decided to forage further afield. She had recently completed the exhausting task of laying five thousand eggs and the new brood would require a considerable amount of feeding when they hatched.

The ordinary everyday giant hornet is a ferocious hunter with a stabbing stinger some five millimetres long. Capable of stinging repeatedly, their venom is toxic enough to kill human tissue and each year a few dozen Japanese citizens pay the extreme penalty for under-estimating the power of this airborne killer.

A veritable killing machine, the mutated version had a stinger some fifty millimetres long. When pummelled hard and deep, it was long enough to puncture the heart of a human being; and when this sting-ing organ was powered by huge abdominal muscles, it was capable of ramming the stinger into flesh at an incredible rate of ten times each second. One such sting and a mere drop of the highly toxic venom would kill a full-grown elephant in less than a minute.

Turning back towards the entrance to his thatched house, Tatsujiro placed his hands on his waist and spread his elbows wide in a charac-teristic posture of domination; and opened his mouth to shout a break-fast order to his wife. First to die in the hornets' campaign, blackness enveloped him; it was as if a blanket had been pulled across the open-ing to his house or the Sun had been blacked out by an eclipse by the Moon.

Mercifully, he did not see the huge wasp clamped firmly over his face, nor did he live long enough to have any further thoughts on the matter. Within five seconds he was dead and sucked dry of blood twenty minutes later. Within ten hours the man's body tissue and bone structure would dissolve into a venom-saturated soup and the wasp, together with a few of his companions, gorged themselves on Tatsujiro's blood for the few minutes that it took to complete their meal.

Hours later, Tatsujiro's clothing flapped in the stiffening breeze like a desiccated skin. Strangely, although empty it still retained the outline of a man. Having soaked up some of the juices oozing from the carcass, the breeze had stiffened the drying clothing like a sheet of wrapping paper.

The huge orange and black hornet had withdrawn its sucker from the body of the dead man, raised its huge head and looked around for more prey. Only partially satiated by the few litres of blood and venom soup that it had extracted from the man, it was looking for more opportunities to feed.

At that moment the dead man's beleaguered wife ducked out of the house. Her eyes registered the orange and black ball, lying on what her quick glance assumed was a discarded piece of her husband's clothing and, as she turned her eyes away, looking for her lord and master, she too died almost instantly.

Yet more of the mutated giants had arrived on the scene. The hornets were patient predators and formed an orderly queue around the body of the woman. And there was not the feeding frenzy normally associated with the animal kingdom, for the instruction from their Queen was to return with food; and any fighting for a share might render them incapable of foraging further - which was certain to incur the wrath of their gigantic leader.

Over the next few days many more incidents of attacks from giant wasps were reported. Becoming a little unnerved and jittery, the majority of the Japanese population did not at first register fear at the news reports.

Attacks spread over all four of the main Japanese islands, from Hokkaido to Honshu, Shikoku and Kyushu. Large city and town populations were decimated, for the rampaging mutated wasps treated such large conurbations as their normal sized cousins would treat the nest of the honeybee.

Alfred Leonard

Attacking with an unbelievable ferocity, tearing their prey to pieces and casting them aside to curl up and die, the attacking hordes knew not what they were hunting for. The usual prize of the honeybees' larvae did not exist; but their killing instinct forced them onwards until every living thing in sight had been stung to a standstill.

Few humans escaped such attacks. When all was still, the area was marked with a highly concentrated secretion from the hornet's stomach and a messenger sent back to the main colony. The human carcasses were then reduced to venom soup, which the flying food baskets sucked up and carried back to feed to their own larvae.

Those humans that did survive this holocaust were those that remained still or could not be seen, hidden from view underground or trapped in lifts or frozen to the spot in fear. For the marauding insects attacked only what they could see and then only if it was moving. Even the slightest movement did not escape the huge visual sensors on the nodding heads of the predators and triggered an attack.

Windows were no barrier. The heavy body of the giants easily burst through the heaviest of plate-glass to spend hours stalking the corridors and rooms of buildings, searching out their prey. Normal wooden doors did not stop them, for they combined to smash through such flimsy obstacles; only very thick metal doors withstood their fierce and determined attacks.

In the first week the death toll was as unrealistic and improbable as to belie understanding. Unbelievable to the population of the Japanese islands, the sixteen million population of Tokyo was reduced to ten million in continuous night-time attacks.

The military were powerless to stop these attacks, for the blood-hungry creatures had incredible flying capabilities and their inbuilt radar system was able to identify the approach of a bullet and take avoiding action, even if crawling along the ground. The predator seemed immune to smoke, gas, fire and chemical sprays; and the frantic Japanese scientists were unable to find a means of deterring the hornets, who seemed intent upon clearing the islands of all human presence.

Protective clothing was useless, for the fifty millimetres long stinger could penetrate up to twenty-five millimetres of solid steel. Attacks on other Japanese cities followed relentlessly and, just two weeks after Tatsujiro's death, the Japanese population of about one hundred and sixty-five million souls had been reduced by a third, when the attacks suddenly ceased.

Deep underground in the Queen's lair, the monstrous creature surveyed her kingdom. Lined up in front of her were her seven hand-picked husbands, promoted to regimental leaders, each of whom would eventually command an attack force of a thousand hornets.

Similar in size to a huge aircraft hangar, the small cave had been enlarged to such an extent that it could now accommodate a Squadron of jet fighters. A sixth sense seemed to warn the occupants of this enormous structure whenever the air quality deteriorated; which instigated yet further digging within the honeycombed fissures and cracks of the mountain, flooding the occupants with fresh supplies of the lethal agent which produced their extraordinary growth.

Within the confines of this large structure, gigantic banks of larvae in various stages of development were engorged with sufficient food to feed both the existing colony and the five thousand larvae reaching their chrysalis stage; soon the Queen would indeed have a kingdom.

Of the five thousand larvae about to pupate, she had decided that only seven would be born female and each of these junior Queens was to be attached to a hornet Squadron to establish new colonies across the world.

Food was no longer the Queen's overriding consideration. Human bodies in various stages of decomposition littered the streets and buildings of every Japanese city. The remaining human population had not been able to clear up the dead but had left them where they fell and retreated into their homes, frantically attempting to dig underground shelters to protect them from further attacks.

Above ground the stench was worsening with each day and would continue to increase until the giant hornets finished their occasional return visits to suck up the contents of the cadavers; or the bodies had been successfully buried.

Such visits did not include any further attacks on the living. Even if inadvertently caught moving in the open such carelessness did not invoke an attack. What the Queen needed now was time. Time to transfer her knowledge to the pupating junior Queens, and instruct her Generals where to establish new colonies. She ceased all attacks on the colony's human prey and initiated a policy of cleaning up the partially processed food that littered the Japanese islands.

It seemed to the Japanese survivors that their harrowing ordeal was over. They started the business of creating a new government, reorganizing the military and generally starting again. The task was Herculean; the remains of some fifty-five million bodies littered the four large Islands of Japan.

Bulldozers worked 24-7, digging burial pits for the dead and bulldozing the human remains carelessly into them, the work interrupted only by the return of the hornets to harvest their crop, when every single person ran for cover.

The human instinct to rebuild is probably stronger than that of the ant. And this instinct, combined with the indomitable spirit of the Japanese people, enabled them to re-establish control very quickly.

In many parts of most Japanese cities there were scenes of total devastation, mainly caused by aircraft which had been attacked by the hornets crashing to the ground, sometimes starting horrendous fires which quickly spread, totally out of control, through the surrounding area. Gas mains, fuel pipes and fuel depots exploded in the intense heat, causing yet more damage and spreading the fires to other areas of the cities. In many places, these fires were still burning and the bulldozers razed each area to extinguish them all.

In some areas, the overall effect was similar to that after the nuclear attacks during the last World War. Almost total devastation, and lack of human occupation. Smouldering debris with gangs of feral dogs and cats picking over the bits and pieces of human bodies left after the passage of the bulldozers.

In other areas, all was peace and calm, such a peace that is seldom seen in a large metropolis at any time of the day or night. The population appeared to have simply evaporated into thin air; and all that remained were piles of clothing, blown into piles in every corner and doorway. It was an unnatural peace; the silence was intense except for the noise of the soft breeze whispering through the abandoned vehicles that littered the streets.

For a little over four weeks until the end of August, 2056, the Queen held her developing hordes in check, whilst she briefed the new Junior Queens and Generals. The seven hornet-impies were instructed to follow the movement of the Sun, pausing to rest only at night. Moving ever westward with each new day but never moving further west than an imaginary line linking the White Sea to the Black Sea. They were to establish seven new colonies, never moving further north than the Arctic Ocean or further south than the equator.

Within this enormous land mass lay the vast populations of China, Russia, North and South Korea, the Middle East and India. From these easy pickings, the Queen instructed her junior leaders, the new colonies could feed to their hearts' content, establishing yet more colonies until she instructed otherwise.

The new colonies were to live a peripatetic lifestyle, remaining in one place for not more than a few weeks and constantly sending out marauding patrols to establish the location of future temporary camping sites. She, the guiding Queen, would remain in the vast complex on Hokkaido Island and a chain of communication stations would be set up to link each new colony with her main base.

Since the first major strikes by the killer hornets, the rest of the world had promised much but provided little. The finest brains in the known world could hardly accept the existence of such creatures, never mind explain how they had evolved; or indeed how to deal with them. Not a single specimen had been captured for examination and study. No one knew their capabilities, limitations or nesting sites. Most Japanese experts predicted that the nests must be located on Honshu or the two southern islands, believing that Hokkaido would be too cold for the giant insects to survive.

Despite enormous satellite coverage, diverted by the USA from their normal surveillance activities, not a single sighting was made of a large number of predatory insects leaving any part of the Japanese Islands, nor from the neighbouring countries of North and South Korea. The reason for this failure was of course quite simple; the giant Queen dispatched her armies during darkness, with instructions to fly a terrain-hugging pattern and not to return until the black of night returned once again.

In fact, the world and its leaders had not the slightest inkling of how to deal with this new menace and they were happy in the knowledge that only Japan seemed threatened. The body count, claimed by the Japanese to top fifty-five million, staggered most minds into disbelief. The mind of the average man found it difficult to cope with the number of deaths claimed and even more difficult to accept that such devastation could be produced by a swarm of bees! The maths, however, were simple. At an astonishing rate of fifty each minute, a single normal-sized Asian hornet can kill thirty thousand honeybees in a ten-hour day. The Queen had an original army of two thousand killing machines capable of dispatching around sixty million people in the same single ten-hour day. Of course, the killing rate of fifty every minute was only possible in very large cities and where the density of the population permitted; and the final body count had taken almost a week to achieve.

The army of giant hornets had been carefully instructed by their Queen not to waste effort by multiple stings and full, fifty millimetre penetration; a simple prick of the stinger and a mere drop of venom would do the job on each human. At first, the hornets attacked blindly, temporarily forgetting the orders from their Queen. Stabbing deeply and inserting massive amounts of venom, tearing and ripping flesh in the sheer joy at being free; lost in a red mist of destruction similar to a Zulu-impi on the rampage, their assegais greedy for a first taste of blood.

Not a few hornets, once again, paid the ultimate penalty for disobeying their Queen and the lesson was quickly learned by the remainder of her army. And in the midst of this human destruction, not one single body of a hornet was left for discovery, all returned to their secret nest.

In the month since the attacks ended, the leaders of both China and Russia had been looking towards the east, hungry for the now virtually undefended lands of Japan. Acting as gawping window-shoppers, the Russian leaders, however, could do little more than look. They no longer controlled the where-with-all in terms of manpower or weapons to strike, take and hold any new lands. Their national rise in fortunes and their expansionist success in 2015 had been another brief window of heady power, for depleting supplies of fossil fuel and lower than anticipated yields had wiped out their Soviet empire once again.

And to add fuel to their woes, the population of Russia had fallen by about thirty percent to approximately one hundred million. With this shocking fall in the country's birth rate over the preceding fifty years, allied with the associated drop in the nation's economy, they could only bemoan their inability to sustain an empire - and that such an opportunity for re-expansion should arise but could not be grasped.

In China, however, the political and economic situation was quite the opposite. A soaring birth rate had seen the country's population explode to over three billion. Deep below the surface of the Earth and circling a vast new inland sea, its new capital of Chang Jiang had been purpose-built to accommodate some two hundred and fifty million people.

Created by linking the original lakes and waterways that surrounded the city of Wuhan, in Hubei Province, the building of the inland sea and the new capital had been the largest building project the world had ever witnessed; and took twenty years to complete from 2030 to 2050. In the process, and in addition to old Wuhan, the cities of Xiantao, Huangshi, Xianning, and Puqi were demolished to make way for this huge new water reservoir. Designed to provide all the power that the city could possibly need for the foreseeable future, mammoth generating stations on the eastern shores of this man-made inland sea were fed by the tremendous weight of water falling into new river beds which led eventually back to the original course of the Yangtze.

A fast growing banana shoot leaping from a fertile jungle, China was vibrant. Its economy was booming and marching blindly onwards towards an inevitable burst, as had every other raging economy before it. Its leaders and people were intent on enjoying their moment of power and influence in the world. They were the world's richest and strongest nation and they were not shy about letting others know about this fact.

To the Chinese leaders the unfortunate events in Japan were not considered to be a gift from above but the reward for decades of hard work, solid leadership and a common goal. For a considerable number of years expansion had been at the top of their national hidden agenda and they saw Japan's misfortune as an invitation to occupy the islands. With a bit of luck they might take North and South Korea on the way. Plans had been in place for many years to expand in any direction, it was simply a case of activating the Eastward Plan.

To this end China's fifty million strong military might was placed on alert. Twenty battle Corps, each of fifty thousand men, was to be assembled around the nation's new capital. From here, they would be transported to gigantic air-trooping aircraft to parachute on to Japan's four islands in two waves, each twelve hours apart.

It was to be a typical cleansing operation by the Chinese. In line with their new concept of waging war and involving huge numbers of troops, the physical invasion was scheduled to follow the initial bombing campaign, designed to bring their target to its knees. Planned to the last detail, the operation was well within the capabilities of China's military leaders. Since time immemorial, military leaders around the globe have connived amongst themselves and cajoled their political masters to wage war. China's Generals were no different and they welcomed this opportunity to flex their combined muscles.

For centuries after this day's brutal experience, the Chinese people would bemoan their nation's infernal bad luck and the failure of their army of superbly-trained troops to achieve their latest expansionist attempt. On the morning before the planned air strikes on Japan, the first hornet scout found the huge city of Chang Jiang, ringed by one million troops awaiting their movement orders.

Thirty hours later the population and its army lay in vast droves of dead, awaiting processing by their predators. The guiding Queen had dispatched all seven of her new colonies to stop the invasion of her homeland. With orders to continue attacking until every single one of the two hundred and fifty one million humans were killed, the impies were unleashed without restraint.

Ravenous after their long flight, attacking hornets smashed into the city's population, thrusting their stingers deeply into their victims and hopping from one body to the next as if anointing each with a heavenly touch.

The latest communications systems, especially devised for China's new capital city, had given every single citizen a picture of the attacking hordes of hornets. Images from space communications satellites were projected on to miniature screens implanted behind each person's ear, which transposed the image into what the brain saw in sixty-centimeter TV screen size. Useful to the Chinese in establishing and enforcing communist ideals and doctrines into the masses, the system had been invented in Britain. Stolen, modified and produced for Chang Jiang, it was a virtual telepathic information system and the first to be installed anywhere in the world.

And the pictures that the population of Chang Jiang saw caused large numbers of Chinese citizens to freeze in fear.

At a depth of eleven kilometres, China's new capital of Chang Jiang was of course not within the mantle of Earth. However, China's engineers had made extensive probes much deeper and these had provided some surprising discoveries. China's ever-inventive scientists had found that the mantle, when ground and mixed with water into a paste and allowed to set, formed a construction material of amazing strength, which they subsequently marketed as Mantellium. They had further developed a series of drilling machines, completely autonomous and remotely controlled that could drill through the mantle, mix and apply the Mantellium to leave a perfectly symmetrical circular tunnel up to a width of one hundred metres and in the process lifted any unused mantle waste to the surface.

At Chang Jiang, above the nuclear storage and heavy engineering levels and supported by towering Mantellium columns, rose the remaining levels of the complex, each designed for a specific use.

Above ground there were no roads and the whole surrounding area out to a diameter of one hundred kilometres was replanted with indigenous trees, with wide open spaces around the many large lakes, rivers and streams, scattered amongst the huge agricultural systems, with sporting facilities available for every conceivable human activity. From space, the facility gave the appearance of a paradise and, to its inhabitants, it most certainly was.

The underground transport level provided links to all other parts of the complex. Dozens of termini linked this internal system to the external high-speed rail network, providing access to the surrounding agricultural and recreational facilities, and the rest of China.

The picture of the attacking Hornets, relayed over Chang Jiang's communications system, was available to all two hundred and fifty million residents simultaneously. And the Chinese authorities within the underground city would soon wish that they had built the doors to the city from Mantellium when the attacking hordes of hornets burst through them.

The temperature was stupefyingly hot within the small cockpit of a hovering army helicopter. Once again, its design origins had been in Britain during the 2040s and it pioneered the use of a solar-generated energy plant which powered a system of total thrust for lift and motion, rather than rotors. Britain's engineers were no less inventive than the rest of the world and this brilliant concept would be cast aside by the British for lack of funding, a degree of pessimism and fierce opposition from the American and Middle Eastern oil companies.

Supremely confident in his new machine, the pilot had a passenger for this morning's aerial inspection of the neatly arrayed battalions below. General Hu Gan was China's most senior military Officer, reporting only to the Chairman of the SAC, Li Tu-hsiu. Both pilot and General had been gazing below, dreaming of the honours that would be won over the next few days. From the ambitious General's point of view, such honours might even include the ultimate honour of being elected chairman of his beloved country.

A sudden warning bleep from the helicopter's main console drew the attention of both occupants away from the ground below and each was struck speechless by the picture in the heads-up display before them.

What appeared to be seven waves of very small aircraft were approaching Chang Jiang. Flying low and slow, virtually terrain hugging, each wave some thirty minutes apart. Immediately suspicious, General Hu Gan was well known for his relentless and tireless quest for the complete picture. Leaving nothing to chance he ordered the pilot to turn towards the approaching Squadrons and instructed his aides on the ground to come to battle stations. An unscheduled call to readiness would prove a useful exercise, should the approaching threat be found to be nothing more than a natural occurrence; perhaps a huge flock of Khaki Combell ducks moving to new grazing areas or escaping from a combined fish and duck farm.

At the same time, a picture of the slowly advancing threat was relayed to the army's main operations room on the military's restricted bandwidth. Slowly the helicopter closed with the hornet Squadrons. No panic or sense of unease was felt either in the air or on the ground at this time, for the consensus of opinion was that the threat could not be anything other than a natural event.

This scene of calm was short lived and the Officers on the ground looked at each other in total confusion as the picture from the helicopter disappeared. The last image had been that of a large object smashing through the cockpit roof before a blank screen turned their guts to ice water.

Brigadier Hwang Lo was second in command to General Hu Gan. He immediately launched seven helicopters to check on the approaching threat and to determine whether or not their Commanding General had survived what must surely have been a catastrophic crash.

Seven helicopters, each identical to that assumed downed, were airborne in less than fifteen minutes. Far too slow a reaction to provide any further information. The lead helicopter had reached a height of no more than thirty metres when it made contact with the approaching enemy hornet Squadrons, which gleefully stabbed the pilot into almost instant death.

However, the pilot had looked up as the hornet came through the roof of the helicopter and the ferocious face of the predator appeared gigantic on the large-scale screen of the operations centre; and the sight chilled all to the bone.

Sudden panic overwhelmed all control and in this panic, a switch was made enabling the output of the still active helmet from the dead pilot to be relayed into the civilian information system.

Added to the dying screams from the other six helicopters and the panic-stricken comments from the military operations centre, the scenes relayed to the citizens of China's new capital city were horrifying indeed.

As the citizens shook off the state of frozen fear, general panic erupted within the layers of the city; but this lasted for only a few minutes before the usual calm returned to most of the city's inhabitants. The people had supreme confidence in their leaders and their military. Nothing could withstand their national might and everyone was familiar with the city's evacuation plans. Each individual citizen was assigned an evacuation exit, which ensured a panic-free draining of the population to the above ground areas and to predetermined muster points, from where transport would be provided to other parts of the country.

In the operations centre, overhead sensors saw the swarms of hornets from the first Squadron swoop towards the city. Each citizen witnessed the attack of the first wave as one thousand killing machines swarmed over the aboveground level. Appalled at how quickly, and evidently painfully, a human being died from what appeared to be a gentle stab from these ferocious creatures, Brigadier Hwang Lo ordered an immediate evacuation of the city.

A silly and dangerous decision, since once the switches were thrown the exit doors locked in the open position, which subsequently allowed the invaders unencumbered routes into all levels.

At first in a controlled manner, as they had done on so many routine exercises, the population moved towards their exits. However, it did not take more than a dozen horrifying deaths to overwhelm the usual calm of the Chinese people and push them into stampede. The scene inside the city's underground levels was one of total panic and bloody carnage.

Successive waves of hornets had descended upon the doomed population, smashing their way through outer and inner defences and had managed to reach most areas of the city. The dead lay everywhere and the stench of dying bodies voiding their waste systems, mixed with the cloying smell of large quantities of venom-polluted blood, was suffocating.

Residents of the city escaped in their millions, at least as far as the above ground and surrounding areas. Just one collective thought filled their minds - escape, run, hide!

And as they ran, some frantically clawed at their heads in an attempt to remove the implanted communications system, heading for none knew where. But there was to be no escape and vast circles of dead bodies lay motionless in the surrounding area. For the hornet Queen's instructions were clear, no survivors!

Fists white with the strength of his grip, Ng Jianguo had clung to his mother as the single-parent family attempted to make their escape from the underground capital. They had been lucky. Their apartment was situated quite near to one of the city's emergency evacuation exits and they had dashed towards it as soon as the order was given to make an escape to the surface.

Neither Jianguo nor his mother bothered to check if the door to their apartment had closed properly, nor did they make any attempt to take any of their belongings with them. Speed was their most urgent consideration. 'Be quick,' Jianguo's mother had screamed, over and over again at her son. 'We must get to the exits before they are blocked.' Clear in the memories of both mother and son was the speed at which the evacuation exits could become jammed with people, even when the event was merely for practice.

Not even when clear of the bottleneck and out into the open air and bright sunshine did Ng Xue slow her pace. Mind in a turmoil of panic, she dragged her seven year old son behind her. Heading for the safety of a copse of trees in a nearby park, she twisted her head to and fro, looking for the first sign of the attacking monsters. Occasionally her eyes swivelled up into the sky and she cursed the unfamiliar heat from the Sun.

Her neck was bloody, as was that of her son, for she had nicked the implanted communications system from both with quick, slashing strokes with her kitchen knife. The scenes were simply too terrifying. She would rather not know what was going on inside the capital and for some unknown reason she harboured a deeply-rooted fear that the fearsome creatures were using the implanted communications system to home-in on to their targets.

Mother and son must have been among the earliest to vacate the city, for there were very few people in front of her. However, they were rapidly being overhauled by fitter and faster escapees. The hard surface of the paved path grazed her hands and knees as she fell to the ground, one of the passing youths, eyes searching the skies, had bludgeoned her off her feet as he careered, panic-stricken, out of the city.

Jianguo took one look at the horde of escaping city dwellers and reached for his mother's hands. 'Come, mama, be quick. We must hurry or we will be run down by the mob.' The fear in his voice galvanised his mother; she screamed, over and over again, as she pulled herself to her feet and fled towards a large, overhanging tree. The obnoxious smell from the blossoms on the tree identified it as a Chinese chestnut but both mother and son ignored the unpleasant aroma and fell gratefully beneath its shelter.

Breathing heavily now the pair lay on their backs, desperately trying to calm their racing pulses and thumping hearts after the near fatal fall. Both knew that had she not managed to regain her footing she would have been trampled to death by the escaping mob. Sheltered now by the large tree, eyes squeezed tightly closed, Ng Xue asked for protection from Tu Di Gong, the patron saint of villages and farmers, and the deity to which her own parents had sworn allegiance whilst working on the tiny allocation of land from which they had gleaned sustenance.

Had the communications implant remained in place, Ng Xue would never have risked praying to any person or any thing; stories abounded amongst the common folk about the information that the authorities could extract from a person's mind and she knew that religion in any shape or form was taboo.

The hordes of people escaping from the underground city were now spreading towards the sheltering mother and child. They were in danger of being stomped underfoot but Ng Xue felt exhausted and was unable to move much further. Jianguo looked around and spotted a large rock behind which he and his mother might shelter. He dragged his mother to her feet and partly pushed and partly dragged her weight behind the rock.

Screaming, shouting, cursing and swearing, the human stampede passed them by. Hundreds; thousands; who knew how many? Mother and son could not join the fleeing community, they had both reached the limits of their endurance and could go no further; their only option was to wait for whatever might befall them.

The beat of many wings thwacked the air. Like an attacking flight of tiny helicopters, the giant hornets emerged from the same city exit that Jianguo and his mother had used. Looking up at the attacking air-borne monsters, mother and son thought that there were so many of them that they must collide with one another in the tightly massed Squadrons.

There appeared to be no order in their formations, individual insects acted independently in flight; and the sunlight cooled beneath the closeness of the huge swarm. As if controlled by a single brain, the swarm gained altitude and extended along the line of escaping humans, seemingly waiting for some command to attack.

Fascinated, Jianguo watched. The eyes of a child view some events in phantasmagorical outline, unconsciously assigning comic book capabilities to raw nature. And Jianguo saw the attacking hornets as miniature jet fighters ready to exact revenge on those that had harmed his mother. He waited for them to strike and watched with mounting glee as the formations dropped on to their victims below. But his joy turned to horror when he saw the brutal stabbing-sting penetrate deeply into the flesh of man, woman and child. Time seemed to stand still in his mind and for many long hours, the boy simply watched. He pleaded with his brain to close his eyes, remove the awful sights in front of him, but his wilful brain would not comply and his eyes stopped blinking whilst the terrible scenes were played out before him.

A hornet landed not more than a couple of metres away from Jianguo. The giant insect settled on to the face of an old man who was heading for the shelter of the same rock behind which mother and son sheltered. The body of the hornet was already shiny with blood; wings outspread as it balanced upon the man's face, its huge eyes gazing into the eyes of its victim.

Clearly, Jianguo saw the stinger emerge, massively thick at the end nearest to the body of the enraged hornet but tapering to a wicked-looking tip. In slow motion, the boy watched the stinger, already dripping venom, stab viciously into the chest of the old man. Not once, twice, nor three times, the stinger must have penetrated the body of the man at least a dozen times in the space of a fraction of a second. The old man fell to the ground, dead long before his body made contact and the killer-hornet looked around for fresh victims.

With her eyes held tightly closed, Ng Xue had seen nothing of the horrors of the attack. Both arms were wrapped firmly around the legs of her son, she was determined that they would not become separated.

'Mama, we must run again.' The hornet had spied the woman on the ground, grasping her male child's legs in a fierce embrace. Slowly the beast advanced; unblinking; soulless eyes; like those of a snake, fastened upon its next victims.

'Mama, Mama, please! Get up, we must flee. One of them is here, very close. Come Mama, let me go.' The bodily strength of the young boy was no match for that of his mother and no matter how much he squirmed and twisted he was unable to break free.

'No, no, no!' The fearful screams, from the very core of Jianguo's being, finally burst into his mother's mind and she opened her eyes. But it was too late. Already the creature had settled on his mother's head and was turning quickly to line up its tail with the woman's chest.

Locked in his mother's restraining embrace, the young boy watched the blood spurt from her chest, drenching the body of the hornet whose stinger was no longer repeatedly stabbing but deeply implanted within her as if sucking up her internal organs. Desperately he tried to grasp the body of the insect, pull it off his mother; but his feeble actions seemed only to enrage the creature and it pushed the stinger even more deeply between the woman's breasts as if anchoring its hold more firmly.

The flesh-sucking plop, as the stinger was dragged from his mother's chest, filled the boy with a mind-numbing, terrible, cold fear that he had never before experienced. He knew that he would be the insect's next victim.

His mother was motionless, dead already, and he could see the blood bubbling still from the wound in her chest. An overwhelming sadness drained the strength from his small body and seeking to die as closely to his mother as was possible, he draped himself over her motionless body.

The hornet felt no compassion for the boy. It was in the killing zone, it could smell the blood and body fluids all around and wanted only to kill, kill and kill again. The beast did not spare the boy's life, at least not intentionally; it simply preferred to kill whilst looking into the eyes of its victims. The boy had collapsed face down across the body of his mother and the hornet had simply walked away, looking for more suitable victims.

Jianguo lay motionless for many hours. The lingering warmth

from his mother's body tricked him into believing that she might still be alive, despite the fact that he could not feel her breathing. Mind in shock, he did not know what to do. Tired, hungry and thirsty, he drifted in and out of sleep as the time passed.

When finally the boy returned to total sanity, it was cold. His mother's body was also cold and rigid. He could not see the ferocious hornets busily sucking up the venom-soaked contents of their victims but he could hear them and his young brain made the correct interpretation of the obscene, slurping noises.

Jianguo knew that he must move but his heart sank at the thought of leaving his mother. He knew two things; he knew his mother's fate and he knew he was still alive.

As gently as he could the boy freed himself from his mother's arms. He fell to his knees and, for the last time in this lifetime, lowered his lips to his mother's face. The coldness of her skin was alien to him; it also frightened him and his first thought was to pull away in distaste. But he forced himself to extend his final kiss and remained so until he glimpsed a movement in the darkness that surrounded him.

'Goodbye, Mama,' the boy whispered and sensing exactly why he had not been killed by the hornet he crawled away over the body-strewn ground, face pressed closely to the cold earth, searching for a place to hide and maybe even survive.

In reducing the capability and blunting the enthusiasm for war in the two antagonists foreseen by the Verunians to be involved in World War 3, the hornet campaign was successful beyond my wildest dreams.

At the time of the event and within the area bounded by the restrictions imposed by the hornet Queen, population numbers exceeded six billion. Of these, more than two billion died, a figure that exceeds double the total death toll for both previous world wars combined.

In loosing the hornet-impies I felt no remorse. As was the case for those other human beings, who were not directly involved in the widespread and indiscriminate massacre of so many of Earth's burgeoning population, the heartache and suffering heaped upon the relatives and friends of those that died created little more than a passing interest once the marauding killers ceased their migratory path to the east.

Alfred Leonard

It is easy for students to review the details of Earth's previous global conflicts, namely The Great War and World War 2, and to list thoughtlessly the losses in their history exams in tens of millions. And into the young minds of the majority of those students will seep precious little sympathy for those that forfeited their lives; and when separated from the violence by time and distance, the macabre details of such conflicts are - just data.

And such were the feelings in most other parts of the world, especially when after ninety days the swarms of Asian Giant Hornets themselves gave up their lives. For they too had a weakness - they could not survive longer outside the radiation saturated atmosphere of their cave.

When next I overlooked the ageing Queen she was totally alone. Lying on her back with legs twitching skywards, she was fading fast. My familiar voice burst once again into her consciousness and I saw her make a huge effort to revive herself.

'Your armies have done well in reducing the burden upon this planet. Many humans have died and my voice speaks to you for the last time. Your colonies have also died, for they cannot survive long without the special mixture of air that made you grow.'

Painfully, like an upturned beetle righting itself, the old Queen rolled her body once more and struggled to raise herself on to her feet. Unsteady, she rested her head on the floor of the cave to maintain her balance and gazed about her kingdom. Surrounded by the remnants of thousands of dead larvae she looked utterly forlorn and she turned her huge eyes towards the direction from which she fancied she heard my voice.

She knew that her time had come and I in turn had the distinct impression that for the very first time I heard a response from the creature's own innermost being; and her words troubled me greatly for the rest of my present life: *'But I have been, and having been, I may be again.'*

CHAPTER 26
AND A LITTLE MORE NATURE

THREAD:

Africa. That Dark Continent. The physical aspect of this vast area of land on the surface of our planet had changed very little during the first few decades of the 21st century. Apart, that is, for the continuous insidious creep of the huge desert areas, seeking to achieve nature's intention of covering the entire planet in sand.

At one time in fairly recent history, ownership of this second largest continent in the world was divided between the European nations, with the greater shares held by Great Britain and France. But by 2050, over fifty separate, independent countries occupied the area where man is believed to have taken his first step.

For the people of this land there exists a bedrock of history consisting of two constants - pain and suffering - and death has been their constant and ever-eager companion. Dominated, suppressed, enslaved, uneducated and subdued beneath ruthless dictatorial rulers, nonetheless the people of this land increased their numbers against all odds.

Dictators came and went; internal tribal differences festered; and each fuelled the death toll, as would a gigantic cancer. Financial support by the tonne had been lavished on this continent throughout the 20th century and continued as each new decade followed the last into the new millennium.

Aid organisations, charities, the schoolchildren of the western nations and a host of religious foundations sought to relieve the suffering of Africa's indigenous people. But little improvement was made to the stability of precarious political systems that governed the continent and which greedily absorbed the never-ending aid.

For the vast majority of the population, living conditions in terms of adequate housing, clean water, medical treatment and education remained well below world standards. And to ease this suffering a multitude of missionaries had flooded into the continent for hundreds of years, confident in their promises that Christ will help the African people. 'Put your faith in Our Lord; he will raise you up from your poverty and lead you to the Promised Land.' The average Mr Africa might well be forgiven for welcoming both the existence of a True Holy Father and His promises, and at the same time wonder why blessed release from their suffering was taking so long.

But the terrible diseases from the womb of Mother Nature just love the conditions in which the people of Africa live; and she needed no help from me in taking her fair share of responsibility in reducing the ever-growing numbers of humans on the face of the Earth. Spread by human contact, at times by careless Lotharios both ignorant and heedless of the risks, and at others by rampaging, rapacious and raping troops during the many conflicts, AIDs had mutated itself time and again to thwart the efforts of the world's most brilliant scientists.

And if mankind has not yet learned to trust in neither nature nor god, then it has not learned anything of any real value.

But what lies dormant can sometimes be more dangerous than what is active.

REPUBLIC OF CONGO. 2059.

A tiny man standing barefoot, just a few centimetres over a metre in height. His skin is black, gnarled and wrinkled; and lies under a grayish layer of dirt, smoke and general grime accumulated from years of life in a dense equatorial rain forest.

Thick, curly black hair adorned his head and his near-naked body with its protuberant stomach proclaimed his own hunting and fishing skills with bow and poisoned arrow; and testified to the cooking skills of his plump wife.

He stood now, under a tall Kola nut tree reaching twenty metres into the canopy, chewing contentedly on a slice of the coffee flavoured Kola nut. Beneath his eye-line his stomach bulged, a happy sight for this cheerful member of the Bantu tribe, who sought nothing more from life other than to be left alone in his family's remote shack, some thirty-five kilometres upstream along the Ngoka River, south of Ouesso in the Republic of Congo.

At last protected in perpetuity, the forest was safe from any further logging incursions and preserved forever as one of the World's Preservation Zones. It was home, for as long as they wanted it, to its indigenous people and it provided all that his family of eight daughters required in terms of food, shelter, medicinal preparations and essential clothing.

The fast flowing river Ngoka, which made its way into the Sangha and eventually fed the mighty Congo river itself, provided water for his wife's meagre maize and vegetable crops and an abundance of fish which happily answered his hunting prayers by jumping on to the end of his arrows or long stabbing spear.

Whenever visitors or other more nomadic distant relatives from his extended family called at his house, Juma Eduni's family spoke the local Bangandu derivative of the Bantu language. Not that such visits occurred very often; in fact, the family rarely saw other human faces.

Although Juma as a young man had travelled into Ouesso, not one of his children had yet made the break from the family ties or, indeed, shown any inclination to do so. His wife had responded to his vigorous and numerous implantations of seed every year since they had left the homes of their parents and the children, ranging from a few months to eight years of age, had been a product of that combined effort. Juma also suspected that the blood might cease flowing once again this very month and he wondered idly how many more years his wife would remain so fruitful.

As a family, and in the conditions that they had always known, the small group was sublimely happy. Well fed, they were protected from the elements and totally at ease in the sometimes dangerous rain forest, with its deadly snakes and predators.

Alfred Leonard

Several weeks later on the 15th August, 2059, Juma felt a rumble beneath the tightly stretched skin over his bulging stomach. He had recently devoured a large portion of his wife's maize porridge and a handful of bananas; a normal breakfast for him and on this particular morning it had been supplemented by the remains of last night's *beef* stew.

The wud-wud-wud of a watery fart gently coughed from his rear and he felt the warm liquid run down his legs. Startled, he looked down at the mess at his feet and recoiled at the sudden stench; in the rain forest, happiness and health are signified by a firm stool and he hastily flicked a light covering of soil over the offending deposit. Juma did not know it but today was the Congo's celebration day, when his city-dwelling countrymen rejoiced in all manner of expensive parades and parties to commemorate their independence.

Reaching downwards with a gnarled hand, Juma used his jagged, dirt-filled fingernails to scratch at his crotch; and watched as the escaping fleas fell to the ground. Instinctively his hand moved to the injury on his cheekbone. Still sore and weeping with pus, his fingers gently investigated the injury and he shuddered with horror at the memory of how he had received the wound.

It had been just yesterday when he had left his house, having told his wife that he was going to hunt, and wandered down to the water's edge. Having just bolted down a huge portion of his wife's delicious vegetable stew, which contained the bones of a small monkey that the spirits of the forest had provided for the family, Juma was lethargic.

With no intention of hunting this day, he intended instead to laze in the warmth of the day, a few kilometres downstream in a favourite spot under the shade of a huge African Teak tree.

The journey to the tree did not take long, for the nimble Juma could move surprisingly quickly when necessary, and he flopped down in the shade with a sigh of grateful satisfaction. Loud snores soon rattled from his throat; his dreams were sweet indeed and included much fornication with beautiful young girls, none of which resembled his wife and all of which bore him male children.

Rudely awoken from his journey into paradise, Juma felt a stabbing pain in the side of his face. At first, he thought that he had been stabbed by one of the boat-traders which occasionally peddled their wares up and down the river but his eyes filled with terror when he managed to focus on the furry lump attached to his face.

He recognised the animal immediately. It was a Giant African river rat which Juma identified as *beef* and which provided much of the meat for his family's food bowls. These rats are normally docile, friendly creatures; and being about the size of a European domestic cat make good pets. Weighing in at about four kilograms and breeding at a prolific rate, they also provide an easy meal.

Juma felt the wetness of the animal's fur; it had obviously recently climbed from the river. *'But why had it attacked him?'* he wondered idly. He was totally familiar with the forest and the habits of its inhabitants and he had never before heard of such a creature attacking man.

Leaping to his feet, Juma dragged the animal from his face, leaving a jagged strip of skin and deep puncture marks from the bite. Twirling his body he smashed the rat's head against the tall tree, killing it instantly; at least he could justify his hunting claim for today.

Occasionally wiping the blood from his face, Juma returned to his home. The pain from the bite did not trouble him too much; such injuries were a way of life in the forest, but he felt somehow troubled by the experience. *'Why had the normally docile rat attacked him?'* He could not erase the question from his mind. But in the way of the simple people of the rain forest, Juma did not, however, worry himself too much or too long over this vexing problem. More concerned that the rat had infested him with the irritating fleas which lived in its thick furry coat, he was scratching vigorously by the time he reached home and threw the *beef* at his wife's feet.

The voraciously hungry fleas that had so willingly transferred themselves from the already dying rat were infected with a particularly virulent and deadly version of pneumonic plague. The stomachs of the fleas were blocked by the plague bacteria and no matter how vigorously they fed, they were unable to satisfy their hunger. Eventually, their throats became so engorged with blood that they vomited into the bites in their hosts, transferring the deadly bacteria in the process. For this previously unknown strain of pneumonic plague, the bacteria were particularly fast acting and the incubation period was just a few hours.

Thus, Juma found himself unsure of what to do next. His nostrils flared at the strong smell from his still soiled legs and the powerfully pungent aroma offended his senses. He wanted to move down to the river to wash but he found that he had extreme difficulty in breathing. He felt chilled. His skin appeared to acquire a yellowish tinge and he had war drums pounding inside his head.

Suddenly his strength left him, a frightening experience since he had not known the like before and, as he collapsed to the ground, fresh eruptions spurted from his rear.

Juma's wife, hearing the groan from her husband, appeared at the entrance to the house. She saw his body on the ground, curled into the classic foetal position, which told her of his pain, and she felt her nose tingle at the smell of excrement. A moment of anger overcame her and she opened her mouth to admonish her husband for defecating so close to the house but a sight of the vomit pouring from Juma's mouth quelled her reprimand.

A quick fear entered her heart as she knelt at her husband's side. As she rolled his body on to his back, she noticed how hot the skin felt to the touch of her fingers; and she reeled back in horror as a loud belch and whoosh of air came from Juma's lungs, straight into her face.

The African, who lives an isolated life in the very depths of the jungle, has his or her mind polluted early in life by the strange mythical stories of the forest. Kneeling by the side of her husband, the woman remembered these stories of jungle evil-spirits related by her parents, stories of monsters which caused such fast acting, deadly diseases, and she knew that such ailments were usually associated with the giant rat.

But she had not seen any sign of their multiple deaths along the riverbank, a sight which usually preceded any outbreak of disease. Frightened now for her children, the whole family had relished the meat from the rat that Juma had brought home yesterday and she was desperately afraid that the meat was tainted with whatever spirit had entered the body and was even now attacking her husband.

Hurriedly she stood, called for her brood, snatched the baby from her eldest daughter and led the family to the river. Evil spirits tend to dwell for long periods once they have found a host and Juma's wife knew that the only saviour for her children was distance.

Just six hours later the whole family was dead and Juma would never know of, or see, the son forming inside his wife's womb.

The last to die was Juma's pregnant wife. She had been standing in the shallows at the side of the river trying to wash the filth from her body when the pains overwhelmed her and she lapsed into unconsciousness. As her body floated downstream, her muscles became so weak that she was barely able to keep herself afloat despite the effort of her fevered mind to compel her body to respond.

Total awareness returned to her just once more, as she felt the bite from the small crocodile as it fastened on her leg. The crocodile was too small to devour the body but sufficiently powerful to drag it under the water until it drowned, mercifully relieving Juma's wife from any further discomfort or pain.

Released from the jaws of the crocodile, the lifeless body of Juma's wife floated downstream. For the most part it remained just below the surface and, surprisingly, it did not attract the attention of further predators.

Some days later the body was spotted in the Congo River, just before it entered the capital city of Brazzaville. A patrolling police boat pulled the remains from the river and the two rescuers were immediately infected by air-borne bacteria escaping from the still intact lungs of Juma's wife. Within a few hours both Officers were suffering from flu symptoms.

Unknowingly the two police Officers carried the disease into the centre of their city, thereby exposing its inhabitants to the hell-on-earth that is nature's dark side. A firestorm fed by the wind, the unseen killer was transported in all directions at the will of the seasonal air currents.

Within a week, some ninety-five percent of the city's population of just over three point two million souls had succumbed to this air-borne menace.

In relatively quick time, the flu-like symptoms and multiple deaths were identified by World Health Organisation officials as a new variation of the deadly pneumonic plague. A variation in which the majority of victims did not respond to the known treatments or the most modern of medicines. Spreading from Brazzaville at tremendous speed, the outbreak swept through the population and over the course of the next month had travelled north as far as the Tropic of Cancer where it struggled to find new victims in the vast desert wastelands and was mercifully halted in its move towards the northern hemisphere.

The news of this powerful and virulent new threat to mankind spread almost instantaneously around the world on Freinet. The shocking news of the re-appearance of this life-threatening disease prompted various medical and scientific organisations to search for a more effective treatment - and quickly.

Throughout the previous century there had been minor outbreaks of the more common bubonic plague, all of which claimed just a few thousand lives, but each outbreak was quickly brought under control by powerful new drugs. Scientists worked feverishly to find a treatment that would provide a vastly reduced mortality rate for this new strain. Whilst they worked towards this goal, the whole of the continent of Africa was physically isolated. Except for migrating birds, few of whom survived the flight across the Mediterranean to Europe, nothing left and nothing arrived.

So it was that this new and extremely virulent strain of pneumonic plague was halted in its progress to the north by the vast deserts and sparse populations of North Africa. To the south, however, lay the enormous populations of Southern Africa and nothing could stop the disease until it met the southern oceans.

In its frantic haste to annihilate all human life in its path, the disease scythed the human population of the numerous African countries as if it were an avenging angel.

A continental population of some nine hundred million souls at the beginning of the 21st century had increased to an horrendous figure of over one point five billion. Herded together in huge conurbations, the vast majority of these people were susceptible and vulnerable to any new diseases in one way or another; but especially from the high levels of population density or infected water and food.

The Black Death rolled unstoppably onwards and resembled a gigantic herd of feeding elephant, grazing, heads down, through a field of succulent green grass. The demise of the original carriers, those infected fleas on Juma's body, should have heralded the end of the epidemic. However, the new strain of plague transmitted itself by air and took a terrible toll. In the final count, some twenty-five percent of the population, around three hundred and fifty million humans, fell victim to this terrible plague.

Humanity and nature usually combine to provide a plus to counter the majority of minuses in the grand scheme of life and the Universe, and such was the case in the African plague disaster. For in one fell swoop the passage of the disease virtually obliterated AIDs from the African continent, if only temporarily.

Prior to the plague, this other human disaster had spread throughout Africa at an alarming speed. At the time of the plague, neither the source nor a cure had been discovered for this dreadful and debilitating condition, and there were some one hundred million AIDs sufferers throughout Africa alone.

The list of the world's most successful killers in terms of numbers of victims does not include the dark side of nature. But nature has killed, is killing and will kill again; on and on as long as man places himself in nature's way. Even the most demented of human monsters eventually feels that enough is enough. But nature does not feel constrained by the bounds of reason; it has no feelings and does not know that it kills; and those that so easily dismiss such dreadful loss of life as an action that could reasonably be expected by the will of a kind and merciful god must surely be the greater monsters.

CHAPTER 27
THE JOLT

THREAD:

Space exploration. The words have always excited man's senses. The first sighting of the far side of the Moon in 1959 was a huge milestone for earth-bound mankind. It sparked the biggest waste of earthly and human resources that this planet will ever witness.

Mankind has always been intensely interested in space. The desire to know what is out there has been an enormous driving force, encouraging man to push the boundaries of his knowledge to the very limit. Huge risks were taken, both in terms of human life and of financial investment. Spin doctors from around the globe used a variety of rationale to support such huge investments, the favourite of which was 'To advance the frontiers of man's knowledge; and to ensure the survival of humankind'.

Claptrap and bullshit. What man really wants is to find a safe haven to which we can all migrate when we have blown the crap out of this planet.

The more pragmatic human being might argue about the value of such commitment. Has mankind actually learned anything of any real value from the vast amount of resources poured into this endeavour? Would it not have served mankind much better to have concentrated their efforts on improving something as basic as a world bank of medicine and beneficial drugs? Or found answers to much more urgent existing problems, such as finding a cure for HIV, cancer or heart disease? Perhaps a much more realistic space programme would be to let anyone else *'out there'* make the effort to find us. Earth's bright-blue albedo must be a glittering beacon to other inquisitive eyes in the Universe. Surely if other life forms exist, we are not alone in our curiosity.

And with what does man's knowledge of space really help us? Most of what has been discovered is open to interpretation, causing more questions than answers. And what do we actually agree upon, in terms of how the Universe was created, how it will expand or decrease and just how the end might occur? For it took the world's scientists over two thousand years to agree finally that dinosaurs were actually wiped off the face of the Earth by a collision with an asteroid or meteorite. To say the world's scientists finally agreed is also stretching a point, for as long as a century after the acceptance of this theory in 2106 there was still doubt and controversy surrounding the 'big bang' theory. Thought to have occurred some sixty-five million years ago, an asteroid or meteorite is supposed to have created the one hundred and ten kilometre wide Chicxulub Crater in the Yucatan and subsequent tsunamis, landslides, dust-clouds, violent storms and earthquakes were thought to be responsible for wiping out the huge prehistoric animals that roamed the Earth at that time.

Certainly, such a sudden catastrophic calamity is capable of wiping out large numbers of people and animals. But was it really possible for a single asteroid or meteor strike to wipe out a complete species of animal?

The 20th century saw the development of the means to space travel, powered by the invention of large liquid-fuelled rocket engines by Germany during the Second World War. At the end of this violent conflict, both the USA and USSR *obtained* this rocket technology and the engineers from the vanquished foe. Throughout the remainder of that century, mankind probed our Solar System, searching for that which most probably does not exist. Literally hundreds of spacecraft managed to achieve the escape velocity from Earth, a little over eleven kilometres every second, and blast themselves into space.

Between the decades that straddle the halfway point of the 21st century, the effects of what the people of the Earth called global warming increased dramatically. Extreme temperatures, natural disasters, high winds, together with the encroaching effects of rising seas and deserts.

Our planet has faced a whole host of problems during the billions of years since our Solar System was created. Some of these problems have been earth shattering, violent and extremely frightening to the inhabitants of our planet. But the most frightening and catastrophic event that standing-up-man has so far witnessed awaited the dawn of the year 2062.

It is not only what we all understand as nature on Earth that is possessive of a violent temper. Cosmic nature, space nature, the nature of the Universe; call it what you will. Whatever you choose you can be certain-sure that it too has a character defect; it is also a demoniacal killer.

What is sown is what is reaped. And after four decades the world was about to pay the price for the Russians' nuclear space test. Way back in 2018, when the Russian leadership had felt rich enough, bold enough and careless of world opinion sufficiently to re-arm and re-expand, they had put a train of events in motion that would have disastrous effects upon many of those people on Earth not yet born.

Only memories remained for the feeble, former President of the CSSR. At eighty-six, Voloshin was nearing the end of his days on Earth and would soon be the proud possessor of his rightful few square metres of planet Earth, over which he would no doubt have total domination. But neither he, nor anyone else on Earth, could possibly know that the course of the approaching asteroids, hell-bent on inflicting such terrible damage on the citizens of Earth, had been engineered by man.

The passage of an object on Earth is resisted by air and gravity. But in space, no such resistance exists and the nuclear explosion that destroyed the ISS reached deep into the outer regions of the Solar System. The tentacles of the explosion touched two large pieces of space-flotsam, or asteroids, and changed their trajectory on to a course that would eventually bring them to threaten the survival of our planet.

Linked in tandem for the next forty-odd years, the pair circled the Sun in an ever-decreasing orbit that would bring what we now know as Upsilon and Ombre into contact with Earth. But unknown to everyone who waited for this extra-terrestrial contact, the two asteroids had already been touched by man and carried still the fruit of that union in terms of high levels of nuclear radiation.

DEEP SPACE. SATURDAY 17TH SEPTEMBER, 2061. LAIKA.

Julien Gelert was on duty in the brand spanking new astrophysical observatory, recently incorporated into the ageing Laika space laboratory. He had been in space, completely alone for a little over eight of the twelve months he was expected to remain on station.

Laika was a most suitable name for the space laboratory that doubled as an early warning system. Named after the first animal to travel in space, the original Laika had been a Soviet dog that flew into history on 3rd November, 1957. The idea of a barking dog giving early warning had appealed to the space agency that launched the laboratory.

Boredom was Julien's most fearsome enemy. That, and the strangely weird effects of being totally alone, weightless and at times in fear of his life, made his existence very hard to tolerate. An orbiting laboratory, his life was contained within an egg-shaped spacecraft, similar in size to a small one-bedroom flat.

Blasted into space on 1st June, 2061, Julien's first three months aloft had been virtually trouble free. His body was strong and healthy. All of his nutritional requirements were provided from the three small tablets that he swallowed each day.

But muscular inactivity for any extended period can produce some very strange effects on the human anatomy. Bodily functions involving the discharge of waste products slowly decreased in frequency and after some twelve weeks of virtual inactivity, ceased altogether. His first reaction to this reduction in normal bodily-functions was the appearance of several large boils on the back of his neck. The very worst place as far as Julien was concerned because he was unable to reach or manipulate the swelling to treat it.

In the weightless environment, he found that his muscular development deteriorated rapidly. His body had been honed through a daily combination of physical sporting pastimes and boosted further by strength and isometric training. The space laboratory was not fitted with a mirror; the designers knew of the muscular deterioration and had deliberately not provided the duty personnel with any means of viewing themselves. In carrying out his daily duties, he had little opportunity for exercise; his tasks involved little effort. Banks of monitoring computers would inform him of any strange or unusual events in the huge expanse of space surrounding his tiny world. And this was to be the last of the manned stations. In future, such deep-space watch-keeping vehicles would be unmanned and stationed much further away from Earth.

For Julien, life had been easy. Blessed with a superb brain, he had literally breezed through his early school life. Examinations had tested him not at all and he had consistently finished at the top of every class. University followed and his huge brain absorbed a mass of information about every subject under the Sun.

During his studies to graduate as a cosmic physicist, he had become intensely interested in the Universe as a whole. And his knowledge was vast, and spanned many sub divisions of science; sub-atomic particles; Newton's laws of motion; Maxwell's equations; quantum mechanics; chemistry; classical physics; astronomy; electricity; magnetism; optics; and nuclear and solid state physics. Since graduation, Julien had pioneered the understanding of our Universe to new horizons and had contributed greatly to mankind's knowledge of his environment. It was he who had designed the revolutionary astronavigation system that automatically returned any outgoing space craft to Earth, navigating through space and the Earth's atmosphere to a safe landing on the surface. Dubbed the Core Navigation System (CNS), it was based on the magnetic core of the Earth as a reference position. This point is identifiable from anywhere within known space limits and the direction of the magnetic core was indicated by a beam along which any spacecraft, fitted with a tiny magnet, homed into its parent base, anywhere on the surface of the Earth. Working alone in space provided ample opportunity to study and Julien was currently working on his latest project, that of isolating the individual spectrums of light emitted from other planets and using these as a navigational aid for space vehicles trying to find their way to the hundreds of other new planets discovered in deep space. Man still dreamed of finding other life forms, other intelligence or other entities somewhere in the vastness of space. But no such life forms had yet been found.

It was almost time for his final meal of the day. Julien floated across to his food store, picked up the tiny pill and popped it into his mouth. At the precise moment that the pill started its journey down his throat, the collision sensor sounded a strident alarm, filling Julien's heart with sheer panic. The pill stopped in his throat and he had to cough and spit for several precious seconds to expunge it from his body. Eyes streaming, he finally managed to reach his computer console. His eyes flashed across the screens, looking for the reason for the alarm.

There! The screen told him that his laboratory was on a collision course with an unknown space object. 'Unknown?' Julien whispered to himself. His heart soared. 'How wonderful, *tres intéressant*,' he whispered again. 'I hope it is something new to study.' Talking to himself was becoming a habit.

A lifetime of study. Julien often took a retrospective look at his life. And in this backward view it often struck him that he had spent most of his life studying the work of the past. Newton described his laws of motion way back in the 17th century; Maxwell outlined his equations in the 1800s; and quantum mechanics were pioneered in the early 1900s. Julien wanted to look into the future, to discover new laws of physics and to leave his own mark on the world.

But he was to be disappointed once again. The fast approaching satellite was an old, if irregular, visitor. Unknown to Julien, however, was that on this occasion his well-known visitor was concealing a greater danger. Similar to the Flying Dutchman, the legendary spectral ship supposed to be seen in the seas around the Cape of Good Hope, the sudden reappearance of MP89107 was to be an omen of disaster. But Julien was, as yet, blissfully unaware of that fact.

Asteroid MP89107 appeared and disappeared seemingly at will. Several sightings had been made since its first discovery in 2026. More correctly termed minor planets; asteroids are small worlds that move around our Sun in what are known as heliocentric orbits. The majority of these small worlds have orbits that lie between Mars and Jupiter, at a distance of between about 220 and 780 million kilometres from the Sun.

Since the early 21st century, new minor planet discoveries had been made each year. The number in our Solar System now totalled some one hundred and fifty thousand. Very few measured more than a hundred kilometres in diameter; and until the discovery of MP89107 the minor planet Ceres (designated MP41609 in 2052) was the largest with a diameter of about four hundred and fifty kilometres. Similarly, very few were afforded an individual name, since finding names had become too much of a chore for the astronomical community. However, the larger asteroids were usually afforded this honour and the irregular visitor measuring twenty-five kilometres in diameter was certainly big enough to be awarded one. MP89107 was also known as Upsilon, because there existed an unknown factor of why it appeared and disappeared so suddenly on each occasion of its sighting; and the Greek letter upsilon (y in the English alphabet) was thought to be a fitting name to represent this question. Worryingly, Upsilon had been the subject of two near misses on Earth but Julien decided not to get too excited about what might or might not happen; the asteroid had always veered away from Earth in the past.

Chuckling merrily, Julien programmed the avoidance coordinates into his computers. There really had been no possibility of danger to Laika, the computers had given him plenty of time to re-programme and would have made their own decisions if he had failed to do so. The settings he programmed would allow Upsilon to pass Laika in a very close flyby; and he was hoping for some exciting photographs to download in his next *comms* schedule.

Fixed schedules to mimic the working day of a person living on Earth had been discarded many weeks before. Controlled by his body, Julien now worked until he was tired and slept until he awoke. His calculations revealed that he would most probably be asleep when Upsilon passed in flyby. There was no real need for him to be awake; the computers fitted in the lab were the best that money could buy and they could be relied upon to do their work. But he wanted to see the minor planet; it was a sight that few other living persons had seen before and a first close-up sighting of a really large asteroid for him.

In space, the established and recommended method of sleeping involves strapping oneself into a small cot. At first, Julien had followed established safety procedures and had diligently lowered the cot when retiring each night. Over time, he found it much more convenient to allow his body to relax and float in space. Sleep came much more easily and he awoke feeling more refreshed and revived.

Normal sleeping patterns for Julien involved his drifting into a restless slumber for about four or five hours and he was therefore surprised when his eyes flew open. Instantly alert, he noticed that he had slept for a little over two hours and there were no audible alarms. What had disturbed him? He searched his mind for some clue.

There was something. Nagging quietly at some as yet unknown part of the human brain. In the deep recesses of his mind, there was a tiny fact that he had overlooked. He was sure of it now but he could not put his finger directly on to the problem.

Slowly, so as not to disturb his train of thought, he hoisted himself over to his bank of computers. The only thing that had disturbed the uneventful day had been the collision alarm. A starting point, at least. Programming the computer to replay the recorded image of the approaching Upsilon took but a few moments. The image looked quite normal and he gazed at the screen for several minutes, seeking further clues. Nothing further occurred to the brilliant cosmic physicist and he forced his body to relax again in search of sleep.

SPACECOM.

Like an eagle's eyrie, Spacecom sits on the top of Mount Whitney. At a touch below four point five thousand metres, this is the highest peak in the Sierra Nevada range of mountains. It is also the highest mountain in the lower forty-eight states of the United States of America. The peak is remote, accessible only to the finest and fittest climbers and it sits inside a large area of the Earth's surface that is completely free of human occupation. It is therefore clutter-free, in terms of radio, TV, radar or any other electrical emission. A clean footprint, where signals inbound from space are most unlikely to be distorted by human intervention. The facility is permanently manned, shifts changing on a two-weekly rota by air.

Earth had gone space crazy. Hundreds of probes were seeking information. Man was desperate to discover the secrets of the Universe; how it was formed; are we the only life forms; and how, if ever, it might die? Are we all heading towards the antonym of the Big Bang, known as the Big Crunch, when the Universe is supposed to stop expanding and implode?

Spacecom monitored all of these probes. It contained the equipment necessary to control and manage them and the resources to deal with any problems, whether manned or not. The equipment cost a great deal more than an arm and a leg; and the running costs were astronomical. Fortunately, the agency was funded by a multi-national consortium; but as usual, and despite being classified no longer as a superpower, the USA provided the greater share.

Expensive communications equipment does not react well to lightning strikes. A gigantic Faraday cage, the inside of Spacecom was a lightning-safe area and its backup power and computer capacity ensured that nothing failed. It also guaranteed that not the tiniest piece of datum was missed from the space probes. Its remoteness also ensured that not too many visitors called at the facility.

Bioastronautic equipment monitored every conceivable bodily function, from every human and animal in space. Checked and rechecked every second of the day, the slightest change in a person's stress levels was instantly downloaded to Spacecom. Akin with its namesake, Laika was known by other names within Spacecom, Muttnik, Curly and the Pointer being the most commonly used; and as Earth's early warning system, Julien's bioastronautics were routinely presented to the senior on-duty personnel.

One might be forgiven for envisaging the inside of Spacecom as a peaceful place. But this could not be further from the truth. Whilst not quite bedlam; it was not far short of this. At least twenty situations were being dealt with. From course corrections, navigational problems, malfunctioning equipment and power failures to personal problems - the list of possible human, electronic and mechanical problems was virtually endless.

LAIKA.

The space lab Laika was regarded as a fairly high-priority mission. Very little went wrong; it required little in support apart from the occasional short surge of power from its ion thrusters to maintain its geosynchronous orbit around Mars. Routine *comms* schedules were established each evening but there was normally not much of interest to download.

The excitement of the flyby by Upsilon had also caused little excitement amongst the staff at the monitoring ground station. Standard operating procedures (SOPs) demanded that routine surveillance of the fast disappearing asteroid be continued for as long as it remained in view. After his brief few hours of personally monitoring the minor planet, Julien set the computer systems to comply with SOPs and settled back into his routine.

The mind can be a very tiresome organ. Few can have failed to experience a situation whereby a required piece of information escapes one's total efforts to recall. On the tip of his tongue, but out of reach, the elusive scrap of data tugged at Julien's mind and would not let him rest. No matter how hard he tried, he could not recapture his previous sleeping habits. The nagging worry was still with him. Had he in fact missed something? Laika's systems did not find any problem with Upsilon's flyby; so why was he so on edge?

Countless times Julien reran the pictures of the fading asteroid, watching it intently until it faded from view. Nothing strange there, completely in accord with previous sightings; one minute there, the next - gone!

LAIKA. 22ND OCTOBER, 2061.

The asteroid's flyby had been several monotonous weeks ago. Tired did not begin to describe Julien's exhaustion; he felt weary in body and soul. No comment came from the Spacecom, although the monitoring ground-station did record some slight deviation in his stress levels and also noted his inability to sleep for very long. 'Space orientation' was listed against each logged event.

At about two hundred and fifty million kilometres away from Earth, Julien was a long way from home. Fixed in areocentric orbit, keeping station with Mars' other two moons, Phobos and Deimos, he was entitled to feel lonely at times. Interest in the brief visit of Upsilon should have dwindled in his mind weeks ago. But still he could not completely satisfy his mind that he had not missed some tiny detail that would explain his constantly feeling on edge.

Awakened suddenly after only an hour's rest, Julien was wide awake yet again. Whilst the human body sleeps, the brain whirs in

constant activity; and it often happens that if the human mind con-
centrates on a given problem for long enough, the answer is usually
found whilst asleep. And this time when he awoke, he had a glimmer of an idea.

Moving suddenly from fitful dozing to complete awareness, his
senses were zinging with anticipation. Floating down to the chair
in front of the computer terminal, Julien rapidly issued commands.
'Bring up Upsilon. Show me the final day before contact lost.' Familiar
shots lit up the screen in front of him; he had watched these countless
times before.

And then it hit him. Upsilon filled most of the screen but the area
of space that closely surrounded the asteroid was completely black;
there were no signs of other stars to break up the blackness. A few
fast computer commands and the camera panned out. There, in front
of him, was his answer. Behind Upsilon, there must be another huge
mass, much larger than the asteroid. There could be no other explanation for the large dark ring around it. Another minor planet, following in Upsilon's wake.

For the first time in his life, the cosmic physicist panicked. His
heart began to thump in his chest and his fingers twitched; he knew
not what to do!

SPACECOM.

But the sudden and massive increase in Julien's heart and respira-
tion levels set the alarm bells ringing in Spacecom. Inside the her-
metically-sealed and temperature-controlled interior of Laika, Julien's
body levels slowly returned to normal. However, Spacecom could not
ignore the sudden increases - somebody would have to check.

'Are you OK, Jules?' The need for identifying call signs did not
exist; everyone in the Spacecom knew the voice of the space lab astronaut; and Julien knew the voices from Spacecom equally as well.

'Yeah, I'm getting there.' A few last deep intakes of breath to calm
his racing senses. 'Thanks for the call, Jim. I was just about to give
you a shout.' Julien was quite happy with the diminutive used by
Spacecom but he always thought of himself as Julien. It had been
what his recently-departed mother had always called him.

'You got a problem up there, Jules?' The voices from Spacecom were consistently calm, pitched low and full of reassurance.

Julien took a few moments to compose his reply. 'Without wishing to be too melodramatic, Jim, I think the whole planet has a problem.'

'What you got, Jules?' The voice had gone up a notch and Jim sat up a little straighter and leaned towards his console. He knew that Jules was an extremely intelligent man, a man who did not make wild statements or hurried decisions. If he said the Earth had a problem, then by God you better believe him.

'Downloading to you now Jim. See what you make of this.' Jules hit the send button and the data zipped into Spacecom's central analytical systems some half a minute later. Radio transmissions, travelling through space at the speed of light, took quite a time to travel the half billion kilometre round trip to the Muttnik and back.

Jim was impressed; he noticed that the monitors checking on Jules' body status had quickly returned to normal. *'The man must be made of ice,'* thought Jim. *'One minute he is reporting a danger to our planet and a few seconds later he is as calm as a cucumber.'*

For several long minutes, Jim studied the download from Laika. 'I don't see the problem, Jules,' he finally admitted.

'Neither did I at first,' agreed Julien. 'But pan the camera as far out as it will go, then have another look.'

'Christ almighty! Is that what I think it is, Jules?' Jim's excited voice; many decibels higher than any other conversation in the room, together with the frowned upon blasphemy turned all heads in his direction.

'Jules, let's be sure about what you are calling in. Can you recheck your systems and confirm what we see?'

'Merde, damn, shit, sod.' Now it was Jules' turn to swear; he was often inclined to throw in a few French words in recognition of his Gallic ancestry. 'I have already double-checked every last detail, Jim. Believe me, the equipment does not lie.'

Taking a few seconds to catch his breath and to compose his words carefully, Julien continued. 'What I am saying is that Upsilon has not disappeared, as I at first assumed. It is still there but it is being pursued by a much larger piece of space junk that is hiding it from our view.'

'I don't want to call this one, Jules. You say it, man.'

A very deep and tired sigh preceded the earth-shattering announcement from Jules. 'What I'm calling in is that there are two space objects out there. They are running in tandem and if both asteroids continue on their present course, and if neither is deflected by Earth's atmosphere, then there exists a very real probability of an asteroid strike on the surface of Earth. Is that clear enough for you?'

Time seemed to stand still for long seconds. 'Thanks, Jules. Don't go away; I gotta let Pash know about this one.'

All was strangely silent inside Spacecom, no one had overhead the announcement from Julien but they all knew that something was going down. Jim threw down his headset, leapt to his feet, turned and smashed headlong into his watch supervisor. 'Pash! I was just coming to look for you. We got a humdinger from the Muttnik and I think you better deal with it yourself.'

Pashkeesh Prahma took the recently vacated and still warm seat. Her soft voice trilled swift instructions to the central computer. She spoke in fluent Hebrew and of those few people who were close enough to hear the instructions, none understood. Pashkeesh could have used any one of the nine different languages in which she was fluent, the computer cared not; it understood every language ever devised by man.

In between bursts of what sounded very similar to gobbledy-gook, Pashkeesh told Jim that she had been monitoring Laika for sometime and had overheard the conversation with Jules. 'Jim, you are entitled to know what I am doing about this problem. But I would take it as a personal favour if you will keep the entire conversation to yourself. Just for the time being until Washington has had a chance to decide a course of action.'

'Yo! Understand Skipper.' Jim was a retired US Navy man and he had managed to regain his usual composure.

'I'll take Laika in my office.' Brunneous, deep and dark; the almost black eyes bored into Jim. 'I will push it up the line as soon as I have sufficient information.' The ultra-slim and extremely shapely body of the beautiful Sioux Indian from South Dakota rose elegantly from Jim's chair.

'*Pash by name and pash by nature?*' Jim would dearly love to confirm his thought. '*Hm, and I might just be running out of enough time to give it a go,*' he smiled as he realised that a decision had been taken.

Back in her office, Pashkeesh was all business. Before contacting the National Security Advisor in Washington, she had some preparations to make and some facts to check. Had the follower of Upsilon been sighted before? Was it there and been missed at Upsilon's previous sightings? What information existed about Upsilon's previous sightings, apart from the near-miss angle? Just how close had Upsilon's near misses been? Confirm Upsilon's projected course. Get some figures for the new intruder; size, estimated time of impact, possible damage to Earth in the event of a collision. But above all, be absolutely certain that on this occasion, Upsilon will strike the Earth if it remains on its present course. And perhaps more importantly, will the second, bigger asteroid also strike Earth? Angrily she admonished herself. *'Think squaw!'* First, give it a reference number for the computers and a name for the media. MP151603 for the bit-crunchers; Ombre, the shadow, for Julien and the media.

An hour later, she had most of the data that she needed. Jules had downloaded his own estimates and conclusions together with a mass of other information that he had been able to coax from his onboard sensors. Jules could do no more; both intruders were far beyond his range. More would be available as the pair closed towards Earth's defensive ring of sensitive equipment.

It looked bad. First indications for Ombre hinted at a diameter of about double that of Upsilon, as much as fifty kilometres. Records showed that the new intruder had not been sighted before; but there were some indications that it might have been present during previous sightings of the smaller Upsilon. Now that they knew what they were looking for, there was definitely a hint of a shadow around the previous sighting of the original infrequent visitor.

As for the likelihood of an impact with Earth? Very difficult to predict with any degree of accuracy but Pashkeesh understood that Julien had really had no other choice than to highlight the probability of such a strike. Earth's atmosphere deflected or burned-up a large percentage of intruding space particles, whether large or small. Both the computers and Jules predicted such an impact with Earth as probable, rather than possible. They also forecast that should an impact occur, the crash site would be somewhere within the vast landmass of India.

In the back of her mind, Pashkeesh knew that she was pushing the boundaries of incompetence. She was already way past the right time to push the situation up the line. But hot lines are just that; you have got to be ready to have something hot and tangible to talk about when you hit the button.

America's NSA was very close to retirement. He was fighting it but it would not be long before he was forced to vacate his chair. Protecting his country had been a lifetime work for Conrad Karnag and he had occupied his chair through the two terms of the present POTUS. A dedicated man he virtually lived in his office, particularly since his wife of forty-seven years had recently died.

'Speak! Pash.' Con Karnag was a busy man. At the beck and call of both POTUS and his staff, Karnag did not have time for social niceties on the hot-line telephones. Such lines were person to person, he knew who would be speaking on each of the many-coloured instruments on his desk; and his manner was persistently blunt to the point of rudeness.

The pair knew each other well, although they had never met. Several similar conversations had taken place over the previous few years. 'Con, our little Yankee pain-in-the-ass is back.' She waited in vain through the short silence for a response from the NSA. 'And this time she has brought a pal.'

'Predictions?' The NSA was already late for an appointment with some 'army-brass hat' and he relied on his finely-tuned instincts to prioritise initial reports from a host of inputs.

'On your desktop, under mid-year financial estimates.' Pash knew that hiding her report in some boring budget report, encrypted in a private one-to-one space-noise crypto system and marked 'NSA eyes only' might well be seen as overkill by the NSA. But she would rather that than be seen as the shepherd that let the pig out of its stable to space-hop into a maelstrom of media attention. The mixed metaphors in English always pleased her and tended to both relax her mind and enable total concentration on the problem at hand.

'Back in five, Pash.' The NSA was already talking to his computer before the line went dead.

The young body of the American Indian relaxed. She had just about got away with delaying her report through the chain of command. Should she wait for the NSA or speak with Jules? Shrill ring-tones from the hot line made the decision for her. She silently cursed her hands; they always seemed to feel hot and sweaty when she was under pressure. The slim, darkly brown left hand, moist with per-spiration and completely free of rings, reached forward to engage the recording system. Despite the apparent friendliness of the NSA, she did not entirely trust him; but then she did not entirely trust anyone. 'Connect hot line,' she gave the quiet command to connect the call from the NSA.

'You predict eighty-six days to impact, Pash. That is the 16th January, 2062. How accurate is that?'

Blast! The NSA had an uncanny ability to latch on to the weak-est point in any report. 'The best we can do at the present, Sir. We estimate the range to be in the region of about half-distance between Mars and Earth; say 130 million kilometres. Its speed, estimated at about sixty thousand, gives us the space-journey time.'

Although the NSA had clearly downgraded the situation by speaking of an impact, Pash was still trying to maintain some form of cryptic speech. They were both well aware that the speech sys-tems between them were susceptible to an invasive attack by any one of a dozen or so determined knowledgeable and very wealthy organ-isations. Government secure speech systems used the best availa-ble digital inversion algorithms; they were split-packaged and splat-ter-propagated randomly over thousands of satellite channels, micro-wave links, dedicated fibre-optic cables and a variety of frequencies throughout the radio spectrum. But conversations were just data; and computers can work miracles with data. And any national newspa-per would pay a small fortune for such information. 'We will be able to make more accurate predictions when we can light them up on our sensors,' Pash added lamely.

'When will the intruders enter capture-range for our sensors, Pash?' They both knew the basic parameters of Earth's sensors; out to one hundred million kilometres. What the NSA wanted to know was when the pair of asteroids would reach that point.

'About three weeks, Sir.' Pash was on solid ground again and was beginning to relax.

'Form a small team, Pash. You will lead it. Rest them for a cou-ple of days, then I want some facts; and no more of this *in the region of, about* or *estimate*. I want facts and options so get some rest yourself. And I'll want to hear what assessment Jules has made.'

Silence reigned as both conversed inwardly with their own thoughts for a while. Finally, the NSA closed the conversation. 'From now on we will refer to them as the Shadows. I will brief the President after our next chat.'

'Aye, Sir.' Pash acknowledged her orders and broke the connection. It was odd. Somehow, whenever such situations developed, almost everyone switched, quite unconsciously, to a military vernacular.

LAIKA.

He could feel his eyes drooping. His eyelids seemed to weigh a ton; another of the strange effects of weightlessness that Jules had noticed. Eyes sore from constant rubbing, Jules remained awake. His body craved sleep but he could not switch off. Absolute fatigue had nullified his ability for coherent thought and he was unable to make any decisions. He remained awake, waiting for Pash to decide what he should do.

Three hours had elapsed since he had made his report. During that time, he had realigned his sensors to look back towards Earth, hoping to re-establish contact with the two asteroids. But at more than one hundred and thirty million kilometres distance, they were way beyond the capabilities of his systems.

Julien knew this but it did not stop him from looking. He was beginning to regret his decision to remain awake; he should have tried for sleep again, at least for a couple of hours. But he was his own worst enemy. Once his interest was piqued, he could not let go. In the background, oddly loud, he could hear the clickety-click of increased activity within his computer systems as his onboard laboratory sensors crunched the numbers once again. A mass of information had been eagerly gathered about Upsilon as it had passed in flyby. Pash had requested a recheck, she was hoping that there might be some information about Upsilon's new escort; but the sensors had been concentrated upon Upsilon and there was nothing on the newly-discovered Ombre.

Laika's sensors were first class. It was often quoted by the manufacturers that the system was so sensitive that it could track the passage of souls, birthing and dying on their journey from and to heaven. Julien thought that there would be plenty of opportunity to test this theory in the near future when Upsilon and Ombre touched down.

MONDAY 16TH JANUARY, 2062. ALTON, HAMPSHIRE. TOUCHDOWN.

'It *is* out of bounds, you ignorant old git!' The shorter of the two elderly golfers shouted at his partner, his voice rising in tempo and anger with each word.

His partner, much larger in build and with a fierce and determined look on his face, cast a withering glance at his old pal.

'Have you gone blind or are you just having an old fart's senior moment?' His voice was filled with venom and contempt. 'Can you not see that the ball has not gone beyond the last white post and therefore, according to the rules of golf, it is not, I say again, it is not, out of bounds.'

David Caless, the larger of the two golfers, looked down at his lifelong friend. He missed not a single opportunity to quote the rules of golf. Blood began to course through his veins and he could feel that little prickle of excitement that heralded the onset of a really good argument. The pair, almost inseparable over the past fifty years, enjoyed nothing more than a good squabble, the noisier the better and preferably with a large audience. In fact, they disagreed most of the time, sometimes apparently to the point of coming to blows, about everything and everybody; but mostly about any statement the other made.

'I knew you were half blind when you drove into that bog in East Meon!' Again the shorter of the two golfers spoke. Bob Monger, allowing his eyes to swivel upwards in a gesture of long-suffering annoyance added, 'And I'm telling you, as sure as your bottom looks downwards, you are out of bounds; so play three off the tee and let's get on with the game.'

With a lifetime of shared experiences between them there was no shortage of material with which to embarrass the other. The incident involving the bog had occurred many years before, shortly after they had first met. In the same watch, they had been temporarily serving in some long-forgotten peacetime naval exercise in the RN Dockyard at Portsmouth way back in 2014. Dave had momentarily dozed off whilst driving to their homes in Alton. Following a long and exhausting night watch the conversation had slowly dried up, David's attention had drifted away and the car had veered pilotless into a very smelly, marshy area at the side of the road. The human brain does not function on all cylinders in a state of extreme tiredness and the pair had made many fruitless efforts to push the car out of the stinking mess, up to their knees in sludge, before finally admitting defeat. Abandoning the car, they had thumbed a lift home and left its retrieval until the following day.

'I can play a provisional ball.' Dave looked belligerently at his friend, knowing even as he spoke that he was wrong.

'No, you cannot.' Bob reached for his copy of the rules of golf, tucked away in his golf bag, ready for just such an event. But both men knew that it was a pointless gesture, since neither could see well enough to read the small print, even with their spectacles.

The golfers had enjoyed many happy years of retirement; they were golf fanatics and still managed to play two or three times a week. Not rich but comfortable, they managed on their meagre pensions, which provided them with the necessities of life.

Completely insular, the pair had relinquished their interest in the world many years ago, handing it into the seemingly uncaring hands of the next generation. Daily newspapers had struggled for some time to compete with the instantaneous information available on Freinet and were rendered almost obsolete many years before. Neither bothered to access the world news on their Pewis, nor cared sufficiently to watch the news broadcasts on TV; and the contents of modern radio broadcasts were casually dismissed as 'Nothing more than a load of trite and piffle'.

To their combined relief, neither of their wives played golf. However, they were mindful, occasionally, to invite the ladies to accompany them, certain in the knowledge of a refusal. Much akin to a husband teaching his wife to drive a car, a marital team on a golf course was apt to develop into a battle zone; and the two old chaps took great delight in watching a domestic develop between other husband and wife teams during a round.

To the rest of the golf club female membership, the wives of Bob and Dave were generally regarded as suitable candidates for canonisation. A minimum reward, for a lifetime of looking after the two old, cantankerous and religious reprobates, whose souls would surely be damned and turned away by St Peter towards the hotter climes of hell.

'Bloody women golfers, should be home cooking the dinner!' Spoken loudly in the clubhouse, in the hope of inciting a response from anyone and which might just escalate into a good shouting match, was a common sprat to catch a mackerel. It was one of their favourite expressions of worldly wisdom, one which never failed to raise a chuckle from some of the male members and scornful glances from the female members.

Notwithstanding their age, they were both sharp-witted and sharp-tongued, if not sharp-eyed. Of an earlier age, they did not find it easy to tolerate the new liberal attitudes of society; the constant noise of personal games and telephone systems; the new wave of social misconduct; and deliberate avoidance of the laws of the land. Of one accord in their battle cries 'Reinstate the death penalty, hang the bastards (of murderers); stand 'em against a wall and shoot 'em (of terrorists); off with their knackers (of sex offenders); bring back National Service (of the lazy, unruly young); make 'em all walk back to their own countries (of those immigrants not willing to adhere to Britain's social order); and send 'em all to hell and damnation (of clerics, seen as the perpetrators of all mankind's problems)'.

Despite their irascible characters, the pair was well liked amongst their golfing peers. The two other golfers which made up the four-ball leaned casually on their golf buggy, waiting for the pair's latest spat to subside. They knew better than to voice an opinion; one was apt to get one's head chewed off in return for an ill-timed comment.

Finally resigned to the possible loss of two strokes, David accepted that the ball was most probably out of bounds. He smiled and bent forward to place another ball on its tee.

A groan, and a quick exhalation of breath that was almost a sigh emitted from David as he stood up from placing a second ball on the tee. He glared at the other three members of his four-ball, daring them to make some comment. Obviously content with the total silence, he readdressed his ball, ready to commence his swing. As is usually the case in such circumstances, the second ball took the same trajectory as the first and came to rest out of bounds.

Unable to remain silent, Bob was forced to make some comment. 'Well, I don't think I would have done it quite like that, David. But since you seem determined to make a prat of yourself, I suggest you give those bottle-tops in your glasses a good clean and put another one down,' adding under an obvious, gleeful chuckle, 'and this will be five off the tee!'

'You little wizened gnome! You did that on purpose. You moved as I started my swing.' David was looking for excuses and hoping that someone might suggest a mulligan.

'Christ, David. The cold up there must be freezing your brain. Nobody moved and you would not have seen it had they done so, you half-blind, half-drunk, lanky excuse for a human being!' The withering comment from Bob was accompanied by an outstretched hand, clutched within was yet another can of beer.

'Ah,' sighed David. 'About time you got the beer out; I was beginning to think that you had forgotten to bring any.' Grasping the offered can, he smiled contentedly and drained a large gulp.

Unwilling to risk losing further golf balls, David decided not to play another off the tee. 'I'll just drop one somewhere down the fairway; and call it three off the tee!' No one argued, it was only a friendly game.

All four golfers clambered into their buggies. Resembling miniature hovercrafts, the buggies hovered just above the ground; and they were completely enclosed, fully air-conditioned and usable all year round.

Halfway down the fairway, the buggies slammed into the ground. Or, more accurately, the earth seemed to leap up and smash into the underside of the buggies. All around was chaos. As David and Bob's buggy shot back towards the sky, both hung on as tightly as they could. Suddenly the buggy hit the deck again and slipped towards a small copse. Trees were falling all around and in his peripheral vision Bob saw the clubhouse slowly crumbling like a house of cards.

The buggy was upside down in the midst of a chaotic landscape of fallen trees and David was lying on his face next to Bob. Neither was seriously injured but the buggy looked much the worse for wear. Glancing at his friend, Bob quipped, 'Well David, if you feel that strongly about it, perhaps you were not out of bounds after all!'

The two old friends looked around for their playing partners. They were both quite dead and lying under the huge oak tree that had squashed the flimsy buggy as easily as it would have a ripe melon.

Neither was prone to panic. Approaching their dotage both were staring eternity in the face and had little fear of death. They walked back to the remains of the clubhouse to give what assistance they could to the dead and dying. And perhaps this might not be an appropriate day to wind-up the lady members.

Calls had already been made to the emergency services. But there would be no response on this day, for the nearby town had been flattened by the strange phenomenon. The emergency services were concentrating on stemming the numerous fires and gas leaks that further threatened the town. The dead could wait; and those that survived could look after the injured until help arrived.

16TH JANUARY, 2062. JARWA, NORTHERN INDIA.

The streets were deserted. The silence was total and not a breath of wind disturbed the remanent garbage that littered the streets, a sure sign of a hasty departure. Not a single soul remained in the town. The population of almost twenty-one million had flown, almost as if they had been vaporized. Second only to Mumbai (Bombay), whose inhabitants now exceeded twenty-five million, Jarwa baked in the Indian Sun; and awaited its fate.

The people of this town had packed whatever they could carry and fled. Situated in the State of Uttar Pradesh in northern India and close to the Nepalese border and the mighty Himalayas, this once busy town had become the hub of the western world's cheap source of information technology assistance. Wherever in the world the '?' button was pressed, the question or cry for help found its way through a labyrinth of communications networks to the thousands of hectares that made up M?E. The headquarters of this mega-corporation was surrounded by hectare upon hectare of huge blocks of flats, purposely built for the workers.

The occupiers of Jarwa did not leave because they wanted to.

Although very poorly paid, those that worked for M?E were still the highest paid group of workers in India. They were comfortable in their tiny flats, which were not much larger than rabbit hutches. M?E took care of everything. The company owned the shops, provided the necessities of life and built whatever the community needed in terms of schools, transport and medical facilities. Almost every rupee paid out in wages by M?E was subsequently recovered through company-owned stores and utilities.

The eyes in the sky, as the population of Jarwa referred to the over-head satellites, had predicted that their own town was to be obliter-ated by a killer asteroid. Fatalistic workers had fled in all directions; much as would a colony of ants departing their nest when boiling water is poured into it.

And just as would a gigantic swarm of locusts taking flight in search of new feeding grounds, the twenty-one million souls left a trail of debris in all directions as they discarded those possessions that they could no longer find the strength to carry. The vast major-ity headed south towards the heartland of their own country. The air-ports at Lucknow, Patna, Kanpur and Varanasi, already overwhelmed with millions of people attempting to obtain international flights to safety, were the scenes of ferocious fighting. As were the hundreds of railway stations in the surrounding area.

Jarwa was not the only town in danger of annihilation. Many oth-ers in the vicinity of the crash site were in dire danger. But only Jarwa was left totally empty. Across India, there were scenes of mass hyste-ria, mass evacuation and mass fear.

India's population had exploded during the 21st century's first five decades from just over a billion to a little over two billion and ninety percent of this mass of people were attempting to leave their homes or their country. Depending on their individual assessment of the dan-ger attached to the approaching mini-armageddon, they made a deci-sion to go; go somewhere; go anywhere; get out of the way - escape from the approaching Shadows.

Pakistan, China and Myanmar lined their borders with tanks and troops. Two billion people represented a lot of extra mouths to feed; and all three countries were struggling to feed their ever-growing pop-ulations. Millions crossed over the Indira Gandhi Canal to the west of Rajasthan, heading for the Thar Desert and the perceived safety of Pakistan. The blood flowed freely along the Pakistani-Indian border; the would-be escapees had no chance against the heavily-armed Pakistani army. Three days later the smell of decomposing bodies, rotting in the intense heat, wafted eastward towards Delhi, a clear warning to other itinerant refugees.

Many thousands died attempting to cross the mountain ranges into China. Many thousands more perished under the fierce reception of the Chinese troops along its border. No quarter was given to the advancing hordes of cannon fodder. Fast-moving tanks rampaged through the multitudes of refuge-seeking Indians, crushing the packed humanity beneath their old-technology but murderous tracks. Bodies popped like pricked balloons; blood and body parts sprayed over ground, tanks and the still advancing army of escaping safety seekers. From high above, precision bombing created yet more ghastly scenes of man's unforgiving nature.

Warplanes strafed the massed battalions of escapees along the Myanmar borders. Pilots dive-bombing their co-planetarians willy-nilly, pressing home their attacks with tears in their eyes. Raised high in unison, the massed voices of the refugees sang their national anthem. 'Jana, gana, mana', the words of the anthem referred, and gave salute, to a long-dead King George V, who with his Queen, Mary, was crowned Emperor and Empress of India some one hundred and fifty years before.

COLLISION.

161307UTC-JAN-2062 converts to 19.07 on 16th January, 2062, India time. At that moment in Earth's history, a cataclysmic event occurred that was felt by every person that lived on our planet; but was witnessed by few.

Mankind had at last been granted its dearest wish, that of contact with another member of the space community. Similar to a monstrous snooker ball, the black intruder kissed the multi-coloured ball of the Earth in the most humungous explosion since the dawn of life. Ombre struck Jarwa exactly as predicted by Pashkeesh's advisory team and exactly on time.

As in the case of the curate's egg, it was not all bad news. At least the Earth had a single collision to contend with; true to previous form, Upsilon veered away at the last moment and disappeared back into the loneliness of space to await its own individual moment of glory.

Freinet was flooded with graphic descriptions and photographs of the flaming orb that was Ombre. During its descent through Earth's atmosphere, the giant asteroid had lost a little of its speed and mass. The surface of the fifty-kilometre diameter siderite reached fantastic temperatures during its transit through Earth's shield and huge, fiery lumps of liquid metal dropped to the surface of the Earth - molten, nuclear-infested teardrops intent upon wreaking their own havoc.

The track of the flaming blackball was also as predicted. Across Brazil, watchers saw the phenomenon, at first difficult to spot in the glare of a setting Sun but slowly increasing in size to become the monster that it was. The globules of molten siderite caused panic, destruction and death wherever they struck the Earth. Brazil, a huge tract of Africa from Cameroon to Islamia and most of western India suffered hundreds of hits. Whole cities were razed to the ground and millions suffered *the* most horrific death by being burned alive.

As the fiery visitor appeared alongside the setting Sun, people fell to their knees and awaited whatever fate had in store for them. To many, it was if the Sun had given birth to an unruly child and sent this vengeful son to deliver the final judgement on mankind. If the makers of Laika's sensors were to be believed then they would shortly have plenty to analyze, as millions of burning souls took what must be a well-trodden path into heaven.

When the news of the approaching Shadows assailed the incredulous ears of the people of the Earth, the reaction of mankind was threefold. Those who trusted their religious leaders accepted their quiet assurances that 'The Heavenly Father, in His infinite mercy, will protect you from danger'.

Others, who obviously suffered from some deficiency of the brain, trusted their politicians; and waited for their leaders to tell them what to do.

Yet others pinned their hopes of survival on Earth's all-knowing scientists, who claimed that there was most definitely an answer; all they needed was a little more time to find it.

Some made their own decision. And if religious dogma were to be credible, many hundreds of thousands would be turned away at heaven's gates this day. Those who chose to decide for themselves the time and method of their death might well face an even greater decision when their knocking on those Pearly Gates was ignored.

Societies, clubs, associations; all had been formed in the weeks leading up to the 16th January. All these groups preached freedom of choice in the manner of their deaths; and men, women, and children activated whatever mechanisms they had chosen during the morning of the asteroid's collision. In some cases, whole villages were as one in making this choice. The sound of gunfire rippled around the globe during that morning, as those who chose to be the first to depart pulled the trigger.

Others went more quietly in gas-filled rooms; some chose to die by going down with a sinking ship; or by crashing an aircraft; or by jumping from a high place; or by imbibing of some potent potion. Yet others saw the occasion as a golden opportunity to indulge in their own private drug hell, completing what must be every drug-user's dream of over-dosing: to the max, man!

The vast metropolis of Jarwa was, quite simply, utterly destroyed. Not a single brick or piece of glass was ever found. The size of the impact crater was huge when compared to any other hole on Earth. The blast at impact hurled billions of tonnes of the Earth's crust into the atmosphere, creating a vast stream of shooting stars, clearly but briefly visible in the night sky as they burned up.

The dimensions of the Barringer Meteorite Crater in Arizona, previously the largest hole in the Earth caused by a collision with a terrestrial interloper, paled into insignificance when Ombre's effort was measured. Some thirty kilometres across, two thousand five hundred metres deep and fifteen kilometres long, it put to shame the Barringer site. Huge rocks, mixed with great lumps of tektite, surrounded the gaping edges of the elongated crater to a height of some fifteen hundred metres.

But that was just the first strike. The flaming Ombre ricocheted off Indian soil and at the same time it was diverted slightly from its original course. The few degrees to the east placed the ascending and still flaming asteroid on course for Mount Everest. A fateful day indeed for that most majestic of Earth's mountains. Like a cosmic-sized firework, the top twenty-one hundred metres of Everest exploded into dust and it too became a skyrocket to oblivion in the heat of Earth's atmosphere.

The double kiss, like the cheek kisses of a French-person's greeting, slowed Ombre to about forty thousand km/h. It next touched down just north of Lanzhou in China and hopped off towards the southeastern foot of Russia. Each time the burning sphere touched the Earth, it immediately bounced away again, as if reluctant to stay.

Slowing rapidly after the touchdown in China, it made contact again in the central wastes of Mongolia, again at Tugur in Russia and finally slid into the Sea of Okhotsk. On entry into the water, Ombre had lost a considerable amount of its bulk. It now measured some thirty kilometres in diameter and when it belly-flopped through the almost two thousand metres of seawater it was a white-hot poker slicing through butter. Eventually the asteroid came to rest, burrowing some one thousand metres below the seabed. In passing, it displaced billions of litres of seawater, creating wave after wave of mega-tsunamis in all directions.

The effect of the final landing was to create the newest and highest point on Earth. At about twenty-eight thousand metres high, this new earthly mountain reached into the stratosphere. It formed a sister island to Sakhalin and was claimed as Russian sovereign territory on 13th February, 2062.

The newly-dubbed Tugur Island, named after the last city that it demolished, took five years to cool sufficiently to allow man to set foot upon it.

Ombre's massive divots created several side effects. The touchdowns were so violent that the tectonic plates of the Earth's crust shifted suddenly and violently.

In its normal state, the Earth's crust moves continuously, very slowly and almost unnoticed. This is known as aseismic creep. Ombre's little nudges bowled normality out of kilter and caused chaos around the world.

Earthquakes resounded around our planet. Volcanoes that had been declared extinct hundreds of years before suddenly blossomed once again. Mountain ranges rose and fell, creating the illusion of the back of a monstrous whale breaching the surface of the ocean. The clouds of dust and debris settled into rivers, stopping their flow over hundreds of kilometres and creating new flood plains further upstream. These gigantic clouds of meteoric dust tainted with nuclear particles irradiated the planet, changing weather patterns, creating a multitude of health problems and playing havoc with worldwide communications. They blocked out the Sun completely, lowering the temperature of our world by twenty-five degrees Celsius. A mini ice age descended upon our planet; and the only part of the globe free of ice and snow was Tugur Island, a place where man could not yet live.

And two golfing fanatics lost their footing thousands of kilometres away from India.

Even more damaging were the unseen dangers, chief amongst which was that the atmosphere had been irreparably damaged. Cosmic rays come from far beyond our Solar System; they penetrate deeply and are known to damage human tissue. Most of these rays are rendered harmless by mixing with elements within our atmosphere but holes of indeterminate size appeared in our heavenly shield, allowing the passage of these rays to make contact with the Earth's surface. The holes were not centred upon fixed positions on the surface; they were influenced by unknown and unseen forces and moved around touching all areas of the globe. The effects on the human body included changes to DNA structures and huge increases in the risk of cancer, cataracts, neurological disorders and coincidentally, increased incidences of lightning.

The Earth's surface changed dramatically. Scientists have always predicted that Africa would eventually split into two continents. The massive division occurred during the months following the asteroid strike. The mountains of Islamia (formerly Ethiopia) were originally divided by the Great Rift Valley. And this huge depression, formed by faults and weaknesses in the Earth's crust, was up to ninety kilometres wide. It extended about six thousand kilometres north from Mozambique, through East Africa and the Red Sea, into Syria.

As the giant continent separated, the Suez Canal was blocked solidly throughout its length and the Bab el Mandeb, which gives access from the Gulf of Aden into the Red Sea, also closed, creating a new inland sea. Smaller islands all over the globe disappeared forever and were replaced by newly-born replacements. Some of these slipped quietly above the waves; others thrust belligerently towards the sky, bursting into volcanic activity beneath the surface and exploding masses of additional volcanic waste towards the already heavy cloud cover.

The devastation caused by the tsunamis was even more damaging than the effects of the asteroid's hop, skip and jump across the surface of the Earth. The huge waves swept around the world, increasing the death count by many millions more. The unbelievable power and energy in these waves was doubled when the Sea of Okhotsk refilled again when the seas poured into the Great Rift Valley and thereafter by spasmodic contractions and expansions of the Earth's crust.

But our Earth had suffered a much more damaging consequence of the asteroid strike. Above and beyond the mind-blowing known effects of the strike lurked a far greater danger.

THE AFTERMATH. ENGLAND, JUNE 2072.

The ice age was beginning to thaw. Large portions of the more temperate areas of the world had begun to warm up over the last few years, revealing larger and larger areas of greenery. Ten years after the formation of the Great Rift Sea, separating the two African continents, when the world had changed in so many ways, the two old codgers could only manage a single round of golf each week.

Both octogenarians, David and Bob found walking eighteen holes of golf much too demanding. But with the aid of one of the old, wheeled and solar cell powered buggies, they could just about manage it. Controlling the new-style sky-buggies was completely beyond them. And as for the modern, computer style whizz-bangs that afforded the golfer with whatever information he needed, from wind speed and direction to predicted spin, direction, softness of landing, etc., well, forget about it! For the two old codgers such frivolities of golf paled into insignificance alongside the concentration required to prevent oneself from peeing down one's trousers when taking a leak.

There had been an abundance of times during the most recent decade when they had spoken of the day of the jolt. The day the world went crazy. They recalled the tree falling on to the buggy occupied by their playing partners on that day and the terrifying events that followed.

Their golf course and the nearby town of Alton sat in the bowl of a valley to the east of the Hampshire Downs, some fifty kilometres inland from the south coast of England. The initial, gigantic tsunami had penetrated inland as far as the town but the full force of the wave was absorbed by both the Hampshire and South Downs.

Even so, the town did suffer considerable damage to its infrastructure, in terms of electrical fires, bursting gas mains and falling trees and buildings but there was surprisingly little loss of life. The water quickly drained from the town, only to re-flood as the retreating waves gathered themselves for further attacks. Tsunamis abhor any landmass but particularly any low-lying landmass; and the repeated attempts to flood one of Hampshire's prettiest valleys bore witness to the destructive nature of this most fearsome phenomenon. Thirty-two times the town flooded and thirty-two times the waves returned to the sea.

Around the coasts of the UK, other towns did not escape so lightly. Many were flattened and all signs of previous human habitation washed out to sea. Millions died that day. The population of the UK mainland had been approaching a staggering seventy-five million and growing. A nationwide census taken one year later, as the only means to discover exactly who had survived and who had died, revealed that in excess of twenty-five million had bowed their heads to nature's mean streak and paid the ultimate penalty demanded of us all.

But the worldwide figures flabbergasted all and sundry. The population of our planet had soared once again to almost eleven billion by 2060. Of these, only six billion remained. The world had been restored to the population levels of the year 2000 in one fell swoop.

Those with religious inclinations saw the death and devastation as the will of whatever spirit they worshipped. They argued that man deserved this punishment. Humankind should have expected nothing less from a spiritual leader intent upon protecting his creation. Less certain of their convictions, others may have thought that the world's most merciful deity must surely have been having a bad-hair-day to have inflicted such a death toll.

Homo sapiens were slowly destroying His world, which He had flogged for six whole days to create, and He was not about to sit around watching those made in His image destroy everything. His world could not possibly support the ever-growing numbers, requiring ever-larger amounts of food and water and hurling the obnoxious fumes towards His heaven, destroying the protective shield that He had put in place. A cull of Earth's numbers was necessary; and only one being could do it: the Supreme Being Himself, God. Donning His cloak of condemnation and having wagged an admonishing finger at his multitudes, He had waited until the collection plates had been passed around and let loose His armoury of natural nastiness.

The whole episode was a godsend to the church. Like a young puppy returning to a half-gnawed plaything, the macabre scenes of thousands of mass burials with a single vicar standing over the hastily bulldozed pits, full to overflowing with thousands of twisted bodies, were played endlessly over Freinet. People flocked to the churches like sheep to the slaughter. Once depleted congregations swelled and the collection plates overflowed with the donations from repentant sinners. In the face of such obvious heavenly intervention, religious fervour reared its ugly head once again and the numerous destroyed and damaged churches were the first in line for restoration. Those that had felt their religious convictions slipping into abeyance had suddenly reassessed their beliefs and most jumped down from the fence of indecision straight on to their knees in front of the pulpit - and into the joyous open arms of the priesthood.

It was to be eight years after Ombre's strike before radiation levels fell to a point that allowed outdoor activity to recommence; and the two old golfers still retained sufficient *joie de vivre* to attempt a few holes of their favourite pastime.

'Here we go again, David.' Bob's feeble voice attempted to sound indignant but managed only a croaky squeak. 'I expect we will get hit with more tax demands to rebuild the bloody churches.'

Suddenly nervous, they were approaching the eighth tee. It was whilst playing this part of the course that the catastrophe had occurred and they never failed to get a tad nervy whenever they subsequently teed-off for the hole.

'It'll be the thin edge of the wedge too, Bob,' David finally replied, having safely negotiated the fairway down to the eighth green. 'You mark my words, my boy. The blasted clerics will drain the coffers of every nation around the world. Just look at what's happening around the midlands.' David was four years older than Bob and therefore felt entitled to call his friend 'my boy'.

The death toll in the UK had created a new social order. Over the years, as immigrants flooded into the country, they tended to settle in the large conurbations of the midlands - Coventry, Birmingham, Leicester, Stafford, Nottingham, Stoke, Sheffield, Manchester and Leeds. These were the mainly Muslim strongholds of Britain, a brotherhood that paradoxically had suffered least from the effects of the tsunamis.

Protected from the east by the Pennines and by Ireland and Wales from the west, they were the least damaged of the UK's cities and townships. And they suffered the smallest number of casualties. Nonetheless, a number of mosques had been damaged and the Muslim community used this excuse to demand huge sums of money with the intention of building many new mosques. It was this unjust demand on the Nation's finances that so infuriated the old sailors.

'Somebody ought to do something about it,' Bob replied. Neither had retained sufficient of their faculties to suggest quite what could, or should, be done about the perceived injustice. But they both felt entitled to have a good moan about it.

Changing the subject David said gruffly, 'Bit warmer today, eh?'

'Yes, I think you are right David.'

'Bloody hell!' The two old boys fell to their knees, felled by a sunbeam, the first that they had seen for over ten years. And there, right above them, the dark and oily mass of cloud cover cleared. The perpetual drizzle of muddy, ash-filled sleet or snow suddenly stopped, revealing the impossible blue of the sky; and they had to shield their eyes from the fierce glare of the Sun.

'Looks as if Ombre's finally shot his bolt then.' David could not resist an attempt at humour.

The mini ice age was over. Slowly over the course of the next few years, the Earth's weather systems returned. But they were not quite the same. Violent storms appeared out of nowhere and the smallest of clouds might herald the onset of violence. A veritable roller coaster of extreme weather conditions bombarded every continent. Floods, droughts, heat waves, hurricanes, glacier retreat, reduced stream flows and a general rise in sea levels; all contributed to a dramatic fall in agricultural yields.

The dense cloud cover came and went but at least it was no longer a permanent fixture in the sky. From cloudless skies, huge lightning storms lashed the planet and it seemed that the jagged, dazzling forks of God's wrath came directly from space; or heaven.

The world rejoiced at the return of the Sun. But the rejoicing did not last for long. For a still vengeful Maker had waited until this moment of rising hope before allowing His people to discover Ombre's most devastating effect: planet Earth had been jolted out of its heliocentric orbit around the Sun.

With each rotation, the journey was completed in a slightly quicker time. In 2073, our planet's anticlockwise rotation of the Sun took just 364.9 days. Earth was moving inexorably nearer to its mother star as each year passed. Predictions and opinions poured from the world's experts. Most agreed that eventual destruction was Earth's inevitable fate but all differed in the timing of this fate. The general consensus was that it would take anything from a decade to hundreds of years before Earth became untenable.

David died just three days before Bob. Neither lived to witness the terrible consequences of Earth's diminishing orbital path. The closing distance between Earth and Sun, allied to the known rise in Earth's temperatures as a direct result of greenhouse gases released by the use of fossil fuels, saw daytime temperatures climbing to well over forty-five degrees Celsius. And around the equator: ten to twenty degrees more.

CHAPTER 28
JOSH - CHANG JIANG

THREAD:

As one of the gifted people that had attracted my overlooking atten-tion, Li Tu-hsiu was well suited for his eventual role as the most pow-erful man on Earth.

Described in his biography as a gated-person, the author intended to describe his subject as a person with a variety of personalities, any one of which he could affect at will - and thus the perfect politician. Soft; charming; beautifully mannered; an attentive listener; family ori-entated; and someone apparently always ready to compromise: when speaking with females or children his feminine side controlled his every body action.

With men, he became decisive; with his political colleagues on Earth - unbending, ruthless, blinkered, and uncompromising; amongst China's military, dominating and dictatorial; and of lover, wife, fam-ily, or religion - there was none. The man was a chameleon of human behaviour, controlled by a logic circuit providing a single output from multiple inputs as and when he chose.

But the man also possessed two attributes that were both trou-blesome and useful to me as the Verguide. The ability of a person to resist my mind-bending abilities appeared to increase in parallel with each individual's intelligence. Li Tu-hsiu was simply brilliant and in controlling his mind, I could do little more than make suggestions. But with this huge intelligence came an openness to new ideas and none were discarded until they had been subjected to complete assessment and evaluation. And it was through this medium that I managed to implant the idea of mankind vacating the surface of the Earth and moving to a safer environment below ground. Once the seed was planted, the tree started to grow until China accepted the move as part of their future. One of the branches of this tree was China's new capital, Chang Jiang.

2062 to 2070. In the eight years following Ombre's strike when radiation levels were at their most dangerous, restrictions on outdoor activities precluded many activities: air travel, holidays, sporting events - all were curtailed.

Slowly, new protective screens were provided for vehicles, powerful potions and clothing were invented to protect humanity, allowing a return to some sort of normality.

The Verguide Team were of course exempt from the restrictions placed upon other mortals. Using our shrouds we could travel in the open without regard to outside conditions and our method of overlooking enabled us to keep in touch with the rest of the world. This was fine assuming we had no reason to travel normally; but of course there were times when it was necessary to behave as ordinary people.

ABBOTSTONE, ENGLAND. 2070.

The Verguide team suffered very little discomfort from the many devastating effects of the collision with Ombre. Since early in 2012 we had lived almost exclusively below ground. By the time of the arrival of the visitor from outer space, we had managed to extend the depth at which we could comfortably survive to about two thousand metres.

At this point, we had constructed a small community, about village size. Mainly composed of living accommodation and office space, with a few laboratories and manufacturing levels, this area was used as an evaluation point. At two kilometres, deep below the raging surface and whilst still within the Mohorovicic discontinuity, all was peace and calm.

Our original intention had been to descend to a depth exceeding thirty-two kilometres, which we anticipated would be a safe depth where the terrible effects of Earth's climatic changes would not reach us. Thirty-two kilometres would take us just inside the Earth's mantle.

The completely autonomous excavation machines, developed by the Chinese whilst building their own underground capital, were exceptionally efficient and reliable. However, whilst extracting Mantellium from depths up to thirty kilometres, they were recording temperatures in excess of one thousand degrees Celsius. The team had been worrying about how to insulate our own proposed city from such extreme temperatures; and similar to the Church, *le bump* with Ombre was to prove beneficial to us.

Joe was the first to recognize the significance of the peace in the Verden. 'We may not need to go very much deeper, Boss.' Joe spoke, shortly after a deep rumble was heard. Our laboratories monitored, evaluated and recorded every tremble from within our planet; every belch from every belligerent volcano; and every crack of complaint from the troubled crust. But, apart from the noise, we seemed to be suffering no other inconvenience.

'So how far down do we now consider might be safe?' I asked the question but not necessarily of Joe; anyone was quite free to toss in an answer.

'Hey, Boss. Why don't I sidle off to Chang Jiang?' Josh's forehead was creased in deep furrows; he was in a *brown study*[31]. 'I could see what damage they sustained. The city is at eleven kilometres as we all know.' He paused as he gathered his thoughts. 'I could take some monitoring equipment, a camera - and perhaps one of those pretty geologists from the lab.' I saw the tiny smile grab at the corners of his mouth; Josh was on the make! 'See what effects the Shadow has had from close up and maybe sneak around the gook experts - see if they have any fixed plans to cool deeper excavations.'

Notwithstanding Josh's lecherous intentions, it was a good idea. 'I think you are probably right, Joe. It may well save a great deal of excavation; and it would certainly give us a little extra time, just in case

---

[31]Brown study. Australian, deep in thought.

another bird from space pays us a visit.' I turned to Josh, and winked. 'And a second pair of eyes can never be a bad thing. Go, take a look - but don't be gone forever.'

Chang Jiang was truly impressive. Josh looked around at the undamaged underground city. Its population, restored to pre-hornet attack levels by the simple process of enforced relocation, had survived the tremendous first touch of Ombre. Chang Jiang also provided shelter and survival to a further five million. Handpicked by the Chinese leadership during the weeks leading up to the asteroid's arrival, they came from all walks of life. Those best equipped to rebuild China, should the ball-of-fire destroy everything, were squeezed into an already tightly packed city. Vast storage areas were hastily dug to accommodate China's wealth and everything that her experts decided might be useful for a rebuilding program. Some elements of Chang Jiang's society were evicted prior to the bang; they became the 'disappeared' of China.

These criminal elements were considered to be the least value to the nation: the gangsters; drug dealers and users; those unable to work or support themselves; those suffering from any illness or incapacity; and those whose voices were raised in any form of dissent. In fact, anyone who was deemed to be of no use to the leadership was systematically eliminated by the Chinese military.

Three weeks before the first strike, the entrances to Chang Jiang were sealed. Access was denied to all and no one was allowed to leave. The doors were not reopened until a year after the tsunamis had finally ceased; and as quickly closed again, when the occupants of the city discovered the deep snow, the bitter temperatures above ground and the high roentgen levels.

But when Josh arrived the entrances were not sealed and access to and from China's capital had been resumed.

The giant Australian arrived on Thursday 17th April, 2070, some eight years three months after Ombre's first touchdown; and with his very pretty associate, Linda Jenkins at his side. At almost half a metre short of Josh's two metres, she was a perfect foil for the giant man.

At thirty-seven years of age, Linda was a tri-di. Married and divorced three times before she was twenty-eight. On all three occasions, her chosen man had obviously hankered after a tall, slim blonde, since each had departed with such a woman at his side. She knew that the possibilities of another marriage were slim, she was 'knocking on a bit', as her large companion repeatedly informed her. *'And he was big,'* she thought. *'Big hands, big feet; and goodness-knows what else of similar proportions.'*

Uncontrollable giggles erupted from her tiny bosom. Her thoughts had amused her; and annoyed her escort. Josh glared down at her. The government official briefing them before their visit had been very clear on this point. Female occupants of Chang Jiang, whether part of the population or as visitors, were expected to maintain a demure expression on their faces at all times. Absolute peace and tranquillity was demanded; and if you were unable to live within these constraints, then one was invited to purchase a pair of skis and a good pair of gloves and expelled to the still frozen wastes outside the city.

Theirs was not a clandestine visit. As ambassadors of England's Coalition Executive (CEE) on a fact-finding mission, they had flown to Hong Kong in first class seats. From there they had been airlifted on a Chinese military flight to the recently reopened Chang Jiang domestic terminal. The international facilities had not yet been reinstated and it would be many more months before the runways would be capable of dealing with larger international aircraft.

Super-fast lifts dropped the visiting duo down to the administration level of Chang Jiang. It was time for Josh to be careful. He must not display too much knowledge of this wonderful underground city. Neither his travelling partner nor the Chinese leadership knew of his alter ego visits to the city and he must keep this in mind at all times.

Prior to the visit, the Team had considered carefully what we might wish to gain from Josh's visit. Apart from a real-time, close-up look at the city, we needed a powerful ally in preparing the world for drastic measures and strange happenings. And Li Tu-hsiu, as Chairman of the Superpower of Atheist China, known in diplomatic circles as Chang Jiang CSAC, was the man who could help us most.

Born in the year 2024 in Qingdao, a large city in China's eastern Shandong province, the boy had spent his early years on the sun-kissed beaches of his native city, alongside which the apartment building in which he was born was located.

Indoctrinated from an early age into China's dogma-liberated principles of life and government, Li Tu-hsiu was an ardent supporter of his country's refreshingly new religious and political beliefs. Educated at the University of Beijing, the articulate youth came to the attention of the country's leaders, whose own children numbered amongst Li Tu-hsiu's contemporaries.

Earmarked as a future leader, the ambitious young man courted the favours of these high-ranking contacts, disdaining any personal social life in favour of studying his peers, moulding himself in their image. And what endeared the young man above all else to his masters was his concept of waging war. Making much of America's earlier failings in Vietnam and the Middle East, he refuted the idea of God being on the side of the big battalions. In Li Tu-hsiu's opinion, such fortuitous assistance is only forthcoming when the big battalions are committed fully; holding them in check by the pressure of public opinion was a grave mistake.

Dedication delivers and Li Tu-hsiu became the youngest Chairman of the SAC in 2055, just one year before the nation's capital was to suffer the horrors of the hornet attacks.

Such national catastrophes require strong leadership allied with total obedience. Li Tu-hsiu provided the strong leadership in full measure and the inhabitants of China obeyed.

Interested only in food, the hornet attacks had not damaged the capital city. Apart from broken doors, shattered glass and blood-stained floors and walls, there was very little other damage. And quickly making full use of the opportunity, Li Tu-hsiu gave his orders that the city was to be repopulated by drawing people from all parts of the country and from all walks of life.

Occasionally the Team considered it best not to influence a particular world leader directly but to achieve our aims in a more subtle manner. And to get to Li Tu-hsiu we decided to use our own political leader in England. But when manipulating the thoughts of this leader of England's civil administrative body, I no longer visited such a personage as a prime minister.

Twenty years before in 2050, England discarded its bicameral system of government. It was just too costly to operate for such a small country. National plebiscites using the power of Freinet replaced general elections and each individual cast a vote for whichever candidate wore a necktie of their chosen colour. From this voting, a thirty-seat Coalition Executive was formed, led by the Mediator who held the casting vote. From this thirty-man executive, one from each of the main Liberal, Labour and Conservative parties was sent to Europe to represent England at the European Parliament. At home, the primary role of England's Coalition Executive was to implement the decisions from Stuttgart. In 2050, England's first Mediator (MCEE London) was Liberal Mr Lesley Murrell.

In preparation for Josh's visit, I had visited MCEE London on several occasions during his sleeping hours. And it was through Mr Murrell that the ideas about the future of planet Earth began to appear on political agendas across the world. After the shocking revelation concerning the Earth's shrinking orbit around the Sun, political organisations were beginning to accept that some very radical precautions might be required to ensure the survival of mankind. All it needed was a bit of stirring up in the right places and some support and practical suggestions from some respected person in high office.

Soft, almost feminine; the grip that clasped the hand of Josh was surprisingly weak. And from his towering height, the forty-six year old Chinese leader reminded Josh of a gnome. Completely bald, bespectacled and slightly stooped it was almost inconceivable to Josh that this inconsequential little man could be the most powerful human the world had ever seen.

Li Tu-hsiu was not impressed. This giant envoy represented a tiny country and would not normally have been entertained by the great leader of China. But the man's country was part of a much larger and more powerful alliance and as such, Li Tu-hsiu had agreed to receive him personally.

Now a highly skilled manipulator, Josh analysed the thoughts of the great leader, gently turning his mind to the danger that our planet faced. The plush and opulent surroundings of Li Tu-hsiu's cabinet offices were unnoticed by Josh, as over the next several days he convinced the Chairman of the Superpower of Atheist China to support the idea of humanity moving away from the Earth's surface. Already the Chinese had the expertise and resources to demonstrate and prove this concept; and the mind of Li Tu-hsiu filled with a vision of himself as the leader of the new underground world.

Even at only eleven kilometres deep, the city of Chang Jiang had suffered only superficial damage from Ombre's strike and virtually no damage at all from the mini ice age and natural phenomenon that followed. A few cracks and crevices in walls and floors, some occasional flooding and air filtration foul-ups, and a few interludes involving blocked drains that pretty much sickened the giant Australian. But as at Abbotstone, the underground city had remained warm and cosy during the never-ending raging storms on the surface.

Each night in the quiet of their VIP suite, Josh gently turned aside any discussion concerning the reasons for his visit to Chang Jiang and the amorous advances of his travelling companion. Who knew what surveillance systems monitored every single action or sound from within the apartment? There would be a stopover in Hong Kong on the return journey; and anticipation of an amorous encounter can sometimes greatly enhance the act itself.

Josh learned little of any real value from his visit. The Chinese engineers had not provided any means of air-conditioning or cooling, other than that powered by their hydroelectric schemes. And no matter how deeply he delved into China's future plans he could find no intention to go deeper. The transport system was an absolute marvel and Josh stored the details within the databases inside his brain to be downloaded into Abbotstone's computer systems for possible improvement. What appealed to him most was the general atmosphere of a gentle lifestyle, a place where its people were able to move about freely without the worry of criminal activities, traffic noise or pollution; and a haven from the temperamental forces of nature on the surface.

CHAPTER 29
NATURAL DISASTER

THREAD:

Mother Nature cares not about repeating herself, nor about how much damage this world has already suffered, nor how many have already died. She is relentless, vindictive and cruel, particularly when her domain is subjected to unexpected hazards over which she has no control.

Rising temperatures produced rising seas. Gradually over a period of several decades, global warming had itself produced a considerable rise in sea levels. And the warming effect of our planet increased dramatically when aided and abetted by the newly-discovered trajectory change of Earth, which produced even warmer temperatures and even higher sea levels.

Another side effect of Earth's collapsing orbit around the Sun was that the Moon's orbit also changed. At its perigee, it now came much closer to Earth and this pernicious closeness of our nearest neighbour in space had a much greater effect upon the tidal actions of the rising sea levels. Regular higher tides had forced people to move away from the coastal and low-lying areas; and cities all over the planet waited with bated breath for a natural disaster that might trigger the giant waves of destruction that were capable of reaching even further inland.

In some parts of our planet, there exist accidents just waiting for an opportunity to happen. And sometimes the trigger that sets a catastrophe in motion is not witnessed by man.

But the effects most certainly are.

BOSTON, MASSACHUSETTS. SATURDAY 8TH SEPTEMBER, 2074.

Hated names! Standing in front of a huge congregation in the Roman Catholic cathedral of the Holy Cross in Boston, Massachusetts, Engy Scrivener allowed his mind to wander while he awaited the arrival of his bride. Calmly he waited, whilst next to him stood his best man, Jim Stenson, who appeared much more nervous than he did. Named by his 'Oh, so last century' parents, the young man would not have chosen his given names in a month of Sundays.

Whilst he waited in the cool interior of the intensely holy place, in the centre of his beautiful hometown that is known as the Athens of the New World, he allowed himself a moment or two to review his life. *'What a mouthful you saddled me with,'* he thought. Adolphus Scrivener had never quite found it in his heart to forgive his parents for assigning him such old-fashioned names. His bride had saved him from a lifetime of embarrassment, for it was she who had dubbed him Engy, shortly after they had first met.

More formally Adolphus Engelbert Scrivener, he hated his name; but he really should be more grateful to his parents, since it had been his bride's dislike of her own name that had first brought them together. Both recent law graduates from Harvard and expected to spend a lifetime serving bench and bar, they were twenty-five years of age having been born just two days apart in October, 2049.

The familiar notes of 'Here Comes the Bride' and a nudge from Jim dragged his mind away from his pet hate. *'Stunningly gorgeous,'* the words leapt into his mind when he first saw her and he watched with a huge lump in his heart as his wife-to-be approached him. The vast majority of couples suffer doubts about marriage right up to the point of saying 'I do'. Adolphus was no different and the sight of his lovely bride calmed his fears.

When Adolphus had first been introduced to her at Harvard she had replied 'Fanny Evadne Hogsbottom' and waited for the usual tittering to subside. Recognising a kindred spirit, Adolph had suggested an acceptable diminutive, 'I'll call you Anny,' as he reached out and took her hand.

Entirely pleased and happy with this suggestion and amazed at the thrill of his touch she had replied, 'And I will call you Engy.'

At that precise moment in time as their fingers first entwined, the bond was made. A bond that would last them for the rest of their lives, they had no doubt about that. In the days that followed their nuptials, in the first flush of matrimony their love deepened; and they both knew that each had found a soul mate.

Their commitment to one another was total and their desire to be married was almost overwhelming; but they were both dreading that part of the wedding ceremony that called for the announcement of their names, in full! The marriage blessing had been simplified and reworded several times during the preceding decades and they both blushed a deep shade of red when the priest asked, 'Will you, Adolphus Engelbert Scrivener, in the eyes of God and this congregation, take this woman, Fanny Evadne Hogsbottom, to be your lawful wife, and lifelong partner?' Engy had glared belligerently at the Roman Catholic priest during this question. *'Just the slightest giggle and I'll deck you, so help me Lord,'* was the message in his eyes.

It was over. The ceremony, the reception - where every speaker had been firmly instructed to use Engy and Anny or Mr and Mrs Scrivener - and the departure; until at last they found themselves alone on the flight out of Logan International to Jamaica.

Sublimely happy they had taken charge of a twelve-metre yacht, the *Caribbean Queen*, which belonged to Anny's father. Desperate to be alone they sailed that same day for a three-week honeymoon around the islands. Expected to return to Boston and take their rightful place in the Scrivener Legal Advisory business, they fully intended to enjoy what might be their last opportunity for an extended vacation; at least for some time.

But fate is a fickle taskmaster and they had no way of knowing about the maelstrom that a cruel Earth was stirring up for them.

For the happy couple the beginning of the end came in the form of a tropical storm, a week or so after they left Jamaica. This storm, which might or might not blossom into a full-blooded hurricane, forced the inexperienced sailors to head for the nearest refuge.

Deep below the warm, calm and amazingly blue salt water of the Caribbean Sea, lies the Caribbean tectonic plate. For billions of years this tiny section of the Earth's crust had been subjected to the enormous pressure of its huge neighbours, the North and South American plates. Inexorably and unnoticed over that vast period of time, the pressure had taken its toll deep below the surface of the Earth. For the unremitting pressure had been forced downwards, towards the centre of the Earth.

Deep down, through the Moho, below the crust of the Earth, lies the upper mantle. Generally accepted as being made up of hard and stable rock, this mantle can be softened and rendered unstable by heat and pressure.

Basking in this tropical paradise just north of the equator, lie the beautiful islands of St Kitts and Nevis. In reality, these two islands combine into a single entity below the surface of the sea and as the newlyweds sailed the *Caribbean Queen* into Charlestown, the population was attempting to sleep through the noisy tropical storm.

As a volcano, Nevis has not been active for hundreds of years and is technically extinct. But Nevis is not a true volcano; it is a parasitic cone providing an alternative route for magma flow, on the side of what was once a much larger super-volcano. Throughout the passage of time, the rim of the original volcano had crumpled inwards and slowly washed away by the grinding action of the sea, leaving what is now called Nevis perched at an acute angle above the ocean.

Under normal circumstances, the Earth's upper mantle starts at about an average depth of some one hundred kilometres below the surface of the Earth. In some places, its borders commence much nearer the surface, particularly under the world's oceans. But nature abhors a status quo and unknown to science, Mother Nature had softened and liquefied the mantle up to a depth of some two kilometres below the island of Nevis. And above this weak spot, the enormous weight of the island perched precariously on its unstable platform.

Nature would not have to wait long to change the face of the Earth yet again, just a small slip of the Caribbean tectonic plate would produce an earthquake: and that small slip happened just eight days after Engy and Anny's wedding.

Consistent in her efforts to remove humanity from the face of the Earth, man's unforgiving mistress - Mother Nature - has never failed to experiment with her witch's stew; and on this night she chose this unstable, liquidised mantle, and a heavy island teetering directly above it, as her ingredients for madness, mayhem and death.

'Six bells,' yelled Engy, energetically ringing the bell.

A landlubber all her life, Anny had adapted quickly to life at sea. She understood the sailing terms and knew how to handle the yacht, whether under sail or power. But she had still to come to terms with the sailor's-clock and it took her a few seconds to convert the tintinnabulation into actual time.

'Got you, oh three ring bolt,' with a smile, she used her young husband's nautical phraseology.

'The seas should calm soon, we will be in the lee of Nevis very shortly.' Engy was still worried that his young wife would suffer another spell of seasickness, which had torn at his heartstrings when they sailed from Jamaica just a few days ago. He was immensely proud of his beautiful young bride and she had proved her mettle over the past few days.

'Quit worrying about me, honey. When we get alongside I am going to cook you an early breakfast.' Unable to prevent herself, she giggled at her husband's groan. She was a notoriously bad cook, having been sheltered from such mundane tasks by an extremely wealthy family.

'But what I lack in expertise, I more than compensate for with my enthusiasm and passion.' Her voice took on a sultry note and a soft exhalation of breath with the final word.

Suddenly all was calm, or at least relatively so. The yacht no longer rolled and dipped into the deep troughs of the sea and Engy eased the throttle back. All fears left him, he felt at ease and he knew that the peace and safety of Charlestown harbour was only a few minutes away. It was 03.23 and he was ready to give Anny's bacon and eggs another try.

Above the shriek of the storm force wind, they both heard the sound of the mainmast crack; but when they looked up it was, surprisingly, still in place. Almost immediately, the yacht dropped beneath their feet and Engy's heart leapt into his mouth. Something was badly wrong.

'Get below, Honey,' he called to her. She obeyed instantly and started to move towards the hatchway. At the last moment she paused and looked into her husband's eyes; and watched as they filled with fear and dread. She did not have time to turn and see what had filled those eyes with such terror. Had she been able to do so she would have seen the lights of Charlestown sliding beneath the sea in front of them.

The yacht did not have a chance. Sucked under the waves, it accompanied the huge island mass all the way to the bottom of the Caribbean Sea. With not the slightest pause, the island mass slipped through the Earth's crust and continued ever downwards until finally settling in the mantle. The young lovers, dragged beneath the warm surface of the sea, tried desperately to reach each other; but the suction was too great. They could see one another quite clearly but they could not swim towards one another or strike upwards towards the surface.

Engy was the first to die. Anny knew that she could not survive and she felt her eyes fill with tears as she watched the life drain from those of her husband. Finally resigned to death, she stopped trying to swim to the surface and allowed her body to relax, opened her mouth and let the salty water flood into her. She almost giggled at her last thought, the reading out-loud of their hated names, included in their formal declaration of love, 'Will you...'

The never-ending darkness engulfed her.

It was the 19th September, St Kitts and Nevis' Independence Day, and what should have been the start of a day of dancing and celebration turned instead into a mass burial for the twenty-five thousand inhabitants of Nevis.

In a matter of three minutes and twenty-eight seconds, the island mass slipped beneath the stormy surface of the Caribbean Sea. Imitating a doomed Titanic, the mass began to disintegrate as it rapidly increased speed; and to the deep-sea divers that subsequently surveyed the area, the seabed resembled the pockmarked surface of the Moon.

Craters and rocks of varying sizes covered the seabed but of the main bulk of what was once Nevis there remained no visible sign. As the huge mass hit the bottom, smashing its way through what remained of the Earth's crust, the world received its first notification of impending disaster. Extremely sensitive seismic instruments located around the world indicated a cataclysmic event of over nine on the Richter scale.

Ten minutes later the crack in the Earth's crust, through which Nevis had disappeared, slammed shut; an action which caused the larger American plates to subduct one below the other and this almost imperceptible movement created a domino effect in Earth's tectonic plating. Although the initial movement of the American plates was small, it was sufficient to trigger a chain reaction of earthquakes around the globe.

At first, orbiting satellites offered little further information other than the precise location of the disaster. The incident, as with all other major happenings in the world, was automatically broadcast on Freinet, '9.1 cataclysmic seismic events, St Kitts and Nevis, Caribbean Sea 19:09: 2074:03:26:28UTC'. The whole world knew that judgement day had arrived for many millions, if not billions of people; and fear and panic blossomed quickly in the landmasses closest to the disaster.

A heavy object falling through water accelerates at a frightening rate and by the time the huge mass of rock crashed into the fragile crust of the Earth, it had reached some 150 km/h. It crashed into the thin crust of the Earth with such force that the impact was felt on every landmass in the world.

Those living on the continents above the North and South American tectonic plates felt the most noticeable jolt. For those asleep it felt much like waking from a bad dream and feeling the bed walking around the room; or for those on their feet it was similar to a person trying to descend a ship's ladder in rough seas and missing out a step.

Of those that felt this jolt, all asked the same question. 'What was that?' Within minutes, Freinet displayed the answer and those who found themselves to be at some risk accessed the network's databases for information on the possible consequences of the disaster.

None were too reassured by the information they received. Maybe a tsunami at best, or even a train of tsunamis; otherwise that most fearsome of all natural cataclysmic events - a mega-tsunami. For many of the Earth's population it made little difference, whichever choice butcher-nature had planned for them they were dead, living on borrowed time. Just a few hours to get to high ground. Burrow below ground or make some other escape from the approaching wall of water.

But any escape had better be very high, or very deep, and very soon. Tsunamis do not wait upon the convenience of mankind, they have a harvest to reap, work to be done; and travelling at just below the speed of sound, they are in a great hurry to get started.

A small boy throws a pebble into a pond, the rippling circles spread rapidly and harmlessly to the very edges of the pond. The world faced a very big rock in a very big pond, and from space the ripples seemed widely spaced and totally without menace. However, on this occasion sneaky Mother Nature had manufactured a double whammy. Not just the movement of tectonic plates under a deep ocean that creates a tsunami, or the falling of a large landmass into the ocean, which might generate a mega-tsunami. No, this time Mother Nature had combined the two, a combination never before witnessed by mankind, with the ferocious power to raze the huge cities of the world, stripping the surface of the globe down to bare bedrock.

As other earthquakes rattled around the world in sympathy, their power either supported or attempted to counter the power of the initial tsunami-whammy, as the media named this new phenomenon; described as a rugby scrummage fighting for possession of the ball.

Along the west coast of the USA, the North American tectonic plate nudged against the Juan de Fuca plate. Within a week, fourteen of the High Cascades, a string of volcanoes, which form part of the Pacific Ring of Fire from Washington State to California, erupted with unprecedented force. Other volcanoes over the entire land surfaces of the globe also decided to vent their spleens once again, causing scenes of chaos at every point of the compass. Mount Colima in Mexico's Sierra Madre mountains; Italy's Mount Vesuvius overlooking Naples; Mount Etna at the southernmost tip of Italy; Mauna Loa in Hawaii; Merapi in Java, Indonesia; Nyiragongo in the Democratic Republic of the Congo; Sakurajimaon on Kyushu Island, Japan; Mount Taal near Manila, in the Philippines; Mount Ulawun, Papua New Guinea; and many more.

With giant waves reaching to over one hundred metres in height, the mega-tsunami is a slow mover. Restricted also is the distance over which the waves can travel and damage is more localised. Nevertheless, the landmasses encircling the Caribbean Sea suffered incredible damage and loss of life from this initial battering and on most, the huge wave washed across the whole island range. Most of the coral reefs amongst the string of Caribbean Islands were covered in a deep layer of sand and mud, as the huge frontal wave hit the shoreline, hurled itself into the air and burst inland, unhindered as would be a herd of sheep finding new grazing.

The tsunamis that followed were even more devastating. Caused by the earthquakes, these fast-moving waves left the starting gate at St Kitts and sped away in all directions. Racing across the Caribbean at well over eight hundred km/h, these monstrous phenomena struck the isthmus connecting North and South America. Supported by the combined weight of the ocean, the gigantic mass of in-rushing water shoaled more than forty metres into the air and continued inland, taking the form of a giant spring tide. As the seas slowly subsided, the Panama Canal was no longer recognisable as a separate sea-passage, since Lake Gatun had formed as a new inland sea. The Gatun Dam and Locks at the northern end of the canal were consumed by the tsunamis, as were the Bridge of Americas, Centennial Bridge and the Miraflores Locks at the southern end. Passage through this inland sea from the South Pacific Ocean into the Caribbean Sea and the Atlantic eventually became recognised as international waters.

Other waves swept into the Atlantic, passing across thousands of kilometres of ocean almost unnoticed, searching for victims further afield. It was not until these innocuous ripples hit land that the carnage began.

In many ways Adolphus and Fanny had been amongst the lucky, for many millions of others the waiting was mind-blowing.

CHAPTER 30
PRIMARY TASK

THREAD:

In the red corner Atheism. In the blue corner the deeply-rooted religious fanaticism of Islamic belief. The eyeballing, name-calling and general strutting about and badgering associated with pre-fight posturing, was done.

The troubles had been brewing for a very long time. Probably the two most powerful men on the face of the planet, they did not have much regard one for the other. Whilst apparently engaged in meaningful discussions of worldly matters, Li Tu-hsiu had met with Rasul-Allah on a number of occasions in the cabinet rooms around the globe.

The national global ambitions of both leaders had been widely discussed, dissected, analysed and reported over a considerable number of years. The basic precept of each man was identical; our world was only big enough for a single leader. They differed in one single detail, the answer to one simple question; to whom will that single world leader bend his knee? As far as Li Tu-hsiu was concerned, the answer was no one; and for Rasul-Allah, the answer was Allāh. At least *pro tem.*

Founding principles of social life for each camp formed a broken bridge that could never be repaired. China's population control methods of monogamous marriages coupled with fixed family size restrictions inflamed the Islamic beliefs in free-breeding polygynous human relationships involving multiple wives and concubines. Under the rule of Li Tu-hsiu, the women of China worked alongside their men in every way, open-faced for all to see; equal in terms of stature within their social structure; and engaged in all trades and professions. The dictatorial Rasul-Allah demanded that the faces of Muslim women be hidden from the view of other men; their choice of profession be severely limited; and their activities be confined mainly to the kitchen, the zenana, and the marriage bed.

Of middle ground, compromise, concession or negotiation, there was none. The line had been drawn in the sand and neither party was willing to straddle it. Bear-baiting tactics from both sides had been going on for some time, from small-scale incursions and guerrilla attacks aimed at small villages and settlements, to deliberately destructive attempts on nationally-esteemed shrines and buildings. Chinese forces attacked mosques and religious sites throughout the Middle East and Saladin's Scimitar units made repeated and damaging attacks deep into China but most especially on the Great Wall, which infuriated the Chinese leader and the Chinese people.

The people of the world saw it all in graphic detail on the updated Freinet system. Renamed Glosys and introduced in 2080, the system was now powerful enough to provide communications to other planets. Using a method of superimposing information on to isolated sunbeams, the system also provided thought transference between Pewi and user.

Populations of the world were now at acceptable levels, ready for the people of the Earth to vacate the surface. The attacks by the Hornets, the Plague, le bump with Ombre and the terrible effects of nature's contribution with Nevis had all contributed to an existing world population of about twelve billion. But in achieving my primary aim of averting World War 3, I needed to introduce the world to Belial First.

Alfred Leonard

ABBOTSTONE, UNDERGROUND CITY. 2080.

The twins and I were mulling over our plans in the Verden. Around the room were large projections from Glosys showing the ramifications of the world's media systems, complete with translations. Occasionally the silence was interrupted by a tiny bing-bong, indicating an item of interest on one of the screens.

We had three needs. Inform the world of its fate; convene a meeting of world leaders; and introduce them to the Small Person.

'Time to move my children and in this enterprise we must have total concentration and complete dedication; for in this one aspect of our plan we must not fail.'

Over the next few minutes, I outlined my requirements. 'I will influence the Mediator and convince him to call a political convention of world leaders. Ana, we will host the meeting here. Please make a list of who best to invite and make the local arrangements. And Joe, please make and finance the necessary travel bookings.'

Joe nodded. 'Assume you mean first-class for everyone?'

'We can't take it with us.' I smiled at my little witticism and added. 'Better recall Josh. There might be some persuading to be done.'

The Team swung into action. Arranging the convention was not difficult. Given the Mediator's sponsorship, Ana would simply speak her orders into her Pewi. 'Order. Contact list xray of world leaders. Meeting 21st March, 2081, Abbotstone, UK. Chairman Mediator England. Agenda: Global warming. Travel arrangements to follow.'

In the blink of an eye, Ana's brief outline of the meeting arrived in the operations rooms of each and every known national leader; none would be able to resist a world convention to discuss global warming. And not a single addressee declined.

'From Washington, USA, for Mediator England. Delighted, will arrange preliminary chat soonest.'

'From Chang Jiang, China, for Mediator England. Excellent, we must talk before meeting.'

'From Canberra, Australia, for Mediator England WMP.'

'From Buenos Aires, Argentina, for Mediator England. We will attend.'

Every time I walked into the grotto, my mind instantly flitted backwards to an earlier time. One hundred and nineteen years ago, to a time when I had fallen behind the rock in Singapore and ended up in that strange but wonderful cave to be confronted by Belial First.

The cavernous and purpose-built auditorium was constructed deep below Volly's Folly at Abbotstone. It was a very impressive space. Excavated some three thousand metres into the mantle of the Earth, it was the size of a small Hampshire village. Hemispherical in shape, the structure included a high ceiling, or rather an artificial sky that was some one thousand metres above floor level. Presently a brilliant pale blue, almost identical to that of a summer day in Australia, where the blueness appeared to slowly darken from an almost *claire de lune* into a cobalt blue, giving an impression of a gradual descent into the blackness of space; and infinity.

At one end of the huge dome-like structure, a small dais had been installed. Standing on this structure, looking out at the rising tiers of seats in a huge semi-circle, the space resembled that of a Roman amphitheatre. In a few short hours, some ten thousand of the world's most important luminaries would be seated there to listen to the words of the first visitor from space.

Except for the Verguide Team and myself, no other person on Earth had knowingly met a representative from another world. Behind this dais, an enormous screen had been assembled, measuring some one hundred metres square. It would soon show a picture of both Belial First and me as we addressed the assembled leaders of planet Earth - and through the power of the latest communications system, to every other occupant of planet Earth.

Currently the huge backdrop displayed a representation of the solar system, that tiny portion of the Milky Way galaxy graphically displaying Earth's position in the Universe. In this representation, our only star was shown as a menacing liquid ball of fire, with gigantic solar storms bursting into space to all points of the compass. Our Sun was depicted as huge, dominating and appeared to threaten the planets. The picture was designed to instill a feeling of intense fear in the Earthlings that would soon set eyes upon it; and those earthly dignitaries that entered the auditorium would be seen to tremble at the sight, sickened by the message portrayed before them.

Those who looked really closely saw an additional small planet, hidden behind Earth's moon, Veruni.

The auditorium was empty, totally silent; not a sound could be heard. Not a whisper of wind or the sound of a falling drop of rain. Eerie, and not a little unnerving. My mind went out in sympathy for both Belial First and myself, both of whom must shortly stand on that tiny dais and address the thousands amassed before it.

Of the two tasks, mine was the easier. For me, all that was required was an introduction for Belial First. But as I stood on that dais, looking up at the rising semi-circle of seating, my feelings must have mimicked those of a gladiator, awaiting the raising of the restraining bars behind which the lions watched, in gleeful anticipation of being let out on to the killing-ground before them. My eyes swivelled through 180 degrees, imagining the faces of the audience; and with a lump in my throat, I attempted to rehearse my small speech. I opened my mouth to speak but no sound came from my fear-constricted throat; and I felt as if I was a large dog on a very tight leash, straining so hard against its collar that its vocal cords could not function properly.

This was a totally alien feeling for me. I had been around for a long, long time and my normal imperturbable manner was not easily disturbed. 'For Christ's sake, get a grip, Volly!' I shouted the words and at that precise moment, Belial First chose to appear at my side.

'Fear not, Verguide.' Belial First's soft and sibilant voice greeted me. 'I shall be with you when you speak to your world.' The well-remembered voice soothed me instantly and boosted my confidence once again. 'Free your mind of all thoughts when you face your peers, I will speak through you.'

A slight sound from the main entrance heralded the arrival of the first of Earth's ambassadors. Instantly, Belial First retreated behind his cloak of invisibility, followed just a split second later by me.

England's Mediator, currently Conservative Mr Roderick Jay, was accompanied by half the Coalition Executive. The president of the United States and his team of advisors; First Ministers; and heads of states from every country in the world; and the last to arrive was the Chairman of China together with his team of almost one hundred immaculately-uniformed military advisors. The timing of China's arrival and the size of its contingent reinforced that country's dominant position in the world. The only remaining super power.

There was not a single member of royalty present. For the dissolution of the world's last royal households had taken place during the 2060s, taking their outdated and emotionally provocative honours systems with them. The last to go being the royal Windsor household in 2070, when on Commonwealth Day, 10th March of that year, the nineteen year old Queen Ann II abdicated her throne. An inevitable conclusion since Her Majesty was Queen only of the tiny country of England. The remainder of the British Isles had gone their own way. Scotland, Wales, Northern Ireland (renamed Ireland in 2049) and Southern Ireland (readopted its previous name of Eire in 2049) were now autonomous countries in their own right. And the British Commonwealth had jointly agreed to dissolve its alliance some sixteen years ago, in 2055.

England could no longer afford to support a royal family. The royal collections of jewels and artifacts donated by world leaders as 'gifts to the nation' had been shared between the five small countries and England's share was now housed in a massive museum in London. A plebiscite conducted via the power of Glosys confirmed the people's choice from England and the Commonwealth countries. A worldwide general decline in support of monarchism, supported by a general realisation that such grandeur could not possibly be supported by such a tiny country as England, forced the role of royal families into antiquity, bringing to an end the one hundred and sixty-year dynasty of the House of Windsor.

The huge screen at the rear of the dais was blank. I had been caught daydreaming and unprepared for the first arrivals. Hurriedly, I formulated a thought in my mind, which would be transmitted to my Pewi to cancel the representation of our Solar System on the auditorium's screen.

At our previous evening's planning meeting, the Team and I had decided to force the visitors to walk the six hundred metres from the Verden to one of the secondary entrances to the underground auditorium. Mid March, and above-ground temperatures were expected to be about forty-one Celsius; and the intense heat would reinforce our radical argument about global warming. Many of the visiting dignitaries were overweight to the point of obesity, which suited our plan very well, since we wanted them to be instantly aware of the pleasant coolness and generally peaceful ambience of the underground auditorium.

Alfred Leonard

Ten thousand voices make a great deal of noise but total silence followed the blast of sound that emitted from the hidden loudspeakers around the auditorium. Many had been wiping sweaty brows with large handkerchiefs, which were suddenly rammed into ears as a single bugle note lasting some ten seconds stopped all chatter. The images on the huge screen whirled in a confusing, meaningless kaleidoscope of flashing colours and slowly zoomed into the picture of our solar system, showing what appeared to be the view through the frontal screen of an approaching space vehicle.

Several minutes were allocated to allowing the visitors to ponder the huge screen. Some of the scientific community quickly noted the 11th planet; and not a few of the more blinkered experts scoffed at its appearance.

Bright spotlights cast a single golden sunbeam, in the centre of which I allowed myself to materialise. I had decided at the last second to appear seated before the audience; I was still feeling a little overwhelmed by my task and I was worried that my legs might inadvertently give an inopportune demonstration of the Elvis syndrome! The posture would also give an impression of relaxed equality and a firm visual indication that any delusions of self-esteem or hierarchy would not be appropriate in this auditorium.

I had also decided, again at the very last moment, not to speak. I would implant my introduction into the mind of every single one of the ten thousand strong audience. No 'good mornings' or 'good days' or any form of salutation.

In the total silence, I began. *'Some of you might regard my sudden appearance as a devious, theatrical gimmick.'* A slight pause, to allow my first thoughts to enter their minds. *'I urge you not to doubt my powers, or those of the Verunian ambassador, who will shortly be joining me on this dais.'*

My thoughts were transmitted to each individual using that person's mother tongue. *'You will note that I am communicating with you individually.'* A slight pause and I continued by speaking out loud. 'You will also notice that I am the only person in this auditorium wearing a Glosys Pewi. I will switch the system on when Belial First commences his presentation, so that the rest of the world will know what is said. And I reserve the right to switch it to broadcast mode at any time during the question period that might follow. I believe that the people of the world are entitled to be aware of their ambassador's comments, if any, following the Veruni presentation. As a small demonstration of one of my more minor powers, I will name two ambassadors who have already broken the terms of this presentation. You will all be well aware that everyone was asked to leave their Pewi sets in the Verden. Perhaps Washington and Canberra would be kind enough to remove the Pewi sets from their jacket pockets and bring them to the dais.'

Both leaders thought to remain in their seats and send an aide forward with the offending items. A quick mental intervention saw them both rise to their feet and head towards me, accompanied by much tutting and sighing from around the auditorium. As they made their way forward, I spoke again. 'You will also notice that I am expressing my thoughts and speaking in English. But each of you is aware of my words in their own national tongue. We all know that this facility is one of the parameters provided by Glosys but you can all see that my Pewi is switched to the off position.' Here I held up my wrist for all to see and a picture of the wristband appeared on the giant screen for a few seconds.

As the two world leaders deposited their Pewis on the dais, I looked them in the eye. 'I owe you both an apology,' I surprised them with my words. 'You will recall that it was only at the very last moment that you decided not to leave the equipment in the Verden as requested. It was I that persuaded you otherwise, so that I could stage this demonstration; however I would be most grateful if you will both indicate that no previous collusion took place between us to stage this display of my powers.' The two leaders clearly miffed at being singled out nodded curtly and started the walk back to their seats.

Very slowly, I allowed my head to traverse the auditorium, my eyes settling on a few of the more anxious faces returning my gaze. Most suspected that I had other nasty tricks up my sleeve. I started to speak again. 'Firstly, a few words about me. Although most of you will know me as Timothy Yewly, my real name is in fact Victor Yewly. I was born in 1941, which makes me some one hundred and forty years old.'

Preposterous! Utter rubbish! What nonsense! I heard the disclaimants voicing their opinions in no uncertain terms and loud voices, from all points of the auditorium. Not a flicker of emotion or annoyance passed across my face. I simply waited until all comments had ceased.

'I have another name. I am also known as the Verguide, appointed by the ambassador from Veruni some one hundred and eighteen years ago. Their planet, similar to ours, is under threat; and it is my task to ensure that Earth is ready to accept the people of Veruni when their planet becomes uninhabitable. All of my powers, including longevity, come from them. And preparing the Earth to share with the Verunian people is not my only task but I will leave my friend to explain that.'

Many long seconds I waited, allowing each person a little time to absorb what I had said so far. Those who believed that the Earth was flat must have felt exactly the same doubts as did the world leaders who sat before me, when they discovered their error. 'It is now my pleasure to introduce someone that I have known for a very long time, someone that I have come to trust implicitly. He is the leader of the Verunian council and is known to me as Belial First.'

A second brilliant sunbeam miraculously appeared and Belial First slowly descended within it, materialising in a dramatically slower way than normal. He was exactly as I had first seen him, totally naked and very obviously totally genderless. He did not sit, neither did he stand, he remained poised a metre or so above the floor.

Again, no salutation, perhaps Belial First had taken a tip from me!

'Thank you Belial Second, or as I have come to know you, Verguide.' The vision on the dais nodded briefly towards me. My cue to disappear and I left him.

'We have watched you evolve. From the time before life began on your planet.' Belial First paused for several long seconds between each of his statements. 'We were overjoyed when the first signs of life stirred in your storm-tossed oceans. We watched in fascination as the landmasses of your Earth changed shape and the various branches of mankind developed. From little more than a blob of slimy mucus with a single cell, we watched as man battled through the various metamorphoses of Australopithecus; Pithecanthropus; Swanscombe; Neanderthal; Cro-Magnon; to the people that you are today. Thinking man. The fair-skinned Caucasoid of Europe, the Polynesians of the Pacific, the mongoloids from Asia and the dark-skinned Negroid from Africa. And we look ahead to the man destined to walk this Earth in the future; a single race, with a single colour and a single reason for existence.

'What is this future-man? I can hear this and other questions tumbling around in your brains. What would you not give for an ability to look through a window into the future, a goal that Earth's man has struggled to achieve for millennia? We Verunians have that ability and just three of your many questions I will answer for you today. What race of people will you be; what colour will your skin be; and what will be your *raison d'être*? I have chosen to answer these three simple questions, amongst the billions that man has asked in the past, and the thousands that I see in your minds today because they will eventually lead mankind to the single most important level of blissful co-existence. That pinnacle of human cooperation that mankind has not yet managed to achieve and what has so far been your greatest human failure. The attainment of global peace.'

All eyes were glued on Belial First. 'But I will save these revelations until the end of my talk.'

The audience was stunned. Not a sound, not a single word of reproach or disbelief; and I knew that Belial First had formatted their minds to listen to his words.

Belial First's voice took on a wistful tone. 'Many, many millennia in the past, we Verunians were much as you are today. We too worshipped deities, demons and devils. We too waged war amongst ourselves. We also reproduced in the same way that you do. We fought our battles with deadly viruses. We too changed the geological composition of our planet by depleting the stocks of precious metals, minerals and fossil fuels. Verunians had all the faults of Earthmen; we murdered, tortured, committed adultery, stole, lied, cheated, deceived, envied, fornicated and corrupted - all in the name of what you know as money.

'Of much more relevance, we too saw the beginning of the end of our original planet. Like you, we recognised the symptoms but we misdiagnosed both the condition and the cause and foresaw the wrong prognosis. As on Earth, the primary symptom was clear for all to see - that of increasing temperatures around our planet. We diagnosed the illness as global warming caused by the use of fossil fuels. Our tiny brains were blinkered and we imposed draconian taxes on anything associated with the use of those fossil fuels, just as you have been doing for many of your decades. We also placed all our eggs in one basket. We believed that a reduction in the use of fossil fuels would be our salvation. Just as you have been doing we tried to make our people aware of their own personal carbon footprint and outlined ways in which individuals could help in a reduction in the use of fossil-fuels; but to use one of your fabled adages, you cannot educate pork, and our people were only interested in their own lifestyle and survival.

'But we were wrong. Just as you are now. Our planet could not be saved. Fortunately, we had the technical expertise to manufacture a new home and millions of years in which to provide ourselves with a new planet. How we achieved that feat you do not, at this time, need to know. I can see the questions in your minds. Why do we need Earth? Why can we not manufacture another planet? Why can we not populate another planet?

'You are all leaders of this world and you will know that hindsight quenches the self-recrimination associated with poor decisions. At some time in your lifetime, you will also all have wished for second sight. Today I will outline a glimpse of your future.

'With our forward looking capabilities we have seen the destruction of Earth; and here I would ask you to use your imagination. Think of this planet as a freshly-picked apple, at first so firm and green, that develops a small crack when it reaches a certain temperature in a pot of boiling water. The tiny split expands at frightening speed and the apple eventually disintegrates and turns to mush. And what might cause this Earth to react in the same way, you may well ask? We see the greedy aspirations of two power-hungry persons - Li Tu-hsiu, Chairman of the Superpower of Atheist China, and Rasul-Allah, the leader of the Islamic nations, marching boldly towards bloody confrontation and eventual extinction in a new global conflict.'

The tiny finger of Belial First pointed directly at his accused but both were too shocked to make any reply and remained bug-eyed in their seats.

'World War 3 will evolve into a terrible nuclear battle, where both sides will commit their entire arsenals of nuclear weapons at the other. After this monstrous act of destruction, the death toll will be almost total. But there will be some survivors. And given time, man will be able to repopulate this world. But time is not at the beck and call of man and the effects of the nuclear explosions will resonate around the globe causing huge cracks in the crust until eventually a monstrous earthquake in California will create one gigantic split that extends to the very core of this Earth. Unstable, out of control and without atmosphere or gravity, what remains of Earth's population will take a step into space that no one can prevent or retract, spinning in free-fall through space and destined to suffer a lingering death from suffocation. Earth will break up and collide with the other ten planets in our Solar System; and in a cosmic representation of a shattered snooker triangle of balls lasting millions of years, the collision will continue until there remains nothing but space dust.' An extended period of total silence followed this bombshell.

'The Verguide's main task was to find a way to avert this war. In doing so, we could have chosen to dispose of the two greatest leaders on the face of this planet and this would have been easy for us. But there are always others seeking the same goals of global dominance and we feared that whatever we managed in the way of assassination and mind control, we might miss one tiny scrap of intelligence that could confound our intentions.'

The Small Person's voice dropped as he continued. 'Neither combatant has yet crossed the Rubicon. Should we manage to provide sufficient doubt in the minds of Li Tu-hsiu and Rasul-Allah as to persuade them to step back from the precipice of extinction, we will have achieved our primary aim. But even if we do, your world is still in great danger.

'As you know, it has now been proven that your Earth is moving nearer to the Sun. As it does so, it warms more quickly with each orbit and we see the melting of Earth's ice deposits as we enter the next millennium. Your own scientists have always predicted such an occurrence but their predictions have been too conservative. Sea levels will rise to heights far in excess of those forecast and the planet will be completely covered in seawater in your year of 2115.

'And before that interesting development occurs, we will have need of those two great leaders; for if you accept my peep into the future as fact, you will all have to make decisions about how best to survive as a species.'

Except for a little mind control to accept and listen to the Small Person's talk, we had agreed not to influence each individual's decision. On this occasion, we would leave them to arrive at their own conclusions.

'The acceptance of my vision of the future will help you to make decisions over the coming years for your own people but in the final analysis those decisions are yours alone.'

An edgy silence filled the auditorium; people were beginning to fidget until Belial First spoke again.

'In conclusion, I will fulfil my promise to you and describe the person destined to walk this Earth. Before me, I see a tall man, over two metres in height, his skin is a pleasing light-brown in colour.' A picture of Belial First's vision appeared on the screen. 'He is perfect in all aspects, healthy, free of disease or handicap; and most importantly, he is smiling and content with his lot. History will dub him Capomone Man and he has a single aim in life.'

Belial First paused for a much longer period. 'And that purpose is the safety of his planet.

'Before departing I will leave you with a cryptic puzzle, for I am aware of your love for such things. But I urge you to both solve the puzzle and heed the message within.'

Digit by digit the symbols of the puzzle filled the screen as Belial First climbed the sunbeam and faded from view.

$$(\male \div) = (\dagger \rightarrow \infty)$$

CHAPTER 31
DECISION TIME

THREAD:

Within the world of automated message transmission systems, in those long-ago days when messages were sent using codes perforated into paper tape, certain parts of the beginning of each message had to be completely error-free. In preparing messages for dispatch, operators had a simple procedural instruction when dealing with any errors before the crucial cut-off point. Ditch the imperfect tape and start again.

When any rational human mind reviews the management of human population on our planet, perhaps that mind might conclude that we have reached such a point. Perhaps it is time for us to ditch and start again.

Evidence of man's early existence below ground is widespread throughout the globe. Homo sapiens, or intelligent man, have been in existence for some one quarter of a million years. Not even the blink of an eye in spatial terms.

Man-made dene holes, excavated throughout Britain and Europe from as early as 70 AD, are thought to have been made to reach deposits of chalk, which was hauled from depths of about twenty metres and spread over the land to improve soil fertility. Later they were used as storehouses for grain and other farming produce; or as places of concealment for smugglers, highwaymen or the displaced persons of the day; and possibly dwellings. Whatever their use, they provide evidence of man seeking to descend into the earth for shelter. Wise man was already seeking to extend his borders and knowledge of his planet; and it is fascinating to wonder if he also raised his eyes to the heavens and beyond?

Certainly, our predecessors made good use of caves, which provided them with a place to practise their leisure activities, from cave painting to cannibalism. Places in which to shelter from the elements; places to rest, eat, and defend themselves from nature's predators. At up to two kilometres deep and ranging in length from a few metres to some five hundred kilometres, they must have been regarded as a gift from above to the inhabitants of our planet some forty thousand years ago.

More recent occupants of our planet have managed to extract extreme enjoyment from exploring cave dwellers' early apartment blocks. Cave exploration; base-jumping by parachute; cave diving; all provided a variety of dangerous pastimes for those members of our society dubbed reckless or foolhardy: those adrenalin-junkies engaged in an endless quest for the thrills of living on the knife-edge of the unknown. For those of a less adventurous spirit, caves were cleaned, floored, heated and lit with colourful displays of artificial light: tourist attractions like St Michael's Cave in Gibraltar or the Lechuguilla Cave in New Mexico.

NO SPECIFIC PLACE. POST VERUNIAN VISIT.

Life as we know it on the surface of our planet was about to become untenable.

The people of our planet were stunned by the revelations of Belial First; but he, rather pointedly, had refrained from offering any suggestions as to the methods by which the population of the globe might survive. Glosys was flooded with information from around the globe. News articles; endless questions, meetings, and debates; scientific ravings from 'ologies' of all shapes, sizes, and colours; religious interpretations from a countless number of bible thumping, ranting theologians; and the opinions from those who think they know everything, attempting to cloud the judgement of those that do.

At last. It slowly dawned upon the diverse peoples of the Earth that man must hoist himself out of the mire of petty squabbling; there was a higher plane or category of existence which man must find the mental ability and moral strength to reach. A leap of faith in himself.

Survival. The core of man's existence, his most primordial sense, was under threat. The subject shaded every other worldwide event and provided a catholicon for the troubles of our world. The high fences of deeply-rooted distrust, hatred, religious differences and the mindless feelings of revenge and retribution drifted away and died - like the contestants in a brutal rugby match hugging and kissing after the violence ends. Arms finally yielded to the gown and violence finally gave sway to reason.

A final solution. For five long, wasted years, the world talked and searched. Sifting through history and the totality of man's knowledge, the combined effort of mankind sought an alternative El Dorado. The search for a solution was researched, discussed, theorized, speculated upon; and a pragmatic solution was prayed for in every conceivable language, demanding the exclusive attention of man's total resources.

The Verguide Team was kept especially busy during this period of uncertainty. Our minds flitted around the globe like butterflies on an ocean of salt water, silently eavesdropping on *in camera* and secretive meetings, whilst attempting to influence the decisions of the world's political and religious leaders. Finally, in late 2086, the leaders of the world agreed to the composition of a New World Committee. This committee would be apolitical and based upon the religious beliefs of mankind, whose leaders would be expected to provide guidance to the people of the Earth when making their choice to vacate the surface.

Religion is a minefield to human understanding. In the one hundred and ninety or so countries of the world, there exist twenty-two main religious groups, with an enormous number of minor denominations within each group. Christianity alone, the largest group, has some eighteen denominations.

A list of man's religious sects is a real tongue twister to read. The underlying principle, common to almost all the higher religions, is that of salvation. But the meaning of the word varies greatly for each main religious group. For Christians, it is the concept of being delivered from sin, or the consequences of such sin through the death of Jesus Christ on the cross. Wisely, world leaders recognised that a committee with representatives from the following twenty-two groups would be unworkable and unmanageable:

1. Catholics; Christians.
2. Muslim - Sunni, Ahmadiyya and Druze.
3. The Secular, irreligious, agnostic, atheist, antitheistic, antireligious groups which include humanism, deism, pantheism, free thought and Juche.
4. Hindus - Vaishnavism, Shaivism, Neo-Hindus and Reform Hindus.
5. Chinese folk religion, which includes elements of Taoism and Confucianism.
6. Buddhism, which incorporates the Mahayana, Theravada, Vajrayana and Tibetan sects.
7. Primal indigenous beliefs, a wide range of primarily Asian traditional or tribal religions, including Shamanism and Paganism.
8. African traditional and diasporic teachings, which include several traditional African beliefs such as those of the Yoruba, Ewe, Bakongo and Voodoo.
9. Sikhism, mainly in India and Pakistan.
10. Spiritism - a system of belief based on supposed communication with the spirits of the dead, especially through mediums.
11. Judaism which includes Conservative, Unaffiliated and Secular; Reform, Orthodox and Reconstructionist.
12. Baha'i Faith - emphasises the essential oneness of humankind and of all religions, and seeking world peace.
13. Jainism, which includes Svetambara, Sthanakvasi and Digambara.
14. Shinto. A Japanese religion incorporating the worship of ancestors and the spirits of nature.
15. Cao Dai - whose ultimate goal is of freedom from the cycle of birth and death.
16. Zoroastrianism, including Parsis and Gabars - a pre-

Islamic religion of ancient Persia founded in the 6th century BC.

17. Falun Gung - Chinese religion consisting of five sets of meditation exercises.

18. Tenrikyo - Japanese religion advocating a life of charity and abstention from greed, selfishness, hatred, anger and arrogance.

19. Neopaganism, including Wicca, Asatru, Neo-druidism and polytheistic reconstructionist religions.

20. Unitarian Universalism – Christian-based religion, teaching a free and responsible search for truth and meaning.

21. Rastafare - a religion that accepts Haile Selassie I, the former Emperor of Ethiopia, as God incarnate, whom they call Jah.

22. Scientology - has as its goal that of making the individual capable of living a better life in his own estimation and with his fellows.

But twenty-two religious delegates, enclaved in meaningful theological discussion, would be too much like a murmuration of starlings, twittering in unison amongst the numerous branches of the religious tree. Such a committee would make the decision-making process much too cumbersome. In a bid to reduce the size of the committee, world leaders elected to consider a more classic view of religious groups, which lists twelve major religions. In alphabetical order they are: Baha'i Faith, Buddhism, Christianity, Confucianism, Hinduism, Islam, Jainism, Judaism, Shinto, Sikhism, Taoism and Zoroastrianism. Still too many, in my view, for a single padre could usually talk the hind leg off a donkey and, in a bid to create an ideal situation, world leaders continued to search for a way of producing a committee consisting of a chairperson and a maximum of four delegates.

The adhoc committee had but one simple objective; decide the options by which man would achieve his salvation or survival. It was further decided that the composition of the committee was also to be kept simple; a small group of representatives was much more likely to achieve agreement. After considerable discussion agreement was reached and under the auspices of a pragmatic sanction, the committee was to be chaired by the Verguide and made up of a single member of the clergy representing each of the four main religious groups around the world. One delegate representing Atheism from China, where twenty-five percent of the world's twelve billion population worshipped not a single deity and occupied a single country. Another delegate representing the Abrahamic Christian religion, mainly Catholicism and Christianity, where twenty-six percent, or some three point two billion people, was spread over the surface of the Earth. A third delegate represented the Abrahamic Islamic religion, which numbered some twenty percent of the world's people, that is, two point four billion Muslims, living mainly in Africa and the Middle East. And the final delegate, representing the Dharmic religious group - Hinduism, Buddhism, Sikhism, etc., currently twenty-one percent of the population and numbering about two point five billion souls, mainly in the Indian subcontinent.

In terms of individuals, the Atheist representative (AR) was none other than the revered leader of the Superpower of Atheist China, one Li Tu-hsiu. At sixty-two years of age, he was the single most powerful man on the surface of the Earth. No man had ever wielded such immense power and no man would ever do so again.

Batting for the Abrahamic Christian religion, the ACR, was the Pope. Despite a strong challenge from the Archbishop of Canterbury, there really could be no other choice. A former Italian Cardinal from Genoa, Giovanni Saverio Piccolomini had been elected as the Bishop of Rome in 2084 at the tender age of seventy. As Pope Celestine VI, he was now an extremely fit seventy-two year old, in total charge of his faculties and highly respected by the world's leaders and clergymen. As the Vicar of Christ and absolute monarch of the Vatican City, he saw his enormous flock of Christians as his Holy See.

A gilded state barge used by Muslim rulers in the Middle Ages was called a *Dahabeah*. Placing his hands on the tiller of the Muslim religious *Dahabeah* and representing the billions of Muslims around the world, was The Prophet of Islam, Rasul-Allah. This most worshipped of a long list of Muslim Prophets had burst from the womb of his illegal immigrant mother in a small house in the back streets of Birmingham in 2003. His parents had named him Saladin-Hakim Salah. The world had learned of his atrocious war of violent extremist activities in the name of Islam; but he was untouchable in the eyes of every known security organization. At eighty-three, his eyes still burned with the steely glint of the true fanatic and he was now the Abrahamic Islamic Representative (AIR) on the New World Committee.

The Ocean of Compassion, or the Ocean Monk aka the Dalai Lama. The Dharmic religious group could not think of a more suitable delegate (DR) to decide their religious salvation. For almost seven hundred years, the Buddhist monks have ensured an unbroken succession of this personage. As each Dalai Lama departs this earthly world for his richly deserved heavenly nirvana, his loyal monks embark upon a search for a young boy - one who displays the special attributes of the dead Dalai Lama - and select him as their God's representative on Earth. Dragged from obscurity in 2025, the infant Lhakpa Dorjie was uprooted from his native Tibet and secreted across the border to Dharamsala in India. There he became the 16th in a long and illustrious line of Dalai Lamas, taking the name of Pemba-Appa Gyatso.

In addition to inaugurating the New World Committee and deciding its composition, the combined might of the leaders of the world also set out a clear and unambiguous manifesto. The NWC had but one aim - deciding which of the available options their religious adherents would take when the time came to leave the surface of the Earth. They were allocated a time frame, within which they must return the numbers choosing the following options:

- Moving to underground cities within the Earth's mantle.
- Colonize the Moon, in similar underground cities.
- Leave the Earth in space habitation vehicles, in search of other habitable planets.
- Remain on the surface of the Earth and place their trust in their Maker.

Every citizen of Earth, capable of reading one of the 7,891 known living languages, was aware of the predictions of Belial First. Their information came directly from the vast amount of information available on Glosys or by word of mouth from other human contact. Each individual knew the problem and knew the options; but he did not yet know how to register his choice of option.

Five years; the period allocated by the world leaders to the New World Committee in which to make a decision as to which option the bulk of their followers should accept. This theological decision would be advisory only; individuals could, in the final resort, choose whatever option appealed to them most, providing they adhered to the laws and social requirements associated with that option.

Global trading ceased worldwide on 1st January, 2087. At the same time, the world began constructing the means of providing accommodation to meet the four options. Monetary systems were of no further use to mankind and were declared extinct. All production for profit was ceased and whatever resources the world could still provide, both human and material, were used to construct the means to man's salvation. Every single thing, either on, in or above planet Earth, whether natural or man made, was declared a world asset to be used for the benefit of all mankind.

Most of the surface of our globe is already uninhabitable; of the five hundred and fourteen million square kilometres available, seventy percent is covered in water and the vast majority of what is left is accommodated by less than one person per square kilometre. Underground accommodation need not be constrained by its physical location; and in order to construct one thousand underground cities in the Earth's mantle, at least two thousand of the gigantic automatic drilling machines would be needed. This alone, at the highest level of density, would provide accommodation for up to fifty billion people and could be regarded as the place where the buck stops for those individuals who believed that there was only Hobson's choice available.

Drilling below the surface of the Moon was expected to be more damaging to the giant machines. A steady flow of visitors during the 21st century had revealed much more information about the planet and its structure and from a drilling perspective the new knowledge was not all good. Much like a hazel nut, it was found that the Moon had a very hard shell and a soft, porous centre. Excavations proved that the shell was badly cracked. Crevices, cracks and fissures extended hundreds of kilometres below the surface and branched off in all directions, covering thousands of square kilometres like a huge spider's web. But the worst news of all was that the waste extracted by drilling operations would not produce a useful building product. Such waste was only useful for filling up some of the crevices around the drilling sites but Mantellium for support and strength would have to be transported from Earth. It was expected that an additional two thousand drilling machines would be required to drill in the hard shuck of the Moon. Initial, wet-finger-in-the-air estimates indicated a requirement for no more than one hundred underground cities on the planet. But it was decided to transport the extra machines; just in case.

Much bigger problems faced the team involved in the free-space accommodation project. It was thought that the numbers electing to accept the possibility of spending the rest of their lives floating endlessly in space, hoping for a life-supporting planet to appear over the horizon, would be very few. But as the previous POTUS stated somewhat recklessly in private conversation 'There are bound to be *some* pond-life willing to take the chance'.

Space technology had evolved in leaps and bounds over the last fifty years. New and more powerful propellants allowed man to thrust an all-up weight of ten thousand tonnes into space orbit. Built using the ultra-lightweight Mantellium. These spacecraft would each be capable of providing living space for about forty thousand people. No definitive limit was placed on the build programme; a simple instruction to build as many as they could in the available timeframe was all that was given.

For those wishing to remain on the surface of the Earth, the build programme was much simpler. The principles of building giant cofferdams were both well known and well understood. Many such tourist attractions had already been built on the seabed, following tried and tested methods used in extracting undersea oil deposits. Built beneath the oceans, they would not have to withstand the fury of nature leading up to the deluge. However, few understood the long-term danger associated with this choice and the numbers selecting this method of survival were thought to be quite high. Each cofferdam was designed to accommodate about fifty thousand people. Linked by Mantellium reinforced glass tunnels, the seabed would eventually look like an Arctic landscape dotted with hundreds of thousands of igloos.

In 2091, the New World Committee assembled for its final meeting. In striking contrast to me, the four representatives looked drained. For five exhausting years they had berated, cajoled, reasoned, threatened and bribed; and talked. Talk, talk, talk; the human organism has never yet, and will never, learn to keep its mouth shut. Incessant talking at meetings, with all levels of the priesthood within their own persuasion and at ecumenical meetings around the globe. They talked until their throats ached with the effort and strain; and all suffered from metaphorical bleeding ears after listening to endless theological and physiological discussions and points of view. More than simply dog-tired, or weary of the subject, they had reached their level of endurance; they could go no further and were thankful to their spiritual godheads that they had managed to stay the course.

As chairman of the NWC, my base was of course at the Abbotstone underground city, the ABUC. A nice twist on my part, since a similar acronym was used in the proposed underground time system.

By mutual agreement, all previous meetings of the NWC had been held in Volly's Folly. But for this final meeting, there had been a great deal of controversy and disagreement about the venue and all representatives had some convincing reason for convening the meeting in their own territory. And there was a very good reason behind each of the claims.

Travel by air was becoming increasingly more dangerous and the world had seen a vast increase in the number of nervous flyers. Huge storms could blow up in a matter of minutes and sudden, vicious wind shears created many a skid mark on the underwear of pilots and passengers during landing and takeoff.

And it was this fear of flying which prompted the delegates to suggest that the final meeting be held in their own country.

Since Rome is the centre of the Catholic Church, Pope Celestine VI considered it his God-given right to host the meeting in Italy's capital.

Now short and thin, the frail frame of the leader of the Chinese superpower had stopped short of demanding that Chang Jiang be chosen as the hosting venue. Staying his raised fist as he prepared to pound it on to the table in emphasis of his demand, I managed to divert his thoughts to a less dictatorial direction. 'As the most powerful nation on Earth, it is of course China's right to host this last meeting, but...' The hand had gently lowered to the surface of the table and the squatly-framed Li Tu-hsiu continued: 'During our forthcoming discussions many compromises will have to be made by each of us. Chang Jiang will lead the way in this new spirit of cooperation by acceding to our chairman's decision.'

The oriental features of the sixteenth Dalai Lama did not display an ocean of compassion. It would be many years before the Ocean Monk would be able to tolerate the close proximity of the Chinese leader. Anything Chinese upset this normally gentle personage, and twisted in hate and anger, the face of Pemba-Appa Gyatso belied the peace and tranquility associated with his religious group. 'Surely you will all agree that India is, at this moment in time, the closest place on Earth to heaven. And, as you all know, our Lord's most recent message from the heavens arrived in the form of Ombre. Since He directed that messenger to India, then I suggest that the final meeting of this committee be held in Dharamsala.'

Beneath all these claims was, of course, a natural desire to be on one's own turf. Surrounded by a familiar culture and lifestyle and free of the tiresome drudgery of being expected to abide by the rules of social intercourse in a foreign country.

Of all the delegates, Saladin was the least vociferous in his claim to entertain the NWC in Birmingham. Demurring to my demand, which was supported by a chairman's prerogative, Saladin was content that he would not have to take to the air to attend.

It was Friday 15th June, 2091. We, the New World Committee, had come together for our final meeting. Each delegate had brought with him an official document stating the chosen route by which his calling should seek survival from the deluge. The document was of pure gold and would form part of the fabulous legacy that man planned to leave on the surface of the Earth; the golden cartouche.

'*Like two plain old ducks in a muster of peacocks,*' my thoughts mirrored those of Li Tu-hsiu. The Chinese leader and I were plain-Janes in comparison to the other three members of the Committee.

Each of the religious representatives had dressed to impress. Forsaking the traditional Episcopal mitre, the immaculate pontiff wore the triregnum or Triple Crown. He was dressed in the traditional long, white cope, reaching down to his ankles and with a pallium around his neck, which was worn over a sleeveless chasuble. In a move from tradition, Pope Celestine VI had decided to have the symbol of the keys to the Kingdom of Heaven embroidered on the chest of his outer garment. The silver and gold keys reflected the artificial sunlight, and cast small dots of light around the room when he moved. His Holiness wore the Fisherman's Ring, which he nervously twisted when under any pressure, and had ceremoniously laid the pastoral staff of his office on the circular table.

No less impressive was the Abrahamic Islamic Representative. Saladin, the Rasul-Allah, had managed to achieve that pinnacle of Muslim expectation previously only dreamed about by his predecessors. *Ummah*, the entire worldwide Muslim population had united behind a single leader. In recognition of this unique achievement, the Muslim Grand Faqihs had persuaded Saladin to accept a new honour and title, that of The Prophet. Recognised throughout the Muslim community only he, and he alone, was entitled to rewrite or reinterpret the Islamic Holy Book - the Qur'an - and the billions of followers carried his reinterpretation in book form, which was known as The Prophets *Resalah*.

The royalties from this book exceeded the dreams of avarice. It contained a considerable number of changes, new rules and regulations to which the Muslim nation were required to adhere. One such rule was introduced to protect his extremist armies. Muslim men were instructed to wear the *niqab*, the black, full-face veil previously only worn by Muslim women that revealed only the eyes of the wearer. Hidden behind this headdress a man's features were almost totally obscured from view; it was almost impossible to identify one man from another.

Saladin stared at me in stony silence. He had fixed his attention solely upon me on several occasions and each time I spoke his head dropped slightly towards his right shoulder, a sure sign that he was concentrating hard. I knew that he recognized my voice and I also knew that it worried him greatly; but I would not allow his mind to make the connection to what he heard as the holy voice of Gabriel. He wore a dazzlingly white, full-length cope, similar to that of the Pope, except that the cuffs at the end of each sleeve were much more voluminous. Over and above the *niqab*, he wore a black turban which ended in a long sash flowing down his back. It was well known that he wore neither ring, chain nor earring; certainly none could be seen but who knows what lurks behind the *niqab*? He appeared to obey his own rules; all Muslims had been ordered to donate such worldly possessions to their mosques many years before. Prior to the cessation of monetary systems he had been fabulously wealthy; and in terms of possessions he still was. He could not have put a figure on his wealth but he did know that if he could see it, he could afford it.

Old age had not diminished the timbre in his voice or softened the look in his bright-blue eyes; neither had it lessened his ambitions. He had achieved more than any Muslim leader before him but he had not established domination over his planet; and despite his agreement to step back from another world war, he harboured still his dreams of achieving a lifelong ambition. There was still much work to be done.

India had proved to be a most kind and generous host to the Dalai Lama. Listed first in a catalogue of the new Seven Wonders of the World is the traditional home of the Dalai Lama, the Potala palace. Located in what was known as Tibet, the beautiful palace and the town of Lhasa is regarded as no-man's land by the Chinese leadership and is the place to which millions of Buddhists make pilgrimage each year. India could not duplicate this wondrous palace but it came close. The new Potrang Karpo palace was built in the hills outside the town of Dharamsala in the Northern India state of Hamachal Pradesh, close to the Himalayas. It was to this place that Buddhists from all around the world trekked thousands of kilometres to stand outside the palace and await a glimpse of their spiritual leader. Completed in 2057, the palace was extremely lucky to survive the asteroid strike in 2062 with little more than superficial damage. Located northwest of Jarwa, it was sufficiently far away from Ombre's strike to escape coming to any real harm.

Continuous Indian pressure had secured the return of some of the treasures stored in the Potala palace. China happily agreed to return the sacred Buddhist scriptures, known as the Kangyur and the Tengyur, together with devotional offerings which included elephant tusks from India, porcelain vases and a pagoda made from over two hundred thousand pearls. But they robustly refused to return the tomb of Thubten Gyatso, the thirteenth Dalai Lama, a giant *stupa* which contains over a tonne of solid gold and priceless jewels.

Bare headed and dressed almost entirely in yellow - almost ochre-coloured - vestments trimmed with red, the sixteenth Dalai Lama oozed charm and charisma. His shaven head glistened in the artificial sunlight and he neither wore nor carried any insignia of office, except that is, for his lightweight spectacles. The wearing of spectacles was still preferred by many of the older generation, despite the availability of the latest surgical techniques for eye transplantation. 'It gives me something to do with my fingers', was a common reason given, particularly by those who had finally weaned themselves from the tobacco drug in the face of worldwide criticism.

Politeness, supported by the world's newly-discovered sense of oneness, had been the watchwords of our meetings. At this our final meeting, there was one item on the agenda. It was decision time.

Reiterating his country's dominance as the only world superpower, the Atheists' representative always spoke first, followed in alphabetical sequence by the Dalai Lama, the Pope and The Prophet.

Without a word, the leader of China's three billion atheists handed the golden sheet to me. On the A4-sized sheet was printed a single word; 'mantle'. The people of China had indeed had an opportunity to express their choice of destination in a national ballot but the result of that ballot was decided by Li Tu-hsiu. It is surprising how easy it is to massage, mould or manipulate the results of a computerised ballot, particularly when you have control of the computer. Complying with the decision of their leaders was pre-programmed into the Chinese psyche. The population of that eastern superpower would, to a man, dutifully follow in their leader's wake; leave the surface of the Earth and live in the vast, underground cities, nearing completion beneath their huge landmass. Brilliant Chinese engineers and scientists willingly shared the plans for their cities with the other nations of the world and they were largely responsible for both the weather and transport systems used underground.

'Thank you Li Tu-hsiu.' I felt that an acknowledgement of the document was required from me. It had been almost a racing certainty that the Chinese would elect to reside in the underground complexes, for they had pioneered the way many years before with the building of their new capital, Chang Jiang.

I looked across the table to the Dalai Lama. A brief nod and, politeness personified, he stood to read from his golden document. His soft, melodious voice spoke for about thirty minutes, during which I felt my eyelids become increasingly heavy. His soft, soporific drone seemed to hypnotize my mind; so much so that I actually missed the bottom line and was grateful that the Buddhist decision was clearly stated on the last few lines of the golden page. 'The Dalai Lama and his monks will continue life after the deluge in the cofferdams at the bottom of the ocean. However, the Dalai Lama will appoint a representative to lead a second group in the free-space venture. Buddhists are, however, free to make a choice from the full list of options available to the people of the Earth: in the certain knowledge that our beloved Buddha will be amongst his followers, whither they disperse.'

Not an unexpected decision by the followers of the Enlightened One, for they believe that Buddha is present in all beings; and it therefore follows that it matters not where his subjects are because he will be with them.

For the first time in many, many years I wished that the religious deities actually existed. My gift of foresight for much of the period after Earth's migration from the surface had been blocked by the Verunians. But deep within myself I felt that both the free-space and cofferdam options were fraught with extreme danger. No matter my own feelings or opinions; theirs was the decision and may their Gods go with them.

The Pope had popped his pop-bottle before the meeting. Backed by a phalanx of Princes of the Church, Pope Celestine VI had jumped the gun earlier that morning. Standing on the balcony overlooking St Peter's square, he had read his decision to the assembled mass of adoring Catholics, standing in the rain below him.

After five years of discussion amongst the Fathers of the Church, the Catholic Church could not agree with the Church of England. Each side offered compromise, counter compromise, concession and conciliation and made every effort to find a way forward. Possible solutions were penned by the other branches of the Abrahamic tree. From the wise Rabbis of Judaism, and from representatives of the Hands of the Cause, the controlling committee for the Baha'i Faith.

Just one point stuck in the craw of the Catholic Church; they could not condone the use of non-natural methods of birth control, neither could they accept the possibility of cloning. A last ditch meeting between the Archbishops of the Church of England and the College of Cardinals had this very morning stumbled upon the unforgiving rock of human propagation.

The whole Christian faith wished to remain on Earth and migrate to the underground cities. The wish list for the Christians included separate cities for Catholic, Church of England, Jewish, Baha'i Faith, Atheist and Verunian communities. But a real fear existed; that an increasing birth rate over many thousands of years might overwhelm the space and resources necessary to sustain life available in the mantle. A blind man could see that at some time in the future, birth control must become an issue.

The Verguide Team worked overtime. We could not allow the leaders of the Abrahamic Christian churches to fudge the issue or make the move underground without some irrefutable evidence of accepting non-natural methods of birth control. Tirelessly we attended meetings all over the globe, in our alter ego state and protected within our shields of invisibility, bending minds as best we could. But there were simply too many of them.

Of late, either by intention or by design, the Princes of the Catholic Church had muddied the waters even further by arguing over terminology. They could no longer accept the term birth control; it smacked of drugs and test tubes, the rational intervention of man in a divine act and, heaven forbid - cloning. In contrast, they were much more comfortable with the use of the term family planning, since this term allied the natural act of conception with the marriage bed.

With the two sides at loggerheads and without a leg to stand on, the Pope had no option than to act unilaterally. I too had no choice, I had been with him for his early morning prayers and when His Holiness left the room I went with him. He had left the Cardinals and Archbishops deeply entrenched in their traditional views and had returned to his private suite. He had heard the words of the Almighty enter his head whilst at peace during his early morning First Hour of the Divine Office; he knew what he must do to break the deadlock.

The words seemed to flow on to the sheet of paper, almost unbidden by his mind, exactly as if drafted by the Holy Father in Heaven Himself. The voice within his mind, silently dictating the words, seemed vaguely familiar; and the chosen words did not exactly follow the contemporary ecclesiastical syntax with which he was so familiar.

I had lost him. His mind had drifted back to happy memories of his days at university. His mentality was drifting towards the shore of senility; I could not hold his attention for any length of time. Eyes closed, he saw himself young again; regarded as a brilliant student by his tutors; carried aloft by his contemporaries on prize-winning presentation days; gifted with a natural, forceful, and convincing oratory skill far in excess of his years; fluid in the romance languages - he stopped suddenly in full flow. 'No!' He had shouted in English. 'That's wrong - *fluent* in the romance languages. For Christ's sake!' Often, when alone, he allowed himself verbal access to the expressions of the common man.

Confused, the old gentleman looked down at the sheet of paper. He read the text and was suddenly angry.

'I heard the will of God, so why do I feel so discontented with these words.' His head dropped to his chest in fatigue. 'I feel pressurised - but who by? Those CofE Archbishops are assholes! Ranting on about Catholics; accepting their share of the responsibility of restricting a population explosion. And those bloody Rabbis; who gave them the right to declare themselves as His chosen people? Claiming first hand knowledge of an exodus and dictating where their cities should be located, acting as a boisterous group of children vying for seats in a game of musical chairs!'

Anger did the trick. He was back with me. '*Servus servorum Dei.*' One of the Pope's titles: translated from Latin it means 'The servant of the servants of God'. I pushed the words to the forefront of his consciousness. The familiar language that he had mastered so early in life focused his mind on the document in his hands.

It was a *motu proprio*[32]: effectively it added an addendum to the *codex juris canonici*[33]. Although he was not entirely happy with the wording of the document, the Pope felt the turgid words sufficient to pacify the argumentative clergy of the Abrahamic Christian churches. 'And it's certainly good enough for government work.' The old man smiled at his final statement. Used frequently, it signalled to all that a subject was closed and cleared his mind for battles new.

Since reading the papal decree in St Peter's Square, the words had been transferred on to the golden material which the Pope handed to me.

'This is the final decision for the Abrahamic Christian Religious group.' His shaky voice and unsteady stance showed clearly that he was feeling every one of his seventy-six years.

---

[32]*Motu proprio.* A decree issued by a Pope acting on his own initiative.

[33]*Codex juris canonici.* The official code of canon law of the Roman Catholic church.

It had been translated into Latin. No problem to me; a knowledge of the languages of the world had been programmed within me many years before and I had no difficulty in reading the document. For the benefit of Glosys, I read aloud the decision of the Pope.

'This decision is imposed on the Abrahamic Christian Religious group ex cathedra. It will become extant at the actuality of an all-engulfing flood; and remain extant for as long as man is prevented from occupying the surface of the Earth. As The Vicar of Our Divine Lord on Earth, I recognize that limited accommodation and worldly resources might require a limitation of the number of souls returning from heaven.

In recognition of this fact, the Roman Catholic Church reiterates:

- Its faith in the sanctity of marriage, and
- That it regards the use of non-natural methods of birth control as a sin.
  However, during the period of The Second Deluge, I Pope Celestine VI, in the name of Our Holy Father and the Holy Catholic Church, temporarily rescind objections to the use of all such non-natural methods of birth control. Subject to the following conditions:
- The use of such non-natural methods of birth control will be regarded as a venial sin; but the committing of this sin alone will not extend a sinner's period in purgatory.
- The Recording Angel will assign such acts to the middle ground.
- Sinners must avow this sin in confession, in the certain knowledge of absolution.
- The Pope's personal guarantee is freely given: that using such methods will not deter God's Grace and Indulgence on the Day of Judgement.

This edict is to be included as a separate prayer during the Canonical Hours of the Divine Office and spoken at each of the Daily Offices; at Prime, Terse, Sext, None, Vespers, Matins, Lauds and Compline: that The Holy Catholic Church will not forget its original teachings.

The followers of the Abrahamic Christian religion will reside in the mantle of the Earth.'

Underneath his Papal signature, the Pope had added a final, hand-written note. 'I, Pope Celestine VI, make this decision for the good of all mankind; and I alone accept this venial sin for all Christianity. I will answer to my Lord, in His own good time.'

A deathly hush filled the room. Even the eyes of Saladin had glowed with a fierce concentration during the reading of the Pope's decision. He was elated; none had chosen the option of colonizing the Moon. It was inconceivable to his advisors that no other religious group would wish to attempt life on our nearest planetary neighbour. Silently he admonished himself; he should have believed the words of Gabriel, spoken so softly to him those many months ago. 'None will take the Lunar option; it is yours.' Joy, exceeding that felt during the many hours in his harem, filled his heart. A hidden smile beneath the jet-black *niqab* accompanied his thoughts. The beat of his heart might be a tad erratic these days but it still beat.

No other but himself could admonish him for his distrust in the Angel's words; as punishment he would resist temptation this very night and refrain from visiting his many wives.

Not one single ethnic or religious group had ever managed to hold sway over all the inhabitants of a whole planet. Many had attempted to gain such power; even more had dreamed of the unlimited rewards to be gained from such a conquest; but none had reached that pinnacle of man's desire.

Later that evening, Saladin sat amongst his closest Lieutenants in his favourite mosque in Birmingham. These were silent affairs, an opportunity to explore one's own mind, formulate ideas and plans, make difficult decisions, and decide who shall live and who shall die. After delivering the tersely-worded Abrahamic Islamic religion's decision to the New World Committee, Saladin had hurriedly left the underground city at Abbotstone.

Excited almost beyond endurance, his heart was aflutter, his pulse raced and his blood zinged in his veins. A crystal clear picture of himself was held close within his heart; he could already see himself on his diamond-encrusted throne of solid gold, blessing the multitude of worshippers bending low before him. Rejuvenated, he felt the weariness drain from his bones. As his thoughts continued, he fingered a

---

[34]Noi. Nation of Islam.

fillip to the Lord Gabriel, who might well have to consider bending a knee to The Prophet. *'I, The Prophet Rasul-Allah, will be the only God on Noi. I do not need the good graces of any other deity; I will leave this place and spend the night with my wives.'*

Res communis: international waters; a weapon and nuclear free zone. At two percent the size of Earth, and recently renamed Noi[34] at the insistence of the Islamic leadership, it was still free of human habitation. Virgin territory, waiting only the hand of a strong leader to mould it into a Muslim paradise. Allāh had clearly intended that the Moon be rendered habitable by His special people; for its astronomical symbol was that of the Islamic faith. *'Very fitting,'* thought Saladin. *'The followers of the crescent will rule the star of the crescent.'* The megalomaniac had already upgraded Earth's small moon to star proportions.

No one, other than Saladin, dared make any broadly based decisions concerning policy or method. The eight Scimitars had a much different role to perform now; and all who would make a decision without a nod from The Prophet risked almost certain death. The Prophet issued his proclamations to his inner sanctum of Grand Faqihs who controlled the massive workforce of dedicated Muslims. 'Prepare the spaceships.' 'Build the tunnelling machines.' 'Construct the underground cities on Noi.' 'Ensure we have sufficient weapons and ammunition to take with us.' 'Make all things ready for a nuclear capability on Noi.' 'Two hundred and forty-one cities will be built.' 'A single Grand Faqih will control a group of twenty cities, answering only to me.' 'We will land on the Far Side.' 'Commence construction in the crater Daedalus.' 'Build our cities away from the prying eyes on Earth, on the far side of Noi, under the dried up seas called Maria.'

And with a much more sinister tone in his voice: 'Bring me the names of those who do not obey, or who seek to obstruct our efforts.'

A force of two point four billion workers can produce almost anything, especially if forcefully fed on clap-happy pills. Galvanized by the universal fear of The Prophet, the demands of their Grand Faqihs and kept happy by the mood enhancing properties of their daily intake of drugs, the Muslim population set to with a will. The story of their incredible achievement is not for inclusion on these pages; but a detailed chronicle of their efforts is included within the pages of the golden cartouche.

The Islamic nation had already decided not to wait for the rest of Earth. They chose to leave their home planet as and when the cities were completed. First occupied was The Prophet's magnificent spacious and luxurious quarters in the principal city of Saladin, located precisely in the centre of the encircling two hundred and forty subsidiary cities.

Rasul-Allah blasted off from Earth on 8th June, 2105, atop the stupendous thrust from the latest Zeitgeist rockets, exactly 1,473 years after the death of Muhammadpbuh; and a single year after the life preserving systems had been proven effective on Noi. Before stepping across the threshold of his chariot to destiny, he turned, raised his hands above his head with six digits exposed and waited for the single trumpet to sound. He was *Israfil*, the Islamic archangel who will herald the end of the world by sounding a trumpet on judgement day.

In contemplative mood, The Prophet settled into his comfortable chair after being launched towards space. His seat was in the leading spaceship of the Muslim First Fleet. His thoughts drifted back in time to his parents who had conceived his earthly body whilst awaiting their passage across the English Channel. He clapped his hands. 'Send for three of my wives.' Perhaps the short trip to Noi need not be as boring as he had expected; and who could deny a future claim on his throne from a firstborn son, begot by an untainted conception without contact with the infidels on Earth.

CHAPTER 32
WORLD IN 2100

As our world staggered hesitantly into the 22nd century, its people faced a most uncertain future.

The most recent one hundred years of our planet's history had followed preceding centuries with little change in terms of how its inhabitants viewed their world. Each violent, painful and bloodthirsty year followed on from the last, with precious few bright windows of peace and harmony.

Many aspects of man's existence on this planet had changed. The physical shapes of the landmasses were different, altered by the movements of unstable tectonic plates. Mountain ranges had fallen and replacement high peaks had taken their place. Coastlines had squeezed inland, reducing the available living space in almost all countries of the world. Weather patterns had altered dramatically, forcing people to be more wary about spending time away from the protection of their homes. But by far the most noticeable change was the basic essence of life on our planet.

Most of the world had been furiously digging, excavating and tunnelling for over two decades from the late 2080s; and during the subsequent twenty-odd years man managed to revert to a previous existence, at least in terms of where on planet Earth he chose to live.

It had been a century of build and bust.

The start of the 2nd century of the 3rd millennium saw the dawn of a world that would be unrecognisable to the people of Earth that witnessed the beginning of the 21st century. By 2085, many of the people of our planet finally started the long road to enlightenment and lifted their eyes to a higher level of existence, free from the mindless depravities into which the search for human self-gratification had reached during the earlier part of the century. Others saw a greater reason for increasing the depths to which their depraved minds might take them.

In our world in terms of transport, nothing had been discovered to supplant man's greatest invention of the wheel. Many disastrous efforts were made to take to the air in small vehicles but all had failed due to the effort to overcome gravity. And man had not yet invented an anti-gravity system.

Hydrogen-powered vehicles had their moments in the early decades of the 21st century but were found to be very limited in their power output and range. Their only redeeming feature was that they were perceived to provide a 'green-system' and therefore helpful in reducing individual ecological footprints by emitting only water and heat into the atmosphere. However, this source of power still relied upon electricity to produce the hydrogen, which itself was generated mostly from fossil fuels. The hydrogen-filled fuel cells were cumbersome and difficult to fill; and the expense of providing the retail outlets for the hydrogen proved to be too great.

Moving personal transport into the air awaited the arrival of the solar-powered fuel cell. These cells were similar to the popular financial credit cards used during the first decade of the 21st century and could be used to power anything from a space lander vehicle to a hairdryer. Extremely cheap to manufacture, they were recharged either by plugging into a household electrical socket or by simply being left lying on a windowsill. Unfortunately, at the time of their successful development, man had other things to occupy his mind and which would totally negate the need for personal transport.

Alfred Leonard

Throughout the early decades of the 21st century, conventional air travel ballooned on a massive scale; and the reason behind this expansion was bad news for the American aircraft giant Boeing. In 2007, the European consortium Airbus introduced the A380 Superjumbo, which spelled the end of American air passenger supremacy. An absolute joy in which to fly and enormously successful, the original jumbo-jet, the Boeing 747, had ruled the skies for well over forty years.

Despite the imposition of swingeing global-warming taxes, the advent of the giant A380 passenger aircraft reduced costs to such an extent that air travel became almost as cheap as travelling by train. By 2015, some sixteen hundred of these giants circled the globe and in some countries, notably India, inter-city travel was by A380 aircraft. Stripped to the bare minimum in terms of facilities and comfort, the aircraft was able to accommodate some 850 passengers; and air travel had virtually replaced the rail network in some areas.

Most international airports required updating to handle the A380. Of these, almost all had plenty of spare acreage to spare for new runways and terminals to deal with the explosion in affordable air travel. London, however, suffered badly. The new Terminal 5 opened shortly before 2010 and although two new runways were installed during 2014, the groundside facilities remained hopelessly inadequate. For the travelling public, a journey through Heathrow was a nightmare; it just could not cope with the numbers.

But the A380 also rekindled the international race for aviation supremacy. The mighty USA was not about to relinquish its bragging rights so easily and decided to settle the argument in terms of atmospheric travel once and for all.

In terms of size, airframe technology had just about reached its limits; but in terms of speed? Well, that was a whole new ball game.

Aviation designers had long dreamed of building an aircraft that was capable of flying above Mach 3, or three times the speed of sound. Of those successfully built and flown to date, each one had been for military purposes. Designers of such aircraft have faced one common problem; that of finding materials to cope with the enormous heat generated when an object flies through the atmosphere at great speed.

For the 1960s military experiments, titanium was the answer. But titanium is an exceedingly expensive commodity and the first

American XB-70 Valkyrie bombers cost some seven hundred and fifty million US dollars each. But they did achieve their design speed, reaching Mach 3.1, or about 3,800 km/h.

At about the same time, America's charismatic young President, John F. Kennedy, asked Boeing to design and build a passenger-carrying aircraft capable of Mach 3. History shows that Boeing failed but associated huge development costs were not entirely squandered because out of that program was born the remarkably successful Jumbo.

Possibly the sole remaining world superpower during the early part of the 21st century, America had yet to fail to rise to any challenge or adversity. They were not about to allow the Europeans to steal their thunder and they were also aware of China which was busy building huge aircraft engineering plants with exceptionally long runways. The secretive Chinese were obviously up to something and a passenger aircraft capable of three times the speed of sound would swell the coffers of the first nation to build one.

The search for a suitable metal that was light enough and strong enough to cope with sustained Mach 3 flight continued; but it was to be many years before a routine drilling operation provided America with the means to achieve its dreams.

In 2012, painfully aware that the A380 was cornering the market in aviation orders and not wishing to lose their national bragging rights, POTUS asked Congress to allocate covert funding to build such an airliner. The project, codenamed Phoenix-3, was unanimously endorsed by Congress. The most telling persuasion for Congress was the remarkable discovery of a new metal, the only known deposits of which were found deep below the San Joaquin Valley in California. Beneath the long dried-up bed of Lake Tulare, into which the rivers from the adjacent Sierra Nevada Mountains once drained, were found deposits of a new ore. Once processed, the ore produced a surprising material; similar to titanium but much lighter; many times stronger; and almost oblivious to the most extreme of temperatures.

Since the discovery, which was made during routine drilling associated with the study of earthquakes, the search had begun throughout the USA for further deposits but the wide-ranging explorations proved virtually fruitless. The decision was therefore taken to restrict the use of this remarkable material for military purposes, a decision quickly overruled when POTUS called for the reinstatement of America's commercial aviation supremacy.

Boeing was of course delighted. At last, its vast team of aeronautical engineers had a material that could easily withstand the incredible heat of multi-Mach flight. They rejoiced in their find and set out to design an aircraft that would wipe the smile from the face of Airbus.

Just five years later, the first sleek Boeing 833, dubbed the Tridecker, rolled off the production line. At the rolling-out ceremony lavishly staged by Boeing, a collective gasp was clearly heard from the world's media as their eyes settled on the airliner. The material from which it was built was called Tularium and in its final form, it took on a natural, deep cerulean blue. Boeing had decided not to add some seventy tonnes of paint to their new aircraft; and against a bright-blue sky, it became almost invisible to the naked eye. A simple American Airlines logo on the tail-section was the only adornment.

For the first five years, the aircraft was restricted to American-owned airlines. Capable of carrying some fifteen hundred passengers at the design speed of Mach 3, America was ready to do battle and intended initiating a fare-cutting campaign that would see many world carriers teetering on the brink of bankruptcy and clamouring for the right to buy the Tri-decker.

But it was not only the speed and load capacity of the new aircraft that was so impressive; it was also capable of landing on runways used by the first Jumbo. In fact, in terms of airport management and facilities, it required little more than was required for the 747. Most airports coped with relatively minor inconvenience but for those airports with no additional space to provide the required increase in docking areas and service stands, it was a different problem.

No heavier, but about one third larger than the last series of 747s, the gleaming aircraft was an impressive sight when it made contact with the Tarmac on landing. Four powerful ramjet engines slammed into reverse and brought the huge aircraft to a safe stop in any conditions. Spacious, quiet, economical and quick; it was a worthy replacement for the first Jumbo. And, as an added bonus for Boeing, a commercial freight version dubbed the Blue Whale boasted specifications that outstripped any other freight-carrying aircraft ever produced.

This triumph of American technology and resourcefulness was to remain as the market leader for some thirty years until a new metal was discovered which exceeded the exceptional qualities of Tularium.

Once again, Heathrow needed more terminals to accommodate both the Tri-decker and the enormous increase in passenger demand; and the furor over the airport's demands for more land transcended all other national issues for several years.

But landing space for Heathrow was not the only pressing national problem for Britain. For many years, it was common knowledge that water was becoming a commodity in very short supply; and once again, it was the shortsighted attitude of British leaders that had produced this problem.

House-building had largely been concentrated in the southern half of the country and by the early 2030s, there was very little green space south of Birmingham. This disastrous building policy had produced a host of problems in terms of jobs, communications and social behaviour; but most of all from a lack of water. Year on year rainfall figures dropped and with each succeeding year came harsher water restrictions. Standpipes became commonplace and hosepipes had virtually disappeared from the shelves of Britain's shops.

Successive weak government administrations underpinned Britain's penny-pinching and shortsighted attitude towards solving what was a major national problem. Summarised as 'if you don't know how to fix it, compromise' or 'give it a good buzz word name and sideline the problem' - a nice way of saying 'botch it' - it was the constant fallback position for UK governments. And this attitude stemmed from a common malady, the same resource and financial mismanagement when faced with other national problems of road, rail and other public travel systems.

A typical example of this head-in-the-sand attitude was that of on-street parking. Most towns and cities, particularly in the south of England, suffered from the start-stop syndrome. Vehicles were allowed to park on any road, in any direction and in defiance of local road regulations. Journeys were fraught with short bursts, followed by long waits to clear on-coming traffic. Most Councils did not have a clue about how to deal with this problem so they burrowed deeply into the sand, called the problem 'traffic calming' and dismissed the item from any further discussion - and at the same time took their cut from the additional fuel used by combustion engines working at their lowest level of efficiency.

As is the case with all problems, there is an answer. But it was to be late into the 2030s before a simple solution to the parking problem was found. Removing the pedestrian pavement from one side of each residential road and introducing a carefully planned one-way system finally cracked the problem.

As for the travel and water problems, it required long hours of overlooking and mind bending by the Verguide Team to convince the British Government to act. But finally, the Cabinet agreed to approve the creation of the biggest construction project that the United Kingdom had yet seen.

Completed during the third decade, this joint project finally solved two national problems; that of Britain's inadequate water supply and storage; and the lack of suitable landing facilities for international air travel.

Built across the Thames Estuary, the construction consisted of a new man-made coastline between a point just east of Sheerness on the Isle of Sheppey, and north across the Thames Estuary to Shelford Head on Foulness Island. Some ten kilometres long and five wide, this new coastline provided several other benefits. An outer flood protection for the city of London, relieving the pressure on the Thames Barrier from rising sea levels; a new outer ring-road and high-speed rail network running beneath the first sub-level airport facilities, relieving the pressure on a hopelessly inadequate bridge and tunnel crossing for the Thames; and a large inland sea for aquatic sporting activities that rivalled anything else in the world known as the London Htwozero Playground. Not to mention freeing up many acres of valuable building land around London.

As an added windfall, this newly-created inland sea was salt free. Massive desalination plants and electricity generating machinery had been installed in the new North Sea Barrier. Fed by a mixture of fresh water from the Thames and seawater from the North Sea, the facility provided ample power and water for the whole southern half of England and, when linked to the newly-built underground water distribution system and the national grid, provided a back up for the rest of the country.

The infill for this massive reclamation venture came from excavating gigantic fresh water storage facilities deep under the Pennines. Similar to the Snowy Mountains Scheme in southeast Australia, these huge water storage caverns were interlinked with an underground system of tunnels, pipes, pumping and cleansing stations that could transfer clean, fresh water to any part of the mainland. Every rooftop, every road and pavement and every river and stream throughout the country fed into this system - and when precipitation occurred, not a drop was wasted. Storage facilities for a year's supply for the seventy-five million population, based upon one hundred litres per day per person plus an additional fifty percent for emergency agricultural purposes, was provided in the system; the excess pumped to the source of each river and stream to boost the natural flow.

London Thames East (LTE) was born, the brainchild of Ana Templeton, member of the Verguide Team. Built along the top of the new coastline, the above ground area provided twelve runways, each some five kilometres long. Four ran on a north-south line, four on an east-west line and four more on criss-crossing diagonal lines. Each runway, taxiway and loading area was covered by a poly-tunnel structure protecting each from cross winds or adverse weather conditions. Landing and take-off was completely computer controlled, as was total control of the aircraft whilst on the ground during taxiing and docking. All aircraft movement on the ground was completed without the aid of aircraft engines, power being supplied from an overhead system of electricity very similar to that used on European trains in the early part of the 21st century. Expert opinion believed that the facilities would be sufficient to take Britain from atmospheric travel to space travel without the necessity of further building or costs.

Airport terminals and other facilities were provided immediately below the runway level, with roads and rail links running below that.

Other huge building projects took their turn to materialize, not least amongst which were road and rail links to bridge the three continents of Asia, Europe and the Americas.

Principal among these bridges was the North Atlantic Bridge. Prominent engineers have long dreamed of providing a connecting bridge across the North Atlantic Ocean to finally link east to west.

Only one feasible route has ever been suggested for this bridge but the methods of construction have been numerous.

And it was the successful completion of the Bering Peace Bridge that rekindled interest in the Atlantic crossing. Built along the route of the ancient Bering Land Bridge, the construction was designed to cater with up to twenty-meter sea swells in the Bering Straits. Linking USA (Alaska, Cape Prince of Wales) with Russia (Cape Dezhnev, Siberia), it utilised the Big and Little Diomede Islands as stepping stones and support islands. The bridge was in effect three bridges crossing the eighty-five kilometre span in waters up to fifty metres deep.

Following the successful completion of this bridge, an American engineer, Simon Altwhistle from Denver, Colorado, proposed a land link across the sometimes inhospitable seas of the North Atlantic. This brilliant engineer, best known for his revolutionary construction principles used in the building of the Gibraltar Bridge across the Straits of Gibraltar in 2045, suggested a floating, sectional bridge anchored by typical oil rig structures embedded deeply into the sea bed, similar to those employed on the Bering and Gibraltar Bridges.

Unfortunately, most engineers were sceptical about presently known materials being strong enough to withstand the constant bombardment from the sea, considering the depth of water and the length of the span; and most countries feared the huge financial implications.

Spanning firstly the Davis Strait between Baffin Island in Canada to Greenland; thence across the Denmark Strait to Iceland; finally hopping across the North Atlantic gap using the Faeroes, Shetlands and Orkneys as stepping-stones to Scotland; the idea was to provide a rail link that would not require any form of fossil fuel power. To serve this bridge, new rail links were built across all land masses to provide a continuous line between Washington and London; and extending eventually to Europe using a similar English Channel Bridge.

The design of the floating sections of the crossing were similar to those used on all aqua ducts however wide the span, ever since the Bering Strait was finally bridged. In the late 2020s, a British engineer pioneered the production of Flexisteel, an immensely strong, lightweight and totally flexible sheet material that provided the construction properties of some six hundred millimetres of solid steel. This fantastic material did not rust; did not require painting or sealing in any way against the ravages of the elements; and was impervious to water and chemicals. During the manufacturing process, which consisted of laminating together various layers, a sensor network was introduced between the two outermost laminations for connection to controlling computer systems as required. A single thirty-metre diagonal circular section of aqua duct measured one hundred metres in length. Sections were joined by a two-metre flexi-joint, and when four such sections were joined together side by side and with an additional four sections above, provided four passenger tunnels and four freight tunnels in each direction - all completely protected from the elements. Such a combination of eight sections became known as an octatunnel.

But this enormous building project awaited an anchoring system that did not involve the high costs of drilling into the seabed. Jon Sullivan, a young engineer from Inverness in Scotland, suggested in 2055 that it would be possible to anchor such a floating aqua duct using powerful thruster motors controlled by satellite-based station-keeping computer systems. A further enhancement was added by Mr Sullivan; that of a large, air-filled, aquadynamic wave-suppression base for the octatunnel and smaller outrigger tunnels on each side of the octatunnel to act as additional wave-dampening systems. Air pressure within these wave suppression systems was monitored continuously and reacted to the force of each wave via a complicated system of computer-controlled compressors.

The whole project, finally completed in 2061, was entirely green; and the system was completely automatic. It was provided with numerous back-up systems and was powered by free solar energy collected from solar panels in the roof of each octatunnel.

But in our build and bust scenario, the busting was a much more painful and costly process. As far as England's protection was concerned, there had been some major changes. The Royal Navy continued its decline by reducing the numbers of operational ships year on year. And by 2030, only a single battle group remained, consisting of a single aircraft carrier (HMS *Queen Elizabeth*), with two destroyers and one nuclear submarine. As a maritime fighting force, the Royal Marines, aka the Jollies, were disbanded after failing to protect the nation's monarch earlier in the century. And England could not support an army of land troops. By 2070, the Navy had been disbanded and the country depended upon its nuclear capability and a missile defensive system, supported by a few ageing jet fighters to deter suspicious interlopers. England could not act unilaterally and military plans did not include the word offence, for such a tiny country could rely only upon insular and defensive policies.

One contributory factor in the bust scenario was the problem of displaced persons. What or who was stirring up the problems associated with the flood of refugees into Europe? No one actually knew. Wild theories abounded; some suggested a Chinese or Islamic plot to support their dreams of worldwide domination; others suggested that it might be the Germans striving towards the phoenix of a Fourth Reich; and yet more people blamed it all on extremist activity.

Whatever the root cause, the never-ending river of discontented, displaced persons was the only flow that did not dry up throughout the era of the 21st century. And as more developing countries became better educated, their people demanded better living conditions; and in almost all cases resorted to extremist activity to achieve their ends.

The following is a small selection of the most bestial of these acts, in no particular order or time frame:

a. An attempt to pollute the new water storage facilities under the Pennines; and attacks on water facilities around the globe including the Itaipu Dam in South America and the Three Gorges in China.

b. The destruction of large sections of the Bering Bridge.

c. Horrendous damage and loss of life associated with continuous attacks on the North Atlantic Bridge.

d. Always easy targets, other bridges around the world provided fodder for the extremists' table. Attacks on the Gibraltar Bridge; the Rion-antiron in Greece; Verrazana-Narrow in New York; Lupu, Runyang, and Sutong in China; English Channel Bridge; and the Golden Gate in San Francisco.

e. Frejus tunnel in France.

f. Churches, Cathedrals and Mosques in almost every

city of the world.

g. Assassinations by the cart load.

h. Attacks on sporting fixtures, including the Tour de France; the Monte Carlo grand prix; Isle of Man TT races; Le Mans 24-hour; Nevada gambling centre; and countless football, rugby and cricket events.

i. A spectacular explosion in the restaurant at the top of the Courcheval pistes in France, followed by devastating avalanches into the valleys below.

j. Countless vehicle bombs; hand-held missile attacks; and body-bombs.

k. An A380 downed by hand-held missile attack whilst departing London Thames East; followed by many other such attacks.

In the field of human endeavour, the arts had also suffered badly. Many of the world's finest museums containing the artistic riches of past civilisations, artists, poets, authors, sculptors and the like were destroyed by extremist activity and natural calamities throughout the century. 2100 saw a world where the existing human brain had reached the *full* mark, a world where not even its powerful computers could invent more stories, paintings, music or sculpture. Man was, temporarily, replete.

Music had reached its zenith in the early 80s, at which point every conceivable variation of musical notes had been used and copyright claims exploded throughout the courts of the world. Every single composition was fed into the copyright computer system and none failed to find a match from previous composers. The same applied to books, films and plays and, again, very few new ideas were forthcoming that could satisfy the copyright computer that it was a fresh idea.

Sporting events declined during the 2070s and 80s. To some extent the people of the world had become bored with all the outside sporting pursuits - golf, cricket, football, rugby, athletics, cycling and all other activities involving personal effort. Temperatures had become just too high and there was little spare water to maintain grass surfaces in the major towns and cities throughout the world. Synthetic surfaces and underground air-conditioned facilities were experimented with at vast expense but to no avail. However, boredom, in itself, was not the real reason for the decline of sport; any public gathering was a dangerous place to be and a favourite place for media cameras to await the antics of some drug-crazy bunch of hooligans to inflict their worst on to the peaceful minority.

Supporting the bust camp were natural and man-made disasters. We can do nothing about the natural events such as acid rain or Athens smog. And the world had witnessed its fair share of terrible man-made disasters, most foolish among which were the needless nuclear accidents that added to the pollution of our Earth. Fledgling nuclear countries strove to emulate established nuclear powers and several experienced accidental reactor meltdown or China syndrome. Also mindlessly stupid was a decision to allow the storage of carbon dioxide under the sea beds in what were known as subcardi dumps. Earthquakes had fractured the dumps in the earlier part of the century, releasing untold amounts of the main greenhouse gas produced whilst burning fossil fuels. Gigantic bubbles had risen to the surface, where they exploded into an already toxic atmosphere and added considerably to the deterioration of our shelter from the Sun.

But at the same time, man was tireless in his efforts to degrade himself.

Drugs had changed considerably over the preceding century in terms of their usage, their legal status and their capabilities. Frightening, mind-warping new drugs became readily available throughout the world and countless thousands went to an early grave in the drug-induced belief that they could fly, exist underwater, overcome wild animals, stop bullets and bear the pain of self-dismemberment or torture. Mind enhancing, body enhancing, sexual performance enhancing, sporting ability enhancing - the list of concoctions became as diverse as they were dangerous.

Freedom of choice - these were the buzzwords of the controlling liberal influence on society during the last half century. Available on demand from national health budgets, the use of drugs expanded as would a giant balloon sucking in the obnoxious element that was air and greedily absorbed over eighty percent of the planet's gross national product in the fiscal year of 2077.

A new wave of sexual freedom had been inexorably spreading around the world, bringing with it yet another upsurge in immune deficiency diseases that the medical fraternity continued to find so hard to control.

No known antibiotic existed to counteract the terrible symptoms of a new sexually transmitted disease known as penii-tremendii or penni-rot. Contracted unknowingly, untreatable and morally offensive, this affliction developed with remarkable speed and involved a massive swelling of the male genitalia prior to its being devoured by flesh-eating bacteria that decomposed live flesh. Equally as dangerous, usually consensually contracted and known colloquially as a purple nose job, a new and powerful mixture of drugs was injected into both male and female, either in collusion or surreptitiously. The effect on the human body was instantaneous. Females show a short-term increase in the aphrodisiac pheromones emitted from their sweat glands and emit a sweet-tasting odour that is impossible to mistake by a male. The effect upon the male is frightening. The male receptor of the female pheromones, the atrophied Jacobson's organ, is slowly reawakened. With continued use of the drug, the organ grows bigger and bigger, and with each increase in growth the intensity of the man's reaction to the female pheromones increases in proportion. Over a period of just a few months, the drug-stimulated organ grows quickly. From the base of the neck, it spreads downwards into the thorax and reaches upwards into the nasal passages. In the final stages, the nose bulges up to four times its normal size, eventually splitting asunder, exposing the dark purple mass that resembles haemorrhoids at the end of the alimentary canal, which eventually prevents the body from breathing. Death follows almost instantly.

Even more degrading for man was the depths to which he would descend to pass the time.

Alfred Leonard

From as early as the beginning of the century, humankind had searched for new ways of satiating the seemingly endless search for more vile ways to degrade himself, seeking always the holy grail of *entertainment*.

Cage rage. Initially an extension of various unarmed combat techniques, it manifested itself into all-out physical confrontation in an enclosed arena, from which there was theoretically no escape whilst each bout took place. And it quickly became an event of gladiatorial proportions. Man versus wild animals; some events where the animal's killing instincts were suppressed by powerful drugs, or the removal of teeth and claw; and some against animals in full control of their faculties and flesh-tearing weapons.

Other events where man, at times alone and sometimes in teams, overwhelmed their opponents in spectacular fashion, using high-powered, automatic weapons which blasted the animals to a mist of flying, blood soaked offal. During these early tournaments, only the animals died but as time progressed and man's search for 'something to do' exhausted the minds of those most recently having climbed the steps from hell, then man fought man, or woman, to the death. So-called reality TV shows showed every gory detail of a contestant's death, in so many different ways but none more gory or profane than that of crucifixion during which the cameras remained hungrily glued to the unfortunate participant until the drugs wore off and the screaming started; at which time the whole spectacle became pay per view.

Yet other shows recreated the most macabre murders and shootouts of the 20th century, the most popular of which was a re-creation of the mafia and cowboy gunfights from an early USA. Depraved and warped minds from all over the world queued up in their droves to take part, achieving their single moment of fame as they slipped into the show's incinerators having met a bloodthirsty end.

Amidst this butchery, censorship was a toothless crone, prone to verbose condemnation but incapable of stopping the flood of such material through the world's entertainment satellites.

In many ways, the impending disaster of the world flooding was heralded as the saviour of the soul of mankind. It is amazing how focused the human brain can become when its species is forced to face the end of life. Contrary to popular belief, most elderly people do not change overnight into ill-tempered, fractious, self-opinionated old farts, with an inbuilt answer for all the world's problems. They can no longer see the long, shining road of extended life stretching before them; and they find it difficult to cope with the wilful waste and ruination of life. As people grow older, they feel a deeply-rooted sense of desperation. Inevitably, their known world is changing: people are more educated; they want more control of their lives; they extricate an ever increasing slice of the public sector cake; and demand a utopian society where handouts of drugs and money cost them zilch.

As a human approaches the end of life, everyone can see the change in its body - the wrinkles, bent and aching spines and limbs, failing eyesight, hearing and vocal ability. The databases of the brain are full, symptoms of which are an inadequate short-term memory but a crystal clear recollection of events over seven decades in the past.

However, none can see the changes in the mind. An older person becomes more tolerant of the mischief-makers; more willing to give way to the young and strong; and strives to mend the bridges of disagreement, blasted away during a long life of work and social intercourse. No longer able to fight, the older person *always* looks for compromise; *never* allows a discussion to descend beyond a point of no return; and attempts to find *something* good in all things, whilst *fearful* that they will not. Many turn their faces from the world, refusing to read or listen to the news reports on Noosnet of change for the sake of change; prices spiralling out of control; ever more levels of government and taxation; political intrigue; war; famine; flood; and natural disasters.

Noosnet shows a graphic picture of a drug addict, lying curled in the foetal position in a filthy gutter. Viewers can almost smell the stench of the unwashed body. A young person looks at this picture and sees someone who has 'Trod his own path in life; made his own decisions; rode the bucking bronco of a fix or joint; had a purple nose job, flown with the eagles - man!' A person more advanced in years views the scene and feels desperation at a life wasted - discarded thoughtlessly and somehow diminishing the orderly state of the womb that nourished him - without giving life a chance to mould the drug-user into a useful member of society.

In a sop to this new liberal social order, there was an underlying aspect to the emigration policies decided by the religious leaders in 2086. Everyone, of whatever creed, nationality or colour, was entitled to make an individual choice from the four available options designed to provide continuing life. During the period from 2086 and right up to the actual day of vacating the Earth's surface, freedom of choice was undeniable. Access to a public or private Pewi was available to all inhabitants of the planet and the numbers electing to take the available options changed on a daily basis as each individual's perception of the future altered or their personal circumstances took an unexpected turn. The ineffably large and powerful databases within Noosnet cared not for the fickleness of its input, nor how often it was asked to provide analytical reports.

Having obtained religious guidance in 2091, world leaders formally announced the dissolution of the adhoc New World Committee. In its place, an Earth Congress was formed, with representatives from each and every country. Having been advised of the software by which man could expect the religious salvation of his soul, the mission of the Congress was to provide the hardware by which man might ensure the survival of muscle and bone. The building of the required accommodation had started in 2087 but when a more informative indication of numbers was available, building the spacecraft, cofferdams and underground cities could continue in earnest.

It is generally accepted that man's most powerful basic instinct is survival. When that survival is threatened, mankind is capable of bonding together as never before. Working for a common cause is a driving force that can propel mankind to unknown heights of achievement. The two world wars of the 20th century proved this fact.

Resembling a giant colony of worker ants, the people of the world worked tirelessly for almost twenty years. By 2107, the work was virtually complete; all that was needed was to allow everyone a final chance to change his or her mind and determine the day on which each city would open to the public. To this end, Noosnet had replaced Glosys in 2095 and had been crunching the numbers ever since.

In summary, it was not a nice world. Not a world in which one would choose to live or bring up children. It was a dirty, spiteful, filthy world of selfish humans. Is it possible that the total civilisation of a planet might burn itself out or implode? Reach a point where its very essence becomes so old-hat as to be anathema to the people who created it?

A world of pressures, whereby one absolutely must excel at school and at sports to satisfy parental expectation; marry at a young age to ensure the production of healthy children; crumple at the knees under the weight of a mortgage; climb the corporate ladder to the pinnacle of success; keep up with the Jones'; run a luxury car; take expensive holidays; pay bills on the due date; make some contribution towards a pension - and hope to survive the obligatory heart attack and live through the stress long enough to enjoy it.

Would it not be a refreshing change if we could make a singular global choice to change it all? Live a different lifestyle free of stress and expectation? Live amongst similarly-minded people in harmony and trust in a world free of backstabbing, money grabbing, robbing, cheating, murdering and all the other *ings* in our sick civilisation?

Perhaps we can.

CHAPTER 33
MOVING DATE

THREAD:

The decision to vacate the surface of the Earth had involved years of discussion, disagreement and discord. Making that decision opened a Pandora's Box of related questions to exasperate the people of our world.

Almost as controversial was the choice of a suitable date on which to move. Selecting a single date on which each individual was to make his or her way below ground was of course impossible. In a determined community working together as one, nothing is impossible in terms of logistics but actually agreeing on a suitable date was a different matter involving mutual consent and compromise; and each underground city was eventually left to make its own arrangements. But the world could agree on one important detail; the date by which the move should be complete.

For every country of our planet history provides ample examples of auspicious dates from which a departure date might be chosen. Literally, millions of dates were suggested and each country made their choice.

From those suggested in the USA by far the most popular was 7th October. It was on this day some five hundred years before that Admiral of the Ocean Seas, Christopher Columbus, had, somewhat rashly, changed the course of his Squadron of small ships consisting of the Niña, the Pinta and the Santa Maria. In doing so, he missed discovering Florida. However, the population of the USA eventually forgave him and each year on the second Monday in October this great race of people celebrates Columbus Day.

But, of course, England does not participate in these celebrations and the 7th October was chosen for a much more personal reason. A census conducted in 2107 threw up a few surprising facts about life on our island. One of these revealed that more people were born on this date than on any other. Probably as a direct result of new-year celebrations where bellies full of wine, beer and whiskey, and the feel-good factor of a new year, anticipated the coming spring and new beginnings.

Each underground city in every individual country made their choice and their arrangements.

Literally thousands of suggestions had been offered for a suitable completion date; Noosnet had been inundated with proposals. Some represented personal choices; others were suggested to mark some highlight of a famous person's career; and yet others that marked a turning point in world history. But from the shortlist of dates, the most popular was that of 11th November, 2111. Remembrance Day, a date to which the whole world readily agreed. Armistice Day; Monday 11th November, 1918. The date, on which Germany finally surrendered at 11.00 on the Western front, bringing an end to four years of bloody conflict and ending World War 1. There could be no more suitable date to herald the dawn of a new world, a new life and more importantly, a new beginning.

Slightly further down the pecking order in Pandora's Box of difficult problems was if, and how, each group would communicate after the departure. Glosys was not up to the challenge. The system needed a bit of a boost - a few tweaks and a tad more speed.

Noosphere: the totality of information and human knowledge.

Anoosbyte (AOB): data handling speed of 1048.

Noosnet: the network designed to provide noosphere at the speed of AOB.

Consisting of access to a network of supercomputers, that is propagated internally using the Mantellium shells of the underground cities around the world and externally via highly sophisticated transmission systems capable of passing through the oceans, through the atmosphere and into space. As such, the network was capable of linking those who had chosen to remain on or below the surface; those who opted to leave Earth and live in huge spacecraft; and those who had elected to transfer to the Moon. In this one small way we differed from Veruni's first exodus in that we did not wish to sever contact with the departing groups.

Powered by solar energy, the system is capable of doing anything and everything, from deciding what and when anything is built, repaired or maintained to the extent of managing a complex re-cloning program to maintain a sustained level of population.

ENGLAND. TUESDAY, 29TH SEPTEMBER, 2111.

Precipitation. Designed to ruin a person's wish for a perfect day but rain can also be fun if the temperature is warm enough.

But since the return of the Sun after the mini ice age it had been raining for over thirty years and contrary to the beliefs of those people occupying the desert regions of the world, it is possible to have too much of a good thing, especially rain. At least it was warm enough and the rain in England fell on to a country that had evolved into primordial jungle.

She had been awoken early, to wait once again for the onset of yet another violent storm. The heat and humidity was incredible and she lay on the sweat-soaked mattress in fearful anticipation of what might be in store.

This was not a new experience in her life. The past twenty years had brought increasingly terrifying weather conditions and her fears for the safety of her children, her house and her planet was a continuous ball of ice-cold terror in her stomach.

At her side were her three small children, cuddled in closely for the reassuring protection of their mother's body. In the flashes of approaching thunder she could see the outline of their heads, incongruously misshapen by the large pieces of cotton wool stuffed into their ears. When a storm threatened it was the only way to get some sleep. Gently she reached down and removed the wads of cotton wool. *'Once a child is asleep, nothing on this Earth can wake them.'* Her thought produced a small and rarely seen smile on her face.

Uncomfortably hot, she desperately wanted to change her position in the bed; but unlike sound, movement can disturb a sleeping child and she did not want to wake them yet.

Huge claps of thunder crept ever closer. The woman did not fear this sound; it had been part of her life for a long time. Subconsciously she counted the seconds between each clap of thunder and the flash of lightning that followed. *'Getting bloody close,'* she realised.

Sleep evaded her and the closeness of the slippery bodies suddenly annoyed her. But it was not really the heat or the proximity of her children that bothered her. It was the approaching storm. Worry was a constant companion to a woman with three young children and she was quite accustomed to that emotion. But this was something different. Worry had deepened into something infinitely more terrifying, a feeling that engulfed brain and body and deep within her stomach she felt the gnawing, grasping tentacles of horror.

What filled her ears had not been heard ever before. An underlying grinding, scraping sound rumbled beneath the howling of the wind. Similar to the sound of two huge corn-grinding stones, it was growing in volume with every second. It sounded and felt as if jet engines were vibrating behind her brain; deafening now - and she reached up to place her hands over her ears.

The urge to look was too great to be denied. Carefully she left the bed and felt the welcoming slight decrease in her body temperature as she moved across the room. Peering into the jet black night she could see nothing except the flashes of the approaching storm. With a glance around at her children the woman reached to move the net curtains that covered the window. In a flash of lightning she saw the wall of sludge rushing towards the house but she did not see the tree that smashed through the glass as her bedroom window imploded. Her last coherent thought was, *'Jesus! That's going to cost a lot.'*

As storms go, this one exceeded the normal methods of measurement. Born in the Atlantic, the gigantic mass of water vapour had risen high in enormous clouds that filled the skies. Blown ever east by the prevailing winds that exceeded even hurricane-force, the storm

hit the coast of England. And because everything must have a reason, the storm gladly accepted the challenge of obliterating any landmass that it found. Winds were so strong that they lifted the soil from
the surface of the Earth, throwing it high into the sky to mix with
the snowball-sized raindrops and fall to the ground as giant mud
balls. Soil, trees, hedges, buildings, vehicles; everything that could be
moved was blown before this wind. Piled high in the form of a huge
wave, this porridge of sludge rolled across England, searching for a
place to dump its contents. Any low-lying area provided the dump-
ing grounds and once freed of restriction the wind bullied onwards,
tearing yet more earth from the surface.

The woman awoke. It was still pitch dark and she awoke into a sea
of pain. Total silence; almost painful in itself after the fearful sound
of the storm. Slowly her senses returned and she heard the sounds
of the world settling back on to its feet, timbers creaking, noises that
indicated disturbed items finally losing their grip and falling to the
ground. Natural sounds but nowhere the sound of a crying child
or the noise of a distressed animal. Freezing cold and soaking wet
she seemed unable to move, weighted down by some unknown substance. Mentally she searched her body for damage. She was bleeding from multiple minor injuries, mainly cuts and bruises, but as far
as she could tell she was not seriously injured. But despite this mental examination, she could not move. And this return to consciousness was to be only a short visit; and her final thought was that she
felt cold. She was unaware that her body temperature had fallen to
about twenty-eight degrees and she remembered that, 'I haven't been
cold since I got shut in the walk-in fridge.'

Whimpering, snickering and panting; a wet and warm tongue
flicked at her face and returned the woman to her senses. The puppy
was hungry, it had been trying to remove the pile of ice-cubes covering its mistress for what seemed a long time. Finally the heat of the
gigantic Sun had both melted the ice and warmed the woman's body
and small movements from the puppy's mistress hinted at the possibility of food. The puppy saw cognition in the woman's eyes; he
yelped with delight and started to pull at her clothing.

Her body felt warm again. She felt as if she was lying in a warm
bath and for once she welcomed the power of the Sun. But with her
returning senses came a dreadful realisation and she felt fear once

again. She could not hear her children and she turned to stroke the whimpering puppy into quietness. Slowly she dragged her aching body to its feet and staggered through the wreckage to where her house had stood.

Very little remained. The house had been virtually levelled by the storm. Quite how she had survived she knew not; but when she explored further afield she discovered that the deep river valley surrounding their acres had been filled with sludge and rubbish. It created an illusion of a newly-opened rubbish dump.

The woman was distraught and she slipped in and out of rational thought. At times she heard the children crying, at others the playful, yapping puppy seemed to hint at a discovery. *'My ears must be deceiving me,'* she thought, hearing the sound of the approaching storm once again.

As she turned to search the horizon for the return of the killer storm, she saw the tractor come into view. Perched in its cab were four people, her husband and three children.

The storm had provided a turning point for the family, a fulcrum upon which a decision could be made. How the couple had wrestled with making a decision. For years they had discussed their options, hardly believing what the media was telling them. They were told that life on the surface of the Earth would become untenable in a few short years. They must leave their farm; decide which option would provide the best future for their children. From farming stock they were outdoor people; how could they move underground?

Over the years the family had made several visits to their underground apartment. Yes, it was large, comfortable, warm, cosy and sheltered from the elements: but it was indoors. How could they be expected to live such a life? But the woman now knew that life underground would be safe. They had been lucky and she had lived through the most frightening experience that any mother can possibly face; the fear that her children were lost.

The woman no longer feared the move and three words that described life underground confirmed their decision; it was safe.

CHAPTER 34
ANA UNDERGROUND

THREAD:

Following the visit of Belial First in 2081, the populations of the world began to accept that his extraordinary peeps into the future were accurate, particularly concerning the fate of both mankind and his planet. The great underground cities had been constructed deep in the mantle of the Earth and occupied in the year 2111 (AUC0001).

Another of Belial First's predictions materialized in 2115 (AUC0005). The world was, once again, engulfed by a deluge. But this time the world would not need Noah and his Ark, for the underground cities provided a safe retreat from the rising waters.

To early 21st century man, the polar ice sheets were one of the new Seven Wonders of the World. Covering millions of square kilometres of both land and sea, they were thought to hold more than ninety percent of the fresh water on Earth's surface.

As Earth was drawn relentlessly nearer and nearer to the Sun, these polar ice sheets began to liquefy more rapidly. Meltdown had begun. The glacier of Mount Kilimanjaro faded away in the intense heat of the Sun, as did the Larsen B ice-shelf in Antarctica. Vast areas of Siberian peat lands thawed, releasing enormous quantities of carbon dioxide and methane into the already heavily polluted atmosphere. As the ocean temperatures increased and the sea levels rose, animal species waded inexorably towards extinction. Colonies of sea birds thrived in the midst of this catastrophe, though for only as long as the higher ground remained above water level, when they too faced their Waterloo. Agriculture declined to the point where only genetically-modified crops of maize, corn and soybeans could be grown in heavily-armoured shelters. Meat was unobtainable; there was just insufficient pasture to feed cattle, sheep, or pigs. Needs must and man adjusted quickly; he learned to be content, the sea hath fish enough; and the bounty from this watery world became his staple diet.

In the early part of the 21st century, a hundred years before the final great flood of 2115 (AUC0005), the seas covered about seventy percent of the Earth's surface. Eminent hydrologists of the day predicted sea-level rises of up to about eighty metres, if all of Earth's ice melted. During January of 2115 (AUC0005), the population of the world finally discovered just how wrong those early experts had been. There was far more water than expected. Encapsulated beneath what proved to be a relatively thin crust of ice, the polar ice caps concealed huge reserves of fresh water, descending some twenty thousand metres below the surface of the Earth. A eustatic rise in sea levels of about two hundred metres was expected to wash over the British Isles, leaving only the very highest points above sea level. When the final chunk of ice fell victim to the Sun's increasing heat, the seas rose to an incredible three hundred metres. Very little of the surface of the world existed in breathable air; nor felt the power of the Sun.

During the period between the move underground in 2111 and the great flood of 2115, life above ground became increasingly more difficult. Exceptionally violent storms rampaged across the globe; coastal towns were razed from the ground; perpetual hurricane-force winds that blew the top off the Fujita scale battered the Earth, uprooting all in their path. The last of the animal species succumbed to the demands of nature, as did those human beings who could not accept one of the other three alternative methods of escaping the onslaught of nature's violence and had elected to remain on the surface of the Earth to await whatever fate nature or nurture had in store for them.

Below the wind-tossed surface of the seas the giant, reinforced cofferdams were ground into the paste of the ocean depths by the incessant grinding movement of the huge volume of water around them.

Alfred Leonard

As I had feared, the people within these cofferdams were the second group to die; very few were picked up by patrolling submarines and brought to the safety of the underground cities.

Except for a few inland seas and lakes, such as the Caspian Sea and the Great Salt Lake, the oceans of the old world were in fact a single World Sea. Following the great flood there remained not a single isolated pocket of water on Earth; one mighty ocean covered the entire surface.

In the underground cities, all was peace. Man's sub-abyssopelagic existence provided huge benefits, the greatest of which was that humanity need no longer fear the idiosyncratic ways of nature. Unpredictable weather extremes, sunburn and skin cancer, flooding, tsunamis, killer ice storms, damaging winds, lightning-storms; all these things wiped out life, crops and buildings - and were events of the past. For the first time in his history, man was finally safe; for the foreseeable future.

Within the ocean depths below the hissing roar of gigantic tornado funnels, fish stocks increased year on year and easily outstripped the demands of mankind. Succulent *fruits de mer* were harvested automatically by unmanned, aquadynamic, deep-sea fishing vessels which were programmed to take the biggest specimens in quantities sufficient only to satisfy the needs of the population. These fishing vessels could operate at any depth and discovered never before seen demersal life forms, some of which tasted remarkably similar to beef or chicken.

To the mind of a human being, the life of a mole must appear to be absolutely abysmal. The Stygian darkness, the unremitting dampness, cold and hunger, the confinement, lack of open spaces and the loss of the heat from the Sun. In reality, as far as the little gentlemen in velvet are concerned, life is probably sweet. This underground creature is protected from marauding predators such as the fox and the stoat. Food, in the form of worms, might be a little lacking in variety but the mole has its own private environment; and has known no other.

Similarly, life below ground for a 22nd century human was also quite bearable. For it was life; survival, and man had to learn to cut his cloth according to his means. In fact, life deep in the mantle of the Earth was more than simply bearable; it was much less dangerous; and far less stressful than had been life above ground.

ABBOTSTONE UNDERGROUND CITY.
2121 (AUCO011).

Ten years had elapsed since the population of our globe had moved to a safe haven beneath the surface.

Still young, lithe and very beautiful, the one hundred and forty-four year old woman awoke with a start and sat bolt upright in her bed. Perspiration was dripping from her body, the bed linen was soaking wet, and her hair was dank and bedraggled from her constant twisting and turning.

However, it was not heat that had forced the perspiration from her body. The interior of her room was not dark. Ana Templeton could not abide darkness; it frightened her and invoked unpleasant memories from her childhood. Sucking in air in noisy gulps, Ana slowly calmed her racing pulse. 'One day,' she whispered to herself, 'I will pop off during one of these.'

Nightmares are the product of vicious demons. Or so the lovely young woman's Mauberian ancestry believed. She well remembered the stories told by her grandmother, whose given names Ana had answered to for the first eleven years of her life. 'Ana Carla.' Akin with most other humans who lived alone, Ana spent most of her days talking to herself.

She knew that Hayley Templeton had convinced her to drop the middle names that linked her adopted twins to their Portuguese and Timorian roots. Wishing to give her new family the best chance of integrating into Australian society, Hayley had advised the twins to discard Carla from Ana's name and Vincente from Joe's. But when alone, the twins occasionally reaffirmed their background by addressing each other using their mother's chosen names.

For Ana, her most vicious demon was a regular visitor. Always during the dead of night and never quite the same. Her nightmare starts as a heart-warming dream. Ana is looking down upon her mother in a large bed and with a man who wears the face that Ana associates with that of her father. With her back to her husband, her mother has pushed back hard into the arms of her father, in the characteristic sleeping position of a happily married couple. All is peace and apart from the ticking of a clock, there are no other sounds to be heard. In the large bed, there is no movement; no sound; none of the snoring, grinding and dribbling that is usually associated with a person who is deeply asleep.

Silently, and without the slightest creak or groan, the door to the bedroom opens. Two children enter the room. One a girl; the second a boy. Uncannily, they look remarkably similar in shape and build. The girl leads, as she would for the rest of their lives. Ana cannot see the faces of the two children; there is a fuzzy haze round their features. She cannot actually see that they are boy and girl; she just knows them to be so.

Tiptoeing towards the bed, the girl turns and holds a single finger in front of her lips. *'Keep silent,'* the silent sign commands. *'Do not disturb Mama and Papa.'* Both children wriggle between their parents, the girl behind her mother and the boy in front of his father. Suddenly each parent tickles the nearest child. They were awake all the while, waiting for their children to join them in the huge bed.

The haze around the children's faces clears. Ana can now see the features clearly. They are those of herself and her brother at about seven years of age. The tickling stops and the family lie in the bed enveloped in warmth, love and safety. Protected always by the wonderful elasticity of family, that can stretch to limitless limits but can never be broken.

It is then that the vicious demon strikes. The door is kicked from its hinges. Pieces of the door burst into the room, imitating a cloud of wooden shrapnel in slow motion. Jackbooted men, faces dark and menacing with eyes glowing with fanaticism and hatred, carrying blood-spattered machetes and cudgels, follow the exploding door into the room. Her parents sit up in bed to face the intruders. Ana and Joe hide beneath the bed-covers. They cannot watch. Sometimes the imagination is more acute than eyesight and in Ana's mind she clearly hears and sees the meaty thumps of the machetes. Her parents make not a sound. The gruff breathing of the attackers and the same sounds that Ana remembers from her visits to the butcher's shop with her adoptive mother are the only sounds.

Silence follows a few short minutes later. There is a deathly hush in the room; and all movement has stopped. Joe has disappeared. She is alone in the bed but she feels more, she feels alone in the world. She is lying on her back, inside the small tent-like shape of the bed linen.

Bright red blood is dripping through the sheets on to her face and chest; the smell is nauseating; and her throat, constricted with fear, gags at the awful stench. Her eyes are blinking rapidly, like a window opening and closing during a storm, and the trembling jerks of her body seem to synchronise with these optic movements.

She is so frightened. Each time she opens her eyes, there is light above the bed covers. Suddenly, this light is extinguished. Darkness. Instant terror. Her body suddenly rigid with expectation, fear and loathing. Rough hands grab at her arms and legs, holding her in the classic X position of sacrifice. She struggles; the cords in her neck bulge, but no sound comes forth; she cannot scream. She feels the pain; the ripping and tearing of her flesh; the warmth of the blood turning to icy cold; just as her heart does. She feels the coarseness of the military uniform chafing her skin and the man-stink of her violator will live in her memory for the rest of her life.

'You evil, cowardly, bastard!' The words exploded from deep within Ana's body. They were the catalyst, which never failed to return her mind to the present.

Ana stood upright. The nightmare always unsettled her for a few hours following its unwelcome visitation. She stretched, and marvelled at her body. 'One hundred and forty-four years old and not a single wheeze or blemish.' The mirror told her that her beautifully formed and delicate features were those of a twenty-something year old young woman. Each morning she expected to see the first signs of ageing; but none appeared.

Set on a single floor, her living quarters are standard issue. A large apartment with two en-suite bedrooms, living room, dining room, kitchen and utility room. Each room is reached via a long, wide hall.

Located within the lithosphere of the Earth, her apartment is part of the city that lay between ten and thirty-two kilometres deep. It consists of twenty levels. Each level is twenty-five kilometres long, one kilometre wide, one kilometre in diameter and separated from adjacent levels by one hundred metres of solid rock. Each level is crisscrossed with enormous Mantellium beams, set in a complicated honeycomb structure, giving the complex both strength and flexibility.

Ten of these levels are dedicated to accommodation. Although designed to accommodate an initial population of five million people quite comfortably, the population density of the complex can easily be increased to cater for as many as fifty million.

On the ten accommodation levels, the main tunnel houses the recreation amenities: sports pitches, golf courses, swimming pools, skate parks, ski slopes, etc. These main tunnels are constructed along the line of a gentle declivity, which levels occasionally to form small plateaus and gives the impression of a descending series of valleys. Tree-lined streams cross and re-cross the valleys, which resemble a multitude of anabranches leaving and rejoining the main channel.

Drilled at ninety degrees to the main tunnel are the apartments, built in smaller tunnels of five hundred metre diameter, extending outwards for at least one kilometre.

Levels 1, 2, 19 and 20 are filled with circulating seawater. These four tunnels, together with similar vertical tunnels to each side of the complex, act as a cooling barrier. The chiller system continuously circulates water to and from the single massive ocean covering the Earth's surface.

Level 3 houses the social areas, restaurants, bars, shops, work places, information technology areas, learning establishments and communications facilities. The accommodation levels are located on levels four to twelve and fourteen. Level 13 does not exist; man has come a long way since the azoic period but numbers and colours considered unlucky are still avoided. Level 15 is used for transport systems, sixteen for military and tunnelling activities, seventeen for agriculture and eighteen for heavy engineering and waste disposal.

The sliding door at the end of the hall in each and every apartment gives access to the underground city's transport system. An absolute marvel of design and engineering, it not only links every single apartment, level and amenity but also provides access to the thousands of such cities throughout the mantle of our planet. Within each city, at a constant speed of 50 km/h, a continuously rotating band of compartments circles day and night, with individual compartments leaving and rejoining the main loop as and when required. The transition from horizontal to vertical movement is seamless, as is that to faster inter-city travel.

Passing through the hall in her apartment, Ana glances out of the virtual window. In the main tunnel of each accommodation level, where normal human social activities are concentrated, an artificial weather system has been installed. Ceiling levels are at about eight hundred metres and weather systems are programmed to mimic automatically the seasons of spring, summer, autumn and winter. The artificial sunlight so accurately resembles real solar rays that grass, shrubs and trees grow as realistically as they had above ground.

Without light, life underground would be impossible. And the law of ancient lights is unintentionally preserved by providing virtual openings in the walls. Within the confines of each apartment, the virtual windows display whatever light or weather system the occupant desires. Ana's was currently programmed to show a bright, sunny day and subtle dimmers diffused the light into softening sunbeams throughout the apartment. The sunbeams do not appear and disappear, as in the blink of an eye, but seem to possess a mystical effluence and appear to gently flow into the walls of the apartment under some unknown, intangible influence.

'What's it like in Town?' The main tunnels in the city under the Hampshire Downs are known collectively as the Town. In response to the spoken command, the skyscape in the virtual window changes slowly to display a cloudy and wet day. *'Suits my mood,'* Ana decides.

In the kitchen, Ana goes straight to the coffeepot, already simmering on the work surface. She prefers to drink her own rather than the automated version. The walls of her apartment are the same uniform colour throughout the city. Adamantine, as bright as a diamond and with an adularescent milky-blue sheen, the walls reflect and react to the light within each room; and the colour succumbs to an albescent reaction as they near ceiling level.

Kitchen utensils are made from a different Mantellium metalloid, deep blue in colour, which resemble azurite, that colourful mineral consisting of hydrated carbonate of copper. The lines of kitchen tools glisten in the artificial light, matching the appearance of a washing-line pegged with crystal glass ornaments or gemstones, each diffracting light in a multitude of directions.

She sees her face in the reflective surface of the coffeepot and watches the sudden, unbidden tears fall from her eyes. The nightmare has upset her greatly, as it always does; and just for a brief second she allows her thoughts to descend towards morbid reflection. 'Maybe even death will not shield me from this hellish nightmare.' She speaks the words to the reflection in the coffeepot.

Her birth mother had raised her to be a staunch Catholic and for several of her early years she had supported Catholicism and all its beliefs. But after one hundred and thirty-seven years, she now understands that such beliefs are nothing more than false hopes; nothing more than the doctrines, dogmas and policies invented to counteract early man's belief in dragons, ghouls, ghosts, demons, heaven, hell, Satan; and Those Almighty. Calling upon the mercy of a heavenly being to help her had died in her heart during the seventh of her long years of life when a mindless creature had also robbed her of her hopes of love, marriage, children; all those things to which a woman is entitled as her birthright.

For her nightmare did not entirely reflect the truth. When the hand that encased her tiny child's throat was removed, she had managed to scream three words, 'God, help me!' In her direst moment of need, that entity had chosen not to hear her plea; and in that very moment, she had known that He did not exist. No God could possibly ignore such a plea from a child. In the years to come, her intelligence scoffed at the various religious leaders who attempted to postulate reasons for her hypothetical questions. She never called for such help again, not even when her mother disappeared with the sinking Tetum in the turbulent waters of northern Australia.

The air is fresh and clean. Ana breathes deeply of it. Her mind assesses this realisation. She remembers how polluted the breathable air in the above ground major cities had deteriorated over the last century.

That obnoxious chemical sulphur dioxide was the main pollutant associated with large, above ground manufacturing cities. By the year 2100, half the world's population lived in urban areas, where sulphur dioxide concentrations regularly reached damaging levels. Towns and cities were usually built in valleys or low-lying areas, and this together with the millions of people burning fossil fuels, running engines, and the outputs from millions of factories, produced the almost lethal cocktail that man breathed. Attempts to wean mankind from the use of fossil fuels failed miserably. At the time these fuels were still in abundance and man was not about to make too much of an effort to replace them as a fuel, at least not until supplies became dangerously low. And certainly not, whilst there was a profit to be made and taxes to be extracted from the population.

Added to this were the still lingering effects of the asteroid strike in 2062, increased tremendously by the terrible effects of the island disaster in 2074. Volcanic activity had exploded around the globe in the years following these catastrophic events. Each eruption hurled billions of tonnes of the loathsome mixture, smelling of burning sulphur, into the atmosphere; and for years it circled the globe, adding to what were already dangerous levels of this choking pollutant.

Ana is happy in her underground apartment. She breathes deeply once again and slowly sips at her coffee. Completely hairless, she looks at her reflection in the full-length mirror. She and Joe are almost identical in their features; particularly more so now that they had both elected to dispense with body hair. She was quite simply a smaller version of her brother, with somewhat different body features. And even these she keeps flattened under her tightly fitting siren-suit.

CHAPTER 35
JOE UNDERGROUND

ABBOTSTONE UNDERGROUND CITY.
2121 (AUC0011).

His eyes look upwards at the synthetic sky. He never ceases to marvel at this wonderful invention and he feels forever grateful that such a system of light production has been possible; a system that so accurately mimics the real thing.

'You are a child of the Sun.' Joe, too, remembers his mother's words. He also has a huge hole in his heart, ripped out when his mother had died. Identical to his sister in so many ways, he has spent a long lifetime wishing for something. He does not know exactly what; he can never quite fully explain it to himself.

His early years had been spent in sunny climes. He had always loved the feel of the Sun on his skin, even as a small baby. One of his fondest memories is that of his mother rubbing the smelly concoction of mashed vegetation into his skin that served as a barrier against the fierce Sun, whilst in the camp on Timor. It was the only protection that his mother could provide; and her calloused hands rubbing this mixture all over his body usually lulled him to sleep.

Since moving underground, Joe's role as the financial wizard in the Team had come to an end. Money no longer existed. And he had found a kind of peace for his troubled heart and mind on level 17, the agricultural level.

Maintained at a constant twenty-two degrees Celsius, this arable farming level is a pleasant place to pass one's time. It is a beautiful and impressive area of the underground city, huge tunnels filled with the natural colours of life-supporting crops.

Joe's eyes look around at the other people working in one of the side tunnels. He finds that he is happiest in this underground farm-yard and he spends many solitary days metaphorically studying his navel.

Level 17 has been expanded to include numerous such side-tun-nels, some much longer and larger than the side-excavations for accommodation. The purpose of these extra long side-tunnels is to provide a method of extracting two of the three basic requirements for plant growth: heat from the magma and irrigation from the circulat-ing cooling shields of water.

'And the third element for growth comes from our artificial Sun.' Joe looks at his companion as he speaks. She is of medium height for a woman, a little over a metre and a half and a little on the plump side. At seventeen years old, she has the rounded proportions of a well-formed woman, startlingly obvious in her skin-tight siren suit.

'What did you say Joey?' Her impossibly blue eyes fill with love when she looks at the man working next to her. She feels a strange affinity towards this quiet, unassuming man; but she does not know whether to believe the story of the Verguide Team. *'How could they have lived for so long and still look so young?'* Paula Enfel had often asked her-self this question, especially of late when her thoughts seemed to be constantly centred upon the young-looking object of her affections.

The occupants of the underground cities are not forced to work. Every man, woman and child is entitled by right to the underground version of LSD; man's Life Sustaining Decadal. A decree which pro-claims that the basic necessities of life are free - thus food, shelter, water, heat, power, communications, transport, freedom, respect, and burial are fundamental basic rights assigned to each person from his first cry at birth to his final death rattle. Individuals choose to com-mit themselves to whatever pastime they are most suited to, or most inclined towards. The sole aims being those of human survival and the safety of planet Earth.

Alfred Leonard

The agricultural level provides light work for a huge number of people. But perhaps work is not the right word to describe the activities on this, or indeed on any other level. Given the latest crop producing methods, it would have been possible to fully automate the food-producing processes. But gardening had been a much-loved pastime for people all over the above-surface world, and more especially for those people who had occupied the islands of Great Britain.

'I was admiring our artificial sky, Paula.' Joe dragged his mind back to the present. 'Life is so much more agreeable when you can feel the Sun on your back.' His voice sounds odd in his ears, as his eyes slowly cast over the shape of the young woman at his side. His feelings towards her are different than his feelings have been towards any other woman. *'Was this young woman the missing link in his life; the missing part of him for which he had searched for so many years; was this love?'* Thoughts tumble over and over in his mind. His stomach feels queasy; his hands suddenly become sweaty; and he senses tiny beads of perspiration break through his scalp.

Not wishing to analyse his turbulent thoughts too closely, Joe surveys the huge gardens around him. The use of soil is kept to an absolute minimum. Whenever soil needs to be used, a system of no-tillage is utilized; but most crops are grown hydroponically on lofty, vertical frames. Irrigation is completely automatic; there exists an abundance of water; and Joe never tires of watching the huge drops of crystal clear water dripping down the huge walls of produce.

In its true sense, the underground cities no longer have access to meteoric water. Man's lifeblood comes from recycled sewerage, desalination, dew point and hoar frost systems. Gigantic quantities of potable water are stored below ground, using existing artesian and man-made wells; and the life-giving substance is distributed using a system of aquifers and karsts.

Each tunnel is packed with produce, a huge aquaculture system that self-generates crops for both food and seed. Planting, harvesting, pruning and the clearing out of old crops; every process is completely automated. The huge mass of vegetable waste is converted into pristine compost, which is used extensively in the ubiquitous terrariums, scattered liberally around the accommodation and social areas.

But suddenly all thoughts of the Sun, the sky, vegetables, food, had gone. Obliterated from his mind by the closeness of this young woman. She has turned to face him and is standing very close to him; so close that he can almost feel the warmth from her body. Shapely arms rise from her sides like those of a ballet dancer; she seems to lift into the air as she pushes herself upwards on to her toes. The world has shifted into low gear; everything is happening in slow motion. Joe is struck dumb, he is incapable of moving a muscle, he cannot even blink - and his eyes are glued to hers, as her face appears to float towards his own. So soft, so warm, so alive, the two closed lips press against his tightly closed mouth. Joe's eyes are wide open but they close when he feels the sweet lips open slightly. He moans softly as his own mouth opens in response to the slow, exciting circular movements of her mouth and his rigid body regains the power of movement when he feels the tip of a moist, sweet-tasting tongue. His arms circle her body and he draws her to him. She presses closely to him and her heart soars as she feels the male response that she has hoped for.

It is a first time for Joe. Throughout his long life, he has had similar opportunities with members of the opposite sex. None had flourished; none had gone beyond a quick hug and an embarrassing, hastily abandoned attempt at kissing. Without fail, his own memory was the mental assassin that withered his feelings, long before they had a chance to blossom. Each time the memory of those strong hands groping at his small body and the dreadful smell of stale alcohol and tobacco on the breath of the drunken man killed his own responses.

Fate had dealt a cruel hand to the siblings; and both brother and sister had suffered the same fate. For Ana's dream was not accurate on a second point. She was not alone in the room when the attack on her took place. Her mind had erased some of the more unacceptable memories to protect her sanity. Joe too had been there all the while and had witnessed the brutal sexual attack on his sister. He had turned away when the painful grip on his face, which forced him to watch, had relaxed sufficiently to allow him to move his head; just moments before the excruciating pain as the man violated his body.

At a loss as to his next move, Joe holds the young girl in his arms. *'One hundred and forty-four years old and I don't know what to do.'* He looks into Paula's eyes as his thoughts tumble through his mind. *'I have the entire wisdom of this world and Veruni at my disposal; but still I do not really know how to deal with love.'* He knows it is love, he can look into the mind of this girl; he can see her thoughts; he sees himself through her eyes: and feels elated.

'I have a story to tell you, Paula.' Joe takes her hand and leads her to a nearby arbour, set into the base of one of the towering walls of vegetation.

As her chosen man speaks, Paula holds on tightly to his hand. She knows some of the details, for rumours about The Verguide Team abound, both in the underground complex and throughout the world before the mass departure from the surface of the Earth. Joe opens up his heart and his mind.

He tells her everything about himself; the good; the bad; the evil; the fierce hatred; and the terrible uncertainty of his masculinity. He also tells her that it is different with her; he is able to see into their future. At their single attempt at natural childbirth, before the advent of cloning, the couple are destined to produce a set of twin boys. He even knows their names and can see their family tree, growing strongly, spreading in the form of a huge oak tree for generations to come.

Wisely, Joe withholds the details of their children within himself. *'A young girl should be allowed her dreams,'* he thinks, pulling her close again and kissing her passionately. He is getting the hang of things quite quickly now!

It was some time later when Joe suddenly remembers that he is expected at the midday Verguide Team planning meeting. 'Come with me, Paula. There are some people that I want you to meet.'

A new serenity, a quietude of assured composure, has settled around Joe. Recent thoughts of relinquishing his Verunian gift of long life are discarded, tossed aside with the knowledge that he now has someone to walk beside him. *'I have a future.'* Joe embraces this wonderful feeling and squeezes the soft hand in his.

CHAPTER 36
JOSH UNDERGROUND

ABBOTSTONE UNDERGROUND CITY.
2121 (AUC0011).

10th December, 2121 (AUC0011). It is his birthday and he is one hundred and fifty-five years old. His large body aches, especially first thing each morning. At such an advanced age, Josh Templeton's large frame is beginning to give him some gyp.

The carefree Australian stretches the muscles in his large frame. Living underground is not a problem for him, despite having been raised in the wide-open spaces of New South Wales. The Team has become quite used to such living conditions over the previous century; and in many ways, they prefer their underground lifestyle.

'Another day, another obsolete dollar.' Just like everyone else who lived a solitary existence, Josh speaks aloud to himself; and his words are usually accompanied by expressive hand and arm movements to punctuate his statements. 'Long, lonesome soliloquies, just like an old speckledy hen, rousting around in the *chook-run* at home.' He spots his reflection in the coffeepot and his words conjure up a deep-rooted and well-loved memory of his mother.

Alfred Leonard

The life of Hayley Templeton had been a busy one. Up from her bed early each morning, she set about feeding and watering man, bird and beast. Vividly, Josh recalled the morning when he had accompanied his mother to the *chook-run*. At about eleven years of age, he was already large-framed, almost as tall as his mother. Whenever his father was away from the property, Josh saw himself as the master of the house, responsible for his mother's safety.

Snakes had been a part of life in Australia. Both mother and son knew very well that these creatures just loved a free meal; and the *chook* eggs provided the means to some easy pickings. In most parts of the property, the large number of dogs, cats and horses kept the snakes at bay. But in the *chook-run*, it was an entirely different environment. This was a large enclosed area, fenced with chicken wire. In the corner of the *chook-run* was a tin hut, inside which the *chooks* laid their eggs.

Inside this protected area, the ground was pockmarked with small holes. The *chooks* attracted other visitors looking for food - mice and rats. The *chook-run* became a small, almost self-sustaining ecosystem where Hayley fed the *chooks*; the mice and rats scavenged on the leftovers; and the snakes feasted on the free-range eggs; and the free-range rodents.

Deep rumbling belly laughs erupt from Josh. His whole body jiggles as he giggles, trying to suppress this laughter. The whole Team are able to overlook each other and Josh does not want the Boss to see him laughing to himself.

But his mind cannot block the wonderful memory of his dear mother. And his mind lights up when he remembers her dashing out of the *chook-hut*; bucket and eggs flying in all directions, mouth agape as she gasps for air, wind milling arms and legs going fifteen to the dozen as she scrambles for altitude. Her high-pitched screams bring the dogs running to her side and she desperately tries to leap over them as they impede her escape.

'Get out of the way! You bloody-buggers!' Her voice is filled with panic as she trips over one of the dogs and falls into the sloppy mess that Josh has recently deposited for the *chooks'* breakfast.

'Sod, sod, sod and bloody Bognor!' Hayley can really swear when she is wound up. But she is ever mindful of her language when her children are close by.

'What's up Mum?' At the time, Josh was not laughing. He was concerned for his mother. Something had happened inside the *chook-hut* and he needed to know just what it was. 'There's a bloody great snake in there.' His mother's breathless words did not frighten the young boy. 'Ok, Mum. I'll sort it out later. Let's go back to the house and have some breakfast.' Josh kept his voice low and controlled, as he lifted his mother to her feet. 'Hope there are some eggs left over from yesterday; the bloody dogs have eaten that bucket full.'

Tears are streaming down the giant antipodean's face. The memory of his mother stirs such mixed feelings within him, hilarious humour, and the bitter regret in the knowledge that he will never see her again. 'She may be gone but she'll never be forgotten.' Josh whispers the words, his heart bursting with his love.

A faint hiss, as the door to the shower opens at his approach. The lukewarm water sprays his body from head to toe and from all angles. Josh still favours the old-fashioned water showers; he somehow does not really feel clean after using the ion-showers. 'Cold, please!' There is no shortage of hot water; the desalination plants and heating systems provide an unlimited supply. The spray of water slowly chills and he recalls dealing with the snake.

He did not tell his mother of his intentions. On his way to wait for the school bus, at the end of the long, twisting driveway, Josh picked up the long-handled shovel from the barn. Gingerly he pushed the door to the *chook-hut* inwards; he was not afraid of snakes but he was very careful around them. 'It's bloody red-back spiders that put the fear of Christ in me.' He said the words very slowly, spacing them out with each carefully placed footfall, allowing his eyes to become accustomed to the dim interior of the hut. There was nothing there, his eyes searched every nook and cranny on the floor of the *chook-hut* but there was no sign of the snake.

'*Perhaps Mum had imagined the snake?*' Perplexed, and not a little disappointed, he allowed his eyes to lift to the roof, anticipating the sight of a few nasty little spiders in the many cobwebs. 'Wow!' Josh leapt backwards out of the hut. He could now see what had frightened his mother. 'You're a bit of a *boomer*, pal.' Josh had stepped back inside the hut and was looking up at the huge, coiled, Australian Brown snake. The roof of the *chook-hut* was also covered with chicken wire, above which had been fixed the sheets of tin to provide shade. It was between wire and tin that the snake had found a warm spot.

The Brown was a big specimen, it looked huge. Josh had tackled several of this species over the last year or so but none as big as this one. In an ideal world, he would have walked away and left the snake to move away in its own sweet time. Tangling with this most dangerous of snakes was not recommended; when they are left alone they are quite docile but when attacked - they fight back. Killing the snake was illegal, Josh knew this; but he also knew that the snake had taken up residence and it was unlikely to vacate its well-stocked larder.

'You'll have to go, blue. Can't have you putting the wind up my Mum.' And Josh swung the long-handled shovel.

'But it was a *bonzer* dance, Mum.' Josh stepped out of the shower and briskly dried his body. Automatically, his hand reaches out for his electric shaver, an instinctive action born from years of repetition. But there is no need to shave anymore; the daily vitamin supplements include a hair-growth suppressant and his body is completely devoid of hair.

'Tea, please.' The command is issued as Josh steps into the small kitchen area. Almost immediately, the large Mantellium mug of tea appears on the work-surface, made exactly to his taste: light-brown, weak, with just a hint of sweetness and not too hot.

Pyjamas and any other sort of sleeping garment have always been uncomfortable for Josh. He sleeps naked and has always done so. Noisily, he slurps at his tea as he falls about the room, attempting to dress with one hand. Finally, he steps out of the front door of his apartment into the transport system. His naval training is inbred and he hates being late for anything, particularly a Team planning meeting.

CHAPTER 37
THE BOSS UNDERGROUND

ABBOTSTONE UNDERGROUND CITY.
2121 (AUC0011).

Modern day troglodytes; Modtrogs. First coined by an article on Noosnet, the name stuck.

My mind was flitting from subject to subject, changing tack as quickly as a leaf floating on the surface of a pond, its path dictated by a fickle wind.

One hundred and eighty years. It sounds quite a short time when the words are spoken quickly. Almost certainly, every man and woman that had walked this Earth would gladly accept a few more years of life, in addition to his or her allotted time.

Lowering my eyes, I look down at the lumps beneath the sheet that make up me; and I marvel at my physical condition. But within this body of a twenty-five year old, there resides the mind of an old-age pensioner. Or so it appears to me this morning.

Gazing up at the ceiling, I am fully awake, yet not quite totally aware of my surroundings. I am lying on my back, peering up at the beautiful blue of the artificial sky. It seems quite normal to me but of course, it is nothing more than a computer simulation. No more than five metres above my body but truly realistic. The software engineers of the 22nd century are extremely proud of their simulated weather programme. Strange! It is almost as if I am lying in an open field, with the warmth of a balmy summer evening enveloping me. Illusion city, this is how I think of this man-made sanctuary. Above me, the sky appears to extend higher and higher, deepening in colour and blackening as it merges with space. In my focal illusion, my eyes seem capable of seeing through the atmosphere that surrounds Earth. The programme is so good that it changes the depth perception of my eyes, so much so that if I concentrate hard enough, I can see what I take to be infinity.

Time. Possibly man's greatest obsession. Clock watching. By the clock. If time permits. Given time. Early, late, punctual. All of these words and expressions have almost disappeared from Modtrog's vocabulary. The passage of time is no longer measured against the movement of the Earth around the Sun or by the movement of the Moon around the Earth. For they are no longer visible, except through the power of Noosnet.

'We measure time in a different way below ground.' My mind clings to this thought. I cannot move away from that single thought. It circles around in my head endlessly; and I seem incapable of dismissing it. To drag my mind away from this single, pointless brain activity, I force myself to consider our new method of measuring the passage of time.

AUC. *Anno urbis conditæ.* A Latin expression, which roughly translated means 'in the year from the time that the city was built'. Almost three thousand years ago, the Roman Empire measured time from the date that the city of Rome was built. It seemed fitting that those moving underground should follow a similar system. The basics of the world's old celestial system of keeping time had changed.

Even before the move underground, man could no longer see the heavens; the permanent, dense cloud cover had obscured the bright stars from his view. The Earth's ever-decreasing orbital path around the Sun had also destabilized the Moon's orbit around Earth and our nearest neighbour in space now took almost five weeks to complete its orbit. Also, as an atheist community, we considered it entirely inappropriate to base the passing of the years on the birth date of a fantasy being.

Noosnet still tracked time in the old world's conventional way. But the new system is used for all day-to-day practical purposes and by mutual agreement in every underground city throughout our planet. We still measure twenty-four hours as one day, use the existing days, weeks, months, and allocate three hundred and sixty-five days to each year; but discard the 366th day in leap years. Today, Noosnet informed me when I asked for information about any special events concerning me, was Wednesday 10th December, 2121, in old money; Josh's birthday. In our new timing system, it is day number three hundred and forty-four of our tenth year below ground; therefore 344AUC0011. It is 08.30, and my Pewi displays the time as WED-0830-344-AUC0011. And this is the standard time on planet Earth; time zones and seasonal adjustments have also been discarded.

Thinking of our new time system terminates my cranial inability to register more than one subject. Slowly, the lids descend over my eyes. All is blackness. I can feel my visual acuity leaving my body and venturing into the labyrinth of apartments that make up the bulk of the underground city. Something had disturbed me and I knew that I would not be able to rest until I discovered the reason.

My mind's eye saw many things whilst floating on my visual magic carpet. I was able to look into each and every compartment in the city. Nothing blocked my vision, I could see through anything. I eavesdropped on private conversations; witnessed every human activity; and sometimes I could even tune into the dreams of my fellow Modtrogs.

And in the daydreams of one man, I found the problem. About thirty-five years old, over two metres tall and sporting a full-length beard. Both his beard and the long, skimpy hair are white; the kind of bright white that normally comes with extreme old age.

The daydreamer is smiling. The kind of self-satisfying smile that comes from a mind that is content, fulfilled, trouble-free and passing along a well-trodden path to a known conclusion.

But the words are those that I had wished not to hear in our city. They are out of place and very much a potential problem for me. 'The cross of Christ is my light. Lord, hear my prayers, I beseech thee. I have renounced you to my peers, but you know that I am a true believer; and that I will never accept the religious demands of this place.'

Resting in the palms of the man is a small bible. I feel a sense of shock and for a few moments, I am unable to understand how the man had managed to get the book into the underground city. Almost as a second birth, everyone who migrated to the underground cities had agreed to enter completely naked; just as they had been born. They arrived empty handed, without a single possession. The city would provide all their needs and there was no place for individual wealth or possessions.

Turning my mind back in time I searched for the moment that the man emerged from the ion-shower and took his very first step out of the cleansing station. He walked away briskly, towards the underground city's transport system and his new home. He was just a very tall man, with a long beard and long hair. But the bible must have been concealed somewhere and as I forced my vision to penetrate the hair on his chin, I saw the small book taped to his neck.

'What do you think, Boss?' The quiet voice startles me for a moment. I am still hovering over the tall, bearded stranger. Josh has joined me; he too had felt uneasy and had ventured forth to find a reason.

'I think he must have hidden the bible beneath his beard, Josh. That is the only way he could have carried the book into the city.'

'Yep, I think you are right, Boss. And he has broken the pledge.'

Entry to the underground cities was purely voluntary. Of the thousand or so available around the globe, most were non-religious. Each city had its own simple oath stated by all who chose entry, together with an equally simple set of rules. The pledge and rules were decided by a Noosnet survey amongst all who wished to live in each city. For the Abbotstone underground city, the pledge taken by all who entered was: 'The City is terra nullius. There are no Gods. I will obey the rules of the City'.

And the rules of the city are: 'The City, and everything in it, is res nullius. All persons are equal. All persons are atheist. All persons have suffrage on reaching the age of twenty-one. There will be a decemviral committee (The Committee) elected by the population, and a single primus inter pares (The Governor) elected by the Committee. The first Governor will be the Verguide.'

'Meet me in the Committee Room, Josh. The others will be there shortly; we will have to deal with this person.' Reading my thoughts, Josh left our celestial meeting place and returned to his body.

Reunited with my own body and without conscious effort, I reel in my wandering alter ego. 'Call a Committee meeting,' I instruct my Noosnet Pewi.

I step out of my apartment and dial level three. The city is designed to isolate completely each individual's living space; the better to ensure the eradication of any neighbourly disputes. Noisy neighbours are rarely a source of irritation in our underground world and garden fences to argue over no longer exist. Superbly sound-insulated, each apartment is identical, again to diminish man's natural traits of jealousy and envy. If a family is too large for a single apartment, then it is assigned sufficient contiguous apartments to satisfy the family's needs.

In the Town, the simulated weather system is that of a grey, overcast day. Heavy clouds, dark and ominous, float overhead. Occasional light showers wash over the floor, giving it an allusion of being highly polished. A glow of continuous light lay beneath my feet, produced by forcing huge shoals of noctiluca from the surrounding ocean through the floor levels of the city.

Although the weather is inclement, it is not cold; the temperature below ground is never allowed to drop below a comfortable twenty degrees Celsius. I am sitting at a small table in one of the many piazza cafés scattered around the Town. A large, multi-coloured umbrella shelters me from the showers and I watch in fascination as the huge droplets of water fall from the clouds above. My vision slows each droplet, to such an extent that I have time to follow each fat globlet as it falls through the air, hits the floor and shatters into oblivion with a meaty-sounding blop.

I am the first of the Team to arrive. Josh will be along in a few minutes and I delay ordering breakfast until his arrival. Most of the

younger members of the population choose to survive on food capsules; small, colourful pills that contain all the protein, trace elements
and carbohydrates required by the human body to survive. The older
generations still prefer more solid fodder and usually eat their meals
in their living quarters, with occasional social visits to the cafés and
restaurants.

I feel on edge, unsettled. What was about to happen is the first
occurrence of this kind; the first person found to have broken the
pledge. We, that is the five million people in the city of Abbotstone,
had been living deep below the surface of the Earth for ten years. Our
numbers had not increased during this first decade; the expected gradual accretion in numbers had not materialised. And this trend was
duplicated in almost every other complex around the planet, much to
the consternation of the various City Governors.

Maybe it was little more than a metagenetic phase but mankind was
slowly dampening down the raging fires of his carnal desires, especially amongst the younger generations. Genetically identical organ-
isms, or clones, produced by fully automated systems from a single
parent by asexual means: this is to be the new order. The human race
no longer trusted in nature and confidence in the traditional method
of reproduction had diminished slowly during the past decade. Ever
since the first Rhesus Monkey, called Tetra, was successfully cloned
in the most recent millennium, man had been striving to perfect the
cloning method of propagating our species. The haphazard fusion
of male and female gametes was considered too inefficient and produced too many defects. The natural child came without a guarantee;
it might be deformed or mentally defective; or develop into a sub-class
of killer or criminal. GIGO, as the old computer adage claims, if you
put garbage in you will get garbage out. And the garbage of humanity
were the flawed individuals who seemed to lack, or suppressed, the
genes that provide each human being with the attributes of personal
control and discipline necessary to behave as normal, rational people.
They became self-centred solipsisms, 'I want, me - me' morons, totally
selfish and totally oblivious of the feelings of their fellow Earthlings.

Attitude suppressive additives, intended to reduce man's natural
appetite for violence, social disorder and general troublemaking, are

included in our food pills. But not all choose to consume this type of nourishment, so the ASAs are also added to drinking water. They help - a little. And incidents of unsocial behaviour are rare. Of those incidents that do occur, most are incited by one man's relationship with another man's woman. Cloning is seen as the means to a utopian existence for mankind in a place of harmony and peace; a Shangri-la or synergetic paradise.

Noosnet contains an enormous amount of information on the subject of cloning, commonly known as the Twigging System. The scientific sector had been claiming enormous breakthroughs over the past century; and mankind, weary of the criminal antics of the social miscreants in its midst, appeared to be in a state of limbo, intentionally restricting the natural method of reproduction whilst awaiting the phoenix of Twigging.

Thunder rattles in the distance. I count thirteen seconds before the strike of simulated lightning flashes overhead. The lightning is completely harmless and as it strikes the plankton-filled floor, it triggers a countless number of bright beams of light to explode upwards, emulating a huge silver firework blasting off in all directions or a gigantic diamond reflecting the Sun. The sound of the thunder and the amazingly bright rainbows produce an incredibly beautiful, almost attention-grabbing, *son et lumière*.

My eyes look down the long township. The Committee room in front of which I presently sit is located on the highest tier; and the town appears to lie at my feet as a series of escarpments, or hanging valleys, sloping gently downwards. The cooling of humid air, cresting over this gently rising landscape, produces orographic precipitation - rain, snow, fog, whatever the weather system is programmed to simulate. I can see fountains of warm water, spraying high into the air, surrounded by small wisps of steam as the warmer particles of water meet the slightly cooler air, attempting to copy small Gibraltar *levante* clouds. Through the trees, I can see a large swimming pool, a golf course, a school and a funfair: and I know that a whole host of other amenities, available to our people, are hidden from my view.

I know Josh is there before I see him. Forcing myself to become invisible, I attempt to hide from him. *'Don't try that trick with me, Boss.'* I hear his thoughts. *'I know you are there.'*

The giant figure ambles towards my table. He is light on his feet, almost ethereal, and as he approaches me through a sudden shower, the lightning cascades around his feet. For a few brief seconds he disappears and re-materializes suddenly, giving the illusion of man given life by the fiery bolts from on high.

'Happy birthday, Josh.' I greet the Australian giant. 'And how does it feel to be one-hundred-and-fifty-five years old?'

'Thank you for remembering, Boss. As for how I feel, we must have a chat later.'

We had known each other for a very long time. I did not need my gift of entering another person's mind to know what was troubling him. Similar to my own feelings, he was considering the possibility of ending his stay on Earth. A chat with Belial First would decide the future for both Josh and me.

We sit in companionable silence for some minutes. The aviculture enclosures are alive with small birds, twittering in the branches of the trees once again now that the thunder had stopped rumbling in the distance. Much of the fauna and flora from the Earth's surface had proved impossible to bring underground, particularly the large and dangerous predacious animals. But smaller versions of birdlife, such as sparrows, tits, robins, yellowhammers, etc., appear to thrive. All require artificial feeding, since butterflies are the only species of insect brought below; and there exist far too few of these to feed the birds.

Birds are a messy species. They spray food in all directions when taking sustenance from the feeding stations and their droppings splatter the floors of their aviaries. But a nightly wash through with fresh, warm water quickly restores the areas to their former pristine state.

'But not yet, Josh.' I speak aloud. 'We cannot desert the Verunians, they have not failed us, nor lied to us. We must make sure that there are no attempts to impede their joining us here on Earth.' I think for a few moments and add: 'Who knows, maybe old Belial First's claims of transmigration might be an additional option.' Josh gives me an odd look, obviously disappointed in the direction my thoughts are taking him. 'How do you feel about a couple of thousand years in the cryobank and being reborn in another body, Josh?'

'I will have to think about that one, Boss,' Josh replies. 'Sounds like a load of *borak*[35] to me. And frozen ruddy solid doesn't do a lot for me!'

'And, Josh.' I hesitate when I spot Ana coming towards us and add hastily, 'We still have to deal with Saladin. He must be well over a hundred years old now and we cannot allow him to go to his maker without telling him the truth.'

Josh chuckles wickedly. 'Yes, Boss. I am really looking forward to that little job.'

'Looking forward to what?' Ana had heard the last few words from Josh as she arrives at our table.

'Saladin.' The single-word reply tells Ana all she needs to know; but at that particular moment in time, she has no wish to think of the leader of al-Shamshir.

The still radiant girl sighs, 'Hi birthday boy.' She speaks, as she seems to float on to the huge lap of Josh. Gravity below ground had been reset to a much more comfortable level. Everything weighed much lighter than it had on the surface of the Earth; and the human bone structure was subjected to far less strain.

Over the years, Josh and the twins had become a second family to me, almost as if they were my own children. I allow my eyes to scrutinize Ana. She is dressed in a shocking pink siren-suit, which emphasises every womanly curve of her slim body.

Although the siren-suit is the only mode of dress available in the Abbotstone complex, individuals do, at least, have a choice of colours. Worn for a single day at most, most men opt for the colours of nature; brown, fawn, green, black or white; whilst almost any colour is chosen by women. Dhobying is a thing of the past and at the end of each day, the siren-suits are dumped into a gash-shute, one of which is fitted into every compartment of the city.

Nothing is wasted. Every item of waste material, both human and natural, is discarded into this disposal system. Again, the whole system is completely automated; whatever can be recycled - is, and the

---

[35]*Borak*. Australian for nonsense

system provides a number of bi-products for the community. The siren-suits, delivered automatically on demand, are just one of these bi-products. Anything that can be liquidized is returned to our drinking water systems as fresh, potable water. Activated sludge helps to cleanse the mass of excreta egested from the body and also the manufacturing effluent that passes through the huge sewage system.

Many of our people had found it difficult to accept this recycled water. Although our cleansing systems produce a product that is completely odourless and tasteless, free of viruses, bacteria or hormones and with zero risk to human health, it is the knowledge of its origins that deterred many. Generally known as the disgust reaction, people knew that this *l'eau de toilette,* or recycled effluent, had passed through a variety of human bodies and had been mixed with human wastes, urine, faeces, blood and gore. Disregarded was its multi-stage refinement process, including ultraviolet disinfection, advanced oxidation, reverse osmosis and ultra filtration. The end product is most probably more pure than desalinated or rain-water. But in the final analysis, primal instincts often overwhelm scientific blurb; and humankind felt uneasy about drinking the water, believing that once water has contacted something 'nasty', it retains the essence of that contact.

'And how many years young are you today, Josh?' Ana knew exactly how old Josh was; she was simply filling a gap in the conversation. 'One five five and counting,' Josh answered. 'But I am not as old as the Boss. One hundred and eighty!' Josh shouted the number, imitating the call of an old-time darts commentator.

'Let's order a drink.' I changed the subject. 'Joe will be here shortly, with the rest of the Committee, and you both know what a ticklish problem we have to deal with.'

'Yes, we most certainly cannot allow this man to get away with his deceit.' Ana paused in mid sentence; and rose to her feet. 'Here comes Joe and it looks like he has got his arm around a girl!' Ana's voice sounded incredulous.

'Well strike me pink, the boy's blushing.' Josh also climbs to his feet and holds out his hand to an embarrassed Joe. 'Who's this pretty little thing, Joe?' Josh continues, wrapping his huge arms around the pair of them.

Regaining his composure, Joe introduces Paula to his family. 'She has consented to declaring a lifetime commitment with me.' The religious ceremony of marriage is no longer performed since the move underground and the general acceptance of atheism.

Instead, a simple ceremony is performed, where couples agree to live together as the basis of a new family unit; and the union is shown on the city's records as a dyad. Banns are not called in any churches; parental permission is not necessary: all that is required in terms of formality is the acceptance of the man's proposal by the female. The only official requirement is that the short enactment of the ceremony must be broadcast on Noosnet. Every action or word on this communications medium is filed and recorded and thus becomes the official record of the union.

At such times, when in the company of the very young, I often feel like a creature from another world. 'Welcome to the family, my dear.' I feel a bit of a prig, holding out my hand to the child which, to my complete surprise she ignores, throwing herself into my arms instead. 'I have so wanted to meet you Verguide.' The whispered words in my ear somehow fill me with a warm, fatherly feeling; a sensation not felt by me for many long years.

The future Mrs Templeton is not in the slightest bit awed by being in our company. She turns from me and launches herself into Josh's huge bear-hug. 'You have got to be Josh.' She pauses for a few seconds, thinking deeply. 'And I think that I am to be your sister?' The question was asked of herself, which was fortunate because at that time the Team did not know the answer.

Lowering her heels to the floor, Paula turns to stand in front of Ana. The two women look at each other for several minutes, not saying a word, until Paula finally walks very slowly into Ana's embrace. 'And a sister too.' The words are spoken almost in awe of the fact, as the realisation of the new family that her marriage will bring to her dawns into her consciousness.

Much later, inside the committee room, I look around at the Decemviral Committee. This is not a specially built place; simply the lounge of a vacant apartment. Five men and five women each hold a single vote. As the Governor, I do not vote unless a casting vote is required.

Alfred Leonard

During the last few years, our city had required very little in the way of hands-on government. Policing is no longer necessary, since there is very little crime; and the military deal with any unruly behaviour or domestic disturbances. Our people do not have vehicles in which to flout the rules of the road or maim and kill their fellow road users; neither personal valuables nor money exist to be stolen; and there are no banks or building societies to attract those seeking to improve their lot by dishonest means.

Obviously feeling a little peckish, Mrs Gabriella Maston popped a food-pill. She had been elected to the Committee on the day that it was formed. A prolific sculptor, she had been both extremely wealthy and extremely famous in the above-ground world. In the past few years, she had become the leading exponent of a new art form, hydrothermal sculpting, and had already produced some startling examples which were displayed throughout the city. Today, she looks trim in her siren-suit. Gone are her piles of money and gemstones. Gone too are the enormous wrinkles of fat that had pushed the needle on her scales to a point opposite the one hundred and forty kilogram indicator.

The human stomach grows larger in direct proportion to the amount of food stuffed into it. And our food-pills have several other common benefits, in addition to their behaviour control and drug-dependency override effects. Eating disorders have been eliminated. There are very few fat people in the underground communities and none at all amongst those that choose to extract all of their nutritional requirements from the small capsules. The long sought after cure for the common cold and all forms of the influenza virus had been discovered as long ago as the 2020s. At first, the formula had been purchased by the multinational drug companies and quietly hidden away from the public in fear of diminishing returns on existing remedies.

Not surprisingly, Mrs Maston is extremely happy with her new slim-line shape. She does not mourn the lost trappings of wealth and privilege; as with her eight husbands, they were gone and forgotten. Since moving to the underground city, she has reduced in size by almost eighty kilograms and is now a shapely size fourteen. Allied with the reduction in gravity, her feelings are of lightness and echo those of being reborn. Where once the simple task of climbing on to the scales required as much effort as climbing a mountain. Now everything is a breeze, from shopping antics to bedroom antics.

Forming a frame with her fingers, the sculptress focuses on Josh. *'Now there's a challenge for any woman - wow! What I wouldn't give for that!'*

'Methinks the sculptress turneth temptress,' I muse, eavesdropping on the lady's thoughts. At forty-two years of age, she is a most attractive woman and her bubbly, girlish character belies her intelligence. I allow myself to dally in her thoughts for a few moments longer. As an ex-matelot, very little shocks me but her mind filled with lascivious intentions towards every man that her eyes rested upon! Reminiscent of a young child in a sweet shop, she wanted to try them all.

'Watch out Josh, you might be husband number nine.' I wink at Josh as I send him my silent message. *'Buckley's chance, Boss. Buckley's chance.'* After all these years, Josh still loved to throw a few Australianisms into his manner of speech.

Suddenly the room is full of people. The final five members of the Committee have arrived together. With Ana and Gabriella Maston, Fiona Lyson, Abigail Fullerton and Jane Ashcroft make up the five lady representatives. Josh and Joe are joined by Andrew Petrie, Gordon Chaworth and Nigel Nimes, which completes the male section.

Josh receives much of the early attention and is offered a shaken hand or a kiss from each of the new Committee members in turn; in addition to numerous birthday wishes. Each had received a reminder from Noosnet that it is Josh's birthday.

The Committee know each other well. From the hips upwards, Fiona Lyson is a strikingly attractive woman but she is a woman with a fish's tail. Her spindly legs are painfully thin and bent outwards at the knees. She has spent over fifty years soaking up the cruel jibes from her fellow human beings. 'Where's your horse, missus?' 'Hey lady, you'll never catch a pig with those.' 'Wow, you must have been a busy town-bike, gal.' But it was only those that did not know her, or the very young, that teased her. Fifi, as she prefers to be called, is the person on whom the hopes of the entire underground world are pinned. For she is the leading geneticist of the day, and the main contributor of articles on the Noosnet twigging site.

Tobacco is not banned in the city. Anyone is quite at liberty to light up a cigarette, pipe or cigar, wherever and whenever they choose. And for the first six or seven years below ground, the habit proved too difficult to shake for many people. One of these people was Abigail Fullerton. A sixty-a-day addict for over fifty years, she is lucky to be alive, for her lungs are lined with a terrible black, slimy secretion, which produces a continuous tickle in her chest. Abi's ancestors originated from the West Indies and her bald scalp glistens under the bright artificial sunlight. A professor of engineering, she designed the teach yourself education system for all ages, in use throughout the world. She coughs continuously but since the inclusion of a habit-repressant in the food-pills, she has managed to quell her lungs' demand for tobacco: even her cough is not quite so harsh and incessant.

The cleanliness of the air is the reason why smoking is not banned; and also the main reason why Abi is still alive. Hugely efficient pollution extractors suck every single tainted air molecule from the cities. Black-smokers and blow-holes, gigantic caverns built just below sea-bed level, provide a route for polluted air through air-pressure release valves into the sea. Fresh air is produced by subjecting seawater to an electrolysis system, which automatically takes in seawater, dissolves the seawater into its component parts and gives pure, fresh air to the inhabitants of the underground cities.

Her ladyship. The nickname with which we tease the fifth female member of the Committee. By her first marriage, some forty-odd years ago, she had metamorphosed from plain Jane Smith into Lady Jane Fenchcoombe-Ashcroft. Despite coming from an ordinary working class family, Jane had not married for money. She had loved her husband dearly for the three years that their marriage lasted. A wealthy landowner in Berkshire, her husband had met his untimely demise in the wreckage of a glider which struck a church steeple whilst attempting to land in a pea-soup fog. During her three years of marriage, her ladyship had delivered three healthy children, all boys. It was to these three boys that she had dedicated the rest of her life, refusing the considerable number of subsequent offers of marriage.

Her ladyship does not regret the loss of her lands and money; neither does she yearn for a return to the class system of her above-ground life. It is said that death levels all distinctions; the move underground had the same effect. Only one person in their city answered to a title. The Governor. All other persons are equal in status; there are no lords, ladies, barons or earls. None consider themselves to be of a better quality; none expect others to act as servants or affect grandiose behaviour because of their perceived birthright; or amass land and wealth to reflect those affectations.

She is comfortable with what she sees reflected in her mirror. Plain Jane, once again, suits her just fine. Two disappointments mar her ladyship's otherwise perfect life. Firstly, on each and every day since his death, she wishes that her dear husband had lived to grow old with her; and secondly, she feels a deeply-felt desire for a grand-daughter. Nine boisterous grandsons are a joy to her but how she longs for a girl.

A man of fine wine and fine wit. Andrew Petrie had been born in Scotland but had chosen to live in the south of England. Previously CEO of the largest chain of food shops the world had ever seen, he now devoted some of his time to overseeing the food production system below ground. At the peak of his company's world dominance, there had been a branch of Gastros in almost every town or city.

At eighty-two years of age, he is the oldest member of the Committee, apart of course from those of us who no longer count the passing years. A renowned viticulturist, his knowledge of fine wine is legend, as is his capacity for consuming it, and his happiest moments are when messing about amongst the grapevines on the agricultural level. He possesses a mordant tongue and can, if he wishes, reduce a person to the point of tears with his withering comments. The old gentleman also has at his command a wonderful sense of humour and has amassed a huge collection of comical stories and jokes, a selection of which trip off his tongue at the slightest provocation.

When not involved with food or wine production, this man helps with programming the system that keeps the shops stocked with the basic, everyday necessities of human life. Computer-assisted manufacturing techniques controlling a workforce of androids ensure that the simple things in life such as combs, nail files, tooth brushes, toothpaste and the like are readily available. In each shopping centre or mall, there is at least one large emporium which offers a wide selection of various goods, from toothpicks to toilet paper.

Such goods are manufactured either by the android force or by the voluntary efforts of the people but all are offered for the benefit of the population. The people of the underground cities take what they need, when they have need of it and without payment. Noosnet identifies the location of any particular human necessity and whether or not that requirement is accessible to those in the cities. 'Pre AUC' is the answer given by Noosnet to any request for items no longer available or needed by the below-ground communities.

Unfortunately, there is usually at least one bad apple in every barrel. As a retired professional politician, Gordon Chaworth had performed within his political world with a total lack of distinction and a total disregard for his constituents. But of the people inside the room, only myself, the Verguide Team and one other know this fact. To all others, he gives the impression of a man who cares passionately about all things under the Sun. In the past and in common with almost every politician, he knew how to placate the masses; how to turn aside the awkward question by launching himself along party lines about a completely different subject; how to appear to say the right thing; how to phrase a statement that included a hidden get-out clause; how to appear attentive to his audience without actually listening to a word being spoken; and how to drone continuously about the 'blasted Whigs', who were responsible for all his party's failures. 'There will be no tax rises during this Executive's period of office', appears to be a categorical statement of an intention not to increase *any* type of taxation. But it offers an opportunity in the future to claim that the statement referred only to direct taxation; and thus allowing Brobdingnagian increases in indirect taxation.

Sneaky. The word perfectly described Mr Chaworth. As a young man, he had been almost a saint. The first and only son of a Bishop, he had been ordained into the priesthood and served for a few years in the parish church of St Just. When he retired from the church at the age of twenty-five, he gave as his reasons that he was 'Weary of this ritualistic life', adding that 'I am reassessing my faith' and the age old chestnut 'the Holy Father has a different path for me to tread'. In truth, he was inordinately fond of fondling the young girls in the church choir. His bishopric father had turned a blind eye to the cries of indignation from his wayward son's parishioners and destroyed the letters of complaint. Defrocked in the eyes of his father, the young Chaworth turned his face to the nation's capital; turned his hand to poetry; turned his expensive education towards drinking, and debauching around the sordid clubs of London; and turned his life into a continuous state of grossness and vulgarity.

Thus perfectly prepared for public office, he entered politics. A glib tongue, a ready wit, allied with a devious tendency and natural cunning, backed by a last-ditch financial donation from his father, propelled Chaworth into a Labour seat in England's Coalition Executive in 2080. There is a fine line between truth and deception and the newly-elected member of the CEE quickly acquired the essential skills to extract huge personal gain from the public purse. Opportunities for free travel around Europe were virtually endless and each opportunity was eagerly grasped by Chaworth, who managed to justify enormous expense claims during his many 'fact finding' trips.

Involved in many of the *chronique scandaleuse* so prevalent in late 21st century politics, Chaworth somehow managed to extricate himself from any real punishment when carpeted before his Mediator.

In his latter years, the retired CEE member turned his efforts towards writing. Firstly his memoirs followed by a collection of fictional novels that miraculously managed to satisfy the terms of the copyright computer and were eagerly turned into print by publishing houses starved of new ideas. Whilst not receiving rave reviews from the general public, they served to occupy the time for the old bachelor as he headed towards his day of atonement.

As an old man, Gordon Chaworth is a lecherous old devil. An excessive and compulsively tactile old man, he cannot resist caressing the female body. Small girls remain his favourite target but of late almost any female was acceptable. I watch him now as he stands behind Fifi Lyson, his left hand resting on her upper arm as he leans forward to whisper a greeting; as he moves away his fingers pass lightly over her breasts in the briefest of contact. Some day, we will have to deal with this man.

In contrast, the final member of the Committee is a thoroughly good man. A barrister in the above-ground world, Nigel Nimes at forty-two is the youngest member of the Committee. An absolutely brilliant academic, Nigel had excelled in all things. A tad under two metres tall and strikingly handsome, he chose to retain his full head of curly hair, worn at shoulder length. No one is perfect and a single vice marred Nimes' perfect character; vanity. Unconsciously, he continuously runs his powerful hands through his hair, drawing attention to his flowing locks and pleasant facial features.

Nigel is a good listener. Whenever a point is made by another member of the Committee, his powerful body remains erect and perfectly still; and his eyes bore into the speaker with an unnerving intensity. He detests Gordon Chaworth. Normally a mild-mannered man, Nigel's antipathy towards his fellow councillor is obvious to all; and the venom in his voice when he speaks of the disgraced clergyman is unmistakable.

On the very first occasion of my being in the company of both Nigel and Chaworth, I had sensed the presence of bad feelings. Chaworth's opening statement whenever he met someone new was invariably, 'What do you think of my books?'

The answer from the laid-back barrister had surprised me; and set Chaworth back on his heels. 'Well, Mr Chaworth. In my opinion your books are little more than offerings of episodic ineptitude. But that, of course, is a purely personal opinion.' By an extreme quirk of coincidence, Nigel had dealt with the Bishop's estate after his death. Chaworth's father had left a codicil to his last will and testament, from which Nigel had learned the truth.

The ex-barrister has one claim to fame; he is the reigning and undefeated Acrostination champion of the underground world. This new game has captured the imagination of every city. Excerpts, passages, lines or words are taken from poems, songs, nursery rhymes, books, films, famous quotations, etc. They are placed on Noosnet and from these clues participants are required to use a certain letter from some of the words to form another word or phrase. The game is a killer of time and an endless subject of conversation.

When not involved in solving the latest Acrostination brain-teaser, Nigel feels somewhat frustrated by the simplicity of the City's laws. Forsaken forever is the legalese associated with the law in the old-world. The tongue-twisting jargon with which Nigel is so familiar, and which is so misunderstood and mistrusted by lay people, is considered to be far too archaic to be of any use in the simplified systems employed in the modern world. NADR, the Noosnet Alternative Dispute Resolution system, has access to every legal case in Earth's history. Each individual case has been de-legalised, converted to the language of ordinary men and can be accessed by anyone with a Pewi.

It is in fact difficult for the population of the City to find very much to argue about and therefore a complex legal system is not necessary. The absence of any monetary system; the complete amortization of all property; the automated production systems; the lack of personal treasures, precious stones and other *objets d'art*; the simplicity of the transport system; and the fact that all their needs are provided at zero cost, cohabit in perfect harmony to produce a near perfect society of modtrogs. But it is entirely probable that the Angels in heaven occasionally find something over which to disagree. And such will always be the case for man.

All disagreements of whatever nature are initially dealt with by the NADR system. Complaints are made by individuals directly into the system from their Pewis. In almost all cases, NADR is the sole judge. After negotiation, mediation and arbitration, the NADR system requires either the plaintiff or the offender to make a public apology. Most people know when they are in the wrong and in the vast majority of cases, the apology is freely given. As time passed, this public arbitration system became the foundation of a more altruistic society and the number of cases reduced year on year.

Every square millimetre of the City is subject to 24-365 surveillance and every thing that moves is tagged in some way or another. NADR can produce photographic evidence to support its decisions, no matter how minor the circumstances of the case. In more serious cases, that is those involving violence, NADR refers the case to the Committee and the military. Within seconds of an act of violence occurring, the NADR system compiles the evidence and sends it to the two organisations. The military pick up the culprit and hold him or her on their dedicated level. In cases of assault, a 'two strikes and out' rule prevails. And the word out has a very clear definition, for the word is also included in the sentence for murder.

An unchanging law, one permanently fixed in the very fabric of a society, is known as a law of the Medes and Persians. In our City there exist two such laws: 1. You must not deprive another human being of life; and 2. You must not breach the rules of the city. The penalty for transgressing these laws is equally as simple: for killing, death; for breaching, expulsion or death. The decision is unambiguous: no ifs, buts or what-if's; no mitigating circumstance or excuse is acceptable; and the use of action-stimulating substances as a reason for committing any offence is considered irrelevant by the Committee.

Arraigned before the Committee, the tall, bearded man sits in a comfortable chair, his legs crossed and arms folded across his chest. Inside the committee room is a large crescent-shaped table. Around the convex side sits the Committee and in the centre of the concave side is the accused. His appearance is that of a modern version of Jesus; long, wispy, shoulder-length hair and a long beard achieve the image that he wishes to project. In his hands he carries his bible, openly now, defiant in his belief that his Maker will save him.

Not a word is spoken. NADR presents the case for the prosecution. The information is spoken and also displayed on an otherwise unseen screen between committee and accused. The words and pictures appear to hang in the air and the clipped and precise voice of NADR reveals no emotion as it speaks the words.

> WED-1332-344-AUC0011.
>
> | | |
> |---|---|
> | Accused: | Ernest Arthur Vidgen. |
> | COA[36]: | 49601236. |
> | Born: | 6th May, 2086. Manchester, England. |
> | Residence: | Apartment number AN58847-11. |
> | Accusation: | Violation of the City's pledge. |
> | Detail: | Involved in religious activity. |
> | Evidence: | (a few minutes of footage from the NADR surveillance system is shown here, clearly showing the accused praying on repeated occasions; and his attempts to persuade others to join him.) |
> | NADR recommendation: | Out/Expulsion. |

'Have you anything to say?' I ask Vidgen. His eyes lift to mine and he holds the bible in front of his face, his outstretched arms apparently offering the book to me.

The man's reply is obviously well rehearsed, he is performing before the cameras of Noosnet; his moment of fame has arrived. Our Lord above had selected him to be the new Jesus, He had sent him to remind mankind that He was the only true God; and he now had a Noosnet audience and the chance of a few converts.

His voice is full of confidence now; his mind convinced that the

---

[36]COA. Citizen of Abbotstone

Committee will not overrule the recommendation of NADR. 'As heaven is my witness, I swear that I entered this City without any religious convictions and without possessions.' Vidgen pauses, awaiting confirmation of his claim by the NADR system. He obviously knows the system and the procedures of the Committee very well.

'NADR sensors did not identify any possessions when this man entered the City and took the pledge.' The even-handed voice of NADR supported the man's claim.

'Only recently have I heard the call from God,' The bearded man continues. Each time he mentions his God, his voice extends the word and the tone of his voice rises by a few notes; as if the word itself conjures up a vision of Him in his mind's eye. 'I left our City just a few short months ago and journeyed to the Christian City of Chester.'

NADR confirms:
Date of travel: 212-AUC0011 (31st July, 2121).
Destination: Chester.
Duration: 7 days.
Other details: on request.

'The right to err belongs to all men.' Religion's latest recruit was beginning to sound more and more like an old-style member of the clergy. An all-knowing, pompous inflection in his voice indicates to all his listeners that he, and he alone, has a direct link with Our Lord above. 'The word of Our Father is within this book.' He shakes his hand, waving the book under the noses of the Committee. 'I found myself to be living in the midst of a city of unbelievers and I brought His teachings with me when I returned to our city.'

He bows his head and kisses the cover of the bible. His voice softens as he speaks his final words. 'Yes, I have breached the Pledge of the City. But I am now a true Christian and as such I no longer consider myself subject to the rules of this city. I am subject only to the Divine Law and His holy law overrules the powers of this committee. I demand that you accept the decision of the City's legal system and expel me to a nearby Christian theocratic city.' Ernest Vidgen closes his eyes and adds: 'In thee, O Lord, have I put my trust. I am the anointed one and You have named me Jesus. Amen.'

Several long seconds elapse whilst I wait for Vidgen to continue.

There being no further utterances, or claims of godly parentage, I look at the two military men. 'Please take Mr Vidgen to the waiting area.' The two military men escort the accused from the room. NADR will continue recording the proceedings, logging every word and movement; but the accused is not entitled to listen to the deliberations of the Committee.

The Decemviral Committee asks NADR many questions. Where Vidgen had stayed in Christian city; the names of the people he had met and spoken to; recent contacts in our own city; times, places and conversations. But the crucial point was the man's entry into Abbotstone when he had taken the pledge. Did he, or did he not have the bible in his possession at that moment? Was he in fact lying about obtaining the book from his recent visit to Chester? The Committee seem to agree that if the bible had been obtained recently, then NADR had the right of the matter. But if the bible had been brought into our city on the day of Vidgen's pledge, then it was a premeditated act and might well conceal an intention to subvert our peaceful existence underground. In this case a harsher sentence might be called for. NADR runs the moment of Vidgen's pledge many times but none, other than the Verguide Team, can see anything secreted on the man's body.

I take no part in the questioning of NADR. My role is to exercise a casting vote and I listen carefully as the afternoon wears on. Finally the discussion dries up. They all look at me. 'Have we all finished?' They each nod in turn. 'Time to vote then.' I pause, looking into the minds of the seven non-team committee members. '*Blast!*' My thought reflects my consternation. I can see that the vote will be equally split. Five for the death penalty, and five for expulsion. The final decision will be mine.

The occupants of the committee room know me and they also know of my powers. 'Before I call for a vote, I wish to show you something. NADR, please re-run the moment that Vidgen entered the City.' The familiar scenes are re-enacted in front of us once again but this time I arrange for the NADR software to temporarily erase the beard. Nestling underneath, now clearly in view, is the Bible.

Gasps of dismay and disbelief can be heard from the Committee members. 'But why did you not reveal this information when we were discussing the case?' The law-man asks the inevitable question.

'For a very good reason.' I pause and look pointedly at the non-team members. 'You may have noticed that neither myself nor the rest of the Verguide Team questioned NADR. I specifically asked Josh and the twins to refrain from doing so. I know that we are not experts in questioning the accused, nor are we skilled at asking questions of NADR. But I was rather hoping that one of you might ask the most important question of all.' Again I pause, and I see comprehension dawn in the eyes of Nigel Nimes.

'Of course, the Bible. We did not ask to examine the Bible ourselves; neither did we ask if NADR or the military had examined it.'

'I'm sorry, Tim,' interjected Fifi, using the forename by which she knew me. 'Fleetingly it did occur to me to have a look at the book; but like most other atheists, I have a strange aversion to actually handling the bloody thing.' She giggles and smiles at me. 'But I did not attach any particular importance to my passing thought and it did not occur to me to ask NADR if it, or anyone else, had made an examination.'

'What would we have found if we had examined it?' Chaworth drags eyes and thoughts from Fifi's chest and manages to ask the obvious question.

'On page 107 there is a blank half page. Here you will find a note, handwritten by Vidgen's father on the occasion of Vidgen's twenty-first birthday. The inscription reads 'Keep the Holy Trinity close within your heart'.

'But all that proves is that the book was in Vidgen's possession on his twenty-first birthday, it does not necessarily prove that he brought it with him on the day that he entered our City.' Nigel is a little rusty maybe but he is used to playing the devil's advocate. 'Without your special gift of being able to give a photograph a digital shave, we might reasonably have assumed that he could have somehow located it in Chester and simply gone to pick it up.' Nigel is speaking his thoughts aloud.

'NADR. Examine the records on the days that Vidgen both left and returned to the City. Analyse Vidgen's person and belongings and report any differences.'

The City's surveillance system is ultra sensitive and ultra efficient. It monitors every single movement in and out of the City, weighing, measuring and recording every person and every piece of baggage. It can zoom in to provide a readout of documents, etc., and instantly highlights any anomalies to the military.

'There were no differences,' the computerized voice replies and shows the contents of Vidgen's pockets and small handbag. There, clearly in view, is the small, unmarked bible.

'The book has no markings on its cover,' I point out. 'And this is why the surveillance system did not highlight a religious document entering or leaving our City.'

'But why didn't NADR provide this information?' Chaworth is beginning to whine, and seeks to heap some blame on to NADR.

'You did not ask.' The computerized voice has the last word.

'Assuming there are no further questions, it is time to vote. A show of hands in favour of expulsion please.' No response, not even a twitch of uncertainty. 'And for death?' Ten arms are raised high and I clearly hear the faint hiss of activity from the NADR system as it records the moment.

When Vidgen is escorted back into the Committee room, NADR has already displayed the case details.

WED-1703-344-AUC0011.
Accused: Ernest Arthur Vidgen.
COA: 49601236.
Born: 6th May, 2086. Manchester, England.
Residence: Apartment number AN58847-11.
Accusation: Violation of the City's pledge.
Detail: Involved in religious activity.
Decision: Guilty.
NADR recommendation: Out/Expulsion.
Sentence: Out/.

Very similar to a wagging, threatening finger, the small curser next to the word out/ pulses expectantly. The system is waiting for the Governor to officially inform the prisoner of his fate; at which point the final word will be added.

The bearded Christian is a mess. His earlier composure and self-assurance have evaporated. Eyes rimmed with black circles, face grey with worry and uncertainty, and with a newly acquired twitch in his left eye, he faces the Committee. The NADR printout tells him that he has been found guilty and he knows that he will be leaving the City; but what is the final word going to be? *'By what right do these heathens judge me? Christ! They had taken a God-awful time to reach a decision. By all that's holy, I would love to give them a severe tongue lashing.'* His angry, almost blasphemous thoughts calm his raging emotions a little and he drops into the chair at my invitation.

'Was it your intention to come amongst us as a missionary?' I begin a series of questions, mainly for the benefit of the NADR record.

'No.' The single word reply bursts from the throat of the Christian man.

'Did you have your bible in your possession when you visited Chester?'

'No. Definitely not.'

'Did you have your bible in your possession when you took the pledge?'

'No, Sir, I did not.'

'Do you accept that all men are entitled to their own opinions?'

'Yes, of course I do.'

'Do you accept that all men are entitled to their own beliefs?' The bearded man looks directly at me. He gives a very tentative 'Yes, but...' in reply. I wait. He cannot resist it; he is a true fanatic.

'All men are equal in the eyes of Jehovah. There is only one true God, who gave His son to save mankind as a whole. There is only one true religion, Christianity. Christians are His chosen people; and the whole of mankind must one day bend their knees before Him. The Decalogue from *Heaven* is the written law, by which mankind shall live. Unbelievers are the antichrist and I pronounce the anathema of God's church upon you all. Only he can grant you absolution. Fall on your knees and praise His name; for He is forgiveness and He is the light. Desert Him and His holy ways and His wrath will be terrible to behold. This city and all within will be cast into the depths of hell beneath His retribution.'

'An old story and old threats; cabbage warmed up again.' I can see that my thoughts echo those of the Committee.

Deeply red in the face and perspiring freely, Vidgen not only has a bad case of religion; he also has a bad case of high blood pressure. He raises his hands above his head, once again waving the small bible under our noses. 'Forgive these sinners, O Lord, for they are blind. Amen.'

'Was it your intention to recruit others to your faith?' My voice does not convey any response to Vidgen's attempted religious rhetoric.

As if suddenly losing all heart or hope, the bible-waving Vidgen allows his head to sag on to his chest. My questions continue for several more minutes but no response comes from the man who sits before us.

'In this case, NADR has concluded that an expulsion sentence be imposed upon you.' I see a flicker of hope spring into the man's mind.

'We the Committee overrule that conclusion. We believe that you obtained entry to our City with the intention of recruiting others to your belief. We have seen proof of your dishonesty and deceit.'

The now familiar shots of Vidgen's movements flash on to the screen in front of us.

'Therefore, it is the decision of this Committee that you pay the ultimate penalty.'

The cursor on the screen moves and prints the word 'death'.

In all cases, the decision of the Committee is final. Appeals are not allowed and the sentence is carried out immediately. In our old world, administering capital punishment was usually an unwatchable, messy and upsetting event; and those ordered to witness suffered a much greater level of distress than those who chose to watch. In our society, the condemned person dies alone. Two methods of execution are available: the choice of which method to be used is offered to the person about to die. Down the gash shute or go for a swim; burn or drown.

Vertical tunnels reach deep into the barysphere of the Earth. As hot as the fires in hell, temperatures reach extreme levels of about four to five thousand degrees Celsius. On level eighteen, the heavy engineering and waste system level, several rooms are provided for the disposal of larger items of waste. The disposal procedure is quite simple - place the unwanted item in the room, vacate and press the button.

The alternative to dying in the core of the Earth is by drowning in the sea. Unmanned and unarmed submarines patrol the ocean. They collect enormous amounts of data from the sea, from the surface and from space, all of which is automatically downloaded into Noosnet.

Vidgen elects to take a ride in a submarine. I watch his mind as he reasons that he just might have a fighting chance if he is released on to the surface of the ocean. What he does not know is that the submarines are designed to eject any foreign matter every five minutes, a design feature to prevent any unauthorized use of these machines. This facility cannot be de-programmed without the agreement of a full gubernatorial meeting.

The holy man reaches his Calvary at three thousand metres below the turbulent surface of the ocean. Clutched in his hands is his bible, open at the page containing his father's inscription.

CHAPTER 38
WEARY MIND, DOUBTS AND FEARS

THREAD:

There comes a time in everyone's lifetime when the act of living becomes a burden. And if you are really unlucky there comes a time when you have outlived all of your close family members.

My daughter Alicia had died in 2030, almost a hundred years ago. Having lived long lives, my three granddaughters, Kacey, Ruby and Lydia, had passed on between the years 2070 and 2083. Being part of their lives had been denied to me and even though this denial had been self-inflicted, continuing to overlook them had become too painful a process for me.

But I missed them. And as each day passed the memories returned to haunt me and cause me pain.

ABBOTSTONE UNDERGROUND CITY (ABUC). 2122.

My job was done. The Verguide no longer had a task to fulfil. For some years I had been feeling my age and after one hundred and eighty-one years of life I had good reason to do so. I was also beginning to fear for my sanity. So many had died as a result of my actions.

Was I merely a pawn, manipulated by the Verunians to achieve their own aims? Was it really necessary to contain the explosion of human life on our planet? Could the Earth have coped with a population of fifty to sixty billion? Only time will answer these doubts and only time will reveal who or what might judge my actions.

Years of life stretched ahead and for me the years looked empty and lonely. Trial and error had proved the accuracy of Belial First's stated limitations placed on my ability to move within time, forward to the year 2130 and always back to the present. Within these constraints, I was able to move quite freely and at will. For most of my life the ability to look forward into the years ahead had been a boon but perversely my restricted forward vision flustered me. With only eight years until 2130, I felt as if I was approaching the end of my life; but no matter how heavy the burden of life becomes, few welcome the end.

Even in the relatively free existence within the underground cities, people still chose some pastime or activity to justify their period of life. For me, the future looked bleak and short. I had no wish to make a lifetime commitment with a female. I had no hopes or desires. I had lived many lives already; there was little of interest for me that I could foresee. Others sought my company and life in the underground cities was rich in so many ways; but my problem was more of a feeling. A sense of not belonging; being out of context by virtue of my old age; out of place - like a comma in the wrong place that makes a sentence meaningless. And the feelings left me somehow unbalanced and unsettled. Nothing grabbed my interest; not one thing excited me; naught fired my imagination; and the butterflies in my stomach had died long ago. For me, the sum of my existence could be expressed very economically with words; I had been born, I had lived and I was waiting for death.

Loneliness was my sole and most constant companion and I spent most of my time isolated, entrenched in my memories of the past, usually with a gormless smile on my face, remembering the times spent with my wife and family all those years ago. I could not contain my longing or hide it from Josh or the twins. They knew what was in my mind, my unhappiness and discontent; and some of what I was thinking of doing; but I dare not allow them to know all of my plans for fear of their attempting to dissuade me.

For some reason, my mind kept returning to the first meeting with Belial First. There was something said at that first meeting that I needed to rethink. I knew that it was important to me but I just could not remember the actual words. Odd really, since I had almost instant recall of any other conversation throughout my long life.

'Belial First, we wish to speak with you.' Ana and Joe forced their minds to concentrate on contacting the Verunians. They had not attempted to do this before and had left this aspect of their enterprise to the Boss. They knew it was possible, they had the same powers as the Verguide and he seemed to be able to make contact at any time.

'I am Belial First. Ana and Joe, I have been expecting your call.' The quietly assured voice entered the minds of the twins, together with a vision of the speaker. But this vision was totally different from that fixed in their minds, that of the body of the visitor on their thirtieth birthday. Gone was the bodily form of a child-like figure, in its place was a golden orb, gently throbbing and floating freely in space. The orb did not have facial features, nor arms or legs. Rather, it oozed an impression, or a feeling, of pleasantness and a benign acceptance of them. The vision seemed to control their own feelings, calming their fears and inhibitions and encouraging them to speak what they felt.

'Speak, Ana. For I know, that you are the one who loves.' The words did not come as any surprise to Ana, it was almost as if she had some pre-knowledge of what Belial First was about to say.

'The Verguide needs your help, Belial. We know that his mind is in the past, he feels that in completing the Verunian task he has missed his true existence. His need is great and we wish to help him.'

'We too know the Verguide's mind, Ana. And we know that you ask out of love for him. I will speak with him. As for you and your brothers, we know also your minds. We see that Joe is happy with his new life, new wife and happy future; we know that he will be content to remain on Earth for the foreseeable future. But we see that he is concerned about outliving his wife Paula. We can grant him a lifespan to match his wife if he chooses. For yourself and Josh, we make a different offer. A life on Veruni awaits you if you wish it. You can learn of the new discoveries that our scientists have made and of how we plan to help the people of Earth render their planet a safe haven for both our civilisations; for all time. Be with us when we migrate to the underground cities that you have prepared for us. There are a great many problems facing planet Earth in the next several thousand years and we will welcome your human participation in dealing with them.'

I was still wrestling with the problem of Belial First's initial conversation. Several times I had the answer within my grasp but just could not bring it to mind. Quite suddenly, as if the information had been deliberately unlocked in my mind, I had it. Something about the human brain. *'Yes!'* I remembered clearly now. The Small Person had said: 'The human brain is infinitely more powerful than man is yet capable of understanding and its retrospective capabilities are almost unlimited.' Way back in the 1960s, I did not pay too much attention to, nor indeed understand, the meaning of the words. But now I was beginning to realise the significance of them.

The Verunian people are different from Earthlings in many ways. They live in another dimension of time. As such they have lived the years that is the future of our world and have the ability to see much further ahead. I also knew that their ability to travel freely in time was a slight misconception, for there were boundaries beyond which even they could not cross. And these boundaries were those of their existence. Mimicking my own limitations, they could go forward but only as far forward as they have lived. However, their abilities differ from mine in that they can go back in time, beyond the present, as far back as they wish; and there they can materialise and exist.

And Belial First had said that the human brain had unlimited *retrospective* capabilities that man did not as yet appreciate. In other words, it is possible for man to go back to an earlier time; and maybe even live another life. Perhaps to atone for a carelessly wasted first attempt; or for wantonly taking the life of another; or to correct a personal habit that threatens a normal lifespan?

'Good God!' I was so flabbergasted that I spoke aloud. My thoughts were mere assumptions but what I had just thought was the closest I had been to a religious notion since the old king had died! At times such as these I automatically slipped back into the vocabulary of an earlier naval life.

Perhaps man's long ago devout belief in super humans and deities was in fact a sub-conscious understanding of the power of his own brain. Man somehow knew that he had more than one chance at leading a good and rewarding life. Maybe what he did not know was that his God was not some external magical being, it was already within him; all that he needed was to learn how to use it.

Impious thoughts overwhelmed the spiritual significance of my newly-found understanding. My thoughts were more of the secular kind. I knew now what I wanted to do. I would ask Belial First if I could go back.

'Your wish will be my command, Verguide.' The words of Belial First burst in to my mind; the Verunian must have been overlooking me. Golden and softly pulsating, the glowing orb appeared in front of me. Slowly it changed and became the same Belial First that I had met in the cave.

'Verguide, dear friend, loyal and true man of planet Earth. You have indeed fulfilled your mission and we Verunians are grateful. I know of your wish to return to a previous time and your desire to lead what you might describe as a normal 20th century life. When you are ready to go, think back to the moment in time from which you wish to re-live your life, exactly as you would return your alter ego from a trip into the future. As a small token of our appreciation, we will send you back with a small gift, a capability of which you will be unaware until the time comes for you to have need of it. We will not communicate again, dear friend. You will live a long and happy life, Victor Yewly.'

'Open.' I gave the instruction for the door of my apartment to open. 'Hello Ana - and what problems have you brought me today?' Strangely, she was alone. Usually she would have one or more of the Team with her when she came to visit.

Something had changed. The minds of Josh and the twins had always been open books to me. I could block some of my thoughts to them but they could not do the same to me. As soon as Ana stepped into my apartment, I knew that there had been a major change in our relationship. She had reversed our roles and was blocking my mind from looking into her own.

CHAPTER 39
KILL SALADIN

THREAD:

My cup was running over, I was bubbling with high spirits, exuberant, totally ebullient. Following my talk with Belial First, I was on cloud nine. I was to be granted the option of going back in time, given a second chance to relive my life as a normal human being. The Small Person had confirmed that going back in time was indeed possible and involved only a small risk. Very occasionally it was possible to get trapped in the time transfer system, especially if some catastrophic event should occur whilst one's alter ego was attempting to rejoin its solid form.

ABBOTSTONE UNDERGROUND CITY.
TUESDAY, 18TH AUGUST, 2122 (TUE-230 AUC0012).

Wandering the deserted areas of my underground city, I was indulging myself with a nostalgic and final walkabout. Enjoying the crispness of the air, the gentle breeze and warm sunshine on my face, my mind was drifting over the details of the time transfer and the arrangements for the next few days. At no time had

Alfred Leonard

it occurred to me that the Team would have overlooked the personal meeting between the Small Person and myself and I assumed that they knew nothing of my decision to accept the slightly risky return to the 1960s.

In concluding our conversation, Belial First and I had agreed that there was a final task that required attention before I returned to the 1960s. A task that had been at the forefront of my mind for some considerable time. We had to deal with Saladin.

Each of the Team knew what lay ahead for each of us. We had all thought long and hard about where and how to spend the rest of our time on Earth. We had acted as a team for so long that making personal decisions was an unusual event. But the Team had made those decisions and I knew some, but not all, of what they had decided; and my reduction in powers no longer allowed me to overlook them. The Team had decided that tomorrow, Tuesday, 18th August, 2122 would be D-day, departure day; and the day that Josh and I would make our way to Noi.

There we would reveal ourselves to Saladin and send him on his way to his anticipated joyous welcome into his Muslim paradise. It was much more likely, however, that his credentials might be considered to be lacking in certain respects; and he might find himself turned away by *Ridwan*, the angel guarding the gate to paradise. In which case, he had best make his peace with *Maalik* who, with his staff of nineteen angels, oversees the punishments in hell.

Later this evening, however, the Verguide Team had arranged for a final dinner together to learn of each other's decision for their individual future and to express our farewells. Emotional goodbyes unman me; I have always found them to be extremely upsetting and I avoid them as often as I can. I was not looking forward to the event but there was no dodging this evening's trying soiree.

A difficult few hours it was most certainly going to be and I was not especially looking forward to the forthcoming events. We had been a closed user group, or a closely knit family, for many, many years. The gift of overlooking each other's thoughts had conditioned our minds to be open in all our personal dealings and mutual trust dominated our relationship.

Whatever the moral rights or wrongs of our manipulation of Saladin; he had been a most willing, if unknowing, accomplice. In so doing, he had amassed an enormous amount of the shiny baubles that were so worshipped and valued by an earlier mankind. He had also revelled in his role. He had killed, or been responsible for the killing of, millions of people and he took joyous pleasure in this bloody task. But he lived under a delusion; a belief that a real Almighty God existed and that this supernatural being had directed his hand in all things; a belief that he, as a man, was not responsible for his actions; and we felt obliged to disillusion him while he still lived. We also knew that Saladin, as Rasul-Allah, had elevated himself to that of a godly deity and ruled Noi in an unforgiving reign of terror.

Wandering aimlessly through the various levels of the ABUC, I had revisited most parts of Abbotstone during this, my last day of living in the future. Sitting in a quiet arbour on the agriculture level, I was trying to keep my mind firmly on the subject of Saladin; but I found it impossible to thrust aside the thoughts of this evening's leave-taking and was slowing slipping into morose despair.

Soft footsteps stopped in front of the bench on which I sat. I looked up and saw Paula. 'You must be feeling sad, Verguide?' Paula had refused to address me by any other name since the moment we had first met. She used it as a term of respect, almost as a child would call a grandparent. For a few minutes I could not answer, I had choked up at the sight of her. 'Joe has told me much of your life story and I have learned much more from the Noosnet databanks but I know little of your life before you met Belial First.' Imitating the actions of a small child the pretty girl reached out and took my hand; it felt small, dry and very smooth and she leaned forward to gaze into my eyes. 'Please tell me about those years.'

In the recounting of my early life, my happy childhood and schooldays, my teens, marriage to Tracey and the birth of my daughter Alicia, and my life in the Royal Navy, I felt a change waft through my mind. Almost as if in the telling of my story my whole being had been reprogrammed to operate in those long-ago times; the beginning of a gradual process of metanoia preparing me for the return to a previous life. Much as would a gentle breeze, it cleansed my soul, cooled my fears for this evening, raised my spirits and rejuvenated my body. A pre-apostate version of myself as a child might well have thought that God's forgiveness had descended upon me. Maybe this was to be my day of atonement and as the thought entered my mind I saw the wings appear behind the head of the young Paula. I heard the tiny ripple of laughter; Paula had seen my vision of an imagined angel in my mind. It suddenly occurred to me that this girl was either extraordinarily fey or had been invested with some Verunian powers by the Small Person. 'Come on, Verguide. You have wasted most of the afternoon wallowing in the mire of your guilt. You must bathe and change for this evening's celebrations. Tomorrow will be Tuesday 230-AUC0012, which you well know equates to 18th August, 2122. And Verguide, we both know that it was upon that very date in 1962 that you fell into the cave in Singapore and met with Belial First.'

The lovely girl who was the highway to Joe's happiness rose elegantly to her feet; she stood in front of me and lowered her face to mine. Placing her hands on my shoulders she kissed me on both cheeks, turned abruptly and walked away. Tears were in my eyes, we both knew that we would not see each other again; that small ceremony had been Paula's farewell.

Later, although not a particularly happy group, we were nonetheless a party of four people determined to make the most of our leave-taking dinner. As I had expected, Joe's young wife had yet again displayed her remarkable insight and refused to attend the Team's final farewells. 'It is a time for the Team,' she had explained to Joe.

'*My powers must be weakening,*' I thought, realising that I could no longer read the thoughts of the Team as they entered the dining room. Of late and on decreasingly rare occasions I felt addlebrained and acted as would an elderly man struggling to make decisions. Intuitively, I knew that I was returning to the mental and physical state that I had enjoyed in former times.

'Don't worry, Boss. The Team will look after you.' Strangely it was Joe that seemed to have assumed the role of leader. 'And to prepare you for your return to the 1960s, we have arranged a rather special meal for you.' '*I must be losing my wits as well,*' I thought. For I suddenly realised that the Team had indeed overlooked my personal meeting with Belial First and therefore knew of my decision to return to 1962. But they could not know of my other decision, that of the exact time of my departure; I had refused to think of it, closing my mind to the subject so as not to upset the Team.

'Roast beef and Yorkshire pudding.' Ana announced part of the menu, as the team of helpers entered the room with the dishes.

'And apple pie and custard for pudding,' added Joe.

'*Et plusieurs des bouteilles de vin blanc.*' Josh's French accent was terrible but we all got the message.

'The beef might taste a bit fishy but use your imagination.' Joe was clearly enjoying himself and felt it necessary to hint that the synthetic beef might not live up to my expectations.

Sometime later, after consuming several glasses of the delicious wine, I broached the subject of our departure. 'We are all aware of Joe's decision. He could make no other than to remain here with his wife. But what of Josh and Ana? What decision have you arrived at for your future?'

It was immediately apparent that Ana was to assume the leadership in her new partnership with Josh; for it was she who replied to my question. 'We have decided to accept an invitation from Belial First. He has recognised that life here on Earth for both Josh and me will be somewhat less fulfilling without you. Although I dread leaving my little brother, I know that he will be more than content with his life and will make a fine Governor and Chairman of the Decemviral Committee. But Josh and myself have other needs and Belial First will require human representatives when the population of Veruni join us here. Josh and I are to be Earth's ambassadors on Veruni, until and beyond the date on which they are ready to move. Until that time we will live on Veruni; learn all that we can of their advanced civilisation; come to terms with their technology; and if necessary find a way of dealing with Noi.'

Tears sprang unbidden into my eyes, my emotions were running away with me and I was finding the events of the evening very upsetting. After several deep breaths I continued. 'From Paula's reaction this afternoon I am now sure that you all know of my decision to return to a previous life. And since you can all read my thoughts you will know that tomorrow Josh and I have a final task to perform. Belial First has made all the necessary arrangements.' Tears ran down my cheeks, I could not suppress this indication of my deeply felt emotions and for several long minutes I remained silent, desperately trying to compose myself and also regain control over my speech functions. I sensed that the other three members of the team were in a similar emotional state and I could hear quiet sniffs from Ana and Joe. With croaking voice, I tried to carry on, one sentence at a time, gathering myself between each. 'You will all know full well what is in my mind. And I am sure you will also know what is in my heart. As a team you have been my willing associates, my right hand and on many occasions my guiding light. But more than this you have been my surrogate family. Although I know it to be impossible, I still hope that if I am allowed any memory of my years as the Verguide, then that memory be of you.'

It was too much. I could not go on. Pushing myself to my feet, I held out my arms and we came together in a group hug, sobbing uncontrollably.

The room was large and ornate. Strangely misty, it was as if a very heavy fog had recently been warmed away by the heat of the Sun. Liberally scattered around the room were examples of old-world treasures that only vast wealth can afford. The kind of wealth acquired from a grateful nation of dutiful subjects, every one willing to donate their time and strength in providing lavish rewards for their much-loved leader.

At one end of the room stood a throne. Made from solid gold it was supported by eight massive statues of angels, each one cast in solid gold and festooned with glittering jewels. The throne appeared to sit upon a trilithon suspended above the heads of the eight angels, barely touching the fingertips of their raised hands.

The roughly-hewn walls were covered with thick, colourful carpets and the floor was jet black, smooth and shiny, made from some marble-like substance mined on Noi.

The room was filled with people but there was total silence. Wielding archaic automatic weapons, stern-faced guards stood with their backs to the four walls. Apart from these guards, and irrespective of gender, each person was dressed similarly in white one-piece garments; long loose-fitting robes reaching down to the floor, with voluminous sleeves but without a hood. All were bare-footed and of veils and *niqabs* there was no sign. Clearly there was little need for purdah or any necessity to hide one's face in this modern all-Muslim community. Huge doorways at each end of the room provided a single access and exit. Heavily guarded, these doorways controlled entry to the throne-room; as one person left, another was admitted from the other end of the room.

To one side of the vast room was a small alcove. A simple, brightly-white silk curtain served to conceal the contents from view. Inside this alcove the aroma immediately identified it as the personal living space of a very old person. Surrounding the body on the bed, the air almost crackled with the pungent smells of faeces and urine. What remained of the person on the bed had lost all control over its bodily functions.

Bones as brittle as matchsticks and joints riddled with arthritis, the old man could barely move. Sparse, silver strands of hair jutted from the skull and from the beard on the chin. On each side of the gaunt, heavily wrinkled face, the ears stuck out, emulating the handles on a saucepan; and they too were festooned with long grey hairs. The ears were overly large and elongated, as if weighted down in a deliberate attempt to increase their length. The gaping, perpetually open mouth mimicked baby-chicks in the nest squawking for food; and revealed but two stumpy black teeth.

Visitors kept their distance from this gaping orifice, for the evil-smelling air escaping from the bulging stomach hinted of death and pestilence. Hair follicles in the eyebrows had ceased to grow many years previously and a carer had pencilled-in large, young-looking replacements; which gave the face a bizarre mummy-like appearance. Barely perceptible, the very slight up and down movement of the chest was the only visible indication of life.

Until that is, the eyes opened. Visitors to this most revered of Muslim leaders could still see their own fear reflected in the steely, intensely blue orbs. The eyes of man are the gateway to his brain and emotions; the collectors of information; and the window through which others may deduce hidden secrets and feelings. They can lie with consummate ease; display every conceivable human emotion; set traps for trusting and unwary watchers; and when set within the picture frame of a pretty female face; they are sometimes able to lead a man to a lifetime of pain, heartache and grief.

Blazing still with the fanaticism honed from a lifetime of self-belief, the eyes of this old man bore witness to the sharpness of his brain. As such, the man was dying the most horrible of deaths; that of a continuing mental functionality that could not be translated into kinetic movement.

Alfred Leonard

During the period of the Team's relationship, only occasionally had it been necessary for me to play the role of leader and insist upon a certain course of action. In the methods and planning for the assassination of Saladin, I was to exercise this prerogative one last time.

Visitors were *persona non grata* on Noi. An absolute monocracy and ruled by the iron fist of The Prophet; its borders were closed to the Universe and access to the underground cities was denied to all unless sanctioned by its tyrannical leader. A two-class nation of priesthood and proletariat, all Noians worshipped one Maker in heaven and answered to one mortal man on Noi. They worshipped Saladin, Rasul-Allah in this life, and dreamt of the day that they would walk in paradise with the one true Allāh in the next.

Countless space probes from Earth had visited the Moon during the 21st century. Some were manned and others were not; some under the guise of peaceful scientific exploration and others seeking a more sinister advantage for one or other of Earth's war-mongering nations; some looking for benefits for mankind and yet others with an eye on the main chance. Much of the Moon's surface had been sold to gullible Earthlings by shifty entrepreneurs preying upon the dreams of mankind. But from 2105, when Earth's only moon was permanently occupied by the Muslim race, all previously-issued deeds were revoked, the international *terra nullius* agreement cancelled, and Moon exploration ceased.

At the same time, Earth witnessed the nascence of a new policy on space exploration. For as long as Earth was capable of supporting a human population, man would refrain from seeking out other planets and the possibility of discovering other life forms. There were still the sceptical amongst us who could not accept the Verunians' claim that no other life forms existed within the known Universe. And we kept our fleet of spaceships circling our planet and our early warning systems far out in space, largely as a sop to the sceptics but also as a warning to Noi that we were not a harmless and defenceless sitting duck.

The people of the Earth, however, continued to trade with Noi. There was little to gain for Earth in this arrangement, the Moon provided nothing of use as far as Earth was concerned. And the transactions were not in the traditional ethos of trading, for monetary gain; but simply because the Muslims of Noi were part of mankind and they had a need of something from their original homeland. In the eyes of the Muslims, Earth had a surplus of two very desirable commodities that could not be provided by Noi. Mantellium and gold. By supplying these essentials-to-life on Noi, the people of Earth sought to ensure their peace and safety. Confrontational policies of denial can swiftly breed violent conflagrations; best to set one's feet on the soft approach; let the tongue speak the words of friendship; offer the hand of help and assistance; but do not turn your back nor close an eye.

Neither planetarian wanted the other to set foot upon his homeland, and a system of half-way storage bases was set up to enable trading. As long as the extraction of these two commodities did not weaken our planet, the storage bases were filled by Earth and emptied by Noi.

Dual purpose and mutually beneficial, the storage bases doubled as a surveillance system for both nations. Saladin's military had built an extremely effective defence and monitoring system around the circumference of the Moon, part of which doubled as the half-way storage depots. The rest of this monitoring system was sown as dragon's teeth in the form of a nuclear armoury of neutron bombs. Quite why the people of Noi had deployed these weapons was a mystery to those living on Earth. For there was not the slightest chance of such a weapon getting anywhere near what was once the blue planet; it would be detected and destroyed long before it got close enough to do any damage.

Nevertheless, the monitoring ring of satellites gave both Noi and Earth a total picture of any space vehicles nearing either world. It was completely impossible for a visitor from another world to make a landing on Noi without the Muslims being aware of the event; and the only method of gaining entry to Noi's underground cities was by way of the cargo shuttles from the space storage facilities.

The Team thought that my travelling to Noi to dispose of Saladin was a dodgy business and all three wanted to accompany me. During the previous evening's dinner we had discussed the proposed venture to Noi and with my diminishing powers of reading the thoughts of the others, I was worried that the Abilene paradox might produce a decision that I did not want. It was time to put my foot down. 'I'm sorry people but I have made my decision. I cannot allow Joe to become embroiled in this risky enterprise. He will remain here with Paula and take over the role of Chairman of the Decemviral Committee.' I allowed a certain edge to surround my words, emphasising that my decisions were not up for further discussion.

'We will use the new shuttle with the latest Verunian cloaking systems installed. Ana will pilot the shuttle and deliver a payload of Mantellium to one of the storage depots. From there we will make a normal departure towards Earth but with the cloaking system enabled we will turn back to the dark side of the Moon. Once in geostationary orbit over the crater of Daedalus, Josh and I will alter ego down to the City of Saladin.' I waited for a few seconds, letting it all sink in, and finally added: 'On no account are you to close Noi, Ana. I want to know you are there as my lifeline.'

Throughout the issuing of my orders and during the many hours leading up to this moment, I had steadfastly refused to think of what I was about to add. I knew that if I had allowed myself to think of my intentions, the Team would have found some way to deter me from my chosen course of action.

The lovely face of Ana was looking at me, a puzzled expression and a briefest hint of pre-knowledge lit up her beautiful eyes. 'When Josh and I have done the deed, I will *not* return to the shuttle. It is my intention to return directly to the 1960s. As you know, we have not attempted to do this before; we have always returned to our solid-selves in the time zone in which we left them. But the Small Person has assured me that the procedure is relatively safe, involving only a very slight risk, and that no harm should come to me.'

'But what if it doesn't work, Boss?' Ana's voice was filled with concern.

'That is why I want you in the shuttle, Ana; as my lifeline. If something goes wrong with the time transfer I may need to come back to the ship; so please remain on station for a couple of hours after Josh returns. How you will know if the transfer was successful or not, I do not know. But I will leave it up to your good sense whether or not to contact Belial First for assistance.'

Hovering above the reeking body of Saladin, Josh and I uttered not a word. In alter ego mode we remained hidden from view; and no one had any idea of our presence. But the old man below us sensed something. Sometimes advanced deterioration of the body can heighten the awareness of the mind and Saladin's fleshless arms and legs twitched with sudden alarm.

'Saladin, do you hear me?' Josh projected the thought into the mind of the old man.

Since leaving the shuttle, my original powers seemed to have been partially reinstated and I was able to read the minds of both Saladin and Josh with ease. Obviously Belial First had reprogrammed parts of me for this final mission. A gust of fetid air wafted upwards from the lungs of the old man as he struggled to speak. 'Who is there?' he whispered.

Some heavily pregnant, and all very young and strikingly beautiful, the eight female attendants surrounding the old man's body reacted as one to the words. 'There is no one here but us my lord. We have stopped the visiting faithful whilst you rest.' Soft hands caressed the wrinkled brow of the old man, washed his wasted limbs, cleaned away the mess from the fork of his legs and lifted his head to replace the black turban.

'Gabriel! I hear you.' The sudden blast of sound from the comatose body caused the eight hand maidens to reel backwards. Shock at the unexpected and tremendous vocal noise, combined with a desire to escape the accompanying stench of decaying internal organs, forced them to take a backward step.

'Gabriel! I hear you.' The excited shout from Saladin sounded once again, more clearly now. 'Lord, I thought that you had cast your loyal servant Rasul-Allah into the wilderness. It is many years since I have heard your voice.' The old man's strident voice gained strength and clarity with each new sentence.

Screams from Saladin's young wives brought the guards into the alcove. Assault weapons at the ready, their faces wretched with fear and anticipation, the four guards clad in black now stood motionless in the silence of the room.

Eyes wide and glinting with religious awe, Saladin appeared to be looking beyond the women and guards, focussing on some point in the far distance.

An eerie silence filled the room as Saladin cast his mind back over the recent years. Not once since the Muslim community had occupied Noi had he heard the voice. Many hours had he spent considering this fact and many reasons had occurred to the old zealot. The elderly man's mind had been in turmoil; perhaps Allāh was an earthly god, capable only of influencing the lives of those living on Earth. Maybe the Creator could not project his voice from paradise to the far-distant planets. Alternatively, he might be angry at Saladin's decision to move his chosen people to another world. Possibly he might be upset by some action of Saladin or the Muslim nation. Or maybe Allāh, in his infinite wisdom, had decided that The Prophet Rasul-Allah was Lord enough on Noi.

Whatever the reason, Saladin's heart rejoiced at the well-remembered voice. Aching joints rebelled at his unaccustomed movement as the aged body struggled to find sufficient strength to rise from the bed. Back bent low, the old man tottered towards his throne room, wobbling unsteadily on his feet, much like a toddler taking its first steps.

Guards and female assistants rushed to aid him but he stilled their advance with a withering glance. The entire congregation had fallen to their knees as he entered the throne room, lowering their foreheads to the floor in obeisance.

From some unknown final reserve of energy the crone-like body managed to make its way to the hidden staircase leading up to the throne of solid gold. He lowered his creaking body slowly on to the seat of the throne, lifted his head and looked over his flock. He waited patiently for Gabriel to speak again.

The ear-shattering voice crackled in the air above the cowering assembly. Saladin thought that Gabriel had decided to personally address the church of Noi and every single being expected some new honour to be bestowed upon their illustrious leader.

'Hear me! Faithful Muslims of Noi.' The faintly Australian accent was more apparent when raised to a point where all could hear.

'This man who calls himself The Prophet is a false messenger. He has lived a long and comfortable life as your spiritual leader; secure in the absolute conviction of your unfailing support. He is already in the valley of the shadow of death and has not for much longer to endure his deceitful existence.' An extended pause followed these words, allowing time for the listeners to make their own minds up about possible trickery. 'Saladin Salah! For your sins you will be regarded as a *Jinn*; and banished to hell for your arrogance and disobedience.'

'You can hear a voice,' Josh continued. 'The voice appears to come from the air. You may imagine that it comes from the Bosom of Abraham or you might think that it is that of a Jinnee, sent from hell to frustrate the lives of Allāh's true believers here on Noi. But this is not the case. In a moment or two I will reveal myself and you will see that I am an ordinary man, albeit invested with a few rather special powers, but a simple man nonetheless.'

Slowly, Josh materialised. His shimmering outline gradually took shape, solidified and stood at Saladin's side. Raised high upon the golden throne, Josh looked down upon the assembled Muslims. He smiled his broadest smile and in an outrageous and deeply affected Australian accent said: 'This man is not a God. If you pinch him he will squeal like a stuck pig.' The cry of anguish from the wizened frame of Saladin supported the claims of the large human at The Prophet's side, as Josh searched for sufficient flesh to grasp.

Wearing an Akubra hat draped with dangling corks, Josh epitomized a typical Australian male. Around the vast room assault weapons were raised and pointed at Josh but the distinctive guards, dressed in their jet black copes, dare not open fire for fear of hitting their Noian spiritual leader.

Hands held high and facing the crowd, Josh spoke again. 'Hear me out; do not judge me so soon. With me is another person who some of you will remember from your time on planet Earth. You will know him as the Verguide.'

Theatrical dramatization is not my thing. Throughout my long years I have had many experiences of dramatic-Annies over-reacting to some minor lifestyle problem and each experience has left me with a deeply felt sensation of extreme embarrassment.

But in revealing myself to Saladin, I decided to ham it up a tad. I allowed myself to solidify above the head of the old tyrant, legs folded beneath me as if I was indeed sitting on his head, taking the form of a resting Buddha.

'It is he!' I heard the voice from the silent crowd in front of the throne. 'It *is* the Verguide.'

'Saladin Salah. Do you recognize my voice? Am I not Gabriel, who first spoke aloud to you in the Quba mosque in Medina? Is my voice that which fed you information on targets for your extremist Scimitar groups around the world; kept you informed of miscreants within your own organization; advised and guided you in your nefarious operations; led you to vast riches; and suggested the Muslim move to Noi?'

Unblinking blue eyes gazed straight ahead and the old man nodded his head in a gesture of affirmation. 'Yes,' he croaked.

Slowly I allowed my body to turn and lowered myself to face the old man. He gasped in instant recognition. Old memories flooded into his mind. Memories of the voice that he had listened to so often but to which he could never quite make a human connection. Now he knew. Knew for certain, that he was not the prophet of Allāh; merely a man who had been duped into working for an infidel. The blue eyes blazed into mine. I knew them as well as I know my own. Saladin's pain was clear to see and I could see understanding tearing what remained of his insides apart.

The eyes of the congregation were centred upon me as I rested in midair in front of their religious leader. Amongst these people were numerous members of The Prophet's own family. Throughout his long life he had acquired many wives and concubines. With little thought to the consequences he had sown his seed with gay abandon and had managed to father over a hundred children. In taking his pleasures with women he had no regard for age and droves of very young girls willingly succumbed to his power and charms. Human beings reach an age of discretion at different times; but Saladin rarely waited for his many young concubines to achieve this mental age. 'Old enough to bleed, old enough to breed,' was his maxim.

I could feel the eyes of the congregation boring into me and I attempted to hold their attention by ignoring them completely, my back turned to them as I gazed into Saladin's eyes.

With the attentions of the congregation distracted and with extreme slowness, Josh moved to take up a position behind Saladin; and with equal caution removed the garrotte from his pocket. We had agreed that Saladin had earned both a painful and bloody death and the garrotte, when applied correctly, achieved such an end.

But not all eyes were on my back. Qassim Salah was Saladin's latest and youngest Scimitar leader. Promoted to Masjid-Imām and in command of the Seventh Scimitar, he was Saladin's current favourite amongst his one hundred and twenty-one children. The last male issue of Saladin, Qassim was just sixteen years old. The boy had been conceived during the passage to Noi in 2105 and filled a special place in the old man's heart.

Although a boy in stature, he was a man in every other respect. An in-bred sanguinary character defect, incisive intelligence, and decisive command authority, allied with the deeply disturbing gaze of his father's eyes, made the boy a natural leader. He was the first to react when the garrotte slipped around his father's neck. His weapon may have been old-technology but it was certainly serviceable and the rifle whined as bullets streamed towards the trio on the throne, tracers from the rounds clearly visible in the faintly misty atmosphere.

It is amazing how much detail the human brain can absorb during the shortest passage of time. In the few milliseconds between the sound of the first shots and the first bursting pain in my back, I saw the face of Saladin collapse, eyes bulging and mouth agape in his vain attempt to inhale. Mixed with the sputum from the old man's lungs, blood splattered from the ruptured veins and arteries in his neck, spurting over my face and chest. Consciousness slipped away, I could not arrest the flow of awareness from my brain. Had Saladin died? Had Josh been hit? Darkness was my only answer.

Whenever my alter ego went on its journeys, I had always been aware of not being totally alone. A strong feeling of someone or something watching over me accompanied me wherever I went. I had always assumed that it might be my old friend the Small Person but at no time was I ever given any supporting evidence of this.

And now, after the numbing shock of the striking bullet, I saw the outline of a figure. The shape faded in and out of focus, never really settling into any shape that I could identify - but something was definitely with me.

Colourful whirls of light, fascinating shapes of colour, merging and melting into a visual cacophony of prodding nuisance into my brain. The experience reminded me of my unbalanced, slightly tipsy feelings when gazing into a kaleidoscope as a child.

My eyes opened. Above me, both Ana and Josh peered into my eyes. 'Volly! Wake up, wake up - you must open your eyes.' Concern over-spilled from their eyes into their hands and each attempted to brush the hair and blood from my face and pulled gently at my clothing to more clearly inspect my injuries. 'How badly are you hit - can you speak - can you move your arms or legs?' The questions annoyed me, there were too many of them; and my brain could not deal with more than one thing at a time.

My tongue filled my mouth and was frozen to the back of my lower teeth; I could not utter a word. Desperately I tried to answer the questions and I had some burning questions of my own to ask. Had Saladin died? Was this to be my own death? The fact that Josh was uninjured was not a surprise to me; he had obviously sheltered behind his protective shield and the bullets had been cast aside. This thought raised further annoying questions in my mind. Why had my protective shield failed and what was I doing back on the shuttle; or had the strange outline of another being sheltered me?

But my time in the future had ended. The shapes of Ana and Josh flickered for a few seconds and blackness claimed me once again.

The scene was a sad one. A deeply-shrouded space-shuttle orbited the planet Noi. Within, two forlorn people gazed down at the body of a third, their faces streaming with tears and sobbing uncontrollably. The body on the deck of the shuttle was covered in blood. 'He is going, Josh. The Small Person has him.' Ana could only whisper, she had never in her life experienced such deep emotions and her throat felt gorged with the intensity of her feelings. The body of the Verguide appeared to be passing through a series of amoebic reactions, pulsing and fading as it continually changed shape. The colour of the skin faded to a transparent, chalky white and the limbs twitched and shook, like the body of a soul in torment. 'Goodbye, I love you.' Ana whispered as the body evanesced and finally disappeared, leaving only a discarded siren-suit.

Nothing remained of the Verguide, not even a speck of blood. Wherever the body had gone, it had gone complete. And Ana hoped with all her heart that it was back in time, to where she knew he wanted to be.

EPILOGUE

CONEY ISLAND, OFF SINGAPORE.
18TH AUGUST, 1962.

A crowd of tanned young men stood around a large slab of concrete, their skins glistening with sweat from the hot tropical Sun overhead. The nearby screams and shouts from their wives and children rang in their ears, indicating that the boisterous game of hide and seek was in full swing.

The men were naval communicators, resting between shifts. One of their group had been missing for hours and they had become concerned for his safety. 'That bloody Volly!' The acknowledged leader of the group had spoken with anger in his voice. 'He's never happy unless he is poking around with a bleeding stick.' Brow wrinkled in deep thought, the leader of the group hesitated for a few moments. 'Right, I suppose we had better go and look for the pillock. Let's give the kids a game of mobile hide and seek, that way we can cover the whole island and still enjoy ourselves.'

'Mums and kids, off you go and hide. We will count to one hundred and then come to find you.' Yelping with glee, the children left with their mothers seeking places to hide, their toes kicking up the sand as they raced away from the banyan beach.

It did not take long to find the hidden women and children. There were plenty of places to hide on the small, deserted island but none wished to venture too far from the safety of the beach. They had spied the remains of the buildings shortly after finding the last hidden mother and child and Dicky had extended the game as far as the fallen piles of rubble.

Someone had spotted a leg protruding from under a slab of concrete. The men had quickly surrounded what they thought resembled a grave. The slab of concrete looked very heavy and must surely have killed the person buried beneath it. 'Keep the women away.' Dicky had sent a couple of his watch to send the women and children off in different directions. 'And not a word to Tracey.'

'One, two, three - heave!' Not one of the lifting men could believe how easily they managed to shift the slab of concrete. It seemed to levitate of its own accord. Below was the body of Volly. After a quick check of vital signs, Dicky pronounced him to be alive and apparently uninjured. Dicky gave his friend a prod with a meaty finger. 'Come on you sleeping beauty, you're in the rattle for getting your head down on watch; and scran's up!'

The body did not respond. 'Go fetch Tracey,' Dicky ordered. And while he waited his brow puckered into a puzzled frown. *'Something odd here,'* he thought, looking down at the pale body. *'He is as white as a pongo stepping off the plane at Paya Lebar airport. Whatever happened to him must have frightened the bejesus out of him; he has lost his tan.'*

My eyelids felt heavy. Although I could hear voices, I had no idea where I was. I felt reluctant to leave the dream. I could feel a strong pulse in the veins of my neck; my fingers twitched; goose pimples spread over my arms and legs; and I sensed the warmth of soft female skin warmed by the Sun.

With a huge effort I opened my eyes and looked up into those dark brown eyes that I loved so much.

Struggling with a strangely constricted throat, my tongue felt heavy and I could not speak. The words, when they came, were assumed by those close enough to hear to have come from me.

'Thy name is Belial.' And those few softly spoken words, drumming into my consciousness, would trouble me for many years to come.

ADDENDA

Author's note.

In the telling of this tale, I realise that its ending is somewhat incomplete; and I have a personal detestation for such stories.

Set upon a trajectory of diminishing orbit to certain obliteration, our Earth has been catapulted towards the Sun; what happens?

My hope is that the following addendums might provide a more satisfactory conclusion.

ADDENDUM 1
GOLDEN CARTOUCHES

THREAD:

A single gram of this ductile metal can be hammered flat to provide a sheet as thin as paper and covering a full square metre.

Gold. The very word raises the hackles at the back of a man's neck. At the birth of the second millennium, simply finding the auriferous deposits, which contain this rare and beautiful metal, was becoming more and more difficult. Ever deeper, man's lust for this metal knew no bounds; and the unquenchable thirst for this almost indestructible treasure forced those who sought to wrench it from nature's grasp to take more and more risks.

If man had wings, he most certainly would not be an angel but would undoubtedly be a jackdaw. For both have an undeniable tendency to hoard bright and shiny objects. For the jackdaw it is milk bottle tops, pieces of glass, pretty stones and pieces of shiny paper which the bird carries back to its nest. For man it is gold, the noblest of metals. But unlike the jackdaw, which leaves its treasures on view for any passing feathered flyer to see, man hides his from the view of all but a few.

Strangely, having risked life and limb to extract the shiny yellow metal from its deep hiding places, man shapes the malleable metal into uniform blocks - and stores them in vaults, protects them with unbelievable security systems and allows entry to a very short list of trusted people.

Mankind could not get enough gold. The alchemists' dream of manufacturing this precious metal from other substances lived on; as did their determination to extract the beautiful metal from sea water. Both dreams were as bright and shiny as the metal itself and had filled the minds of man for thousands of years.

The demand for AU79 outstripped supply, every year from 2015 to 2050. That is until a safe method of mining below the deepest sea beds was discovered. Its uses are manifold, from coinage to cleavage. Records show that the world's first known coinage dates from about 650 BC; whilst more recent uses include the infamous, 24-carat sex costume worn by Karat Klondike, the notorious porn star of the 2070s.

National archives also indicate that by the year 2050, some quarter of a million tonnes of gold had been extracted from the earth. Valued at 2050 prices - three hundred trillion US dollars. Of these, about fifty thousand tonnes rested in national gold reserves supporting monetary systems around the globe. And by any known human yardstick, China was the richest nation on Earth; having amassed an enormous declared reserve of 26,492.4 tonnes.

SOMEWHERE WITHIN THE OUTER CORE OF THE EARTH. IN THE YEAR OF OUR LORD 4552. (AUC2442).

No person willingly wishes to vacate his or her space on Earth. Most human beings spend a lifetime searching for a method by which they can leave their mark on our planet when their time to depart is thrust upon them. Striving for recognition in all walks of life, from tiddlywinks to time travel, all have the same goal; find some way for history to at least know your name.

No sound came from the two men. Although quite capable of vocal activity, they usually preferred to communicate using a process of thought transference.

'Heh Uppy, how long have we been out this time?' Ets' thoughts passed into the mind of his friend. Exchanging thoughts was not difficult

for modern man; the necessary methodology and transmission media was programmed into each child clone at birth. But learning to direct one's thoughts to a specific individual and blocking unwanted incoming transmissions required many years of practice.

'I don't know, Ets; couple weeks, maybe more. Or do you want something more accurate?' Uppy spoke his reply in his distinctive high pitched voice. Ets turned to face his friend, a mark of common courtesy when vocalizing occurred. 'No, I was just wondering how much longer we can spend searching this time.' The two men had not voiced their words for some time and it was a mark of their growing frustration that they had spoken now.

'If the Old People could see you now, they would certainly have a good giggle.' Old People was the colloquial expression for the first version of sub- abyssopelagic man to occupy the underground cities, way back in AUC0001. Uppy voiced his thoughts once again, chuckling and lowering the tone of his voice as much as he could. 'First sub-abbo man might well mistake you for a girl.' Both roared with laughter at this suggestion, for they stood well over two metres tall, were slim and lightly muscled, and completely hairless; even nostrils and ears no longer needed the protection of hair, since the air in the Alluvium Probe (AP) was as clean as that in the underground cities. Their bodies were not encumbered by clothing, nor did they wear any adornments or equipment. Everything they needed was provided by their implants or the AP. Information and communication came from the minuscule implants in the head, whilst sustenance was provided by connection points built into the chairs in the AP.

'*Can you guys keep the noise down, please?*' The last of their AP team flashed an angry thought. '*I think I might have found something.*' Silence followed her command; she was the leader of the group. Ets and Uppy felt their heartbeat increase with excitement - finding anything in what was now the Earth's external crust was a rare event.

'*Nice shape,*' Uppy contained his complimentary thought. His leader had stood, revealing her body. As tall as the men, she was definitely female. Similar to the male version she was hairless and did not have any outward indication of a sexual organ; but her ultra-slim, finely boned, shapely outline and petite breasts gave ample evidence of her femininity.

Zand Dwy had occupied her space in her underground city for

forty-two years. Females no longer needed breasts to feed their young and they were cloned without them. Most women, however, elected for a simple addition to their shape before their eleventh year; and the implants were put in place. Perfectly formed and similar in appearance to a breast within a bra of fine silk, they were unmarked by nipple or areola; and most women opted for a small, less cumbersome size.

'*What have we got?*' Ets grew impatient and finally zipped his thought to his two colleagues. '*AP is still evaluating.*' Zand still looked ruffled at the intrusive question. '*She's got a ratty on about something, best keep shtoom.*' Uppy isolated his transmission so that only Ets could receive it, glancing away to hide a brief smile.

Time passed slowly whilst the AP completed its detailed examination of the object. The inside of the AP resembled the interior of a pale-blue egg; and was probably just as quiet and peaceful. Three comfortable chairs, which reclined fully to form beds, were the only hardware in sight. All control was by thought transmission, with the various requested information displayed on fade-away ion-air-screens throughout the vehicle.

'*Time for a top-up then.*' Ets seemed to require considerably more sustenance than his two team-mates. Food entered and left the body in liquid form but not by way of any conventional orifice. For the usual human orifices were no longer necessary on these hi-tech bodies. Human shapeology still found a use for eyes; ears, mouth and nose; but all other entries or exits had ceased to exist.

The almost unconscious concentration of the mind toward a given command was received by the AP's sensors. Confirmation was requested and when given was regarded as the executive command. At the word 'food', a crystal-clear concoction, shaped like a round malleable tennis ball, rested briefly against the stomach and was absorbed through the skin. At the same time, any waste product was extracted from the stomach and disposed of by the AP's systems.

Lying comfortably prone on his command chair, Ets allowed his mind to wander. The AP would give them ample warning of its conclusions. The story of the Verguide never really left his mind and it was an unending subject of conversation between him and his friend.

Humanity still took gold from the Earth. But the risks involved in ripping it from the rock-hard fist of planet Earth no longer existed.

Vast deposits of liquid gold had been discovered hundreds of years before, bubbling gently within the fiery grasp of the inner core. And man no longer took for the sake of taking; he no longer regarded the yellow metal as some sort of trading token or as a means by which one man might rise above another.

And so it was that the search for the casket containing the missing golden cartouches had nothing whatever to do with a quest to obtain fabulous wealth. The two young men had seen detailed plans of the artefact, even knew the secret of obtaining entry, but in their minds they saw it as a fabulous fantasy building, with the spirits of their long-departed ancestors surviving, awaiting their arrival; even to this very day. What the two young archaeologists really wanted was to actually see the cartouches; examine the build process; assess the skills required to build it; read the inscription of worldly knowledge; and the list of names from a bygone age. Not that the wisdom on the golden sheets would be of much value to 46th century man but it would be interesting to see just how primitive their forebears had been. As children on their mothers' knees, they had listened to the story of the Verguide and later they had delved within the archives of the world for further, more detailed information. The deeper they dug, the more intrigued they became.

A Full Life Span Clone, Uppy Urpen had chosen his name about twenty-four years ago, whilst just eight years old. His date of re-cloning as a child was 267-AUC-2410, a date that his archaeological brain instantly converted to 24th September, 4520. He had spent the first fifteen years of his life with his *parents*, the young couple who had made a lifetime commitment to each other and to whom he had been allocated. Not formally schooled in any way, all the information he would ever need was in his regularly updated implant; and any questions answered by his more experienced guardians. At some point he would be allowed to choose his own name, select a career, chase and win a female and eventually be allocated a child clone of his own. His overriding principles were those of obeying the rules of society, extending the boundaries of human knowledge and ensuring the continuity of his planet.

He and Ets had been friends since the naming ceremony. Uppy had no idea how his chosen name had leapt into his mind; it was there and he was happy to accept it. Similarly, Ets Xcrece had made his own choice of name. Neither had wanted to take a name already used and they had made their somewhat outlandish choices based solely on that fact.

Best friends from that day forward, they had chosen a career of discovering and studying the past. A past rich in the written word stored in vast historical databi but the detailed descriptions could never fully compensate for the paucity of artefacts.

Viewed from outer space, the blue planet could no longer be looked upon with the naked eye. To do so, risked permanent damage and necessitated an immediate eye transplant. Still moving nearer to the Sun, the temperatures on the surface of Earth precluded all exposed activity; unless sheltered by one of the super-efficient heat shrouds. Scientists were busily investigating systems to allow the reoccupation of the surface but few really wanted to live in the sweltering temperatures and perpetual fierce winds.

The Earth had now been moving closer to the Sun for about 2,500 years. It had taken only half that time to dry up the huge ocean that covered the surface. During those thousand years, the grinding action of the sea had crushed every feature into sand. This cycle of erosion scratched first at the higher areas of ground still above water and the sawing action of the sea slowly flattened them; and as the thickness of the alluvium deposits increased to a uniform depth the seas reached ever higher, devouring the high mountains as if they were nothing more than mole hills.

No longer blue, our planet appeared jet black to visiting space craft, as the shimmering surface reflected deep space. Earth was now completely enclosed within an outer layer of alluvium that extended to a uniform depth of 6,428 metres, the outer five hundred metres of which had been caramelized by the Sun and formed a solid ring of glass from which the screaming winds removed every fleck of dust.

But there remained various bits and pieces of human occupation located in the accumulated silt. Huge whirlpools had at one time drained the final remnants of water from the surface, leaving spiralling adits deep into the alluvium cover, with huge caverns at their base. Sucked into these whirling masses of water were debris deposits, some tiny and some quite large, akin to the spilled contents of a sunken ship. Whatever their size, they were prized as a glimpse into the past.

Driven by reaction motors, it was the business of the Alluvium Probe to pass through this sea of sand, searching carefully for whatever solids that may have escaped the grinding action of the sea.

'Cavity, cavity, cavity.' The warning from the AP's sensors was vocalized in a calm and measured tone. There was no danger of the sand-machine falling into the cavity, for its own systems would take control in the absence of human intervention. Built of a much improved Mantellium, the craft could withstand any impact or fall.

'*Take us in at the base, please Appy.*' Zand's thought command was acknowledged by both males and the AP. Humankind still loved to assign nicknames to their tools. Although the AP made a sharp downward change in direction, the crew did not feel the move, nor were they aware of any change in their physical attitude inside the hull of the machine.

The AP was perfectly designed to move effortlessly in the sand. By magnetizing the surrounding alluvium deposits and maintaining the AP at the opposite polarity, the vehicle glided effortlessly through its region of uniform magnetism or domain, similar to a snake emerging from the ecdysis of an old skin.

'*She seems a bit happier now,*' Ets sent the thought to Uppy, '*and I mean our illustrious leader and not the AP,*' he added hastily.

Zand was talking aloud. Not for the benefit of the AP's recording system; it routinely copied all thought and voice transmissions and sifted out the personal comments during back-up periods. She was simply excited and spoke without thinking.

'Obviously it must be a new shute and it must be quite deep.' They all knew that the AP had been travelling vertically for some minutes and the machine was programmed not to respond to a previously-explored hole in the sediment.

'Appy is stationary, in free space.' The AP had learned its nickname but reserved the use of it for known happy occasions. Finding a new cave, Appy knew, was such an event.

The crew of the AP felt no indication of their silt-tractor's stop. Standing operating procedures required that they don heat shrouds whenever they left the safety of the AP.

'*Activate shroud, full protection.*' Each gave the order for the protective shield to assume its highest level of cover. '*You never know what's out there.*' Zand Dwy flashed the thought to her companions.

Outside the AP, the crew were invisible beneath their shrouds. As far as the human eye could see, the only indication of their presence was a brilliant circle of gently pulsing amorphous light. A soft blue in colour, the pulse seemed to match that of a heartbeat.

The three circles of light were suspended in the air, floating effortlessly and emulating feathers in a soft breeze. The crew looked back at their craft. Shaped like a bullet but with a snub-nose at each end, it was perfectly smooth; not a single join, seam or external projection could be seen. Neither were there any doors or windows; the crew simply passed through the shell of the vehicle using their 'you-can't-see-me' cloaks. It too floated in the air, its magnetic propulsion system emitting intermittent, corposant signals of light, trying to repel the air as it did the sand.

That electrifying sense of human excitement usually nullifies good sense and judgement, leading man by the hand into all sorts of dodgy situations. Notwithstanding the inbuilt intelligence and common sense of modern man, he was not infallible; and the AP, when switched to guard mode, stayed close to its three crew members. If they split up, the AP remained with the leader and dispatched rescue modules to closely accompany the other two, ready to intervene at the slightest indication of danger or stress.

The chamber was huge, like a vertical oceanic trench. High above them they could see the narrow base of the volute, the first few whorls illuminated by a faint glimmer of light. *'Wow! This is the biggest we have ever seen.'* Uppy was thrilled. *'Look! Over there.'* A flash of brilliant light focused into an intense beam and pointed to a cone of debris about five hundred metres in front of them. At least two thousand metres high, it had the appearance of a small hillock, littered with enormous rock segments, lumps of metal and shiny deposits of unknown origin, the whole covered with a thick layer of dust.

'Breathable air, gravity set to normal surface level, temperature acceptable, environment stable. You may materialize if you wish.' AP reconfirmed its original assessment of the cavern.

'OK, let's give it a whirl. Shed the shells.' Zand gave the order to assume their natural shape. The first few gasps of natural air produced a few moments of coughing and spluttering until their lungs readjusted to less than pure air. Xcrece was mindful to retreat behind his protective shroud but obeyed his leader's quickly flashed thought

command. *'Wait, Ets. You will soon get used to it. And please don't worry about the dust, it will not harm us.'*

As their feet made a gentle touchdown with what was to them the surface of their planet, the three archaeologists felt the weight of their bodies. The AP had adjusted gravity to normal surface levels but these levels differed considerably from those used in the underground cities. The slight difference was felt by the crew members in muscles and joints. They had all been in caves before and were familiar with what to expect but the reaction of their bodies never failed to surprise them. They felt heavier, sluggish, and aware of tiny twinges of an almost unknown medical sensation - aches and pains. Strangely, their mental capabilities seemed to have slowed in time with the heavier movements of their bodies; they felt fuzzy-heady, unreal, misty and somehow different - almost as would aliens in another dimension. It was almost as if time itself had slowed and they had returned to the past and, like ecads, they had been changed by their environment.

They did not walk for long. Moving under one's own steam required too much kinetic energy; and they all agreed to reduce the level of gravity even further to allow them to move more easily. *'We need some help with getting around, Appy. Please fix the gravity level.'*

With the gravity levels reset, the trio had simply to focus their minds to move freely in any direction. Moving swiftly now, they reached the base of the central mound in a few seconds and sank slowly back to ground level.

Peering up at the ectopic mound, the trio were speechless. The pile of rubbish was extraordinary and they stood gazing up at the rising heap in amazement. Similar finds had been made in the past but none as large as this.

'We will need the shrouds now,' Zand advised her two male colleagues. *'We must move carefully, disturb nothing, and allow the sensors to complete a survey.'*

Eight hours later the survey was complete. Sitting in the AP, the team was focally locked-on to the images displayed before them. The comments from the team, both voiced and thought, were recorded by the AP's sensitive systems. *'Unbelievable, indescribable, monumental, at last - jackpot, how do we open it?'*

The AP's systems had peeled back the outer layer of rocks, debris and dust to reveal what lay beneath; and the reason for the height of the mound. The gleaming bright yellow outline of a perfectly proportioned pyramid, revolving in the 3-dimensional perspective provided by Appy. The feelings of the team were mixed, from elation at their discovery to disappointment at the completion of the long quest. They were not the first to search and as in the case of mankind's search for the Ark of the Covenant, many had attempted to find the lost container of golden cartouches for hundreds of years. But theirs was the glory; and theirs would be the names set against the record of discovery, names that would live in history for eternity.

Awed at their achievement, the team waited. Surely the Committee would afford them the honour of opening the golden pyramid and be the first to set eyes upon the cartouches for over two thousand years. The archaeologists had no conception of possession, or individual ownership of anything, anymore than they had any idea of converting the artefact into a monetary value. It was simply something from the past, a part of their history as humans, a tangible example of an item that existed before the last great deluge. Undoubtedly, the consensus of public opinion would demand that the pyramid be recovered and returned to one of the underground cities for further examination.

'Zand, this is the Chairman.' The team were not to be kept waiting too long for a decision. 'The people applaud the achievement of you and your team. The public require that the monument remain in situ. There it will remain, unopened until yourself, Uppy Urpen and Ets Xcrece have completed a detailed examination of the remains of the mound, the cavern and the shute. Our people further require that when the time comes to open the pyramid, Zand Dwy will lead.'

The Chairman waited for a few seconds, to allow time for his bombshell to sink in, before adding: 'My own personal congratulations also go out to you, Zand. And to you Uppy and Ets. I am sure that I do not have to remind you not to hasten the detailed survey of the cavern; there could be other relevant finds to be made. When we have read the cartouches, we will ask you to draft additional pages; and your own colophon. In time, the cavern will be rendered safe for visitors and will form a monument in honour of the Verguide.'

Zand and her compeers returned to work. They needed no other equipment to sift, analyse and catalogue the huge pile of debris covering the pyramid. Appy was quite capable of dealing with it, even lifting the enormous lump of solid gold and placing it on a level surface would not be a problem.

For ten months the team laboured, carefully measuring, numbering and plotting the entire cavern, the shute and the mound. The people of underground Earth watched from afar, goggle-eyed at every new revelation. The team discovered algal remains taken from a diverse number of specimens of underwater life, from diatoms to giant kelp. Strangely shaped rocks, twisted into weird shapes by the actions of water and heat. Diamonds, rubies, pearls, gold, silver; the pretty pieces of glittering rock that early man found so fascinating and over which so much human blood had been spilled. Bones from animals, birds, fish and man. All were regarded as world treasures.

'*Bagged, tagged, tested and posted.*' Ets claimed the last word as the final parcel of specimens was shipped back to their base by the AP. The team had become quite used to walking on the surface and their muscles had grown stronger over the months of activity. By unspoken agreement, they felt obliged to refrain from using their new technology as the golden pyramid was revealed. Apart from a few scratches and gouges, the soft metal seemed to have suffered little from its exposure to the elements. And initial analyses indicated that the golden artefact had not moved far from its original location.

At last, after months of painstaking work, the golden chalice appeared in all its glory. The three archaeologists stood in silence, gazing at the blazing spectacle before them. They each felt the same distortion of perception and memory, a feeling that belied what their eyes could see; almost as if what they were looking at had never been seen before. 'I feel like an old-world person with a psychiatric disorder.' Zand spoke her words aloud but softly, in awe of what confronted her. '*Jamais vu?*' The two men searched their memory banks and nodded agreement.

The vertical height from base to tip was one hundred metres and its base was an exact square measuring one hundred metres by one hundred metres. The AP listed its weight at one hundred thousand tonnes of pure, 24-carat gold. Inside the pyramid could be seen the outline of a large room, about twenty metres square, the contents of which were strewn about the floor.

Entry was via a tightly fitting doorway, centred precisely on one of the sloping sides. A small inscription was etched into the golden door. 'This compartment was automatically sealed at 0001-001-AUC0002; which indicates the beginning of a new day - on the first of 365 days in a year - in the second year of man's vacating the surface of the Earth'. It was signed 'The Verguide'. Behind the door was a passageway that led to the central chamber.

There were no lists of contents or instructions how to open the pyramid; but the AP had already downloaded what it needed to accomplish entry. From above, a broad spectrum of sunlight flashed downwards from the whorls of the shute and illuminated the golden pyramid. The AP concentrated this sunlight on to the golden entrance and waited. It took but a few minutes for the ancient 22nd century software to whirl sluggishly into life, awakened by the power of the Sun and a boot up signal from the AP.

Employing its complement of androids, the AP had constructed staging around the pyramid, from which a narrow set of steps led up to the door. One or two of the worker androids remained on station, awaiting any further tasks. Suspended in the air, they were not fashioned in the image of man but a simple Mantellium central ball, surrounded by multi-implemented arms. They were capable of lifting colossal weights and handling the most delicate of objects.

'*Are we ready, boys?*' Zand was intoxicated with excitement. Her eyes glowed with a burning desire to issue the order that would open the ancient sarcophagus. '*Go, Ma'am.*' The two young men had taken to calling their leader by a new nickname since the discovery of the golden pyramid.

'*Appy, please open the door.*' The command from Zand was witnessed by almost every pair of eyes on Earth; such was the interest in this fabulous artefact. The three archaeologists waited, fidgeting, muscles twitching, unblinking eyes glued to the door, waiting for the AP to manipulate the 22nd century software.

With a huge sucking noise, the door opened. Air rushed into the hermetically sealed compartment and all three of the would-be entrants felt the draught of its passing. Zand led the way, visible, walking normally and unprotected by her shroud. The solid gold floor felt forgiving to the hard underside of her archaeological boots as she walked along the short passageway towards the central compartment. Well lit and of a pleasantly warm temperature, the inside of the pyramid quickly filled with air. The ceiling height was about thirty metres and the impossible blue of the facsimile sky was that of a 20th century spring day.

As they neared the entrance to the core of the pyramid, Zand ordered a stop. Some of the cartouches had come loose from their binders and were scattered about the floor of the passageway and the central area. *'Drone, record what you see.'* Zand gave the order to the worker android to record the interior. While she waited, she issued her final orders to her team. *'Please do not step on the cartouches; pick up those that are loose and place them on the central table. When the Drone has finished recording the interior, we will make our own examination. I am doubtful of any funny tricks or surprises but please be on your guard, just in case. And finally, without teaching a droid how to take pictures, please restrict comments to facts and brief descriptions by thought will do for our initial sweep.'*

'Finished, Ma'am!' Even the Droid had picked up its master's new name.

A resigned lift of her eyes signalled a wry acknowledgment to the Droid. Had she had eyelashes and eyebrows, they too would have lifted but the wrinkles in her forehead confirmed her meaning.

A brief examination of the contents revealed the following. Millions of bound cartouches, each sheet of A4 size and covered in minute printing and pictograms, outlining the worldly knowledge of 2111 (AUC0001). Details of the religious practices of early man; copies of the Christian Bible; the Jewish *Torah*, *Nevi'im*, and *Ketuvim*; the Islamic Qur'an; the Laws of the Bahá'í Faith included in the *Kitáb-i-Aqdas*; the Buddhist scriptures in the *Tripitaka*; and a host of other religious doctrines and dogma.

Every language, nationality, custom; every academic discipline, together with minute drawings of every known patented object under the Sun. The DNA from each and every species known to man; miniature specimens of eggs and seeds from every known bird and plant that once flew or grew on the planet from a tiny blade of grass to the giant Redwood tree; and images of the wonders of the world before the deluge.

The labour of love to copy the writings and drawings into present day computer systems, analyse and check every formula and compare findings with the data already held would take years to complete. In the final analysis, very little new information was found but it did serve to confirm the information already held.

For the crew of Appy, it was their last mission. No more would they endlessly sift through the Earth's new crust, searching for whatever might have survived the grinding seas: that task had been reassigned to lesser mortals. Zand Dwy, Uppy Urpen and Ets Xcrece dedicated the rest of their lives to their partial Augean labour of love; for the work was difficult but not unpleasant.

Each year they added new cartouches, updating the store of information to include present day knowledge, using miniaturized sheets of gold.

ADDENDUM 2
VERGUIDE TEAM'S CARTOUCHES

THREAD:

Ten years had passed since the discovery of the golden pyramid.

MAUSOLEUM OF THE VERGUIDE.
4562 (AUC2452).

The Presence floated down the whorls of the long ago desiccated whirlpool. It was in no hurry, for it had made the same journey on many previous occasions. The smoothness of the gently sloping twists and turns were amazing and the Presence found it difficult to accept that such a precise formation could have been produced by nature.

Arrested in mid air, at the point where the last curl of the shute opened up to reveal the huge cavern below, Liet Armst felt cooler inside his heat shroud. Inside the shroud was the glow of his invisible presence, which in itself did not reveal any information about the occupant. In solid form, his shape left no doubt of his manliness, despite the lack of any defining genitalia.

Full Life Span Clone (FLSC) 310-75-1610 looked down at the wondrous scene below him. It was at the quiet time of the night, when most occupants of the underground cities were resting; and he was alone in the cave-like grotto. 'Just the way I like it.' He raised his voice and projected the words outside the shroud. 'The sound of my own voice pleases me.' He shouted the words and waited a few brief seconds for the echo.

'Hail, Verguide. I visit your spirit once again.' And, as the echoic words returned to him, he thought: *'It's like talking to myself.'*

He never tired of this view. In the ten years since its discovery, the cave had been completely redesigned. Huge stalactites hung down from the roof, covered with the pretty stones of diamond, emerald, ruby, etc., that could still be found within the deep layer of alluvium covering the Earth. Similar stalagmites rose majestically from the floor, seeming to reach up to join with their opposites above them. Boulders of all shapes and sizes littered the ground; flower beds blazed in an abundance of colours, and filled the air with an exotic aroma; trees and vines vied for the space above them, gently bending this way and that in the soft, warm breeze; footpaths paved with solid gold wended their way to the many arbours scattered around the cavern; streams, waterfalls and ponds glittered in the bright sunshine; animals of every species known to man roamed freely in their own, separate enclosures; and birds of every variety flitted amongst the foliage.

But the eyes of Liet Armst could not for long stray from the golden pyramid. He loved the natural look of the cavern but it looked much the same as any underground city. The very uniqueness of the Verguide's monument thrilled its visitor to the very core of his existence and he gazed down upon it for many long minutes.

Emphasising its importance, the monument was raised high above all else. Its surroundings of rock, tree, flower and waterfall blended artistically around its footings and its gleaming surface reflected the sunlight to all points of the compass. A wide, golden verandah had been built around the base of the pyramid; and from this verandah, a single set of stairs led up to the entrance.

As a mark of respect to their long departed hero, people tended to materialize before entry. Most made the transition without being aware of their intention, sub-consciously appearing before the Verguide as they felt he would prefer to see them. Naked and open-handed in the time-honoured gesture that declared that they carried no weapon, their hearts full of love.

The door opened at Liet's footfall and closed automatically behind him. The mausoleum was a world heritage site. Open to visitors at any time, it was never locked. The contents were quite safe; the people of the world no longer vandalised, desecrated, craved or coveted that which was public or beautiful to behold.

Walking tall and proud, Liet had, over the years, become used to the heaviness of his body under the downward pressure of Earth's normal gravity. Eyes wide with wonder, he looked again at the familiar contents of the monument's main chamber. Fingers gently caressing the golden pages, he turned to the opening words of the story that he knew so well. 'Thy name is Belial.'

The well-known story fascinated him. For several hours, the 46th century Earthman read the story again, as he had done so many times in the past. He stood, feeling the unfamiliar twinges in his knees, and turned towards the secret opening.

Discovered only recently, the opening led to four small rooms. Each hardly high enough for a man to stand, the rooms contained the golden statues of the Verguide Team. At the foot of each statue was a simple inscription, enclosed within an elaborate cartouche, identifying the statue.

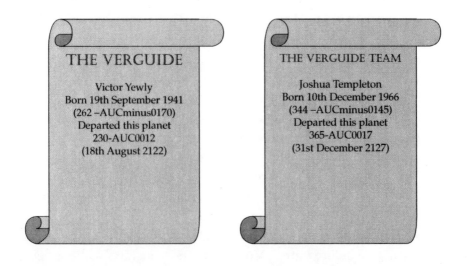

THE VERGUIDE

Victor Yewly
Born 19th September 1941
(262 –AUCminus0170)
Departed this planet
230-AUC0012
(18th August 2122)

THE VERGUIDE TEAM

Joshua Templeton
Born 10th December 1966
(344 –AUCminus0145)
Departed this planet
365-AUC0017
(31st December 2127)

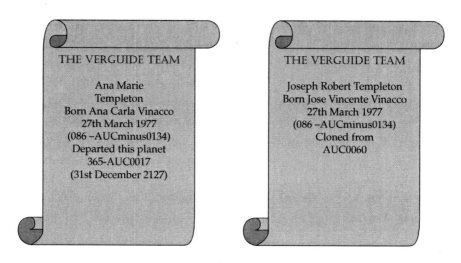

THE VERGUIDE TEAM

Ana Marie
Templeton
Born Ana Carla Vinacco
27th March 1977
(086 –AUCminus0134)
Departed this planet
365-AUC0017
(31st December 2127)

THE VERGUIDE TEAM

Joseph Robert Templeton
Born Jose Vincente Vinacco
27th March 1977
(086 –AUCminus0134)
Cloned from
AUC0060

Liet Armst wiped an arm across his eyes. He always read the story before entering the crypt and the words engraved upon the coffins never failed to wring a flood of tears from his eyes. He felt a strange empathy with the Team and how he wished that he could go back in time to meet them; but the way back had been irrevocably blocked for all time. The events of that era in Earth's history were not to be altered by future generations.

Mentally geeing himself up, Liet wiped the last vestiges of liquid from his face. He had dallied too long once again. He had duties to perform and must record the measurements from the sensors in the cavern. Liet left his favourite spot on planet Earth and started his routine checking of readings from what was one of the world's monitoring stations.

Hovering over a particularly large rock, Liet ordered the system to reveal its findings. 'Maximum surface temperature 148[37] degrees Celsius - Anemometer indicates surface wind speeds of 250 km/h, with occasional haboobs - Actinometer rising - Orbital speed indicates 85,000 km/h, and slowing - Radial velocity plus 0.01.'

Liet's heart missed a dozen beats. Orbital speed slowing! The system had never before qualified its estimation of Earth's speed through space. Dismissing the myriad of other data, Liet went for the jugu-

---

[37]Water boils at 100 degrees Celsius.

lar. *'Show orbit, assess radial velocity.'* The system responded to his cranial instruction and gave its reading, together with a graphical representation. 'Radial velocity at plus 0.01 indicates orbit at zero inbound, moving away.'

Had Liet been sitting on a chair, he would have fallen off it. Zero inbound indicated that the Earth had stopped moving nearer to the Sun; its orbit had stabilized and their planet was now moving away from the dreadful heat of their G-type dwarf star. Into his mind sprang a vision of a blue planet, with deep oceans and life-giving green forests, lush verdant pastures and the vibrant colours of nature.

And into his heart sprang a fierce determination that given a second chance, he and his fellow Earthlings would not make the same mistakes again.

Depigmentated, emasculated but not dehumanised. Liet was an avid student of cosmology and ontology and was partly Earthman and partly Verunian. As such, his character and physical state reflected parts from both cultures, following a natural process of acculturation, and his actions were always tempered by several acquired characteristics. Excessive caution and a pedantic attitude towards rules and regulations were part of his Verunian inheritance and the chimeric being asked for confirmation of the system's readings. When the monitoring apparatus repeated the self-same response, the man felt something that had been missing from the hearts of Earth's occupants for a very long time. A part of human nature that perhaps exceeds even that most powerful basic urge to survive; **hope**.

ADDENDUM 3
ROYAL MARINE JARGON

ace	good, excellent
airy fairy	a member of the Fleet Air Arm
all the fours	Portsmouth whores
bandies	Royal Marine bandsmen
beer coupons	money
bimble	casual walk
birds	helicopters
bivvies	field shelter made from a poncho
bombed out	exhausted
bootie or	
bootneck	Royal Marine
brown-hatter	a gay man
church keys	device equipped with both bottle and can opener
coffin-shute	body-bag, recovered from the air
comms	communications or communications systems
crab-air	RAF
crabs	RAF personnel
dig out blind	make an all-out effort

down on your chin straps	exhausted
fat knacker	overweight and unfit Marine
gannet	one with an insatiable appetite
glimp	brief sighting or peep
globe and buster	the Royal Marine Corps crest (the globe and laurel)
heads up	prepare to move
hoisted inboard	received, understood, taken onboard
jack-up	arrange, organise
janner	a person from the west country of England
junglies	jungle fighters
lizzie	HMS *Queen Elizabeth*
nappies	disposable towels
noddy	green recruit
O Group	an operational orders meeting or briefing
OD	Ordinary rating, someone who perhaps does not know any better
old man	Colonel or Commanding Officer
ooloo wallah	jungle operator
Oppo	friend, or the opposite number in a two-man team
percy	soldier
plum	posh-speaking; Officer's mode of speech
rabbits	presents for family members
ring bolt	double zero (i.e., 05.00)
run-down period	last few months of military service
secure	cease work
shreddies	underpants
silent running	maintain silence
sod-buster	Private soldier or Marine
snappers	homosexuals
sneaky beakies	intelligence staff or their operations

snotty	very young, inexperienced Officer
snurgle	advance warily
ssss	silence
stand-easy	short rest period, tea break
sweating neaters	very worried
the Corps	The Royal Marine Corps
time out	endex, end of exercise or end of current activity
troop bible	book containing details of individuals in a squad
turn to	begin work
yap-yap	resume normal communications
yomped	forced march with heavy load